W9-BMS-007

"A huge novel that combines power and politics with the personal lives of its heroes. The suspense was terrific, the characters just dandy."
—Susan Isaacs

"Front-line legend Colonel David H. Hackworth proves in this gripping tale that he is as accomplished a storyteller as he is a soldier. With vivid, powerful combat action and a terrific band of brothers in arms, *The Price of Honor* is one of the year's outstanding military thrillers."
—W.E.B. Griffin

"Not many men in America could have written a story like this, but Colonel David H. Hackworth is one of those few. This is a sprawling, fast-paced, and damned good novel about the legacy of war, truth, honor, and courage, and about lies, cover-ups, and cowardice. For all those who served in Vietnam, and those who lived through that terrible and interesting time, this is a must-read."
—Nelson DeMille

"Expertly told by a man who's braved the heat of battle time and time again, *The Price of Honor* is tell-it-like-it-is, epic storytelling that's as exciting as it is suspenseful. There is little more that Hackworth could put into a gripping yet thoughtful thriller."
—Clive Cussler

continued . . .

"The battle scenes, settings, and political maneuverings all ring true ... Hackworth now joins the host of authors behind Tom Clancy in the military thriller genre ... *The Price of Honor* is a worthy entry into that race."

—*San Antonio Express-News*

"If you're into action, adventure, and taking on the 'system,' you'll get off on this book. Plus, it's a damn good story!"

—*The Airborne Quarterly*

"If there's any problem with David Hackworth's *The Price of Honor*, it's finding a good point to take a break once you start reading. From its opening punch-in-the-gut combat scenes in Vietnam and Somalia to its evocations of political action in Washington, D.C., this book sizzles like a broiled sirloin—albeit a very bloody one ... This book is one that you may not want to miss."

—*El Paso Times*

"A slam-bang first novel ... the battles scenes generate the kind of excitement that makes you turn the pages with Gatling gun speed."

—*The Berkshire Eagle*

"A success ... Strong, well-developed characters move the narrative ... Even minor characters ... are well-drawn and distinctive ... Very definitely not standard-issue macho old devices, these people are the creations of a good writer."

—*Southbridge (MA) Evening News*

Also by David H. Hackworth

★ ★ ★

HAZARDOUS DUTY
**America's Most Decorated Living Soldier Reports
from the Front and Tells It the Way It Is**

with Tom Mathews

ABOUT FACE
The Odyssey of an American Warrior

with Julie Sherman

BRAVE MEN
with Julie Sherman

THE VIETNAM PRIMER
with Samuel Marshall

THE
PRICE
OF
HONOR

★ A NOVEL ★

David H. Hackworth

BERKLEY BOOKS, NEW YORK

THE PRICE OF HONOR

A Berkley Book / published by arrangement with
Doubleday, a division of The Doubleday Broadway Publishing Group,
a division of Random House, Inc.

PRINTING HISTORY
Doubleday hardcover edition / October 1999
Berkley mass-market edition / September 2001

Visit our website at
www.penguinputnam.com

ISBN: 0-425-18064-6

BERKLEY®
Berkley Books are published by The Berkley Publishing Group,
a division of Penguin Putnam Inc.,
375 Hudson Street, New York, New York 10014.
BERKLEY and the "B" design
are trademarks belonging to Penguin Putnam Inc.

PRINTED IN THE UNITED STATES OF AMERICA

10 9 8 7 6 5 4 3 2 1

For all the unsung heroes of the Vietnam War.
And for those who never returned.

★ ★ ★

This book is dedicated also to my partners,
Eilhys England, cherished wife, best friend, soul mate,
and Tom Mathews, great good buddy, without both of whom,
truly, The Price of Honor would never have crossed
the line of departure.

ACKNOWLEDGMENTS

This book could not have been written without the help of a bunch of folks who always answered when the bugle called.

I want to offer special thanks to Colonel Dave Hunt, U.S. Army, Sally Allen, Lucille Beachy, Shawn Coyne, Joan Kuehl, Henry Morrison and Michael Schiffer, who lived with the story from beginning to end.

I am also deeply grateful for the help and support of Major General Donald Hilbert, U.S. Army; Colonel Carl Bernard, U.S. Army; Lieutenant Colonel Roger Charles, U.S. Marine Corps; Major Brian Grattan, U.S. Army; Major Eric Haugland, U.S. Air Force; Captain John P. Nelson, U.S. Army; Captain Stacy Starbuck, U.S. Army; Captain Mike Suessman, U.S. Army; Captain Larry Tahler, U.S. Army; Chief Warrant Officer Kyle Grogan, U.S. Army; Master Sergeant Donald Linton, U.S. Army; Corporal Robert McMahon, U.S. Marine Corps; Cadet Todd Dicaprio, USMA; Jim Bartlett; Giralti Cisternas; George DiOrio; Elizabeth England; Melissa Firdman; Dr. Gerald Haidak; Bert Jocovino; Julie Lynch; Lorena Morales; Juan Ocampo; Janice Pangrazzi; Sara Rowan; Charlot Schwartz; Chuck Spinney; Dr. Henry Tulgan; Vicki Voll; Dr. Robert Woodbury; and Linda Woods.

It is difficult to keep errors out of any story about soldiers, harder still to keep a love story honest. To the degree I have succeeded, I owe an enormous debt to all of these friends. Any blots that remain are my own.

'Tis a fault to Heaven,
A fault against the dead,
a fault to nature . . .

HAMLET, *Act I, Scene 1*

THE
PRICE
OF
HONOR

PRELUDE

"Burn 'em, for Christ's sake, burn 'em—they just blew the wire."

Through the gray fog hiding the firefight, the cry rose like a hot red tracer.

Circling at 1,500 feet over the Central Highlands, Colonel William Augustus Buell flipped from the Fox Mike radio to the intercom of his command and control Huey and ordered his pilot to make another orbit of the battlefield. Far below him, mortar and artillery rounds exploding on the Lang Vei Special Forces Camp smeared red across the clouds.

At the side doors of the chopper, two gunners crouched over their M-60 machine guns cursing the weather. In front of them, the young captain at the radio console was switching channels, twisting the dial, trying desperately to raise the beseiged camp.

"Three-Five-One, this is Brandy Six Alpha, over."

He twisted the dials furiously.

"Three-Five-One, come up, over."

Nothing from the ground.

Below the chopper, four hundred Montagnard Strikers and the eleven members of Operational Detachment Alpha 351, all Americans—one captain, one lieutenant and nine highly trained NCOs—were looking into the guns of at least two reinforced North Vietnamese regiments.

The captain spun the dial again and again, back and forth, like a faith healer praying for the strength of his fingers to raise the dead.

"Three-Five-One. Come up, come up."

No answer.

For an instant, the clouds parted. Colonel Buell flipped the intercom switch again and told the pilot to drop another 300 feet. Through his field glasses, he watched A1E fighters sweeping in to drop their 500-pounders. As the A1Es veered off, greasy black smoke seamed with crimson flames rose around the camp's dog-bone perimeter.

Gus Buell was flying above ODA 351, listening over the Fox Mike while his men were dying because in the middle of that firefight was the son of General John Pershing Caine, Commander, United States Army, Pacific.

The colonel told himself to concentrate on the action, the color code of battle—the scarlet explosions of the demolitions ripping away the wire, the green helmets of North Vietnamese regulars scrambling through the gaps. They reminded him of death beetles falling on a corpse.

The camp's Montagnard Strikers were throwing down their guns, trying to surrender. A few of the Bru tribesmen, seeking the protection of the bush, were sprinting through their own minefields. But the North Vietnamese were taking no prisoners. With short, accurate bursts from their AK-47s, NVA infantrymen cut down everyone the mines didn't blow away first.

Colonel Buell swept his binoculars to the right. A few Americans were still alive, fighting their way back toward a wooden footbridge over a deep trench protecting the inner perimeter and commander bunker.

Suddenly, a figure in tiger-striped trousers and a brown tee shirt darted into the colonel's field of vision. Crawling out of the command bunker, he ran over to a sandbagged fighting position on the near side of the bridge and plunged a detonator.

The bridge splintered and disappeared in smoke and flames. For a second, the stranded SF warriors, cut off from the inner perimeter, stood there paralyzed. Then a stream of machine gun fire tore into them. Colonel Buell's gut clenched as he watched them spin, pitch forward and crumple like blood-splattered burlap bags.

After that, nothing moved but green helmets.

Another mortar barrage, even heavier now, began to pound the camp. The command bunker vanished in black smoke. As the clouds closed in, he heard the forward air controller's final call.

"Come up, guys. I got all this good stuff for you and I don't know where to put it. Where are you, for Chrissakes, where are you?"

Silence.

The young captain shut off the radio. Above the grinding whine of the chopper's rotor, he yelled over to Colonel Buell: "Fuck—it's all over."

ONE

Dumb. Dumb. Dumb.

Anger beat a familiar cadence in Sandy Caine's head.

Sprinting off the training ground, he headed into the dry riverbed that ran alongside police headquarters. Some moat. You could drive a herd of goats across it. Or a truck filled with plastique.

Dumb, dumb, dumb . . .

Running harder now, the heels of his worn-out soccer shoes kicking up little puffs of dust in the wadi.

What was it that made General Rushman such a jerk? If they gave out oak leaf clusters for stupidity, the guy's ribbons would be sagging down there right next to his double-digit IQ.

It was only 0800 hours, but already the August sun hanging in the cloudless blue sky over Mogadishu was bringing the city to its morning boil. With each stride he felt the hot desert air tearing at his lungs.

Dumb, dumb . . .

Chest pounding, sweat coursing down his back, he no longer felt much like a Special Forces officer. He damn sure knew he didn't look like one. For the day's mission he was wearing a pair of chinos cut off at the knees and a faded blue soccer jersey in the colors of the Honduran World Cup team. As he scrambled up the far bank of the wadi, he could smell the pepper gas oozing from the jersey. It clung to his short, dirty-blond hair like bad perfume.

Dumb . . .

And suddenly it came to him.

General genes.

That had to be it. Evolution rolled the dice and out came these corporate types who could care less if they got you killed.

Until the summons from Rushman, the morning's mission had been relatively simple. All he had to do was convince Major Mustafa Kalil that even in times of national crisis it wasn't necessary to grease every enemy of state in sight. Not always. Sometimes you could tear gas them.

The major and the green recruits for the new Somali National Police were just starting to get it when Sandy heard Sergeant Santana's voice come crackling over the walkie-talkie.

"Hawk 6, this is East LA. You need to get back here. Over."

Sandy punched the button and identified himself. "Come on, Sarge. Give me a break."

"I'd move it, sir. Excelsior is pissing in his boot."

Excelsior was the radio handle of Colonel Willard Jenkins, General Rushman's executive officer and brown-nose-in-chief. Which figured. Cursing softly, Sandy punted his gas mask ten yards down the training field.

SOS—Same Old Shit. One minute you were doing your job, the next you had your heels locked in the commanding general's headquarters, taking crap from a perfumed prince who could ruin your life if he didn't like your attitude.

Damn right, he had an attitude.

That's what it all came down to, he reflected, slowing to a trot. Attitude protected his mind the way a sheath protects a fine knife. It was essential to his survival, like wound dressings in a medic's kit. He was pushing thirty. A brooder. On the days when he thought he should bag the Army, it occurred to him that he knew a dozen ways to kill a man for every way of being one.

He was a captain with a golden name and a platinum future. Five years out of West Point and he spent half his time wondering why he didn't quit and get a life. He came from a tradition— eight generations of Caine warriors, six from the Point. But he was no traditionalist. He broke things, rules, icons, not just gas masks. Before the voice of authority, what he felt was a trickle of contempt, not the terror that made lifers grovel.

For a moment he stood there, waiting for the anger to cool. On the far side of the wadi, he saw Summar the mop man coming out of the command post. Summar was wearing the same faded cotton shirt and torn trousers he put on every day. Most of the time he went around barefoot. This morning he had on a new pair of Air Jordans.

The sun and wind had mummified his face. When he saw Sandy, he gathered his skinny body into a travesty of attention and saluted. Nice old guy. Mopped the floors every morning with muddy water from an old bucket, swirling fresh arabesques of filth over the patterns he had laid down the day before. After work he went over to the Bakar Market and reported the day's intelligence from police headquarters to the Somali National Liberation Front. The Nikes had to come from somewhere.

Summar's treachery was transparent, perhaps even useful. Sandy used him to spread disinformation. From across the wadi, he returned the mop man's salute. Soaked in sweat, he double-timed it to the rear of the four-story building that housed his command post. The rest of the Bakar Market district consisted of colonial villas faded to soft brown, mud houses with earthen roofs, and thousands of wooden shanties. Towering above them, the walls of police headquarters reminded him of a castle looking over a medieval slum.

The concrete walls were scarred from old battles. On the second floor, the dark smudge left by an exploding RPG round looked like the bruise circling a black eye. Sandy pushed open a steel door and went down a splintered flight of stairs to the cellar. When he came into the command bunker, he found Santana bent over a Sabre MX. The radio was lying on a crate covered by a frayed prayer rug. Talking quickly and softly into the hand mike, the A-Team's commo expert sounded like a man trying to calm a barking terrier.

"Yes, sir. I know, sir. Hawk 6 knows you're looking for him. He's on the way, sir."

Santana was a tall Latino from East Los Angeles. Cool, a little eccentric, even for Special Forces—sometimes the meditation and tai chi got to be too much for the other men. They read war stories and thrillers. Santana read *American Anthropologist*. In his footlocker, he kept a travel-tattered copy of his master's thesis—"The Guayaquil Tribe and the Shining Path"—along with the wooden flute the tribe's ghost talker had given him at the end of his field work. He spoke Japanese and Italian as well as Spanish and English. The CIA was always trying to steal him. For his mind, and for his other assets. He could do twenty-five one-armed push-ups and kill silently with either hand.

Right now, he was just trying to buy Sandy some time.

"Yes, Colonel. He knows who's looking for him. Sergeant Caldwell went over to the training field himself to get him."

Panting as if he'd just run the Boston Marathon, Sandy leaned against the wall of the bunker and let Santana play the spluttering colonel. On the wall behind the radio, two lizards were hunting flies. Sandy watched them until his breathing returned to normal. When Santana gave him the hand mike, he hefted it gingerly, as if it were a live grenade. Then he pressed the push-to-talk button.

"This is Hawk 6," he said. "Is Thundering Eagle having a nice day?"

Colonel Jenkins registered the jab at Rushman's handle but saved it for later. "Cut the crap, Captain. Where the hell have you been?"

"Across the wadi, sir. Training. East LA told me you called."

"You're damn right I did. Twenty minutes ago."

Over the hand mike, Jenkins sounded like an air horn in an end zone—pompous and a long way from any danger on the field. Sandy drummed the top of the Sabre. Gray dust covered his slender fingers. "I'm here now, sir. What's this all about?"

"What it's about, Captain, is Abu Bakar." Jenkins paused for effect. "We've got twenty-four dead Pakis and four Americans KIA over the last ten days. You are aware of that, I assume, Captain Caine?"

"That I am, sir."

"Well, the little bastard's right out there laughing at us. Thundering Eagle wants to talk to you. And the word he used was *now*. I suggest you get here ten minutes ago." He clicked off.

Sandy passed the dead handset back to Santana and sat down. Absently, he ran two fingers over his chin. A three-day beard stubbled his jaw, a pale blond mustache was advancing above his lip. Stubble chic wasn't Thundering Eagle's thing.

Screw Thundering Eagle.

Sandy's eyes moved to the short stack of mail sitting on the crate next to the radio: a letter from Lieutenant Atkinson's wife—you could tell by the green ink—and a purple envelope from Sergeant Mayemura's girlfriend. The two soldiers competed over the number of letters they got from home. After four months, Atkinson was ahead by two letters, but the purple tide from Waikiki was still running strong.

Sandy also saw the May issue of *Bon Appétit* magazine. Three months late, but that never bothered its most loyal reader. Eddie Mayemura, master of good chow and bad vibrations. Blow up that bridge, Eddie, but don't let that soufflé fall. Mayemura could do it all.

At the bottom of the stack, Sandy found a note from Melba, the envelope square, feminine, the address in bold script. Shoving it into his pocket, he tossed the rest of the letters to Santana. "Mail call, Professor. Better get these out."

He stood up and stretched. Santana was already halfway out the bunker. "Ask Sergeant Caldwell to meet me out front in five minutes," Sandy called after him. "And tell him to fire up the Blue Deuce."

★   ★   ★

Up one floor in the squad room, Master Sergeant Nathan Preston Caldwell, the A-Team's senior NCO, was taking Friday off. Caldwell had it all worked out. The Muslims got Fridays for prayers, and that meant the A-Team had to work Sundays. So it was only right for him to take Friday off, too. But not for praying. When Santana found him, he was pressing the only cold beer in downtown Mogadishu to his cheek.

No one ever wrote Sergeant Caldwell letters. The married NCOs on the A-Team carried pictures of their wives and kids in their wallets. In the cobra-skin billfold Caldwell had taken off a dead Cuban in Angola, he kept pictures of his favorite guns.

At forty-four, Nate Caldwell left the impression on weaker men that he could crush them with one hand. That perception was accurate. He had learned the art during four combat tours in Vietnam—what he had to show for it were a trio of Silver Stars and two Purple Hearts. By his reckoning, that put him ahead of the game.

He was sitting in the squad room next to the minibar Mayemura had scrounged, nursing a Bud. Breakfast time in the 'Dish. Outside, the temperature was nosing toward 100 degrees.

"Hawk wants you and the Blue Deuce out front in five," Santana said. "Something about Abu Bakar."

"No shit?" So much for the day off.

A six XXXL-size tee shirt, red, black, and green with the call letters of a Harlem radio station embroidered on the back, lay crumpled on Caldwell's cot. He looked at the gold Rolex on his wrist. He had won it staying with a five-high straight against a sergeant major in Panama who made the mistake of trying to bluff him with a busted full house. Bad idea. You didn't play poker with Nate Caldwell unless you wanted to contribute to his retirement fund.

In the morning heat, his dog tags, dangling from an 18-carat gold chain around his neck, stuck to his heavily muscled chest. The tags were solid gold. One side said, "Nathan Preston Caldwell, African Methodist Episcopal Zion, DOB 8/16/49, Blood Type O." On the other side, it said, "If you find these take 'em and have a blast, motherfucker. I sure did."

For a few seconds, Caldwell pressed the beer to his other cheek.

Santana knew better than to tell him to hustle.

Caldwell drained the beer, crushed the can and tossed it aside. Grabbing the tee shirt from the cot, he tugged it over his head and came up through the neck hole looking like a grumpy sea lion. From the holster attached to his webbing, he took out a 9-millimeter pistol. Chambering a round, he flipped the pistol off safe and slipped it in the space between his jeans and the small of his back.

"Okay, Professor," he said. "Out of my face. Got bizness."

Santana watched him go, moving out as relaxed as a man setting off for church. Caldwell's eyes had gone dead. The way they always did when he went into combat.

TWO

The Hotel Selim was a dump, but the only other choice was to sleep on the ground with the creepy crawlies. Abigail Mancini had checked in feeling jumpy after the flight from Nairobi. Pocketing the $50 bill she shoved over the gritty desk, the night man had taken her to a room with no blankets, no sheets, no towels, no toilet paper. The one small window had no glass. Its broken louvers beckoned to every winged insect in east Africa.

A mosquito net fell in dirty folds around the narrow bed. When Abbie was working in hot countries, sleeping under a gauzy white canopy made her feel like a princess. But this net was filthy, full of holes. The mosquitoes had whined around her ears all night while she slapped and dozed, wondering bleakly if she had remembered to bring her malaria pills.

Now she felt the sun streaming through the window, warming her naked back. Her tee shirt and bra were hanging off the end of the bed. Rolling over, she drew her knees to her chin. Sand fleas had put bracelets of little red welts around her ankles.

I'm getting too old for this.

It didn't show. Although she was coming up on thirty, bartenders still carded her. Her hair, tawny red and curly, was shot with golden highlights. Her long legs made her look taller than she really was and she carried her narrow shoulders easily, as if she were just coming home from dance class or the gym.

Her tongue felt thick. Sweat was trickling between her

breasts, leaving a white line in the brown dust that covered her entire body. No water for drinking or a bath. She looked at the stainless-steel TAG Heuer on her wrist. Fifteen minutes until the meeting with the ambassador.

She slipped into her bra. Her tropical-weight khakis hid the curves of her round hips and trim waist, leaving everything to a man's imagination and nothing for the locals to grope. Pulling her backpack out from under the bed, she unzipped it and rummaged through an inner pocket. Good. The malaria tabs were there, so were the vitamin B-12 capsules, the Lomotil and a tube of Benadryl. Her trusty joss. Her balm of Gilead. All set. Pen and pad, shits pills and itch cream. All you needed to report for the *Washington Chronicle*.

She was stringing for the *Chronicle*, working for a day rate and expenses. That was the price she paid for quitting her safe job on the domestic staff to gamble on herself in Africa. No salary, no benefits. Better to starve in Somalia than feed from the media trough in Washington. Some days she was sure she'd made the right choice. Some days she wondered.

The Hotel Selim made her wonder.

She looked around the room. A sleek brown rat slithered out from under the bed and disappeared through a large crack in the floor. Her stomach knotted. Why didn't she just go home? No way, Abs, she told herself. No way.

From the backpack, she took out a fresh white tee shirt and pulled it over her head. Then she dragged an aluminum suitcase from under the bed. Inside was a Voyager satellite phone and transmitter, the components all neatly packed in form-fitting rubber compartments.

As she was examining them, she heard a tremendous thumping at her door.

"Hey, love, wake up. Gotta get going."

Kurt Phillips was standing there in his vest of many pockets screwing a 300-millimeter lens into a Nikon F5. The lens looked like a grenade, one of the old-fashioned German potato mashers. The photographer looked like a bouncer between shifts. His face was oddly angular. He was an ex-pat Rhodesian who lived in Paris between gigs. Some days Abbie thought he looked Oriental, other times Afro, sometimes like an American Indian. His features had an uncanny way of taking on the coloring of the stories he covered.

"Come on, babe. I found us a four-wheel drive."

Macho man. Lean, hard, six-foot-two, built for action. Nice ass, she thought, watching him bolt for the street.

From time to time she had toyed with the idea of getting it on with Kurt, but she always decided against it. One night after they'd both had too many beers he had said to her, "I find 'em, fuck 'em, forget 'em." She'd clicked bottles with him and said, "Me, too." She liked guys, but she didn't trust them enough to love them.

Especially Kurt. He had a woman waiting in every combat zone. Abbie didn't like lines. She wasn't going to stand there holding a ticket for Kurt or any other man.

When she finally caught up with him he was throwing his gear into a beat-up Toyota Land Cruiser. "You drive, I'll shoot." He climbed into the back of the Land Cruiser, wedging the toes of his boots under the front seat so he could stand and focus his cameras. Abbie craned around and shook her head. "No way, cowboy. I'll drive, you'll sit."

"So glad you care, babe."

"Look, we don't have a story unless the ambassador opens up. So humor me."

He waggled his eyebrows at her as he dropped into the passenger seat. "The American embassy's behind the Kisenyi Hospital," he said. "Take the K-4 circle. You've got five minutes. And here's a question for Howett. Mr. Ambassador, sir, I saw a shitload of special ops troops come off a C-141 at the airstrip about an hour ago. What's the deal? Are they here to boil rice for the hungry?"

"For that one, my love, I owe you."

Kicking the Land Cruiser into gear, Abbie headed north across the city. She passed a small whitewashed mosque where half a dozen boys were sitting in the dust reciting Koran verses to an old man in a brown robe. Bullet holes scarred the front of the mosque. The gaps in its crenellated roof looked like missing teeth. Circling the shell-torn parliament building, she found the hospital, turned and pulled up in front of the American embassy at exactly eight o'clock.

Behind a sandbagged security post, one of the two Marines standing guard stepped out to check her credentials. Glancing up from her passport and press card, he scanned the rest of her, obviously liking what he saw. She ignored the leer. She was used to it. It came with the territory. The Marine waved her through the front door.

At the front desk, a middle-aged woman in pearls, a neat white blouse and black skirt was sitting behind a computer monitor. An iron handmaiden.

"We're here to talk to Ambassador Howett," Abbie said. "Breakfast interview, I suppose you could call it."

The woman tightened her narrow, perfectly rouged lips and took her time opening the appointment book. Her nails were freshly manicured and polished. Looking down, Abbie saw little crescent moons of dirt under her own. She resisted an impulse to hide her hands behind her back.

"Umm, yes. Please have a seat."

"Look, Miss Congeniality," Abbie snapped. "I don't have my needlepoint with me this morning. The appointment was for eight o'clock. It is now three minutes past eight. I suggest you ring the ambassador and stop wasting our time."

The woman flushed, but before she could reply, the door behind her swung open and a tall, thin man with a silver mustache stepped into the room. He was wearing a tan, tropical-weight suit. He looked like a man who'd just choked back a laugh.

"Miss Mancini? The *Chronicle*, isn't it?"

"Yes, Mr. Ambassador."

"Glad you could make it so early. I've got to be out the rest of the day."

He led her through a large office fitted out with the usual flags and photographs to his private dining room, where the mahogany table was neatly set for two. "You're one short, Mr. Ambassador," she said, nodding toward Kurt. "This is Kurt Phillips, my photographer."

Ambassador Howett made a signal to a Somali maid in a white *futa*, who set a place for Kurt and brought in a large silver tray with coffee, rolls and scrambled eggs.

The ambassador unfolded his napkin. Knifing a blob of raspberry jam onto an English muffin, he handed it to Abbie.

"My private stock. Flown in from Rome this week."

"A bribe, Mr. Ambassador?"

He looked at her over the tops of his glasses. "A rather crumby one, wouldn't you say, Miss Mancini?" She smiled politely at his little joke. "All right," he said quickly. "Call it a bribe. I want to sell you a story." He put down the knife and looked at her earnestly. The old I'd-never-bullshit-you eye contact.

"The story, Miss Mancini, is war and peace."

Ambassador Howett chuckled. Somehow Abbie kept from rolling her eyes.

"Let me be more precise," he said. "The Somalis are good people. I know them and I like them. They are fully capable of putting their country back together if we give them the right help. Feeding them was only a stopgap. We've done that. Now we need to do something else."

"And what would that something be?"

"They need a first-rate police force."

"You're kidding," she said, brushing a crumb off the table and dropping it onto her plate. "Is that the story? Wow. Page one for sure."

To her surprise, he stood up and began pacing up and down. "Look, Miss Mancini," he said, stopping next to her chair. "This country deserves a chance. It can recover. But order can only come from an efficient police force. We've got a Special Forces team running a model program. I really think you should go out and take a look at their work. It's a very hopeful sign."

"What about all the bad guys outside, what about all their guns, Mr. Ambassador? You can't go ten meters around here without somebody sticking one in your face. What about them?"

"Guns aren't what it's all about, Miss Mancini. Americans are getting a totally distorted view of what's happening. Go look at that SF team. They're the best we've got, jumpers, HALO trained to land on a manhole if there's trouble underneath it. But they're here to keep us out of combat. I'm giving you the real story. There's an interesting young officer running the program."

Was that supposed to seduce her? She felt a prickle of annoyance.

"He has strong opinions. The idea for the program came from him."

"Great."

The ambassador sighed. "I can see I'm doing this all wrong," he said. "Just go down there and talk to Captain Caine. Take a look at what's going on. Make up your own mind."

She had held her fire long enough. It was time. "Here's the deal. I'll go talk to Captain Caine. And now you owe me one, right? So what's going on with the special ops troops you off-loaded at the airstrip this morning? That looks like the real story to me."

Ambassador Howett sat down and reached for his coffee. "You know how they overreact in Washington, Miss Mancini.

Somebody decided we needed more security, so they sent us a few Rangers. The State Department talks peace, the Pentagon sends us warriors. That's all it is, the left hand not knowing what the right hand is up to—very old story, don't you think?"

The guy was good. Very good. "That's all?" she asked him.

"As I said, Miss Mancini, no more combat here. Not on my watch."

A buzzer sounded near the head of the table. Ambassador Howett rose quickly. "Let's do this again after you've seen Captain Caine."

Ten seconds after he left, the door flew open and the woman with the pearls rushed in, a look of victory on her face. "I'll show you out," she said.

Abbie scooped a large forkful of eggs onto her muffin and took a bite as she stepped into the vestibule. Survival issue, she told herself. I came for breakfast. I'm leaving with breakfast. She was still chewing as she climbed into the passenger seat. Kurt rested his hands on the wheel.

"Okay, babe, what do you think?"

She looked down at her nails. "Well, shooter," she said, tossing him the keys. "I think we should accept the ambassador's kind invitation and cover the wedding."

THREE

★ Mogadishu ★

The Blue Deuce was the ugliest truck in town, an old clunker that blended right in with Mogadishu's advanced state of decay. Six wheels and a diesel engine that ran on faith and a quart of oil every other day. Sergeant Mayemura had found it parked behind the tanner's souk at the Bakar Market. He bought it for twenty-five bucks and hired a dozen red-eyed Somalis to roll it back to police headquarters. Caldwell took one look and said it was worth about as much as a blue deuce in a busted heart flush. But Sergeant Heinrich Kruger, the A-Team's fixer, found enough chewing gum and WD-40 to give Mayemura's old derelict the hug of life.

Caldwell was behind the wheel when Sandy came down the front steps of police headquarters. "General Rushman's got a wild hair up his ass, Nate."

"Yeah, I heard," Caldwell replied. "Maybe someone else does too."

"Who are you talking about?"

"You gotta ask, go figure it out yourself."

Easing the Blue Deuce out of first gear, Caldwell headed down Armed Forces Avenue. Just before the Bakar Market, a crowd of women, kids on hips, baskets on heads, surged up and around the truck. They were carrying the few scraps of food they'd been able to find at the filthy stalls just up the road: carrots, yams, a few small handfuls of rice. Trussed and dangling from the wrist of one of the women, a scrawny chicken clucked out a wild protest against its last ride.

Who was better off, the woman or the chicken? Sandy asked himself, watching the two of them disappear up the dusty street. Somalia was the pits. Its leaders were crooked. They'd gone to school in Europe, bitched about colonialism, then come home after independence to rip off everything that wasn't bolted down. They were the ones who had opened the way for Abu Bakar and the Somali National Liberation Front. Bakar promised justice. Right. The guy who'd gotten his training in Moscow with another crowd of corrupt bastards who stole everyone blind in the name of revolution.

Either way, the woman was screwed, but at least she was still alive, Sandy reflected. That put her one step ahead of the chicken.

At the K-4 traffic circle, he saw a kid no older than twelve sitting at the end of a pile of discarded tires. In his lap he was cradling an AK-47. Next to him, he had a small radio and a rocket-propelled grenade launcher. A little girl with long black hair braided in the style of the Dir clan crouched by his side. Her hand was resting on the neck of what appeared to be a dead goat. Flies swarmed around its open eyes, but the goat didn't move.

"Who the hell created this place?" Sandy said out loud. "Couldn't have been God."

"When you gonna quit that shit, Hawk? Look, you wanna talk religion? Okay, keep five yards and do unto them before they do unto you."

Nate drove on in silence, his eyes sweeping the road for trouble. Sandy kicked himself. What did he have to bitch about? He and the A-Team had come in country to provide security for Archer Howett, the President's special representative. The ambassador had done two tours with the infantry in Vietnam before going into the Foreign Service. He wasn't the problem.

The problem was General Rushman. A two-star with four-star ambitions. Rushman liked air mobile assaults. A battalion here, a regiment there. What else did you need to pacify a dipshit country like Somalia? Howett knew better. The Somalis were good fighters. Push them, they shot back. "We'll do this my way," Sandy heard him tell Rushman one morning. And since Howett was the President's special representative, the general had no choice but to comply.

So they had opened the country peacefully: first the arid

scrubland of the Guban to the north along the Gulf of Aden, then the richer Shebele River region from Marka and Baraawe down to Kismayu.

One morning Sandy went along with Howett to inspect a warehouse where Somali gunmen had murdered two UN relief workers and carried off five tons of rice. All that was left were the dark brown bloodstains on the floor. Looking at the mess, Sandy said, "The only way we're going to get this country squared away is if the Somali cops get their shit together."

Howett shook his head. "That's never going to happen." His eyes traveled back to the bloodstained warehouse floor. "You know," he said suddenly, as if he had made up his mind about something, "sometimes the messenger gets killed and sometimes the messenger gets the job. How about *you* whipping them into shape?"

Hell, yes, Sandy said. The A-Team was trained to drop behind enemy lines and organize peasants into combat battalions. If they couldn't train a few cops, they ought to hand in their jump wings. Three days later, he and his men moved into the trashed headquarters of the Somali National Police. For a while, things went well. Out in the field, relief supplies began flowing and the guerrillas from the SNLF hid their guns.

Except that it didn't last. The guns were out. And now General Rushman wanted to see him.

Sandy leaned back in the Blue Deuce and closed his eyes. As they passed through the gate at the airstrip, Caldwell looked across the seat. He didn't like what he saw. The sun playing over the captain's high cheekbones cast a dark smudge of shadow under his eyes. He looked like ten miles of bad road.

*   *   *

Caldwell drove past the 10th Mountain Division's bivouac. Making an arc around the berm shielding the fuel dump, he sped along the edge of a long chopper pad where A-4 Little Birds nestled like chicks next to the larger Black Hawks and Cobra gunships. A little way off, a Spectre AC-130, mother of all gunships, watched over the flock.

General Rushman had set up his command section in a mobile VIP trailer at the northwest corner of the airstrip. The rest of his huge headquarters, a large windowless building nearby, housed the 1,400 clerks and jerks who fought the paper war and directed the other 5,000 logisticians who cooked the beans and moved the bullets. With 1,000 riflemen, Rushman's tooth-to-tail ratio was about as soft in the gums as it could get. No need for Abu Bakar to kick out the teeth, Sandy reflected. Wait long enough, they'd fall out.

Because Abu Bakar didn't have an air force, there had been no need for cammo paint or nets. General Rushman could put himself on full display. In the dusty morning air, the white vinyl siding and roof of his trailer were gleaming through waves of heat. It looked like an egg in a sandbox. A child could smash it.

At 0900, Sandy stepped down from the truck and walked over to the trailer. Through much of Desert Storm, General Rushman had served as chief of staff to an even more star-studded officer, picking up the man's habit of using full colonels as gofers. In the anteroom, Colonel Jenkins was installed at his desk, poised to service his general's every whim.

Glancing at his watch, he gave Sandy a significant look and pointed to the door.

Sandy knocked twice. No answer. He waited a full minute, then knocked again.

"Get in here, Captain."

The voice was a practiced baritone, sure of its power. When Sandy stepped into the room, the general had on his don't-fuck-with-me face.

General Rushman was a gaunt, handsome man, just over six feet, with a touch of gray in his black hair. As usual, he was immaculately dressed. No matter how hot the weather, even in a combat zone, Manuel, Rushman's enlisted aide, starched and ironed his cammo fatigues until they stood at attention in his wardrobe. The grunts knew all about Rushman. They hated his guts.

Sandy snapped a salute and stood at attention.

Taking off his reading glasses, aviators in the Douglas MacArthur style, the general studied the stubble on Sandy's face, then his ragged shorts and soccer jersey.

"Nice look, Captain. Where's your skateboard?"

"Left it with Colonel Jenkins, sir. Heard you didn't like people scratching up your floor."

General Rushman's jaw tightened. "Ambassador Howett told me about your sense of humor, Captain. I don't have one. So I suggest you save your smart-ass talk for the next time you're sucking up to him."

Unlocking a file drawer, he took out a buff envelope with a red cover marked "Secret" and tossed it across the desk. Sandy pulled out two photographs, a close-up of Abu Bakar and a shot of a small white Saab. Satellite photos from the markings.

"Abu Bakar's new limo," General Rushman said. "He likes things Swedish—machine guns, transmissions, pornography. He's the one with the big beak in the other picture." There was a transcript along with the snapshots. Rushman pushed it toward Sandy. "We picked up a scoop last night. The two men talking are Abu Bakar's brother and his security chief. The guy they're talking about is their commander in Baidoa. Colonel Raschid thinks he can run the revolution better than their boss. He's coming into Mogadishu for a coffee klatch at the Hotel Royale. Abu Bakar is going to put him straight. Straight into the ground would be my guess."

The purr of the air conditioner was the only sound in the room. Rushman was enjoying himself. "All right, Captain Caine," he said. "You're the one who talked the ambassador into letting you play cops and robbers. Now you're going to get back in uniform. I have a soldier's job for you."

"What did you have in mind, sir?"

"Bring me Abu Bakar."

The idea was dazzling in its stupidity. Even for Rushman. Technically the A-Team wasn't even under the guy's command. SF always hesitated before putting any team under a conventional commander below corps level. Too many fools like Rushman around. But now was not the time to tell the asshole to pound sand.

Sandy propped the blurry head shot up on the desk. Abu Bakar looked like a carp with five o'clock shadow. The fish he swam with had very sharp teeth. "Abu Bakar never goes anywhere without guns and grenades," he said. "We can't get near him unless we take out his bodyguards. They could also kill us first."

Rushman nodded. Sandy looked at the two stars on his shoulders. Caldwell was right. This guy meant to go all the way. No matter who had to die for it. He began feeling his way forward like a man probing for mines with his trench knife. "Our recruits are looking pretty good, sir. But if we task them with this one, they'll fold."

General Rushman tapped his gold pen on the desk. The pen made a sharp noise, as if its owner were a teacher prompting a dim student.

"I'm not asking the Somali police to do this job, Captain Caine. I want you to do it."

"But, sir—"

Rushman cut him off. "Let's call it an order. You're only two blocks from the Hotel Royale, so nobody will see you going in. That gives you the best chance of getting out."

Or getting blown away. "Okay," Sandy said tightly. "Miracles happen, and my guys are good. So let's say we make the snatch. How do we extract him? He's got two thousand trigger pullers and maybe fifty thousand true believers out there. The place won't last ten minutes once they're on to us."

General Rushman pushed his chair back from the desk. "You know, Captain, I've been listening to you carefully and I don't like what I'm hearing. If I had any brains, I'd remove you from command, but I have too much respect for your grandfather."

Sandy reddened.

"What's the real problem here? You having a little trouble with your nerve?"

Before he could say anything, General Rushman moved in for the kill. "You asked about the extraction," he said. "We can't use birds to pull you out because they'll be expecting them. So we're going to keep this operation on the ground all the way. I've got the 10th Mountain saddling up two companies to escort you back to the airstrip."

"With respect, General, aren't there any other options? Have you checked this out with Ambassador Howett?"

Rushman exploded. "Look at your chest, Captain—down there where your uniform should be. Do you remember what it says over your pocket—or what it would say if you weren't wearing that getup?" He jabbed a finger at his own chest. "It says U.S. Army, the same way it does on mine. Remember, mister, you are still subject to the Uniform Code of Military Justice."

The Tiffany desk clock struck the half hour as Rushman tossed the photograph to Sandy. "I don't give a damn how you do it as long as you get him to your playpen jail alive. The little bastard's car is going to pull up in front of the Royale at 1430. That gives you five and a half hours to work out the details. If I were you, Captain, I'd throw it in fifth gear. Dismissed."

*   *   *

The first thing Sergeant Caldwell noticed when the captain came out of the trailer was the locked jaw. Caldwell tossed aside a dog-eared copy of *Guns and Ammo* and turned on the ignition.

The captain got into the Blue Deuce. Gray eyes stormy. No way he was going to talk. Caldwell drove out of the base and headed up the Mogadishu Mile past burned-out Soviet trucks, the charred bones of the American Black Hawk, a mangled Paki APC. War surplus from all the best brokers. Coming out of the K-4 circle, the captain finally broke radio silence. Leaning forward, he pounded so hard on the dash, Caldwell had to jam in the clutch and drop down a gear.

"You gonna share the good news, Hawk?"

"Try a snatch and grab, Nate. Abu Bakar's coming to the Hotel Royale at 1430. All *we've* got to do is bring him back to NPHQ."

Sandy banged the dash again, harder this time.

"How stupid can one white man be?" Sergeant Caldwell shrugged. In his own mind, he had settled that particular question a long time ago.

"Okay, so we snatch him. Maybe the 10th even gets across town. What happens after that? We can kiss everything we've been trying to do good-bye. You think Kalil and his boys are going to hang around until the bad guys come to slit their throats and murder their families?"

"Like I been sayin', Captain, maybe two times twinkle twinkle little star ain't doing it for General Rushman no more. Put yourself in his place. What would you do if you saw a chance to go for number three and all you had to do was send out a few grunts to get their asses greased?"

Caldwell had on his Ray-Bans with the gold mirror lenses. The captain couldn't see his eyes. That was good. Caldwell didn't give him advice often, but when he did, he expected him to take it. "Way I see it, Captain, ain't no good bitchin'. Only choice we got is to figure out how to get in there and back with our cocks still in our jocks."

Sandy shook his head.

"Hey, great, Nate. All we need now is a secret weapon."

"We got one, Captain."

"What the hell are you talking about?"

"The Deuce, Captain." Caldwell floored the accelerator. The truck lurched forward like a drunk in a waterfront bar. "We got us the Blue Deuce."

FOUR

New York ★ Shelter Island

Eight time zones and 9,000 miles to the west, the moon hung like a white lantern over Shelter Island. In front of the old summer house, the wind had fallen and the sea was calm, ebbing like a sigh from the rocky beach.

On the porch, two men sat in white wicker chairs talking quietly. A silver tray on the small table between them held an antique seltzer siphon, a bucket of ice, two crystal glasses and a tall bottle of Johnny Walker Black Label. Neither man reached for the bottle. Both waited, certain that a steward would materialize, perhaps out of the surf, to pour their last scotch.

The first figure, the older of the two, was Senator Jefferson Kenefick Taylor. Handsome in a black Irish way, just losing a well-developed summer tan, he was a shade over 6 feet tall. From time to time he extended his right leg out in front of him, easing its stiffness. He had draped his navy blazer over the back of the wicker chair. Pinned to the lapel was the blue-and-white rosette of the Medal of Honor.

The second man, a few years younger, was running out the clock on his forties. Taller than the senator, broader across the shoulders. Softer in the gut.

"Thanks for coming," he said. "I didn't give you much time."

"Your helicopter made it easy, sir."

Coming from the older man, the word *sir* sounded odd. But

Taylor had been a soldier a long time before going into politics. And the man in front of him, watching the moonlight rippling toward the beach, was the President of the United States.

The war hero and the policy wonk. The cut and thrust of their rivalry transfixed Washington.

Senator Taylor had made a national name for himself as a defense reformer. Around the Pentagon, ticket-punching generals and defense lobbyists groaned at the name of the junior senator from Ohio. Unlike the assorted liberals and bean counters of the post-com-symp left, when he attacked an inflated budget, a cost overrun or the latest weapons system that couldn't hit the side of a barn, people listened to him. There was something else about him that drove the defense crowd nuts. Taylor was always talking about the individual soldier, the grunt, his rifle, his boots, his chow. All of them chump-change items. Not a $100 billion contract in any of them. Besides, who had to use a rifle any more? Satellites, smart bombs, missiles that see in the dark. That was where the future lay. And the contracts. They thought Senator Taylor ought to shut up.

Voters saw it differently. They loved him. He was a Republican, a fiscal and social conservative, but Democrats crossed over regularly to keep him in Washington. When the people around town who kept count took their private polls, the numbers showed that if Jefferson Taylor ever chose to, he could clean the President's clock.

Senator Taylor wanted to. The more cogent issue was when and how. There were two ways—carefully or flat out. Both had their attractions.

Right now, the senator and the President were observing Beltway Rule Number One: pick up the phone if breaking bread with an enemy will keep him from eating your lunch.

The invitation to fly up to Shelter Island had arrived four hours earlier. Senator Taylor had been expecting the call for over a week. On the Hill, where Republicans in the House and Senate were administering their own brand of Rose Garden spray, hoards of the administration's self-righteous, poorly advanced initiatives were dying like aphids.

Around the defense establishment, the Old Guard was grumping that a draft-dodging skirt chaser could never act as an effective Commander in Chief. Their deeper fear was encrypted. What really worried them was his weakened grasp on power. Democrat or Republican, it didn't matter who occupied the White House so long as nothing upset the orderly flow of contracts.

No one saw the President's growing vulnerability more clearly than he did himself. The West Wing was abuzz with survival scenarios, including the one that had spurred Senator Taylor's night flight to Shelter Island.

The smart money was telling the President to can Robert Lassiter, his Secretary of Defense. Too liberal, too inflexible, too committed to budget cutting, they all said. He just didn't get it. The good news was that Bob had health problems. Spin the dweeb's execution as a personal necessity, they said. Spare everyone the embarrassment of firing him. Offer the job to Jefferson Taylor. Name a war hero, a Republican for godsakes, to secure your right flank. Consider the icing on the sticky bun. You shut the guy up, you keep him from using the Senate Armed Services Committee to blow you out of the water.

Only a matter of time, the power players all said. Senator Taylor knew it, too. For a week he had been asking himself whether the better part of valor would be to accept the job, broaden his base and leave the *mano a mano* with the President until later.

The President thought all of them might be right—unless he could think of something better. Then he did. And tonight was the night.

Settling deeper into his chair, he said, "I invited you here tonight, Senator, because I've done some things today I wanted to tell you about myself."

Not good, Taylor thought. Not like a job interview. The man sounded almost smug.

"As you know," the President went on, "we're having some trouble with Somalia. Bush thought he could send in a few troops and some Wheaties and do God's work. What crap. Now those little pricks in Mogadishu are trying to chew up the missionaries. Well, they're not going to get away with it. I've ordered General Rushman to get out the muzzle and leash. Can't give you the details until tomorrow morning, but you'll get them first. I hope you'll explain the setup to your colleagues on the committee."

"You can count on it, Mr. President."

"I was hoping you'd say that, Senator Taylor. Thank you."

So much for the appetizer, Taylor thought. What's the main course?

The President looked up at the moon, drawing out the moment.

"I'm sure you've heard Bob Lassiter's not well," he said.

"Yes, that's what I hear."

"He's going to stand down."

"I'm sorry to hear that. His heart's in the right place."

"His heart's going to kill him. I can't have that on my watch. Too much going on."

Taylor kept a poker face. "Stand down?" "My watch?" My ass. Was this the guy's idea of command presence? Where did he get all the military clichés? How could he ever work with this asshole? Hell, what's the difference? It didn't have to be for very long. Just long enough.

Then it came. Right between the horns.

"I'm going to ask Hal Bonham to take the job. You know him? He's been up at Harvard. The Defense Institute. Good man, full of ideas."

The President was looking at him like a kid pulling the wings off a butterfly. Getting off on it. Senator Taylor felt a muscle begin to cramp above his knee. "Fine choice, sir."

"Will the Senate confirm him?"

Twisting the knife now, the sonuvabitch. "I can't speak for the Senate, Mr. President. Bonham doesn't have much hands-on experience. Could be a problem."

"Will *you* support him?"

Goading him now. The sonuvabitch. Rising stiffly, Senator Taylor took his jacket off the back of the chair. "I'll think very carefully about it, Mr. President. Thank you for the briefing."

"You'd do the same for me."

Out in the drive, a car was waiting to take Senator Taylor back to the helipad. The helicopter rose slowly and whumped off south toward Washington. Somewhere over Chesapeake Bay, he took his cell phone out of his briefcase and punched in the home number of his chief of staff.

"Patrice? That you?"

"Here I am, Senator. How'd it go?"

"Why don't you put up some coffee. After I fill you in, you tell me."

FIVE

All that Caldwell had told them was "Be there."

It had to be big.

Just before 1100 hours, they piled into the squad room. Santana passed the time examining body armor, the new stuff, black not green, heavy, awkward as a corset. After a few minutes he tossed it aside. Maybe they wouldn't be testing it that day. Maybe pigs fly.

One by one the rest of the team arrived. Blowing off tension, they jabbed at each other like boxers, cracked jokes, guffawed even when the punch lines were lame.

Against the front wall, Lieutenant Boyd Atkinson, the team's executive officer, was trying to look older than he felt. Atkinson was the kind of clean-cut guy you see singing in church next to his wife: brown hair, clear hazel eyes—decent, fairly bright, gung ho. It was Nancy Atkinson, his wife, who wrote the green ink progress reports on their two-year-old, Timmy. "Hey, Mayemura," he called across the room. "I got mine today, did you get yours?" The men laughed and Atkinson felt better, though it puzzled him why they thought mail call was so funny.

At exactly 1100 hours Sandy and Caldwell walked into the room. The nervous chatter stopped. Everyone pushed forward to hear better. "All right, listen up," Sandy said, skipping any small talk. "General Rushman wants us to invite Abu Bakar back to his trailer. Maybe he figures his air conditioner will cool off this civil war."

Sergeant Reginald Wilson spat the gum he was chewing into his hand and stuck it to the wall. Wilson was a weapons expert. He wore his feelings on his sleeve. "Yeah, I know. It sucks," Sandy said. "But we've got a mission and we're going to do it. Sergeant Caldwell will fill you in on the details."

Caldwell stepped forward to outline the plan. Standing in front of his makeshift blackboard, he looked straight at Wilson, a skinny kid from Baltimore, always cracking wise, always on his shit list. He had made it his purpose in life to smoke the kid's ass, to shape him up before he got anyone hurt. "Okay, Wilson," he said, "you and Doc Carter are light, bright and damn near white, so you gonna pass for Somalis. Doc's gonna drive us to the Royale Hotel and you're gonna ride shotgun. I want you to walk like a Somali, talk like a Somali, dress like a Somali, and shoot like Dirty fucking Harry. You got that?"

Wilson nodded gloomily.

"And Wilson," Caldwell snapped. "Somalis don't chew gum, you hear me?"

"Yeah, Sarge. I got it." Wilson looked at the ceiling, pulled out another stick of gum and jammed it in his mouth. Doc Carter, the team medic, said nothing.

"Okay, Strunk, Mayemura, Santana, you'll be ridin' in the back of the truck with the captain and me. If we get lucky, no one will ever have to know we're there."

Sergeant Mathew Strunk nodded. Before the Army, he had worked for his father as a lobsterman. He was a born hunter, of deer and black bear back then, more recently, of men.

Caldwell pressed on, pointing to each man as he laid out his job.

"Doc Carter and Wilson are gonna unass the Blue Deuce, take out Abu Bakar's security and throw the prisoner into the back. Then we haul ass back here. Any questions?"

There were no questions.

"Good. We got three hours to get squared away. The 10th Mountain's set for the extraction. But if we gotta fight our way out, we start right here. So we gotta bunker the shit out of our positions. I want sandbags at all the bottom-story windows and firing ports all over the building and on the roof. We need wood to block the doors, water for drinking and putting out fires."

He stopped. "One more thing. The trainees. We can't count on 'em. The captain is gonna tell Major Kalil that we're getting ready for a class tomorrow in static defense. You can use 'em to help prepare the building, but don't blow our cover."

When Caldwell finished, Sandy told Lieutenant Atkinson that he wanted him to stay behind with Kruger, Gomez and Hassan. The police recruits could man the bunker. Nonessential jobs only. The four Americans would provide cover for the Blue Deuce's line of retreat.

"If there's no place to come back to," he said, "we're all dead."

Atkinson started to protest. He knew he would be babysitting and he didn't like it. But he saw the cobalt in Sandy's eyes and shut up. He was left with only one pro on his stay-behind team, Sergeant Kruger. Sergeant Jesus Gomez was a twenty-two-year-old kid from Puerto Rico, and Sergeant Sejdi Hassan was only twenty-one. Both of them were pulling their first hitch in SF. They looked like babies to Atkinson. But the lieutenant nodded to the captain and got to work preparing the building.

Sandy felt sorry for him, but he had no choice. Green lieutenants get good men killed. The axiom had been wired into Sandy's brain as tightly as his own name. He could hear his grandfather drilling him in the catechism. Green lieutenants. Don't trust them. Liabilities. The whole purpose of the U.S. Army is to put a rifle platoon on an objective, but the guy in charge is the most inexperienced guy in the whole defense chain.

Sandy left Caldwell in charge of the assault team while he went back into the bunker to organize air support and check for intelligence updates.

The men lined the bed of the truck with sandbags. When the firing positions were finished, Caldwell took out his trench knife and cut ports in the canvas on each side of the truck bed. He slashed another slit in the rear flap, then taped the tarpaulin back into place. To the innocent eye, the Blue Deuce looked harmless. But if they had to shoot their way home, the tape came off, the blinds came down, and the guns came out. If the engine and transmission could handle the weight of the sandbags, they'd be all right. If they couldn't, he didn't want to think about it.

Half an hour later, Sandy was back. "Looks good, Nate. We all set?"

Caldwell tossed a case of machine gun ammo into the back of the truck.

"Almost there, Captain Hawk. This Trojan Horse is gettin' ready to roll."

"Hey, Nate, I didn't know you were a reader."

"Saw the movie, Captain." Caldwell adjusted the rear flap. "We're good to go," he said. "Let's do it."

SIX

Patrice St. Jean stood next to the stove watching his egg timer, counting off the seconds.

Two minutes 40 seconds, 41, 42.

On a stool next to the kitchen island, Senator Taylor sat reading the first edition of the *Washington Chronicle*. "Nothing in here about Bonham." He frowned as he turned to the op-ed page.

Forty-three, 44, 45.

"Courage, *chér*." The southern accent softening Patrice's New Orleans French patois eroded the *g* in courage.

Forty-nine, 50. Finis.

With a quick flick of the wrist, Senator Taylor's chief of staff turned off the flame under the soft-boiled eggs. He took two Limoges egg cups from the warming shelf above his Wolf range and put them on a small aluminum tray, art deco.

Five A.M. The kitchen in Georgetown was redolent of the French Quarter, the sweet aroma of beignets out of the deep fryer, snowy with powdered sugar, mixing with the darker note of chicory coffee. Patrice arranged the power breakfast on the tray and took it over to the island. "So the White House suddenly gets balls," he said, handing Senator Taylor a linen napkin. "Where did they come from?"

"General Rushman. Old Drop-'em and Mop-'em Rushman. Gordie thinks he's got the answer in Somalia. The President bought it."

"Which is?"

"Kick butt. Move some boys, use some toys."

"Think it'll work?"

Senator Taylor took a last bite from one of the beignets. For a moment he had considered dipping it into his egg, then he saw Patrice watching him and thought better of it. "We should know in an hour or two. He said he'd call this morning. Asked me to sell it to our side."

"Not bad," Patrice said. "He really shoved it up your ass, didn't he?"

"That he did, Pat. That he did. Pass the beignets."

For a while the two men concentrated on breakfast. The first pale light of morning began to glow on the top branches of the Norwegian maple out in the garden. Through the kitchen window Patrice watched the sunlight working its way down toward the ground.

Ground zero, he reflected.

"What's going on in that war room of yours, Pat?"

Senator Taylor watched, knowing that whatever came out, it would be original. Patrice Michel Alain St. Jean, the wizard of Georgetown. He might have a junior varsity body, but tucked in there was the mind of a Jesuit. In a city of supercharged dunces, Patrice was a genius, of course. But he was something even rarer in Washington. He was loyal.

The division of labor between them was quite clear. The senator walked the walk, talked the talk. Patrice did the deals. They went together like butter and eggs.

"This could work for you," he said, beginning his spin. "All it does is make things happen faster."

They had discussed it before. The Defense job presented two lines of march on the White House. If the President succeeded in restoring his own strength, the senator could sit out the next election, then swoop down to destroy the Vice President four years later. If the President faltered, he could move sooner.

The trip to Shelter Island had made the choice moot.

"The money's there," Patrice said. "Same as always. We need to do some sampling. I'll put Strong and Carver on the phone banks this morning."

He aimed his spoon and gave his egg a sharp crack. Removing the top, he peered in at the goo. Ten seconds short of three minutes. Perfection. Anything less, he would have dumped it in the disposal.

"How long?" the senator asked.

"We need to wire this thing right. I've got to talk to a few people, do a little sniffin' around."

"How long?" The repetition came sharply, automatically. Patrice ignored it. You could take the man out of the military but not the military out of the man.

"A few months. Gotta grease the skillet, *chér*."

"I want to be ready before the first of the year."

The sun was up now. Patrice rose and turned off the kitchen lights.

"Just out of curiosity," he asked, "what do you think he's up to over there?"

"He didn't say."

"Think you could find out? You could always call Sandy, *chér*. He might as well be your nephew."

"Come on, Pat. You don't just ring up an SF team on AT&T." The senator had to remind himself that if anyone could, Patrice could. But as a matter of day-to-day reality, the military wasn't Pat's thing.

"Isn't Archer Howett a friend of yours?"

That was true. They had served together in Vietnam. When Howett left the Army to join the Foreign Service, Taylor's father was Assistant Secretary of State for European Affairs. He saw to it that Jeff's bright young friend met the right people on the seventh floor at Foggy Bottom.

"I don't think Arch knows."

Patrice put down his spoon and looked across the island. This was interesting. "Not too swift, considering Ambassador Howett is the President's special representative."

"Rushman was the only name that came up."

Patrice grinned as if he had just been handed a brightly wrapped present. "Why don't you give Howett a call?"

The senator looked at his watch. Well past noon in Mogadishu. "What's the point?"

Patrice pushed the basket of beignets across the island. "Well, let's say for the sake of the argument that the President didn't tell his own special representative. The ambassador's a peacenik, you know that. What's he gonna do when he finds out that Rushman's bitten off the big one?"

"He'll shit."

"And then?"

"He'll try to abort."

Patrice watched as it began to sink in.

"We might save some good guys."

Pat waited.

"And if Howett calls it off, the President's back to square one."

Patrice wiped a spot of powdered sugar from his chin. "That's right, *chér*."

"And he'll be asking the Senate to confirm another Harvard idiot who doesn't know the business end of an M-16 from a hole in the ground."

"Uh huh."

"And we'll ram this one right back up *his* fanny."

Senator Taylor pushed aside his plate and walked over to the wall phone. Taking a small black book from his jacket pocket, he punched in the number of the East Africa desk at the State Department. "This is Senator Taylor," he told the duty officer. "Please patch me through to Ambassador Howett."

SEVEN

Ambassador Howett looked out the window. Two thousand feet below his helicopter, the brown desert of Somalia was unfolding like a bad dream. Why were so many people willing to die for it? He was on his way to Hoddur to talk the head of the Teflis clan into standing up to the Somali National Liberation Front. What the Teflis and the Dir hated more than Europeans, Americans, and Soviets was each other. The Teflis could help contain Abu Bakar. Maybe they would listen to him.

He closed his eyes and listened to the whump of the rotor. A red light flashed on the instrument panel in front of the pilot. He flicked the switch on the intercom. "For you, sir. It's a patch from Washington."

Howett groaned silently. "Thanks, Major. Put it through." Hard to hear anything over the clatter of the chopper's engine, but the voice was unmistakably Cincinnati. "Hey, Arch. You there? It's Jeff Taylor."

"You got me," Howett said, brightening. "How'd you do it?"

"Connections 'R Us, Mr. Ambassador. Where the hell are you?"

"Two thousand feet up. Coolest place in Somalia. What about you?"

"Just got back from Shelter Island."

Howett frowned. The summer White House was the curse of a

diplomat's warm season. Too much time for golf, bright ideas. "They must be cheering in the E-Ring. When do you move in?"

"Ain't gonna happen. He wants Bonham."

"You're kidding me."

"Wish I was, Arch. Harvard's our bridge to the twenty-first century. West Point doesn't do it for the man."

"Sorry, Jeff. I . . ."

"Doesn't matter. Listen, something else came up. That's why I'm calling. If you can't talk, just say so."

"No encryption necessary, Jeff. I'm just breezin' along to Hoddur. Some wheeling and dealing with the Teflis."

"I'll be damned. That's not what the man said."

Howett stiffened. "What did he say, Jeff?"

"He told me a few hours ago he was sick of having his missionaries chewed up. Said he's ordered General Rushman to do something about it. The operative words were 'leash' and 'muzzle.' "

"Don't know anything about it."

"I guess I'm not surprised. He didn't mention your name. Hey, how's Betty?"

"Chafing to get me out of here, believe me. My tour's up in three months anyway. Thanksgiving at the Cape. Why don't you come up?"

"Bet on it, Arch. I'll tell Pat to book it. Call when you get back."

"You're first on the list. Listen, what are you going to do now?"

"Oh hell, I don't know. Maybe I ought to be choosing my own SecDef. You interested?"

Howett chuckled. "Who would've guessed? Watch your back, Senator. Talk to you later."

Flicking off the line, Howett reached over and got the pilot on the intercom. "We're diverting, Major. Back to the strip. I want you to land on top of General Rushman's trailer."

"Yes, sir."

"And Major, I'd like you to observe radio silence. I think it's better if General Rushman is not expecting me."

EIGHT

★ Mogadishu ★

Sandy was still dressed for soccer. Shaking his head, he went into the small, sandbagged room where he had his cot. Kicking off the running shoes, he stripped off his shorts and jersey, folding them neatly before he put them in the laundry. Reaching over for the basket, he felt the envelope in a pocket. Message from home. All's well. Wish you were here. Christ, wouldn't that be nice? He sat down on his cot and put the envelope on his knee. The paper fluttered in his fingers. Adrenaline rush. Good, he thought.

It wasn't fear that was bothering him. He'd lived with fear all his life. Doubt was worse, much worse. What sense did it make to stick his dick in the electric socket for the greater glory of a phony prick like General Rushman? What gave Rushman the right to order Nate and Mayemura and Atkinson and the others to follow him on this stupid rat fuck? Okay, sure, Rushman had the right. The Army gave it to him. It demanded obedience. But why should a good A-Team get blown away just so one more numbnuts with stars on his shoulders could go for another promotion?

Oh man, Sandy, he warned himself, now is not the time. He tore open the envelope. The note inside was wrinkled—his sweat had blurred the ink—but he could still make out Melba's confident handwriting:

Caro halcónito I miss you, little hawk. Arlington in summer is death. Too hot, too boring. The General must be getting old. I beat him twice this week. Bishop 7 to King's 4 both times. He was a very bad sport. The second time he knocked down all the pieces.

He felt the tension in his body ratchet down a notch. Melba to the rescue. In his miserable room he saw her brown face, warm, wrinkled with concentration, leaning over the little table where she wrote her letters and studied her stock reports. Melba Casadero.

Love had never been one of his assets. He felt about it the way disbelievers felt about God. He had no faith. Love's proud atheist. Except for Melba.

He had been a sulky, hostile three-year-old who'd chased off half a dozen nannies before Melba arrived. His grandfather hired her as a stopgap while the agencies continued the search for a nanny strong enough to handle him.

Around the General's fine old house in Virginia, there were no other women. His own wife, Elizabeth Putnam Caine, had died giving birth to Sandy's father. She was a Boston Putnam and she should have been in Boston Lying-In. But she was also a good Army wife, so she had gone to an Army hospital, where she died because an incompetent couldn't stem a postpartum hemorrhage.

The General had promised her that when their son was born, he would be there. But when the baby came in 1942, he was in North Africa with the only boys that really counted for him. Elizabeth Putnam had died calling his name.

Sandy had always thought of her as killed in action, a martyr to love, while the General was busy winning the war. Another part of the Caine family tradition. His own mother had driven her car off a cliff in Hawaii six months after his father bought it in Vietnam.

Given the track record, Sandy's view of women was that even the best tended to vanish. The conclusion was obvious: disappear on them before they disappear on you.

Except, of course, for Melba.

He kept her letters in a tin box that had once been full of almond candy. From Melba, of course. Reaching for the box, he saw the small black book wedged next to it in his footlocker. The cover was soft, pebbled to look like leather, and blank. You couldn't tell whether it was a soldier's Bible or just another collection of hot phone numbers.

On the flyleaf was a faded stamp: *Printed in Accordance with Wartime Restrictions on Paper.* On the title page, it said in the same economical spirit: *The Soldier's Shakespeare. Henry V.*

The General had bought the little volume from a stall outside a used bookstore in London during the Blitz. He had carried it with him across Europe on the plunge for Berlin. The night before Sandy left for West Point, he gave it to him as a going-away present. When Sandy came into the dining room that evening, he saw it lying next to his fork on the polished mahogany table where the General drilled him every night over dinner.

"It's about you, son," the General said. One of the few times Sandy had ever heard a crack in his voice. "The choice you're going to have to make in life."

"Sir?" Sandy had mumbled.

"In all of Shakespeare, only two princes really count. Prince Hal and Prince Hamlet. Who are you, Alexander? Which one are you going to be? The prince of action or the prince of dithering around?"

"I'll have to think about that one, sir."

"Think long and hard, Alexander."

Then Melba came in with the standing rib roast. From that night on, whenever Sandy thought about that evening, what he saw were the old man's powerful hands around the antler handles of the carving set. What he heard was the snick, snick, snick of steel on steel.

At first he had thought the choice was easy. Hamlet, Jerkoff of Denmark, worst wimp of all time. Play Hamlet and everyone dies. Prince Hal was his man. "We band of brothers." He could believe in that. "Once more, dear friends, into the breech." He believed in that, too.

But then. But then. When he started soldiering for real, it turned out the job wasn't so simple. No one fought with swords. Shit, since Vietnam hardly anyone fought with guns. At least theoretically. The Pentagon wasn't interested in weapons. It was interested in weapons systems. Big Bangs. Big Bucks. It could care less about your boots or your rifle.

To act or to doubt, wasn't that the real question? To lead or be led? Goddammit, man, get a grip, he told himself, looking again at the note from Melba:

No more news, except I shorted Microsoft as soon as I heard they weren't going to get Windows 95 out on time. So we'll go for a good dinner, maybe El Parador, when you get home. Be careful over there. Go with God, hijo mío. Melba. P.S. Wear your medal.

Sandy opened the tin box. At the bottom, under the stack of letters, was a Saint Christopher's medal the size of a silver dollar. Melba had given it to him the day he left for Mogadishu. He took it out and looked at it. Melba believed in protective powers, miracles. He believed in training, guts, luck. When Melba had taken him into the kitchen to give him the medal, he had teased her mercilessly. Now, he slipped it onto one of the chains around his neck, letting it clink against his dog tag. If he was lucky, Caldwell would never notice.

NINE

★ Mogadishu ★

Kurt eased the Land Cruiser around a corner just beyond the mosque of Fakr al-Din, pulled up in front of police headquarters and turned off the engine. "Here comes the bride," Abbie hummed. After the embassy, this place looked relaxed. Whoever was inside was getting along better with the locals than the people uptown. She pushed open the door and walked into a long room running the entire length of the building. A wide staircase led up to the higher floors and down to the cellar. Turning, she heard footsteps pounding up from the basement.

An apparition appeared at the head of the stairs.

Green and brown smudges darkened his forehead, cheekbones and chin. In one hand he was carrying a set of body armor. In the other he had a submachine gun and a helmet.

"Who are you?" he snapped. "What are you doing here?"

She stuck out her hand as if she were poking her fingers through the bars of a cage. "Abbie Mancini, *Washington Chronicle*. Ambassador Howett told us to come over here. Insisted, really. We had breakfast with him early this morning and, umm . . . here we are. You must be Captain Caine. The ambassador told me all about you." Okay, Abs, she told herself. Now try for the innocent smile.

The soldier stared at her blankly. "We're tied up," he muttered. Before he could throw her out, she began rattling off questions.

"What do you mean, tied up? How so?"

"We're just about to take off on a training mission." His voice was guarded, as camouflaged as his face. Her internal radar went on triple scan.

"Great. I'll tag along."

"Sorry, it's classified."

"Oh really? Ambassador Howett's already told me what you're doing here with the police. He seemed proud of the program. He practically ordered me to do a story." Captain Caine smiled faintly. "Sorry," he said. "Come back tomorrow."

Okay, Abbie. Time to regroup. "Sure, I'll do that," she said. "Nice meeting you. See you in the morning." Pushing her sunglasses up on her forehead, she turned and went out the door. Kurt came bouncing up, on his toes, like a tennis player about to return serve.

"What was all that about?" he asked. "Since when do you paint up to play cops and robbers?"

"Bingo, shooter. Since when?"

They got back into the Land Cruiser and she told Kurt to take a swing around the Bakar Market.

"Let's give them ten minutes," she said. "Then we'll come in the other way."

*   *   *

Eight minutes later, Caldwell emerged from the rear of police headquarters and tossed a backpack radio into the Blue Deuce. Strunk had muscled an M240-G Belgian machine gun over the tailgate and was setting it up on a platform of sandbags. Mayemura was hunkered down behind him with an M-16. Nothing fancy, but serviceable. The captain was carrying the MP-5SDK he liked to use for close-in work. It was compact—about the size of a Sten gun—it fired 9-millimeter rounds, and its silencer made it the weapon of choice for today's surprise.

Santana came out of the building with his M203 over-and-under and trotted to Caldwell's side. "Brought your pee bringer, Professor?" The Latino slapped the stock of his double-barrel cannon. The barrel on top was the working end of an M-16 set on automatic. Underneath was a launcher that could drop a 40-millimeter high-explosive grenade on a pie plate at 200 yards. A weird smile flickered across Santana's face. The Professor always looked that way before a firefight. Sometimes Caldwell wondered if he was nuts.

There was one extra machine gun back in the building. Caldwell decided to bring it along. As he headed for the rear door, he heard the low growl of a vehicle crawling toward him in first gear. From around the corner, a Toyota Land Cruiser came creeping, heading straight for the Blue Deuce. He grabbed the walkie-talkie strapped to his webbing. "Better get down here, Captain. We got visitors."

Before Caldwell could do anything else about it, a redhead in a white tee shirt and baggy pants got out of the Toyota, then a tall dude covered with cameras.

"Where you think you're going?" Caldwell shouted. "This ain't fucking Disney World."

The rear door of headquarters flew open. Captain Caine came out looking deeply pissed, but the redhead just kept coming. Now she was right in Hawk's face.

"Hi," she was saying. "Me again."

Hawk was looking at her like a man considering the best way to break her sweet neck.

"I've decided I'd better tag along," she announced, as if she was GI Jane. "It just doesn't seem right to miss you guys doing your thing."

"Not today."

"Why don't you check with Ambassador Howett? He told us to talk to you, to get some pictures."

"Not today."

"I'm coming."

"Not today."

"Look, Captain," she was saying, going slower now, as if she were talking to someone deaf or stupid, "I'm a journalist, I'm accredited here and I can go where I want to go. I have a right to find out what you're doing. My readers have a right to know what's going on in this country."

"Arrest them, Nate."

"You can't arrest me." The redhead, really pissed now. "I'm a civilian. I'm an American. You don't have the right to arrest me."

"I just did. Bust her, Nate."

Caldwell was carrying two pair of plastic manacles in his pocket. He had brought them for the raid. Whipping them out, he snapped them on the mouthy redhead and the photographer. Then he shoved the two of them toward the back door of headquarters. The dude with the cameras took it well. The redhead went bitching all the way.

"Kurt, do something."

"They got us, babe. Relax and enjoy it. Take notes."

Caldwell hustled them through the door and down to the lockup. Atkinson was checking three cells in the rear. "The captain says for you to stow these two, Lieutenant. Don't let 'em out." As he turned to leave, the photographer said, "Would you mind getting our gear out of the car, Sarge? I can't leave the cameras out there. There's an aluminum suitcase in the back. We need that in here, too."

Cool motherfucker. Give him credit for that. It got the woman's attention. She finally shut up, waiting to see what he was going to say.

He nodded to Atkinson.

"Send Gomez out to get his stuff. Lock her in with Mr. Candid Camera. We're gonna need those other two cells."

*   *   *

A few minutes later, Caldwell got back to the Blue Deuce with the backup 240-G. They now had more firepower than the LAPD. Oughta be enough, he thought, jumping into the rear of the truck and lowering the canvas over the tailgate. Better be enough.

Up front in the cab, Doc Carter pumped the brake pedal a couple of times to test it. Without thinking, he reached out to adjust the side mirror and grabbed air. The corroded frame was empty, shot out with the windshield a million years ago.

"Didn't wanna look back anyhow," he said to Wilson. "Too fucking scary, man."

Wilson had two MP-55 DK's on his lap. "Shut up, Doc," he said. "Drive."

At 1420, Doc Carter nursed the Blue Deuce onto Armed Forces Avenue. At five miles an hour, he rolled slowly for one block, then turned left. The Royale Hotel was about 200 meters dead ahead of them. It was a two-story building with pink walls and metal shutters. From the dusty courtyard in front of the lobby, a dead palm stuck up like a busted finger.

Deserted. We're in luck, Carter thought. Maybe this won't be so bad.

Even in the shade of the dead palm, it was 105 degrees. The morning crowds were gone. Anyone with sense was hiding from the sun, sleeping off lunch. Keeping the truck in second, Carter drove 100 meters, then swung in a broad U-turn and pulled to a stop directly across from the hotel. He left the engine idling.

In the back of the Blue Deuce, the heat under the canvas was stifling. Sweat dripped from the Professor's glasses, trickling across the stock of the M203. He looked over at Strunk, who was moving his lips silently, counting breaths, rationing the superheated air.

At 1428, Doc Carter saw the white Saab stop four blocks up the boulevard. Wilson saw it at the same time and tossed over one of the MP-5SDKs. Slipping out of the Blue Deuce, the two men crossed the street and squatted under the desiccated palm.

At exactly 1430, the Saab began moving slowly down the boulevard. In front of the Royale, the driver came to a halt and the doors flew open. Two bodyguards with AK-47s stepped out to scan the street. Wilson and Doc Carter pulled their guns from under their baggy white shirts and started walking forward. The bodyguards swung around toward them, leveling the AK-47s.

The first burst from Doc Carter's MP-5SDK caught bodyguard number one in the chest. *Pfffft.* No more noise than an air gun. The Somali spun around and slammed against the Saab. He slid slowly to the ground, leaving a long red smear on the sedan's white hood.

Wilson fired twice. His first burst hit the other bodyguard in the leg. Lurching forward, blood spraying out of the wounds, the man peppered the front of the hotel with a few wild rounds. Then Wilson iced him.

At the sound of the shots, Sandy and the others tore open the gun ports, and the Blue Deuce bristled with steel.

Caldwell jumped out and ran over to the Saab. Carter was hauling one of the passengers out of the car by the neck of his business shirt. The second passenger, a short man in fatigues, was struggling to free the Czech CZ75 strapped to his hip, the kind the SPETZNAZ carried. Deadly. Fifteen rounds, 9-millimeters long, the same parabellum used by NATO. Kill a NATO guy, you got a new stash of ammo. Before the dude could pull it out, Caldwell hammered his left hand down. There was the sound of bones snapping. Reaching through the door, Caldwell wrapped an arm around the prisoner and yanked him out as easily as if he were lifting a duffel bag. "Get these clowns in the truck," he yelled to Wilson and Carter.

Strunk pushed aside his 240-G to make room, and they shoved the two hostages to the rear of the Blue Deuce. The prisoners were just disappearing headfirst over the tailgate when Caldwell heard a pistol crack twice. An officer in the blue uniform of Abu Bakar's Revolutionary Guards came running out of the Royale.

Who's the fat dude? he wondered. Must be Colonel Raschid. Save the Revolution Raschid. Raising his own 9-millimeter, Caldwell squeezed off a single shot that planted a small red rose in the middle of the colonel's chest. He pitched forward, collapsed under the palm.

Caldwell spun around. Doc Carter was back behind the wheel of the Blue Deuce; that gun-chewin', duck-screwin', shit-for-brains Wilson had frozen at the door. No choice. Caldwell banged him on the side of the head with the butt of his pistol. Wilson sagged. Caldwell lifted him like a stuffed toy, threw him onto the front seat and piled in next to him. "Move it, Doc," he shouted. "Let's get the fuck out of here."

The Blue Deuce burned rubber, rumbling down the boulevard like a rhino. Just before the intersection at Armed Forces Avenue, they had to slow for the corner. Two rebels waving AK-47s came running out of an alley. Strunk took them out with two short bursts from his machine gun.

They came around the corner and headed for home.

Lieutenant Atkinson was standing outside when the Blue Deuce roared up. Ignoring him, Caldwell jumped out of the cab and ran around to the tailgate as Strunk and Santana dumped out the two prisoners. Caldwell grabbed them—his huge hands made it easy, almost as if he were palming two basketballs. He shoved them toward the gaping young officer.

"Lock these bastards up, Lieutenant. Get 'em out of my sight before I smoke 'em."

Sandy took a quick look up and down the boulevard. The sound of the gunfire had blown their cover. Grabbing Doc Carter by the arm, he told him to run the truck back up the street and toss a thermite grenade under the gas tank—no point in leaving the Blue Deuce to Abu Bakar's men. They'd use it as a battering ram.

A few minutes later, the Blue Deuce disappeared in a blinding eruption of red and yellow flames. Doc Carter came running out of the inferno with his hair smoldering, fire licking at his clothes. From the school yard far up the boulevard, a kid stepped into the street with an RPG launcher and pegged a round at him. The shot missed, but the concussion from the explosion as the RPG slammed into a wall behind police headquarters knocked him to his knees. Automatic fire was kicking up dust all around him.

"Cover me, Nate."

Firing the MP-5SDK from his hip, Sandy ran across the boulevard and dove for the medic, knocking him over, rolling him through the dust. When the flames were out, he slung the MP-5SDK over his back, lifted Carter in a fireman's carry and hauled him back to the headquarters building.

Crouching at the front steel door to provide covering fire, Strunk and Mayemura saw Sandy running toward them. They jumped forward and carried Carter into the building.

"You all right, Doc?"

Sandy propped Carter against a wall away from the windows. The shaken medic's face was smudged with dirt and smoke. Wrinkling his nose at the acrid smell of his burned hair, he began patting himself down quickly, looking for wounds. Finally, he stood up and dusted off his arms.

"Shit, first guy in the aid station is me," he said. "Better get it set up."

He waved Hassan and Kruger over to help him collect his medical gear. When they were gone, Sandy went to the vault to check on the prisoners. Atkinson had dumped them in separate cells.

Fuck it. What difference did it make now?

He walked over to Atkinson.

"Where the hell is the 10th Mountain?"

The lieutenant hesitated. Fog of war time. "Ambushed at the K-4 circle. The TOC says some little kid zapped the lead Humvee with an RPG. They're in one hell of a mess. They're trying to make it back to the airstrip now. TOC says we should go to Plan Bravo."

"What the fuck is Plan Bravo?"

"They didn't say."

A current of rage shot through Sandy's body. He fought it down. The bars on one of the cells began to rattle loudly. Wheeling around, he saw the reporter beckoning to him. She didn't look scared. She looked as if she were in complete control, as if all that was left was for her to assume command.

"Great exercise," she said. "Did you use all that blood to make it look real?"

What a pain in the ass. When she turned up he had felt like taping her mouth and FedExing her back to the *Chronicle*. But she obviously had guts.

"What about letting us out?"

Atkinson had a bunch of medieval-looking keys six inches long hanging from a leather thong wrapped around his hand. Some things in Mogadishu hadn't changed for a thousand years.

Sandy nodded to the lieutenant. He fumbled through the thong until he found the right key. The cell door swung open. The reporter stepped out and walked over to Sandy.

"Sorry, Miss Mancini," he said. "The mission was classified. You can leave now, if you want, but I think that might be a bad idea. It's going to get wild out there."

"We'll stay."

"Up to you."

"But we want our gear."

Sandy nodded, examining the woman more carefully. Her eyes were very large. He saw small flecks of gold mixed in with the brown. He put her at about five-foot-five. She looked like a tomboy. But not butch. Headstrong but smart. And she had needled him without quite busting his chops. Not bad.

Atkinson came back with the bags. As he was handing them to the photographer, the radio on his web gear began to squawk: "Gomez to CP." Sergeant Gomez was up on the roof, where Atkinson had positioned him. "Go ahead," Atkinson snapped, struggling to regain his bruised sense of authority. "The crazy *pendejos* are buzzing like flies on shit out there. Everywhere you look." Atkinson looked pleased. "Roger that, Gomez. Keep me informed and stay alert. I'll be up there ASAP."

★   ★   ★

The walls of police headquarters were four stories high and two feet thick. Sandy did some calculations. The closest enemy position would be 50 meters across the avenue, and it had only a ground floor and roof. Abu Bakar had maybe two thousand fighters. He had ten. But at least his guys had good observation, good fighting positions.

There wasn't much time. "Tell Caldwell to put the guys in position," he told Atkinson. "I'm going to find out what fucking Plan Bravo is all about."

He found Sergeant Santana on the second floor putting old Soviet helmets on makeshift dummies and propping his limp reinforcements next to unmanned windows. "We've got to move the radio," Sandy said. "If we lose commo, it's all over." Down in the basement, they bundled up the Sabre and moved it into the vault on the first floor. When the radio was hooked up, Santana raised the TOC and passed Sandy the handset.

"Lion, this is Hawk 6," he said. "Give me Lion 6, over."

"Wait one."

Lion 6 was the call name of Colonel Grady Harrison, a southerner from Alabama. Harrison was an old Delta Force warrior. He had started as a grunt in the Ia Drang Valley and moved out to every other hot landing zone in sight. He had seen them all and lived.

"This is Lion 6. What's happenin', young man?"

"Tell Thundering Eagle the good news is we've picked up the mail. The bad news is we're looking at deep shit out here."

"How deep?"

"One foot in it. You want it all?"

"Affirmative."

"Okay, no attackers so far, lotta angry noise. We need gunships, like now. Then reinforcements by chopper ASAP. The roof's cool as an LZ. Perfect for a wham-bam insertion. But no way we can do a fast bug-out. Too many people. The prisoners, the police, a reporter and photographer. We're stretched way too thin. We could use more people and another medic, night vision stuff and a dozen strobes."

"Got it. What else?"

"An eighty-one-millimeter mortar with HE and ILLUM and a couple more 240s with a shitload of ammo. It wouldn't hurt to get another ten walkie-talkies, spare batteries and a backup radio."

"Roger on the take-out."

Sandy laughed. "What's Plan Bravo?"

There was a long pause. Harrison's disgust came in loud and clear. "Thundering Eagle wants to call in the Marines. They're at sea. ETA two days."

Command post chicken shit. Fort Leavenworth training exercise. Computer driven. Unfucking believable.

"How about UN tanks?"

"Thundering Eagle is working it. The UN's playing rat fuck. The Pakis say they can't move out until they get a green light from home. We're talking Christmas here. A lot longer than the Gyrenes, anyway."

A burst of automatic fire suddenly splattered the front of the building. Sandy heard the whine of bullets ricocheting off concrete.

BEEYOW. BEEEEEEYOW.

"Yeah, well, if we're at two days, Lion 6, we're talking thirteen body bags."

        ★   ★   ★

Atkinson was on the roof assigning sectors of fire. He told the men to harden their positions with timbers and concrete blocks torn from the walls of the building and to keep their heads down. The roof was where they would live or die.

On the ground below, Abu Bakar's irregulars were buzzing like August locusts. From time to time, Gomez popped off a round at anyone who looked like a leader. Kruger held fire with his 240-G, saving ammo, waiting for bigger game.

Toward the front of the building, a wooden platform fitted out with a flagpole jutted out from the roof. The police used it each morning to run up their colors, avocado green on a field of black. The rotting base that supported the pole was hidden by a low wall of planks.

Studying the platform, Atkinson got an idea. Turning to Gomez, he said, "Hey, Jesus, a sniper out there could control the whole street, east to west. Go on out and see what you can do."

Gomez looked up and down the street, then he looked at the platform. Fucking yo-yo lieutenant wouldn't be there to screw things up if they had enough warrant officers.

"There's no cover," he shouted. "It's suicide."

In Atkinson's book, the only thing worse than a chicken shit was a chicken-shit young sergeant. If he let Gomez buck him now, he might as well turn over the whole show. "Bullshit," he snapped. "Look at that wall. Get behind there and no one'll ever see you."

Then he stopped. Bad leadership, he reminded himself. Ordering a man to do something you wouldn't do yourself. He had heard it a thousand times in ROTC, had it beaten into him at the Infantry School. Follow me. Follow me. Follow me.

"I'll show you," he yelled over to Gomez.

Crawling forward on the platform, he inched his way behind the boards and stretched out to shoot prone. Up the street he saw two gunmen dragging a machine gun into position.

Blaap. Blaap. Two shots. Two bodies crumpled on the ground.

Atkinson smiled, leaned over and waved at Gomez to join him. From behind the corner of a building across the street, a machine gun rattled. A stream of bullets tore through the wooden platform and ripped open his belly. Atkinson reached down and felt a warm wet pudding where his stomach had been. The second volley lifted him up and spun him over. He was falling. How slow it all seemed, a long, slow dive like the ones he used to make in the Moline River back home, showing off for girls. "Nancy," he called out, "watch this." Down, down he dropped, and then, where the river was supposed to be, he landed on the hard-baked earth and blackness swallowed him.

Gomez felt sour bile rising in his throat. He bent over and retched.

"Christ," he said, wiping his mouth with his sleeve. "I warned him not to go out there."

Kruger grabbed his shoulder, shook him hard.

"Not your fault, Gomez. Dey give poetry lessons at Vest Point. Dese *scheissköpfe* don't learn to stay alive."

Almost as if it were rising from the earth, a yell went up from the Somalis and a dozen men started racing across the street toward Atkinson's body, a trophy to strip, flay, drag through the market. Kruger had the target he'd been waiting for. Opening up with the 240-G, he poured lead into the street in short, accurate bursts. When the machine gun stopped sputtering, a dozen bodies, red as sides of beef, lay broiling in the sun.

★ ★ ★

Ambassador Howett stared at General Rushman. The American commander was leaning over a table in his trailer studying a map. He was talking to Colonel Jenkins as if the two of them were engaged in a map exercise at the Infantry School. On the acetate overlay of the map, he drew a neat blue circle around the 24th Marine Expeditionary Unit on station in the Indian Ocean.

"What do we have to do to get Colonel Charles to move his Marines faster, Willard?"

"If they leave the supply ships to catch up with them, sir, they can pick up eight hours."

"Excellent, they could still go in before sunup the following day."

"You're right on target, General. As usual."

A revolting wet kiss.

"General Rushman," Howett said frigidly. "I think your little raid has just come unstuck."

He spoke each word precisely, clipping the syllables as if he were using scissors, leaving nothing General Rushman could misconstrue. The two of them had gone to the National War College together. But that was a long time ago.

The general's answer was what he'd been expecting.

"Come off it, Arch. You don't really think this was my idea, do you?"

So Jeff Taylor had it right. "Well, Gordie, I don't know what to think. Who could be stupid enough to dream this one up?"

The general laughed. And Colonel Jenkins was smirking.

"Okay, Arch, here it is. Early this morning I got a call from Shelter Island. You know, Shelter Island, where the President likes to ride around in that little golf cart of his? And guess who was calling me?"

"Why don't you tell me, General?"

"It was the President, Arch, you know, the Commander in Chief. He told me he couldn't find the Secretary of Defense. He was off Hilton Head looking for marlin. And he couldn't find the Chairman of the Joint Chiefs. He was on his way to get a good citizenship award somewhere. When he couldn't find you, either, Arch, that's when he decided to call me."

Colonel Jenkins snickered.

"And do you know what he said to me, Arch? No. I bet you don't. But you do know there's an election coming, don't you? And you do know that Senator Taylor is always on the news breaking his balls."

Howett held his fire.

"You know what the President said to me, Arch? What he said was 'I want you to nail that little cocksucker, and I want you to do it today.' So I asked him, 'Have you talked to Ambassador Howett about this?' and he said, 'Howett's off somewhere playing Lawrence of Arabia. That's why I'm talking to you.'"

That's what this was all about? A presidential tantrum? A campaign ploy? A photo op?

"Why didn't you stop him, Gordie?"

"Goddam it, Arch, this is what I know how to do."

Howett had heard enough.

"Okay, Gordie," he said coldly. "Let's take a look at what you've accomplished so far. You've destroyed our best chance for rational progress toward law and order in this country. And now you're about to get eleven of your best men killed."

The ambassador hadn't lied to Miss Mancini about the Delta Force Squadron at the airstrip. Not exactly. The Pentagon had sent them to do special ops without being precise about what those operations were going to be. He had a mission for them now.

"Here's what *we* are going to do now, Gordie," he said. "*I* am going to call Washington to sort this all out. And while I'm doing that, I think it would be a good idea if *you* got that Delta Force parked outside your trailer onto birds as fast as they can get their shit together. And then you are going to send them into that firefight."

General Rushman threw his pen on the table. It made a feeble snap, like the crack of a .22 in an empty desert. The ambassador ignored it.

"Get your head out of your ass, Gordie. You've got the Marines arriving before their tanks. Without the tanks, they're just dismounted infantry. Maybe you think Marine light infantry is more bulletproof than the Army's, but they're not going to be any better off than the 10th Mountain, and the 10th has already gotten its clock cleaned. They couldn't even get through one road block."

"Now, look, Mr. Ambassador—"

"No, *you* look. You get those Delta people moving now or you're going to retire as the major in charge of the bowling alley at Fort Drum. You screw this up any more and I'll arrange it today. *That*, General Rushman, is what *I* know how to do."

★　　★　　★

Behind a sandbagged window on the ground floor of police headquarters, Caldwell tapped Sandy on the side of his helmet and pointed his finger to the roof. Lieutenant Atkinson had fallen directly in front of them. It crossed Sandy's mind how perfectly choreographed the slaughter had all been, like a demented dance: the brassy music of the automatic weapons, the falling bodies, the silence after the finale.

A useless thought. The point was the roof. They couldn't afford to lose it.

"Yeah, get up there," he said to Caldwell. "Check out Gomez and Kruger. Tell me if you need another man."

"Okay, Captain. You the stud down here, I'll be the main motherfucker in heaven." He sounded almost happy. Staying low, he ran across the floor and took the stairs two at a time.

From the vault, the radio crackled to life.

"Hawk, this is Lion 6. Over."

Harrison's voice sounded about two feet away. Santana had arranged the Sabre in a corner, facing out in a way that turned the vault into a booming speaker. Sandy grabbed the handset.

"Go ahead, Lion 6."

"Delivering your goodies. Gunships will be over you in five minutes followed by Black Hawks with Delta trigger pullers. You're getting two birds with the trigger pullers, then two with sling loads they'll drop on the roof. You want the Delta guys to land or fast rope in?"

"Land. Have the gunships suppress fire on all four sides of the building. And have the chopper drivers come up on my frequency. I'll control the OPs from the roof."

"Wilco. ETA Three Zero for Delta. How's it going?"

"Still a rat fuck. We've already taken one KIA, and it's not getting any better."

Sandy signed off. Across the bunker, Santana had on his eerie smile. "Keep 'em coming, Professor. Relay any messages." Sandy signaled to Strunk and they ran for the roof.

When they got to the top, they saw the reporter crouching behind a low wall of sandbags. She was tuning up a small satellite feeder. The aluminum suitcase was open on the deck beside her, and by the time Sandy reached her she was already operational.

"Sat phone," she said. "Want to phone home?"

"Jesus Christ, Miss Mancini. What are you doing up here?"

"Just looking for the powder room, Captain. As in gunpowder. You going to send me back to jail?"

Wild child keeps her head under fire. Give her that. "It's your story, tiger," he said. "Don't let me get in your way." Bending low, he started across the roof. From behind, he heard her call, "Hey, Captain, thanks."

Abbie cranked up the phone. Two false starts, then the desk assistant said, "Foreign," as clearly as if he were just up the street. "Give me Julian," she said.

A few seconds later, the *Chronicle*'s deputy editor came on the line. "What's happening?" he said sourly.

"Can you still get me some front-page play?"

"Depends."

With Julian, everything had a price. "The balloon's gone up in Mogadishu. I've got American snake-eaters kidnapping Abu Bakar. The town's ready to blow."

"Who told you that?"

"No one."

"Don't jerk me off, Abbie."

"I'm on the roof at police headquarters, Julian, Abu Bakar's in a cell three floors down, and the shooting's already started. You want more?" She held the receiver up. A burst of machine gun fire ricocheted off the front of the building. That got Julian's attention.

"All right, I heard it, you can quit showing off. I heard it. Empty your notebook to Cam. I'll get you the space." She heard him starting to pass the phone to the desk assistant.

"Julian."

"Yeah?"

"What do you think?"

"I'm busy, Abbie. What are you asking me?"

"No 'Great stuff, Abbie, thanks for the scoop.' "

"Give us the feed."

He handed her off. No changing Julian. The guy gave away nothing.

*　　*　　*

Interlocking bands of plunging fire, Sandy thought as he worked his way around his defenses. Out at the edge of the wadi, the Claymores with their electric detonators would slow a broad attack down some. On the east flank, Caldwell had positioned Strunk with one 240-G. Kruger was covering the west flank with the other machine gun. Now they could lay suppressing fire down across the wadi and the soccer field to the west and the low buildings across the street.

The sun was beginning to sink toward the horizon.

The choppers would come in on a north-south vector. The machine gun and gunship fire would force the Somalis to keep their heads down while the birds came in. If it worked, the whole thing wouldn't take more than three minutes. To the north, he could hear the *THWUMP, THWUMP, THWUMP* of the approaching choppers. Over the air-to-ground radio, the voice of the lead chopper driver came through the static.

"Hawk, this is Raven. Inbound. Give me a vector and pop smoke."

Sandy glanced across the roof. "Come in on a hundred and eighty degrees, Raven. And have your guns work over that soccer field. I saw a couple of Technicals out there with crew-served weapons. Two choppers can land at the same time. We'll put down a shitstorm of suppressing fire."

"Roger, Hawk. We're zero-three mikes out. Start your rock and roll."

Sandy motioned to Kruger and Strunk, and the machine guns roared. Red tracers stitched the soccer field. Bakar's men were skittering away like mice running from an eagle. As the gunships moved in, blasting the flanks of the building with miniguns and rockets, the earth shook. Sandy saw the Black Hawks flare and hover while nineteen Delta warriors bolted out. As they hit the roof a sergeant major waved them to their firing positions. Within forty-five seconds they were all in place. Lifting off, the two Black Hawks headed for home.

The odds were looking better.

A few seconds later, two more Black Hawks began hovering over the roof. As neatly as a surgeon implanting a pacemaker, they set down cargo nets loaded with weapons, ammo and supplies. The gunships escorting the cargo ships hosed down the rebels. The rockets went *Whooooosh*, then exploded in flames.

"Hawk, this is Raven. We're away clean. I'll have a minimum of two sets of guns over you until you're outta there. Call signs are Raven 1 and 2. Good luck."

"Tell your crews thanks, Raven," Sandy shouted into his radio. "They do good work."

He scanned the roof. The reporter was huddling over her sat phone. She gave him a wave, then went on talking. Did she take a phone to bed? he wondered. Maybe he should find out. He called Caldwell over. "Let's get her a helmet, Nate."

*　　*　　*

In the slanting rays of the afternoon sun, the percussion from the gunships died out and a lull fell over the battlefield. The black, oily smoke from the burning truck mingled with the burnt-sulphur smell of cordite. A dark haze drifted around the building. Picking his way through the jumbled cargo nets, the Delta sergeant major, who had expertly deployed his reinforcements, walked up to Sandy and saluted.

"Sergeant Major Dan Perkins, sir. Was that plain or with pepperoni?"

Sandy laughed. The man's sleeves were rolled up. When he saluted, a long white scar snaked from his wrist up past his elbow. He looked to be in his late forties. His eyes were a washed-out blue and his skin had weathered to rawhide.

"Thanks for dropping by," Sandy said. "Let's get these supplies out of here, then you can help me and Sergeant Caldwell over there figure out how to defend this shithole."

Perkins looked across the roof to where Caldwell was untangling the nets. "Could that be Nate Caldwell? Master Sergeant Nathan Preston Mojo Motherfucker Caldwell? I think I know the man." Trotting over to Caldwell, he grabbed him from behind as if he were picking up a box of mortar ammo and dumped him on the deck.

No one ever touched Caldwell. Sandy saw his hands flatten as he wheeled around. But when he saw Perkins, he roared with laughter. Then he jumped to his feet, hit the new man with an open-handed slap on the chest, got a leg behind him and rode him down to the roof.

"Steely Dan," he sang out, pinning the sergeant major's shoulders. "Where's your fuckin' band, man?" Scrambling to their feet, the two of them stood up and ambled toward Sandy like a couple of foraging bears. "Knew this dude in I Corps, Captain," said Caldwell. "And in Angola, and in El Salvador. Only white boy I ever met who could dance. Like, 'Tea and me, GI—long time, short time. Steam and cream.' Remember that, Dan? We tore up every whorehouse south of the Seventeenth parallel."

Perkins had stopped listening to Caldwell. He was staring at Sandy.

Sandy had pulled off his helmet to wipe the sweat from his face. For an instant it looked as if the old master sergeant was going to ask him something, but then he seemed to change his mind.

"Come on, Sarge," roared Caldwell, dragging Perkins off toward the cargo nets. "Ain't no time for pussy right now. You gotta shoot 'em before you kiss 'em here. Let's get your boys tucked in for the night."

★   ★   ★

Sandy scanned the bodies strewn in front of his fortress. Abu Bakar's men weren't the world's best shots. But they obviously believed in their leader. And they knew how to die. How many American generals could make the same claim? He remembered a quiet day in Baledogle when he and Ambassador Howett had sat in the shade behind an old mosque weighing relative force levels: theirs and the SNFL's. Howett told him that Abu Bakar kept a copy of General Giap's memoirs next to his cot. Superpowers didn't impress the man. American firepower didn't scare him. "Put him in a room alone with Rushman," Howett said, "five will get you ten on who comes out alive."

Abu Bakar's real name was Colonel Mohammed Mustafa Khalid. He came from Baledogle, but he had named himself after the market in the poorest quarter of Mogadishu. Abu Bakar. Son of the Bakar. More than a little show business in the nom de guerre. Khalid's father had been a rich landowner, rich enough to fly to Egypt and start over when the revolution came.

Khalid himself was an intellectual with a wife in Baledogle, another wife in Cairo and a mistress in Moscow. But he knew how to inspire other men to fight and he knew where to send them. Right now he had enough of them outside the building to kill everyone inside.

When Sandy came in, he saw that the Professor had moved the prisoners from their cells. He'd tied them up with nylon cord and stashed them in the corner, where he could keep an eye on them. The prisoner in the torn business shirt was slumped over, silent. The small man in fatigues was nursing his arm and babbling wildly in Italian.

"I think we have a problem, Captain."

"Yeah, right, Professor. We got a basic shitload of problems."

"Not like this one, Captain."

"Okay, Santana," he said tiredly. "Let me have it."

"This guy says he's not Abu Bakar."

TEN

The little man with the busted wing drew himself up from the floor. His hands and feet were bound, but his eyes were darting wildly and his mouth was working hard.

Raising a hand to stop his babbling, Santana began translating. "The gentleman says he's Abdul Rahman Khalid, Abu Bakar's brother. The other guy says he is Abu Jihad, their foreign minister."

"Bullshit, Professor."

"I told him if he was lying Sergeant Caldwell would fix his other arm. I don't know, Captain. He's a dead ringer for Bakar. Face matches the mug shot. But maybe we do have the wrong guy."

Sandy looked at the photo, then the prisoner. His mind tracked into reverse, sorting through the day's screwups. Nothing about the mission made sense. The intell was all wrong. The plan had fallen apart like a cheap pair of shoes in the rain. "Tell him I don't give a shit who he is. He's going to see General Rushman."

The other prisoner stood up and shot Santana a cagey look. "I think I may have a solution to your dilemma," he said softly.

The accent was English. Upper class. Oxford or Cambridge. "You and your men are just ordinary soldiers," he said. "I understand that. Abu Bakar will understand that. He doesn't want you. He wants his brother. I suggest you release him, or, if you don't feel you can do that, release me. I shall negotiate with Abu Bakar. I guarantee that you and your group will be given safe passage back to your base."

Over in the corner, Major Habib was sitting on a wooden stool, eavesdropping. Santana had asked the Somali officer to watch the hostages while he manned the radio. The major was trembling. "He is right, Captain Caine. We are all going to die. You must release them both."

Sandy spat on the floor. Better cops? What cops? How naive can you get? He'd been dumber than Rushman. "Okay, gentlemen, here it is," he said icily. "Mr. Nobel Peace Prize here and whoever you are"—he pointed to the babbler in the fatigues— "will go out with us. If we get our asses shot off, I'm going to make it my final purpose in life to shoot off yours."

He wheeled on Habib. "Major, you tell any of the trainees who want to split they're free to go. Anyone who wants to stay can stay. But if they stay, they fight."

Major Habib nodded and left. Ten minutes later the entire reconstructed Somalian National Police retreated through the rear door, waving streamers of toilet paper as their white flag of truce.

Abu Bakar's men laughed and jeered, then they let the new National Police, now broken, pass safely into oblivion.

★   ★   ★

Caldwell and Perkins looked down from the roof, watching the recruits disappear.

"Seen it before, Nate?"

Caldwell nodded. Maybe a thousand times before. Like in Nam at the end. A lot more times in a lot more places after that.

The two men returned to their work. They assigned a pair of Delta reinforcements to man the 81-millimeter mortar, ordered four more to help secure the roof. Perkins set up a Delta sniper team, a spotter and a shooter with a 50-caliber sniper rifle, to cover the soccer field. Then they scattered the others around the building, setting up a tight defense.

At 1700 hours, with the sun dipping lower in the west, Sandy's radio squawked again, and the pilot of the Spectre he had seen earlier out at the airstrip came on the air. "Tell us what you need," the pilot said. "We're ready to play."

The Spectre could put a bullet on every inch of a soccer field in a matter of seconds. Sandy asked him to stand by. A few minutes later, mortar rounds hit the field and started creeping toward their position—*boom, Boom, BOOM*—the gunner was searching for the range. Sandy got on the radio.

"Spectre 10. Check to the west and find that mortar position. He's about to make us real uncomfortable."

"Wilco, Hawk. Out."

More thuds. Black smoke. *Ziiip. Thuump. Ziip. Thuuump. Ziip. THUUUMP.* And then a tremendous roar of voices as hundreds of Somali irregulars firing RPGs and AK-47s came steamrolling at the American position.

But when the gunmen reached Atkinson's body, the Spectre suddenly loomed up, a monster flanked by smaller choppers. All the birds opened fire at the same time. As Sandy watched, the mob of advancing Somalis disintegrated. Arms, legs, heads flew through the air, limbs torn from their bodies, chunks of bodies torn from their limbs, a tornado splashed with blood and brains and buzzing with chips of bone.

When the firing died down, nothing was left of Atkinson's body, not even his dog tags. And not much was left of the Somalis. The gunfire had minced everything on the street.

"Yell if you need our services further," the Spectre pilot radioed. "And scratch one mortar. They had it up in a hut. Marked it with a Red Cross. Those boys must have studied with the Viet Cong."

The moon wouldn't rise until well past midnight. Up on the roof, Caldwell and Perkins went through the crates searching for strobe lights. Perkins looked up and shrugged.

"Ain't no pulsers here, Nate."

"Hot pot time, man," Caldwell said, remembering an old night-fighting trick the two used defending CIDG camps in the Highlands. "Think you can get up the fucking mixings?"

When Perkins got back, they mixed oil and gas with the sand they had stored on the roof to fight fires. Then they poured the concoction into cans, setting one fire pot in each corner of the roof. In the center, they arranged a movable line of pots shaped like an arrow. When night fell, they could light the pots and move the arrow to point in the direction of any attack, as if it were a compass needle. The arrow would guide the Spectre in to erase anyone crazy enough to sneak out of his mud hut.

Overhead, the gunships were circling like condors. Every now and then one of them would swoop down and rake an enemy position, or the Spectre would let go a long tongue of flame.

GAAAAARAAAAH, GAAAAARAAAAH. The rounds sizzled like dragon's breath, ripping into the targets, bathing them in fire.

The Somalis fought like men without memories. Whenever their harassing fire seemed to die down, it would erupt again from another direction.

At 1730 hours, an RPG round landed directly on Gomez's position, blowing off a leg and half his face and slightly wounding three of the Delta warriors. Doc Reeves came running up and found the reporter bent over Gomez. Her white tee shirt was spattered with bright red arterial blood. She had her thumb pressed hard on his femoral artery.

"Where'd you learn how to do that?"

"My dad's a surgeon. Taught me ER stuff."

The medic moved in beside her and started putting on a tourniquet. But they were too late to help Gomez. His eyes rolled up, he coughed blood and died.

"Shit," she murmured, cradling him in her arms. "Shit, shit, shit."

After Doc Reeves patched up the Delta warriors, they rolled Gomez in a poncho and stretched his body out gently on the roof. He had managed to stay alive only three hours longer than Atkinson.

At dusk, a 75-millimeter recoilless rifle mounted in a banged-up pickup rolled into a firing position behind a wall at the end of the avenue. The gunner got off two rounds that thumped into the building between the first and second floors.

"Dickhead," Caldwell muttered. "No marksmanship medals today." Grabbing a Viper-AT-4 anti-tank weapon, he rested it on the top of the balustrade, took time aiming slowly and blew the vehicle away with one round.

"How'd that grab, Dan?" he yelled, slapping the roof.

"Do it, Nate. You're the man."

"Deadeye Dick and my gun is quick," Caldwell shouted back. "Come and get it."

Out in the gathering darkness, no one took up his challenge.

An hour later, night came thumping down over the battlefield. Through night-vision scopes, the Delta snipers on the roofs watched the Somalis skittering around like green bugs in a black bottle, but they held their fire. The Americans were outnumbered by at least three hundred to one, but they could see in the dark and they meant to keep that advantage a surprise. The order from Perkins was not to open up unless there was a full-scale attack.

Half an hour before midnight, on the far side of the soccer field, the snipers saw at least five hundred men lining up in three columns. Some were carrying ladders and grappling hooks, others were pushing large trucks toward the building. To the south of the building, a smaller group of gunmen was heading for the rear door where the trainees had slunk away. Caldwell got on his walkie-talkie. "Better get up here, Captain. Shit is about to happen."

Sandy left the vault and ran to the roof. The air was cooler, and the wind had come up, making it easier to think. He squatted next to Caldwell, who pointed at the two Somali concentrations. One was clearly a diversion. They would hit first from the south, hoping to draw the defenders to the rear of the building, then hit the front with their main attack. So those recoilless-rifle rounds earlier in the day hadn't gone wild. Abu Bakar was poking a new door in the place.

Santana was right. It had to be Little Brother down in the vault. Only Abu Bakar would have the brains to dope out this line of attack.

The first thing they had to do was clobber the diversionary force with 81-millimeter white phosphorus and HE rounds. Sandy ordered his snipers to concentrate on leaders, then got back on the radio.

"Spectre, this is Hawk," he said. "Got a juicy target for you. We're ready to laze it now."

"Okay," the pilot called back. "Rope."

From the roof, one of the Delta warriors pointed a laser beam straight up into the darkness and began to wave it. Overhead, the Spectre's infrared TV instantly picked up the beam.

"Sparkle," the pilot called out.

The Delta grunt lowered the beam to the target. At first it looked like a *Star Wars* light saber. Then the grunt wobbled it so that on the gunship's NV gear, it would make the target stand out against other light sources.

"Visual, Hawk. Got your laze. We're good to go. Let me know when you want us to burn 'em."

Sandy counted the seconds ticking off while Caldwell pointed his arrow to the line of the main attack and lit it.

The Somalis began their diversion. On the southern flank, a tremendous noise began. Before the advancing Somalis made it halfway across the street, whining shrapnel from the mortar rounds and long bursts of machine gun fire sliced and diced the diversion. Then a roar came from the wadi as the defense line of claymores started to explode. No longer empty now, the soccer field was full of screaming gunmen launching the main attack.

"Zap 'em," Sandy said into his radio.

The sky exploded in streaks of red tracers. The Spectre's miniguns scourged the open field. There was no place to hide. Hundreds of men went down. They screamed again, this time quivering, drowning in their own blood. Only a few survived to run forward with their ladders and grappling hooks. They were still 20 feet away from the walls when the Americans on the first floor and roof opened up and smoked them.

Now, from beyond the wadi, two long streams of machine gun fire scoured the roof. One of the Delta weapons men went down.

"Medic, medic."

A gurgle more than a cry. Doc Reeves ducked across the roof. The man had a sucking chest wound, but before the medic could do anything for him, his lungs rattled and his eyes turned to glass. Two more Delta defenders were slumped face forward in black pools of blood. Cursing silently, Doc Reeves turned them over. They were gone too. Nothing in his bag could pump life into a corpse.

He looked up and saw the photographer pulling an M-4 out from under one of the bodies. "You know how to use that thing?"

"Yeah, I know how to use it, mate. Four years in the Rhodesian scouts."

Caldwell heard the medic and the photographer whispering and inched over. He saw the M-4.

"You like killing black people, white boy?" he said.

"Only when they're hassling me, Sarge. Or maybe trying to grease you."

Caldwell guffawed.

Across the roof, Perkins was hopping up and down trying to stamp out a fire touched off by an incoming round. Caldwell loped over to him, ripped open a sandbag with his trench knife and began pouring sand on the blaze. "Dance, 'Steely Dan,' " he shouted. "You in the 'Dish, and it's boilin' over, man."

The machine gun chattered again. This time the Spectre whirled around and raked the wadi. On all flanks, the attack stopped as quickly as it had started. To the south, the wounded screamed in the darkness. On the soccer field there was only silence.

Perkins looked down and saw that a bullet ricochet had sliced open his leg. He asked Caldwell to wrap a bandage around the wound. He didn't bother to hit the aid station. When the bleeding stopped, he limped off to check the mortar crew. "Steely Dan," Caldwell muttered. "You are one hard-core dude."

Down in the aid station, Doc Reeves and Doc Carter were working frantically on the wounded. Shrapnel had hit one Delta warrior in the face; an eyeball was hanging weirdly from its socket. Just as they got the IV going and the blood starting into him, he groaned once and died. "Five minutes," Carter muttered. "Five fucking minutes more and we'da saved him. Saved him, man. I know we'da saved him."

Tears streamed down his cheeks. Doc Reeves shrugged.

"I've known the dude for five years. With that face, he wouldn'ta wanted to be saved."

For the next two and a half hours, everything was quiet.

Sandy returned to the vault. It was still two hours before sunup. Rushman wasn't any help. If they waited for the Marines, they'd be lucky to wind up in Arlington National Cemetery. A few more hours and Abu Bakar's men would be dragging their bodies through the streets. Feeding them to his junkyard dogs. Photo opportunity for the media. He did a few quick calculations and told the Professor to raise Harrison on the Sabre.

"Lion 6, this is Hawk. Let's finish this thing. At 0500, send me four big birds. Bird one picks up wounded personnel. Bird two the hostages. Bird three pulls out the KIA and the gear— we'll put them in a cargo net. The trail chopper can extract the rear detachment. We'll blow anything we can't take out."

"Roger that, Hawk. Good go-to-hell plan."

"Christ, I hope so. Also request you do a slicky slicky on the bad guys twenty minutes before we start doing our thing. Put a shitload of fire on Abu Bakar's headquarters over beyond the market. Run a few fake helicopter insertions. A little Sun Tzu. Noise in the East, attack in the West."

"Wilco. Not bad for a West Pointer, Hawk. The Zoo was quite a guy. Southern China, right?"

Sandy laughed. Only Harrison could make Sun Tzu a good ole boy.

On the roof, Abbie piled half a dozen more sandbags around the antenna of the sat phone, then leaned back against them breathing hard. She had a world-beat scoop. She was in the right place at the right time, she'd never do city council meetings again. Let Doctor Dad and all her brothers suck on that one. The day she'd left for Africa, Dr. Mancini had congratulated her for moving up from the idiotic to the insane. "Shut up, Dad," she whispered to herself. Don't let him sneak up on you now.

Then she remembered the dying soldier's face.

Her father and brother had the skill to save lives. The best she could do was act as a witness to death.

It wasn't enough.

Nothing she could do would ever be enough.

ELEVEN

The stars had come out over the battlefield. The shooting had stopped, but the moon was still down. Perkins was propped up against a sandbag, thinking.

"Hey, Nate," he whispered to Caldwell. The sergeant had just returned from checking the perimeter. "How long've you known Captain Caine?"

" 'Bout a year. Since he took over the team."

"He any kin to Alexander and J. P. Caine?"

"Papa and granddaddy."

"Yeah, figures."

Landing on the roof had been like looking into the past. The young captain's face had startled him. He looked like someone nearly thirty years dead.

"I knew his dad in I Corps, Nate. Saved my ass once near Lang Vei."

"That right?"

"My first tour in the Nam, he was a lieutenant on my A-Team. I was pulling point on a recon patrol and walked right into an NVA ambush. That's how I got this."

Perkins raised his scarred arm.

"The motherfuckers were hugging the belt, keeping me alive so they could chop up the rest of the patrol. If Wolf hadn't charged them all by his lonesome and pulled my ass out, I wouldn't be here saving your black ass. I didn't know he had a kid. The captain looks just like him."

"Well, if I was you I wouldn't bring it up."

"Why not?"

"The captain ain't no family man. Got a lot of baggage."

"What're you telling me, Nate? The kid's got it. You think the Caines got another four-star there?"

"I don't know, man. Great soldier. But sometimes, looks to me he wants to get his ass tossed out. You ever hear about the Night of the Jackasses? Up at the Point?"

"I didn't know they only came out at night."

"We're talkin' just one night, man. Spring of Caine's last year. He's lookin' to outdo Douglas fuckin' MacArthur, man. Same kind of shit as when MacArthur put a reveille cannon up on top of Pershing Barracks. Five floors up. Took the Corps of Engineers two weeks to get it down.

"Anyway, this kid Caine beat him."

"What'd he do?"

"The way I heard it, he kidnapped the mules—you know, the West Point mascots—and put 'em on top of Pershing Barracks. Perfect mission. Had one team of strikers do the snatch, one team of engineers to build a pulley hoist and a knock-down pen. Took 'em a week to smuggle the parts into the barracks and hide 'em.

"Night of the raid, the strikers hit the stable, engineers set up the rig. Snatched Traveller, Trooper and Ranger, all three big motherfuckers, man. The engineers lowered a girdle, pulled those big suckers up on the roof. Took maybe seven minutes.

"Sunup, Sandy pulls the muzzles off and he and his guys rappel down the back of the barracks. Three jackasses start brayin'. Whole fuckin' Point woke up. Cracked up."

"He get away?"

"No. Candy-assed little plebe ratted him out. Inquiry, hearing, whole nine yards."

"So why's his sorry ass up here with us tonight?"

"That's my point, man. He was an accident lookin' to happen—half the Point's calling him the Caine Mutiny, the other half's callin' him the Hawk 'cause he had such sharp eyes for tactics. Commandant didn't want to lose a man like that. Busted him to private, gave him a bunch of demerits, let him walk it off."

Nate looked out into the darkness. "Didn't change him any.

He's always right there on the edge. A lotta times he just doesn't give a shit. There's this time we're doin' an exercise down in Panama. The mission's to build an assault airstrip. Like whack the jungle down with machetes. So we cut the shit out of everything and when we're finished, the Air Force comes in to pick us up."

"What's your point now, man?"

"Fuck you, I'm gettin' there. The captain tells us all to strip, except for our boots and our weapons. When the aircraft stops at the end of the strip, we come out of the jungle and stand there buck naked. Eleven dicks at dress right dress, present arms. Salutin' the Air Force. The crew was blown out, man. Laughed so hard the plane shook."

"You're shitting me."

"No way, man. Story was the hit of the week when we got back to Bragg. Until it got to the Commanding General. This new Army, you even fart in the barracks you're out. If J. P. Caine wasn't the captain's granddad, he'd been out on his ass right then. Weird thing, he seemed almost relieved. Like gettin' canned wouldn't be such a bad thing. Might solve some shit."

"What shit?"

"You ever hear those stories about ODA 351? Like, after you left?"

Caldwell picked up another M-4 magazine and started to reload it.

"Everybody greased except Captain Taylor?" Perkins said.

"Yeah, right. So some people say it was Lieutenant Caine's fault. Maybe the kid thinks so, too. Fuck it, man, I don't know."

Caldwell turned away. Plenty of time, Perkins thought to himself. Taking out an old toothbrush, he cleaned the bolt of his weapon. Then he stuffed a pinch of snuff under his lip and looked up at the stars.

★　　★　　★

At 0400 hours, Sandy made the rounds again. He told the men they'd be back at the airstrip in time for a hot breakfast. Before he left, he asked Perkins, Caldwell, and Strunk to meet him in the vault in ten minutes so they could chalk-talk the pullout. Caldwell and Perkins set off around the perimeter to reinforce the message.

"We ain't running, we're attacking to the rear," Perkins said to Strunk.

Caldwell shook his head. "Hey, man, since when did *you* start stealing lines from the Marines?"

Thirty minutes later, the world fell in on them.

The motion detectors went off, but before anyone could respond, the trip flares shot into the sky. A huge explosion rocked the first-floor west wall near Wilson and Hassan's position. Two enormous holes opened up. Concrete, splinters and debris shot across the room like grapeshot, and a dozen Somali sappers roared through the holes, firing as they came. Before either of the Americans could raise their weapons, the hot barrage of automatic fire cut Hassan apart—his body fell on the floor like a child's puzzle—and wasted Wilson.

The explosion knocked Sandy and Caldwell, Perkins, Strunk, and the Professor to the vault floor. Strunk stayed down, crushed under a slab of broken concrete. Sandy shook himself off and charged, firing his MP-5. *Once more, dear friends.* Only this time it was Somalis pouring through the breech. Figure that, Prince Hal.

Perkins was right behind him blasting with an M-4.

The fighting was close, dirty, hand-to-hand. Caldwell took a point-blank shot into the front of his Kevlar helmet. Sinking to his knees, dazed, he zapped the Somali who had fired at him. For a moment, he knelt there, wagging his head like a shell-shocked sheepdog, saying, "Damn, damn, damn." Then he rose and waded back into the fight.

From one of the holes a grenade arced in, bouncing slowly toward Sandy and Perkins. For a split second, they both froze. There was the sound of metal rolling on wood. Then Sandy reached down like a shortstop and flipped the grenade out through the crater in the wall. It exploded on the heels of the fleeing sappers.

"Jesus Christ, Captain," Perkins said quietly. "You fight just like your old man."

A torrent of adrenaline shot through Sandy's body. His heart was pounding and his mouth went dry. He spun around and pointed the MP-5 at Perkins's face. For one crazy second Perkins thought the captain was going to waste him.

"Fuck that, Sergeant. My old man was a loser who got himself killed. And if you don't quit running your mouth, same thing's going to happen to us."

"Easy, Captain."

"Can it, Sergeant."

"Okay, skipper," Perkins said. With a finger, he pushed the barrel of the captain's submachine gun to one side. "You organize the PZ and I'll clean up down here."

Sandy lowered the MP-5.

He could hear gunfire somewhere above him. As the retreating Somalis crossed the dry wadi, two Delta warriors shooting from a window were picking them off like deer bounding through an open field.

Sandy started walking away. From over his shoulder, he heard Perkins's voice following him.

"See you on the roof at 0500, Captain. When we get back, let's have a beer. We called him Wolf. Coupla other things about your daddy you maybe ought to know."

★   ★   ★

Caldwell was on the roof when Sandy got there at 0450. The sergeant said, "You feelin' lucky, Captain? Five-card stud? Still time before the birds come in for a few hands."

Perkins was sending up the dead: Wilson, Strunk and Hassan, all killed during the sapper attack. With Gomez and Atkinson, that made five. Then Sandy saw Doc Carter bundled in a poncho. Six warriors down from the A-Team, four from Delta.

Ten men.

Down the rathole.

For nothing.

At 0455, he heard the roar of gunfire to the north beyond the Bakar Market. Long tongues of flame from the Spectre were licking down toward Abu Bakar's underground command bunker. Sandy could hear the rumbling explosions of rockets and cannons. He looked through his night-vision gear and saw hundreds of gunmen running toward the sound of the guns.

At 0500, the first Black Hawks reported they were three minutes out. Sandy turned to Caldwell. "Round up the wounded and the journalists. I want them out first." A few minutes later, the sergeant came back, the reporter barking at his heels.

"I'm not ready to leave yet," Abbie said hotly. "You still haven't told me what the hell is going on."

"That's right, and I'm not going to."

"I'm staying."

"No, you're not, lady. Show's over."

The photographer walked over, put his hands on her shoulders. "Come on, Abbie," he said. "We have what we came for. I gotta get the pictures back. Julian's gonna eat lunch on this one all over town."

"Oh, screw you, Kurt."

The chopper fluttered down; she shook off Kurt's arm as she crawled aboard. After Sandy and Caldwell helped the Professor and Mayemura load the wounded into the cargo bay, the first Black Hawk lifted off. The second was inbound when General Rushman came up on the radio.

"Hawk 6, this is Thundering Eagle. Where are those hostages?"

"On the way, sir. I sent our wounded out on the first bird."

The news went down badly with General Rushman. "That was a mistake, mister," he shouted. "I need those hostages. The wounded would have kept."

"Some of them were hit pretty bad, sir."

General Rushman brushed it away. "Put the hostages on the next bird, Captain. That's an order. And you come with them. Don't buck me." The voice disgusted him, the order disgusted him, the whole fucking operation disgusted him. But there was nothing he could do. At least he'd gotten the wounded out first.

He clapped Perkins on the shoulder. "I'm out of here, Sarge." He paused. "Look, I'd really like to have that beer tonight."

As Sandy's Black Hawk came down, Perkins and his four-man rear guard and the gunships laid down a blistering wall of fire to cover the withdrawal. Then the bird wheeled and headed for the airstrip. Sandy leaned back and closed his eyes.

"Captain, you're bleeding."

The voice came from a Delta trooper sitting next to him. A large splotch of blood was spreading across Sandy's shirt. He hadn't felt anything during the fight. He tore open the shirt and felt blood on his fingertips. A trickle was running down his chest. A piece of shrapnel no bigger than a small finishing nail had passed through one of his dog tags and Melba's Saint Christopher medal. The dog tag and the medal were nailed to his chest. The shield of Saint Christopher had kept the needle of shrapnel from penetrating his heart. He put his face in his hands. *Gracias, tiita.*

★   ★   ★

The last bird dropped down and picked up the cargo net like an eagle snagging a salmon. Perkins hit a detonator switch. As he and his men hauled ass into the bird, the bottom floor of police headquarters exploded.

Spectre and the other gunships scorched the earth with covering fire. Legs dangling out the chopper door, Perkins watched the ground recede. The extraction was flawless.

He didn't hear the RPG round that caught him in the chest and blew him back into the cargo compartment. A dud. Looking down, he saw the stabilizer sticking out below his ribs. There was no pain. Reaching back he felt the blunt nose pushing through under his shoulder. Strange. He felt himself starting to drop through blackness. Like a night jump. "Lieutenant Caine," he mumbled. "Wolf, where are you?"

*   *   *

At the airstrip, Sandy ordered Caldwell to take the hostages to General Rushman's trailer.

"General's gonna want to see you, Captain."

"Fuck him."

Caldwell saluted, pushed the two blindfolded prisoners into a Humvee driven by an MP and took off. A few minutes later, the last Black Hawk, flying low and trailing smoke, dropped hard on the airstrip. Sandy threw off his body armor and started to run.

Perkins was lying on the floor of the chopper. His chest was covered with blood. His eyes were fixed on the cabin bulkhead. In his hand, he held an empty can of snuff.

TWELVE

Indian summer in Washington. The grass on the parade field at Fort Myer still as green as the fairways at Burning Tree Country Club, the trees along Jackson Avenue turning to gold.

In the warm yellow light of the afternoon sun, the Stars and Stripes drifted in the languid October breeze. From the towering white flagstaff, a long shadow pointed like a finger to four rifle companies marching onto the parade field in full dress blues. The Third United States Infantry Regiment. The Old Guard.

In the reviewing stand, two dozen green metal chairs were arranged in three lines behind a neatly lettered sign that read FAMILY AND HONORED GUESTS.

At five minutes to four, General John Pershing Caine made his way to the stand, passing through a large crowd of military officers, wives and VIPs. Gus Buell, once General Caine's executive officer and still his chess partner, was standing among them, his face glowing from the three martinis he had downed at lunch.

The General was well into his seventies, lean, remote, not the sort of older man people call fatherly. In a city where power players so often slump to disguise their sucker punch, his ramrod bearing made him look taller than his five-feet-nine-inch frame. His eyes were blue, intense, impatient; his silver hair was still full.

The General was fit, rich and independent, above politics. Unlike so many of his old friends, he didn't need money, so he had not been drawn into the mire of the defense lobby. He had chosen instead to serve on advisory boards and the occasional blue ribbon panel on national security. Years of these good works had made him a regular visitor in the offices of the Secretary of Defense, the military chiefs of staff, the Director of the CIA and the National Security Advisor. He had met President Wilton when Wilton was still a green first-term congressman looking for honest advice.

Normally the General wore a dark business suit, but for this occasion he had put on his Army greens: four stars stood out on his shoulders, and nine rows of ribbons from World War II, Korea and Vietnam rode high on his chest. As he walked up, a platoon of colonels and one-stars who knew more about selling weapons systems on the Hill than leading men on killing fields saluted and made room for him to pass.

His uniform stood out from the off-the-rack stuff all around him. It came from Thompson and Squires, the Savile Row tailors who did his business suits. They also cut the riding breeches he wore every afternoon during his ritual daily session with Black Jack, his Morgan stallion.

The woman with the General didn't look like anyone from horse country. She was not quite five feet tall and she almost had to run to keep up with him. She was not so much plump as sturdy, in the way of Central American Indians. Her jet-black hair was threaded with silver, her skin, still smooth around the corners of her dark eyes, was nut brown. She was wearing a bright blue wool coat over a yellow dress embroidered with tropical red flowers.

Melba Casadero, daughter of a fisherman, a Marxist, dead long ago in Honduras, was the General's housekeeper. To her mind, all revolutionaries were demented fools and the soldiers who killed them, animals. But she had come to look on the General as an exception, an odd but acceptable American king of beasts.

She loved his grandson as if he were her own boy. Her worst fear was that Sandy would die the way her father and brothers had died, like his own father and great-grandfather. Whenever the talk around the General's house in Arlington grew too military or ideological, Melba withdrew to her own room. What did it matter which side a man was on when the guns exploded and you spit blood and cried for your mother?

As they took their seats, the General looked over the row of officers quartered beyond the parade field. A deep sense of satisfaction came over him whenever he found himself at Fort Myer. Something sturdy and earnest about the place. Something decent. It always moved him.

The U.S. Army Band struck up a Sousa march, and the guard of honor began to advance across the parade field, polished brass gleaming like burnished gold. The General took out his dark glasses and settled in his chair. In precise ranks, rifles at right shoulder arms, Bravo, Charlie, Delta and Echo companies came down the field toward him in all their glory, the taps on black patent leather shoes adding thunder to the sound of marching feet.

One by one each of the four companies peeled off and marched to their positions in front of the assembled guests. Between Charlie and Delta companies, the colors of the nation and the Army rippled through the autumn haze.

Out front, the Commander of Troops studied the formation, then nodded to his adjutant.

"Preeeesent H'arms," the adjutant bellowed.

CRAAAAACK.

The sound reminded the General of a lightning bolt. The members of the Old Guard had metal wedges sewn into pockets in the palms of their white gloves to double the noise when they slapped their rifles.

The adjutant shouted again.

"Order H'arms!"

CRAAAACK.

For thirty years General Caine had waited for this moment. The pleasure he felt was sharp, fierce, like standing over the fallen on a battlefield, breathing in the grace of being alive. The boy had acquitted himself well. Extremely well. Jack Church was about to pin the Distinguished Service Cross on him. For the Caines, West Point had always been their finishing school. Duty, Honor, Country was bred into their bones. But before Sandy, no Caine had ever gotten his first award for valor straight from the Army Chief of Staff.

"Persons to be decorated, front and center, H'arch!"

A drum roll, a burst of brass from the Army band. Sandy and three of the four survivors from his A-Team executed a column left and marched to the reviewing stand.

"Sir, the persons to be decorated and the colors are present."

As the Commander of Troops made his report, Melba leaned over toward the General. "He looks just like the pictures of his father," she said, beaming. Everyone on the platform could hear her. The General nodded patiently, wishing she'd had the presence of mind to whisper. But he said nothing. The boy looked good. Damn good.

The Commander of Troops snapped a salute to General Jackson Church. What was left of the A-Team stood face-to-face with the man whose job put him four steps down from President Wilton in the chain of command that had gotten the rest of them killed or wounded.

The band broke into "The Star-Spangled Banner," and everyone in the crowd stood up as General Church moved forward. One step to the Chief's rear and exactly 15 inches to his left, the sergeant major assisting him carried a tray of medals.

The strong voice of the lieutenant acting as narrator came over the public address system:

"Attention to Orders. General Order Number 51. Department of the United States Army. The Distinguished Service Cross is awarded to . . . Caine, Alexander Grant, 844-66-0575, Captain, Special Forces, United States Army, August 21 to 22, 1993, Somalia. For extraordinary heroism in connection with military operations involving conflict with an armed hostile force in Mogadishu. With total disregard for his own safety . . ."

Rolling across Summerall Field, the battle honors echoed off the brick barracks of the Old Guard as the narrator recited the details of the firefight. Then the Chief of Staff pinned a blue ribbon with an attached cross to Sandy's chest. Again the lieutenant's voice boomed like a howitzer:

"Caldwell, Nathan Preston, 748-49-7772, Master Sergeant, Special Forces, United States Army. His extraordinary heroism and devotion to duty reflect great credit upon himself, his unit and the United States Army."

General Church was shorter than Caldwell; he had to reach up to pin the DSC on the sergeant's green tunic. Caldwell looked pleased. The public address system made a high-pitched *EEEP*. The narrator, breaking through the static, said:

"Perkins, Daniel, 886-47-0705, Sergeant Major, Special Forces, United States Army. Distinguished Service Cross— posthumous."

At the announcement, a ripple of surprise ran through the military and political guests. The review was to honor the living heroes of Mogadishu. With general elections not so far over the horizon, the dead were already a political embarrassment. Strictly according to regulations, as well as what passed for good political judgment, the right way to honor Sergeant Perkins was quietly, privately. The White House Chief of Staff looked at the National Security Advisor, who looked at the Secretary of Defense, who held his hands palms up and shrugged.

Rising from a green chair in the first row, a tall young woman stepped down the stairs to the parade ground, her short, butter-blonde hair bobbing slightly as she moved. Her legs were bare and tan, and her Blahniks were patent leather black and quite high. Her name was Carrie Perkins. A gray silk jersey dress clung to her tightly, stopping several inches above her knees. Shining in the sunlight, her hair and pale gray eyes obviously transfixed General Church. For a moment, it looked as if he were considering pinning the medal on her chest. Pulling himself together, he handed her a small flat blue box.

"Your father was a brave man," he said, adding inanely. "He would have been proud of you."

"I'm the one who is proud, General," Carrie Perkins replied, flashing "thank you" and "drop dead" in equal parts. Taking the box in one hand, she pressed it against her breast as she returned to her seat.

More flourishes from the band as General Church pinned Silver Stars on Mayemura and Santana. Kruger was still in Walter Reed Hospital with a leg full of pins, recovering from the burn grafts. Earlier that morning, the Chief had gone to the hospital. Kruger's wife, Sigrund, had stood by his bed while Church pinned the Silver Star on his pajama pocket.

After the last award, Sandy said, "Right, H'ace. Forward, H'arch," and the four warriors marched back to their places. The Chief stepped forward, the Commander of Troops bellowed, "Pass in review," as the third herd moved down the field. When the American flag floated by, everyone stood, soldiers saluting, civilians holding their hands over their hearts. As Echo Company passed in review, the band broke into "The Caissons Go Rolling Along."

In the last rays of sunlight, the guests and dignitaries rose, exchanging small talk. Working through the crowd, Sandy came up to the General and Melba. Bracing like a plebe, he snapped a salute. The General's hand shot to the brim of his cap.

"Well done, Captain," he said. He sounded more like a tac officer at West Point than a proud grandfather. But then he slapped Sandy on the back. "Damn good job. I'm proud of you, son."

Sandy saluted again, and as if he had suddenly remembered something, wheeled around, took three quick steps forward and kissed Melba on the cheek. Then he was gone.

The General looked across the crowd until he spotted Gus Buell. Buell's suit jacket was unbuttoned. A thin band of white lining could be seen where his paunch had turned the waist of his trousers over his belt. Buell had his hand up, flashing a V for victory.

From the first day, before the body bags were zipped in Lang Vei, they had both known what had to be done. For twenty-seven years they had done it, done the right thing.

Now it was over.

For just an instant, the General allowed the possibility to enter his mind. Then, he felt a surge of revulsion welling up inside him like black blood oozing from a severed vein.

It would never be over.

THIRTEEN

At the same moment, on the other side of the Potomac, a vintage silver Porsche purred out of the garage beneath the Dirkson Senate Office Building. Senator Taylor was running late. The Senate Armed Services Committee hearings on the F-44 fighter had dragged on past four. When he had seen that he would miss Sandy's award ceremony, he had looked restlessly at his watch. As usual, Patrice had materialized out of nowhere "It's an eight-billion-dollar contract, Senator," he had whispered. "Stop worrying. I'll get you there in time."

So Senator Taylor had relaxed. Sandy's parade would be different, of course, but he was no fan of awards ceremonies. Half the medals the Pentagon sowed among its favorites were phony, like the senior clerk's good conduct medal they were now handing out to desk officers, mocking up the ribbon to make it look like the Silver Star. And when a real one came along, the narrators read from their scripts and never knew what hell the winner had seen. Absently, he raised his hand to touch the rosette. They never knew. No one knew.

Patrice aimed the Porsche down Independence Avenue and made a hard left onto the approach to the Fourteenth Street Bridge. Threading his way through the gathering rush-hour traffic, he crossed the river, drove past the Pentagon and turned into Fort Myer. He was wearing Gaultier sunglasses and a good Versace knock-off in a taupe color that matched the fall foliage.

Looking over at Pat, Senator Taylor allowed himself a fond smile. You could tell he'd never lived on a military base. Ten minutes in boot camp would have killed him.

Slipping by the carefully manicured lawns of the officers quarters, the Porsche came to a stop under the portico of the Officers Club.

Patrice checked his instruments. The readout on the digital clock said 4:50 P.M. "Plenty of time for a drop by."

"You park the car," Senator Taylor said, picking up the attaché case from the seat beside him. Inside it were the latest R and D reports of the F-44. Some problems in there. He'd have to look them over again tonight.

Opening the door, he unfolded his lanky frame and eased out of the bucket seat. As he passed under the silver portico, he slightly favored his right leg.

Seven titanium pins held the shattered bones together, but the rest of him was perfectly fit. Before breakfast each morning, he did one hundred laps in the Senate pool. Three days a week, he followed his swim with twenty minutes of weight lifting in the Senate gym. His hair was still dark. His voice was surprisingly low. To hear him better, women unconsciously leaned toward him.

He had a gray Borsolino in his right hand as he reached the door. The hat was a prop, a tribute to his grandfather, Jefferson Kenefick, mayor of Cincinnati, poker crony of Harry Truman, "the mug in the beat-up fedora," as the newspapers affectionately called him. The senator had resurrected the symbol when he entered politics. People remembered the hat, liked it. It helped neutralize the surprise Democrats felt when he told them he was a Republican.

At the door, the NCO stiffened to attention and saluted when he saw the blue rosette. Inside, the familiar feel of the green carpet underfoot gave him a momentary twinge of nostalgia. After the MOH, the Pentagon had wanted to show him off. For two years he had served as aide to the Commanding General of the Military District of Washington, headquartered at Fort Myer.

The introduction to Washington had been instructive. After the Tet Offensive, he had watched from the Pentagon while the White House and the politicians on the Hill—the same crowd that had been so eager to pass the Tonkin Gulf Resolution and go to war—cut and ran. And if twelve years in Congress had taught him anything, it was a sure bet they'd do the same damn thing the next time they got a chance.

He could hear the friendly murmur of the reception drifting down the stairs. Find the General first, he thought. Make amends. They'd known each other for more than forty years, from the time he was just skinny Jeff Taylor, Alex Caine's best friend. He idolized the General, a man of action, uncompromising on matters of principle, so different from his own diplomatic father, always an art-of-the-possible man, always a trimmer.

He was a year older than Alex, Sandy's dad. The General's son had trotted amiably after him through Andover, then West Point and finally into Special Forces, and ODA 351 until a foggy morning up in I Corps when North Vietnamese Regulars came screaming through the wire.

Including Lieutenant Alexander Caine. Including Captain Jefferson Taylor.

That was the way it had been until Captain Taylor woke up three days later at the 121st Evacuation Hospital in Nha Trang to discover that he alone was still alive and that General William Westmoreland was flying up to pin an interim DSC on his chest. The Medal of Honor would come later.

Shaking off the memory, he looked up at the full-length portrait of George Patton guarding the doors. It was the George Patton Officers Club now. More Americans recognize George Patton than George Washington, he reflected. That's what a good movie will do for you.

He frowned. Patton Syndrome. For fifty years the United States had been obsessed with war. Obsessed with preparing for it, obsessed with protesting it, obsessed with everything but understanding it, facing its consequences, getting better at it. What was it the Bible said: The poor are always with us? Yes. And soldiers. And the bastards who didn't give a damn about sacrificing them. After the individual soldier crossed the line of departure, after the guns opened up, there wasn't a damn bit of difference between the warmakers and the peacemakers. On any given day, either or both could get you blown away.

Down the corridor, the edgy noise of clinking glasses and power talk drew him toward the Koran Room. It sounded as if the Army had invited half of Washington to the reception. An unusual honor for one captain and four sergeants. Wilton wasn't the only one playing games. Mogadishu had been a classic rat fuck and the Army was out in force to redeem it.

The double doors were open. To his relief he saw the shag end of a line in front of the coat room. He was late but not beyond redemption. As he gave the Borsolino and the attaché case to the attendant, he spotted the General beyond the buffet table talking to General Church. The Chief of Staff had served as a junior aide when the General was the four-star Commanding General of CONARC in Virginia. Now they had eight stars between them, but Senator Taylor knew the younger man still felt like a captain in front of General Caine.

He ordered a cranberry juice spritzer from the bar and walked over to them. "Sorry I'm late, General Caine." He tried to make the apology sound contrite without actually cringing. "The chairman kept the F-44 hearings going right up to the last feed for the evening news and I couldn't sneak away."

"Then, of course, it couldn't be helped," the General replied evenly. "Sandy will be glad to see you."

General Church finished the scotch in his hand and signaled a passing waiter to bring him another. "Good to see you, Senator," he said. "I was just telling General Caine that the operation may have been a disaster but the ceremony today has turned into a public relations dream. Sandy looks like a young Robert Redford. His men are heroes right out of central casting. We're going to score big time."

Good Lord, Senator Taylor thought to himself. How much of this crap would the old man tolerate? "Not that we deserve it," General Church nattered on. "They went nuts up the road when Sandy refused to accept the DSC because his men were getting Bronze Stars. He said give him the same thing."

Excluding himself from the faceless "they," the Chief of Staff waved his free hand in the general direction of the White House. "The citation had already been drawn up and leaked to the *Washington Chronicle*. We had to get those goddamn body bags off the front page. And the hero was saying, 'No way.' If you hadn't given us a hand, we would have been deader than the Commander in Chief's balls."

Senator Taylor shrugged. Disrespect for the President had started among the enlisted men. Obviously, it had shot up as far as it could go. "I'm up there to help, Jack."

"We all know that, Senator, but how the hell did you bring him around?"

None of his business, actually. But even Senator Taylor, once the youngest major general in the U.S. Army, didn't sass the

Chief. "He trusts me, Jack. I just told him he *might* be able to get the DSC for Caldwell and Perkins and the Silver Star for the others, but you'd ram a detector up his ass and dispatch him to Kamchatka to clear land mines before you'd go any farther."

The Chief laughed and drained the second scotch.

"That all, Senator?"

"No, sir. Then I called the SecDef and told him if the Army couldn't see its way clear to calling Dan Perkins's name at the ceremony today, I didn't see how I could speak at his son's graduation next spring. St. Albans would have to find itself another mothballed two-star to tell its kids the facts of life."

"Did you also tell him you'd have his job? Until you move over to the Rose Garden."

"Not me, Jack," Senator Taylor said, holding his hand over his heart. "There are limits in this town." After the Mogadishu fiasco, the President had held off on the Bonham nomination. But Patrice had been busy. His private polls were fantastic. On job ratings, the voters gave Wilton a generous benefit of the doubt. But the support was soft. Six out of ten thought Senator Taylor showed more character, greater leadership ability. Patrice was already talking about a "Draft Taylor" campaign.

"However you did it," General Church said, "I want to thank you. Did you see the camera crews out there covering the parade—the enlisted men getting high awards along with their captain? I gotta tell you, not many officers in the Army today would have done what Sandy did. Particularly the Generation Xers. Self-serving bastards. But now the Army's got a new hero. An officer who looks after his men. His guys told CNN and CBS they'd die for him."

The General cleared his throat. "What about the others, Jackson? The ones who didn't come back. Why did they have to die?"

General Church looked stunned. "Sir, I'm not sure I understand—"

"Why was Mogadishu a disaster? Wasn't it planned adequately?"

"I don't fault our planning. We did everything right. But we had the White House all over our backs. It wasn't our idea to put a price on Abu Bakar's head. They don't know the first thing about the military."

"Why didn't you sound off, Jackson? If you'd stopped it, those men would still be alive and we wouldn't be standing here discussing your brilliant media campaign."

General Church reddened.

"With all due respect, General Caine, I don't think you understand the complexities of peacemaking operations."

"Complexities? This looks quite simple to me, Jackson. You didn't do your duty."

Senator Taylor hid a smile. Score one for the General, one for the grunts. He let Church dangle for a minute or two, then started looking for reinforcements: when the General was on a roll, it took a tank task force to restore order.

He saw a full galaxy of stars twinkling on shoulders around the room. Then he spotted Sandy talking to a huge black guy, master sergeant, and a woman, quite pregnant, with a towheaded little boy pulling at her arm. He caught Sandy's eye, nodding imperceptibly at the General. It was an old signal between them. Gently taking the arm of the pregnant woman, Sandy steered her toward the General and the perspiring Chief of Staff, the two NCOs bringing up the rear.

Always the good tactician. "General Church," Sandy said. "You remember Mrs. Kruger?"

"What a pleasure to see you again, Mrs. Kruger," General Church said warmly, more grateful than she would ever know. "And who is this lad with you? I don't think I saw him at the hospital this morning."

She blushed—"This is my little Wieland"—then beamed when Church shook the hand of her five-year-old son.

Sandy kept pouring it on. He nodded to Caldwell, whose DSC hung above his campaign ribbons and badges where General Church had arranged it half an hour earlier. "General Church, General Caine, this is Master Sergeant Nathan Caldwell. Baddest warrior I know."

"At ease, Sergeant," General Church said cheerfully, the two scotches beginning to take hold. "General Caine and I were just talking about your mission. You and your people fought well. The Army is proud of you. Was there any single piece of equipment you didn't have that would have made a difference in how you fought the fight."

Caldwell thought about it for a moment. "Don't make much sense to me that we had more U.S. Army tanks at Waco than we had in the 'Dish, General. A platoon of Abrams tanks would have gotten us out of there in a New York minute."

"My point exactly, Jackson." A look of panic crossed General Church's face. Turning to Mrs. Kruger, he said, "May I show you to a table? Wives of heroes shouldn't have to stand on an important day like today. Especially since they give us more heroes." Oozing charm, he took little Wieland's hand and made his escape.

Following the Chief of Staff's line of retreat with satisfaction, the General shifted his attention to Caldwell. "I've heard a lot about you, Sergeant. All of it good."

"I've heard about you, too, sir. None of it too bad."

The hint of a smile flickered on the General's face; he subdued it. "Anything else, Sergeant?"

"Well, sir, it's a damn shame Perkins isn't here today. He was a good man. The best. He told me he knew your son."

A small vein on the General's temple began to throb. Senator Taylor took a quick step forward. "Who is that amazing-looking young woman over there?" he asked.

Across the room, a waiter was offering a tray of hors d'oeuvres to a very attractive, very bored blonde. "That's Sergeant Major Perkins's daughter," Sandy said. "I want to talk to her about her dad."

"I can see why."

"It's not what you think."

"We should make sure she's worthy, just in case."

"Okay, okay. Just don't give me a hard time."

They walked over to where Carrie Perkins was standing with Eddie and Keiko Mayemura, his wife of one week, and Betty Mayemura, his mother. A clap on the back for Eddie. A few quiet words with Miss Perkins. Then Sandy led all of them back. Senator Taylor smiled. More tactics. Mass forces and overwhelm.

Sandy introduced the Mayemuras. Then he turned to the young woman.

"Senator Taylor has asked to meet you," he said. "It is my duty to warn you that old soldiers never die. He is armed and should be considered extremely dangerous."

"Captain Caine exaggerates, Miss Perkins. I'm completely harmless. May I get you a drink?" He offered her his left arm. Carrie Perkins laughed. "It is my duty to inform *you*, Senator Taylor, that I only advance. I never surrender."

At precisely that moment, Patrice materialized for the second time that afternoon. It was as if he had come up through the maroon carpet. The gossip columns liked to cluck over Senator Taylor as the town's most eligible bachelor. The truth was that while he appreciated a beautiful face, he felt awkward with most women. His chief of staff was usually hovering somewhere guarding his flanks.

Patrice had Julian Lynch in tow with a frizzy redhead Senator Taylor had never seen before. Carrie Perkins took in the black suit and the vintage Gucci scarf at a glance and looked away. The Washington dress code for professional women obviously bored her as much as the official canapés.

"Senator Taylor," Patrice said, "please meet Abigail Mancini, the lady on the roof in Mogadishu, the *Washington Chronicle*'s own woman of the year." For a moment the four of them stood there awkwardly. The redhead's black silk blouse showed just a hint of cleavage below the scarf. She, too, seemed more interested in soldiers than senators. Suddenly Senator Taylor felt old.

"Meet my boss, Julian Lynch," the reporter was saying to Sandy.

"Where's your press pass?" Sandy said abruptly. "I didn't know you were on the list."

"Badges?" Julian Lynch said in a fake Spanish accent. "We don' need no steeenking badges—we're the national press." When they looked at him blankly, he rushed to recover. "General Church gave me a call," he stammered, dropping a name where references to an old John Huston movie couldn't do the job. "He thought we should be here."

"Congratulations, Captain Caine," the reporter said, ignoring her boss. "I see you have a new medal."

"Old news, Miss Mancini. You've already written about it. Why don't you ask Senator Taylor about his Medal of Honor?" Before she could reply, Sandy turned away from her. "Miss Perkins," he said, "your father told me something that surprised me. I'd like to talk to you about it. What about that drink?"

A kiss-off. The senator's eyebrows rose slightly. The redhead's eyes were smoking as Sandy and Miss Perkins walked off, navigating the circles of power eddying around the Koran Room. "I admire your work, Miss Mancini," he said. "You remind me of Gloria Emerson and Dickey Chappelle in Vietnam. They both covered combat as well as a man. Did you know them?"

"I was two years old, Senator."

He cleared his throat, tried again.

"Of course. Please forgive me. But I have been reading your work. It's very impressive. The *Chronicle* is lucky to have you."

"Indeed it is," Julian said. What he offered, he just as quickly took away. "We're sending her to Bosnia this week. Let's hope Somalia wasn't just beginner's luck."

"People tell me you're presidential, Senator Taylor."

"People say lots of things in Washington, Miss Mancini. Maybe you'd like to hear my version?"

She laughed. "Any time." He saw her looking at him, checking him for flaws as confidently as any man sizes up a new woman. Her eyes passed over the rosette as if it didn't register. Perhaps with her, it didn't count.

"What about right now? If you're free for dinner?"

"Be careful," she replied. "I may take you up on that interview."

"I thought that was the point. Shall we go?"

★　　★　　★

Like Sherman through Georgia, the General thought, watching them leave. Shifting his gaze, he looked at the Mayemuras. "You're from Hawaii, I understand. I spent three years there a long time ago."

"Well, aloha, General," Mrs. Mayemura said, winking at him. She was a big woman with black eyes and retouched hair, but she must have been lovely when she was young. Mrs. Mayemura said, "My father owned the Lanai Club in Waikiki. Did you ever go there?"

The formality returned instantly to his voice. "No, Mrs. Mayemura," he replied. "I never had that pleasure."

That was not entirely true. The General had never been through the doors of the Lanai Club, but he knew the name. The Lanai Club was where his daughter-in-law had gone for her daily anesthetic after Alex was killed. He had been furious with her, always knew she was no good. But after the wreck he had them carve a beautiful headstone for her anyway: *Barbara B. Caine, 1942–1967, loving wife of First Lieutenant Alexander Grant Caine, Killed in Action, Lang Vei, Vietnam, 1966*.

Her grave was in a remote cemetery for civilians out beyond the Pali. Next to Alex. After what had happened in the Highlands, he couldn't bring himself to see his son buried in Arlington National Cemetery.

There was no way the Mayemuras could know anything about any of that.

"Too bad you didn't check us out, General Caine. Best fish and pork in the islands. Best mai tais."

To the acute embarrassment of the perfectly turned-out younger woman, Sergeant Mayemura then began to tell the General the best way to dig a luau pit. "Just like a foxhole, sir, but not so deep. You could do it with your entrenching tool."

Sandy had come back with Carrie. He laughed and draped his arm around Mayemura's shoulder. "I doubt that the General has had an entrenching tool in his hand since World War II. I hate to break up a good luau, Sergeant Mayemura, but the General's got to leave and I see a lady behind him who needs a life preserver. Why don't you and your wife take Carrie over to the bar? I'll join you in a few minutes."

Sandy had caught a glimpse of Melba standing alone by a potted palm, both hands clutching her purse. No one was talking to her. Putting his arms around her sturdy waist, he lifted her in a hug that left her feet dangling six inches above the floor.

"Dios mío, halcón," she cried. "Put me down or I'm going to spank you."

The General watched impassively. It no longer bothered him when Melba sounded like the boy's mother. Why shouldn't she? She had done so much more for him than Barbara "B for Brakowski."

Lowering her to the floor, Sandy planted another kiss on her cheek. Then he grabbed her hand and headed back across the room to where Sergeant Santana was sitting at a table, deep in conversation with an old guy whose rumpled suit and tortoise-shell glasses flashed: Standard Issue, Yale, O.S.S., CIA. When he and Melba came up, the old guy, already in advanced schmooze mode, was saying in a clipped Connecticut accent, "We really need you for this one. We can arrange everything. You should give it a try—you could do yourself some good."

"Why would I want to go to Afghanistan again, man?" Santana was saying. "Once was enough."

"Excuse me," Sandy said icily.

Flushing, the spook rose quickly and disappeared.

"So, Captain, *quién es la señorita?*" Santana, now standing, asked Sandy, putting on his best East LA macho.

"No es señorita," Melba said, wagging her finger. *"Es su tiita."*

"Professor," said Sandy, putting one arm around Santana's

shoulder and the other around Melba's waist, "I want you to meet the woman who gave me a life."

"Auntie," Santana said, bending to squeeze her hand. "You saved one *mal hombre*."

FOURTEEN

At the General's house in Arlington, breakfast was only slightly less formal than dinner. When Sandy came into the dining room at seven the next morning, showered and shaved after a five-mile run along the Potomac, his grandfather was sitting at the head of the dark Chippendale table reading the Pentagon *Early Bird*. He didn't look up from the daily news digest.

"Maybe this isn't a good time, sir," Sandy said. "Maybe we should talk later."

The General took off his reading glasses and put them down next to a small crystal glass of grapefruit juice. The crystal, the china egg cup in front of him, the silver and the table had all come with Elizabeth, a Brahman on both sides of her family, Boston Powells and Putnams. She had been dead more than fifty years. He never remarried. Melba called him the Monk. "If you have something you need to get off your chest, go ahead, spit it out," he said.

Sandy unfolded his napkin. Melba had put out a small dish of her guava jelly to go with her special banana walnut coconut muffins. The General had one slice of unbuttered toast next to his soft-boiled egg. Spartans versus Persians.

"Perkins said I fought just like Alex. I don't get it."

Sandy didn't use the word *father*. He always said *Alex*.

"What is there to get?"

Sandy looked down at the muffin, hesitated, then plunged ahead. "Alex didn't exactly cover himself with glory."

"True."

"Look, there was something about the way Perkins was talking."

"Sandy, this is nonsense."

"We were going to have a beer later, but there was no later. He never made it back."

"Are you saying you got him killed? You didn't, you know, so make an end of it."

"No, that's not it."

"So we're back to Prince of Denmark? Well, it happened, it's over. All the brooding in the world is never going to change it. Not for Hamlet, not for you. Let it go."

"This is about Perkins, sir, not me. Alex crapped out. He got himself and everyone but Jeff Taylor killed. You know it. I know it. Gus Buell knows it. Everyone but Sergeant Major Perkins knows it. So what the hell is going on?"

The kitchen door suddenly flew open and Melba came out holding a pot of coffee in a padded cozy that looked like a duck; the spout arched out under the duck's bill. Leaning over the General's shoulder, she refilled the Spode cup.

"Good morning, Sandy," she chirped, craning over to look at the news reports. "General, did you see what they are saying about that airplane? Very fast. Very, very fast. So fast it can't stay over anything long enough to hit it."

She had been standing behind the swinging door listening to them.

"Why, Melba, I didn't know you were an expert on Mach 1.6 aircraft and war fighting," said the General, pretending to glare at her. "The first reports on the F-44 look good. Gus Buell gave them to me a week ago. Now, you go back in the kitchen and leave us men alone."

Melba stiffened to attention and raised her arm in an exaggerated salute. "Yes, my General," she said, picking up the coffeepot and marching to the kitchen. Her small feet thumped across the polished wooden floor. The door swung closed behind her.

"Look, Sandy," the General began, less brusquely this time. "Perkins wasn't there when your father was killed. Okay, your father could have saved his life. Perkins would have idealized him after that. It's only natural. Probably no one but Perkins even remembers that firefight. He might have built it up in his mind."

Sandy spread some guava jelly on his muffin. "I don't think so, sir. You're the one who taught me to trust my gut," he said, putting the muffin down uneaten. "What was it you said? 'Good military instincts, the Caines are born with them.' Wasn't it something like that?"

The General flushed.

"You're going off half-cocked again. I thought you'd out-grown it."

"Begging your pardon, sir—"

"Forget the pomp and ceremony, young Captain. When you made the fuss over including Perkins in the awards ceremony I asked Jack Church to run a check. And you're right about one thing. Perkins had balls as big as watermelons. He was there in every scrape we've had for the last thirty years. Vietnam, El Salvador, Grenada, Panama, Desert Storm. I suspect he caught too many incoming rounds."

"That's a crock."

"Believe it, Sandy. The word on the man was that he'd lost his edge, he was battle rattled."

"He had enough edge to save our ass. You've been talking to the wrong people. I fought with him."

"Let it go, Sandy."

"Look, sir, I know I'll never begin to have your combat experience. No World War II, no Korea, no Vietnam. But I've been through enough to know a guy like Perkins. And I know he *wasn't* battle rattled."

The General smacked the table with his open hand. "I said, let it go. You're listening to the wrong bugle call, Sandy. You're hearing *charge* when it's sounding retreat."

Sandy stood up and walked down the length of the table.

"I think you're wrong," he said to the General, "and let me tell you something else. There is no way I'm going to let it go."

He pushed open the kitchen door. With a little gust of air, the door swung shut behind him.

* * *

Melba was sitting at the kitchen table bent over a copy of *Money* magazine folded back to the week's cover story: *You and the Mutual Fund Revolution—Start Small Win Big*. Sunlight angling through the window fell across her square brown hand. She was annotating a chart with a Magic Marker. Sandy saw a tiny green check next to the Vanguard Fund and a rather large question mark next to the Magellan Fund. "It's all about leadership," she said without looking up from the magazine. "Stocks, bonds, whatever—you got it or you don't."

Shoving aside the magazine, she aimed the marker at his chest. "Don't be angry at him, *halcón*. He thinks only of you." Clearly, she had heard every word. Her antenna was better than anything they had out at Langley.

Sandy put his hands up in surrender as he sat down next to her. "How do you know what he's thinking? I can't read him. I don't have a clue. I thought he'd be happy to hear that his son wasn't a total flake. But he just tore my head off."

"He lives with much pain in his heart."

"What about me? Alex was my father, not just his son."

"You act like two little boys." Melba shrugged. A Pop Tart jumped up in the toaster. Reversing field, she fingertipped it out and handed it to him. "I saw you go off with that Perkins girl yesterday, the one with the yellow hair and the skinny legs. What did she tell you?"

"*Nada*. Not a damn thing. She's a designer. Doing something with the architects working on the Korean War Memorial. She told me guns 'weren't her thing.' It's hard to believe she's Perkins's daughter. But I liked her."

"I like the other one better, the one with the crazy red hair."

He brushed a tiny sliver of icing off his arm.

"Too strong for me, not my type."

"The redhead is smarter."

He reached over and patted her hand. "We're talking dating, not breeding."

"Jus' be careful. You are my *halcón*—I see how the women look at you. One day you will think you are dating, but the woman, she will think you are breeding."

He walked over to the butcher-block counter next to the refrigerator. "You going to quit worrying and let me borrow your phone?" Picking up the receiver, he punched out a number.

"Cajun Central. What can we do for you?" At the other end of the line, Patrice St. Jean's voice sounded unusually cheerful. "I need to talk to Jeff, Pat. Can you do it?"

"No way, Sandy. He'll be tied up until midday."

"Listen, I know he's busy, but this is important."

"Okay, *chér*, let's see what I can do."

While he waited on hold, he thought about Carrie Perkins. Her father had put all he earned into making her a lady: convent school, Sarah Lawrence, money for the right lessons, the right clothes. They'd never talked about Vietnam. Sandy had taken her back to the Madison Hotel, but when he tried Wolf on her, all she said was "I'm afraid I can't help you."

Then, suddenly, at the door to her room, she had leaned in and kissed him, a hungry kiss that lasted a long time. She was lean and tightly wound—the kind of woman who'd rather fuck than eat. He pulled her to him, which was what she wanted, and she wrapped her hands behind his neck as though she never meant to let go. He could feel the bones in her back, so near the skin, and the heat as she pressed into him. She gave off the scent of fresh figs.

"You smell like dessert," he mumbled to her.

"Good. You can nibble me anytime, starting now," she said, grabbing his tie and pulling him inside the room. He heard the lock click behind them. Carrie Perkins did things her way. Not unlike her father. And her way had been fine with him.

He toyed with the memory until Patrice came back on the line.

"Okay, *chér*, be here Friday around noon and the senator will squeeze you in."

"Come on, Pat, that's three days from now."

"Best I can do."

Sandy rang off and hit a second set of numbers. This time a woman answered. "Mangan and Buell," she said in a voice as crisp as a new $100 bill.

"Morning, Alice, is Gus around? I'm looking for a deal on an aircraft carrier."

"Oh, you," she said. "It's been a long time, Sandy." She put him straight through to the senior partner.

"Uncle Gus, I need to talk to you. What about lunch?"

"Can't today. Remy Fair's up from South Carolina with a couple of our favorite T. C. Johnsons. I'm taking the three of them to The Palm with Jeff."

"What about later?"

Buell cupped his hand over the receiver. Sandy could hear him yelling to Alice in a muffled voice to reschedule his massage. "Four o'clock all right?" he asked a few seconds later.

"I'll be there."

As he stood, Melba looked up from her magazine. "Why

bother asking? You always take my phone, you always take my car. It's out front—if the Geo is still fast enough for you."

"You trying to get rid of me?"

"Why don't you go out and drive around for a while? Do something." Frowning with concentration, she picked up her Magic Marker and returned to the mutual-fund revolution.

★   ★   ★

A few hours later, he was pushing the little yellow Geo into town. Skirting the Beaux-Arts pile of the Executive Office Building, he turned and headed up Connecticut Avenue to a red-brick tower halfway between Lafayette Park and Dupont Circle.

The House That Buell Built.

The building was seven floors high. The windows were dark polarized glass. The architect's intent had been to create a body of elegance around 115 lawyers, lobbyists and rainmakers. To Sandy, the place always looked as if it were wearing shades.

He parked in the private basement lot and took the elevator to the seventh floor. The secretary showed him into the corner office with its view up Connecticut Avenue. Buell came out of the private bathroom mopping his face with a towel, a few strands of silver hair plastered sideways across his bald head. They didn't hide the brown liver spots.

"Come in, sit down, can I get you a drink?" He gave Sandy a hug.

His pink jowls felt smooth against Sandy's cheek, and his breath gave off the smell of breath mints and gin. Sandy dropped into a soft chair covered in black leather. "Not on duty and never before five, Uncle Gus."

"You amaze me, kid. How does the younger generation ever get anything done?" He poured himself two stiff fingers of scotch.

Sandy grinned at him. "Good discipline and the power of prayer, sir."

Buell groaned. "Okay, okay, okay, what was so important I had to delay my massage?"

No point in being cute. "I want to talk about my father, Gus."

"Jesus Christ. What the hell for?"

"I need to hear how he died."

Buell sat down behind his desk. His faded hazel eyes looked relaxed, but Sandy could see that his foot was silently tapping the thick carpet. On the wall beside him, a photograph from

Vietnam showed him as a rangy Special Forces colonel in combat fatigues standing next to a Huey with Captain Remy Fair and General Westmoreland. Thirty years shot to hell, Sandy thought. Buell was now as soft as a blimp with a slow leak. He wondered about Fair.

"There ain't much to tell," Gus said. "Lieutenant Alexander Caine was killed in action in the Central Highlands when North Vietnamese regulars overran his Special Forces camp. I was over the fight when he died. Only one man survived the battle. End of story."

"That's all?"

"That's it."

"Bullshit, Uncle Gus."

Buell leaned over the desk. The eyes were no longer mellow. "You want to explain yourself, young man?"

"Try this. You remember Christmas 1979? Jimmy Carter was living up the street. The Iranians had a bunch of American hostages in Teheran." Buell nodded. "You and the General spent all Christmas Eve talking about how bad it was. The Army was chewed up from Vietnam. Charlie Beckwith's Delta Force blew it in the desert."

"Anyone with two marbles to rattle together remembers how bad things were. What's your point?"

"After dinner the two of you started drinking brandy. The General said to you: 'I can accept my son's death, but never the circumstances.' What about that, Uncle Gus?"

Buell tilted back in the chair. "Christ, you must've been twelve years old."

"I was hanging over the balcony that night. I used to lie up there and listen to the two of you tell war stories."

"I'll be damned." His eyes moved to the photograph on the wall.

"A couple of days later, I asked the General what the word *circumstances* meant. All he said was 'It's what surrounds something that has happened—it's about cause and effect.' You know how he is, Uncle Gus. He can be pretty vague. So I said, 'You told Uncle Gus you were having a hard time living with the circumstances of my dad's death.' He looked like I'd caught him with a twenty-dollar hooker in Elizabeth Powell Putnam's sacred marriage bed."

Buell shifted his weight in his chair, rummaged in his pocket and took out a roll of Certs. "And what did he say?"

"He told me he was disappointed in me. He said good soldiers don't listen in on gentlemen's conversations, gave me twelve demerits, told me to bone up on Napoleon's Russian campaign for our dinner seminar the next night. That was it."

"That's all?"

"No."

The old soldier's mouth went hard. Sandy could hear the mint clicking against his teeth.

"So?"

"So I went and asked Jeff."

"What did he tell you?"

"He said, 'There was a firefight and everyone but me was wiped out. You have your dad's Bronze Star, kid. You know what a medal for valor means.'"

"Anything else?"

"Yeah. One more thing. He said, 'Look, kid. You've got to stop brooding about your dad or it will eat you up, you'll never be your own man.'"

"Good advice."

"So I put the medal on top of my bureau where I could see it and after a week or two I forgot about the whole thing."

Sandy rose from the chair, the soft leather pulling at the seat of his trousers, as if to warn him he was making a mistake. "But I don't think I've ever heard the whole story. That's why I'm asking you."

Gus knocked back a finger of his drink. "I gotta tell you, Sandy, I think you're chasing your own tail." He set his drink down. Putting his hands flat on the arms of his chair, he looked at them as if they belonged to someone else.

"Look, the night before I went to the Point, the General gave me a farewell dinner. Just the two of us. He brought his agenda to the table that night, the way he always does, and he started checking things off. Finally, he said that before I went up to the Point there were things I should know. He told me a few of his golden oldies, you know, every man has a limit to what he can take under stress and there's no stress worse than battle, that sort of stuff."

"Same old BS?"

"Not exactly. The General told me, Gus. He said, 'Buell was flying over the firefight the day your dad was killed. He saw your father shirk his duty.' And I said, 'How'd he get a medal, then?' And the General said, 'Sandy, listen to me. Gus was a good soldier. A lot of brave men died that day and Gus made sure that every one of them was recognized. He lumped your dad in with the others . . . to protect me and our family's honor.' "

Buell stood up and started to raise his hand. For a second Sandy wasn't sure whether he meant to cut him off or belt him.

"I'm not through, Uncle Gus. The General told me something else that day. He said the only people who knew, besides him, were you and Remy Fair. The three of you covered up for thirty years, but I've known about it for the last ten. So stop bullshitting me."

Buell slumped back into his chair. Rain spattered the dark glass window. It was almost black now. Reaching under the desk, he pushed a button that turned on the lights. Then he got up and walked over to the Vietnam photograph.

Backlit by the lamp, the old soldier's reflection appeared on the glass of the framed picture, the soft, lumpish contours of the present superimposed on the hard-core image of the past. Sandy saw the merciless double exposure and felt sorry for Gus. Suddenly, he wished he hadn't come.

"Maybe it is time you heard the truth. It's worse than you think." He paused as if he hoped Sandy would back off.

"Tell me, Gus."

"All right, here's what I saw. I was over that battle, right on top of it, drilling holes in the fucking sky. Remy was with me working the radios. We went down to twelve hundred feet and I could see everyone running around. I saw every damn thing that was going on. And I saw your dad. He didn't perform the way he should have."

"How can you be so sure? You were looking at a fight from almost a mile away."

"Fair enough, but those binoculars weren't opera glasses, Sandy. I'm not sure what your grandfather told you, but your dad did something I'd call despicable."

"That's what I need to know, Gus."

"There was a bridge connecting the outer and inner perimeter where Jeff was running the show. Your dad blew that bridge. To save himself he cut off his own men's escape route. If those guys could have folded back into the inner perimeter, they might have had a chance. We had all that air over them. We could have blistered the gooks with napalm. The relief element was scratching at the wire. Charlie Beckwith was leading a bunch of Rangers and SF guys up there to bail them out. If they could have held out for another hour, they probably would have made it. But your dad's behavior denied them the chance. Christ, when we finally got in there we thought they were all dead until someone grabbed Jeff to put him in a body bag and he twitched. That's the way it was, Sandy."

The old man put his hand on Sandy's shoulder. "Look, son. The issue isn't what kind of guy your old man was. The issue is who you are. Who you're going to be. The way things are going, you're guaranteed two, three, even four stars. You gotta let your father rest and get on with your life. Forget him. You owe it to yourself and the General. Hellsfire, kid, he's been waiting fifty years for a warrior and you're it. You've given him his life back. Don't fuck it up."

Buell reached over and patted Sandy on the back, the way an older soldier might pat a younger man after a firefight.

Sandy cleared his throat. "Thanks, Gus." His voice sounded hoarse.

Buell looked at his watch. "You gotta let me go now. Mona only waits so long."

After the door clicked shut behind Sandy, he returned to his desk and punched one of the memory buttons on his telephone console. The phone rang twice; then, before the voice at the other end of the line could identify himself, he broke in first.

"The boy's been up here chasing ghosts. I thought you'd want to know."

The line went dead. Softly, he replaced the receiver. Looking up at the photograph, he stabbed the intercom button. "Goddamn it, Alice, where's my limo?" He needed that massage.

★   ★   ★

The General put down the phone and tapped the desk slowly with his fingertips. He was sitting in his study, a large, walnut-paneled room with tall windows and floor-to-ceiling bookcases filled with volumes on military history. The desk was made of dark brown oak, with a green leather top and mother-of-pearl inlays. General Sherman Caine, his own grandfather—Army Chief of Staff to William Howard Taft—had used it in the War Department when the Departments of War and State both fit snugly in the Executive Office Building. The security of the nation had been shaped over that desk. The General hadn't laughed the day Sandy came in from Washington and Lee High School and told him it looked like a pool table.

The boy's getting in over his head, General Caine thought to himself, rising and pulling the drapes shut against the early fall darkness. Time had stopped in the room. It conveyed the atmosphere of the early 1940s, the time when he was away with the 82nd Airborne in North Africa, the time when Elizabeth died. He had promised to be with her when the boy was born and he had broken his word. His punishment had been a son who from the first had been nearsighted, graceless. His curse. His eternal disgrace.

The General picked up the phone. An aide immediately put him through to the Army Chief of Staff.

"Yes, sir, General Caine."

"I need a favor, Jackson, and I hope you're not so angry after yesterday you're going to turn me down."

"Never happen, sir."

"It's about Sandy. I'm worried about him. He got himself blooded and now he's moping. We've got to get him back up on his horse. What he needs is more action. Can you find something for him?"

"Sure can. Consider it done."

Mission accomplished. A faint smile crossed the General's face. "Thank you, Jackson, he won't let you down. He's good, Jackson, very good. And Jackson . . ."

"Yes?"

"The next time I tell you what your duty is, you have my permission to tell me mine is to shut my trap."

"Thank you, sir, but you happen to be right. The boy *is* damn good."

*   *   *

A soft tap at the door woke Sandy. Fumbling for the switch on the night-light next to the bed, he checked his watch: 0600 hours, too late to wake up, too early for trouble. He swung his legs around to the floor and sat clearing the fog from his brain.

The tapping escalated into pounding.

"Come out of there, *halcón*. The Pentagon is calling you. Major Hayes from Army Personnel. Maybe you should take it in the study."

Grimacing, he opened the door, kissed her on the cheek and padded down to the phone.

"Captain Caine, sir," he said. "Didn't know you folks got up so early."

"Managing you water walkers is a full-time job, Captain. Report back to Bragg ASAP. The mission is classified. You'll be vacationing somewhere that won't hurt your career."

"Roger that, sir."

He went into the kitchen, where Melba was making French toast.

"So? *Qué pasa?*"

"Beats me. They want me back at Bragg. Like five minutes from now."

Bad roll of the dice. He'd planned on a couple of weeks leave. It had seemed a safe call. The two of them had talked about flying down to Honduras to see her family, do a little fishing, lie on the beach. Now he saw her hiding her disappointment, concentrating on the yellow batter as she poured it over four slices of fresh bread. "I'm sorry," he said. She shrugged, scraping the sides of the bowl. Patting her shoulder, he reached for the phone and called Patrice at home.

"Change of plans, Pat. I can't make Friday. My leave's been canceled. Got to leave for Bragg tonight. Could you tell Jeff I really need to see him before I go?"

"I'll try. What's up?"

"Who knows? They told me the mission's classified and to move my ass."

Patrice clucked sympathetically. "How'd you like to open a restaurant with me?" he said. "I'll do the cookin', you do the bouncin'. Beat hell out of the hours we're keeping now."

"Pat's Big Easy?"

"You got it."

"Where do I sign up?"

"Chez Patrice, boy. We'll kill 'em. Be right back at you, *chér.*"

He called an hour later. "The senator says to meet him at The Cactus Flower. Eighteenth and F Street. You know the place? Southwestern cuisine, stucco on the walls, little stuffed cactuses. Margaritas at seven. Don't order the jalapeño chicken. It's poison."

★　　★　　★

At 6:45 Sandy walked into The Cactus Flower. The maître d' looked dubiously at his jump boots, then brightened up considerably when he asked for Senator Taylor's table.

"This way," he said, steering Sandy through the cozy A-list tables. Sandy sat down, ordered a José Cuervo Gold and studied the room. He had been in The Cactus Flower once before. It was the kind of place with a men's room out of *Architectural Digest*, so modern you didn't know where to piss and where to wash your hands. A perfect metaphor for the entire town.

Jeff came in at ten after seven. He waved at Sandy, then stopped to schmooze with Wingate Tanner, the CIA's veteran number two, who was sitting at one of the tables with an over-dressed brunette in a clinging black sheath.

"Okay, hero, how was it?" he said, slipping into the booth across from Sandy and reaching for the margarita the waiter had delivered without taking an order.

"How was what?"

"Carrie Perkins. Great legs."

Sandy drained his tequila.

"That any way for a United States senator to talk?"

"You wanna hear those guys talk, go sit in the gallery. You won't last ten minutes. Numbnut phonies. All of them." He corrected himself. "Most of them."

"Sounds like you're getting bored, Jeff." He nodded in the general direction of Pennsylvania Avenue. "You thinking about moving up the street?"

"What do you think? Pat says I ought to quit guessing. Get out there and find out."

They both laughed, the same overheated laugh that erupted periodically from the other A-list tables around the room. The waiter came back. Jeff ordered the mesquite mixed grill, blue corn tamales and a pitcher of Dos Equis. They tucked into the meal, exchanged small talk. When the coffee arrived, Sandy said, "You knew my father better than anyone, right? Gus says he saw Alex go to the bottom of a bunker right in the middle of the fight."

Jeff sighed. "That's true. But we were in there together. The shit was coming down all over us. Thought we'd all be blown away right along with the gooks. Then they came in over the wire and that was it."

Sandy stirred his coffee. "You could protect me when I was twelve, Jeff. Not now. Alex didn't cut it."

"Hey, don't tell me you didn't want to shit your pants ten times a minute in Mogadishu."

"More like twenty times a minute, but the point is, I didn't."

He looked over his cup and saw Senator Taylor's eyes boring into him.

"Okay, killer, everyone knows you've got the guts and brains to go all the way. But that firefight of yours was over in less than a day and you had the advantage of surprise and the offense until Rushman got your dick stuck in a crack. We were out in the jungle with the bad guys for six months. Those last four days they were hitting us with everything but Ho Chi Minh's jockstrap. No air support. The fog was so thick you couldn't see the gooks ten feet away, but you could hear them screaming, 'Die, GI.' All you could do was lie there with the rain pouring down your face and take it. The mud caked your boots so bad you could hardly lift your foot. The place smelled like shit, piss and garbage. Then mortar rounds started hammering in, shrapnel buzzed past your ears and the guy next to you didn't have a head anymore—just a bloody stump of a neck—and the guy you'd soldiered with for two years was blown out of his foxhole, lying ten feet away from his legs, spurting blood like a fire hydrant. That's what was going down, Sandy."

"Gus saw him chicken out, Jeff. Gus and Remy Fair."

"Fuck Gus, fuck both of those rear echelon pukes."

"Hey, come on, Jeff. They're the ones who wrote you up for the MOH."

Senator Taylor leaned toward Sandy. "Look, all any of us did was try to stay alive. How do you think I feel, being the only one who made it out? First five years I had sweats and nightmares every damn night. I still can't get Vietnam out of my gut. Okay, I'm glad to be alive, but I don't see any honor in it. The Army pinned the big one on me for the same reason it stuck the DSC on you—to tie a few ribbons around a fuckup."

He yanked angrily at the rosette. "The only reason I wear this thing is because it's put me in position to see we don't do it again. The rest of the glory trip is pure bullshit. After your father and the others were killed, I couldn't bring them back, but maybe I'm alive so I can fight the bastards who got them blown away, who keep getting us blown away. It isn't much, but it beats hell out of nothing."

"Aren't you leaving something out?"

The senator stared at his coffee. "What am I leaving out, buddy?"

"Honor. What about that one, Jeff?"

"No guts, no glory? Come on, Sandy, I thought you were bigger than that."

"Not the same thing, Jeff."

Senator Taylor shot him that pained-father look they always laughed about after their fights—the young officer with no father, the older man with no son, each man testing the breach in the other's defenses. "Come on, do you really think people care about honor anymore? It went out when MTV took over."

"Not a soldier's honor."

"KIA, Sandy. People get honor and victory mixed up."

"Come on, Jeff. Where do you think I got this from?"

"Beats me."

"From you, goddamn it. From the General and you. You're the ones who beat it into me. Do the hard right thing, Sandy, no matter what the price is, Sandy. Even if you have to die for it, Sandy. Remember the Spartans at Thermopylae. How many times did you tell me that one when I was a kid, Jeff? You saying now it was all bullshit?"

"Easy there, buddy. All I meant is you're getting yourself way too hot over the whole thing. Obsessions suck. And I don't want you and your grandfather shooting at each other. All those holes would screw up his Wall."

Jeff knew where to aim. The Wall occupied the west flank of the General's library, eight generations of Caines framed and arranged in chronological order. Some days Sandy wondered whether his life was his own or whether from the day he was born, it had been designed for the Wall.

The waiter came with fresh coffee. When he was gone, Sandy said, "Did I ever tell you what happened the first time the General really told me about the Wall?"

"I don't think so."

"I must've been about seven. Some second-grader was ragging me every day about not having a father. So that night I went in and said, 'How come I only have a granddad and a Melba? Where's my daddy and mommy?'

"He said, 'I know how you feel. I didn't have a father either.' Then he took me into the library, which was forbidden territory, and showed me the Wall."

The memory came creeping back, the past blurring the edges of time. At the far end of the room, the General had hung Gallaway Patrick Caine's commission in the Continental Army in a hand-carved cherrywood frame. The first of the Caines had come from County Cork. He was an indentured servant, hated the British, spent six years fighting in the Revolution. After mustering out, he was given 1,000 acres of bottomland in Virginia.

In 1785, he married Catherine Murphy. A year later, when they had a son, they named him George Washington Caine. After Gallaway's old Commander in Chief. Sandy smiled. "They were all up there, Jeff, every one of them a soldier."

Sandy put his napkin over the salsa spot in front of him. Looked better that way. "He told me he wanted me to know what kind of family I came from, Jeff. I'd never heard him talk that way. He said the Caine tradition always helped him to never feel alone."

Farther down the Wall, beyond the painting of Col. G. W. Caine at the Battle of New Orleans with the 7th Infantry—the Cotton Balers—was another picture, this one in better shape, of Andrew Jackson Caine, the first of the Caines to graduate from West Point. Class of 1830. He had served with distinction in the Mexican War. By then the Caines had in iron their tradition of fathers naming first sons after great commanders.

The first photograph on the Wall was a dark, black-and-white picture in the style of Matthew Brady. It showed a soldier wrapped in the colors of the Union lying dead on top of a pile of corpses. Samuel Houston Caine, A. J. Caine's boy. He graduated from the Point with the Class of 1855. On July 21, 1861, he was serving as a commander in General Irvin McDowell's army when McDowell and 38,000 green Union troops advanced on 12,000 Confederate forces dug in along a little creek near Centerville, Virginia, called Bull Run. The Yankees drove into Thomas J. Jackson's position. When the sergeant carrying the colors fell, Sam Houston Caine picked up the flag himself and led his men forward. If the rebel commander had been anyone but Stonewall Jackson, the battle might have gone the other way. But Jackson's counterattack overwhelmed the advancing Yankees. After the battle, when they found Sam Houston Caine's body, he was still holding the colors.

"That picture was like a job description, Jeff. I never had to ask what the General expected of me. He showed me the picture of his own father. He had him up there with his citation for the Distinguished Service Cross. Terry Grant Caine. KIA November 8, 1918.

"The guy was a captain. Out of the Point, Class of 1916. He was a company commander fighting west of Reims when the Germans launched the Second Battle of the Marne.

"They swept around his unit on both flanks, leaving him surrounded and cut off 15 miles from anyone else. Every other officer in the unit went down. By that time, of seven hundred men, only fifty were left.

"The perimeter kept shrinking. He became battalion commander as the sole surviving officer. The Germans sent a full general under a white flag of truce to talk to him. The guy said, 'Your men are being sacrificed for a piece of dirt that means nothing. Surrender and we will give you safe passage to your own lines.' Terry Caine said they'd die first. They'd never give up. He was wounded six times and down to a few dozen men, but his outfit didn't crack. Rock of the Marne."

Senator Taylor sipped his coffee. "It never changes, does it?"

"Not in our family."

Sandy pointed to the senator's rosette. "Close as the Caines ever came to the big one, Jeff. They sent him to the hospital and put him in for the Medal of Honor. After the doctors patched him up, he returned to the front. He was killed three days before the Armistice. So the war was over and they busted back the medal, the way they always do. That was something I learned later. But I'm telling you, man, by the time the General finished that night, the Caines sounded like something out of the Greek myths. I had forgotten all about Mommy and Daddy. All I knew was I wanted to be a soldier."

Senator Taylor pushed aside his cup.

"Then why are you raising so much dust? I don't see any mystery. You can read it round or you can read it square. It was rough over there."

Sandy reached for the check. "I've got to shove off. My plane leaves in two hours."

The senator brushed away his hand. "No way, Sandy. It was my invitation."

The senator came around the table and put his arm over Sandy's shoulder. "You're pissing in the wind. Be careful, or you'll find yourself drowning in it. Where are they sending you?"

"I don't know. All the assignment officer said was mission classified."

"Sounds like Bosnia."

"That's a UN show. No Americans."

"Where there's a will there's a way, kiddo. I'm getting nothing but doublespeak from the White House and Pentagon on that little number. Look, stay in touch, will you?"

"Sure. Look, one last question, okay? Was there someone in your unit the guys called Wolf?"

The senator thought for a moment. "We had one guy from Arizona they called Puma, but I don't remember any wolves. Why? What's it about?"

"Just something someone told me. I'd better hit the road." He gave the coat check to the attendant, got his bag and flagged a cab.

FIFTEEN

Lumbering along at 15,000 feet, the snub-nosed cargo plane, a C-130 with Italian markings, bumped through the gray clouds over Sarajevo like a boxer probing for a better punch. Sandy took a pull of water from a plastic bottle and snapped on his seat belt.

The A-Team's survivors—even Kruger, still in the hospital—had all volunteered for the mission, but there was only room for two. So Sandy had asked Nate Caldwell to cover his back.

The orders were to proceed to Bosnia and link up with the British SAS. The Brits were doing recon for NATO under the cover of providing commo facilities for United Nations peacekeepers. On the Farm, the CIA's training facility at Camp Peary, the black bag boys had fitted them out with Canadian uniforms and IDs and pointed them east.

Caldwell stared gloomily at the forward bulkhead of the pitching aircraft as it began its descent. The only quick way into the besieged city.

"Be safer to jump out of this sunuvabitch, Captain. Why don't we ask the pilot to circle once and let us leave by the side door?"

The crew chief yelled over the roar of the four engines to strap in. The plane dropped into a sickening dive, plummeting through the clouds, twisting to avoid Serbian ground fire.

Caldwell closed his eyes. "Oh, man, how I love this shit."

Sandy leaned back into his web seat and breathed deeply. The adrenaline made his body feel quick, light, as if it were flying under its own power. He felt a sharp jolt as the plane touched down, the rear ramp opened, and the crew chief began kicking out pallets of food and blankets. "Let's move," Sandy yelled. Grabbing his rucksack and rifle, he hotfooted it down the ramp, Caldwell pounding behind him.

The airfield lay in a valley surrounded by mountains, a saucer waiting to be smashed. *CRUMP, CRUMP, CRUMP*. From the high ground, the Serbs were lobbing mortars and artillery shells at the runway. They dove into an old shellhole. "Fucking Dien Bien Phu, man," Caldwell cursed into the dirt.

Sandy hit him on the shoulder and ran toward the far side of the runway. Gasping like two lathered quarter horses, they piled into a concrete bunker. Behind them, the C-130 was already picking up speed. Racing down the runway, it lifted off and vanished in the drizzle.

Black smoke curled up above the new craters, mingling with the fog and snow. Sandy smelled leather burning. Across the toe of his left boot, he saw a dark crease where a chunk of hot metal had scorched it. "Was it good for you, Nate?" he said.

"Came twice, Captain. Better than Dak To in sixty-six."

All around them, heads began to poke out of bunkers. Men were scuttling across the field. A bulldozer roared, eating into the earth around the edges of a crater near the end of the runway, as an MP in a blue UN helmet and a Legionnaire's uniform came into the bunker.

"Où se trouve votre commandant?" Sandy asked, wincing at the rust on his French.

"Canadians, yes?" Even the cops were language snobs.

Ten minutes later a French armored car pulled up to the bunker. They got in and took the last two seats. On every side, Greek, French, Pakistani and Italian peacekeepers were exchanging horror stories in four languages.

As the armored car ground into gear, the babble trailed off, lost in the engine's growl. Twenty minutes later, the vehicle stopped, the rear door opened and they emerged into the darkening shadows of a late October afternoon. In front of them they saw a very large building with mortar craters running right up to the sandbagged entrance. Skirting the holes, they hit the steps and pounded on the door. A tall young man in faded jeans and a black pullover let them in.

"Captain Caine reporting in, we're looking for Colonel Hunter."

"General *Sir* Sterling Hunter," the young man corrected him. He had a slight accent, difficult to place, and he was wearing his blond hair in a ponytail. Sandy's shoulders seemed to interest him. Particularly the Canadian patch. Sandy groaned silently. A mistake in rank and title. Not one a Canadian would make. "You'll find him back there," the young man said, pointing toward a heavy wooden door down the hall. "He's expecting you." Sandy knocked. A deep voice called out, "*Entrez*. It's open."

The accent was British, upper class. Sandy pushed open the door. The officer sitting behind the scarred desk across the room, just under 6 feet, 200 pounds, no marbling on any of it. His wavy gray hair was neatly parted and oiled down. Despite the Oxford accent, he looked about as soft as a Welsh miner.

"Captain Alexander Caine reporting, sir." Sandy tried his impression of a Commonwealth salute. "This is Sergeant Nathan Caldwell."

The general looked amused. "Stuff it, Captain. I know all about you. Drink?"

From a desk drawer, he pulled out a bottle of Bombay gin and two glasses. Pouring a couple of fingers into each glass, he pushed two across the desk and raised his own. "Cheers," he said. "Confusion to the enemy—Serb, Croat and Muslim— every bloody one of them."

A first test. The CIA briefing officer had warned Sandy about it. General Sir Sterling Hunter was a blueblood. He'd corrected for it at Sandhurst and spent his entire career in the British SAS. He didn't trust the white wine and Brie crowd, men who drank like debutantes. Gin was his measure of character. Sip or gag, you were dead.

Sandy got down half the glass. Nate knocked back the whole drink and pushed his glass across the desk for another.

"You'll do, gentlemen," Hunter said pleasantly. "What did they tell you in the States?"

Sandy put down his glass. "They said the mission was recon for NATO, sir. Gather intell on all factions—Serbs, Croats, Muslims—get squared away to use NATO air, pick targets."

"Go on."

"Canadian cover. But SAS runs the show. They said you'd tell us the rest."

The bull took a deep pull on his gin. "The first thing to know is you can't trust any of these bloody creatures. The Serbs are the worst. The Croats studied with the Nazis. The Muslims are the victims because they're the fewest. But they're the slickest. Give them half a chance, they'll slit your throat, too. So you're not to trust them either. Understood?"

"Yes, sir."

"UNPROFOR is our official cover. Theoretically, we're here to provide communications for UN personnel wherever and whenever they need it. That covers a good deal of ground. I'm assigning you to Colonel LeFebre's unit in Sarajevo. Legionnaires. Tough buggers. You'll be my liaison team there. Colonel LeFebre doesn't know what we're doing and doesn't need to."

"What about gear?"

Hunter studied their Canadian getup. "You can start by getting rid of those bloody uniforms. We wear mufti most of the time. Pick whatever you like. My men wear denims. If you brought a pair, get them out and you'll fit right in. But be careful. The locals are just like the Russians—they'll kill you for your Levi's."

On the desk next to General Hunter's bottle of gin was a trim little submachine gun—Heckler & Koch, semiautomatic, 9-millimeter, with a silencer. He saw how Caldwell was looking at it. Like a new papa outside the nursery window.

"That's what you'll be carrying. See Lieutenant Drago before you leave and he'll issue you yours. Drago's the hippie who let you in."

General Hunter put the bottle back in the drawer. Sandy rose to go. "Just one more thing. I've spent the last five rotten years in Northern Ireland and my own people are still killing each other. This time I intend to do better."

"Understood, sir."

"You're on your own. If you drop out of sight for a few days, I won't come looking for you, but do keep me informed."

They turned to go. "And by the way, old boy," he called after them. "You can drop that tiresome salute. It doesn't become you. You're not going to need it, anyway."

Down in the arms locker, Drago took out two of the little submachine guns. "Best in the world," he said, looking steadily at Caldwell. "Uzis are over, mates."

SIXTEEN

Croatia ★ Zagreb

The gray light seeping through the bare limbs outside the Cafe
Vukovar reminded Abbie of the discharge from an ancient drain.
Zagreb was exhausted. After three years of civil war, the city
huddled in on itself, feeling for its own erratic pulse like a heart
patient waiting for the next attack.

She was sitting near the front of the cafe at a table with a fake-
marble top, studying the rings from the morning's first cappuc-
cino. Outside the window, a rattling tram stopped to disgorge its
passengers. Stolid Croats, men and women bundled in woolen
coats, scuttled off to work. It was very cold. Along the avenues
stretching away from Jelacic Square, the chestnut trees had lost
their leaves.

Abbie picked up the little gold-rimmed cup and warmed her
hands. She was in Zagreb to explain the war to Americans who
couldn't tell a Croat from a Serb and couldn't care less. "You're
going to have to show me you're not just another Miss One-Hit,"
Julian had told her the week before, polishing off a dripping
porterhouse at the Palm Restaurant. He'd given her a ticket to
the Balkans and a month to make him a believer. She looked at
her watch and waved for the check.

Where the hell was Kurt?

Wrapping her scarf around her neck, she stepped out into the
square. From down the avenue, an ancient Mercedes 220 pulled

up next to her. The car had no bumper. Rolling down the side window, the driver began to hustle her.

"Taxee? You like tour? You like dance?"

The voice was high pitched, wheedling. "Buzz off," she said, looking away.

"What about a scoop, babe?"

The window was all the way open now. She saw Kurt craning out, leering at her like an old cartoon of the wolf in *Little Red Riding Hood*. He knew what turned her on. "Get in," he said. "We've got trouble." The word seemed to please him. He always said it with the upbeat accent normal people use when they say fun or hope or money.

"You are such a snake," Abbie said, piling into the Mercedes and falling back in the seat as the car shot across the square. "If this sucks, you're in trouble."

"This is good, babe. I promise. But it took me an hour to find you. Why don't you move over to my place? There's a studio opening up at the Parcewal. You'll like it. We'll save time."

"Sounds good to me. Tell Dava. So what's your big story?"

"Serbs shot up a UN armored personnel carrier."

"You expect me to phone that in?"

"Lotta dead guys in blue beanies."

"Good pictures. No story."

"They had a couple of Americans with them."

"What Americans? Americans aren't supposed to be here."

"Todor told me Americans. He called from Tuzla, said he was driving a load of petrol to the airbase and about ten klicks before Brodinski Brod he nearly slammed into the ambush. Blood all over the road."

"Yeah, right. Todor's got Americans on the brain. He sees them everywhere."

"Because they're here, babe. So why don't we go up to B and B? Take a look?"

The Mercedes had no heater. Abbie zipped up her jacket and rested her head on the dash for a moment, eyes closed, calculating the odds. Five to one no story. But what else did they have to do?

"Okay," she said. "But if this Rhineland Special of yours breaks down on the road, you won't have to worry about the Serbs or the Croats, I'll kill you myself."

"Ain't happened yet, babe." Slipping into third, Kurt jockeyed the Mercedes out of the city and headed east on the autobahn.

The Serbs and Croats were shooting at each other across the Sava River where it separated Brodinski from Slovinski Brod, and they had the road to themselves. Anyone with any brains stayed away from the two bullet-riddled cities. Kurt rode hard on the gas and the countryside passed in a blur: grain fields now planted with mines, blackened acres cratered by shells, empty of life. They drove past the charred skeleton of a church. Its toppled bell tower cast a truncated shadow across a cemetery full of fresh graves. From the chestnuts bordering the cemetery, an old man was cutting limbs for firewood. When they stopped for gas in the village beyond the church, they could still hear the sound of his ax echoing off the walls of a house with no roof. Out of an abandoned bedroom, a startled flock of pigeons flew up through the rafters, whirring away over the dark fields.

As they got nearer to Brodinski Brod, the land became hilly. Under one of the higher ridges, the Croats had set up a checkpoint at a bridge crossing a small stream feeding into the Sava. Kurt leaned on the brakes as two soldiers dressed in Soviet-style gear and carrying AK-47s jumped forward to block the road. The first guard, a kid with dark hair curling out from under his helmet, leveled his weapon at Abbie and cocked his head, motioning her to get out.

She didn't move. "Just do it," Kurt murmured, turning to get out on his own side. "*Journalisti,*" he said to the second soldier, pulling a pack of Winstons from his shirt pocket and offering him a butt. When he reached for it, Kurt tossed him the whole pack. Suddenly losing interest in Abbie, the kid leaned against the hood, and for a while, the photographer and the two soldiers stood there smoking, exchanging small talk.

Abbie looked across the bridge. About 100 meters up the road, a white APC with black United Nations markings lay on its side. Behind it, a white Toyota riddled with bullet holes tilted into a ditch. Two UN peacekeepers in blue berets and a Croat officer were down on their hands and knees looking at the back of the four-wheel. Kurt reached into the Mercedes and pulled out his camera bag. "This is the place, babe," he said, pointing to a hill on the far side of the stream. "These guys say the Serbs whacked them from up there behind the tree line. They say four dead. One American. Both shitfaced. Lotta plum brandy since breakfast."

"Let's go," Abbie said, brushing past the kid who had pointed the submachine gun at her. As she headed for the bridge, tendrils of hair trailing down her black jacket, the boy hesitated for an instant, but then let her pass by. He put his hand on his crotch and grinned at the second soldier. Kurt grinned back, then jogged up the road after her.

When the blue berets saw Abbie, they scrambled to their feet and began brushing the mud off their knees. "Abigail Mancini, *Washington Chronicle*," she said, praying English would work on them. "I thought you guys weren't supposed to have any Americans with you."

"I don't know what you're talking about, lady. What are you doing out here?"

The word *about* came out as "aboot." Canadian. The officer was wearing a green parka, but the insignia on his shoulder straps identified him as a lieutenant colonel in the 22nd Royal Canadian Regiment. Mid-forties. He seemed more surprised than angry.

"Just covering the war, Colonel," she said, brushing a whisp of hair back from her forehead. "Someone I know drove by here right after the ambush. Told me he'd seen a dead American." She turned and pointed back to the Croat checkpoint. "Those two little shits down there say the same thing. So what's happening?"

The name tag on his parka said Allender. He was short, compact. Still good-looking for a guy heading into middle age, she thought. But he was taking his time.

"Come on, Colonel Allender. I've got two sources telling me an American was killed out here today. Are you going to deny it?"

"Maybe you're right, maybe you've got it all wrong," he said.

"No riddles, Colonel."

"Come with me." Leading her over to his white four-wheeler, he drove her up the road a few hundred yards, where he stopped and pointed to the ridge above them. "The Serbs were up there." He swept his arm down the road. "The mine was over there, planted off center. The right track of the vehicle went over it. Set it off. When our men came out, the Serbs shot them first. Then they shot up the Toyota."

He was looking at her calmly, waiting for her reaction. "I don't want to sound heartless, Colonel Allender," she said, "but that happens around here every day. What about the American?" She could see Kurt walking backward, shooting the wreckage as he moved toward them. A thin plume of gray smoke trailed away from the APC.

"There was an American television crew with us. The correspondent was riding in the APC. He got shook up, but he was all right. The cameraman wanted to ride up front in the Toyota so he could get some footage. Bad move. We shouldn't have let him do it." He looked down the road. "Most of you reporters think you're bulletproof."

Abbie looked at Kurt. He was twisting his 130-meter lens back and forth without raising the camera or shooting.

"You know Joel Mintner?" he asked her.

"The guy who did that great piece on the Mostar massacre?"

"Yeah. We were together in Beirut and San Salvador. He had big balls. Big, big balls, Abbie."

Kurt was blinking back tears. She had never seen him that way before.

"We were drinking in the Astoria last night. He packed it in early, about midnight. Told me he had to get up early to come out. He needed to get some bang-bang into New York before noon for a special."

Kurt turned, twisted the long lens savagely and aimed it at the dead Toyota.

"I'd say Joel just bought it, babe."

His voice had shifted back to cockiness. But Kurt was faking it. She touched his arm.

"Come on, cowboy. Let's get out of here."

They drove for half an hour in silence. The sky grew darker and sleet began to pelt the little car. Flicking on the windshield wipers, Abbie peered into the gloom. The blade on Kurt's side didn't work and the window began to fog up. He pulled a bandanna from his pocket. Swiping at the condensation, he only succeeded in smearing the glass until the view disappeared completely.

"What the fuck are we doing this for?" he exploded.

"Truth and beauty," Abbie said. Her heart wasn't in it, but she pushed on anyway. "Look, Kurt, Joel knew what he was doing. We all do."

"Do we?"

"You come around a bend and the bad guys aren't where they're supposed to be. Four hours later it could have happened to us."

"Sure, babe, but that wasn't what happened to Joel."

"What do you mean?"

"I checked out the Toyota. The shots came from the rear. Joel was drilled through the back. The slugs went through the rear door. Then they went through the back of Joel's seat, through Joel and into the dash. The holes in the door were small and clean."

"So what?"

"The Serbs were a good thousand meters up that hill."

"They're good shots, aren't they? Not that they haven't had enough practice."

"Bullshit. A rifle round fired from that distance couldn't have punched through one sorry Toyota and one poor sonuvabitch and then buried itself in the dash. Shit, it wouldn't have gone through the bloody license plate. The holes were pointed up, not down, Abbie. The angle of fire was all wrong. And how the hell were the Serbs supposed to get down there and plant a mine in the road with a Croat checkpoint one hundred meters away?"

"What are you telling me?"

"We're talking about a Croat mine and shots that had to come from those drunks who gave us a hard time at the bridge. They're the ones who waved the blue bonnets into that mine. Then they shot up the Toyota and blamed everything on the Serbs. The Serbs would do the same thing if they had the chance, but that's how it went down for Joel. In this shithole, there's no way to cover your back, because in this shithole, there's no front."

He turned and cocked a finger at Abbie. "Pow, and you're dead, babe."

* * *

They drove the rest of the way back to Zagreb in silence. The city was trapped in a time warp. She crossed the lobby of the Astoria Hotel with its polished brass and crystal chandeliers, the paneling in dark walnut, the Oriental carpets, feeling as if she were stepping into a forties film noir. As she headed up the stairs to her room, the concierge nodded to her from behind his enormous desk. The cashier in his Art Nouveau cage offered her a cheerful wave. Give her a trench coat and a black lace garter belt, she'd rule the world. What a shame all she had was a black fleece Polartec jacket and a Toshiba laptop.

Her room was cold, but the sleigh bed was buried under a huge down comforter. She crawled under it with all of her clothes on. Kurt's studio was looking better all the time. At least she'd be able to leave the stove on for warmth.

Lying on her side, she spread out her notes and riffled through them for five minutes. The telephone looked like something out of the prop room for *Grand Hotel*. She picked up the antique receiver and asked the operator to place a call to Washington. While she was waiting, she drifted off.

The sharp jangle of the phone snapped her back to the present.

"Abbie, that you? What've you got? I'm late for lunch."

"Quagmire II, Julian. Did you hear that Joel Mintner was killed?"

"Yes. We're doing an obit. A couple of graphs."

"Are you saying the Croats killed him?"

"Bullshit, Abbie. It was the Serbs. The networks were all over that one."

"Why didn't you wait until you heard from me?"

"No time. The TV guys got to the story first."

"Yeah, well, they got it wrong."

"What do you expect me to do? File an international protest? I don't have time for this kind of shit."

"Do you have time for the administration running guns into Tuzla?"

There was a short pause at the other end of the line. "The Secretary of State was out at the publisher's house the other night. He said flatly that there was no U.S. involvement over there. Wasn't going to be any. Period."

"And you swallowed that crap, Julian? Listen, from what I hear, Yanks are landing every night at Tuzla and unloading AK-47s."

"Stop it, Abbie. Why would Americans be shipping Russian weapons? It doesn't make sense. I don't believe it. And I'm late for lunch."

"I've got a source, Julian. He's getting us in."

"Lighten up, Abbie. Who do you expect me to believe? You or the Secretary of State?"

"Who are you working for, Julian? The *Chronicle* or Wilton?"

"I don't want you breaking and entering any airbases. Got that?" He paused. "Look, I want you to go down to Sarajevo and soak up the atmosphere. Give me a color piece—winter is a-comin' in, snipers, blood on the white snow, mothers wailing over dead children—you know the drill. Think Sarajevo, Abbie, not Tuzla."

"Julian, don't do this."

"I just did. Get moving."

"Julian, I'm—"

"The car's here. Gotta go."

SEVENTEEN

★ Sarajevo ★

A four-wheel armored vehicle took Sandy and Nate to Colonel LeFebre's headquarters. It was dark now. The streets were deserted. They passed shot-up cars jumbled along the roadside like broken toys. An overturned tram blocked the mainline leading away from the airstrip. Candles flickering in the blackened windows of trashed apartment buildings offered the only source of light. Why in God's name would anyone stay? It was like living in an enormous junkyard.

Colonel LeFebre had set up camp inside a giant warehouse. Using sandbags and crossbeams, the Legion had created a bunker within a bunker. An NCO gave them cots for the night. Nate fell into his and was instantly gone.

There were no lights in the shower room. Sandy groped his way to a stall, turned on the water and relaxed as the warm spray took the stiffness out of his neck and shoulders. As he was drying off, he heard the door to the room open. An old sergeant came in leading a young private into one of the dark stalls. Sandy heard the shower go on and the men grinding, then a low moan.

He waited until he was sure they were gone. Shivering in the blackness, he found his way back to his rack and tumbled in. The next morning, when he told Caldwell what he had heard, Nate shrugged. "Lucky thing you didn't interrupt them, Hawk. Man, the Legion invented 'Don't ask, don't tell.' They would have sliced you four ways. . . ." He paused, obviously relishing what was coming next. "Long," he said slowly, "deeeeeep, wide and free-quent."

Colonel Armand LeFebre was in Paris on leave. They spent the next week reconnoitering the mountains outside Sarajevo, picking the best observation points, spotting the Serb positions. At the end of that time, they'd barely scratched the surface of the mission. NATO was going to need a lot more time and a lot more Sneaky Petes to get the job done right.

Colonel LeFebre got back toward the middle of the second week. When Sandy went in to introduce himself, the Frenchman was standing by the door to his office, a blue cloud of Gauloise smoke floating up around him. He looked like a geek from central casting. Full of Gallic rage. It showed.

"Yes, yes, you are Canadian, *n'est-ce pas?*" he said, dismissing Sandy's cover.

"Oui, mon colonel. Bien sûr. Mais je parle francais."

"Congratulations, Captain, but what I need today is someone who speaks English." He bolted back into his office. When Sandy ducked in after him, he was sitting on the edge of his desk next to a shell casing filled with stale Gauloise butts. For a moment he studied Sandy as if he were a headmaster preparing to examine a dim pupil. "I have this problem," he said. "I am asking myself if you could be the solution."

He went on thinking aloud, clipping his words to fit his logic. "The public affairs *crétins* are sending a reporter to me, an American. This reporter wants to go out with my troops. I want you to take him. Drive him around. Show him a nice cow or that nursery school the Muslims show everyone."

"I may not be your best guide, sir. I've only been here a short time."

Colonel LeFebre stuck out his lower lip. "Phhh, don't be modest, Captain. Just take the reporter and keep him out of my sight."

"Perhaps—"

"Take him anywhere, I don't give a damn. Just get him away from here."

He pulled a rumpled blue packet from his pocket and offered Sandy a Gauloise. "No, thank you, sir. I better find Sergeant Caldwell and round up a vehicle."

"Round up. What is this round up?"

Sandy flushed. "Old Canadian saying, sir. *Un camion, c'est tout.* I'll need transport, that's all."

"Not a problem, Captain. Tell the adjutant of your requirements."

★ ★ ★

An hour later, the armored car came rolling down Vrmensky Prospect. Back in uniform for the little field trip, Sandy felt like a condemned man as he watched the vehicle draw nearer. When the car stopped in front of headquarters, he walked around, opened the steel door and looked inside. The lights were off, and the car appeared to be empty. Then, a small figure rose and turned toward him. Even in silhouette, she was unmistakable.

"Captain . . . Captain Caine?" she said. "Is that you?"

Motherfuckingsonuvabitchingshitalmighty.

She stepped lightly down from the car. "What kind of uniform is that you're wearing?"

"Please, shut up, Miss Mancini," he implored her. "Shut up. I mean . . . sit down. Please, sit down." He grabbed her arm and led her to a long bench outside the sandbagged bunker. "What are you doing here?" he said quickly. Stalling. The way she moved, it would take her maybe two seconds to blow the mission.

"I could ask you the same."

"Don't." Big mistake.

She started to take out her notebook. "Look, I'm sorry," he stumbled, wondering if it would make it even worse to beg. "You're not going to put this in your paper, are you?"

"I sure as hell am." He frowned. "Hey, we're old combat buddies," she said. "Remember? You can level with me."

"You know as well as I do I can't tell you why I'm here. Let's just say I'm working with the good guys."

"Good guys? In this place? Who are they? I'd really like to know. The last American I heard about was dead. And now you show up in a funny uniform."

"Hey, time out. Let me explain."

"Fine." She folded her arms across her chest. "Explain."

A white UN Toyota pulled up, and Nate's head popped out the window. He saw her and grimaced. "G'morning, Miss Mancini." She peered in at him, eyeing his shoulder patch.

"Hello yourself, Nate. You defected, too?"

"Yep, Maple Leaf MREs are the best in the west."

"Isn't that great. So why don't you nice Canadian boys take me to whatever's happening? Let's party."

Ten days in country and they were fucked. Sandy wondered

how long it would take for the Army to can him after the *Chronicle* ran her story. At least he could stop scratching all those old scabs about quitting—he was already on his way out. "You drive, Nate."

"Drivin' Miss Daisy—that's the easy part, Hawk. You just sit back there and sell her on our new look."

Sandy climbed into the backseat of the four-wheeler next to Abbie. Dodging mortar craters and debris, Nate worked his way through town, then turned east on the road to Illiceza. Entering the rocky hills overlooking Sarajevo, they swerved to leapfrog a Pakistani convoy, then moved steadily upward into the mountains.

"You owe me an explanation, Captain," Abbie said, craning back to watch the city drop behind them.

"I don't owe you anything, Miss Mancini. For that matter, you don't owe me anything, either. What we're doing is a matter of national security and I can't talk about it. But maybe you owe your country something."

"Nice try. You don't win the lotto."

"You know how you sound?" he said. "You sound like some tight-assed judge."

"Hey, who do you think you are—Canada's Oliver North? Let's keep things straight. The country doesn't even know you're over here. It doesn't want you here."

"We're trying to find out things. Same as you. Things that might save American lives."

"Save it, Captain. I'm a soldier's daughter. My dad came back from Vietnam saying when the officers start talking the way you're talking right now it's always just before a whole lot of people get killed." She pointed out the window. "Next you'll probably be telling me you're here to burn down those villages in order to save them."

His stomach knotted. Despite the cold, he suddenly felt sweat beading on his forehead. Where was this Vietnam shit coming from? Never should have gone to see Gus Buell.

I was over that battle, right on top of it, drilling holes in the fucking sky. . . . I saw every damn thing that was going on. I saw your dad. He didn't perform the way he should have. It's as simple as that.

"What's the matter, Captain? Am I making you sick?" She was looking at him quizzically. He took out a bandanna and wiped his forehead. It came away wet. Angrily he stuffed it back in his pocket. "Bosnia isn't Vietnam, Miss Mancini."

"Is that right? Then why are you here in that uniform? Junior year abroad?"

He leaned back in the seat and looked out the window. In a cemetery next to a bombed-out church, an old woman in black from her kerchief to her rubber boots was laying bright red flowers on a grave. Where had she found fresh flowers so late in the year? Then he saw they were plastic.

Maybe Buell was right. Maybe this tomboy from hell was right. What was she trying to prove?

Caldwell slowed down and jammed the horn. In front of them, a convoy of three mud-spattered trucks full of Bosnian soldiers was inching up the road. They were approaching a blown-out apartment complex built in the days when Europeans came to Sarajevo to ski. Nate was leaning over the wheel shouting, "Move it, Abdool, git out the damn way."

The lead truck exploded in flames.

A split second later, Sandy heard the zip of an incoming mortar round, then the chatter of machine guns, screams.

Nate slammed on the brakes, grabbed his submachine gun and did a belly dive into the ditch. Half crawling, half sliding, Sandy dragged Abbie to a low rock wall. Facedown, he lay on top of her, shielding her body with his own, the cordite from the explosives mingling with the vanilla scent of her hair.

Rolling off, he rose to his knees and risked a look over the wall. From a crag overlooking the apartment complex, the Serbs were lobbing mortar rounds at the convoy, stitching it with machine gun fire. One gun, by the sound of the fire. The Muslims were milling around aimlessly, not even shooting back. He couldn't tell whether the Serbs were toying with them before greasing them, or whether they were just too drunk to finish the job.

Then he saw Caldwell ducking low, grabbing dazed soldiers, heaving them into firing positions. "Stay here. Don't move," he whispered to Abbie. He ran toward the cursing sergeant.

"Shoot, you motherfuckers," Nate was yelling, windmilling his arms at the Muslims. "Shit *no*, not that way, *that* way."

The panic-stricken defenders couldn't understand him at first, but after a few more heated signals, they began to pepper the high crag, and the Serbs stopped shooting.

Sandy worked his way over to Caldwell. They pulled the wounded out of the burning truck and slid them behind the wall, where Abbie was firing off shots with her Nikon. No way to shut off the story now.

Nate was examining the casualties. "Coupla these dudes in bad shape, Hawk. Gonna check out." Above them the Serbs began shooting again, moving higher, angling for better firing positions.

"We need more muscle, Nate. Take the Toyota. Go back and grab that Paki convoy. Get 'em up here. Use the Satcom, give the CP a sitrep."

"You want the 1st Cav?"

"Whatever tanks you can scrounge."

Tucking his submachine gun into his gut, Caldwell zigzagged back to the Toyota. Sandy blasted out covering fire, while Nate threw the four-wheel into reverse and careened backward 50 yards, disappearing behind a bend in the road.

Sandy finished patching up the worst of the wounded. He gave injections until the morphine ran out. When he stood up, he saw the reporter was no longer taking pictures. "What can I do to help?" she asked.

"What you can do is get back behind that wall and pray reinforcements get here before dark. If they don't, you can forget about partying . . . Ever."

He fired a short burst of submachine gun fire at the Serbs. The Muslims saw chips of rock flying from the crag and sent up a soft, guttural cry. He couldn't tell whether it was a cheer or a call to prayer.

For an hour, the Serbs hung back. As the sun began to drop behind the mountains, he heard a faint growl far in the valley below them. The sound steadily grew louder. Fifteen minutes later, two French tanks heaved around the bend in the road where Nate had disappeared. Behind them was Caldwell in the white Toyota.

The tank drivers horsed their hogs up the incline. Inside, the gunners trained their main guns on the Serbs. *Gaaaaarummm-mmppppp.* Sandy felt the earth shake as the rounds smacked into the Serbian positions. Somewhere up the mountain, a whistle blew. And then the Serbs were gone.

Caldwell stepped out of the Toyota and walked over. "Reporting to General Custer, sir. Everything cool?"

"It is now. Where did you find the cavalry?"

"Fucking Paki chickenshit egg suckers wouldn't move. Even when I stuck this up their ass." He jabbed the submachine gun in the air and spat on the road. "But these French dudes were hot. Didn't have to invite 'em twice."

The reporter was on her feet shooting pictures of the advancing tanks. To get a better line on the tanks, she was edging backward, out onto the shoulder of the road.

"Fucking freeze."

Sandy's shout echoed off the mountain side. Mouth like ashes. Body hurtling toward her. Knocking her to the ground. Digging her into the earth.

Reaching gingerly with his fingers, he started to test the ground around them, starting at their heads, then out for about a foot, working down and around their bodies. Six inches to the side of her breast, he felt the taut trip wire of the mine.

"Goddamn it, when I tell you to do something there's a reason," he whispered hoarsely into her ear. Reaching across her body, he rolled her slowly toward him, pulling her back onto the road.

For a moment they both lay on their backs, looking at the sky. The sun was gone. Flakes of snow floated down toward them, caressing their faces, blowing toward the shoulder of the road.

"Got your story, Miss Mancini?" he said.

She leaned in against him. "You know what, Captain?" she said, opening her eyes, watching the mine disappear under a white dust of snow. "Fuck the story."

EIGHTEEN

★ Zagreb ★

A few days later, the computer and fax were the first things Sandy noticed when he and Nate flew up to Zagreb and checked into the Hotel Astoria. Behind the manager's desk the IBM 386 that processed reservations could still get out e-mail, and anyone with his own paper could still fire off a fax. The Balkans might be falling apart, but the Astoria was still wired.

Hunter had sent Sandy to brief General Yarif Khan, the UNFOR Deputy Commander, in Croatia. The Pakistani was smoldering over the way his men had shirked their duty while the Serbs were shooting up the Muslim convoy on the Illiceza road. It wasn't altogether clear whether he expected Sandy to give him the truth about the lame-dick performance or if he wanted a cover-up. Sandy knew how he felt. His own cover was still in the hands of Miss Mancini. The prospect of explaining a blown mission to the General wasn't something he liked to think about.

The old man who carried his overnight bag showed him to a small room on the ground floor. He stowed his gear. Then he put a call through to Melba and asked her to fax him any stories from the *Chronicle* carrying Abigail Mancini's byline.

"She is *there*? The smart one? Did you see her?"

"She's here. But I'm not. Just send me her stories and don't say anything to anybody."

"Okay, just don't take off Saint Christopher. It sounds very bad where you're not."

The first day, the report from Arlington had consisted of a single word. *Nada.*

Now he was sitting in an overstuffed chair wondering how long his luck could hold. The old brocade of the red upholstery scratched his neck and arms. He heard the sound of the bellman's footsteps outside in the hall and ignored the knock. He ignored that one, too. After a few seconds, an envelope came sliding under the door. He got up to retrieve Melba's fax. Below the fold on the front page, the *Chronicle* had run a brief account of the firefight. He scanned it quickly. The reporter had written a breathless little tick-tock of the shooting as an introduction to a longer story on the suffering of the people of Sarajevo. The Muslim nursery school was there—soldiers listening to Mozart while they hunkered in the ruins of the city, the crack of sniper fire—but that was all.

He read quickly through the story again. Only one sentence mattered:

"The panic-stricken Muslim soldiers owed their lives to the skill and courage of two UN peacekeepers who organized the defense until reinforcements arrived."

She had covered for him. Unbelievable. Fantastic.

But why? Wasn't he the one who had told her she didn't owe him a thing?

It was 9:45 P.M. The tall window of the bedroom was shuttered for the night. On the wall next to the bed, a fake electric candle flickered dimly under its red shade, throwing shadows among the rollicking hunters, stags and pheasants carved into the dark walnut of the headboard.

Caldwell was meeting him in the bar at ten. Sandy took a fresh shirt and a pair of pressed khakis out of the high pine armoire that served as a closet. Pulling them on, he checked his pockets for his key and stuffed in a wad of marks. Then he snapped on the little chandelier in the vestibule. It was made of blown glass, blue as lapis, and it hung from a gold chain. Pretty. He didn't like coming into dark rooms in strange hotels. He left the little blue light on as he closed the door.

Turning a corner, he entered the lobby. He stopped to buy a two-day-old copy of the *International Herald Tribune* from the concierge before he pushed through a heavy set of oak and glass doors that led to the bar. A bartender in a starched white shirt and bow tie was drawing an enormous glass of beer from a tap set into the wall. Another of the huge glasses, this one empty, sat on the top of the bar.

Sitting in front of it was Nate Caldwell.

An overheated combo on a low platform was exuberantly playing an ABBA riff. Sandy made his way through the noise, sat down at the bar and clapped Caldwell on the back.

"Next one's on me."

"May not be no next one, Captain."

Caldwell was feeling good. Across the room, a dark woman with tightly curled hair was sitting at one of the tables with a very drunk Croat in a brown suit. She disengaged herself, walked over to them and held her hand out to Sandy.

"Elena Haltani," she said. Her voice was smoky, as if she had seen too many bad movies. Caldwell draped an arm around her and pulled her next to him.

"Meet Cleopatra, Captain. Queen of the Nile."

Sandy took the outstretched hand and kissed it. "An honor, my Queen."

"Not yours, Captain. Mine. You move on back now."

Sandy laughed and signaled for the bartender to bring over a round.

"Cleo's from Cairo," Caldwell said. He sounded like her manager. "We met in Beirut at the Club Rififi. Out on the corniche. Long time ago. Les' see, I was 'bout ten, she was 'bout three."

"My Nathan has told me you are always the gentleman." Her eyes were heavily rimmed with black kohl. Her breasts spilled over a low-cut blouse of hot-pink Thai silk a size too small. She was wearing a tight velvet skirt, purple, and white patent leather boots. "Did you know Beirut is the Paris of the East, the city of love?"

"How did you get all the way up here?"

"I am the true Islamic fundamentalist, Captain. Fundamentally, where there is war, there is Elena. The bars are full and the money is always better."

She was warm, funny. Nate wouldn't have to worry about catching cold.

An electric guitar started wailing. Sandy could hear the scrape of chairs as people moved onto the dance floor. When the bartender came back with the beer, Sandy looked up in the mirror behind him. A pride of drinkers had taken over a trestle table running along the back wall of the bar. By the look of them, they were journalists. They were making a lot of noise, sending up a lot of smog.

Out of the smog stepped Abbie and Kurt. They started to dance, slowly at first, all hips and hands, then faster as the combo picked up speed. Abbie was wearing tight black jeans and ankle length boots. Sandy could see her breasts bobbing under her tee shirt as she moved in close to Kurt's thrusts, then spun away in a wild swirl of hair, then back in closer.

Christ, no wonder Jeff had left with her.

The reporters and photographers jammed around the trestle table were shouting at the two dancers, above the pounding music, goading them on. "Hot, hot, *hot* . . ." The others cleared the floor to give them more room.

Dog fucking, Sandy thought. He couldn't take his eyes away. She broke away from Kurt. "I gotta pee," she called to him, stepping off the dance floor.

In the mirror he could see her coming his way. Looking down quickly, he bent over his beer like a nodding barfly. For a second, he sensed her standing behind him. Then, from the corner of his eye, he saw her disappear into the ladies' room.

Caldwell was immersed in the Queen of the Nile. He hadn't noticed anything.

"Come on, Nate. Taps. Lights out. We gotta get up early tomorrow."

Caldwell looked at Sandy as if he had lost his mind. The sergeant checked his gold Rolex.

"It's ten-thirty, Captain. They ain't even *made* the bed yet."

"I don't know, man. I'm beat. You and Queenie have a good time. I'm turning in."

As he was rambling on, Abbie came out of the ladies' room. Walking up to him, she flicked her wet fingers at his face. Reflexively, he shut his eyes against the little shower.

"So what's with the cold shoulder, Captain?" she said. "I know you knew I was here."

She leaned across Sandy and tapped Nate on the shoulder.

"You, too, Nate. Don't even think of ignoring me, guys."

"Who could after all the dirty dancing?"

"And the shower," she said. "Don't forget the shower." She

picked up Sandy's glass and took a sip of beer. "So what's with the big welcoming committee?"

"We weren't expecting to see you again." Sandy took back the glass and drained it.

"Get used to it, Captain. You, especially. It's fate. You know what the Chinese say? When you save a person's life, that person is your responsibility. Like forever." She was a little high. She looked at him quizzically. "I'm serious," she said. "It's why we keep meeting. It's not coincidence. *You* are responsible for *me*. You saved my life. Now you're stuck with me."

She laughed, a silvery laugh that made him think of wind chimes.

"I'd say you have enough people taking care of you. The Incredible Hulk over there, for instance. Looks like he's still doing a really good job."

She sat down on a barstool. "Not that it's any of your business, but it isn't what you think. You are completely full of shit. I've always been careful to keep Kurt as a friend. He has a very, very large fan club, practically half the women in the world, and I don't like clubs."

"Well, you two sure looked like a couple to me," Caldwell said. "I mean, the way you dancin'." He reached over and touched her cheek. Sandy saw Elena look away.

The lights suddenly went down and the combo started into a slow dance. Abbie took Sandy's hand. Without thinking, he began to draw back, but she wouldn't let go.

"On your feet, Captain. That's an order." Pulling him onto the dance floor, she took his arm and guided it around her waist. "Okay, you were so quick to diss the Incredible Hulk, let's see what *you* can do."

As they moved slowly into the music, Sandy felt her thighs lightly brushing his. When he drew her closer, she leaned backward and examined his face. "Better. Much better, Captain." She rested her head lightly on his shoulder and let him move her slowly among the other dancers. Through his shirt, Sandy could feel the heat of her body warming his chest.

Her beeper went off just as his shirt began to wrinkle. "Oh shit," she mumbled. "Duty calls. Don't go anywhere." Breaking away, she started to take off for the phone cubicle at the front of the bar. Sandy grabbed her arm.

"You can use the phone in my room. It's right around the corner." He handed her his key.

"All right," she said. "It's just Julian. Won't take long. I'll be right back."

He watched her leave through the glass doors. Then he pulled out his wallet and called an order to the bartender. He came back a few minutes later with a bottle of Dom Perignon and two champagne glasses.

"Going somewhere, Captain?" Caldwell said. "What about taps?"

" 'Night, Nate. A pleasure, your Highness." He headed for the glass doors.

★　　★　　★

The telephone sat on a small square plastic table. Abbie sat on the edge of the bed and called the *Chronicle*. Julian picked up the phone on the second ring.

"So what have you got, kid? More of those ugly Americans?"

"Nope. More of those beautiful guns. A ton of them." A long pause. "Come on, Julian. Let it go. I gave you your Sarajevo piece. Let me go to Tuzla."

"No way, Abbie. No F-U-C-K-I-N-G-W-A-Y."

"We're getting sucked in over here."

"You're the one getting sucked in. Take deep breaths and try to remember I sent you to cover a war, not start one."

"I know how to take care of myself, Julian."

"Yeah, that's what worries me. Time to pack it in, Abbie. Whatever you've got going, pack it in and come home. Now."

"What are you telling me, Julian?"

"Stop trying to read between the lines. I'm not canning you, not yet, anyway."

"What about the guns?"

"There aren't any guns, Abbie. Either you get your tail back here or you *will* be looking for another job. I have something else in mind for you and it won't keep." He rang off.

She put the receiver on the hook and looked down at her knees. They suddenly felt cold.

"Bastard, chickenshit, baby dick."

She drew a deep breath and started to get up. Sandy was standing at the door with a green bottle in one hand and the stems of two glasses sticking out between his fingers. Under the pale blue glow of the chandelier, he looked like a handsome alien.

How much had he heard?

"I've decided to take my responsibility more seriously," he said, walking toward her. "So how about we toast my becoming your guardian angel?" Was the iceman warming up? Or did she like him better with all that burnt cork under his eyes?

He put the glasses on the windowsill. She saw him wince slightly as the cork popped. He filled the glasses, handed one to her and raised his: "To dirty dancing."

"I'll drink to that," she said, raising the glass to her lips.

The champagne was ice cold, and after a half glass, the bubbles settled her churning stomach. Count on Julian. Good old take-no-risks, kick-'em-when-they're-down Julian. Show him a real story and he ran like a rabbit.

From the bar, the sound of the combo, muffled only slightly by the heavy door, filtered into the room.

"Let's finish our dance," she said, putting her glass down next to the phone.

She put her head on his chest and closed her eyes as he stretched both his arms down her back and pulled her gently against him.

"We've been in some pretty bad stuff," he said. The softness of his voice surprised her. She had only heard him barking orders. "Maybe it's time for something better."

She reached up under his shirt, running her fingertips through the hair on his chest. Then she leaned back to unbutton his shirt. He closed his eyes and she could feel him stiffen as she began caressing his nipple with the tip of her finger.

"Does a guardian angel get special privileges?" he asked her.

She pulled her sweater over her head and turned her back to him. From behind, he unhooked her bra, reaching around to cover her breasts with his hands. He buried his face in the back of her neck, breathing in the scent of gardenias, and below the flowers, just a trace of vanilla.

He turned her around slowly until her breasts brushed against his bare chest and her nipples began to swell. Reaching down, she unbuttoned his belt and peeled down his trousers. Then she stepped back and out of her black jeans, and then her bikini panties.

They were both trembling.

He sank to his knees in front of her, running his tongue over the soft curls of pubic hair, kissing the white planes of her thighs, moving his mouth upward along her stomach, licking warm circles around her nipples.

She touched him as he stood and held her face in his hands. Her eyes closed and then he was picking her up, carrying her to the bed. As he entered her, she rose up with a sharp cry, then sank into the soft red and blue silk caressing her back.

NINETEEN

Thump, thump, thump. The rotor dying slowly on the burning chopper. Everything in slow motion this time. Black smoke oozing upward, rising toward the hot white platinum of the sun. Perkins propped against the bulkhead, the dud RPG run buried in his chest.

Christ, make it stop.

Perkins pulling out the blood-blackened round. Handing it to him. Laughing as it turned into a beer can, falling back, dark gouts of blood spraying from the hole in his chest.

Hisssssssss.

*   *   *

Sandy opened his eyes. Gray light washing through the hotel window fell across the old steam radiator percolating near the head of the bed. He was lying on his stomach, face mashed into the pillow, breath coming hard. The nightmare fading to black.

Quarter to five. The window rattled. Sometime during the night the eiderdown comforter had slipped off his side of the bed. He could feel a draft playing across the backs of his legs. Drowsily, he reached under the sheets with his foot, searching for her.

He could still smell the faint scent of her perfume, the stronger odor of sex drifting up from the bedclothes. He remembered the curve of her back and the way it arched up from her tight little ass. When she came she cried out, "Oh God, oh Judas, Judas." Tough little Italian moaning like a Baptist. He pushed his foot over farther to her side of the bed.

Nothing.

The comforter slid off and collapsed in a soft heap on the floor. Groggily, he swung his feet down to the carpet and snapped on the table lamp. Next to the telephone he saw an envelope, Astoria issue, with his name on it. Inside was a note written in quick, slashing strokes on a narrow sheet of blue paper from some other dump in Zagreb. She must have ripped off the pad.

Angel—Hope I see you again sometime, especially if I'm in trouble.

That's all? he thought. Not even an *A* for effort? She had signed it "Your Responsibility."

He hadn't felt her move, heard her dress. She could have taken him out while he was lying there with his bare ass up in the air. Was she laughing at him? What if he'd been snoring?

He looked down at the bed where the pillow still showed her imprint. What was this act? The soldier was supposed to pull a stealth, not the damsel in distress.

A single strand of red hair, long and curling at the end, stood out against the white cover. He picked it up and curled it around his index finger. No question. She had dumped him before he could cut out—on her. Same M.O. Just quicker on her feet.

But then, why the envelope?

He walked back to the night table. Slipping the circle of red hair into the folded note, he put the note back into the envelope, licked the flap and sealed it. Should he put it in with Melba's letters? Maybe he should start a new box: Abbie's kiss-offs.

*   *   *

Caldwell was sitting in the hotel breakfast room thinking about his hangover. The tablecloth caught his eye. Neatly pressed, free of grease spots. Way it is in this crazy place, he reflected. Half the people out shooting each other's asses off, other half home doing the ironing.

It was six-thirty in the morning, he hadn't slept for thirty-six hours.

He felt like he was eighteen again.

The thing about Elena, the woman didn't do sleeping. An hour earlier, when he finally left her, she was lying in bed, hair all over the sheets, eyes smeared black circles, and he was another two hundred bucks lighter after leaving her money "for groceries." He smiled, remembering the time Santana read him the poem about a black soldier locked up in the Munich nuthouse after scoring with a German chick. Black dude had her in the public garden, his dick sparking like a trolley pole. Oh, mama, that's what Elena did to a man. Same way. Blew every circuit.

A waiter sidled up to the table. "*Frühstück?* Breakfast, sir?"

"Listen, don't call me sir, okay? What's your name, man?"

"Georg, *mein* Herr."

"You my man, Gay Org. Here's what I want: half a dozen soft-boiled eggs, two orders of toast light and a big bowl. Big." He gestured with his hands. "Got it, mine hair?"

As the waiter scuttled off, Caldwell saw Sandy coming across the room, moving a whole lot slower than the night before. He hoped the lady'd been as hot in the cot as she'd been on the dance floor. Do the captain some good.

"That was one long phone call, Hawk," he said when Sandy came up. "Reporter callin' Jupiter? Didn't see you back at the bar." Sandy sat down at the table. "Aw, man. Captain's fuckin' blushing. I don't believe this shit."

The waiter hurried up with a pot of black coffee and poured out two cups. Hawk was lookin' at Gay Org like the Croat was a one-man relief column.

"Things got . . . involved."

Caldwell spooned four hits of sugar into his cup and stirred thoughtfully. "With a normal dude and a normal lady, you know what I'm sayin', next mornin' the normal dude comes down and says like 'Aw shit, did I score, man. Lady blew me away.' "

"We had a lot to discuss."

Caldwell blew on his coffee and risked a sip. "Uh huh," he said. By now the captain should have completed the after-action report. Tits and ass and over the pass. The waiter returned. Lifting a cloth from a small tray, he carefully took six soft-boiled eggs in white china egg cups and arranged them in front of Caldwell. Then he came back with a plate of toast and what looked like a porcelain soup tureen.

"Anything more, sir?" he asked Caldwell.

"Nope, Gay Org. That's just fine." Caldwell dumped the runny eggs into the bowl. Then he took a half dozen slices of toast and crumbled them in on top of the eggs. Peering into the bowl, he took his coffee spoon and poked his concoction gently. From his pocket, he pulled out a small bottle of Tabasco sauce and aimed a few shots of red at the yellow mixture in the bowl.

Nate Caldwell's 100 Percent Pure 100 Percent Sure Hangover Cure. Guaranteed. Put you back on your feet or right into intensive care. Five minutes max. Sandy looked away while Caldwell spooned the first serving into his mouth. "You know what, Nate?" he said. "I think I'm going to hang around here a few days."

Caldwell picked up his napkin and wiped his mouth. "Don't be playing with me, Captain."

"No games. Hey, look, man, I want to do a little French leave, a little scouting around. I need you to cover for me. I'll keep the room and you can vet messages."

"Yeah, great. I got nothing better to do than cover for a pussy-whipped white boy who's lost his fucking mind."

"Two days. Max. I'll meet you here in three."

"White boy's in love. Can't even count to three. Man, what's General Caine gonna say when they nail your sorry ass for going AWOL . . . after *pussy*."

He said the word at the volume of a drill sergeant chewing out a new recruit. The delicate glass prisms dangling from the chandelier shivered with the force of the explosion. From the next table, a couple of startled early risers stared at the two of them.

"Okay, okay," Caldwell said, picking up his spoon and eyeing the bowl. Brain food for a bad morning. "Here's how it'll work. Elena and me got something nice goin', so I ain't gonna be dentin' any pillows in this hotel. We'll keep your room. It can be our drop."

"So I'll call in and you'll cover me?" Sandy stuck out his hand. Caldwell nodded.

"Yeah, I'll be coverin' both of us—from Elena's."

★   ★   ★

Back in his room, Sandy took the envelope out of his pocket and looked more closely at the note. On top of the sheet of blue paper he saw The Parcewal with an address and telephone number. Picking up the spindly receiver from the phone, he dialed the number.

"The Parcewal, Dava Smardz."

A woman's voice, sultry, a bit languid for eight-thirty in the morning.

"I'm looking for Abigail Mancini. Is she staying with you? I'm trying to track her down. I'm a friend. I wanted to surprise her."

"She's not here."

"Shit." He knew he was overreacting, but he couldn't help it.

"She left with Kurt."

The image of the two of them dog dancing blew through his imagination like a tropical squall. Get a grip, man. Abbie couldn't be doing old Kurt, too. She'd said he was just a friend. Or was he? It occurred to him that he didn't know when she had left the Astoria.

"Do you have any idea when they'll be back?"

"I think tomorrow morning. They go to Tuzla on a story."

A plan began to take shape in his mind. No, not a plan, he corrected himself. More like a mission. Covert.

TWENTY

★ Tuzla ★

Screw Julian.

Abbie peered through the windshield of the Mercedes. The road crossed the Sava over the bridge to Slovinski Brod. Then they began jitterbugging through Croat, Serb and Muslim checkpoints. At the crossings, Abbie tried to look bored while Kurt laid German marks on the guards as if he were the president of the Deutsche Bundesbank. Their luck held. No one looked twice at their papers.

Abbie put her head back and closed her eyes. Okay, Abs, so Captain Caine was a one-night stand. Maybe. Maybe not. But that's up to him now. Breathing in deeply, she saw Sandy again, lying in the half-light from the window, his hair damp on the pillow, the sloping shoulders and strong back, the lean, strong arms, how tightly they'd pulled her against him when she cried out and came tumbling down.

She remembered the smell and heat of his skin, the hands and long fingers. Even in sleep there was a certain innocence about him. Before she left, she had felt an impulse to lean over and brush her lips across the back of his neck.

Don't go there, Abbie, she'd told herself. Not a soldier. They're even worse than doctors. You'd spend the rest of your life saluting and shining his boots. Let him sleep. Let him come after you.

They reached Tuzla around seven. Kurt parked the Mercedes

in an alley behind the tram barn, leaving it unlocked so no one would break the windows. He didn't give a damn if anyone stole it. Maybe the next one would have a working heater.

Abbie followed him down the stairs into a smoky cellar with a sign on the door that said CLUB TANGO. The place stank of cheap tobacco, boiled potatoes and cabbage, but it served smuggled German beer and Scandinavian aquavit. German truck drivers who horsed UN relief convoys across the ruins of Yugoslavia liked Club Tango. It was a place where they could top their own substantial tanks before hitting the road.

Kurt had met Todor in the cellar a few days before Abbie arrived in Bosnia. After a barrel or two of beer, Todor, listing dangerously across the wooden table, said, "Good, you Americans. All good. Good money, good guns." When Kurt asked what he meant, Todor whispered, "Shhhhh," then fell asleep facedown on the beer-soaked table.

Kurt switched to brandy, keeping up his own voltage. An hour later, when Todor finally lifted his head, the photographer was waving half of a 100 deutsche mark note lazily in front of his nose. "What were you saying about Americans and guns?" The driver then remembered hearing that white planes with American crews were landing at night at the Tuzla airport. He said they were offloading arms for the Muslims. No, he hadn't actually been there himself, but a friend of his had seen the Americans, heard them cursing the Muslims in English.

Kurt gave Todor the other half of the note. After that he'd staked out the field, spending the night on the Tuzla road. Around midnight, he'd heard the planes homing in overhead. When he tried to get past the front gate at the airbase, a squad of military police chased him away.

Todor's lead was golden. When Kurt fed it to Abbie, she kissed him. "So now all we've got to do is get past the gate, shooter. What's the plan?"

That was why they had come to the Club Tango. For money, Todor would move anything anywhere in Bosnia. He had told Kurt he had a plan they would like.

But Todor was still among the missing. Half an hour later, Kurt was packing away cabbage and potato stew as happily as if he were eating four-star back home at La Tour d'Argent. Looking into the greasy bowl in front of her, Abbie fought off nausea. In the smoke and noise swirling around them, her eyes swam and her head throbbed. She looked at her watch. It was nearly midnight. As she was getting up to leave, Todor came bouncing down the stairs into the cellar. He was wearing heavy brown corduroy pants and a black leather jacket. His face was fat but clean shaven, glowing with the happy smugness of a world-class safecracker.

Kurt did the introductions. Abbie waited until Todor had finished his first tankard of beer.

"What have you got for us?" she asked him.

"What you got for me?"

"Whatever it takes."

"It takes one thousand deutsche marks."

Abbie pointed to her bag.

"How will you get us in?"

"Come with me."

Draining off the second tankard, he wiped his mouth on the sleeve of the leather jacket and bounded up the cellar steps, Kurt right behind him. Abbie, juggling her coat and gear, had to take the stairs two at a time to catch them. The men in Club Tango nodded at one another beerily as they tracked her in the tight black jeans, all eyes saying, I'll take a piece of that.

It was dark outside and colder. Todor led them down the cobblestoned street, across a small park, through a lot strewn with broken glass and used condoms. He stopped in front of an old warehouse. Taking a key from his jacket pocket, he unlocked the front door and waved them inside.

The place had once been a machine shop. An overhead crane rolling on two tracks was attached to the side walls with rusting bolts. The rest had been stripped clean. In the darkness at the rear of the building was Todor's rig, a Mercedes tractor with an 850-horsepower engine. The rig was hitched to a long white trailer painted with the blue markings of the United Nations.

Todor raised the rear door, and they all scrambled into the trailer. It was completely empty. Four aluminum panels stretching from floor to ceiling made up the trailer's front wall. Each panel was attached to the frame with eight screws. Todor pulled a screwdriver from his pocket. Working quickly, he unscrewed one of the panels. Behind it was an empty space about one foot deep and three feet wide, just enough for a stack of boxes or two very good friends. He pointed at the hiding space, then he pointed at the two of them.

"Are you crazy?" Abbie started to turn away. Kurt grabbed her arm.

"It'll work. The drive only takes twenty minutes. We can make it."

"No way. What if they bust him? What if we get stuck in there?"

"Won't happen. This is a UN rig. We can get in there tonight and be back in Zagreb before noon. It's front-page stuff, Abbie. 'Neutral America Gunrunning in the Balkans.' Lynch will cream."

"All right," she said. "Let's do it. When do we go?"

Todor tapped the screwdriver on his thigh.

"Now."

Kurt helped her wiggle in and get settled, then he eased in beside her while Todor replaced the panels. In the darkness, they heard the cough of the engine, then the trailer began to move. Five minutes passed as Todor wheeled the semi out onto the main road to the airbase.

Kurt muttered, "Oh shit."

"What is it?" Fear stabbed her like an ice pick.

"The beer. I've got to piss."

"You what?"

"Forget it."

She giggled as a crazy feeling of relief spread through her body. Reaching into her backpack, she pulled out a bottle of mineral water. She drank what was left and handed the empty bottle to Kurt.

"Go for it, big boy. Wouldn't want your dear little dick stressed out tonight."

"Little isn't the word," he said grumpily. "You want to check it out?"

"No thanks, King Kong, just do your thing."

When he finished, she handed him the top. "For you, beloved. Why don't you keep it in your camera bag for any more gigantic emergencies."

Picking up speed, the truck bounced along for another ten minutes, then stopped. They heard voices and the sound of Todor shifting gears. "Guardpost," Kurt whispered. "We're in." A few minutes later Todor stopped again, and they heard the metallic squeaking of the screwdriver.

The panel came away. A gust of cold air blew across Abbie's face.

"Was I right?" Kurt was grinning like Tom Sawyer. He paid Todor, who pocketed the wad of marks and climbed back up into his seat. Blinking his taillights at them twice, he drove off into the darkness.

They were standing at the edge of a long field bordered by a barbed wire fence. Kurt started down the fence line, studying the wire and the ground on the other side.

"Gotta be mines," he whispered.

The ice pick began to explore her central nervous system. The bile was worse this time. She leaned over and threw up. When her eyes cleared, she felt better.

After 50 yards, Kurt stopped and pointed to a loose section of the wire where the perimeter guards crossed the field. Beyond the sag in the wire, a narrow path, tramped smooth, snaked off toward the runway. "Shortcut," he said. "Stay in my footprints."

He stretched the top wire up for her and they began to work their way through the darkness. Ahead of them, the runway and hangars were bathed in harsh white night lights.

Abbie heard the engines of a plane circling, then dropping to the airstrip. Two more transports followed it down. She waited fifteen minutes, breathing slowly, wondering if Kurt could hear her pounding heart. He was peering through his telephoto lens at the three C-130 cargo planes drawn up in front of the hangars. The planes were white with no markings, but their ramps were open. They were close enough for Kurt to shoot the codes on the crates.

"AK-47s, ammo," he said.

He started crawling forward. After 50 yards, he got to his feet and stood in the center of the runway, legs apart, leaning forward, shooting right up the ramp of the closest C-130.

Loud voices with unmistakable American accents drifted toward her.

"Haven't you finished yet?" shouted someone from the back of the plane. She heard the crewmen bitching. Their forklift didn't work. The offloading was a rat fuck.

Radio-pure American. All of them. She could be in Ohio.

"Come on, you guys, move that shit, we gotta haul ass outta here. It's starting to get light."

Hear that, Julian?

Kurt had his pictures. They jogged back across the field toward the barbwire fence. At the gap where they'd come in, they heard the roar of engines. The first of the C-130s was taxiing down the field.

Kurt raised his camera and started shooting again.

A blinding white light shot through the darkness, trapping Abbie in its beam. She raised her hand to shield her eyes. A dozen Muslim soldiers came running toward her. The first, an officer by his insignia, grabbed for her arm. She twisted away, kicking at him. A thin kid in a heavy beard swung his AK-47 around and butt-stroked Kurt in the back. He fell to the runway, clutching his camera to his belly, gasping for breath.

Smirking, the young officer walked slowly up to him. Kurt rolled over, face to the ground, covering the camera. Furiously, the soldier leaned over and tore it away. Holding it up, he ripped out the film. Then he dropped the camera on the tarmac and crushed it with his boot.

"You are under arrest."

He nodded to one of his soldiers, who grabbed Abbie roughly by her coat, then spun her around so hard her knit hat fell off. He pushed her toward a car. The Muslims threw them both into the backseat. At their command post, a colonel came out. His voice was high-pitched, furious. "What are you doing here?" he shouted at them. Abbie's mouth was dry. No words came out. She heard Kurt saying, "We came in on the plane. With the Americans. Go check it out."

Brilliant, shameless Kurt. "That's right," she said, recovering her voice, handing him her ID and passport.

The colonel pointed to the soldiers, who grabbed them and left them in a windowless room with two metal chairs. They heard the deadbolt slide shut on the other side.

"Think it'll work?"

"Only thing I could think of."

"Anyone ever tell you you were a genius, Kurt? I mean, like if they had an Olympics in fast talking you'd get the gold."

"Yeah, well, we'll see."

After half an hour they heard the bolt slide back. When the door opened, the colonel was a different man. "A misunderstanding," he said. "We have spoken to your Mr. Lynch. You are free to go." He took Kurt's smashed camera and Abbie's cap out of a scuffed leather bag and handed them back. "You should be more careful," the colonel said. "It is very easy to have an accident in this country."

Two Muslim soldiers escorted them to the front gate. For ten minutes they ran back down the road toward Tuzla. When the airbase finally dropped out of sight behind them, Abbie stopped. "I know you, Kurt. Where's the rest of the film?"

Reaching down, he pulled a small black roll from his sock. "Lunkhead."

She put her arms around his neck and gave him a peck on the cheek, burning herself on his three-day beard. Who could ever kiss this animal for real? They started off down the road, walking this time. After a few minutes, they saw a small white UN van bearing down on them. They flagged it and got in.

"You know Club Tango?" Kurt said.

"For sure," the driver said, his breath reeking of garlic and cabbage. The Mercedes was still there where Kurt had parked it. Someone had rifled the glove compartment and stolen the carton of cigarettes he used for petty cash and bribes. But the engine coughed once and started right up. Before dark the next day, they'd be back at the Parcewal.

TWENTY-ONE

★ Zagreb ★

Sandy sat on a wooden bench under a linden tree in the park. He'd spent the day before briefing the Paki brass and staff on the Illiceza road firefight. Then he'd returned to his observation post across from the Parcewal.

Was it the Baltimore Orioles baseball cap that caught the cop's eye? Or the rest of his ensemble? He was wearing jeans that fit tightly above his soccer shoes and he had a pair of Ray-Bans dangling from the neck of his parka. On a lanyard swinging from his wrist, he carried a Leica digicam. The little camera could feed forty digitized images directly into a laptop for instant processing. Santana had asked him to check it out as a recon tool. The Professor thought it was better than anything the Pentagon was sending them.

He'd shown the cop his UN identification and the cop had moved on.

Now he had been staking her out for nearly four hours. The sun helped some, but his neck still felt stiff as an angle iron. Give it one more hour.

At three-thirty, the sun began to disappear behind the roof of the Parcewal. Then, at the far end of the park, he saw a rattle-trap Mercedes coming down the empty boulevard.

          ★   ★   ★

Kurt dropped Abbie at the curb a few yards up from their hotel. They'd agreed that he should get a flight out that night and ship the film from Paris. He blew her a kiss and rattled off to book his tickets and return his rent-a-wreck. Abbie watched the car limp around the park and wobble back up the boulevard the way they had come in.

Then she saw him.

The sunglasses hid his eyes and the dumb cap obscured his face, but there was something unmistakable about the way the body was leaning against the wall. How had he found her? Nobody but Julian knew where she was. He was raising a camera now, aiming it at her.

"You sneak," she called over to him. "How did you get here?"

"Come, signorina? Ma sono un fotografo. Non rompermi le scatole."

Don't break his balls?

She stopped in the middle of the road, cars and motor scooters careening around her. How could she make such a dumb mistake? Was she seeing his face everywhere? She might as well be wearing his class ring. Weakly, she walked over to apologize.

"Scusi," she said, feeling like a fool.

Off came the cap, up in the air this time, maybe 20 feet, followed by the Ray-Bans. "I thought the Italian was a nice touch."

Should she throw herself at him or brain him? "I was in the nabe," he said.

Throwing her arms around him, she buried her face in his neck. "Hey, you're all wet," he said, pulling a bandanna from his jeans and dabbing at her eyes. Then he kissed her, a slow kiss, gentle—no tongue, not the usual pit bull trying to clean her molars.

She felt the strong arms around her back. "You do know how to get a girl, Captain Caine," she said.

"Maybe." He was grinning at her like an idiot. "But how do I keep her?"

★   ★   ★

The hair. It was the hair.

As she leaned over to pick up her backpack, her red hair spilled down over her narrow shoulders, catching the sun, glowing in a way that made him think of *stella rossa* flowers spilling over the patio walls in Honduras. She was wearing a black jacket and tight black jeans, high-top Nikes, also black. Adjusting the straps on her backpack, she said, "How well do you know Zagreb?"

"First time."

"How much time do we have?"

"It depends," he said.

"Don't give up, soldier," she said, leading him through the door of the Parcewal.

"I guess I had you pegged as a bolter." She moved behind the empty front desk.

"Takes one to know one," he said.

"Don't you ever stop?"

"Do you?"

She opened the cupboard under the front desk and took out her laptop. "Let's go," she said, starting up a narrow flight of stairs.

At the top, she led him just beyond the vestibule to a dark oak door with iron hinges and an enormous lock. An old iron key was hanging from a peg hidden behind a black-and-white photograph of day lilies. She opened the door and turned, looking at him as if they had never left the bed at the Astoria. He lifted her in his arms. "Which way do I go?"

"Straight down the hall."

He carried her past another black-and-white photograph, this one of a single rose, set over a Gothic side table. The studio was large with high ceilings. It was furnished with one chest, very tall, very wide to follow the sprawling lines of the room with its dining and sitting areas, and a queen-size bed with a green silk cover and black steel frame.

He put her down gently and she pulled off her sneakers. Arching her back, she tugged off her tee shirt, lifted her hips as she slid off the black jeans. Her legs still carried the last of a summer tan. He ran his hands up the inside of her thighs, lightly, teasing, feeling himself stiffen. Keeping his eyes on her, he stepped back and pulled off his shirt. Then he kissed each knee, peeling her panties down from her hips, down over the trim legs to her ankles. She kicked them off and watched him unbuckle his pants.

The fading sunlight caught a white slash of scar tissue on his calf. She sat up and unhooked her bra, threw it to the floor, then leaned back and waited for him. He kneeled between her legs, caressing the soft hair under her navel, running his tongue up her soft groove.

Then he kissed her softly, again and again, running his lips over her forehead, her eyelids, slowly, still kneeling between her thighs, lingering until she surprised him, arching her back and thrusting her hips upward, drawing him into her until they were racing toward the light. And he knew she could feel him going off within her and she was crying "Yes, Sandy, my God, Sandy. Yes."

*　　*　　*

Now she was sleeping and he was the one stealing around the room. He made a quick circuit of the little apartment. More photographs. Flowers, always white. Mannered, arty. But peaceful. She had jury-rigged alligator clips to her modem to connect the laptop. It was open. On the screen he saw an e-mail message. *You must be nuts. Don't F with me again. Julian.* Unclipping the setup, he called and left the number for Nate. He was just snapping the clips back on when he heard her rustling. Slipping across the room, he leaned over the bed. Her hair was lying in long curling tresses across the dark green bedspread. They hadn't taken the time to get under the covers. As he bent down to kiss her, she suddenly sat up, completely awake.

"What time is it?"

He went over to the telephone table where he had dropped his watch. "Five to four," he called back. She had jumped off the bed and was hooking up her bra.

"Good. We just have time," she said, picking up her panties and running to the bathroom. It would take special training to keep up with her. Like a triathlon a day.

"Where to now?" he called over the running water.

"Don't you ever get hungry? The market closes at five."

Twenty minutes later he was trotting down the boulevard trying to keep up with her. She was a dozen paces ahead of him, moving out fast.

"Miss Mancini," he shouted at her back. "Wait."

She spun around and stared at him. He heard his own voice and groaned again. The craziness of it. He had stalked her through Zagreb. They had made love twice. And he had never used her first name.

"Mancini?" she said, exaggerating the syllables. "Miss Mancini?" She was cocking her head, looking at him closely, as if he were a stuffed owl. "You're hopeless," she said, pushing the bill of his baseball cap down over his eyes. "Call me Abbie or I'm not bothering with you." Grabbing his shoulders, she turned him around and aimed him up the block.

They walked down clean streets filled with prosperous shops, the windows filled with goods. It amazed him. In Sarajevo, the bread ration was down to Gulag levels, but here you might not know you were in the middle of a civil war. Here, there was still the illusion of safety.

At the far end of Metlic Street, she led him to an old-fashioned covered market. Wandering among the stalls, they bought sausages and prosciutto from a sweating butcher. From a stone vat full of salty water, they fished out a ball of fresh goat cheese and picked a crusty loaf of bread from a small mountain of loaves piled on a metal cart pushed up next to a barrel of fat black olives. "Let's try these." She bought a double handful, pushed an olive into his mouth as they headed for the door. Outside it was getting colder. As they moved up the street together, she pulled items out of her string bag, feeding him, flirting. In the little park across from the Parcewal, they sat on the wooden bench and she took out what was left of the sausage and cheese. He tore a crust from the loaf, spread the cheese and fed her small chunks with bits of sausage and ham.

"Where did you find the Parcewal?" he asked, looking across the street.

"Kurt. It's one of his hideouts."

"Who's Vampira? The one who answers the phone?"

"Dava Smardz, also one of Kurt's. She owns the place. Inherited it and did some renovations. The flowers are hers. She's a photographer, too. They probably discuss lighting and camera angles from all sorts of interesting positions."

She wrapped the remains of their dinner and put them in the bag. "Let's go back," she said. They made one last circuit of the park. A *digestif*. On the far side, he stopped on the curb. Without thinking, she stepped into the intersection.

Pop. Pop. Pop. Pop.

She heard the sharp staccato sputter and felt herself yanked backward. Spinning violently, she fell on the cobblestone street. The motorbike that had just missed her skidded into a tight circle and came to a stop. She smelled the sharp odor of burned rubber. Dazed, she looked down and saw that the lace on her sneaker was torn where the bike's kickstand had caught it.

The driver, a twenty-year-old kid wearing a brown leather aviator's jacket and sunglasses, was cursing her. Why was he wearing the glasses? The sun was down. He couldn't see a thing.

And then Sandy slammed past her. He was hoisting the kid by the leg, flipping him over the handlebars, onto the piazza, sitting on his chest, smashing his head into the stones.

She saw the first splash of blood on the cobblestones. Then she was up on her feet, running toward them, grabbing at Sandy's back. He looked up as if he didn't recognize her.

"Stop it," she screamed. "You're going to kill him."

TWENTY-TWO

★ Zagreb ★

The sound of her voice brought him out of it. He saw her standing above him, trembling. The biker was bleeding into the dirty cobblestones. With a quick sweep of his arms, Sandy brought the sleeves of the guy's leather jacket up over his head and knotted them. Unnecessary precaution. This guy wasn't going anywhere.

A crowd was beginning to form around the accident. From somewhere beyond the park, he heard the siren of a police car. "We've got to get out of here," she yelled, pushing him hard in the small of his back. They jogged for three or four blocks, the noise of the crowd fading behind them, then collapsed on a stone bench.

The streetlights were on now. Under their yellow light half a dozen long-haired kids were playing soccer, chasing their scuffed ball over the cracked pavement as intently as golden retrievers. They had set up mop buckets for the goal.

Sandy circled Abbie's waist with his arm so she couldn't pull away.

"What was that all about?" Her voice was frigid. "I don't need this kind of shit."

"Hey, Abbie. That sonuvabitch almost killed you."

The tremor in his voice surprised him. There hadn't been enough action for that. It was the girl. He had been afraid for her.

"Right. I just slept with a man who almost spread some guy's brains on the ground."

"Look, you didn't see it. That guy wasn't just going too fast, he swerved toward you. Fucking little smartass. He wanted to clip you, Abbie. He was trying for a quick thrill on the way home."

"So you decided to teach him a lesson and kill him."

"I didn't decide anything. I reacted. He damn near killed you, and *I* didn't like it. That's the way I am."

She considered it, her eyes on the soccer ball bouncing along the street. "I don't go looking for fights," she said.

"Let's see, Mogadishu, Bosnia . . ."

"Okay, so I'm in the violence business, too. It makes good copy. But I try not to get personal about it. You do. It's like you see everyone coming right down on you."

"All right," he said. "Maybe I overreacted, considering you're still alive, but I didn't come here to attend your funeral."

"And I didn't come here to spend all my time bailing you out of some Croat lockup. That's the way life is in this country. You have to adjust."

"I was just trying to take care of you."

"I can take care of myself. I don't need you running around like some kind of lethal weapon."

So much for all that guardian-angel bullshit. Furious, he got up off the bench and headed down the street. From behind, she shouted after him, "Where do you think you're going now?"

"Back for my stuff," he roared, feeling like a moron.

He heard another shout, a boy's voice this time, as a scuffed soccer ball came shooting by him. And then she was rocketing past his shoulder, bumping him aside, bearing down on the ball as it skidded across the pavement. She was running full tilt, easy in her body, lovely.

He sprinted after her, picking up speed until they were side by side, their bodies bumping. Smacking the ball with her instep, she sent it sailing between the mop buckets. Their legs tangled and they fell, rolling over each other onto the round cobbles.

"Back for *me* is where you're going." She kissed his red face. "Now you're doubly responsible."

A tall skinny boy was standing between the buckets, tending goal. *"Brava,"* he shouted, waving to her. Picking up the ball, he thumped it with his foot. In the yellow light of the street lamps it rose and arced down the street and back into play.

★   ★   ★

"So who taught you to score like that? You kick like a pro."

Sandy peered into the kitchen nook, the rage gone from his eyes. Abbie was bending over a sauté pan, inspecting the garlic. She had chopped it fine and was simmering it in olive oil. She had tomatoes, scalded, peeled, cut small, waiting in an earthenware bowl next to the stove.

"Must be in the Mancini DNA," she said, poking the garlic with a fork. "You're looking at Abigail Mancini, St. Helena High, Class of Eighty-three, Most Likely to Be Picked First for Your Team. It didn't hurt that Doc Mancini was coach."

She had a Band-Aid on her ankle. Sandy watched her probing it with a polished toe.

"I can still see him out there in the backyard with me and my brothers and the ball. He'd go, 'Playing the game is not what matters, you guys. Only winning counts. Go for the score.' I hear his voice about a dozen times a day."

With the General, it had been the same: all push, no rewards; nothing ever satisfied him.

"I wasn't just a tomboy," she said, taking out plates and putting them on the table. "I was a killer with boobs. Barely knew what to do with them until I was a senior. I just thought they got in the way. The other girls taped pictures of Johnny Depp in their lockers. I had a poster of Pelé. But, it was like, I didn't dream of Pelé hitting on me, I wanted him to make passes *to* me. You know, so *I* could score. Crazy, no? You must think I'm completely butch."

He came around behind her, watching her toss the tomatoes into the pan. She took the lid off a pot and stirred it, the rising steam mingling with the smell of hot oil, garlic and tomatoes.

"Estivi," she said, leaning back against him as he put his arms around her waist. "Made with *capellini*. The dish that built the House of Mancini." He started to nuzzle her ear, but she broke away from him. Draining the pasta into a colander, she transferred it to a large yellow and white bowl, then poured the sauce over it. "Known far and wide for its restorative powers," she said, steering him over to the dining table. She had set it with blue china plates and a pair of darker blue wine goblets.

After they finished dinner, washing it down with half a bottle of Chiaramonte '89, he put down his glass and said, "I still don't get it, *principessa*. You've got more moving parts than anyone I've ever met."

"They all fit together. I'll give you the short version. One, my grandfather knew more about vines and grapes than any man in Tuscany. Two, there was a killing frost in the Napa Valley in the fall of 1952. Three, the Badoni brothers out there knew about him and hired him to save their business. Four, he did. He took the family and spent two years in St. Helena. My dad went with him. He was fifteen, Mario Antonio Mancini, the kids called him Manny."

He looked at his hands.

"What is it?" she asked, filling his glass.

"That would make him about five years older than my father would have been."

He ran his finger slowly around the rim of the glass. "You said he was a doctor."

"I did. He met my mother in the emergency room of the med school at the University of California, Irvine. She was a theater major, sprained her ankle in a rehearsal, came sobbing into the ER. Love at first splint. He taped her ankle with an Ace bandage and asked her out to dinner. She told me they were in bed doing it by eleven o'clock that night."

"Are all the Mancini women like that?"

"Fast and loose? Are those the words you're groping for? Let's just say I come from a line of women who know what they want and when they want it. Anyway, the Army drafted him in early sixty-six. He had to go down to San Antonio for a couple of months to learn Army medicine. So he's down there a day or two and the phone rings. It's Mom. She says, 'I miss you.' He says, 'Me, too.' So then she goes, 'Good. Because I also missed my period.'"

Sandy laughed.

"And he says, 'Will you marry me?' And she says, 'When?' Three days later they got married in the post chapel."

"Hot. See that Italian blood."

"All that hybrid blood. While he was in Vietnam, she stayed in Los Angeles with her parents. Henry and Ida Benjamin. The Benjamins of Bel Air. He was an agent for William Morris and she was into real estate. They had a little money, not a lot, but more than enough."

"Where did your father pull his tour?"

"I Corps, I think he said. He worked in a field hospital. A mortar barrage hit the camp one night and took off half his foot. He always said thank God it wasn't his hands. So after they patched him up, he took Mom and the baby and headed north on the first bus out. They didn't even have a car. He gave up surgery and took over an old guy's general practice. All he wanted to do was treat normal sick people in a very quiet place."

"And make babies and coach soccer?"

"Not in that order. He's a soccer nut. An absolute freak. Maybe he's compensating for the foot. He may have been a gimp, but it didn't matter. He made everyone else do the running, starting with my brothers, then me."

"Your mother, too?"

"Definitely. She could have been an actress. And she wrote great stories. *The New Yorker* published one of them. But she wound up writing a gossip column for the *St. Helena Vintner*. 'Becky's First Pressing,' she called it. All the dirt fit to print."

Sandy got up from the table. She followed him out on the balcony. It was nearly midnight. In the black sky, the moon hung like a thin crescent of silver behind the cathedral. It was colder now. She shivered and drew him back into the warm flat.

"So where did you get your short fuse?" she asked him after they were sitting on the couch. "What's your excuse?" He was leaning backward, his head propped up on one of the paler green silk brocade pillows. She stroked his dark blond hair, touched the aristocratic cheekbones, the straight nose, the sensual mouth. Put him in a doublet and tights, he could have been a captain for Lorenzo the Magnificent.

"You mean, why I thumped that guy? I already told you. I wanted to ruin his day."

"You can do better than that."

"Okay, how long has it been since we were up there on that road with all those bastards and all that shit coming down? Less than a week, right? Well, I was just doing what I'm trained to do. It becomes automatic. A reflex that keeps you alive, that's with you until it burns out or you're dead. On that road, it was my job to protect you. Today I *wanted* to protect you. Big difference, but the fuse burns the same both ways. Fast. Real fucking fast. And you can't just shut it off. One day you kill a guy, they give you a medal. Next day you take someone out, they put you in jail for life."

She plumped up the couch beside her. "Maybe I can understand," she said when his head was back on the pillow. "Maybe more than you think."

"What makes you so sure?"

"I'm sure of one thing."

"What's that?"

"I don't buy a word of it. You're talking crap."

He leaned on his elbow and looked at her, more startled than angry. "What are you talking about?"

"I'm talking about you, puppy. You're holding out on me."

Suddenly, he buried his face in the couch, his body quaking. "Sandy . . ." she said, reaching over to touch him. Then she saw he was laughing, choking, falling out.

"Puppy! Did you say puppy?"

"That's what I said."

Reaching across her, he snapped off the table lamp. Then he pulled her closer, running his hands down inside her pants. "You want more?" he said.

"Yes."

"The whole story?"

"Yes—from the beginning."

He threaded his fingers through her hair, letting the silky strands curl through his fingers and over his face, breathing in the warm trace of spice and flowers.

"Okay, the whole works," he said. "After."

* * *

It was morning now, the windows shifting from black to gray.

"I had this puppy named Margarita once," Sandy said. He was still in bed, his chest bare, propped up against the black steel frame, half a dozen pillows behind him. "Must've been about twenty years ago. Melba gave her to me."

The room was warm, the smell of eggs and strong coffee floating in the air. Reflected in the dressing mirror, Abbie was holding forth at the stove, short cotton wrap cinched just above her hips, the legs slender, smooth, tan, showing nicely all the way up when she bent over to inspect the pan.

"It was in Honduras. The first time the two of us went down there to stay with her family. I got homesick, I guess, and started to mope. Probably couldn't hack it without the General on my case. Too much happiness. So she bought me this little black mutt with round black eyes, sweet little nose, soft, warm, wet mouth—Margarita, the first female I ever slept with."

"What a lover," Abbie called over her shoulder. "Bide-A-Wee's answer to Tom Cruise."

She deftly folded the frittatas onto a plate and put them on a tray with the gleaming espresso maker, cups and two linen napkins. When she leaned and put the tray on his lap he could see her breasts through the neck of the white cotton top.

"No forks."

"Fingers." She smiled. "You know how to use them."

Green flecks of fine herbs decorated the delicately browned cylinders. "I loved Margarita. Melba gave me something better than love. The thing was, I always knew I could trust her."

Abbie poured the coffee.

"I want to be sure I've got this right," she said. "You're crazy for dogs but with women you think trust is more important than love. How do you know? Have you ever been in love?"

"No. Not with a woman, no. Have you?"

She picked off a piece of her frittata and waved it slowly to cool it. "There was Johnny Sloane, superjock, quarterback, scouted to Berkeley. He gave me his ring, made me bleed the first time, then called me the night before the senior prom to say he'd made a little mistake. Knocked up Claire Wilson, one of the cheerleaders. I told him good luck because he was going to be living with that mistake the rest of his life. Funny thing was, I wasn't mad, just relieved it wasn't me."

She put the frittata to her lips, blew it just to be sure.

"Then there was Hale Latham at the *San Francisco Examiner*. He was pushing forty when I was just out of J school at Cal. He asked me to marry him. I liked him a lot, but it felt like he was trying to box me in, so I ran like a mad woman for New York. The *Times* treated me like a teeny-bop word processor, which is why I wound up covering weddings for the *Washington Chronicle*. At least there I was putting out my own stuff."

"So what's with Julian?"

She poured out two cups of coffee, taking a lot of time. "How do you know about Julian?"

"You left your laptop open this morning. The e-mail was still on the screen. I saw it when I went to the john. Lovers' spat? You said, 'Julian, darling, the guns are real. Got it cold.' Seemed to bum him out."

She flushed. "You're wondering if I'm making it on my back, aren't you?"

"Like I was saying, it's all a question of who you can trust."

"Whom."

"Sorry," he said. "Green-eyed monster. I shouldn't have read your mail."

"Julian's screwing my story, not me. I don't sleep with anyone where I work. I do flirt."

"You do a lot more than that."

"With you, pups. But don't push it."

"Then what's the story?"

"You can read it in the paper. I haven't filed it yet."

"Not even a hint?"

"Nope."

"Are you going back tomorrow? Didn't leave you much choice, did he?"

"Who's Melba?" she said, changing the subject. "So *I* don't have to get jealous."

Sandy took a sip of the hot espresso. "Like I said, Melba's been the woman in my life." He watched her, hoping to break through her control. She didn't blink. Better not to push it.

"Melba went to work for the General when I was a little kid," he said quickly. "He had four stars, ran the Continental Army Command. And I was driving him and a long starched line of nannies crazy. So one night he was talking to General Woolsey about the problem, and Woolsey looked over to his maid and said, 'Cita, what about your sister?' Melba came around the next day. She's been with us ever since. She was nineteen then, I guess I was crowding three."

"Are they lovers?"

"She took care of me. Not him—at least not the way you think. We're talking different generations here. Different worlds."

"You love her, don't you?"

"Caines don't do love," he said. "It's just that Melba's the closest I ever came to having a mother."

"Sounds like love to me. Maybe there's hope for you."

"Give me a break. Melba took care of me for three years straight and the General was so pleased he forgot all about us. He also forgot to give her a vacation. So one day she went in and demanded the summer off. She said she wanted to go home to Honduras. He said, 'What about the boy?' And she said, 'You mean *my* little boy? He's going, too. You don't think I'd leave him here alone with you, do you?'"

Abbie laughed. "Maybe you're right about Melba."

"She kept me from joining the silver spoon gang. Honduras was heat, emotions, jalapeños in the chow, big families, name days, fiestas. The General came from Kill a Commie for Christ and Country and Melba's family were raving Marxists. You had to make adjustments."

Abbie wiped her lips with her napkin. "How did Melba handle it?"

"Melba's always hated true believers. She thinks commies suck and so do Yankee avengers. The communists because her father and two brothers fell for Karl Marx and got themselves blown away, the Yankees because they trained the security troops that killed them. She told me I was better off playing soccer. So that's what I did. Her uncle was a fisherman. I worked on his boat, diving for lobsters. On weekends, his kids taught me to kick and pass and eat paella. I came home thinking the World Cup was more important than the World Series. So there you have it: Sandy Caine, Semi-Subversive."

She didn't laugh. Jesus, he thought, what did she want from him? He was spilling his guts. What happened if she really started to grill you?

"Why are you Sandy?" she asked him. "If you're Alexander Grant II, why aren't you Alec or Alex?"

"That's what they called my father." He drained the last of his coffee and put the cup back on the tray. It made a loud sound. "He was a spoiled, gutless sonuvabitch."

"And you don't take after him?"

"I try not to."

"Maybe you're trying too hard."

"Oh, give it a rest, Abbie. What do you want me to do, sign up with the twelve-step crowd? Children of Cowards? Don't count on it."

He pulled some clothes out of his rucksack. "Where are my shoes?"

"Try under the couch. Let me know when you stop feeling naked."

When he finally ran out of things to pull on, button or tie, he sat down on the couch and put one of the silk pillows on his lap. "Come here," he said to her gruffly. She cinched her cotton shift around her hips and sat next to him.

"The first thing you need to know is that the General's real son is Jeff Taylor, not my dad. He was everything my dad could never be: a jock, a natural leader, all of that. Alex was a total loser; the best thing that ever happened to him was Jeff."

"Jeff's dad was in the State Department, always away, so it was like they set up their own Lost Boys Society. Jeff hated his dad's power grubbing, his compromising. The General looked like God to him. So he decided to become a soldier, and Alex was right behind him.

"Up to then, Alex hated the thought of being a soldier. The General had parked him on Beacon Hill with the Putnams, and they spoiled him rotten. Nannies, governesses, ponies, tutors, the whole trip. Then Jeff won an appointment to the Point and suddenly Alex wanted to go, too. The General pulled every string he had and sent him off to become a man."

Abbie brushed a curl back from her eyes but it bounced down again. Against the pillow, her warm brown eyes were flecked with gold. "I can understand that," she said.

"Understand what?"

"All of it. In my family, if you had a dick, you were a doctor. You had a womb, you were a wife. You wanted a life of your own, forget it."

He reached down and twined the strand of hair around his finger, then pushed it back into place.

"Same way with the Caines and West Point. I wasn't crazy about being a soldier, either. If I'd had my choice, I'd probably be chasing soccer balls or raising dogs."

"So what happened after the General sneaked Alex into the Point?"

"Jeff pulled him through. He even began to show a little leadership ability. Then in his Cow Year, his hair turned gray. Maybe from all the stress. They began calling him Gray. Better than wuss asshole.

"Jeff graduated in the fall of sixty-three, not as first captain but right up there at the top of the class. He was assigned to the 82nd Airborne at Fort Bragg.

"That last year without Jeff, Alex started humping this Polish girl from New Paltz. He nearly blew everything. His grades fell off and he finished near the bottom of the class. And then he went and married Barbara Ann Brakowski. My mother. In the Sons of Poland Hall instead of the chapel at the Point. The General nearly had a stroke."

She laughed. "Dr. Mancini would do the same if I brought home a soldier. You'd be safer in Sarajevo."

"You planning to take me home?"

"I don't want to die young. So then what?"

"Alex followed after Jeff. Ranger course, then into the 82nd Airborne. They sent his unit to the Dom Rep in '65, so he saw a little action and got his Combat Infantry Badge."

"That doesn't sound so bad."

"No, except some people said he kept his head down when he should've kept it up. No big deal, only rumors. Jeff got him transferred to his Special Forces unit. ODA 351. And the two of them shaped it up just in time for Vietnam."

Abbie looked up from the pillow.

"The problem isn't your dad, pups. The problem is you. You don't know who you are."

"Get off it, Abbie. You sound like Dr. Ruth."

"Cheap shot, Sandy. You've got to make up for a father who couldn't tie his own tennis shoes unless Jeff Taylor helped him. And you've got to be a better soldier than good old Uncle Jeff. If you do all that, maybe, just maybe, it will warm up the Abominable Snowman."

"It's not like that, Abbie."

"The hell it isn't."

He walked out on the balcony. After a while she came out and stood next to him. She put her hand on the back of his neck and stroked him. "What's really bothering you, pups?"

The voice gentler now. Why not tell her. Straight on. "You remember Perkins," he said.

"That good-looking chick at your party? The one you were drooling over, by the way."

"No, I'm talking about her father. You must have seen him up on the roof in Mogadishu."

"Bruce Willis in Kevlar? What about him?"

"He told me something that doesn't make sense. Remember when the sappers blew that hole in the wall? Maybe you didn't realize how close all of us were to buying it. After Perkins and I greased them he turned to me and he said, 'You fight just like your dad.' "

"You sure he was talking about Alex?"

"Not at first. I thought he was sticking it to me, telling me I was yellow, too. But he was standing there over a dozen dead Somalis with dust all over his face and gunpowder stinking up the place and I could see that wasn't what he meant at all."

"What did he mean?"

"That Alex was okay, I think, but I don't really know. We were supposed to get it straight over a beer, but he caught an RPG round in the chest. When they got him back they had to take his body out behind a berm and defuse it, for Christ's sake."

Sandy pounded the dirty brick wall of the balcony with his fist. A small puff of red dust drifted down toward the street. "I just don't fucking know."

"Maybe we should find out."

He put his arm around her and drew her close to him. "No maybes about it," he said.

★　　★　　★

Inside the studio, there was the muffled sound of a phone ringing from under pillows, where Sandy had stuffed it the night before. Screw it, he thought. Abbie went and unburied the receiver. When Sandy finally came in, she held it out to him. "For you," she said. "It's Nate."

"I don't like to interrupt a man's pussy eatin', but you're gonna hafta finish chompin' and get your ass back here, know what I'm sayin'?"

"You getting too old for this business, man? You need some help with Elena?"

"No, sir. You the one needs some help with the man. Hunter's gotta job for us. Wants us back in Sarajevo. Like yesterday."

Sandy looked at his watch. It was just past 7:00 A.M.

"What's he want us to do?"

"Didn't say. We got a massacre up near Polidza. Maybe three thousand. Big ditch somewhere, probably. They're still lookin' for it. UN's coming in. Maybe that's it. Maybe not. Like I said, you gotta quit groovin' and get movin', Captain."

"Yeah, I hear you. Meet me at the hotel in five hours. I'll get us seats on the shuttle."

Sandy looked across the room. Abbie was sitting at the table writing something quickly in her notebook. The laptop was still open, Lynch's e-mail message glowing on the screen.

"Thanks for covering my ass, Nate. See you back at the hotel around noon."

Fucking Serbs. Weren't they supposed to be Europeans? Civilized? Last time out, the Serbs had fought Hitler. It was the Croats and Muslims who were allies with the Nazis. Go figure.

As he put down the phone, he felt her touching his shoulder.

She rubbed his neck, then reached over and dropped a folded sheet of paper into his hand. "I'll get dressed," she said, disappearing into the bathroom.

He didn't open the note until the C-130 began its descent into Sarajevo.

"Why do people get all literary when all they're doing is satisfying biological imperatives?" she wrote. "Lots of things to find out. On lots of levels. No maybes about it. amanci@washchron.com."

He tucked the note into his pocket. That made two. He'd have to find another box.

TWENTY-THREE

Through the glass wall of the deputy editor's office, Abbie saw
Julian pick up the phone and turn his back on her. He had on his
blue and red suspenders, the wide ones Yuppie brokers and
lawyers and upwardly mobile editors wore in tandem with their
black tassel loafers. She looked at her watch. Five-thirty. C'mon,
Julian, we're missing the first edition.

The moment Julian saw her, he'd pointed silently to a chair
outside his door, leaving her to figure it out. Seething, she stood
there taking in his act, the blue shirt with the white collar, the
thin chalk stripes on his charcoal trousers, the Mont Blanc pen
in his hand.

Before the flight left from Rome that morning, she'd e-mailed
him the gunrunning story. From Dulles International, she'd
come directly to the paper. Now she could feel the pulse of the
newsroom racing toward the first-edition deadline. She was
going to miss it.

Why are you doing this to me, Julian?

Her confidence began crumbling, the way it always did with
guys who had her number. Make them tall enough, give them a
voice like a doctor's, and she'd start wondering whether she
could shower and sing at the same time. Then she'd begin to
grovel.

After five minutes, he finally put down the phone and waved
her in. He didn't get up.

"What do you call this?" he said.

"I'd call it a scoop. What would you call it?"

"I'd call it bad news."

"That story's good, Julian. I was there, so was Kurt. What's the matter?"

"This," he said, punching a few keys on his computer and waving her around to look at his monitor. The lead story from Reuters said: "Ethnic Cleansing in Mostar—Thousands Disappear."

"And you're in Tuzla? Chasing phantom gunrunners?"

"That's not fair, and you know it."

"All I know is that at the very moment the Serbs are coming on like fucking Nazis you want the *Chronicle* to say the Muslims are the bad guys. Goddamn it, Abbie, the Serbs are murdering, raping, baby-stabbing bastards. Why are you the only reporter in the world who doesn't get it? You've just pissed away your whole trip."

A little worm of fear began to wiggle inside her. The bean counters hated shelling out for dead stories.

"The big picture isn't always the whole picture, Julian. You're right about the Serb leadership, but you're wrong about everything else."

"Is that right?"

"Yes, it is. One—the United States is getting drawn in over there fast and no one over here knows about it. Two—we can't trust anyone in the Balkans. Sure, the Bosnians are the victims. So were the Buddhists in Hue. Three—it may feel good to call the Serbs Nazis and go in to clean them out, but you saw what happened on the Illiceza road. The minute we go, we're going to get shot in the back by our so-called 'friends.' And there's probably four thousand reporters filing the same story from Mostar. My story is exclusive. And new. Isn't that the business we're in? The *news* business?"

"Are you completely through?"

"No way, I'm just beginning. I want—"

"Oh, shut up, Abbie. Look, I'm not going to run any unsubstantiated story about nutsos with AK-47s. Let's just forget your arms bizarro. Do I make myself clear?"

"I don't know what to say."

"*That* is one great big relief," he said. "Now I'll do the rest of the talking. Your problem is you've got more guts than brains.

For the next three months, consider yourself on probation. You're going to grow up fast or get out."

"How am I supposed to do that?"

"Like I said on the phone, I have something for you."

She couldn't remember, and it didn't matter. Julian was incapable of believing anyone could ever forget even one of the precious words he muttered.

"Who's the best-known war hero in this town?" he asked her. "Who do you think is going to be our next President?"

Easy one. "And what do you propose we do about Senator Taylor?"

"Make him our star. Victory Over Vietnam Syndrome. The Power and the Glory. Jefferson Taylor. The Ultimate Blast from the Past. We're coming up on twenty years since the fall of Saigon. Time for another look."

"But that's more than a year from now."

"We'll call it a special project. Our very special project." So that was it. Julian, the Ben Bradlee wanna-be, using Jeff Taylor to play his John F. Kennedy. Butter up JKT now, eat at the White House later. "You're shameless, Julian."

"Absolutely. Packaging is what the game's all about. And timing. The art of timing. You know who I was just talking to while you were out there waiting?"

"No. Amaze me."

"Patrice St. Jean. He wanted to invite me to a dinner party. Until I saw you out there, I was going to blow him off. Now I've got a better idea." He walked around to his Rolodex and wrote a number on a sheet of notepaper. Not the foolscap everyone else used. The engraved logo at the top said: FROM THE DESK OF JULIAN LYNCH. "You take care of the RSVP. Call him and tell him you and I will be coming together. Get him to set you up an interview with Taylor."

"You really want to get in bed with Taylor this way?"

"Why don't *you* tell me? I saw you and Taylor at Fort Myer. I saw you leave together. And when Patrice called just now and I saw you sitting there outside the door with your legs crossed, that's the first thing I remembered. Our Abbie and our Jeffie. Tell Pat if our project goes as well as I think it's going to go, you'll be covering his candidate." He started for the door, then turned around as if something equally momentous had just hit him. "You ever been chez Patrice?"

"Are you kidding? I'm not even on his C-list."

"I can see why," he said, looking at her rumpled blouse and slacks. "Go buy yourself something decent to wear. I'll sign for it. This time." He reached for the door. "And Abbie, no more J school games, okay? I'll be watching you."

★   ★   ★

On the third floor, the doors opened to the teeming newsroom. Making her way through the maze of desks, she came to her own in a cubicle at the rear wall—the Atex monitor and keyboard commanding the work station, the headset telephone on its little hook, everything neat and antiseptic. She tried to remember who had once told her that journalists were a spit-on-the-floor breed. All that *Front Page* stuff. What crap. Most of the reporters she knew in Washington were as tight-assed as MBAs. All suits and blazers and blue shirts and striped ties. They didn't want to stand out. Put a source on guard, it's harder to mug him.

She felt a plump hand on her shoulder. "Yo, Becca," she said. For a heavy woman, Becca had an eerie way of creeping up on you.

Abbie turned in her chair and looked up at her friend. Becca was short and broad across the shoulders, possibly in her middle forties, a size 18 who looked more like a lathe operator than a society reporter. Abbie put her at maybe 170 pounds between diets, although her face was quite pretty. Her eyes were dark green. When she was angry, which was much of the time, they got even darker. She always wore a brown felt beret, even in the office. It covered the spot on the back of her head where her brown hair was beginning to thin. "Male-pattern baldness," she called it.

Becca was a country girl, maybe the only female card-carrying member of the NRA on the *Chronicle* staff. She owned 500 acres of Blue Ridge hardscrabble left to her by her father, but she was letting the farm return to woods. She preferred deer to cows. You couldn't hunt cows. After her second gin and tonic, she'd start saying things like "Penetration is imperialism" and get pissed off when Abbie laughed.

Behind Becca's back, Julian called her Fats Deming. He told Abbie he considered it a tribute to Becca's powers of reverse English and her skill at hustling gossip. Becca's pet name for Julian was Dickbrain. She told Abbie she didn't ordinarily conjoin those two organs, but for Julian, she would make an exception.

"Well, honey, tell me all. Out with it. Why here so late and so blue? What did he want?"

"Mother, forgive me, I have sinned. He didn't like my story."

Becca put her other hand on Abbie's head. "Recite three op-ed pieces, go with God, child. You do disappoint me. I was hoping you'd get into his pants and yank that little tallywhacker of his right off."

"Hand jobs aren't my thing, Becca."

"Spare me," she said, grabbing Abbie's chair and spinning her around to face the black computer screen. "To work. I'm finished with you." Abbie watched her disappear around the cubicle partition, ambling in the general direction of the Style section on what she called her killer shoes—spindly three-inch heels that always made Abbie wonder how they ever held her up.

Nothing from Sandy in her e-mail. Logging off, she went to the morgue and dug out "Taylor, Jefferson Kenefick, U.S. Senator." The guy was doing all right. Half a dozen narrow buff envelopes with the hard news and a large one jammed with profiles. Back at her desk, she stacked them in chronological order next to her computer and began to read.

The Army had sent him to Washington as a White House Fellow in 1971, clearly a young guy singled out for big things, not a one-shot hero. Two years later he'd moved up to battalion commander with the 8th Infantry Division in West Germany. Then he pulled a hitch at the War College before they assigned him to the Department of the Army's Deputy Chief of Staff for Operations. A water walker. Going all the way. Why did he get out?

The answer fell from the next envelope. In the summer of 1983, during a night jump with one of his units, a freak wind gusted up and dragged him across the drop zone, killing eleven paratroopers, breaking half the bones in his body and leaving him with a compound fracture of the right leg. The Army surgeons said he'd never walk again without a severe limp; so his jumping days were over. That meant an end to his Army career. Sitting behind a desk and limping around the Pentagon weren't the way Jefferson Taylor had seen his future.

Abbie went to the cafeteria for a cup of coffee. When she got back, she put the Styrofoam cup next to her keyboard and opened the large envelope. The first feature story, more than twenty years old, came from the paper's old society section, weddings, not just a quick notice and wooden portrait of the bride and groom, but a full-page story with three pictures. In the early seventies, while he was at the White House, Taylor had run into Janine Walker at a cocktail party and screening thrown by the Motion Picture Association of America. The head of the MPAA had wanted to introduce them that night. Or so he thought. As it turned out, they already knew each other.

"You know, you two look like you belong together," he had said, winking at them, his dark eyebrows curling wildly, pushing the deal as usual. And he was right. Janine, the daughter of John Walker, the senior senator from Ohio, was a good-looking brunette with a master's in psychology from Ohio State. The Taylors and the Walkers were old political friends and allies in Ohio Democratic politics. The last time Jeff and Janine had seen each other was at a Fourth of July picnic in Columbus where Jeff's grandmother and Senator Walker were the Patriot's Day speakers. They began spending more and more time together, until, when Jeff was due to go to West Germany, they realized they didn't want to be separated.

For a time, their marriage in the National Cathedral promised to unite the prevailing powers of Ohio's Democratic machine. Or so everyone thought. True to form, Jeff started to make plans to run for the House from his grandfather's old base in Cincinnati while he was still finishing physical therapy at Walter Reed Hospital. Then, to the total disbelief of the Walker and Kenefick families, he announced that he was going to run as a Republican. But after he won by four hundred votes and moved into the House, conservatives who thought they had a new and willing recruit discovered he was obsessed with military reform. In his maiden speech on the Senate floor, he said, "If we're going to build everything bigger, we're going to build it better, by God, or we're not going to build it at all." And he actually meant that one, too.

Too perfect, Abbie thought, sipping her coffee. *What's the hitch? No one was that perfect.* But Jeff Taylor's caissons just kept rolling on, reelection to the House, up to the Senate on George Bush's coattails in 1988 with a spot on the Armed Services Committee, unusual for a freshman.

Then she found a flaw. A small story on slick paper slipped out of the batch of yellowing newsprint clippings and fell on the floor. She leaned over and picked it up. It was a five-line item from the *Time*'s Milestones section in 1986.

Divorced: Congressman Jefferson Taylor, 44, and Janine Walker Taylor, 40, after 12 years of marriage; in Cincinnati, August 1. He to run under a cloud, she to run a bookstore on the Eastern Shore of Maryland. "We're still good friends," said he. "Sure," said she.

That was all. Abbie quickly riffled through the last two envelopes. Nothing. Picking up the phone she punched Becca's extension. "Style, Deming of the Desert," said the bored voice at the other end of the line.

"What can you tell me about Mrs. Senator Taylor?"

"The Good Mrs. Taylor? The Good and Gone Mrs. Taylor?"

"Yeah. That one."

"Well, first she went out and had her tits cut off—"

"Stop it, Becca, I'm serious."

"So am I. First breast cancer, then the divorce."

"What happened to her? Where is she?"

"I don't know. She's still alive or we would have read all about it." A pause. She could hear Becca turning her Rolodex. "Call Anton Dwyer at Black Cat Books. He's an old friend of hers. Maybe he knows where she is. I haven't had any reason to call her, except to offer my congratulations on her divorce."

"You did that?"

"Damn straight. She's tasty, sugar. But I couldn't talk her into moving in with me."

"You did *what*?"

"Joke, Abbie. *Joke*. Although I *was* attracted to her. Aren't too many yummies around. I told you she was a looker. Hang up now, dollface. I'm busy."

Dwyer wasn't at work, but when she said she was doing a story on bookstores, the clerk gave her Dwyer's home phone number. Dwyer picked up on the seventh ring. He sounded annoyed, and when he said she was looking for Janine Taylor, his voice got harder. "Why?"

"I'm writing a profile of Senator Taylor and it wouldn't be complete without my talking to Mrs. Taylor," she said, dropping into her best First Amendment Ms. Responsibility professional voice. "It's clear she knows him best."

He considered it for a while. "All right, she's in Crisfield on the Eastern Shore. Soft Shell Books. But she's Janine Walker again. And that's all I'm going to tell you."

The line went dead.

Abbie wrote the name on a piece of scratch paper, folded it

and put it in her purse. She tossed the clips into the out basket just as Becca's brown beret poked around the partition separating her desk from the others in the section. "I didn't mean to be crabby, puddin'. Anything else I can do to help?"

Abbie leaned back in her chair. "You really want to help?"

"You bet." Becca sounded almost penitent.

"Okay, Wonder Woman, the transmission on my car is shot. How about a ride out to Chevy Chase?"

"For you, even that."

"We're going to Saks."

"Saks?" Becca looked shocked.

"You heard right, Becky Lou. I'm in the market for a dress—one of them right fancy ones."

*　　*　　*

It was a few minutes after 11:00 P.M. The package with the dress was in the backseat and the two of them were roaring down Connecticut Avenue flushing BMWs, scaring away the lesser breeds.

Becca's wheels were a lot more substantial than her heels. The previous summer, a mood swing had led her to the Land Rover lot in Alexandria. There she had sold her soul to buy a '93 four-wheel drive Defender. Pencil yellow with black trim and a safari rack, V-8 engine, five on the floor. The headlights had those little wire cages around them. Under the bumper, a Warn winch with remote controls—good for 9,000 pounds of pull—was bolted to the chassis.

They growled through the quiet tree-lined streets of Cleveland Park, where the city's senior bureaucrats were already soundly asleep in their beds. When they reached the corner of Woodley Road and Connecticut Avenue, Becca turned left and headed down toward Rock Creek Park.

There was a full moon and it was much colder. The moonlight filtering between the bare limbs of the sycamores lit the way toward a small enclave of brick and stone houses set along a narrow street that wound for about a quarter mile along the edge of the park.

Abbie lived in the last house, a two-story neocolonial pile with separate wings east and west. Some long-dead power broker had built it in the twenties before the Crash. It was cut into four apartments. She had the west wing, a small living room with a fireplace, nice old kitchen, big bedroom and screened porch. She had taken the place because of the porch and the park. On cool mornings, she could walk or jog for miles before the rest of the city was awake. During the endless summer she could fix herself a gin and tonic on ice after work and escape the heat out on the porch.

"Drop me off, will you, Becca. I can walk the rest of the way," Abbie said.

"Are you nuts? A backpack and a laptop *and* a shopping bag tonight? You want to attract every thief, mugger and rapist in this town?"

Becca was always ragging her about how stupid it was to wander through the Park. The truth was that Abbie liked the small shiver it gave her to walk the last few blocks home at night. She tested herself against her fear like a child teetering along the top of a wall. It improved her fantasy life.

An old habit. But not tonight; Becca was right.

At the curb, Becca got out and toted Abbie's backpack up to the back door.

"Thanks, Becs."

"Forget it, you dope."

Abbie watched the taillights of the Rover until Becca was gone. Then she unlocked the back door and let herself into the kitchen. Flicking on the lights, she poked the button on her answering machine.

"It's the pups."

The sound of the voice gave her a small rush. She remembered the way he smelled, the way it felt when he touched her. "Check out your e-mail, principessa."

She went into the living room, opened her laptop, fumbled with the modem and punched up her service. His message was there at the top of the list. That meant he had sent it before reveille in Sarajevo.

From: p@santana.net
Subject: sitrep

In Dreams Begin Responsibilities. Did you ever read that one? I'm thinking the guy got it right. First the dream, then the hard part. I miss you. Let's leave it at that. Or this Toshiba might melt in my lap. It's going to get real busy here. You think you can make Julian believe in

NATO air power? No later than spring, I'd say. If you need to reach me, call Santana: 917 899 4224 or hardcore@santana.net.pups

Scrolling backward, she reread the message quickly. Then she hit the reply button and started to type.

From: amanci@washchron.com
Subject: litcrit

You are deeply crazy. If Nate hears you're talking dreams, he'll drag your cute ass off to the shrink. Speaking of which, I miss you, too. And let's *not* leave it at that, soldier. I want to hear more. When will you be back? Call if you can with an ETA, I hope. Still Your Responsibility.

TWENTY-FOUR

"Is there," said the Serb cop, pointing behind him. He beamed at Sandy and Nate. "What you look for is over there."

They had driven from Sarajevo to Polidza looking for a mass grave. The Serb was pointing to the town's brand-new fire station.

Pride of Polidza.

"Think he understood us, Hawk?"

"The bastard understood, all right. Where did Drago go?"

"Said he wanted to do some snoopin' around."

They were standing on the sidewalk in front of the fire station. The neighborhood was fairly new but grimy, run down in the way of cities of the old communist bloc. Never enough money for luxuries like maintenance.

General Hunter had given them a satellite photo showing thousands of men lined up waiting for buses on a street like the one they were looking at now. When the satellite made its second pass, the buses were all gone. So were the men.

Muslims. The Serbs hadn't rounded them up to send them home for Christmas.

From around the corner, Drago suddenly came toward them. He was walking slowly, but his body was taut, a soldier keeping his cool on hostile ground.

"He's got something, Captain."

Drago came up to them and snapped something at the cop, who scowled and walked away.

"What'd you tell him, man?" Nate asked.

"I told him he was a lying son of the great whore of Belgrade," Drago shrugged. "I think you better come with me."

He retraced his steps, moving quickly now, Sandy and Nate trotting after him. He turned at the corner, went down a narrow street for two blocks and stopped in front of a large, abandoned building that looked like a warehouse. The windows were boarded. The front door was big enough to admit a truck or bus.

"What is it, Drago?"

"I was talking to some people down the street, Captain." Drago seemed to be struggling to control his voice.

He pointed toward the large wooden door. "They call this place the House of Death."

He stepped forward and kicked open the door. The sound echoed through the empty warehouse.

"All right, let's take a look," Sandy said, stepping inside. He took out a flashlight and pointed the beam at the walls.

"Holy motherfucker," Nate said. "What we lookin' at, Drago?"

The walls were covered with names. Written out, faded, brown.

"Blood," Drago said. "The Serbs brought the Muslims in here and killed them. They wrote each name in the blood of the dead man."

"That's what they said up the street?" Sandy asked him.

"Why not? They weren't hiding anything. They were proud. They said the building was too small to finish all the Muslims. They killed maybe five hundred of them in here. Then they got the buses and drove the rest away."

"How many?"

"Maybe two thousand. All men and boys."

"Where did they take them?"

"A farm. Somewhere outside the city."

Nate looked at Sandy. "The other pictures, Hawk. Remember? The ones with the trees and the cornfield? Didn't Hunter have a fix on that one?"

"Yep." Sandy had written the position in his notebook. He took the book out of his coat pocket and checked the geo satellite data against his map. "Should be to the northeast of town," he said.

Drago frowned.

"What is it?" Sandy asked him.

"Drina Corps country, Captain. Elite troops. Cut your throat just to watch you bleed."

"Get the vehicle, Lieutenant. We're going to that farm."

They drove slowly through the city, leaving by the east and circling to the northeast where the countryside began. Nothing along the main road conformed to the images from the satellite. They tried three side roads. Nothing there either. Finally, there was only one road left. As Drago turned down it, Nate cursed.

"Sonuvabitch, Captain. No trees."

"Look again, Nate," Sandy said, studying the road ahead of them. On either side of a stretch of road perhaps half a mile long, someone had piled more cordwood than they had seen since arriving in country. Drago pulled the vehicle to the side of the road. Nate jumped out and checked the woodpile.

"Fresh cuts, Hawk. Someone wanted those trees down awful bad."

Toward the far end of the woodpile, they saw a small gate. A Serb trooper was posted in front of it. Piling into the vehicle, they drove up to him and stopped.

"Drina Corps," Drago said, taking in the uniform.

The soldier held up his hand to stop them.

Nate got out and walked over to him. The Serb shoved his rifle against Nate's chest. Nate reached forward, grabbed the weapon and slammed the butt into the Serb's groin. The Serb doubled over and bellowed in pain. Nate's vertical butt stroke caught him in the chin and knocked him backward. He fell on the far side of the gate.

Nate opened the gate and waved Drago through. Then he picked up the Serb's rifle and climbed back into the vehicle. "He'll sleep for a while, Hawk. I gave him something to remember us by. For the rest of his life, know what I'm sayin'? Got me one fine SKS for my wall."

Drago grinned and gunned the engine. They shot up a narrow dirt road that came out on a field that looked to be about 300 yards long and 120 yards wide.

"Cornfield," Sandy said, stepping out. The three of them started across the plowed ground. The stubble looked odd. Irregular.

Drago kneeled down to examine one of the jagged rows.

"Come here, Captain. You better take a look at this."

Sandy kneeled next to him. What Drago had in his hand was no cornstalk. He was holding a human femur.

Sandy ran his hand across the plowed ground. The corn stubble had all rotted toward the soil. The taller spikes were all human bones. He tugged at one of them. It came up through the loose soil with a scrap of torn trousers and a work boot on the end.

"Jesus," Nate whispered.

For the next fifteen minutes the three soldiers crisscrossed the field. Legs poked up through the dirt, hands, arms, entire rib cages, skulls.

"The buses must have brought them here, Nate."

"End of the fuckin' Serbian line, Hawk."

"Let's get out of here. We found what Hunter was looking for."

The ride back was rotten. He thought of Abbie, trying to get the bones out of his mind, but it didn't work. What a story. She would have been all over that field. Should he leak it to her? After she'd protected him and Nate, she deserved a scoop.

It was well past midnight when they got back to Sarajevo. The light in General Hunter's office was still on. He was waiting for them. Sandy made his report, leaving out the part about the sleeping guard at the boneyard gate.

"UN will have to take over this one," the General said tiredly.

"Little late for that, isn't it, sir?"

"Yes, it is, Captain. Far too little, far too late."

TWENTY-FIVE

Washington, D.C. ★ Army Navy Club

"Drinks, gentlemen?"

The steward wore a starched white coat buttoned up to his throat. Where did they get these guys? Patrice St. Jean asked himself. Where did they keep them at night? The Smithsonian?

Against the whiteness of the jacket, the old man's face looked 20 degrees blacker. Affirmative action in reverse, Patrice reflected. Roll the clock back to the forties and keep it there. That was the heart and soul of the Army Navy Club: win World War II, you never get over it. Enough leather chairs, enough bourbon, you rule the world.

"I'll have a white wine spritzer," he said, ignoring the frown Remy Fair directed at him from across the table. Remy had brought a couple of Air Force officers with him. A one-colonel-one-major problem. Okay, let's see what they have to offer.

Remy was the chief troubleshooter for T. C. Johnson, the people who made missiles, planes and more money than God. "Colonel Hollander, Major Jennings," he said, observing the formalities. "What'll it be for you?" They ordered Virgin Marys. Remy waved the old steward closer. "Let me have two fingers of Jack D., Willis," he said, holding his hand out sideways. His index finger and pinky were extended, the middle two fingers curled in. The shot was big enough to stun an ox. "Yessir, Colonel Fair," the old man said. Chuckling dutifully at the old joke, he hurried off to fetch the round.

Remy hadn't been in uniform for three years, but you didn't have to be a shrink to notice his preference for *Colonel* over *Mister*. In the club, rank gave off the same clear ring that had made Remy pursue it all his life. The steward returned with the drinks. Patrice took a sip of his spritzer and frowned; they were using the cheap house table white again, brought in from California in 10,000-gallon tank cars. He handed his glass back to Willis. "Please tell the bartender to use the Montrachet he keeps under the bar for the chiefs of staff."

"Yessir, Mr. St. Jean. You're right, sir. There's a special stash for the flags."

Patrice saw the flicker of contempt cross Remy's craggy face. For a man in his middle fifties, Remy still had the body of a younger man, soldier or athlete. Pat knew he could still knock out the push-ups or run five miles before breakfast, though why any grown man would need to, want to, or actually do it baffled him. He considered it a sign of mental insufficiency. "Come on, now, Colonel Fair," he said mildly. "You wouldn't settle for Early Times when you ordered Jack Daniel's, would you?"

"Yeah, but that's whisky we're talking about, Pat. Not that French soda pop of yours."

The voice was quiet, friendly enough. On closer inspection, Patrice could see that Remy was beginning to lose some of the hard, angular lines he'd always been able to keep in place before retiring from the Army. Another twenty years, he would look just like Gus Buell.

Over the years, Gus had told Patrice everything about Remy. In Vietnam, he served as one of Gus's captains in the 5th Special Forces Group, a water walker headed for two or three stars. The problem was that he bucked too hard for the first one.

One night in the middle 1970s, when Remy was running the U.S. Special Forces in Korea, he cooked up a scheme to capture a North Korean prisoner. Something no one had managed to do since the war. His idea was to send a daylight patrol out along the DMZ right under the nose of the North Koreans. The patrol left behind a rucksack, with an antenna sticking out, as if it were an accident. Then Remy tasked a second patrol to ambush the Northerners when they came to pick up the gift package that night. They smelled something rotten and didn't take the bait, but one of the men on the SF A-Team tripped an SK mine and two of the SF warriors were killed.

Gus told Pat that Remy chalked the fiasco off to bad luck and hid it as a training exercise gone wrong. He got away with it until another member of the team wrote a letter to the American ambassador in Seoul that said: "Fucking Colonel Fair. He'd start World War III to get himself a little glory."

Remy would have been out on his ass, but Gus got him off the hook. True to form, Remy thanked his old mentor for saving his career but never forgave him for not saving his star.

Whenever Patrice saw them together, it always struck him that Remy looked like a man still planning a payback. He'd warned Gus about it once, but Gus was too easygoing to take him seriously. It had been Gus who got Remy the job at T. C. Johnson. After the Gulf War, he had mustered out as a bird colonel looking for a regular paycheck. He went through wives like most men go through socks: three, all into him for their monthly chunk of alimony. Then there was Denise Littlejohn, the blond, high-maintenance Morgan Fairchild look-alike he had promoted from temp in the TCJ secretarial pool to full-time, live-in girlfriend.

During the media circus in the Gulf, Remy had cracked the whip over the Joint Information Bureau—he had half the reporters in the world feeding out of his hand—so TCJ made him Director of Public Relations at $400,000 a year. He had risen fast to become Senior Vice President for International Affairs, the company's best, hands-on troubleshooter.

His portfolio included the F-44 fighter, T. C. Johnson's gilded bridge to the twenty-first century. When Senator Taylor informed Patrice that the new title had come through, Patrice had said with a sigh, "So they finally made Remy Veep for War and Peace—now he can just about afford Denise."

"I want to thank everyone for coming on such short notice," Remy said after Willis brought Patrice his drink upgrade. Pat took a sip. He was handsome in an early Truman Capote sort of way, five-six in his stocking feet. The deep leather chair he was sitting in almost swallowed him up. The three other men looked at him, waiting for him to speak. "What's on your mind, Pat?" Remy finally asked.

Patrice put the glass down. "The senator has developed some doubts about the F-44."

"Is that right?" Remy's voice was glacial. "He told me he was on board only two weeks ago."

"He was, until your last numbers came in. He thinks eighty billion dollars is a little steep. Even if it is spread out over five years. You said it was goin' to be half that."

"We said that eighteen months ago, before the Armed Services Committee started fiddle-fucking around. Times change, costs go up. You know that, Pat. The R and D is killing us."

"Ah, but reform, *mon colonel*. What about reform? What about cost *cutting*? How is it going to look—Senator Taylor, defense reformer, the man who killed the Atticus missile single-handed, running for President with the drag from this ball and chain? Not so good, don't you agree?"

"We had a done deal, Pat."

"Deal? The senator doesn't deal. We had an understandin'."

"Are you fucking with me, Pat?" The voice too quiet this time.

"Okay, let's call it a done understandin'. But it done come undone. He can't go for eighty bil."

Fair looked down at his glass and clinked the ice cubes. They clicked softly, like tumblers falling in the lock of a fine safe. "And how is our senator going to be President if he doesn't have a pot to piss in?" he said, looking up at Patrice and raising the glass. "Not so good, either. Don't you agree?"

The two military officers looked at each other uncomfortably. This was not what they had come for. They rose to leave. "Not a problem, gentlemen," Patrice said quickly, motioning with his hand for them to sit down. "We're all friends here. Colonel Fair is just talkin' in the abstract." He smiled easily, giving it a little time. "Let's keep things in perspective," he said. "The senator is goin' to be President. We should be talkin' about protectin' an asset, not punchin' out his lights."

Fair tapped his fingers slowly on his glass. "What kind of an asset are you talking about, Pat?"

"High grade, same as always. But you don't think I'm goin' to let my man go out there in front of everyone and get himself killed, do you? Come on, Remy. You know the rules. You want somethin' to happen, you gotta make somethin' happen."

Fair waggled his fingers at Willis. "Okay, okay, Pat. Tell us what you need."

"Some new ammunition. You've known him longer than I have. Give me something I can use."

Remy pointed to Colonel Hollander, who nodded to Major Jennings. The major had a green ring binder under his arm about the size of the New York City phone book. He opened it on the coffee table in front of them.

"As you know, Mr. St. Jean," Colonel Hollander began, "the

Department of Defense has ordered us to downsize everywhere. We're almost finished updating our list of base closings." He looked over to the other officer. "Major, what would be the impact on Ohio if we close Taft Air Force Base?"

The major flipped through the pages in the binder.

"Sir, it would take out 16,500 jobs and remove about two point five billion from the local economy."

"Anything else?"

"That's a good start," Patrice said, smiling cherubically. "Thank you, Colonel Hollander. Why don't you leave that binder with me? I'm sure Senator Taylor will find it interestin' readin'." He looked quickly at his watch. "I know you two gentlemen need to get back to the Pentagon. Let's stick Colonel Fair here with the check and we won't waste any more of your time."

When the two officers were gone, Patrice pushed aside his half-finished spritzer. "It's not enough, Remy."

The older man closed his eyes tiredly. "What else do you want from us, Pat?"

"A new number, Remy. Drop the price by ten billion."

"That's a twelve percent cut, Pat. You're asking me to put the profit line near danger red."

"Come on, Remy. The senator gets some glory, you'll still be gettin' half your loaf and you can pick up the rest in cost overruns. You didn't really expect him to swallow the whole thing in one gulp, did you?"

"Is that all, Pat?"

"I hope so."

"It sure as hell better be," said the fixer. Raising his hand, he signaled Willis to bring him the check.

*   *   *

At 8:45 that evening, Adelle Reiner, Senator Taylor's personal secretary, took off her headphones and straightened her hair. She was a handsome woman in her late fifties. Hazel eyes. Straight brown hair just touching her narrow shoulders. A silk scarf knotted in the French style. Locking the transcriber in her desk drawer, she gathered up her purse and coat. She'd missed dinner, but the last tape was transcribed and she could go home.

"Quittin' early, *chér*?" Patrice called across the empty office.

"Even the slaves get to eat occasionally."

"Stay another hour and I'll take you to dinner."

"Another hour and I'll be dead of malnutrition. See you tomorrow, *mon ami*." Straightening her scarf, she put on her coat and left, closing the door softly behind her.

Patrice heard the lock click and told himself to relax. He felt restless. The thing with the reporter bothered him. He had tried to tell Julian no dice on the project, but you didn't just say no to the national press. The following day, Julian had run into Senator Taylor at the State Department. It had taken the editor maybe two nanoseconds of stroking to talk the subject back into the game.

Patrice knocked at the senator's door.

"Give me a minute, Pat. I'm busy."

He looked at the tall grandfather clock ticking loudly at the end of the room. When two minutes had passed, he knocked again, then went in and stood by the window looking out at the Capitol. At night, the dome, bathed in silver light, always reminded him of a giant sugar Easter egg, the ones with an eyehole and a little world of surprises inside. Little men, little bunnies.

"Please listen to me, Senator," he said, turning back to face Taylor. "The reporter's going to be here any minute. Shmoozin' is fine. But this story is a stupid idea."

"Forty acres and a mule in the *Chronicle*? All for free? The timing couldn't be better."

"It couldn't be worse."

"What are you talking about."

"The last thing you need lookin' over your shoulder right now is a woman reporter. She'll get stuck on you, if she isn't already, and then she'll go for your balls when she finds out you're not interested."

"Never happen."

"Trust me on this. What'll you tell her when she asks you about Vietnam, about ODA 351?"

"The truth."

The buzzer rang loudly in the outer office. "Let her wait," Patrice snapped.

Senator Taylor loosened his tie, rolled up his sleeves and sat down behind his desk. He looked at the younger man thoughtfully. "You know, Pat, I can't tell you how much pleasure it gives me every now and then just to see you sweat."

"Bad joke, Senator."

Senator Taylor smiled. "Behind all that slick patois of yours, Pat, you really don't have much of a sense of humor, do you?"

★   ★   ★

Senator Taylor took off his reading glasses when Abbie came into the office. Snapping shut a ring binder in Air Force blue, he rose, walked around the desk and squeezed her hand with both of his. "Nice to see you again, Abbie."

The voice, she had to admit, was great, the baritone deep, the eyes a warm dark brown. "Thank you for seeing me, Senator. Do you always work this late?"

"Only when Patrice puts a pistol to my head. Did you see him outside?"

"You mean the little guy with the attitude? If I were you, I'd do what he says."

Senator Taylor laughed. "Good advice. You want a job?"

"Got one. A story on you. Julian tells me you've talked about it."

"Something about Vietnam? He said you'd fill me in on the details."

"That's right." She consigned Julian to another year in hell. They hadn't even talked about the thrust of the story. "The idea, umm, is to say something new about Vietnam . . . to connect the sixties to the nineties."

He looked at her carefully.

"First we'd have to connect the fifties to the thirties. As you've pointed out, you were only a year or two old when I was over there. What makes you think you could understand me?"

She flushed. "I'd do my best. We might have to spend a lot of time together." The old bait and switch. Use it and they'd hoot at you in New York or Los Angeles or even Dallas, for godsakes. In Washington, they still gobbled it up. He hesitated. Maybe she was reading him wrong. "I've done some extra homework on you," she said quickly.

He sat down on the couch to the left of his desk. "What have you learned so far?" She walked across the room and took a chair facing him. The cushion was soft and she sank in deeply, stretching her skirt tightly above her knees. That left just about everything showing. Nothing to be done about it. Oddly enough, he didn't seem to notice.

"All right, here's the sketch. Diplobrat meets armybrat at Andover. Discovers General Caine as hero and new father figure. Excels at Point. Kicks ass in Nam. Headed for four stars. Bad break. Leg and career. But keeps running, Congress, Senate— next stop, the White House."

She was on autopilot now, racing on with the pitch. "Up to now, military service for a President has always meant World War II. Or draft dodging. You will be the first President forged in Vietnam. That's what makes this story so strong. It's not just about you, it's about the whole country. It's what's in the wind. Out of the quagmire and into the twenty-first century."

He raised his hand. "Okay, okay, enough, Miss Mancini. You really know how to shovel it, don't you?"

Goddamn it, Abbie. Who did you think you were stroking, Bob Dole? He saw the chagrin on her face and laughed, but in a friendly enough way.

"I'm sorry, Senator, I . . ."

"Forget it, Abbie. It comes with the turf. Look, I've spent the last twenty-five years puking over what happened to us in Vietnam. To all of us. I hate to spoil your story, but there it is."

She felt a rush of embarrassment. Rattling on like a dope, forcing him to stop her.

"I apologize," she said.

"No need."

"No, really. Seriously. Sandy Caine has told me a lot about you."

That seemed to surprise him. "When was the last time you saw him?"

"Mogadishu, then that day at Fort Myer when you took me to dinner."

"Is that right? What did he say?"

"He thinks General Caine is the Supreme Being, and you're right up there next to him."

He frowned. "Look, maybe Patrice is right. Why don't we drop this story."

Big one's getting away, Abs. Time for heroic measures. Rising from the chair, she moved over to the couch and sat next to him. "That would be a real shame, Jeff. Modesty becomes you, but it's out of place in a candidate."

"You sound just like Patrice."

"Didn't you say you always listen to him?"

"Most of the time. I listen to General Caine, Sandy, too, sometimes, as you already seem to know. How is he?"

"Fine. But something happened to him in Mogadishu, Senator, and he seems to be brooding about it."

"Do you know what it was?"

"Something about one of his men getting killed. Perkins, Sergeant Perkins. Sandy said he was a lifer. Knew his father. That's all I know."

Senator Taylor was sitting all the way back in the couch now. He reminded her of her father puzzling over a diagnosis when the symptoms were ambiguous. Clearly something was bothering him too.

"Lying doesn't come naturally to you, does it?" he said abruptly.

It shocked her. "God, Senator, what do you expect me to say? 'No, it doesn't come naturally, I have to work really hard at it,' or, 'Boy, are you wrong, I do it like a pro—all the time.' "

"You know what, Abbie?" he said, smiling at her. "They'd eat you alive around here."

"Who?"

For a moment he studied his hands. Then he seemed to make up his mind about something. "Sandy told me all about Perkins. That was a couple of days after Fort Myer. The last time you say you saw him, right?"

"Right."

"I don't think so. Julian told me you just got back from Bosnia. You saw Sandy again, didn't you? Over there."

"I was working on some investigative stuff for Julian."

"Knock it off, Abbie. There are seven or eight senators left up here who can still add two and two and get four."

She started to get up. Julian would be furious, but enough was enough. Blowing Sandy's cover wasn't part of the deal. "Okay, okay, loyalty is a virtue," the senator said.

Leaning toward her, he took her hand. "Okay, you've persuaded me," he said. "We'll do the story. I don't meet many women like you."

Tie him up, Abs, before he gets away. "I thought we might start with the story of your Special Forces team—how you put it together and where it took you."

He smiled as though he had been prepared for the question. "All right," he said, "I'll need a while to think about it. Give me a couple of days. Talk to Patrice. He'll book us some more time."

As if on cue, they both stood up, the impulse wired into them by a city whose central nervous system ran on unspoken signals. Abbie absently reached for her purse. Okay, so the guy's on the far side of fifty and practically Sandy's uncle. But, admit it, Abs, he's very attractive. As she walked toward the door, she felt just the smallest stitch of disappointment that he hadn't offered to drive her home.

* * *

In the old cloakroom next to the senator's private office, Patrice punched a button. It turned off the tape system that recorded everything said on the other side of the wall. He shook his head and slipped back into the outer office just as Abbie came out alone looking pleased.

"You score?" he asked.

"I'd call it a tie, but he wants you to book us some more time."

"I'll get back to you tomorrow. Probably be three or four days before I can find a slot."

"That works for me," she said. "I've got a couple of things I need to get out of the way before we start." She paused. "I'm going to need more than just a sit-down with the boss, Patrice. It's gotta be total immersion, you know that, don't you?"

"Is that what he says?"

"It's what I say."

"For you, *chér*, I'll do my best."

The grandfather clock began to strike ten, an oddly high chime, not the basso gong she expected. "French," Patrice said. "A Bouvier. Paris to New Orleans, 1810. I think the bull-balls WASP kind are oppressive, don't you? All that self-dramatizing *BONG, BONG, BONG*."

She laughed. "You crack me up. Where did he find you?"

"*Au contraire, chér*. I found him. Where can I drop you?"

They got their coats and took the elevator down to the subterranean garage where the Porsche was waiting. "Always makes me feel like Batman," he said as they came roaring up and out into the night. Slamming the Porsche into third, he raced down Constitution Avenue and turned right. He waited until they had shot through the tunnel under Dupont Circle to hit her with it.

"Don't make any mistakes about the senator."

As they started up the hill she looked out the window at the Hilton where the nut shot Ronald Reagan. The Porsche wheeled left, crested the rise and sped past the Chinese Embassy.

"Which mistakes?"

"You've just been Taylored, Miss Mancini."

"What's that supposed to mean?"

"The senator is very charming."

"I'm a big girl, Pat."

He dropped into second and pulled to a stop at the light on Albemarle. "I can see that. You are a very special woman. I mean it. That's the problem. Our common problem—his, yours, mine."

"I don't get it."

"He's been looking for someone like you, Miss Mancini, whether he knows it or not. I'm telling you this because you're going to find out anyway. The divorce really whacked him."

"Million girls in this town, Pat."

"Not like Janine Walker Taylor. Or like you."

"I still don't get it."

"What?"

"I thought you were pimping for him. Wasn't that what you did with me at Fort Myer?"

"No."

"What was it, then?"

"Little matter of control. Handling, I suppose. You work for an important paper. We should know you and you should know us. Beyond that, he's my boss and I love him dearly. I think the country needs him. And right at this moment, I don't need you or anyone else like you running around him with your heart on your sleeve. I don't need it, you don't need it and, if you'll forgive me, the country doesn't need it. He's got to stay focused."

When they came to the corner of Woodley Road, she pointed and he pulled to the curb. Slipping out easily, she came around to his side of the Porsche and leaned down to the window.

"Relax, Pat. Nothing's going to happen. It can't—I'm on a story. Besides, Mancinis don't do love." She patted his hand. "Thanks for the ride."

As she headed down into the park, she allowed herself a smile. Abs, she thought, you are a thief. Stealing Sandy's line like that. Picking up speed, she pushed it as fast as her girlie pumps would take her, wishing she could break all the way out. Run.

TWENTY-SIX

★ Georgetown ★

The cab took a right off M Street and went up Wisconsin Avenue past the singles promenade, working girls and working boys heading for the cozy bars of Georgetown. Abbie looked across the seat at Julian. Julian looked bored.

At Thirty-fifth Place, the driver turned and dropped them in front of a small brick town house. In the light of the street lamps, Patrice St. Jean's place reminded her of one of those little houses you see arranged in toy villages at Christmas: white brick, three stories, with a sharply peaked slate roof and glowing windows. Wishing she'd worn something heavier over her new silk dress, she stood in front of the door watching the silvery contrails of her breath until a maid in a black uniform and starched white apron answered the bell.

Taking their coats, the maid ushered them through the entrance hall to a long room painted a pleasant blue gray. Close to the color of Sandy's eyes, Abbie thought. When he wasn't at war. The walls were hung with watercolors of the French Quarter in New Orleans. Pastel kelims were thrown artfully over wood floors pickled a grayish white.

The entertainment area segued into a professional kitchen, gleaming with a Wolf six-burner. Suspended from stainless-steel racks bolted to the ceiling were enough All-Clad pots and pans to run Lutece. From the middle of this culinary theater, the tenor voice of the host came floating out to the assembled guests.

"Does everyone have a bib?"

She did a double take. The men were suited up in conservative Brooks Brothers gear—most of the women were also playing it safe in pearls and generic silk dresses or suits. All of them were wearing large white bibs. Starched linen with CHEZ PATRICE lettered in handsome blue embroidery. Abbie did some quick calculations. Pat's hand laundering costs for this party would pay her grocery bill for a week.

She had never seen Nina Barrington in a bib. The world-class climber was chatting with Rafe Dolland, builder, fund-raiser, New Democrat. Looking over his shoulder, Nina was scouring the room, less intent on listening to Dolland than looking for her next husband, preferably someone straight this time—a breeder before her biological clock ran out. Children were so validating in photo layouts.

Abbie saw Dick Milton, the Pentagon correspondent for one of the networks, a guy who looked like a cop, bringing a drink to Admiral Collins, the Navy Chief of Operations. The rest of the crowd was made up of power staffers from the House and Senate, military officers, think tank brain trusters and other nongovernmental organizations.

All of them had the host's blue logo around their necks.

Holding a giant silver tray aloft, Patrice St. Jean came out from behind the huge Wolf range with the hors d'oeuvres, baby back ribs, glazed prawns, blackened chicken on small skewers, Cajun by aroma and crust.

A tall man in a short tux coat and formal trousers took the tray and began distributing the appetizers, neatly dropping them onto small white dishes, then slipping them into the hands of the guests. "Hey, Pat," shouted a middle-aged guy in a navy cashmere sportcoat. "No napkins?"

"Use your bib, Gordo. Miss Manners says it's okay. You can look it up."

"I'm gonna mess up my glass here."

Patrice laughed.

"Like I said, use the bib, *then* pick up your glass. CIA rules. If your prints aren't on it, it didn't happen."

He saw Abbie and blew her a kiss. She smiled and wiggled a finger at him as he headed back to the range.

Only six weeks had passed since he met her and introduced her to Senator Taylor. But he made it feel as if they'd been friends forever. She'd checked his bio at the *Chronicle*. Lapsed

Catholic, educated by the Jebbies, degree in political science at Tulane. In New Orleans during the greed-is-good 1980s, his father, Emile St. Jean, opened Scaramouche, the hottest restaurant on Bourbon Street. Around Georgetown, power players and about-to-be's killed for invitations to Patrice's chic little dinners. Emile shipped the crawfish and shrimp up from the Big Easy. Patrice manned the Wolf, putting into it all the intensity he normally reserved for obsessions like back lighting and polls.

Pat was not what you'd call a man of the Establishment. The path he had followed to town was eccentric, full of the same kind of twists that had made spinmeisters out of James Carville and Dick Morris. His people were southern Democrats, but that hadn't stopped him from crossing the street to mix with Republicans. When he heard about Jeff Taylor's congressional ambitions in Cincinnati, he got on the next bus and enlisted with Taylor as a volunteer. In six months he was Chief of Staff.

Julian tugged at her arm and nodded across the room. The General and a shorter, red-faced man in a glen plaid suit were in deep conversation. Standing next to them, a tall man in a charcoal suit with continental vents was staring at Julian. On Julian's behalf, Abbie returned the stare. The guy had a drink in his hand but he wasn't mixing with the other guests. He was the only other guest in the room without a bib.

"Come with me," Julian said. "I want you to meet someone."

Circling past Nina and her latest victim, Julian led her over to the three men.

"Julian," boomed the red-faced man as they came up. "I thought you couldn't make it tonight."

"Wouldn't miss it, Gus," Julian replied, patting the older man's shoulder. It didn't seem to occur to him to introduce the woman at his side. The General frowned. "We've met before," he said, extending his hand to Abbie. As if his suit had been trained, his sleeve drew back, revealing half an inch of starched French cuff and a small gold cuff link in perfect taste.

"Yes, General Caine," she said. "At Fort Myer."

Before the General could reply, Gus nudged Julian forward and took both of them by the elbow. "Would you excuse us, Miss," he said to Abbie. "The boys need to talk about the toys."

He seemed to be excluding the charcoal suit next to them. It suddenly occurred to Abbie that she had seen the man once before. Also at Fort Myer. Standing at the rear of the Officers Club with the same detached look on his face. It had been impossible to tell whether he was a little drunk, contemptuous of the crowd, or just shy. He looked the same way now.

Behind her, she heard Gus bulldogging Julian forward. "Go ahead, man. I want you to ask General Caine what he thinks about the F-44."

"We've met, too," she said, holding out her hand to their silent partner.

"I don't think so."

His eyes were pale blue, remote. His voice sounded vaguely military.

"Yes, I keep running into you." Abbie tried a smile. "What do you do?"

"Security."

"Secure enough to tell me your name? Or is it top secret?"

He didn't smile. Finally, he said, "Forgive me, Miss Mancini. I didn't mean to be rude. I was thinking about something else. I'm Remington Fair."

"Fair and milder. Sorry, couldn't resist. I'll bet you get that all the time."

"That's a bet you'd win." He put his glass down.

"So what do you really do?"

"I keep an eye on things, Miss Mancini. Like you."

The effect was instant. He gave off a low-voltage current, a tingle of danger that intrigued her. She took a step back and looked at him.

"FBI, Secret Service, CIA?"

"Amateurs," he said, but at least she had drawn a faint smile from him. He pointed across the room. "Can I get you a drink?" he said.

He let her lead the way. She took a Perrier from the bartender who reached over to the credenza behind him and handed her the next-to-last bib from the pile.

Remington Fair ordered a double Jack D. rocks, then moved in alongside her. He didn't make any noise. Even the ice cubes were silent.

"Who are they?" she asked him, pointing to two men arguing a few feet beyond the bar, their hands sweeping through the air like two old fighter jocks reliving a raid.

"I'll introduce you," he said.

The two officers were so deep into it their radar didn't pick up the approach of Abbie and her stealth escort. The taller of the two men was right on the other's tail firing rockets up the pipe of the Navy's pet F-18E/F fighter. "That plane won't hunt," he was saying. "Won't hunt, won't fly, won't die. You just can't give it up, can you?"

"Come on, every new system has bugs."

"Bugs? The F-18E/F is Bugs fuckin' Bunny. Go into a dog-fight, you snap off a wing."

"Yeah, well, there was some wobbling in the tests, but they're fixing it."

"Fixing it, my ass. Your guys say no problem, we'll just run a strip of sandpaper down there where we're getting the stress fractures. It's Cripple Creek, Mitch. Only thing that sucker's dangerous to is the guy strapped in there flying it. You can't trust it, and you know it. While you're sitting there wondering what it's going to do next, Captain Poon Tang from Pyong Yang shoots your ass off."

Fair poked his finger in the tall guy's back.

"Freeze, Les. You've got company."

Mr. Tall turned around slowly. "Hey, it's the merry messenger from T. C. Johnson."

"Colonel Randolph, U.S. Air Force, Captain Mitchell, U.S. Navy, I'd like you to meet Abigail Mancini. Better watch what you say, Les. You might read yourself in the *Chronicle*."

"You're talking planes, Colonel?" she said. "What about the F-44?"

"You're setting me up, Remy," the captain replied, throwing up his hands as Colonel Randolph homed in for the kill.

"The F-44 is God's own angel of death, Miss Mancini. The answer to all our prayers."

One last shot from the captain. "Pretty damn expensive for an angel, Les. Eighty big ones over the next ten years."

"Worth it, Mitch, every penny. You know as well as I do the Navy should pack it in on the F-18E/F. What good is a gold-plated blue angel with crippled wings?"

The officer turned triumphantly toward Abbie. She saw for the first time he was loaded. "What's a good-looking girl like you wondering about an airplane?" he said.

"Ah, Colonel Randolph," she said, smiling at him brightly. "A question in return for your question. How good is your angel of death going to be if it gets the kiss of death a little higher up in the heavens? Like in the Senate?"

Out of the corner of her eye, she saw Julian watching her.

" 'Bye, Colonel Randolph," she said, leaving him to scope out her legs. "Perhaps we could get together again, Mr. Fair. I'll like to hear more about the F-44. If you'll all excuse me, I better cover the room. One story a party and Julian sends you back to the bush leagues."

She began working her way toward Patrice's proscenium, where Dick Milton was leaning against the serving island trying to hold his own with Charles Rogers. Milton was notorious for carrying the Pentagon's water dutifully onto the television news each night. Rogers was a retired Marine who ran a small news service that did investigative reports, a whistle-blower. The services chiefs considered him a traitor. Lazy reporters hated it when their editors told them to follow up on his scoops. They put him down.

Milton was bloviating about the hostility of civilians toward the Pentagon.

"The people still stereotype, you know," he was saying. "These guys aren't like Patton. They've got advanced degrees now. Outside, they'd be running big corporations."

"Christ, you think that's good, Dick?"

"Sure do. The world's more complicated than it used to be. These are complex guys."

Charles still had a gyrene's temper and tongue. "You know what's wrong with you, Dick? Brass-ass syndrome. You've got your nose pushed so far up there you can't see straight anymore. You ever a grunt?"

"Navy, Charles. I did my time. Don't give me that civvie shit."

"Navy? Well, I guess that explains it."

Abbie stifled a laugh and moved on. What a shame Rogers was so happily married. He was definitely her kind of guy.

At ten minutes to nine, Patrice yelled cheerfully from the stove, "Last call, everyone. Grab a glass."

Chatting and laughing, the guests began filtering dutifully into the dining room. The tablesettings were silver, old and gracefully French, weirdly complementing the bibs. "Pat's M.O.," she heard someone whisper. "Git'em by the bib, their balls are sure to follow."

A couple in servants' uniforms served from the dumbwaiter. A gumbo, then a crawfish, shrimp and rice thing that was the specialty at Scaramouche. When everything was perfect, Patrice swept into the room. He reminded Abbie of a fashion designer hitting the catwalk at the end of a show, accepting applause.

Sitting next to her, he picked up his spoon and tried the gumbo.

"Too much *vierge púre*," he said, thinking aloud. "I should have been more subtle."

She reached over and patted his hand. "Give me a break, Pat. I cook."

It broke him up. "They told me you were dangerous."

"Who said?"

"Oh, people. People who hate reporters." The abrupt jump startled her, the note of warning, but his eyes were sparkling merrily. She wondered if he did coke.

"Whoever could hate reporters?" she said. "We're just misunderstood."

"True, I couldn't agree with you more," he said, changing directions just as violently. "Julian tells me you're one of his best."

"He tells me I'm a menace."

"You don't look all that menacing to me."

"Are you disappointed?"

"Devastated. 'The prince cannot sharpen his wits on a dull enemy.' "

She looked at the silk shirt and Hermes tie. Good clothes made some little guys look even smaller. Patrice seemed to grow as he talked.

"All right," he said. "What's your pitch?"

"The Vietnam special. Don't tell me you don't know about it already."

"Old chestnut, wouldn't you say? I think Julian's getting geriatric."

"Not if Senator Taylor is the next—"

"You don't have to say it, *chér*. It sounds sort of tacky." He wiped his lips on the bib and picked up his wineglass. "Tell me. What is your opinion of Cabernet Sauvignon? Louis Martini, fifty-eight?"

"The rust was barely off the vines. Good, but not truly great."

He put his hands on the table and stared at her. For once, she'd surprised him. "I'm a Valley Girl, Pat. St. Helena High, class of '83."

"An excellent year for Napa, as I recall. You'll like dessert," he said. "Made it myself, of course." Then, making his third leap as quickly as the first two, "You're in. Julian and I have talked. I've been able to do a little jugglin'. The senator will see you tomorrow. He's got hearin's all day and drop-bys until eight o'clock. He wants you to meet him at his office around nine."

"If you and Julian worked this all out, why dinner tonight?"

"I wanted to check your taste. The dress is attractive. Nicole Miller, isn't it? My respects. Not a woman in here thinks farther than St. John. Except, of course, dear Nina."

TWENTY-SEVEN

Alexandria ★ Virginia

At ten-thirty that same evening, on a dead-end street in a run-down industrial zone near Alexandria, the security lights went on outside Dunbar's Used Appliances. Sodium fluoron illuminators. The best money could buy. In their beams, the display window, covered with six months of dust and grime, took on an eerie greenish-yellow glow.

Inside, John Trask leaned back in his chair and considered the lighting. He liked the way it played across the overalls covering his muscular body. The colors reminded him of the nights with the rheumatic fever. The walls at the Sisters of Charity infirmary. His body burning. The baby oil and powder heavy in the air from the nursery down the hall. Sister Theresa leaning over him with the cool washrag, dabbing at his face. Only time she ever touched him without smacking him. And the walls of the orphanage behind her. That familiar institutional green. Distant, cool. As if he could close his eyes and disappear into them.

Half an hour to go. Almost time. Bed check never came later than eleven o'clock, after that only when Mad Max had a mission.

Trask looked at the window. Masterpiece, he thought to himself. He had filled it from the junk boxes at the Salvation Army: next to an old toaster with a frayed cotton cord, an ancient waffle iron gaped like a scorched clam. He'd arranged half a dozen museum-piece radios from the tube era inside a circle of matching hair dryers, setting the composition off against a broken Hamilton blender, also green in keeping with the dominant color scheme. It would never make another malt. The final touch was the lava lamp. It still worked if you shook it hard before plugging it in. At night, it put out a throbbing light, purplish black, the color of the bruises on a corpse.

Trask giggled. His own little cemetery for the badly wired.

To the window, he had taped a sign that said, YOU FRY IT, WE FIX IT. (NO TVS). He had worked the lettering up on his computer using a streamlined font and a laser printer for the post-modern effect. Sharp. The bit about the televisions was an afterthought. Heavy fuckers. Too much of a pain in the ass to hump around.

Next to the front door hung one of those clock things that said, WE'RE OUT NOW. BACK AT . . . Big hand on 12, little hand on 4. Trask smiled, remembering how the sisters had rapped his knuckles when he had been slow at telling time. He wasn't slow now.

The place had been an auto body shop before Trask leased it on orders from Mad Max. The hydraulic lift was still there, along with a one-car kiln for curing paint jobs. The walls were covered in white tile. The smell of Lysol mingled with the pine scent deodorizer. Everything clean, pure.

Purity of mission. Trask's favorite phrase. He had picked it up in Guatemala from a CIA guy trying to work both sides of the death squads and keep a clear conscience. "For 'em or agin' 'em, you can't do without 'em down here," the guy had said. Something like that. What you had to keep in mind was the larger picture—the purity of the mission. Always worked for John Trask.

Up on the lift right now was a white truck stripped down to the body frame. Propped against the walls was a large assortment of spare doors and panels. The set with the crisp blue and white striping said BELL ATLANTIC. Next to it was a second set done in brown lettering made to look like parquet woodwork. This one said FLOOR IT—BOB'S SANDING & REFINISHING. The telephone number below the name of the company connected to the message machine on Trask's desk. Trask never returned the messages. Lying face up on the floor next to the lift was the latest set, that pale green again: LEDYARD'S WHOLESALE FLORISTS. WEDDINGS, PARTIES, FUNERALS.

Behind the lift, the rear wall was covered floor to ceiling with chromium shelves. The shelves were stacks of sealed plastic boxes where Trask kept his snooping gear: the best bugs from the East and West blocs; all the old pets from the CIA and KGB; pick-ups and transmitters from Japan; an Italian oscilloscope in the best Milanese post-modern industrial design. You could put it in a fucking art museum. In the corner was the telescoping transmitter antennae he had stolen off a news van parked overnight behind the Rose of Tralee Tavern in Norfolk.

Norfolk was for R and R. Standing orders from Mad Max were no mixing with indigenous personnel anywhere inside 100 miles of the District of Columbia. Didn't really matter, anyway. Trask no longer trusted himself to take R and R. He knew he wasn't a looker. His luck, lost along with the parents who had dumped him in the orphanage, had done that to him. *Alopecia universalis*, Sister Theresa called it. He had absolutely no body hair. No beard, no eyebrows or lashes. Nothing. All his life he looked weird.

He wore women's false eyelashes, trimming them for a more masculine effect. Tattooing took care of the eyebrows—it was a good job, you could hardly tell. But there was nothing he could do about the rest. For a while, after the Michael Jordan look came in, and hip dudes were all getting baldies at the barbers, things had been better. He stopped wearing hats and even thought about getting that other place tattooed, if they'd do it. Then one night down in Norfolk, in a hot-sheet joint down the block from the Rose of Tralee, this hooker had laughed at him while he washed up before coming to bed. Called him Mr. Clean. Asked if he came in a bottle.

He broke her neck. Then he took his razor and shaved off her pubic hair until she looked like a little girl, at least as much like a little girl as someone with tits that big could look like. After that he cut out her tongue and stuck it in her snatch. When the cops found her, she could talk from down there. He saved the best for last, sucking her nipples until he could taste the blood. Made the news, better believe it. Best Live-at-Five shit Norfolk had had in weeks. Good he'd worn the mask. Cops said they were looking for a maniac. Cracked him up. Shit, it wasn't even his day job.

That had been two months ago. Since then things had been very, very quiet.

Quarter to eleven now. He started to doze off.

Clack, clack, clack.

Three sharp taps on the window.

Trask jumped up, reaching for the knife in the desk drawer.

Unfucking believable. The woman was standing outside the window with a portable TV in her arms, little white job, pushed up against her belly as if she was pregnant with it or something. Third time today. Once at lunch hour, once at four-thirty. Both times he had stayed back in the body shop and she'd gone away. Now it was going on midnight. And this time she had seen him.

Clack, clack.

Hands wrapped around the set. Knocking on the glass door with her head. Her glasses were making all the racket. No way he could escape. Holding the knife behind his back, he went to the door and opened it a crack, leaving on the chain. The woman was panting from the weight of the set.

"I knew you'd be here," she said. "I get off work at ten and I've had this thing in the back of the car all day. I thought I'd take one last chance on the way home."

Trask pointed to the sign on the window.

"No TVs."

"I know," she said. "Couldn't you make an exception?" She looked down at the set bulging from her belly. "I mean, I fried it, so you fix it, right?" She giggled.

The cunt. Stupid, fucking, pushy cunt.

He felt his neck muscles tighten.

He slammed the door outward with both hands, forgetting the chain. The sound clattered off the empty warehouse across the street. The force of his blow cracked the window. A large shard of glass fell out and shattered at the woman's feet.

"Oh God," she cried. "I'm sorry."

Trask reached for the chain.

Hearing the rattle, the woman dropped the set and ran to her car. When she was gone, Trask stepped out the door and looked at the set. The screen was cracked. Returning to his desk, he took out a pad and wrote, "Sorry about last night. I thought you were fronting for some guy in the car. If you want, I can fix this for you. No charge." He wrote down the number for his message machine, then he took the note outside and stuck it to the front of the set with a strip of duct tape. If she wants to come back, let her.

Closing the door, he reached over and unplugged the lava lamp. Then he returned the knife to the desk drawer and lit a cigarette. Ten-fifty-five.

Brrrrrr. He felt the silent alarm of his pager buzzing softly against his hip.

Not right. The signal always came over the net.

Sonuvabitch.

Trask scrambled to his feet and ran into the back room. Floating across the screen saver on his computer monitor, tropical fish bubbled at him cheerfully. He launched the Internet browser and tapped out an address.

"Come on, come on," he muttered, cursing the machine as it searched for the connection and dawdled over the download.

Then he was there.

"Hogs and Heifers Home Page. Whatever Gets You Through the Night."

H and H was a chat room for bikers. Place to rap about Yamahas, Kawasakis or Harleys. The ultimate in chromium cybersex.

He clicked on a throbbing pink button. The hot link to the private chat rooms. Supposed to be a clit. It looked more like a bunny's nose.

Not many lonely hearts in the lounge. Bad for cover, but MM was there.

Trask started typing quickly.

"Warm, wet and waiting by the phone. Dear John."

The moniter lit up immediately: "Code Silver. Customer Mancini. 363B Woodley Road, D.C. Needs a new sound system. Mad Max."

"You got it MM. DJ."

Show time. Trask logged off. Someone was really gonna get fucked now.

TWENTY-EIGHT

★ Sarajevo ★

"We have a problem, Captain Caine. Take a chair, will you?"

General Hunter was standing with his back to the door as Sandy and Nate came into his office. On the wall map, Sandy saw a large red circle marked on the outskirts of Sarajevo. In the mountains. Near the ski area by the look of it.

General Hunter pointed to the circle distastefully, as if it were a wound.

"Two of our lads have been taken."

"Serb bastards?" Nate asked him.

"I wish it were that simple," Hunter said. "The bastards in this case are Muslims." He paused, letting it sink in. "Does that surprise you, gentlemen?"

"Doesn't add up, sir," Nate said. "We're supposed to be on the same side."

"We are not supposed to be on *any* side as things stand now, Sergeant. The Serbs are the chief butchers in this bloody war, but the Croats and Muslims have their moments, too. Today it's Muslims that we're dealing with." He pointed to the red circle. "Two mujahedeen, three Bosnians. They have Sergeant Forte and Corporal Sprinkles over there in a bloody chalet. Took them this morning on the road. The lads were out running. Overextended their range, I'm afraid."

"I guess I still don't get it, sir."

"Mujahedeen crazies, Sergeant. Inciting Bosnian Muslims.

They've been in here freelancing ever since they ran the Russians out of Afghanistan. They hate the British as much as the Russians. We go back a long way, of course. Long before Karl Marx started peddling his bilge. They want to know everything we're doing here. Suspicious devils. Can't say that I blame them entirely. But we can't have it, don't you agree?"

"How much time do we have?" Sandy asked.

"The way this little game is run, it's highly likely that Forte and Sprinkles will soon be hanging from a tree with their balls cut off. And you can be sure that all the fingerprints will point to the Serbs. We're fortunate we have intercepts on their cell phones—that's how we fixed their position."

Sandy felt a prickle of embarrassment run up his neck. If General Hunter knew what the Muslims said on their cell phones, how hard would it be for him to know what was whispered in the bedrooms of the Hotel Astoria?

"We're going to get those lads back. I've got my best man on the way in here now. Lieutenant Colonel Kevin Speed. None better. Falkland Islands, Northern Ireland. The best. He'll take a team and drop in on our friends tomorrow. You'll lead the support force. I want you for Speed's backup."

"Yes, sir."

"Damn right, sir."

"I thought you'd want to join us on this one. You'll have twenty-four men and six choppers. Three transports, three gunships. I want you out on the PZ, blades turning, ready to launch. At first sign of trouble, you go in and beef up Speed."

Sandy nodded.

"The war room will be right here. We will reconvene at six P.M. this evening. Kevin will be here by then. For the rest of it, you're in charge, Captain. If you have any problems give a shout. We don't micromanage the way your senior commanders do. We give a mission order. I will expect you to execute it flawlessly. Understood?"

"Yes, sir."

"That is all." General Hunter walked out of the war room.

TWENTY-NINE

★ Rock Creek Park ★

The next morning, the clock radio in Abbie's bedroom went off at five-thirty, pulling her up through sleep to the day's first snarl of traffic and weather reports. Normal people had nice alarm clocks. White noise. Surf kissing the beach. Robins singing to their mates. She buried her head under the pillow until the news came on. Three dead in a crack house shoot-out on Sixteenth Street, cars bumper to bumper behind a jackknifed trailer on the Beltway.

She rolled over on her back. Low-pressure area moving up fast from the Carolinas. Great, wonderful, oh what a beautiful morning. She tested the floor with her feet. Shivering, she swung her feet back onto the bed and wrapped her arms around her knees under the shirt's soft protective folds. Lying there she could hear her father's voice rebuking her for chasing bylines instead of diapering babies. Go away, Doctor Dad. You can give up now. Remember triage? Do us both a favor and get off my case.

The self-important bass of the news anchor shifted inanely into happy talk. "There they go again. The Serbs are shelling Bihac. The UN isn't going to stop them. In fact, we have reports that twenty-five UN peacekeepers are now hostages. What do you make of that, Nancy?"

"Amazing, Jim. You just don't know what to think, do you?"

Bihac was within shooting distance of Mostar. They killed

hostages, didn't they? Throwing back the covers, she jumped out of bed. Flicking on the lights in the kitchen, she pressed a button that released the modem on the side of the laptop, jacked in the telephone line and called up her e-mail.

One short message from Becca: "Yep on the car. You know where it is. Set of keys up the tailpipe." Nothing from Sandy. She sent a quick one of her own.

> To: p@santana.net
> From: amanci@washchron.com
> Subject: Missing Persons
>
> Where are you P? You worry me. Gotta lotta stuff for you to think about. Phone home now. YR.

Logging off, she went back upstairs to her bedroom and tossed her tee shirt on the foot of the bed. Patting on a bit of powder where her breasts had been chafing, she stepped into a sports bra, wriggling it up into place, pulled on a red sweatshirt and running shorts, and got down on her knees to search for her cross-trainers. She left the house by the side door. It would be better in the park.

Jogging now. The cold air hitting her face. Much better. Freaking out like that so early in the morning? Not like you, Abbie. Sandy can take care of himself.

A white truck with Bell Atlantic markings was parked in front of the vacant Coorain house, down the block where the concrete sidewalk yielded to a dirt footpath that led into the park. The switching box for the neighborhood was on a pole a few yards down the footpath. The previous summer, when the phone company installed the line for her fax, she had spent a half hour looking over the shoulder of a technician in white overalls who had wired her to the outside world.

The box was full of cables and switches. "Spare pairs," the tech told her, as if she knew all about such things. From then on she had made the box the starting point and finish line of her daily run. An easy mile and a half down to the outskirts of the zoo, then slightly uphill on the way back. Most mornings the circuit took her about thirty minutes.

The door to the truck swung open and a tall guy in a white shirt and black jeans unwound himself from behind the wheel and stepped out. He looked to be in his late thirties, although he had a shaved head, as if he might be a jock. New guy, new look, she reflected as she ran past him. At least the phone company knows how to get something done in this town. She waved and he waved back as she trotted down the dirt path.

★   ★   ★

John Trask waited until the girl disappeared into the park. He needed ten minutes. Moving around to the back of the truck, he opened the doors and took out a scuffed leather bag full of tools. Cutters and clips, a pair of needle-nose pliers, the cordless soldering iron. He also grabbed the small nylon pack with his bugs, pinhead microphones with super amplifiers, crystal, spike and contact mikes, carbon mikes and capacitator mikes, all of them micro and wireless, a little something for every contingency.

He picked the lock on the side door of the girl's apartment. A no-brainer. Took maybe fifteen seconds. The job was a soft tap, quicker, more reliable than the old hard-wired bugs. He took a quick sweep of the kitchen, living room and bedroom. Each telephone had four possibilities, the mouthpiece, earpiece, speakerphone and ringer, and this girl had a phone in every room with separate lines for her fax and computer. Plenty of power for piggybacking, no dangerous follow-up visits to change batteries.

Working swiftly, he installed Infinity bugs on all the phones. When they were connected, you could dial a number and punch in a code from anywhere in the world and turn the whole phone into a high-tech spy. You hit the code first, the phone didn't ring, the target could blab her guts out and he would have it all.

As an afterthought, he went upstairs to the bathroom and hooked a subcarrier current bug to the fluorescent light above the medicine cabinet. He'd be able to track her cellular with his scanner, but it was always better to have a backup when they went to the head. The flush could screw everything up.

The feminine smell of the bathroom—especially the powder—gave him another idea. Shutting the door, he went back into the girl's bedroom. A low chest of drawers stood against one wall. Kneeling in front of it, he slowly opened the drawer where she kept her panties and bras. He picked a nice white Olga, fancy, the day-job kind. She had half a dozen. Never miss it. He held it up, admiring the cups. Then he crumpled it, buried his face in it, ran his tongue over the underwires. When he was finished, he unbuttoned his shirt and stowed the bra next to his stomach.

Nine minutes later, whistling tunelessly, he walked down the sidewalk to the switching box. It was about five feet high, was made of stainless steel with heavy hinges in the back and three clasp locks on the front. The middle lock had a hexagonal rod as an opener instead of a keyhole. Pulling a ring of stubby wrenches from the leather bag, he experimented until he had the right fit. Then he swung open the box and took a look at the neighborhood's nervous system.

Under a sticker that said MIRROR IMAGE CIRCUITS, dozens of pairs of wires were braided together and tied. It took him less than a minute to sort through the web of connections. Poking among them, he found the spare pair he was looking for and jumped the leads for the girl's phone, fax and computer lines over to the Coorain house.

There was a For Sale sign planted in the lawn next to the slate path leading to the front door in front of the place. He pulled it up and tucked it under his arm. Then he used a key to let himself in. Attached to the key with a little chain was a large round label that said HOLDEN REALTY, A POWER HOUSE THAT'S THERE FOR YOU.

The place was empty. Trask tossed the sign into the hall closet and went into a large rear room with a fireplace and windows that gave an unobstructed view up the backyards of the two houses standing between him and the girl's apartment. The setup was better than a lot he'd seen. Multiple phone jacks on the wall. Coorain must have used it as an office. Plenty of room for his gear. It took him twenty minutes to set up. When he was finished, he took another look around the room. The job could take a week or two. He'd have to bring in a chair and a folding bed. Maybe the time had come to treat himself to a new coffee maker.

He walked to the window and looked across the backyards toward the girl's place. It was getting light now. Sitting down in front of a black console attached to a computer monitor and a recorder, he punched a few buttons to test the pick-up on her e-mail.

To: p@santana.net
From: amanci@washchron.com
Subject: Missing Persons

Where are you P? . . .

All there, just right. She must have sent it before waggling her ass down into the park. Who the hell did the bitch think she was waving to him like that? He double-checked the soft taps on the phones. All good to go. He took the bra out of his shirt and hung it above the console.

"Okay, little darling," he said, rewinding the recorder. "You're mine."

THIRTY

That evening, Sandy stood in General Hunter's office examining the map. Nate plunked down on the couch next to Lieutenant Drago. He was about to ask Drago where he came from, when General Hunter walked into the war room.

"Colonel Speed won't be with us tonight, gentlemen. His vehicle hit a mine on the way in. I pray that he will still be with us tomorrow."

He turned and looked at Sandy.

"The show is yours, Captain Caine. My ops officer will fill you in. Captain Thaler will take over the backup unit. Liaise with him. Carry on."

Before Sandy could say anything, General Hunter turned and disappeared.

★   ★   ★

"What time you got, Nate?"

Sandy was studying the pilots, who were bent over the instruments of the Blackhawk. The chopper vibrated as the rotor blades began slowly to spin.

"O dark hundred, Hawk."

"Everyone aboard?"

"Roger that."

Sandy tapped the pilot on the helmet and gave him a thumbs-up. "Let's go."

The bird rose and veered to the east, skirting the edge of the dark city below. The rooftops of Sarajevo gave way quickly to mountains. Dropping low, the pilot followed the contour lines of the ridges, hiding the bird, muffling its approach.

Fifteen minutes later, he dropped toward the LZ, a small field in a valley at the foot of a low ridge. On the far side of the valley, on a low shoulder of the next ridge, was the chalet with the Muslims and the two SAS hostages.

The bird landed. Sandy and Nate jumped out, followed by the six men of the rescue team. It was still quite dark. They checked their weapons, then moved quietly into the forest.

No roads, no trails, no noise. For the next six hours it went that way. The navigation by compass, by guess and by God.

"Not bad, Hawk," Nate said, when the sweating raiders finally came out on the side of the valley away from the chalet. "They teach you that in the Ranger course?"

At 1500 hours, Sandy called a halt on a thickly forested knob about 400 meters above the chalet. While he crawled forward on his belly with his field glasses, the other men lay at the prone in a circle around Nate, catching their breath.

"Hey, Drago," Caldwell whispered. "Where you from, man?"

Drago pointed straight ahead over Sandy's receding shoulder. Then he rolled on his side and pointed north. "And that way, about 150 kilometers."

"You from all over the fuckin' place, Drago?"

"Try Zagreb, Sarajevo and Sandhurst. Out of Liverpool." The lieutenant grinned. "The rest of the family is there," he said, pointing south. "My brother's wife's Muslim."

"Jesus," Nate said.

Drago shrugged. "You Yanks have the Hatfields and McCoys. Same here, since 1389."

"Civil War's more like it, man. Even then, I think you got us beat."

"We practiced. Eight hundred years, a million layers of hate."

"Thought Tito chilled you boys out."

"People were more afraid of him than they were of each other. He died, everyone got back at it. We didn't miss a beat."

The captain was going into reverse now, inching back to them.

"How's it look, Hawk?"

"Hunter was right. At least five of them."

"How we gonna do this?"

Sandy looked at his watch. Three-thirty now. An hour and a half until the call to prayer.

"We'll go in at 1700."

"On their knees, easy to please?"

"You got it, Nate. Tell the others to catch ten. I want to brief them at 1600."

★   ★   ★

An hour before the call to prayer, Drago tapped the five SAS warriors on the shoulder. They assembled around Sandy and Nate.

"Okay," Sandy whispered. "Here's how we do it. We break into two teams. Drago, I want you to take Nate and Ed Clark over there and make a big noise for me out front. The rest of us will come in from the rear. Clark can use that C-4 of his. Prerig the charge and knock on their door. We'll do the same out back. 1705 sharp, got it?"

"Yes, sir." A chorus.

"Okay, set your watches. Once the front door and the two French windows in the back are blown, both teams will toss in a coupla stun grenades. I want those bastards in shock. Understood?"

Nods this time. No need for anything more.

"Let's move out."

Wiggling down off the knob, they split into two groups and worked their way across the last 200 meters separating them from their objective.

The chalet rose above a lawn of brown grass bordered by a bed of withered geraniums. Sandy waited until Caldwell and his team were in position outside the door. Then he slipped around to the rear of the building, where two large French windows opened onto a steep slope leading up toward the crest of the ridge.

At 1700, a reedy little wail went up inside the chalet.

Five minutes later, *Baaaarooooooom.*

Clark's knock came a split second before Sandy's.

Bbbbbaaaaarooooom.

The explosions rocked the chalet as the raiders poured through the shattered windows and door.

Five startled Muslims looked up wildly from their prayers. Their AK-47s were propped against the fireplace.

Thunnkkkk, thunnnnkkkk.

The stun grenades drove the five men to the floor. Three were down, out cold. The two others grabbed for their AKs.

Hard-core motherfuckers. The thought occurred to Nate as the first of the two began to swing his AK toward Sandy.

Blaap, Blaaap, Blaaap, Blaaap.

Drago's burst greased both of the mujahedeen. They spun like dervishes, the AK-47s flying through the air, smashing into the rock chimney above the fireplace.

Nate and Drago were already bounding up the stairs to the second floor.

"Picadilly Three, this is Ringo," Sandy called into his radio. "Cargo secured. Let's get out of here. Place is a bomb factory."

By the time Drago and Nate came back down the stairs escorting Forte and Sprinkles, the roar of two Blackhawks could be heard coming at them across the valley. The rest of the team was searching the chalet. Clark, the demolition man, came up to Sandy with two boxes of maps and documents.

"Make a big bang for me, Sergeant," Sandy said. "Something to send us home right."

Clark gave the boxes to an SAS sergeant. From his jacket he drew out a handful of smaller charges. Working quickly, he attached them to the boxes of ammo and plastique pushed up against the wall farthest from the fireplace.

By 1715, the SAS team withdrew, trussing the prisoners and throwing them in the rear of the second Blackhawk. The birds lifted off and headed back for Sarajevo.

Nate watched the chalet grow smaller and smaller.

BARRRROOOOOOOOM.

A tremendous explosion. Sheets of flame as the building disintegrated.

Another scoop for Abs if Julian wouldn't blow it.

"Nothing left but toothpicks, Hawk," Nate observed, still peering down at the flying wreckage.

"Good," Sandy said. "Let 'em chew on that."

★   ★   ★

"Nicely done," General Hunter said. He opened the drawer and uncapped a bottle of gin.

"As I recall, yours is a double, sergeant." He filled Nate's glass nearly to the brim.

When the drinks were poured out, General Hunter raised his own glass to Sandy.

"Here's to you new boys," he said.

"Sir?" Sandy said tentatively. Catching himself quickly, he knocked back his drink.

"You tots have owed the SAS for a long time," General Hunter said, but his voice was warm, not patronizing. "All that training from us since World War II. We practically diapered you. I must say, you are maturing nicely." He studied Nate's scowl. "In fact, I have to tell you, gentlemen, this time the SAS is indebted to you." He drained his glass in a single swallow. "Another round, lads?"

THIRTY-ONE

Smith Island ★ Maryland

Dawn in Rock Creek Park, mist rising through the trees, the damp air carrying with it the dark rich smell of rotting leaves. Glancing at her pace watch, Abbie saw she was running 8-minute miles. She throttled back. Worry always made her push too fast. Too fast meant mistakes.

As she ran, she replayed the video of her ride home with Patrice the night before his party. The little guy had his own style. She gave him that. It was as if he counted on flair to compensate for size. In a town where enormity of scale was everything—power, ego, greed—there was something almost sweet about him.

But what about the way he'd waved her off the boss? Wasn't it out of character? Uncool? She hadn't expected it. That little cherub busily deflecting the arrows of Eros from Jeff Taylor. The senator knew how to get to a woman, no question. Those sincere brown eyes, playing against the studied containment. The aura of power, not a halo so much as an emanation of the city's peculiar radiation shimmering around him.

Her train of thought suddenly jumped to Sandy standing on the balcony looking out over Zagreb, the way he smelled, the way she loved it when he touched her. She matched those sensations with what she had felt in Senator Taylor's office. The two men were both type-A, silverback males, the older one at the peak of life, the other still a wild child. She brushed a wisp of red hair out of her eyes and thought again about Sandy, the way his face dimpled when he laughed, the taste of his mouth. Jesus, what if the Serbs did have him? Julian had her wrong, she knew exactly what Serbs could do. Bad thought, Abbie. Drop it.

The truck was gone when she came up the homestretch. In the kitchen she put a cup of raw barley flakes and crushed walnuts into a bowl with a handful of raisins and a splash of water and left the concoction to soak while she took a quick shower. Then she put on a rust-colored silk blouse and black slacks. After nuking her breakfast in the microwave, she scanned her three newspapers. Buzzing with endorphins and info overload, she phoned a taxi to take her downtown.

She found Becca's Rover parked at a curb two blocks up from the *Chronicle*. On the passenger seat was a copy of *The Beverly Hills Quick Weight Loss Diet* under a box of Belgian chocolates. She picked up the box and rattled it. Half full or half empty depending on the mood swing du jour and whether or not Becca had taken her Prozac.

Traffic was heavy, but by the time Abbie reached the Beltway, there weren't as many cars, and the drivers ahead of her got out of her way as soon as they saw what was coming up behind them. She swung onto I-95, settled into a comfortable 70 miles an hour and turned east. She crossed the Choptank River at Cambridge and stopped at Princess Anne to get gas and pee.

Half an hour later, she was winding among thickets of loblolly pine and stunted oak, skirting marshes full of graceful widgeon grass bending in the afternoon breeze, Spartina spikes thrusting up toward the sun. As she came into Crisfield, she opened the window and smelled the sea.

At the Smith Island ferry pier, the *Sweet Lucille II* was floating at its moorings next to a small office with a hand-painted sign that said TICKETS. She paid eight dollars for a round-trip and asked the ticket taker where she could find the auto ramp.

"Why don't you park that killer bee of yours across the street in the lot?" he said. "The ferry only takes passengers. You missed the morning boat. Ain't another until three-thirty."

She parked the car and stole one of Becca's chocolates before locking up. A few blocks from the pier she found a seafood place and had lunch. Then she killed another hour walking around Crisfield. When she got back to the ferry slip, a tall, salty-looking guy in navy slacks and a white shirt with blue epaulettes was in the office talking with the handyman. "How far is it to Smith Island?" she asked him.

"Fourteen miles, ma'am," he said. "As the scaup flies. Not too bad. Little over half an hour. Do you have a place to stay? I won't be coming back until tomorrow."

"Do you know Janine Walker?"

"Soft Shell Books? Bed and breakfast?"

Ah. A nice warm feeling began to rise from her boots.

"I didn't know she was renting rooms."

"She don't usually, but maybe you'll get lucky. Just watermen over there in Crab Creek now. The drudgin' started two weeks ago."

"Drudgin'?"

"Arsters. They're drudgin' for arsters and crabs. Be doin' it until the snow hits the water. You like arsters? You busy tonight?"

She told him no and yes politely and he took it well.

At three-thirty twenty schoolchildren dressed like miniature hard hats and swinging lunch pails came pushing and shoving off a bus and onto the ferry. The captain pulled a cord, a whistle tooted cheerfully, and like a small boat in a large bathtub, the *Sweet Lucille II* started bobbing across Tangier Sound.

As the St. James Light to starboard fell astern, the sound of thunder rocked the ferry. Looking upward, Abbie saw two F-18 fighters disappearing behind a puffy white cloud. Sonic boom, Abs, you dope. Two hot jocks out of the Navy's Test Pilot School at Pax River. She found herself wondering how Sandy was going to feel, burrowed into some godforsaken Bosnian hill, lazing targets for flyboys like the ones upstairs.

The low hammock of Smith Island came into view, first the steeple of a church, then the low rooftops of Tylerton. "You'll be wanting to go on to Crab Creek," the captain said. "Janine's place is on Elizabeth Street over there at the end of town. Just keep watching until you see the house with the blue fence."

In Crab Creek, the one main street leading away from the ferry strip was lined with white clapboard cottages, some with green shutters, some with red, facing one another from behind pretty white picket fences.

At the end of the street, the uniform whiteness of the fences abruptly changed to a stretch of blue-green pickets in front of a yellow cottage, a whisp of black smoke trailing away from the old brick chimney. The sign planted in the tiny front yard said SOFT SHELL BOOKS. BED AND BREAKFAST. J. WALKER. HEALING.

Sidelight windows with old rippled glass flanked the wooden door. Abbie pulled a knob under one of them and heard a bell ring. The door swung open and the healer was standing in front of her, beautiful, not fragile in spite of her illness. Glinda the Good, Abbie thought to herself. This one had everything.

"How may I help you?"

"I was hoping you might have a room. They told me on the ferry to come here."

The healer shook her head. "Bart Dize is a nice guy, but I'm afraid I've stowed everything away. No one comes much after Columbus Day."

Then, to Abbie's surprise, Janine reached out impulsively and took both of her hands. "Disturbances in the field," she said, decoding a genuine psycho-neural hum. "I'd say you've got a regular nor'easter brewing in there."

Safe-enough guess. Still, a little spooky. "I guess I'm worried about tonight. All I really need is a bed. Or a couch, even. It's just one night. I'd be grateful for your help."

The word *help* seemed to galvanize Janine. "All right, tell you what," she said, squeezing Abbie's hands then releasing them. "Help me, I'll help you."

"What can I do?"

"Follow me."

A bright yellow windbreaker was hanging on a peg just inside the door. Janine slipped into it and stepped into the yard, leaving the door unlocked. Abbie followed her down a long grassy slope. At the foot of the hill, a small white boat with a lapstrake hull was floating just off the end of the dock, the bow line moored to a cleat, the stern held safely away by the anchor line.

"My dinky skiff," Janine said, pulling on the bow line. "Jump in."

Abbie lowered herself cautiously onto the thwart seat while Janine started the outboard and hauled in the anchor. "A spode," she said. "Doesn't foul in shallow water." The little boat turned and headed for a line of about a dozen red and orange floats a few hundred yards offshore.

"You didn't tell me your name," the skipper said mildly, throttling back the outboard as they neared the floats.

"Mancini, Abigail Mancini."

"Pretty, you must be a Scorpio." Uncanny. How did she do it?

Janine cut off the outboard and coasted up to the floats. When they were halfway up the line, she threw out the anchor, then tugged on it to make sure it would hold. Once she had the boat squared away, she handed Abbie a large pair of rubber gloves, orange like the floats, covered with dark stains and nasty little nicks.

"Do you know what a sook is, Abigail?"

"No, I've never heard of it. And it's Abbie."

"A sook is a sexually mature female crab that has moulted for the last time," she said in the same mild voice. "They live in the shallows until they are ready to be mounted, and the tips of their claws are bright red. They paint their nails."

The tossing of the boat was beginning to make Abbie feel queasy. "Is that right?" she said. "Where do the guys hang out?"

"The watermen call them Number One Jimmys. They hide in deep water and only come into the shallows to mate. That's when you catch 'em." Janine pointed to the line of floats with a sweep of her arm. Below each float, a light line sank to the bottom of the bay. "Crab pots," she yelled. The breeze was blowing stronger now and it was harder for Abbie to hear her. "You pull, I'll steady the boat."

For the next half hour they moved along the line of floats, Abbie pulling the crab pots up, hauling the wire cages up and over the gunnels and spilling the blue-green crabs into the well. When Janine finally threw the last empty crab pot back into the water, Abbie watched her eyes diving after it, tracking it all the way to the bottom.

She was slender, graceful, her body showing a sinewy confidence that was amazing in light of her medical chart. Her thick silver-streaked dark hair had come back after the chemo and she was wearing it long and straight, held back by a tortoiseshell band. The sun was nearly down to the water now and Abbie could see her face glowing happily in the last light. "Where did you learn to pull like that?" she shouted cheerfully, feeding gas to the outboard and pointing the skiff back toward her dock.

"I come from a family of boys," Abbie called back, pulling off the orange gloves and dropping them next to the well. "Four of them, including me."

The sun had set, but from below the horizon, the light—scarlet, orange, rust like the floats marking the crab pots—tinted the clouds floating over the bay. The water was dark now, the island hammocks jutting up like ships in a blacked-out convoy.

Up in the well they had maybe four dozen soft-shell crabs. "I'll take care of the boat," Janine said as they pulled up to the dock. She waved Abbie back to the house. "Won't take ten minutes."

Shutting the unlocked door behind her, Abbie stepped into a small room walled with books, Janine's small shrine to wellness. Cranio-sacral therapy and energy healing, psychoneuroimmunology, negative stress cycles, cognitive restructuring—all the usual suspects were there, the best-sellers on a small table next to an antique cash register.

She saw copies of Ernest Becker's *The Denial of Death*, and J. Konrad Stettbacher's *Making Sense of Suffering: The Healing Confrontation with Your Own Past* (introduction by Alice-the-child-within-you Miller). Next to them was Dr. Susan Love on breast cancer, side by side with Dr. Lila Nachtigall's opposing news on HRT.

Through a door next to the books on affirmation and aggression, she could see the kitchen. A few chunks of hardwood cut to stove-wood size were smoldering in the fireplace at the far end of the room. Taking up an iron toddy heater that doubled as a poker, Abbie was just beginning to improve the fire when she heard Janine's voice behind her.

"You're a reporter, aren't you?"

Not a sound when she came in. Where was the twinkle dust? Abbie put the poker back and turned around, trying unsuccessfully to conceal her surprise. Janine laughed.

"Oh, come on. You've got it written all over you. I watched you come up the street. No reservation, no bag and then you're standing outside the door taking notes with your eyes. Most people just say 'Got a room?' I bet you've already taken inventory out front. You want to look in my bureau drawers, check out the medicine cabinet?"

Abbie flushed.

"Look, you're right. But be fair. You had me out there in those rubber gloves so fast I didn't even have time to say hello."

Janine took off her windbreaker and dropped it on the end of the long pine table that filled most of the kitchen. A large Sub-Zero refrigerator was built into the end of the room opposite the fireplace. A hooded Viking six-burner in stainless steel filled out the picture. Maybe $10,000 worth of Patrice's style of high-end stuff. She wondered if they ever used to cook together.

"You're here to talk about Jeff, I suppose."

"That's right."

"You know what?" she said. "I'm sick to death of Jeff. Like, literally. At least I was, and I don't intend to let it happen again. You know what I mean?"

"You mean cancer."

"Exactly. You don't like to waste words, do you?"

"Or time. I didn't intend to ambush you, Mrs. Taylor. It just sort of happened."

"It's Janine. Janine Walker. I haven't been Mrs. anybody for a long time. Have you ever been divorced?"

"No."

"It's very hard on a body." She laughed. "Hoary cliché, right? The people who use it don't know how close they are to the truth. It very nearly killed me."

There was no self-pity in her voice. She sounded almost matter-of-fact.

"A cancer on the presidency. Jeff's presidency. Is that your story?"

"Your tolerance for crap is pretty low, isn't it, Janine?"

"Zero."

"Fair enough. No, that's not the story. My editor is sucking up to Senator Taylor. I've got a profile to do for next April. I was going to wing it until you fell out of the clips. The divorce is the only blot on Mr. Perfect's record. I'm curious."

Janine got up suddenly and walked over to the refrigerator. After poking around for a few moments, she came back with an armful of plastic containers. Red cabbage and sweet potatoes, brown rice and tofu. One more trip for the distilled water and miso soup.

"Dinner," she announced. "I'll do the crabs. You cut the bread. It's in the box on the counter. I think I'm going to trust you. We can talk later."

They ate in silence, avoiding small talk. When they were finished, Janine cleared the table and came back with a steaming pot of green tea.

"All right," she said, pushing a small cup with a crackled blue glaze toward Abbie. "What do you want to know? The war hero who screams in the night, the sheets all soaked in sweat? *The Deerhunter* said it all twenty years ago.

"Or do you want it tall, dark and handsome? 'Ladies and gentlemen, I give you the next President of the United States'—with all the pretty balloons tumbling down? No one wants the truth," she said. "You should know that by now. The truth is something we can only tolerate in small doses. Maybe never."

Don't let her get away, Abs. "So what's the senator's problem?"

"Which one?"

"You know—the divorce. What happened? How did you find out?"

"I hired a detective. A PI. It was after my operation. Jeff was great when I was in the hospital. The day I finally got up enough nerve to show him, he leaned over and kissed the stitches where my nipples had been. Then he didn't touch me again for nearly a year. At first I thought he was just being considerate, but I mean, how considerate can you be?

"He was spending a lot of time campaigning back home. And campaigns are tough. You're tired but you've got all the instant intimacy floating around. And all those hungry young girls. We were always so close I never worried about it. I thought we were different.

"He had this pretty, twenty-six-year-old press secretary. Sarah Wilder. She always traveled with him. I even liked her. But it took the detective less than a week to catch them."

"What happened?"

"He came in one afternoon and dropped a little present in my lap. The pictures had time stamps at the bottom. Photo Op One: 9:00 P.M.—Jeff and Sarah holding hands by candlelight at the Sherwood Inn. Photo Op Two: 10:35 P.M.—Jeff and Sarah entering Room 42, the honeymoon suite. Photo Op Three: 8:15 the next morning, Room Service wheeling in restoratives, Belgian waffles, as I recall. Photo Op Four: 9:45 A.M.—Jeff and Sarah restored, leaving the room hand-in-hand in jogging gear. Glowing like Gary Hart and Donna Rice."

Janine took a sip of her tea and looked at the fire. No tears, no black channels through her mascara. She wasn't wearing any makeup. Didn't need any.

"Same old monkey business," Abbie said. "How did it make you feel?"

"Devastated. So depressed I couldn't move. I felt totally betrayed. I mean, look at me. I'm intelligent. I worked hard. For him. I was out there. For him. All those white-glove teas with officers' wives, smiling through the Army bullshit, then the campaigns. I worked for him, I really worked my ass off. Just like Nancy did for Ronnie. I'd sit there with him war gaming, strategizing, blowing little kisses to fat cats. I was there for him every step of the way except when he was in bed fucking Sarah Wilder."

"She wasn't the only one, was she?"

"No, you've got that wrong. It was the first time, so I told myself it would run its course and we'd go on. But I was living a lie."

Abbie reached over and refilled Janine's cup. "Political wife's syndrome."

"That's right. The sisterhood. We all know who we are. We see each other at congressional wives things. We never talk about it, but we recognize each other. The secret girls club. The worst is what you do to yourself. Before I married Jeff, I had standing in my own world. I could have done a lot of things, but I sold myself short. I wound up feeling that life as Mrs. Senator Taylor was always more interesting than when I was by myself. Big mistake. Almost fatal."

Abbie nodded. Her mother had made the same mistake—Mrs. Dr. Mancini.

"I just couldn't pull myself out of it," Janine said. "It wasn't as bad when we were in the Army. Jeff loved being a soldier. He was good at it, a war hero, for God's sake. But I always felt when he moved into politics he began to move away from me. These guys all turn into power junkies. They demand more and more stroking and I bought into it, goddamn it, even though I can't tell you how empty it made me feel as a woman. Power *is* an aphrodisiac and I couldn't let go of it until it almost killed me."

Abbie reached over and touched her arm. "You're different now, Janine. Lots different. Anyone can see that."

"Thanks, Abbie, you're kind. But I might as well get this all out of my system." She pushed her cup aside and looked at the fire for a moment. "Rank bait for lobsters, fresh bait for crabs," she said quietly, as if talking to herself. She looked up and caught Abbie's bewildered glance. "It all depends on what you're drudgin' for, Abbie. The turn-on, I mean. Did you ever wonder what public service really means? These guys start out thinking they're serving the country but the way most of them end up, they're only serving themselves."

"I don't follow you."

"Think about it. The moment they get here, they belly up to the table and serve themselves everything on it: power, money, adulation. Serve the country? Uh huh. They serve the country up in big chunks to whoever wants a piece of it. The one thing they can't ever admit is that the buyers are also taking big bites out of them, too. Service with a smile. What goes around comes around. *E pluribus unum.* One for you and one for me. That's their real pledge of allegiance."

"Did you show him the pictures?"

"I didn't have to. Patrice found out about Sarah sometime that summer and fired her. Jeff came in one day and she was gone. I think Patrice shipped her off to Strasbourg with some hotshot economist. She did all right. When Jeff asked what the hell was going on, Patrice said, 'Don't you and Janine ever talk?' So Jeff called and I hung up on him. That's when I realized it was over for us, that I couldn't do it anymore. Then he came home, first time in the middle of the day, swore it was a mistake and all he wanted was to save his marriage."

"What did you say?"

"I told him our marriage was a toxic waste dump. I threw him out of the house. Didn't see him for months. Patrice handled all the details of the divorce, the lawyers, the settlement, everything. He said, 'It's no harda' than cookin' for two hundred, *chér.*"

Abbie remembered the little guy and his bibs, the big-brother talk in the Porsche. "He seems like a prude. What is he, gay?"

"Patrice? God, no. With Pat everything's mental. There's nothing physical about him at all. He's the most asexual man I've ever met. It wouldn't surprise me if he's never gone to bed with anyone. Either sex. Not that I know where he'd find the time. All he thinks about is Jeff and the power curve. Perfect guy for the job. No other life. He's taking care of Jeff eighteen hours a day and he's so charming about it, he usually gets his way."

"It's hard to believe there's no one in his life. Are you sure?"

"What I heard was he got sex scared out of him even before his voice changed."

"What do you mean?"

"He worked for this famous chef in his father's first big restaurant. The guy was AC-DC, AM-FM, a complete universal donor where sex came in. One night after closing he drank too much brandy and told Patrice to suck his willie. Big guy, wouldn't take no for an answer until Patrice tried to cut it off with a bread knife."

"You're kidding."

"It gets worse. The chef was too important to lose, so Monsieur St. Jean sent his son off to Jesuit school in Baton Rouge to learn about compromise. Talk about denial. He told me once that he could never go into the restaurant business because the pay-offs were too big and the take was too small. He liked politics better. 'Little somethin' for everyone makes the world go 'roun', *chér.*' "

Abbie thought about the little Sony TCM-354V nestled in her purse with its cassettes. She decided against it. The first sign of a tape recorder and Janine would freeze up.

"Who told you all that about Patrice?"

"Pat. Toward the end of our first campaign. All that exhausted intimacy I told you about, remember? He didn't have a clue about what he was really telling me. Look, he's a little guy and when he was sexually abused, his own father sold him out. Think what that would do to you. With Pat it's all about being safe. He says he's willing to kill himself working for Jeff so Jeff can make the world safe for democracy. But it's really about making the world safe for Patrice. I don't hold that against him. He's always taken good care of me. I owe him a lot."

"What about those night sweats of Jeff's, the nightmares you were talking about? The story is about how far we've come from Vietnam. What did it do to him?"

Janine seemed to hesitate. "I don't want to talk about vio-lence—I don't think it's good for me. You'll have to ask him yourself."

"But you've told me so much that's worse. Why?"

Picking up the pot and the cups, Janine took them over to the sink. She swished water around in them for a few seconds, then deposited them in the dishwasher. Wiping her hands on a dish towel, she came back to the table and sat down.

"You and I both know the rules, Abbie. You've got one source, me, no notes, no tapes. You can't print any of this unless some-one confirms it. I don't think anyone will."

"Then why tell me anything?"

"He's going to be President, Abbie. Compared to most of them in Washington, he's a good man. He can do a lot for the country. I know it. But if I said that first, you would never have believed me, so I'm saying it now."

"Come on, Janine. Okay, so I believe you, but can't you do better than that?"

"All right, since I left, he's had a giant hole in him. Ask him. He'll tell you. I'm not just flattering myself. You must have seen it by now. Maybe I have some regrets, too. You figure it out. Come on, I'll show you your room."

She got up and tossed the dish towel on the table. Abbie followed her out of the kitchen and upstairs. There were four small bedrooms off the landing. "You'll find sheets and blankets in the chest at the foot of the bed," Janine said. "I'm going to turn in. What time would you like breakfast?"

"About six, I guess. Maybe we could talk some more then."

"I don't think so, I'm just about talked out. Good night, Abbie."

On an impulse, Abbie wrapped her arms around Janine and hugged her. She felt the hard, flat chest against her own breasts. "Good night, Janine," she said, trying to strangle her feelings before they made her cry. "Thank you for all this."

When the door was closed, she got out her notebook and wrote for half an hour. Then she made up the bed. For a moment she looked out the window. The hunter's moon was hanging over the bay. From across the water came the whistle of a goldeneye duck winging down to the marshes. She crawled under the quilt and turned out the light.

*   *   *

The following morning at six, steel-cut oats were already soaking in a glass bowl next to the stove when Abbie came into the kitchen. Janine was slicing. The white cotton nightgown brushing the floor added to the general impression she made of kitchen goddess. Persephone, Abbie decided. Back from hell.

"No Belgian waffles?"

Janine wrinkled her nose in disgust.

"So what did you leave out last night?" Abbie asked.

Janine's expression fell somewhere between amused and embarrassed. "A couple of things."

"What couple of things?"

Warming her hands on a cup of tea, Janine thought about it for a while. "I didn't quite get it right." Abbie waited. "About Jeff and me." She stood up awkwardly and took the dishes to the sink. When she came back, she sat down next to Abbie and looked at her intently, like an egret considering a safe place to land.

"I really am selfish, you know. What worries me is that the minute he starts his campaign, every reporter in the country will be after me. You're just the first, although, of course, you're not like them. I mean, what does Sam Donaldson know about sensitivity? I just can't bear the thought of Barbara Walters sitting there with her eyes swelling up asking me if Jeff should be President."

"Well, should he? What's the problem?"

"*I'm* the problem. And he's mine." This morning the anger was gone. The tone was one of perplexity.

"The past is over, Janine," Abbie said gently.

"It's never over."

"So you do still love him?"

"No," she snapped. Then she threw up her hands. "Okay. Yes. It's just that I'm in a different place now, I have to look at things differently. Jeff has a very good side to him. The whole time we were married I tried to align myself with that good side and to help him stay in that part of himself. Even though the marriage is over, I don't want to sell out all that good. It would be cheap, bad for him and really negative energy for me."

"I don't think I get it."

Janine looked out the kitchen window. "They call this whole area the Isles of Limbo," she said, pulling aside the white curtains to let in the morning. "Captain John Smith gave it the name. They left it out of *Pocahontas*. You have to live here to find out. When I got here, I wasn't quite dead but I wasn't alive, either. So the Isles of Limbo was just the right place for me."

"But not anymore?"

"Not anymore. It's been more than five years since the operation. I'm not going to die tomorrow. The other day I wrote to the University of Maryland for a law school catalog. God, I don't know what got into me, but for the first time it seemed safe to buy into the future, make some plans."

"What's wrong with that?"

"Nothing, I guess. I suppose what I'm hoping is you'll do your story and that'll be it. The country needs him, Abbie."

"But you don't, right?" She meant for the rhetorical question to buck Janine up, not draw her out. Unprofessional, she told herself. But she liked this woman.

"I'll walk you to the ferry," Janine said, regaining her footing. When they got to the pier, she took both of Abbie's hands in her own. "Let me tell you something," she said. "It's not just about Jeff's campaign. No matter what I still feel for him, I'm not going to let a dead marriage kill me."

THIRTY-TWO

★ Sarajevo ★

"Better you step on it—General Sir Sterling is waiting for you."

Drago was waving Sandy and Nate into his taxi, a British Saxon armored personnel carrier mounting a 7.62 machine gun instead of a meter. The door of the APC opened. "Weather's whole lot better in here, Hawk. Think we oughtta move in?" The steel walls of the APC made Nate's laugh sound like something thumping an empty oil barrel. The engine roared, the APC shook itself and rumbled off toward General Hunter's HQ. "What's all this 'General sir' shit about, anyway? Whaddya think they say when Hunter gives them an order? Yessir, Sir. Nossir, Sir."

Up front Drago laughed.

"You know how much time all that takes? Shit, no wonder we kicked their British ass."

They bumped across town, wondering why Hunter had sent for them. Drago didn't have a clue. Fifteen minutes later, the APC ground to a halt and they followed Drago back to the general's office. This time, after knocking, he entered ahead of them. While they double braced in front of the commander, he stayed at the back of the room.

By reflex, Sandy started to hoist another mangled Canadian salute.

"I do wish you'd stop that, Captain," General Hunter said. "You might as well have 'Made in the USA' tattooed on your forehead."

"Sorry, sir," he said.

Nate grinned.

"Something amuse you, Sergeant Caldwell?"

"No, sir. Sir Sterling, sir," Nate snapped.

The general looked at him suspiciously. Detecting the irony, he let it pass. "I have a new mission for you," he said. "Take a look at the map." He walked over to the wall and began searching through the contour lines tracing the hills and valleys northeast of Tuzla. "There," he said abruptly, stabbing his finger on the village of Hamagar. "There's my problem."

He began walking up and down the room. "Muslim village, Hamagar. Tough little bastards. Cut off, but the Serbs can't seem to knock them out of the game. NATO has been dropping them rations. Good practice, that. Drop bundles of food now, bombs later, if we must." He stopped in front of Sandy. "That was the general idea."

"Yes, sir." This time, Nate kept his face straight. General Sir Sterling Hunter was the real article, not another Rushman. Nate had already tested his perimeter and gotten away with it. Another go could be suicide.

"As I was saying, the place has been completely cut off for three months. Two days ago they got a man through to our lines. We asked if they needed more supplies. He said, 'What supplies?'"

"I don't understand, sir."

"Nor do I, Captain. Apparently nothing is getting through. Right now, as it happens, the Muslims have a column pounding the hills around Hamagar. Pounding," he paused, "I suppose you could call it that. At any rate, things seem to be loosening up a bit."

"Okay," Sandy said. "We'll drive up in the morning and take a look around."

"I must say, I admire your energy, but that is not quite what I want you to do. I need a Yank to go onto a Yank base. What I'm asking myself is whether some Sergeant Bilko of yours is stealing those supplies before they get off the ground. So you and Sergeant Caldwell are going to get over to Rhein Main this afternoon. That's where they're loading the food pallets. The next drop is in two days. At night."

"Yes, sir. But why Rhein Main?"

"You are going to follow those rations, Captain. I want you to follow them from the warehouse onto the trucks, from the trucks onto the transports, from the transports down to the ground, and from the ground to whoever the bloody hell is taking them."

Drago stepped forward even though the general had given no order.

"Lieutenant Drago here will go with you."

"We've seen him at work, sir," Sandy said.

"So you have, Captain. Excellent man, Drago. Born in Belgrade, but British to the hilt—everything Sandhurst can do for a chap who has the misfortune to grow up in Liverpool without being a Beatle. He speaks the language. He'll translate for you. If you leave now, you should be able to find a little German action in Frankfurt tonight. That is all, gentlemen. Lieutenant Drago will show you where to pick up your chutes. If you have any questions, I'm sure Drago can answer them. His people were eating with forks and knives when ours were still painting themselves blue."

General Hunter sat down again. This time he left the drawer with the gin shut.

THIRTY-THREE

Suitland ★ Maryland
National Military Archives

It was a pleasant morning with no wind. "You travel light, don'cha, miss?" Bart said as Abbie fell in with the schoolchildren tumbling aboard the *Sweet Lucille II*. As they ploughed back across Tangier Sound toward Crisfield, she looked into the clouds, half hoping to see the F-18s reappear. Guardian angels, she thought, free associating a bit recklessly for so early in the morning. It made no sense, but the sonic boom the day before had seemed reassuring, almost as if Sandy had arranged a sign that he'd be there whenever she was in danger.

She found the Rover where she had left it. Some Ford or Chevy lover had written in the dust on the hood, "Please Wash This Lemon." Leaving the message for Becca, Abbie got in and retraced her tracks north.

She stopped in Easton for gas and a map of suburban Washington. Suitland was the town she wanted. Prince Georges County, about five miles to the west of Andrews Air Force Base. The name had always struck her as inspired. She had never been there, but she saw it in her mind's eye as surreal, a place where all the suits in Washington went home at night, GS-15s and assorted admirals and generals, FBI guys and CIA agents, maybe even media hotshots . . . like Julian.

The reality was disappointing. Clockwise around the Beltway to Exit 11, about 5 miles to the south, she moved from the Isles of Limbo to the Shoals of Recorded History.

The warehouse of the National Military Archives was on the slope of a little hill. The building was low, with stone walls. It looked like an old school abandoned by its pupils, recycled into a repository for paper that was already disintegrating. You didn't even have to pulp the stuff.

The desk clerk, a young man wearing white leather tennis shoes under his tan slacks, gave her a form to fill out. After she forked over $10, he pushed back a little card that said, "Archival Researcher." With the delivery of a bored flight attendant, he started reciting the rules: no briefcases, no pens, no hats, sit up straight in your chair.

"You've got to be kidding."

"I'm sorry, no," he said. "But the documents are fragile, and, in most cases, one of a kind. We expect researchers to be alert and to treat them with respect."

The reading room was huge. A few lost souls sat at the long tables, backs straight, the little carts beside them loaded with manila envelopes. She filled out another form, and forty-five minutes later, a clerk came up to her chair pushing one of the carts.

On top was a single envelope. The label said, "After Action Reports. Lang Vei, Vietnam, August 26, 1966."

"If you want photocopies, you'll have to go to the desk to make sure everything's declassified," the clerk said, as if he suspected her next stop was sure to be the Russian Embassy. "Fine," she sighed. "And I won't slump. I promise."

Picking up the envelope, she unwound the string fastener.

Inside she found one substantial document about an inch thick and five smaller ones. The big one had a table of contents. The paper was thin; the text, batted out on a typewriter at a time when machines could process cheese but not words, looked antique:

Headquarters, 5th Special Forces Group [Airborne]
Nha Trang, Vietnam, APO SF 96834
31 August 1966

SUBJECT:
Lang Vei After Action Report
22–26 August 1966

PREPARED BY:
Major Anthony Rhodes

The camp had been a disaster waiting to happen. She flipped quickly through the summary and main battle report. Bad weather limited the use of the only thing that could have saved them: TAC AIR. Without it, they had been doomed.

She took a pencil and started to write down the names of the American dead. She had to push aside an old paper clip to see the first name.

Capt. Jefferson K. Taylor
1st Lt. Alexander G. Caine
SFC Leonard M. Beckman
SFC Layton T. Shapen
SFC Robert C. Giannini
SFC Thomas B. Lord
S/Sgt. James B. Dunford
S/Sgt. Harris A. Everly
S/Sgt. Lawrence D. Hyduk
S/Sgt. Lincoln L. Naylor
S/Sgt. Jackson W. Prysbekowski

At the second name, she felt a sharp pang. All that Sandy was, the catastrophe that had shaped him, was right there, reduced to a single smudged line on a yellowing sheet of Army onionskin.

Jeff Taylor at the top of the body count? It puzzled her for a moment. Then she remembered there had been a lag of several days between the original casualty list and the final report from Major Rhodes. The document in front of her was the original. Never corrected. How could an organization so in love with lists screw up so many of them?

Putting the pencil down, she ran her eye quickly over the table of contents to see if she had missed anything. Looking at the boldface CLASSIFIED stamp on Annex F, she suddenly realized that she couldn't even remember what was in the document. Flipping quickly through the report, she found the log of radio transmissions, the list of choppers, the dead in Annex E. But when she flipped the page after Jeff's name, nothing was there. Annex F was missing.

She slumped in her chair. The guard cleared his throat. "You'll have to sit up, miss." Groan. They actually meant it. Turning the report over, she examined the staples. A small piece of paper was stuck in the corner. Something had been ripped away.

She now noticed for the first time that while Annex F was typed, the word CLASSIFIED was not. Someone had written it out by hand in block letters. The ink was reddish brown. It looked like something from a marker pen. She looked again. The same marker had been used to obliterate two typed words that followed Annex F, presumably the contents of the annex.

Curious, she detached the page from the rest of the report and took it to the window. From across the reading room, she heard the guard mutter, "Good Lord," as she held the thin sheet of paper up to the glass. She heard him come huffing up behind her.

It didn't matter now. She had what she was after. The sunlight through the onionskin had been powerful enough to backlight two of the words the ancient typing machine had cut deeply into the paper.

The two words were *Survivors Report.*

THIRTY-FOUR

"Die, bitch. Give me one reason I shouldn't kill you."

Abbie shut her eyes. With Becca, cringing only made things worse.

"Grand larceny auto. You know what you can get for that? Three years minimum—even if you cop a plea—and I'm not in the mood for mercy."

Becca's eyes were hidden behind the black polarized lenses of the Oliver Peoples sunglasses she wore in the newsroom to annoy Julian. The day he made the mistake of asking her what the hell she thought she was doing, she told him to fuck off. Everyone did it at *Vogue*. Maybe it would class up the *Chronicle*.

Abbie was standing in front of Becca's desk running the chain with the keys to the Rover through her fingers. "I'm sorry," she said, trying to sound contrite. "I should've called, I just got into some stuff and lost track of time."

"For thirty-six hours? Some day it's gonna be no, and I'll mean it."

"It'll never happen," Abbie said. "You're the original girl who can't say no. That's why I love you." She bent and dropped the keys into Becca's hand.

"I look at you and I see an accident about to happen. And I don't mean on the open road. As far as I'm concerned, you're grounded."

"For my own good, right?"

Becca nodded, but she was mollified. Seeing that it was safe to go, Abbie took off her coat and tossed her notebook next to the phone. Not a bad haul for an overnight run. A dab of ancient history. A few true confessions. One good mystery.

Picking up the receiver, she pecked out Patrice St. Jean's private number. It rang only once before he picked up. "Taylor Take-Out," he said.

"It's me, Pat—Abbie."

"Welcome back, *chér.*"

"Did you miss me?" she asked lightly. She couldn't remember telling him she was going away. "I've been doing some research. I need to talk to you."

"Right now's good, amazin' enough."

For the first time, he sounded almost eager to talk to her. Dutch Uncle Turns into Mr. Congeniality, she reflected. Thinking in tabloid headlines was always a worthwhile exercise. Prepared you for that stranger-than-life stuff you might otherwise not believe.

"I'd rather not discuss this over the phone. It's complicated."

"All right, *chér.* Tell you what. I've got about three hours' work here. Why don't you drop by the plantation later tonight? Buy you a drink."

She looked at the clock on the newsroom wall. It was almost seven. "Have you ever heard of the power breakfast, Pat?" she said. "They invented it for people who haven't totally lost their commitment to sleep."

"The just never rest."

"Sorry I asked. Okay, how about ten o'clock?"

"See you then. You know the way." He paused, as if something had just occurred to him. "Did she tell you anythin' you didn't already know?"

Abbie felt her stomach tighten. "You teach her the tarot, Pat, or did she teach you?" she said, making a face at the phone. "Catch you later, *chér.*" Let him wait.

*　　*　　*

On the way home, she stopped at the Hungry Gazelle to pick up dinner. Then she walked home through the park. Bumping lightly against her body, the shopping bag from the gourmet shop reminded her of the expedition to the market in Zagreb, Sandy's lips nuzzling her fingers as she fed him olives. Could she spend her whole life with someone like that? Someone who would always be sleeping with a rifle when he wasn't sleeping with her? Someone who might jump out and break the neck of any guy who even looked at her? Hey, what is this? she asked herself. Maybe I do really miss him.

She snapped on the kitchen lights. The modem was still hooked up to the laptop. As the machine booted up, she tapped her fingers restlessly until the e-mail log appeared on the screen. Four messages from Becca—death threats for sure. Nothing from Sandy.

She pecked out another please-come-home.

To: p@santana.net
From: amanciawashchron.com

Well you're sure MIA around here. Get back, will you? Talked with Janine Walker, checked out the after-action reports on ODA 351. There was something called a survivor's report, but someone's pinched it. Also found a list of the dead men on Alex's team. Any ideas on the quickest way to track down next of kin? Got a lot to tell you. YR

She hit the send button and watched the message disappear. Hey, what's so bad about falling for a soldier? she told herself. Give her enough time, she'd give great PX.

In the bathroom, Abbie checked the mirror to assess the damage of her trip. Awful. Hair scraggly, face in ruins, clothes ready for the incinerator. She ran a hot shower and pulled herself together. Black silk blouse, black Tasmanian wool skirt courtesy of the Benjamines . . . no, wait a minute. She pulled on a pair of faded black jeans and an old gray cashmere cardigan, found her running shoes, grabbed her banged-up black pea coat. See what casual does for Patrice.

The house was dark when she got there. For the next twenty minutes she sat on the brick steps shivering in the late fall chill. At ten-thirty she saw the Porsche turn the corner. Patrice was driving slowly, no flash, almost as if he were casing his own neighborhood.

"Sorry, chér," he called to her as he stepped out of the car. "You been waitin' long?" He was carrying a thin leather attaché case.

"Long enough," she said, trying not to sound testy.

"My God, you're shakin'," he said, putting his arm around her and escorting her up the steps. "Come on in and ah'll get you somethin' warm." His arm only came around her halfway and his hand on the small of her back felt light and soft.

But he obviously wasn't hitting on her. Janine was right. The only signals Patrice emitted were high-frequency power waves. In the kitchen, he fussed over the stove for a few minutes and came back with a steaming mug of mulled cider. Ordinarily, the stuff was cloying, but this was perfection.

"Family secret," he said. "Don't bother askin' for the recipe."

They sat on stools facing each other across the granite-top kitchen island. Pat didn't seem to be in any hurry. He patiently watched her nurse the hot drink, waiting for her to make the first move.

"All right," she said, when the hot cider had warmed everything down to her toes. "So how did you know?"

"About you and Janine?"

"That's right. Me and Janine. No one knew I was going down there."

He smiled at her pleasantly. "No mystery, *chér*. She called me this morning. After you left."

"Why?"

"I handle a lot of her stuff. Janine and I are always in touch."

Abbie put one hand over the top of her mug and felt the steam caressing her palm.

"So what did she tell you?"

"She said you were very nice. For a reporter."

Abbie wondered how much she would have to give him to get anything back worth the price.

"My turn, *chér*. What did she tell you?"

"She called her marriage a toxic waste dump. But she said you weren't so bad. Made you sound almost chivalrous."

He didn't purr. "Don't show me yours and I won't show you mine? Is that how we're goin' to play it?"

From Patrice, it didn't sound insulting. More like Danny, fencing with her over an FDA attack on something he'd put out on the shelf in the Hungry Gazelle. Wait him out, Abs.

"All right," he said finally. "She tell you anythin' I ought to know about? The thing is, there's always more than one side to a story. You know that better'n me."

"She told me he had nightmares."

"About politics? Godalmighty, so do I. Every night."

"About Vietnam."

"Is that right?" Was he being a little too relaxed? No way to be sure. "What nightmares?" he asked her.

"She didn't want to talk about it. I got the feeling she'd just as soon forget it."

"Sometimes that's the best way."

Moving quickly, she stepped forward to blindside him. "The best way is to check everything out. I stopped at the National Military Archives on the way back to look at the ODA 351 after-action report."

"And?"

"Guess what? Someone has snitched the classified part. Now why would anyone want to do that?"

"Why, indeed, *chér*." Pat's attaché case was lying on the island between them. Unlocking it, he pulled out a manila folder, scanned it for a moment and handed it to her.

She opened the folder and pulled out a document on the same yellowing onionskin she had seen out in Suitland. The typing was also the same:

Headquarters, 5th Special Forces Group [Airborne]
Nha Trang, Vietnam, APO SF 96834
31 August 1966

SUBJECT:
Medevac. Survivors Report

PREPARED BY:
S/Sgt. Charlie Windsor, Senior Medic

26 August 0900 hours received order from ODB-311 HG to medevac Lang Vei survivor. Captain Jefferson Taylor, OF 098137, multiple head and chest wounds. Unconscious. Dusted off casualty to Nha Trang field hospital. Aboard HUEY MED-EVAC ACFT MSN. No. 502, Captain Taylor regained consciousness, delirious, hallucinations, repeated cries "Let me die. I want to die."

"You did it?" Abbie said in confusion, handing the folder back to Patrice. "What for? Why did you rip it off?"

Patrice left the folder lying on the island. "I didn't steal this little sonuvabitch, Abbie. I just borrowed it. It's goin' back."

"But you could have copied it."

"Day I was there, I didn't have one red dime. The change machine was empty, it was nearly five, and when I asked the clerk at the desk for a ten-cent loan, you know what he said? He said, 'You'll have to come back tomorrow.' Do you believe it?"

"But why? I still don't understand."

Patrice was looking at her as if she were maybe twelve years old.

"How many political campaigns you cover, *chér*?"

"None."

"I thought so, but you read the papers, right?"

"Of course."

"So what's the first thing you reporters do when any good man runs for President?"

"We check him out." She heard the tinniness of it and felt embarrassed.

"Well, that's one way of puttin' it," he said. "The way ah'd put it is y'all go out every four years and dig up all the shit you can, and then you dump it on the poor sonuvabitch. Right? And when you get finished, the candidate who's still got his head, or maybe just his nose, stickin' up through the big brown pile wins." He looked at her pleasantly. "Tell me if I'm wrong, *chér*. May be somethin' ah'm missin' here."

"It gets ugly, you're right, but . . ."

"But we're fair game, right?" He started rummaging in a drawer below the kitchen island. "Voilá," he said, pulling out a set of polished steel tongs and snapping them twice—they made a sharp, clean click—then he clamped them on the manila folder and shoved it at Abbie. "This is how I pinched the file, *chér*. Just like this. One of my jobs is to check everythin' before you people start shovelin'. Been at it awhile now, *chér*. If ah didn't know everythin' there is to know about Senator Taylor, I mean, if he had anythin' really bad in his past, do you seriously think ah'd let him go skippin' out there on the campaign trail so you media people could trash him?"

What could she say?

"I know you're honest, *chér*. Julian made you wear that dress the other night, didn't he? You picked it, but he paid. Am I right?"

She felt herself blush. "The paper paid."

"Thought so, that's why I like you. Okay, now, you want to drive out to Suitland to give this report back, or shall I?"

"Over to you, Pat," Abbie said, reaching for her coat. She had come to Georgetown feeling pretty cocky. Now there was just one word for what she felt. And you know what that one word is, Abs, she said to herself as she went out the door.

Lost.

★　　★　　★

The house in Rock Creek Park was beginning to feel like a tomb. John Trask lit a cigarette and surveyed the room. The pizza boxes in the corner gave off the smell of stale garlic. Next to his sleeping bag on the cot, a Styrofoam cup held two days' worth of butts. They floated in the cold coffee like dead roaches.

The Mancini cunt had been away twenty-eight hours. No action except for the message machine. No messages worth shit. Papa Mancini, "Don't blow your mom's birthday this year, okay?" Phone hustlers with deals, the gas company with bills, and that bull dildo from the *Chronicle* going, "Abbie, Abbie, Abbie, where are you, girl?" Every ten minutes. Another night of this, he'd be crawling the walls.

He got up and turned off the lights. It was easier to think in the dark, not so many distractions. If she didn't come home tonight, maybe he'd go over there and poke around. Check the transmitters, get a little adrenaline pumping. Absently he reached up and took the bra off the console. Slipping his hand into his pocket, he pulled out an old straight-edge razor with an ivory handle and flicked open the blade. Slowly he began cutting away the tips of the bra cups. When he was finished, he stuck his index finger through one of the two holes and sucked it. In the red light from the front panels of the recording gear, his face looked like a glowing coal.

At nine-thirty, he heard a high beep and glanced at the table where he had assembled his equipment. The reels of the tape recorder were beginning to turn. Moving quickly, he picked up the Sennheiser headset and pulled it over his ears.

"Hey, Miss Piggy. I'm back. Call me." *Click.*

Score one for the dildo. He reached up and touched the bra. Maybe things would get more interesting before bedtime. He flicked his cigarette into the cup. With the earphones on, he didn't hear its dying hiss.

★   ★   ★

It took Abbie fifteen minutes to find a cab. When she got home, she dropped into a chair in the living room. Why on earth was she stumbling around like this? She got some springwater out of the refrigerator and went upstairs. When she had her nightshirt on and her feet up again, the answer started to take shape. None of this was about Senator Taylor. It was about Sandy. She took a sip of the water and the answer suddenly changed. Course correction time, Abs. It's not about Sandy, either, it's about you. You're not going to trust your soldier until you know why he explodes, but he's not going to understand why he does it until he knows what happened to Alex. No maybes about it. Wasn't that what he'd said?

She reached over to snap off the light. The bright bulb blinded her for a moment, the same way the sun shining through the onionskin paper at the archives out in Suitland had made her squint.

She saw something.

"Jesus." She jumped out of bed and ran down to the kitchen. Grabbing her notebook, she flipped to the entry she had made before leaving Suitland: "Survivor's Report."

That was not what she had seen just now upstairs. What she had seen, the sunlight streaming through the onionskin, was "Survivors Report." No apostrophe. Plural. Maybe it was just a typo. Patrice had the survivor's report for Captain Taylor. But what if what she'd seen wasn't an error? What if Major Rhodes was meticulous?

What if Jeff Taylor wasn't the only survivor?

She was shivering. Bare feet on the cold kitchen floor. Taking the notebook with her, she went back upstairs, shut out the light and crawled under the covers. When the shivering stopped, she picked up the phone again. She counted seven rings. "Come on, come on, come on," she whispered. Just as she was about to hang up, a sleep-blurred voice came on the line.

"It's too damn late, Eddie. Leave me alone."

"Remember me, Professor?" she said, squeezing the phone. "It's Abbie Mancini. I've got an emergency."

★   ★   ★

The console had lit up like one of those billboards in Times Square. When the first phone call came in, Trask had been eating a pizza. He still had a slash of tomato sauce on his chin as he bent over the console, punching buttons, tweaking frequencies, turning on the steam.

After half an hour, the board went dead as quickly as it had flashed to life.

Trask rewound the tapes and considered his catch. Reaching up idly, he took down the bra and ran it through his fingers while he worked everything out.

Quality goods. High grade all the way.

When his thoughts were clear, he started to work. First, he wrote everything out on a sheet of paper. Then he flattened the paper on the table next to the console and studied his results.

> *Mad Max. Code Yellow. Loose cannon time. Girl's talking to everyone. Senator, his boy genius, Senator's wife. Going to Fayetteville. Boyfriend's gonna know it all. Details in T files.*
>
> *Standing by.*
> *DJ.*

Trask didn't know who Mad Max was. No one did. Trask did know that Max liked his alerts fast and hard. No personality. But Trask liked a little color. So he left in the part about the boy genius.

He ran the whole works through the encrypter. Then he fired it into the blue.

THIRTY-FIVE

★ Hamagar ★

Sandy and Nate followed Drago into the hangar. Each man was carrying a Heckler & Koch semiautomatic. SAS weapon of choice. The gun for all seasons. In the white glare of floodlights, their shadows stretched eerily across the apron of NATO's giant Rhein Main airbase toward the waiting C-130. The ramp was down. Forklifts were raising the last of the pallets onto the cargo ramp.

He thought about Abbie. She'd be getting up soon. He wondered what her bedroom looked like. Have to find out.

He'd spent the day tracking the load through a maze of quartermaster offices, warehouses, a marshalling area, and now onto the runway and into the belly of the transport. The paperwork was all in order. The supplies were moving smoothly. But he hadn't expected to find anything wrong at the German end of the supply line. Who would want to steal MREs? Meals Rejected by Ethiopians, wasn't that the joke back in the 'Dish? He checked anyway. Always a chance. Nail a crooked quartermaster, spare yourself a night jump. Yeah, right. Lots of luck.

The wind bit at their ears as they followed the last pallet into the bird. Clear night, moon down. Good for the jump. But colder than a reindeer's balls. The plane lifted off and headed east. It was a little past three when the C-130 began to bounce in the turbulence over the endless ridges of the Balkans. Sandy had been dozing. The jolt shook him awake. An Air Force load master was opening the floor locks securing the night's payload—eight large pallets loaded with rations, poised under heavy, detachable chutes for the slide out the cargo door into the night.

Sandy signaled Nate and Drago to stand up. As they checked each other's gear, no one said a word. A thumbs-up was enough. Everything good to go. When the locks were undone, the loadmaster turned and held up three fingers. A few minutes later, the nose of the plane tilted up; the loadmaster and his assistant began shoving the bundles into the blackness.

With the rear door open, the roar of the engines was deafening, the cold ferocious. "You first, Lieutenant," Sandy said, turning to Drago. "If there's anyone down there, you start the introductions. We'll come in right behind you." Drago nodded and headed for the end of the platform, a whisp of his ponytail sticking out from under his helmet.

"Okay, Nate, let's hit it."

They followed Drago aft. As the last of the pallets slid out, Sandy smacked Drago on the butt, then Nate, and then all three of them were falling through the blackness. Cold air stabbed into his lungs. He heard the snap of his chute opening, felt the jolt as his body swung perpendicular. Then it was down through the night, silently, like a raven in winter.

The drop zone was a narrow meadow, maybe three miles long, tucked among the hills overlooking Hamagar. Good drop. Through the gray light of the false dawn, Sandy saw the dark outlines of the pallets strewn along the meadow. As he got closer, he saw the chutes collapsed on the dark field. One huge breakfast for someone.

A few hundred yards off down the meadow, he could see Nate and Drago rolling up their chutes. Good jump. The adrenaline pumping now. Nate was looking out over the meadow, empty except for the pallets on the ground. No sound. Only a slight breeze. At the edge of the field, a small knoll stuck up, providing cover, concealment and a good view over the drop zone. Sandy began moving toward it, and the others fell in behind. The knoll was craggy, full of stones. When he reached the top, he saw two deep fissures running through the crest and slicing down the far side of the knoll. Both were deep enough to hide several men.

Nate pointed to the bottom of one of the cracks. It was littered with cigarette butts and empty shell casings. Good sign. The locals used it. Sandy waved Drago into one of the two firing positions, then piled into the second behind Nate. He looked at his watch. Quarter to four. Shouldn't be long.

Two hours later, they were hunkered down. Half frozen now. Worse than a fucking polar bear hunt. Sandy was weighing the risks of crawling from the crack to take a leak when he felt Nate's hand on his shoulder.

"Not now. Look."

The first rays of light were just beginning to hit the dirt track leading through the meadow. At the far end of the track, something was moving in the trees. From the second firing position, Drago raised a finger. He had seen it too.

Sandy flicked the safety off his submachine gun as a shape began to emerge from the dark backdrop of the trees.

A mule.

Shit.

He let his breath out slowly. The animal seemed to know the path. It stepped forward haltingly, shaking its head as if in protest. Then it hit Sandy.

Mine detector. The four-legged kind. Then its owner, a few yards behind, came into view. An old man. A farmer by the look of his heavy trousers, coat and gait.

The old guy saw the pallets strewn across the meadow. The frosty silence over the field broke as he yelled at the mule. Goading the animal with a stick toward the first of the bundles, he followed in its hoof prints. For a moment he stared dumbly at the pile of boxes. Then he took a knife from his coat and slit open a bundle.

His shout of jubilation echoed off the hills. Sheathing the knife, the old man swung up on the mule's back. At a fast trot, they disappeared into the trees.

Hidden on the top of the knoll, the three peacekeepers huddled in their holes and waited.

Ten minutes later Sandy saw Nate twitch slightly as the silence broke again.

Pop, pop, pop, pop, pop.

A quick series of small explosions, then a darker roar.

Out of the trees, three motorbikes came sputtering down the track. Behind them lurched a beat-up truck with no muffler. "Ain't troops, Hawk." Nate's whisper was smothered in the echoing roar from the truck's diesel engine. Whoever these guys were, it didn't seem to bother them that everyone within five miles could hear them coming.

Unlike the farmer and the mule, the bikers clearly knew what they were looking for. Passing the pallet the old man had stopped to slit open, the leader on the first motorbike led his irregular little convoy 200 meters farther up the track. At the foot of the knoll, he wheeled around and spun to a stop in the middle of the widely strewn pallets. Stepping off the bike, he unslung the AK-47 strapped to his back. The other two bikers got off and stood next to him.

Nate held up three fingers. Three AKs. How many more?

The truck lumbered to a halt and half a dozen men hidden under a tattered green tarp jumped out. No rifles, no uniforms. A few pistols, lots of muscle. They circled around the guy who had come in on the lead bike.

"Fucking bandits," Nate whispered.

Sandy nodded. NATO's own feed-a-thug program. That's why General Hunter's tough little bastards in Hamagar were starving. The bandit leader snapped an order, and the men from the truck began fanning out over the meadow, cracking open the pallets.

They worked fast. The boxes off the first two pallets were already stowed under the tarp when Sandy heard a loud cry go up at the far end of the field. From the trees, twenty men led by the old farmer on the mule burst into the meadow. For a moment they hesitated, then they ran toward an upended pallet that was lying near the foot of the high ground concealing the three peacemakers.

Pop, pop, pop, pop.

The little motorbike got there first. It fell on its side as the bandit leader jumped off. For a moment he stood there waiting while the old man on the mule rode toward him, followed by his group. The Muslims were shouting now. Lot of noise, not many guns.

For a moment the old man sat on the mule. Then he held his hands out in front of him, empty. The shouting behind him died down as he began to plead with the bandit leader. Begging. The bandit shook his head.

A roar went up from the men standing behind the old man.

With a quick upward sweep of the arm, the bandit raised the AK-47 and fired. The burst hit the old man in the face and chest, blowing him off the mule and into the yelling Muslims. There was a second of total silence. Then wild panic. The other two bikers wheeled up, and the villagers broke and streaked away into the trees.

The mule leaned over, gently nosing the dead man's body. The bandit leader threw back his head and laughed.

Sandy's burst caught him in the chest.

Bright red spray spewed from an artery as he spun and fell on top of the old man. At the same moment, Nate's burst blew the second gunman crumpled against the pallet. The SAS also knew its business. Drago's fire shattered the third bandit's head like a lightbulb hit by a hammer.

Far down the meadow, the sound of the shots transfixed the bandits loading the truck. Sandy heard a soft *thuuuck* as a pistol round clunked into the cardboard pallet at his feet. Drago's submachine gun chattered. A long burst arced down the field and shattered the truck's windshield. The driver jumped behind the wheel. With bandits clinging to the doors and bed of the truck, he skittered the old wreck out of range.

Sandy looked at his watch. It was 0700 hours. Three dead, the smell of sulfur rising through the mist over the meadow. If this was peacekeeping, what would it mean to fight?

Gingerly, the three of them edged out of their firing positions and down to the field.

It was cold, very cold. In the meadow, the only sound was the wail of the wind.

Sandy pointed to the motorbikes. They were lying on their sides in a lot better shape than their defunct owners. Picking up the nearest one, he kicked the starter. "You guys all right?" he called over to Nate and Drago. They nodded. "Okay, let's check out the town."

THIRTY-SIX

Fayetteville ★ North Carolina

The alarm went off like a jammed doorbell. Keeping her eyes shut, Abbie groped for the button: 4:45 A.M. She curled her knees to her chin, squeezing a final thirty seconds of fetal bliss from the night, then threw back the quilt.

A day from hell, she thought, groggily burying her head under a hot wake-up spray in the shower. Her flight left National at six-thirty. She had to be back by eight that night for dinner with Jeff. Her place. Her treat. Her tough-luck schedule.

Stepping out of the tub, she pulled on a robe and rubbed a peephole in the gray steam fogging the bathroom window. Floating in the blackness out by the front curb she saw the soft yellow glow of Marvin Hammer's "Off Duty" light. Bless you, Marv. Hack-in-a-Hurry Car Service. The one guy in Washington who never let you down.

She threw on underwear, a pale gray cashmere sweater and a charcoal pants suit and snuggled into a pair of soft, charcoal-gray goatskin loafers. As an afterthought, she tied a gray, rust and white argyle sweater around her waist. In the kitchen, she grabbed a container of blueberry yogurt. Picking up her laptop and purse, she headed for the door.

As she came down the brick path in front of the house she heard a quick, metallic snap that startled her. But it was only Marv, all six feet four inches and three hundred pounds of him, releasing the door locks.

"Here we go again, I hear those trumpets blow again," he sang loudly—and wildly off-key—as she slipped into the backseat. "Where to this time, Lois Lane?" She had heard the mossy old joke too many times, but she indulged him. Where else could she find another Marv?

"Up, up and away, big guy. National. You've got twenty minutes."

"No problem." He dropped the black Lincoln into gear and barreled out of the park like a buffalo in rut. Sex did it for some guys. For Marv, it was making all the stoplights. Through the park, down the Potomac with only the headlights of the overachievers glaring at them along the way, in fifteen minutes he dropped her in front of the USAir terminal. "How about seven o'clock tonight?" She handed him a twenty.

"I'm yours, Miss Lane."

With coffee money on the meter, Marv flipped his light to "Off Duty" and roared off, ignoring a few early arrivals trying to catch his eye. "The early worm catches the bird," he had once told her. Picking up speed herself, she headed for the gate.

Fayetteville was five hours off by way of Atlanta. A good-looking young soldier with a rolled-up copy of the *Army Times* in his hand took the seat next to her. By the time they reached cruising altitude, he was calling her ma'am and offering her one of the cold strawberry Pop Tarts he'd brought aboard for breakfast. Nice kid. He made her feel good about national security and bad about getting old.

In Atlanta she killed time catching up with the Reuters and AP newsfeeds on her laptop, then hopped the puddle jumper to Fayetteville. The plane bumped down through clouds and a light rain, all gloom outside her window until, breaking through the overcast, she saw the first tall Carolina pines and felt the gentle bump of the landing.

Santana was waiting for her at Gate 1. He was wearing a black tee shirt and chinos and for a moment she didn't recognize him. Then he whipped off his sunglasses and walked up to her flashing a grin that could have melted permafrost. "Are we going to war, Miss Mancini?" He took the laptop from her shoulder, shaking off her protest. "It was nice and peaceful down here until you called, but when I got up this morning they were issuing everyone flak jackets."

You shouldn't hug this guy, she thought—wanting to in a mostly sisterly sort of way—but who's going to shoot you for squeezing his hand? "I am a woman of peace, Sergeant Santana," she said. "Tell them they can stand down."

Santana led her out of the terminal to the parking lot. His car stunned her. It was a black and yellow 1986 Camaro, chopped and channeled and low-ridered until the oil pan was not quite scraping the ground. It looked like some sort of wingless fighter. You can take the boy out of East Los Angeles, she reflected, but you can't take East Los Angeles out of the boy. Becca would kill for it. He caught her surprise and grinned. "It's all a matter of cultural anthropology, Miss Mancini. Think of it as an artifact."

"Call me Abbie."

"Call me José."

"All right, José, let's boogie on out of here."

On the road into Fayetteville, she noticed that he drove more carefully than Marv. Was it because he had more experience with death or simply that he didn't want to scratch a masterpiece? His own finish was as perfect as his car's. His skin was a smooth pale beige. On the wheel, his fingers were relaxed, as practiced as a lover's.

"Where we going?" she said.

"My place. Better commo. I've got a surprise for you."

She could see modern buildings rising ahead of them, giving Fayetteville a skyline where once there had only been pines. Then Santana hit the funkier reaches of the place, mile after mile of fast food stands and filling stations, bars and the occasional tattoo parlor, all the fittings of a good Army town. On the sidewalks were men in BDU, even a few women. Slouching in the passenger seat, looking out the window, Abbie began to pick up some oddly contradictory signals. All around her she could sense the violence that beat at the heart of the place. And yet she felt safe.

Santana drove down a street lined with small stores: a bodega with vegetables, plantains and the season's last withered fruit outside, a shop with bridal gowns, the San Salvador Social Club, a newsstand piled with stuff in Spanish. They parked the Camaro in a small, one-car garage around the corner. Santana locked the wooden doors and she followed him up the sidewalk to the third house on the right, a shingled two-story Victorian with a catalpa tree shading the small yard in front.

"My pad," Santana said, unlocking the door. "José Homemaker."

One wall of the large front room was filled with electronics gear. Black boxes with chrome handles, dials and read-outs, an oscilloscope and something with vacuum tubes that looked early *Star Trek*. It was as if Santana was running a radio station.

On the adjoining wall was a collection of Central and South American masks. Some were carved in wood, others seemed to be made of something like papier-mâché. He had collected animals with gnashing teeth, birds in red and green feathers, demons with bloodshot eyes.

"Get comfortable," he said, "have a seat." He waved her to a chair that appeared to be constructed of bones and covered with the skin of an animal she'd never seen. "Llama shanks," he said, laughing at her expression. "Don't worry. The skin's Naugahyde. I got it at Pep Boys." He went out and came back with two mugs of coffee, light brown. "Mocha Antigua," he said, the faintest aroma of bitter chocolate trailing behind him. "House blend."

"What's the surprise?" she asked him.

"Later." He handed her one of the mugs. "First, let's take care of your emergency."

He spoke with no trace of an accent. His voice was terse, but quiet. If she didn't know better she would have taken him for an Anglo.

"I'm sorry I called so late."

"I thought you were Mayemura. Eddie I might have killed." He raised his mug to his lips, studying her over the rim. "We used to share this place, but Eddie couldn't stand the furniture. Drove him right into marriage. But he still calls home, usually in the middle of the night after he's been hitting the cooking sherry."

"Why? What's bothering him?"

"Same thing that bothers the rest of us. Same thing that bothers Captain Caine."

"What's that?" None of them had talked this way in Mogadishu.

"Being and nothingness." He shrugged. "The soldier's life. Combat and ennui. War and peace. The little things that wear you down."

"I see why they call you the Professor."

He shrugged. "Don't be too sure. We're all philosophers here. The green berets are just for show. They should have issued mortarboards, but the tassels get in the way when you're shooting."

She laughed. "Look, José, my problem doesn't stack up to

yours—existentially speaking—I'm just following the captain's orders."

"What is it?"

"You remember how worked up he got over what Perkins told him in Mogadishu?"

Santana nodded. "He told Nate, Nate told me."

"The paper wants me to do this story on Senator Taylor and Vietnam, right? So my plan was to find out everything that happened to his A-Team. That way I'd learn more about Sandy's father . . ."

Santana was grinning at her. "Sandy?" he said. *"Sandy?"*

"Yeah, well, okay, we've gotten past the Captain Caine and Miss Mancini stage. Anyway, the plan was to find out what Perkins meant and explain all to the Dark Brooding One, who would immediately lighten up and be grateful forever. And we'd all live happily ever after."

"Sounds good to me. What's the hitch?"

"I'm not quite sure."

"What doesn't compute?"

"I found Senator Taylor's ex-wife. She told me he had nightmares about Vietnam, but went to black when I asked her what they were. Then I found the after-action report on ODA 351—all the dope on how Sandy's father was killed. I won't bore you with the details, but I think there's an outside chance the senator wasn't the only survivor."

"I don't see where I fit in, Abbie. I'm not big on recent American history."

She stood up and got the list of dead men out of her purse. Santana examined it and handed it back. "Never served on a burial detail, Abbie. I dig things up."

"Yeah, me, too. That's where I need your help. The next stop is the National Personnel Records Center. The military branch. It's in St. Louis. You know computers. I was hoping you could hack into the center and trace these names. If I can get to wives or parents of the dead guys, maybe I can turn up something new."

"That's all you need?"

She blushed. "Sorry. I know it's tough. Maybe I'm just fantasizing."

"Wrong. This one's easy."

He pushed the coffee mug aside and walked over to his wall of electronics. Punching numbers into a console, he stood back, and Abbie heard what sounded like a phone ringing, then a voice from within a barrel somewhere.

"*Sí*, what the hell you want?"

"Mendoza? This is Santana. I got a dozen KIA, amigo. All our guys, Nam, sixty-six. How soon can you get me everything you got?"

There was a pause. She heard a quick exchange in Spanish. It sounded like a short, hot firefight, the kind that dies out as quickly as it flares up.

"Don't ask," Santana said. "You don't need to know." The disembodied voice died in the barrel as Abbie walked over to the wall. Santana appeared to be concealing something on the counter behind his back. When she reached him, she saw what he'd been hiding.

"Speakerphone, technology circa 1958," he said, grinning at the bewildered look on her face. "You don't need to hack the Records Center, Abbie. You can't. The old stuff's all on paper."

"So, you . . ."

"So you reach out and touch someone. Mendoza and I went to Santa Monica High School. Both Crips, homegirl, before we started looking for safe work. He says give him a couple hours."

"How's he going to do it?"

"They've got this high-tech miracle thing in St. Louis. Ever heard of it?"

"No. What?"

"I think they call it a fax."

THIRTY-SEVEN

★ Hamagar ★

Pop, pop, pop, pop.

Too damn cold to laugh.

Knees up to his chin, Nate was wobbling down the road ahead of them on a rickety little motorbike spattered with mud and grease. Except for the submachine gun slung across his back, he looked like a guy taking his first ride without training wheels.

Pop, pop, pop, pop.

They crested a hill, swung around a long curve and came out on a narrow ridge overlooking Hamagar. Below them, the stone houses and barns of the village huddled around the broad town square. In the middle of the square they saw three very lonely British Saxons.

"Jesus," Nate yelled over his shoulder. "It looks like Hunter's mobile CP."

Drago shrugged. "He likes to keep an eye on things."

Sandy pointed down to the square. "Won't be easy, I'd say." A crowd of villagers, perhaps three hundred men and boys, was swirling around the UN vehicles. All three of the APCs were im-mobilized, their wheels jammed by timbers. The rear door of the lead Saxon opened, and Hunter stepped out. His beret loomed over the crowd, a bobbing blue dot on a field of brown.

"Nice of him to stop by and see how his boys were doing," Sandy said.

"Lot better'n he is," Nate said. The villagers were pressing around the tall peacekeeper, shouting him down. For a while, he tried pushing back, but as the villagers closed in tighter, he ducked back into the Saxon and slammed the door shut. Howling now, the starving villagers he had set out to feed began rocking the APC, trying to spill him.

"What's their problem, Drago?" Sandy said.

"They think the UN's sold them out. It looks like that sometimes."

"Like right now?"

"I'd say so."

Sandy turned to Nate. "We need an army, man. You're gonna be it. Drago and I are going down there. Give us a couple of minutes, then make a whole lot of noise."

"You'll hear it." Balancing on the bikes, Sandy and Drago set off down the twisting road for the village. *Pop, pop, poppity-pop.*

When they reached the square, Sandy stopped just short of the mob. A few men and boys turned and looked at them sullenly. "Tell them to stand down," Sandy said. Drago shouted a few words at the back of the crowd.

No one moved.

Revving the bike's pennywhistle engine, Sandy got the front wheel between two jostling farmers and started wedging his way toward the besieged APCs. He could hear the popping of Drago's bike right behind him. "Tell them they've got the wrong guys," he yelled. Drago started shouting, and Sandy sensed a slight softening in the crowd. Kicking up the engine, he pushed on, knocking aside hands that stretched out to block him.

Suddenly, he heard the pounding on the APCs stop. The villagers split ranks, allowing him to skid forward to the lead Saxon.

Standing next to the door was a small man with a pistol stuck in his belt. Nosing up to him, Sandy stopped the bike and let Drago draw in beside him.

The Muslim's face was deeply creased. He looked at them coldly. But he left the pistol in his belt.

"Hit him hard," Sandy told Drago. "Tell him I'm the commander of a UN parachute force. The man in the car is my boss. We dropped in and we're deployed all around the village. If he doesn't stop this shit, we're going to open fire."

Drago began to translate. The villager put his hand on his pistol.

From the shoulder of the hill, a long burst of submachine gun fire raked across the rooftops of Hamagar. The men and boys in the mob threw themselves to the ground, leaving Sandy and the Muslim to stare each other down. A second burst, this time from farther down the shoulder, clipped the top of a mosque, sending a shower of clay and dust down on the square. The Muslim's hand fell from his belt.

"Goddamn it, we're not here to kill you," Sandy shouted. "We came to feed you, not fight you."

Drago spoke more quietly now.

"There's chow up in the meadow. Tell them that, Drago. Tell them we killed the bandits who were stealing their food. Tell them to check out the bikes."

As Drago began, a spasm ran through the mob. Suddenly, men and boys were running full tilt from the square. In less than a minute, it was empty. Sandy pounded on the door of the Saxon.

"Captain Caine here, sir. You can open up."

General Hunter stepped out. "Not unlike Arnhem," he said, surveying the square. "Except this time the reinforcements arrived on time."

From the road, Nate came toward them, the submachine gun crooked over his arm. Their one-man army glanced at the mosque, satisfying himself that his aim had been high enough to do no damage. "Well done," General Hunter said genially. "Pop in the back and we'll have a toast. I brought the gin." Nate looked out over the empty square, then back at Sandy. "Better be quick, Hawk. We got maybe five more minutes before they find out what's in those MREs."

Sandy looked at him blankly.

"Remember the 'Dish? One in twelve of those suckers is always pork."

Lieutenant Drago was already in the Saxon. The general pointed to the three dusty bikes. "Advancing on bicycles. Stroke of genius," he said. "Follow me, gentlemen. I think there's a more comfortable way to withdraw."

THIRTY-EIGHT

★ Fayetteville ★

Out on the street a car started to honk its horn, three short blasts, three long, then another quick three beeps. "SOS," Santana announced cheerfully, grabbing a yellow LA Lakers jacket and pulling it on. "What is it?" Abbie asked, scrambling to fasten her purse and pick up her laptop. "Santana's Own Surprise," he said. "Follow me."

She fell in behind him as he banged through the door and started trotting toward a coppertone Buick pulled up to the curb. Two men were sitting in the front seat. She saw the window on the passenger side roll down and a hand the size of a catcher's mitt shoot out, beckoning to them wildly. "*Schnell*, José," shouted Sergeant Kruger. "Ve're late."

Santana opened the rear door for her, then slid in beside her. Up in the front seat, Eddie Mayemura craned around. "Welcome aboard, Miss Mancini," he said. "Our ground time here will be short." Then he turned back, stamped on the gas and took off down the quiet street as if they were outlaws racing a posse.

"Where are you nutsos taking me?" Abbie yelled. Above the throaty roar of the engine, her own voice sounded a tad squeaky. "Vait," Kruger said, winking at her. "Von't be two minutes."

They rocketed down the streets Santana had navigated so carefully in the Camaro. Running a red light, they swung left against the traffic and came to a tire-squealing stop in front of the ugliest building Abbie had ever seen. It was low, barely high enough to qualify as one story, and made of cinderblocks. At some point in the remote past, someone had given it a bottom coat of paint in light, desert tan, then splashed it with irregular green blotches of jungle camouflage. It gave the general impression of a North African bunker from World War II ripped up and transplanted to the Ho Chi Minh Trail.

Santana reached for the door. "Welcome to Sweeny's Valley of the Shadow," he said.

"Who's Sweeny?" Abbie asked, edging gingerly out of the backseat. Santana raised his finger to his lips.

"Sweeny's your surprise."

Kruger and Mayemura were already trooping toward the saloon. The low door was timbered at the top and flanked by sandbags. She had to duck her head as her three jostling escorts raucously showed her in.

The walls were painted dark brown. It was noon outside. Here it could have been midnight. A few dim yellow bulbs lit the place, supplemented by the flashing red lights of an old pinball machine pushed in one corner. Over the bar was a large sign that said DE OPPRESSO LIBER. And standing under the sign was Sweeny.

It couldn't be anyone else, she decided. He was as much a part of the decor as the sign itself. He went maybe six two up and down and about half that around a middle that was flat and packed hard as a slab of concrete. She put him in his early sixties, though there was no way of being sure. He had the shoulders of an ox and the eyes of a rhino with a nose in between them that had been rearranged so many times his own mother wouldn't recognize it.

"Sweeny, ma'am," he said, pushing out a hand that made Kruger's look like a seventh-grader's. She watched her own disappear into it and wondered if it would ever come back whole.

"Mancini," she said, praying her voice wouldn't break. "Great place. What does the sign mean?"

"It means grease the bad guys or they'll sure as hell grease you."

"In Latin," Kruger said.

Oh man, she thought to herself, what am I doing here? She sneaked a look at her watch. Still two hours before she had to be back at the airport. Two full hours. Plenty of time to find out.

Santana caught her checking the time. While the others were ordering beer, he sat down on the stool next to hers.

"Perkins wasn't the only guy who knew Sandy's dad," he said. "Sweeny knew both of them. And your senator. That interest you?"

"Jesus," she said. "Who is he?"

"You're looking at Sergeant Major Brian Sweeny. Airborne. Four combat jumps to play with the Nazis. Pusan to the Yalu and back. Ia Drang Valley. I lose track. The Valley of the Shadow's chief barkeep and sole owner. Beer from every battle zone. They fly it in for him. Dying for a cold Jarli from Laos? Gotta have one last Phoumere from Cambodia? Still dreaming about the bargirl who did blowjobs with a Kinga chaser in Angola? Nostalgic for Saigon's finest, Ba Muoi Ba, Beer 33, the best brew ever made from formaldehyde? This is the place to come."

She looked across the bar. Sweeny was beaming at her.

"What can I getcha?"

"I'll have one of those formaldehyde specials, that 33 one."

He exploded with laughter, a deep bass laugh that sounded like it came from one of those 6-foot drums the elephants play at the circus. For a second he swabbed the dark mahogany bar. "You're all right, sugar," he said. Then he went off to get the beer.

"This is how it is," Santana said. He seemed eager to get the story out of the way before Sweeny came back with the round. "Sweeny was the world's greatest warrior except around payday, when he'd get on the booze and turn into the world's greatest lush until his dough ran out. Then he'd be back at reveille ready to kill for God and Country. Nobody better at it.

"That's the way he did it for twenty years. Then came Vietnam and one day this new shavetail right out of West Point saw him turn out still half drunk while they were running up the flag on the parade ground. Instead of looking the other way, this prick pressed court-martial charges against him and went all the way to the top at Division to make it stick."

"Did this little prick happen to be a preppy from Andover?"

"Stop it, reporter lady. You're getting way ahead of me. What happened was this. The Division Commander was a two-star. He and Sweeny had fought in Sicily together. He spiked the court-martial and got Sweeny transferred out of the 82nd Airborne into the 5th Special Forces Group. And Sweeny's ass was saved."

Survivors Report. Plural. "Are you saying Sweeny was with them? That he made it through?"

"Goddamn it, Abbie, there you go again. What is it about you reporters? Why do you always think you know the story before you even hear it? No, that's not what I'm saying."

"Oh," she said, crestfallen. "Sorry. Go on."

"Okay. So it's 1965. Sweeny's back from Vietnam after being shot up, and this shavetail is now a first lieutenant. And he turns up reassigned to the 5th Special Forces Group at Fort Bragg as the skipper of ODA 351.

"We're talking 'irregular Army.' Real irregular. No more by-the-book shit. Sweeny was in heaven. He filled that team with every whacko he knew. Fuck up and you went to ODA 351. They made the Dirty Dozen look like choirboys. The way Sweeny saw it, if the fine young officer was so brilliant, he ought to be able to take his precious book and make warriors out of those fuckups."

"What does that say about Sandy's dad?"

"You're the reporter? Why don't you ask Sweeny?"

She looked up and he was looming over them. It was unnerving. He was huge, but he had come back up without making a sound. He could have snapped both their necks. Instead, he held out two bottles of beer, one brown, one an odd magenta, which, fortunately, was for Santana.

"One Ba Muoi Ba for the lady. I'm not going to tell you what Santana's got there. Still classified. You'll have to rip it out of him yourself."

How much had he heard? Everything, probably.

"So what's the story on Alexander Caine?" she asked, taking care not to wipe the mouth of the bottle before she took her first pull. Sweeny hadn't brought out any glasses.

"A weak starter who finished strong," Sweeny said thoughtfully. "The Dom Rep was the first time he saw combat. I heard he was slow on the draw there, so I put him with Taylor's team."

"What happened."

"Turned out I was wrong. Caine was just a late bloomer. Never had trouble with him. Time he shipped he's the most gung-ho sunuvabitch you ever seen. Had this gray hair. I think the men called him Gray. Got a picture of him and me out hunting together one time. Jesus, that bastard could shoot. He bagged his buck a full six hours before me, then sat there laughing his ass off while I burned down the woods. His buck was eight points, mine was six. Anyway, we got 'em strung up and in the picture he's standing between those two sonsabitches. Tough little fucker. I loved him. Picture's gotta be around somewhere. Probably back at my place. Want me to dig it out for you?"

"That would be great. Did you go with him to Vietnam?"

"Oh shit, no. I did my last 'Nam tour in late sixty-four, back when they were still calling us advisors." He held up the bar rag. "Banged up an arm—I guess someone didn't think much of the advice." The tattoos on the thickly muscled brown forearm trailed off into blank white scar tissue that covered the elbow and disappeared beneath the rolled-up shirtsleeve. "Chickenshit wound," he said thoughtfully. "But it made me slow on the draw. So I wound up training guys like Taylor and Caine to go get their asses shot off."

"What about Taylor?"

"You know, sugar, turned out I was wrong about him, too."

"How?"

"I hated his guts. Still do. But look at him now."

"You mean, being senator, people talking about him for President?"

"Not that bullshit. I mean the Blue Max. I was there the day LBJ put it around his neck. It'd been a year since Lang Vei, but he still looked pretty beat up. And I felt like a turd for what had happened between us. Those boys had put up one hell of a fight and he had led them."

The big man looked down at the bar. Her beer had left a wet round circle. They both saw it at the same time and he wiped it away like a bad memory.

"What did you do?" she said, taking another pull from her bottle.

"I went over there and saluted and shook his hand."

"Then what?"

"I said, 'I've never been so goddamn wrong about one man in my whole fucking life.' "

Abbie finished the Ba Muoi Ba. "Good for you, gal," Sweeny said and he lumbered off to get her another round. She turned back to the bar, where Santana and Kruger were playing liar's poker, calling improbable hands off the serial numbers of folded dollar bills, eyeballing each other like two riverboat gamblers.

Suddenly there was the sound of breaking glass followed by a loud roar at the far end of the bar. A muscle-bound NCO, slightly drunk but in an Irish fighting mood. He was swearing at the top of his lungs and poking the business end of a broken beer bottle at Sweeny.

Santana dropped his dollar bill on the bar and started slowly toward them. Mayemura grinned at Kruger. The two of them leaned on the bar and watched Santana glide forward.

"Motherfucking ugly old pig fucker," the drunk shouted, jabbing the bottle at Sweeny.

"Buenas tardes, amigo," Santana said softly, coming up behind the bottle artist. The man wheeled around, shoving the jagged bottle toward him.

The heel of Santana's open palm smacked him in the chest, knocking the wind out of him, spinning him around toward Sweeny.

The older man drove his fist into the drunk's face. There were two distinct noises this time. The first, the brittle snap of the drunk's nose breaking, the second, the thump as he hit the floor.

Leaning over, Sweeny grabbed him by the back of the neck and hauled him to his feet. Smashing the door to the Valley of the Shadow open with the fallen warrior's head, Sweeny threw him out into the street.

"V'ont be back," Kruger said to Mayemura.

"Not tonight, anyway."

★   ★   ★

The ride back to the airport was like whitewater rafting with a stoned crew. Eddie was running half the red lights and all the yellow ones. Kruger was singing out the window. "Ofur hill, ofur dale, ve v'll hit di dusty trail . . ."

Only Santana was silent. She chalked it up to Latino dignity. But before they poured her out at the terminal, he took off his black shades and looked at her seriously. "You've got friends, Abbie," he said. "You know where we are." He handed her the laptop and looked out the other window.

Turning to go into the terminal she heard the Buick burn rubber. Kruger was singing to the pines.

"In und out, in und out, hear de vagon master shout . . ."

She ran for the gate.

THIRTY-NINE

★ Rock Creek Park ★

Marv double-parked outside the Hungry Gazelle while Abbie dashed in to collect dinner: one fistful of watercress, another of asparagus, some gorgonzola, a king-sized sweet potato and two poached salmon steaks.

Danny Sawyer, the owner, sized up the tiny haul she dumped on his counter. "You trying to seduce the guy or starve him?" He held up the potato as if he were weighing a bad idea.

"Business, all business," she said, scrambling through her purse for her wallet. "The idea is to get him to talk. How's he going to do that with his mouth full? With hollandaise running down his chin?"

"You need help, kid."

"I need a lot of things."

She paid the bill and hurried back to the taxi. Marv was listening to the News at Seven on the radio. Something about Saddam Hussein's anthrax capabilities and Senator Taylor's defense of the F-44 program. "Way I see it," Marv said over his shoulder, "we ought to spray both of 'em."

"Spoken like the true voice of reason."

"Call me the Terminator."

"Okay, Arnold. Just take me home."

It was already dark when they came up the street to her place. The For Sale sign in front of the Coorain house was gone. She wondered who the new neighbors would be. Must've left a light on last time through, she thought absently. Anyone would be better than Hugo Coorain. In a town of cigar fanatics, he smoked the kind with little plastic tips. When the wind was blowing right, you could smell them four houses away.

She dropped the groceries in the kitchen. There was a message from Santana on her machine telling her Mendoza had come through. She looked down the counter and saw half a dozen sheets of paper waiting in the fax. Her clock, a neon number that had TWILIGHT DINER written in throbbing letters around the rim, said quarter to eight. She dropped the asparagus into the steamer and uncorked a bottle of Merlot. By the time the doorbell rang, a few minutes later, the salmon was in the oven, the potato in the microwave.

Senator Taylor was standing at the door holding a small bunch of blue asters, the stems wrapped in red tissue paper and tied with a small white bow. Primary colors, she thought as he stepped through the door and handed them to her.

She noticed that his limp was more pronounced than it had been the day of the reception at Fort Myer. "Tough day," he shrugged. "Look, I wanted to make sure we got together this evening, but I can't stay long. I've got to get back to the office." She wasn't quite sure whether she felt relieved or insulted. A little of both, to be honest.

"Okay, moving right along, would you mind checking the asparagus, Senator?" she said, walking him into the kitchen and pointing toward the steamer. The junior senator from Ohio took off his jacket, rolled up his sleeves, tucked aside his tie and peered over the stove. She handed him a hot pad. He pulled the little steel basket of asparagus out of the steamer and brought it over for her inspection.

"Good," she said. "You get an *A* plus." The microwave beeped, and the oven timer sent up a cheery little domestic ding. The goblets of wine and the rest of the dinner were on the table in two minutes and gone in ten. She fixed them espresso and came back with two small cups and a microrecorder on a black lacquered tray.

"I talked to your wife." She watched his eyes, wondering how he would take it.

"How was she?"

"Not bad. Considering."

"Considering what?"

"Considering that her breasts are gone and her husband right behind them."

"You do get right down to it, don't you? Didn't you ever hear about buttering up the source before you go in for blood? Yes, I was a shit, but I didn't want us to break up. What did she tell you?"

"She said you had night sweats. Bad dreams."

"Is that right?" The voice slightly different now. Stalling or just bored? He reached down and brushed an invisible piece of lint off his trouser leg. "About what?"

"She wouldn't say."

He turned his spoon slowly in the little white cup. There was something appealing about him, the intelligence behind the handsome exterior.

"Without putting too fine a point on it, Senator, what makes you scream in the night? Janine told me I'd have to ask you."

"Good of her." Looking into his cup, he started stirring as if the rest of the answer might lie beneath the surface of the black espresso. "Guilty conscience, I guess."

Abbie glanced at her recorder. It was still running, thank God. This was not the moment to change batteries or flip a cassette.

"How come you said in the chopper you wanted to die?"

"Where did you get that?"

"The after-action report. Come on, you know that as well as I do. Don't tell me Pat hasn't shown it to you."

As if he suddenly felt cold, he twisted in the chair and reached for his jacket. Interview over, she thought to herself. But once he had the jacket on, he turned and rested his elbows on the table. "All right," he said. "I'm going to tell you something I've never told anyone before."

She glanced away for a second, pretending she had missed the urgency in his voice, an old trick, inviting him to keep going. Through the darkened kitchen window she could see out into the park. A light in the Coorain house suddenly went on. Odd, she thought, looking at her watch. Eight-thirty. Must've been on a timer.

The senator's voice fell, veering toward the confessional.

"I thought I deserved to die."

"Why?"

He pressed his fingers to his temples and closed his eyes. For an instant, she couldn't tell whether he was playing to the galleries or whether the moment was genuinely painful for him. Then she saw he was pressing back tears, annihilating them before they could show. By the time he looked up at her, they were gone. But for just that instant, he had nearly broken down.

"Ten men were dead," he said. "I was their leader. I thought I should be with them."

"What happened, Jeff?" she said, more gently this time.

"I tried everything in the book to save them."

"Everyone knows that. You shouldn't blame yourself."

"Nothing worked," he said, ignoring her. "Even air strikes on our own position. Do you know what that means, Abbie? It meant the odds were even up we'd be blown to hell right along with the enemy. But there wasn't any other choice. Our guys had been out on the perimeter all morning with the Montagnards and they were getting torn to shit."

"Where was Lieutenant Caine? Was he already dead?"

"Not far from it. None of us were."

"What happened? Did he wimp out?"

"Don't be so stupid. This wasn't about courage or cowardice."

"I'm sorry, Jeff." But he was already pushing far ahead of her.

"Look, Abbie. Every man, every human being has a limit. There are no heroes the way civilians think of them. Fuck Rambo. He doesn't exist. Push us far enough and eventually we all crack. Alex, me, Sandy. Even you, Abbie. Every damn one of us. Christ, they were killing us with mortar and recoilless rifle fire.

"Have you ever seen a friend of yours shot, Abbie? Have you ever seen his guts come sliding out like a pink hose?"

"No." Technically, she hadn't. Gomez came to mind, but he hadn't been a friend.

"That's what happened to Tom Lord and Linc Naylor. Everly was lucky. He took a direct hit from a recoilless rifle round. There wasn't anything left of him to see. The pieces just sort of flew toward the jungle. So let's not talk about wimping out. They were all dead. Everybody. Zipped in body bags—what was left of them—and squared away for the refrigerator. And I should have been with them."

"I'm so sorry, Jeff. If I had known—"

"Now you do. So, yes, you're damn right I scream in the night. There's only one lesson that came out of that shithole. Don't let it happen again."

It was five after nine. He looked at his watch. "I don't see any point in talking about this anymore, do you?" he said. She followed him to the door. "Sorry I dumped on you," he said, leaving his hand on the knob. She saw it was shaking.

He didn't wait for her to respond. At the curb, his driver was already holding the door open for him. She watched him limp across the sidewalk and get into the backseat. The car pulled away. He didn't wave.

★　　★　　★

When she got back to the kitchen, she sat down and looked at the table. The plates were smeared pink and black with salmon skin and bones. She ran hot water over them and left them in the sink.

She was about to shut off the lights when she remembered Santana's message. The sheets from Mendoza were in the fax. Then she went into the living room, snapped on a table lamp and sat down in her reading chair. The list wasn't very long. The clock upstairs in the hall struck the half hour. Nine-thirty Eastern time, six-thirty on the Coast. Everyone would be home. She looked at the first name on the list. Beckman's parents lived in Detroit. Reaching for a pencil and a notepad, she settled in and began to work the phone.

"The number you called is not in service."

Eight to go. She tried again. Two more wrong-o's for Dunford and Prysbekowski, but when she rang the number for Shapen, the voice of a nurse, as crisp as her uniform had to be, said, "Good evening. Greenleaf Rest."

A few minutes later she was talking to the mother of SFC Layton Shapen, who was eighty-six, deaf and more than a little disoriented.

"Oh, Layton isn't dead. He comes every night to see me. It's Lewis who's dead."

Abbie heard someone whisper to Mrs. Shapen. Then a man's voice.

"This is Lewis Shapen. May I help you?"

It turned out that Lewis had been two when his brother was killed. He told her he didn't know anything about Layton and the war, only that his mother kept the citation that came with the Bronze Star in the drawer next to her bed at Greenleaf. She thanked him and plunged on.

Everly's father asked her if she was another one of those MIA hustlers trying to make his life miserable.

"They vaporized him, lady. They couldn't find enough pieces to fill a body bag. They sent us dog tags and his Bible. He was reading the Book of Ezra. The ribbon was still on the page, stuck right there under his blood."

Four left. She only had it in her to do one more. Closing her eyes, she aimed the pencil at the list. When she opened them, she saw it had landed on S/Sgt. Lawrence Hyduk. The phone was listed under the area code for western Massachusetts. Leaning back in the chair, she rubbed her neck for a moment. Then she hit the numbers.

"Dr. Hyduk speaking."

The familiar tone snapped her out of her gloom. It could have been her father.

"This is Abigail Mancini, *Washington Chronicle*," she said quickly. "I know I shouldn't be calling at this hour—"

"Is this an emergency? It's awfully late."

"It is kind of an emergency. Could you give me a minute or two?" She heard a deep sigh, the same how-can-they-do-this-to-me sigh she knew so well. It always meant, I hate this invasion, but it's what I chose.

"All right, Miss Mancini. But please be quick. I have rounds in the morning."

"I'm working on a Vietnam story for the anniversary next spring. I'm focusing the piece on Senator Jefferson Taylor. I see from the records that before your son was killed, he served with the senator." She heard her own voice and wondered how she could sound like such a cold bitch. "I know how painful this must be for you, but I'm trying to trace all the people who fought alongside Senator Taylor and I was hoping you might remember something about him and your son."

The silence at the other end of the line was arctic. It was as if she had put a call through to a phone hanging on the North Pole.

"He's not my son."

"I'm sorry. I must have the wrong number."

"He's my brother."

"Dr. Hyduk, please forgive me. I feel very stupid, but the

records I have in front of me show that your brother was killed in I Corps on August 26, 1966."

Another silence, then a gust from the Pole.

"Dead? Larry dead? He's too damn mean to be dead."

FORTY

E-mail was so much easier than the phone. No matter what kind of shape you were in, it made you sound in control. When she finished with Dr. Hyduk, she brushed the hair out of her eyes, opened the laptop and began to pound.

To: p@santana.net
From: amanci@washchron.com
Subject: ODA 351

Here's the big one, pups, and where are you? Ever hear of a guy named Larry Hyduk? From Alex's outfit, dead for 28 years? His brother believes he's still alive. It's just no one can find him. The truth is no one really wants to find him. Except you and me, pups. Got any ideas on how to dig up a Green Beret who might be back from the dead? I'm going up to the Red Lion Inn in Stockbridge tomorrow. I'm not doing this alone, so get in touch. Just who's the responsible party here? And whose life is it, anyway? YR.

When she finished, she punched the send button and watched the pulsing light on the computer until the message shot off into cybernight.

★   ★   ★

One last beep, and the recorder stopped.

Trask rewound the large reel and played it again. When he had the beginning and end points marked, he dubbed the conversation onto a DAT cassette. Then he snapped the cassette into a small recorder and slipped the recorder into his shirt pocket.

Good stuff.

The girl was leaving for Massachusetts the next afternoon. The flight bookings, the reservation at the Red Lion Inn in Stockbridge, he had them all. A little late, but there shouldn't be a problem. He turned knobs and punched buttons until his bugs were rolling again on automatic. Then he grabbed his jacket and went out the rear door.

The white truck was on a side street off Connecticut Avenue. He made it in five minutes. The drive downtown was another fifteen. He took it slowly, humming to himself as Yuppies heading home whipped by him in their dumb little Audis and BMWs.

He pulled into the lot behind the all-night diner and parked.

The place was called Waiting by the Phone. Outside, it looked like it had been built by Greeks the old-fashioned way—couple miles of fancy aluminum siding, a lotta plate glass, neon trim. Inside, it was a monument to the fifties. Booths for two, four and six covered in red Naugahyde, the tables topped with fake marble Formica and edged with chrome trim, waitresses in little paper soda-jerk hats.

On every table was one of those little consoles connected to the Big Jukebox in the Sky, he supposed. The little selection cards looked like the real thing, but you never could tell where the music was coming from. The Drifters, the Coasters, the Platters—they were all there. Plug in a nickel, you could punch up Dion and the Belmonts and move right into the Twilight Zone.

Beside each console was an old phone, the kind with a dial, not buttons. That was the gimmick. You could play a tune, look across the room, see who was digging it and call them. Hence the name of the place. Waiting like everyone waited back then before the world got so fucking complicated. Waiting by the phone. He liked it. Sort of an inside joke for a guy in his line of work.

It was where he talked to Mad Max. Their Code Red stop. All the rest of the commo went through cyberspace.

He slipped into a booth for two and ordered a cheeseburger

deluxe, chili fries and a vanilla malt. An evening for a little celebration. The chili fries always took some time but that was good.

When the waitress left, he took the phone and unscrewed the cap on the receiver. Then he took a little cable with a miniplug on one end and a pair of alligator clips on the other out of his jacket pocket. He attached the clips to a metal strip in the receiver, then plugged the miniclip into the microrecorder. When he was finished, he dialed a number, counted to twenty, then hit the play button.

The phone was reassembled, the recorder back in his pocket when the waitress came back with a burger the size of a small manhole cover, a platter of fries hidden under half a pot of chili and a malt big enough to float away two or three Mouseketeers.

The girl had short black hair and a slash of red on her pouty lips. "What's happenin', Slick?" she said, putting the food down and shoving a bottle of ketchup at him. "How ya doin'?" She was looking at his head. Fucking big mouth. See what shit you can pull without your tongue.

When he said nothing, she danced away, shaking her hips as she bumped down the row of booths.

Fifteen minutes later, the phone next to Trask rang three times, then stopped. After 30 seconds, it started again. Trask grabbed it on the first ring.

"Taalllkkkk," said Max.

Max used a scrambler phone with a voice masker whenever Trask patched him through the outside circuits into Waiting by the Phone. The equipment lowered his voice a coupla octaves. Made him sound like fucking Frankenstein.

"Check the dump," Trask said. "There's some important stuff on top."

"It'ssssss laaaaaaate."

"Not for this, sir. I think we got a Code Red." He let the line drift off, cool, like Sam Cooke setting up a phrase. "Do I talk to her? Scare her? What?"

"Folllllloow herrrrrr."

The line went dead. Fucking Mad Max. Keep close but don't touch. Trask looked at his watch. Quarter past two. Eight hours to Stockbridge. He'd still get there before she did.

FORTY-ONE

Stockbridge ★ Massachusetts

Abbie pushed the blue Mercury rental north from Hartford. Skirting Springfield, the grimy, red-brick penitentiary looming up beside her window, she headed west on the Mass Pike. Gray clouds hung low over the Berkshire Hills, adding their promise of rain to the day's general index of gloom.

Dr. Hyduk had refused at first to meet her. She had talked him into it by appealing to medical ethics. At least two men, maybe three, judging by what he had said about his brother, were getting badly wrapped around the axle because of what had happened to their A-Team. Maybe her story could help them. At first he told her she should take the guilt trip to Oprah, but then said, "Oh, hell, I guess you're right. Come on up."

Rain began to splatter the windshield. Reaching forward, she turned on the wipers and peered anxiously through the blur. When the glass cleared, she saw a dead deer on the shoulder of the road, its neck broken, a black sludge of blood and entrails spread onto the pavement. Great beginning, Abs. Just follow the roadkill.

At the Red Lion Inn in Stockbridge, the rocking chairs were still out on the wide veranda in spite of the November chill. Wasp stoicism.

"What have you got for me?" she asked the desk clerk, a clean-cut young guy in a shetland crew neck.

"Well, we're sort of full. There's a seminar at Riggs this weekend and we've got people flying in from all over the place."

There were keys in the boxes marked "Suite."

"What about a suite?"

"It's three hundred a night, ma'am," he said, looking at her backpack.

What the hell. She'd put it on Julian.

"Sold," she said, dropping her Amex on the dark mahogany desk. Waving away the bellboy—think of what I saved on tips, Julian—she got into the creaky old elevator and rode up to the third floor. Suite 7 had a nice sitting room with a fireplace and a small bedroom. She pulled back the quilt on the four-poster and crawled in. Sleep came like an anesthetic—forget local, she fell all the way down the chute.

When she woke up an hour later, it was already five minutes past eight. Dammit, she muttered, throwing back the quilt. Then she remembered who she was meeting and slowed down. Never in her life, not once, had she known a doctor to show up on time for dinner. In the bathroom, she put on a touch of lip gloss and untangled her hair. Then she went downstairs to the Lion's Den.

It was softly lit, very middle-class New England, two or three worlds removed from Sweeny's. Over to one side, a dark-haired good-looking guy was playing soft riffs on a guitar. She ordered a Sapporo beer, closest she could come to a brew from the Valley of the Shadow, and settled in to wait for Dr. Hyduk.

At 8:45, she was halfway through her second bottle when he walked into the bar. He was one of those doctors who take care of themselves. Late forties, maybe five-ten, rangy, with a long, easy stride, his face fresh and scrubbed, as if he had just shaved. Preppy. Too preppy, she thought. Trinity, scholarship, Yale, Yale Med School. Nice guy, low-key, married, two kids probably. Pillar of the community. Shrink. Relentlessly sane.

"Dr. Hyduk," he said. He didn't put out his hand. Maybe he meant to give her a personality test before they began. Instead, he sank into the Windsor chair across from her and put his hand in his pocket.

"Mind if I smoke?"

So much for first impressions. Before she could say anything, he pulled out a mangled pack of Merits and lit up.

"Trying to cut back," he said, waving the filter tip in front of him like a talisman. Smoke curled up toward his light brown hair. "These things shouldn't even count."

"Ah, but they do, Doctor, don't they?"

"Yes, Miss Mancini." He sighed, as if she were reading his medical chart upside down. "They sure do. Now, before I die right here, what do you want to know about Larry?"

"Everything. But let's eat first. It might improve your life expectancy."

He waved over the waitress. They ordered scrod and green salad and a bottle of Chenin Blanc and by the time they had polished everything off, the conversation began to improve.

"I thought Larry was dead," she said. "So does everyone else who served with him."

"I wouldn't know about that. Never talked to any of them. Larry was the warrior, I was the nerd. The war was over by the time I finished at Yale."

"What about Larry?"

"We thought he was dead, too—he disappeared for three years. So did the Army. They sent this lugubrious chaplain up to Pittsfield to tell us that he was 'almost certainly' dead. Almost certainly—an oxymoron, wouldn't you say?"

He shrugged. "If you're trying to understand Larry you've got to go back a long way. He's angry and paranoid—and I don't use the term loosely—but that didn't begin in Vietnam. You could be getting the wrong impression of the Hyduks from the bow tie and the Donegal tweed. Our old man was a cabinet maker. Croatian, blue collar. He had us working for him from the first day we could hold a plane. Beat hell out of us when he wasn't whacking my mom. No way she could protect us, but at least she got away from him eight hours a day. She worked as a seamstress downtown at England Brothers, the department store in Pittsfield, where we grew up.

"So Larry had it hard right from the start. When he showed up for kindergarten, he barely spoke English. Every Irish and Italian kid in school beat the shit out of him until he got streetwise and organized his own gang. By the time he got to high school, he was doing small-time break-ins and robberies. When he was seventeen he got caught hot-wiring a car. That was Saturday night. He spent the night in the Pittsfield jail. On Monday, the judge looked at his rap sheet and said, 'You got two choices, Hyduk. Enlist in the Army or do time.'

"That was fifty-nine, I think. It amazed all of us when he got through basic training. Then they sent him to Parachute Training and he went into the 101st Airborne at Fort Campbell in Kentucky. Said it was the first time anyone had really given a damn about him."

Dr. Hyduk lit another cigarette. She looked over and saw half the pack stubbed out in the ashtray. "Larry wasn't wrong about that, you know. Before he left for the Army, Dad cursed him, for the shame he'd brought on the family. So in a crazy way, when Larry turned up dead in Vietnam a few years later, the old man just figured the curse had worked."

"But Larry wasn't dead?"

"That's right."

"How did you find out?"

"Mom never understood him either. But when he was reported dead, it almost killed her. Then, one day three years later, she was sitting there down at England Brothers sewing a prom dress for some rich kid, and she looked up and Larry was standing there staring at her. Thought she saw a ghost. She screamed and passed out. When she came to, the paramedics were leaning over her waving the smelling salts and Larry was saying, 'Hi, Mom. I'm back.'

"When I got home that night, he told me his unit had been wiped out. They hauled him out in a body bag with the other corpses. He found out later that the soldier who unzipped his bag at the morgue thought he saw his eyelid flutter. Pure dumb luck. The guy checked and got a slight pulse. So they tore Larry out of his bag and hustled him into surgery and pumped him full of blood and his vital stats started to come back. But he was in a deep coma and the medics didn't know what he'd be like if he ever came out of it." He looked up. "Of course, they didn't know what he was like to begin with.

"About the sixth night after he got to the hospital, the Viet Cong mortared the place. They burned two wards, including Larry's. The docs got him out okay, but he had bad burns, so they shipped him out the next day, tubes and all, to a burn unit in Japan. More bad news. All his records were destroyed when the hospital wards went up. He came to after about three weeks, lying there with third-degree burns and his head full of steel splinters. He didn't know who the hell he was or how he got there. Special Forces didn't, the Army didn't."

"And no one else did either." She finished his sentence for him.

"That is correct," he said stiffly. Watch it, Abs, interruptions annoyed this guy.

"It took them three years to patch him up. He was just another John Doe from Nam rotting in a veterans hospital. They sent him to Albany, New York, so he was less than fifty miles from us and the whole time we never knew he was there. Dad used his insurance money to make the down payment on a house. First house we ever owned. Larry made it happen. And then one night he woke up screaming his name, rank and serial number. It took them a month to track down the records. Then they discharged him and the next thing you know he was scaring hell out of my mother."

"Can I talk to him?"

"No."

"Why not?"

"I don't know where he is."

"But you said—"

"I said he was too mean and too crazy to be dead. Look, he was back here for about a month. He got a job in a garage, but he was drunk every night, blown out with Vietnam Stress Syndrome. He was going to wipe the town off the map. One night, the mayor came to the garage to gas up his Lincoln. He told Larry to step on it. Larry hauled him out of the front seat and started bashing his head on the hood. Someone called the cops. The blue-and-whites started screaming up. Larry got out the back way and into the woods. They looked for him for three days before they gave up. Even on Greylock Mountain they never could find him."

"So where do you *think* he is now?"

"He blew town with every cop in the county looking for him. If they caught him he would have been facing serious prison time. No one has heard from him since. I don't know where he is. None of us do. And that's just fine. Believe me, this silence is golden."

He stood up to leave. "You'll never find him."

"That's not much help."

"Thank you for dinner, Miss Mancini," he said. "I assume you can put it on your expense account."

"Some things you assume right."

He reached for the Merits, but the pack was empty. Wadding it up, he stuck it in the ashtray and left.

★   ★   ★

The night staff had laid a fire for her in the sitting-room fireplace. Opening her computer, she jacked it into the wall.

No messages. She logged off, disconnected the computer and picked up the telephone. It rang twice before Santana picked up.

"I'm up here in the Wasp Mountains," she said. "I think I've just been stung."

"Want me to send a medevac chopper?"

"It's good to hear your voice, José," she blurted out. "I mean, don't get any wrong ideas, but it's really, really nice to be talking to you."

"No sweat. Did you get the stuff from Mendoza?"

"That's why I'm here. One of the names panned out."

"Which one?"

"Hyduk. He's still alive."

"Mierda." She heard Santana's voice fall. He sounded like he'd just seen an Inca necklace dropped into the disposal.

"What is it?"

The line went silent. For a moment she thought they had been cut off, but then she heard Santana coughing, as if he had something in his throat. When he came back on, his voice sounded odd.

"Sweeny knew him, Abbie. They were tight."

"Great. He can help us find him."

"No, he can't, Abbie. Sweeny's had an accident."

"What do you mean, José? How is he?"

"Sweeny's dead."

Abbie heard the darkness pawing at the tall window beyond her bed. Over the phone, she picked up Selena singing on Santana's sound system. *"Amor Prohibido."* For the first time, it hit her that Santana had been drinking.

"Sweeny couldn't have been more than sixty."

"He was seventy-one."

"No way. Come on, he looked like the Jolly Green Giant. He had everything but the green chops under the five o'clock shadow."

"He was green enough this morning. They found him twenty feet down in the Scobie Reservoir. Under his jeep. There was a big hole where he went through the hurricane fence, no skids on the road. The cops think he fell asleep driving home last night."

"What do you think?"

"Could be. He had enough brandy in him to fuel a convoy."

"Did they do an autopsy?" She caught herself. "Sorry for coming on like a reporter, José. I liked Sweeny."

"Yeah, me, too, Abbie. A lot. It doesn't make sense to me. The thing is, when Sweeny tied one on, sometimes he got happy and sometimes he got mean. The one thing he never got was sleepy. After you left, I took Eddie and Kruger home. Lucky boys. Nice wives to clean them up and put them to bed. I went to the movies and when that didn't do it, I drove back to the Valley to finish myself off."

What a waste. All those brains, that great face and body. "José Cuervo is not the right kind of friend for you, hombre," she said. "You can do better."

"Thanks for the thought, señorita, but Tío Pepe's a turnoff. Anyway, when I came in I saw Sweeny down at the end of the bar drinking with this other guy, younger than Sweeny, must've been in his fifties, I guess, really stood out. Everyone else in the place was in civvies that night, but real casual stuff. This guy had on a suit with double vents and a tucked waist. Looked like the fucking Duke of Windsor.

"I'm sitting there thinking, what's this dude doing in here? But Sweeny was talking to him like a brother. They were sitting there drinking brandy and soda and telling lies. Turns out they'd been at Bragg together in the sixties. I'm like, 'Sweeny, you're a beer man—what's going on?' and he goes, 'Son, when a case of beer won't wash the shit out of your mind, there's always one thing that will.' And he poured the three of us a stiff round.

"Man, I couldn't keep up with them. One was enough for me. So I went and got into a game of nine ball with a guy who was even drunker than I was. To pay for my night out. Ramón Fernandez, friend of mine. About midnight I look over and see Sweeny and the other guy going out together. They'd killed the bottle, but let me tell you, Sweeny wasn't smashed—looked like he was getting ready to take Ho Chi Minh City back all by himself."

"The other guy, José. The Duke of Windsor. Who was he?"

"He had a weird name. I remember that. The reason is, I beat Ramòn's ass and went over to pay up at the bar. That's when I saw they'd killed the bottle. And I noticed the guy had the same name."

"Remy?"

"That's it. How did you know?"

"We've met. Look, José, Sandy said if I really needed to get him on the phone, you could fix it up. That true?"

"Yeah, I think so. Take a little time."

She looked at her watch. "I'm going to be here until tomorrow." She gave him the hotel's phone and her room number. "Could you tell him to call me at two?"

"Sure."

"I need him, José."

"Maybe Sweeny did, too, Abbie. I'm on it. He'll call you tomorrow."

★　　★　　★

It was too late to go out for a run. Abbie picked up the box of matches and slid it open. Something about the neatness of the little box felt reassuring. Running her finger absentmindedly along the scratcher, she stood and walked over to the fireplace. Under a small pile of birch logs, sticks of kindling were steepled over a crumpled page of the *Berkshire Eagle*. Bending down, she struck a match and lit a ragged corner of the newspaper. The light from the birch logs, burning with the sweet smell of fall, flickered across the sitting room.

She ordered a pot of chamomile tea from room service, popped a valerian capsule and sat in a wing chair by the fire until there was a knock at the door. The bellboy came in pushing a cart with the pot of tea hidden in a jack-o'-lantern cozy. When he left, she took off the pumpkin, poured a cup of tea and went back to the soft chair to replay the evening.

Where was the story? The thread kept slipping away. Every time she reached for it, someone was there to pluck it out of her fingers. Janine with her ambivalence over Jeff. Patrice and his overdue library files. The doctor and his now-you-see-him-now-you-don't brother. And why did Remy Fair show up right behind her at Fort Bragg? What bad luck for poor Sweeny to get smashed with that dude before hitting the road.

Kicking off her shoes, she put her feet toward the fire and closed her eyes. She inhaled the steam swirling off the tea. The soles of her feet were warm now. She could feel the heat running up her legs and thought of Sandy between them. She stared languidly at the fire for a few minutes, trying to imagine Sandy's reaction when Santana reached him. It was getting harder to conjure up his face. She dimmed the lights and sat there, reluctant to go to bed, watching the firelight play over the floral wallpaper. Bad night to be alone.

FORTY-TWO

Stockbridge ★ Massachusetts

Sun streaming through the window woke her. She showered and dressed quickly. When she finished, the message waiting light was lit on the laptop.

> To: amanci@washchron.com
> From: p@santana.net
>
> Sorry for the blackout. Been rocking and rolling over here the last week and didn't catch up with your messages until now. Sounds like you didn't really need help anyway. Anyone ever tell you you were a demon reporter? Call Dominick Abella at the VA in D.C. Old sergeant of mine. Retired. Can track a snake through tall grass. Tell him he's looking for vet benefits, signs of a pension, Army disability list. Talk to you at two. Pups

She saved the message and snapped the computer shut. What about *Are you all right, Abbie?* What about *Hang in there, darling, I'm on the way?* What about *I miss you?*

It was eight-thirty. Old soldiers were at work by then, weren't they? Her finger stabbed the phone. Some android from District of Columbia information gave her some numbers for the Veterans Administration. After a few more calls, she finally reached

Abella. A secretary informed her with a rhinestone sparkle that Abella was in conference.

"Tell him it's Captain Sandy Caine's sister."

She waited while the sparkler conveyed the little white lie to the boss. He couldn't have been very busy. In twenty seconds he was on the line.

"Sandy Caine is an only child," he said. His voice sounded like unwashed gravel. "No brothers. No sisters. So no more bullshit. Who are you?"

"You're right," she said, searching for something that might work better. "I'm not his sister. I'm a friend, and he told me to call you."

"Is that right? What does he look like?"

"Last time I saw him he looked like hell. Face black, blood all over his flak jacket. But underneath it all, well, he was looking pretty good."

Abella guffawed. "Okay, that's Sandy. What're you after, sweetheart?"

Sweetheart? So retro it wasn't even sexist. Abella probably rolled his own smokes.

"Sandy's trying to find a guy who served with his dad in Vietnam," she said, hurrying. If she lost Abella, she might as well bag the whole trip. "It's important to him."

"So what?"

"So he asked me to call you. He needs your help."

"Uh huh."

They were getting nowhere. "Look, Sergeant Abella, you don't know me and I don't know you either. But Sandy said you were a friend. So could you quit giving me the business and help us?"

After a full minute, he finally said, "All right—who we talking about?"

She gave him Hyduk's vitals, everything she had gleaned from Mendoza in St. Louis. He listened carefully. She heard him typing at a computer keyboard.

"Caller ID says you're in Stockbridge, that right?"

"Yes."

"Okay then, you're getting hot."

"How hot?"

"Pretty damn hot. It says here this guy Hyduk is on VA disability. Gets a grand and change every month. Check goes to the

Berkshire Hills Bank in Pittsfield. Direct deposit. Been that way since November of sixty-nine."

She thanked Abella and rang off. That rotten shrink. He'd been lying to her. His brother was just up the road. It took a couple of minutes to throw her things into her overnight bag. Somewhere down the hall a grandfather clock struck nine.

Outside, the morning was chilly but clear. Crossing the veranda, she went down the stairs past the two red lions dozing in the sun. She tossed her bag into the backseat of the car and drove over to Dr. Hyduk's office. It was in a two-story, white clapboard cottage four blocks from the inn. At the desk, a middle-aged woman in a dark blue twin-set told her that she would find him at the end of the hall on the second floor.

The lights were on in his office. She knocked lightly and stepped inside. Dr. Hyduk was lying on his couch, a black eyeshade covering his eyes like a mask.

"Just put the coffee on the desk, Helen," he said tiredly. "No patients until ten."

Abbie slammed the door behind her.

"Good," she said. "That should give you just enough time to explain your compulsion to lie."

He sat up as if she'd given him 100 volts of electroshock. Ripping off the eyeshade, he glared at her.

"You ever heard of knocking?"

"You ever hear of telling the truth? How's your malpractice insurance?"

"That's not funny."

"I know. You're lucky I'm just a wandering reporter, not one of your patients."

He moved to a chair and waved her toward the couch.

"Sit down," he said.

"I'll stand, Dr. Hyduk. You lied to me."

A look of irritation flickered across his face. "I did nothing of the sort, Miss Mancini. I think you better explain yourself." He spoke precisely, no elisions. The tone was like a sharp slap across the cheek.

"Okay, try this. You know the Berkshire Hills Bank up in Pittsfield?"

"Know it well. Bud Jenkins, the president, is a friend of mine. A friend, Miss Mancini. Not a patient."

He was looking at her straight on, meeting her gaze.

"Your brother happens to be a depositor."

"That's not possible."

He seemed genuinely surprised. He picked up the eyeshade and fiddled with it, as if it had been concealing something from him.

"He gets a VA disability pension, Doctor. Once a month. The first check went into the Berkshire Hills account in November 1969. The last, according to my information, would have gone in three weeks ago."

The doctor looked stunned.

"My experience is that when money goes into a bank, it also comes out," she said. "Do you really expect me to believe that you haven't ever seen your brother hanging at the bank with your good friend Bud? Not once? Not in twenty-five years?"

"No."

"Come on."

"But it's true."

He looked ashen. Swiping up the eyeshade, he tore it in two.

"Where is he, Doctor? Where's Larry?"

Dr. Hyduk stood up holding one half of the eyeshade in each hand. Shaking his head, he threw the pieces on his chair.

"That's just what I'd like to know, Miss Mancini," he said. "Let's go find out."

They walked back to her car and headed out of town, passing the Riggs Institute's high Corinthian columns and the horseshoe carriageway leading to the old mansion where the patients lived, sweating out their pasts with an assist or two from Xanax and Prozac. Hooking left to Route 7, they went past well-preserved old houses with fine lawns and on toward Pittsfield. Beyond the old Thistle Inn, they drove through the pastoral countryside with its wooded hills and fields of frostbitten corn.

In Pittsfield, the empty windows of England Brothers Department Store looked out on North Street like a rebuke from blind eyes. They circled the rotary at the common with its Civil War monument, a sweet little park with a fountain, mulched flower beds and benches. From his pedestal, the Union soldier, an old warrior in stone, stood guard over the valley, gazing west toward the surrounding Berkshire Hills. Something about the way he was standing reminded her of the General. What chance had Sandy ever had to warm him up?

As they drove by the old Berkshire Athenaeum, Hyduk pointed up the block to another imposing pile of limestone. A lot of other businesses in Pittsfield might have gone belly up, but the Berkshire Hills Bank had survived.

She parked in front of the building and locked up. By the time she caught up with the doctor, he was arguing with a secretary posted at the president's door.

"I know he's in there, Gloria. Kiwanis is two hours from now. I need to see him."

"He's reviewing Lil Mason's estate, Dr. Hyduk. He told me no calls, no interruptions."

"This isn't an interruption, Gloria. It's an eruption."

The secretary rose, fluttering her hands ineffectually as he pushed open the dark mahogany door. Abbie heard him shout, "Damn it, Bud, why didn't you tell me about Larry?"

Bud Jenkins was in shirtsleeves, his coat draped over the back of his chair. "Now look, Bob," he said, "you can't just come busting in here like this. I'm busy."

"I'll say you're busy. Twenty-five years you've been busy. Busy covering for Larry. Where is he, Bud? Over in a cave on top of Greylock?"

"He told me a long time ago his whereabouts were none of your business."

"I'm making it my business."

"Isn't it a little late for that, Bob? This isn't some blowup after football practice."

"I want to know, Bud."

The banker looked over and saw Abbie. "You two together? Why don't you close that door, miss?" She pulled the door shut. "Now maybe all of us should sit down." He sat at the head of a long table under a tall window, waving the doctor to one side and Abbie on the other, as if they were applying for a mortgage.

"Larry's nowhere around here," he said. "You haven't missed anything. And don't tell me you ever wanted to see him, either. You know that's not true."

"I want to see him now. Today."

"That's too bad, Bob. I can't help you."

"I want to see the records. The deposit slips, the withdrawals."

"You know I can't do that. It's against the law. You want me to get Ed Melvin down from the police station to explain the rules?"

"Cut it out, Bud, this is family."

"No, you cut it out. This is business. If you wanted to find Larry you should have done it twenty-five years ago. I'm not going to help you. I can't."

"Larry has some friends who need to talk to him," Abbie said. "The war's been over a long time. They might be able to help each other."

Both men turned on her, jaws tight. Okay, Abbie. Shut up.

Under the table, Dr. Hyduk was rapidly tapping his foot. He thought for a while, then leaned toward the banker and started talking in a loud voice, as if she weren't there.

"I want to see those records. I'm not leaving until I do."

"I told you, I can't do it, Bob."

"All right then, let's do this the hard way. You've been fucking Madge Warner after bridge for three years now. Your wife still doesn't quite get it. She's paying one hundred dollars an hour to find out why you never get it on anymore. Thinks something's the matter with her. Maybe it's time she knew the truth."

The banker flushed. The redness began at the broken veins on his nose and spread across his cheeks.

"You wouldn't do that."

"Truth is therapy, Bud."

The banker pressed a button, and the secretary came in. She looked miserable, as if she had left the city gates open and the barbarians had burned down Rome.

"Please bring me Lawrence Hyduk's file, Gloria."

She looked surprised but knew better than to say anything. A few minutes later she came back with a heavy brown legal folder wrapped with string.

"That will be all, Gloria. Thank you."

After the door closed behind her, he dumped the folder in front of Dr. Hyduk.

"I'll give you exactly one minute. Then I want you out of here."

The psychiatrist untied the string and pulled out a thick bundle of bank statements. Flipping through them quickly, he set them aside and took out the deposit slips and copies of the canceled checks. Even reading upside down, Abbie could see that there had been only a single deposit and withdrawal each month.

Dr. Hyduk took a pen from his breast pocket and looked over at her. What was his problem? No paper, idiot. She opened her purse, ripped a sheet out of her notebook and silently shoved it across the table. He scribbled something down, then he folded the note and put it in the pocket with his pen.

"All right, Bud, your secret's safe with me. But if I were you, I'd fit in a mercy fuck at home every now and then. Be better for both of you."

"I'll try to remember, Doctor."

"You do that."

When they were back on the street, the doctor stopped her as she was unlocking the car. Looking over, she saw that he had taken out the folded note.

"All yours," he said. "Bud was right. I don't give a flying fuck if I never see Larry again."

He turned and got into the car. Abbie slipped into her seat belt and unfolded the note. It said:

> *L. H.*
> *PO Box 1093, Whitefish, Montana*
> *Flathead Credit Union, Whitefish*

The address was written in letters so small she could hardly read it, the handwriting of a doctor, barely decipherable, skewed by fury. Dr. Hyduk obviously preferred his brother dead.

* * *

At the Riggs Institute lot, there were only two empty parking spaces. From behind her, some idiot in a brown-paneled truck squealed into the first, coming to a stop two inches over the white line on her side. Furious, she leaned across Dr. Hyduk and flipped the driver the bird.

"A little road rage, Miss Mancini? A cry for help? Maybe you ought to come inside."

"What can you do in five minutes?"

Locking the car, she accompanied him back to the institute. In his office she gave him her numbers, promised to keep him informed. He thanked her in a way that made it clear he couldn't care less. Okay, neither would she. Just that much less paperwork.

As she walked back across the parking lot, she saw the rear doors of the truck were open. The driver was nowhere in sight. Asshole. The finger was too good for him.

She looked at her watch. Eleven o'clock. Still three hours to kill until Sandy's call. She unlocked the car, slid behind the wheel and pulled the seat belt over her shoulder. When she turned the key in the ignition, the car radio blared full blast. Some fifties golden-moldies station on FM. She was sure that she hadn't left it on when she locked the car. She tried to twist around, but the seat belt had her trapped.

Something sharp pricked her neck. Her finger fluttered over the radio button. She heard the ocean crashing in her ears, then she was spiraling through black waves, down to the bottom of the sea.

FORTY-THREE

"Why couldn't we have done this in my office, Remy? Do I have to come down here and blow your nose for you every time you get the sniffles?"

"Had some business to take care of, Gus."

Old Gus Buell, firing for effect. Remy Fair had seen it a million times. He let Gus lob a few more rounds, wondering through the entire barrage where the techs had found a set of white overalls big enough to fit the old man. The sanitary outfit stretched like a girdle across his gut. His belly swelled against the zipper, flab bulging over the seams. Standing there in the bright white light of the factory, his red face damp with perspiration, Gus reminded Remy of a distended beach ball bouncing along the shore.

The two of them were standing under an overhead crane inside the vast east wing of T. C. Johnson's Block A-7. Out on the immaculate factory floor, engineers and technicians in matching white bodysuits were anxiously puttering over the splayed airframe of the F-44, the ultimate fighter, everything that science could invent, technology could create and money could buy.

Behind the aircraft, the ultralight titanium panels of the aft fuselage lay like dead flower petals. Its belly was open, spilling its wiring out under one wing in a colorful tangle of high-tech guts, all red and yellow, black and green.

"Come here," Remy said tersely, escorting Gus toward the prone body of the plane. "I want you to take a look at something."

A tech moved aside so they could see the minuscule object of his attention, a small box about the size of a pack of gum with tiny blackened wires disappearing inside the fuselage.

"What is it?" Gus asked, peering at the thing. As Remy knelt next to the box, his pant leg rose, revealing the strap of a leather sheath. Reaching down, he pulled out a knife with a long, thin blade. Using it like a pointer, he started to flick through the charred wires.

"You still toting that thing?" Gus said, looking at the knife. "SAS, isn't it? Aren't you a little old to be playing commando?"

Remy ignored the shot. "An eighty-billion-dollar fuckup, Gus. More like pneumonia than the sniffles. I think it's worth your time, don't you?"

"Mother of God," Gus said softly. Loosening the zipper of his overalls, the older man started walking back to the door where they'd come in. "Let's go to your office," he said. "I need a drink."

Five minutes later, they were sitting in a large room with glass walls on three sides and a view across the well-tended grounds of the T. C. Johnson plant. Remy handed Gus a stiff scotch. He took it and walked over to the windows. In the artificial lake across the way, a tall fountain shot up a plume of water that created its own small arch of colors in the afternoon breeze. Tossing down half the scotch, Gus began to wonder gloomily if they'd just pissed away the pot of gold under the little rainbow.

"What you just saw was only half the problem. The best half," Remy said.

Gus hated riddles. "What are you trying to tell me?" he snapped.

"We're still scraping the other half off the runway at Edwards Air Force Base. Until twenty-four hours ago we had two prototypes, right? You just saw the YF-44. That one's still with us. The chairman took the ZF-44 to Edwards a coupla days ago. First landing, the computers browned out. Exley got it back down. But he left a strip of titanium a few millimeters deep on the runway. I can see you're saying to yourself, 'Hey, that's not so bad,' but, Gus, that strip was two miles long."

"What caused it?"

"Something in the wiring. That's what they were trying to fix out there on the floor."

"How long?"

"Maybe a month, maybe a year."

Gus closed his eyes. Behind them, he could feel the first deep throb of a migraine. The F-44 was an $80 billion project. The power guys on the Armed Services Committee's Air-Land Subcommittee had smiled on the fighter, but a few things still worried them. Like maybe it was going to cost $200 million a pop. Then the bean counters from the GAO who reviewed the development program discovered that T. C. Johnson had only completed maybe 2 percent of the flight testing when everyone in the business knew you had to do at least 10 to 20 percent before Big Bugs came slithering out.

"Shit, Remy, they're going to vote on the project before the spring recess."

"Tell me something I don't know."

"It's going to be hard to persuade them to go for it if we can't give them more flight data."

"Well, duh, Gus. That's not why I asked you to come down. We may be able to get the YF-44 back up in time. We may not. No way we can be sure the hardware will sell your boys up there. So you and I both know what that means, don't we?"

Gus shoved his glass forward. Remy poured out another dose.

"Kill the project, kill the company, Gus. The chairman is unhappy. Very, very unhappy."

"Fuck him."

"Oh no, Gus. No, no, no. Nothing I'd like better, crummy little Ivy League asshole. But as you are so fond of pointing out, fuck him, we fuck ourselves."

Gus nodded.

"Christ, I've got practically every Secretary of Defense going back to Richard Nixon's day on board," he said. "They're all for it. Even the Democrats want it. They're all willing to sign a statement supporting us."

Remy took the empty scotch glass and looked at it for a moment. Then he dropped it on the floor in front of Gus and put his foot slowly down on it. The glass broke with the sound of crushing bones.

"Dropping names won't do it, Gus." His voice suddenly sounded odd, as if the two of them were fixing bayonets for one final charge. "Christ, most of those guys do defense work. They're only signing their own paychecks at the end of the day. Everyone knows that. Look at our own board—it's crammed with retired generals and former senators and governors. So who are we kidding?"

"All right, all right, I hear you."

"Active assets. That's what we need now. Live ones. The biggest. Do I have to spell it out?"

"No." Gus suddenly felt very tired, very old.

"Can we count on him?"

Gus said nothing. It was Remy's show.

"The thing that worries me, Gus, is that the guy keeps wanting to *ask* questions. He oughtta be answering questions, terminating them. What are you going to do about it?"

Gus frowned. Was Remy at it again? Had he forgotten who found him his job?

"Plenty," Gus snapped. "You're not the only one who was busy yesterday." He got to his feet. There would be plenty of scotch on the plane. A tankerful for midair refueling, that's what he needed.

"How can you be so sure?"

"You remember what they told us in Vietnam, Captain Fair?"

To Gus's satisfaction, he saw that the reference to their old ranks and relative power had a Pavlovian effect on Remy. The man damn near straightened his shoulders and checked the shine on his shoes.

"What was that, sir?"

"About winning hearts and minds?"

"I think we—"

Gus cut him off at the ankles. "They told us shit happens, son. But when you got 'em by the balls, their hearts fall right into place. Every fucking time."

Gus picked up his coat and headed for the door. "You know, Remy, you're getting to be a little sloppy," he said. "You oughtta get someone to clean up after you. This place is a mess."

FORTY-FOUR

★ Stockbridge ★

Abbie woke up in total darkness. The blindfold was taped tightly around her head; the gag tasted vaguely metallic, as if someone had used it to polish a car.

"That you, little darling?"

Don't say anything, Abs. Don't move. Let him think you're still out.

The voice was high, but definitely a man's. It came from the front, filtering through the tune on the radio. Something about young love.

But this wasn't her car. She was stretched out full length, head toward the music. Her hands were tied in front of her with something plastic. Felt like electrical cord.

"Don't you fret now. We're nearly there."

The voice falsetto now, crooning along with the Top 40 shit, whatever it was.

How long had she been out? A few minutes, an hour? Jesus, what had he used on her?

She wiggled her fingers and toes. Arms working, legs working, but tingling as if they'd been connected to a wall outlet.

Stay cool, Abbie. If he'd meant to kill you, you wouldn't be here. She forced herself to breathe slowly, counted the ins and outs. He had the heater on. Hard to breathe.

They weren't on a paved road. Whatever he was driving, it

was bouncing like a bumper car. She heard the engine grind down two gears, and suddenly they were sliding sideways, as if he was driving through a mudflat.

They stopped. She heard him getting out the front door. After a few seconds, the doors squeaked open somewhere beyond her feet. She smelled wet leaves, a faint whiff of pines. The woods. Then the doors slammed shut.

"Time to get down, Miss Mancini. How you feeling in there?"

He knew her name. A wail started to form somewhere deep within her. Don't scream, Abbie. Whatever you do, don't scream. Wait him out. Maybe he just wants to scare you.

"There now." His fingers were fumbling with the blindfold, tightening it. Checking the cords around her wrists. An odd odor, distant but familiar, wafted over her. She sensed him hovering, felt something cold pressed against her cheek. She heard a faint *whssss* as it sliced through the gag.

Her cheeks stung as he ripped off the two sides of the gag.

Shut up, Abbie. Wait until you can see him. But the darkness didn't lift, he left the blindfold. She could sense him moving away from her, as if he were taking a survey. For a short time, she sat there in total silence.

That smell. What was it?

Baby oil.

Oh Jesus, what's happening?

He ripped away the blindfold.

"Ta da!" he whispered in her ear. "It's Rubber Jack!"

A rubber Halloween mask covered his entire head. One of those celebrity gag masks. The tousled brown hair brushed back boyishly into the rubber, the flashing Camelot teeth.

Her eyes caught the bare feet first, then worked up over the hairless calves to the smooth crotch and rising penis, swelling up like a pale white tuber from weeded ground.

As if she were no longer inside her body, she heard a scream tear from her throat, then die. She knew she was still shrieking, but nothing came out.

It wasn't just that he was naked. It was the hairless body, sweating in the overhead light. He kneeled in front of her, the smell overpowering, dripping with baby oil.

"Ask not what you can do for your country, little darling," he said. She felt his erection brush against her leg. "Maybe there's something you can do for me."

In his hand was a straight razor. The old ivory handle glowed in the dim light.

"Let's see, now," he said, drawing the open blade slowly across the back of his wrist. The place above his hand was covered with long, delicate white lines. She saw a thin trickle of red blood rising next to the white bracelet of scar tissue.

Crouching next to her, he placed the blade gently between her breasts.

Oh God, don't let this be happening.

He snapped his hand upward.

The top button flicked off her blouse.

She heard it fall to the floor of the truck, quiver.

"Awful hot in here, isn't it? Let's try to make you a little more comfortable."

He flicked off the next button, then the next, taking his time, until all the buttons were gone. With a flick of the blade, he opened her blouse. Slowly, he began to trace a circle around one of her bra cups.

"Oops, sorry," he said softly.

She felt a sharp pain and looked down at her breast. A line of blood began seeping through the white cloth of the bra.

"I didn't mean to diss you," she said hoarsely. Anything that would come out. Anything at all. God, make him stop.

"A kiss for a diss?" he said dreamily.

She felt the razor resume its slide. An electric current somewhere in her brain shorted out, sending showers of sparks through her body. Her knees shot upward like the drivers of an ancient locomotive, smashing into Rubber Jack's groin.

A roar of pain came out of the mask as he fell back, doubled over.

"Fucking cunt."

She saw the razor start down and she had no more time for screams.

"Fucking . . ."

She closed her eyes. Felt nothing.

There was a soft, slurping sound.

Her eyes shot open as Rubber Jack's oiled feet were sliding out from under him. He sprawled backward, thumping his head on the rear door.

The truck shook with a deep bass note, as if someone had struck a gong, and Rubber Jack slid to the floor.

The razor dropped out of his hand.

A jack was strapped to the side of the truck. Abbie grabbed it with both of her hands and brought it crashing down on Rubber Jack.

He groaned once and rolled on his side.

Christ, I've got to get out of here.

It didn't occur to her to look under the mask. She didn't care who he was.

Shaking, she picked up the razor and cut the cords binding her hands. Then she grabbed the door handle.

Locked.

WHHHHeeeeeeeOOOOOOOeeeeeeeee.   WHHHHeeeeee-OOOOOeeeeee.

She stared dumbly at the shrieking doors. Then she pushed the jack between them and heaved. The lock popped, the doors swung open. She was outside.

He had parked in a thick stand of hemlocks.

FLOOR IT—BOB'S SANDING & REFINISHING.

A wild laugh of relief at the sign. She wasn't dead. Rubber Jack and his crazy truck were doing the screaming now.

*   *   *

Gray clouds were scudding above the trees. The sun suddenly broke through them as she sawed at the cords binding her wrists. Pulling off her blouse, she shucked away the sullied bra. Then she slipped back into the torn blouse, tied the ends at the bottom and took a quick scan around her.

Not the road, Abs. Anything but the road.

She sucked in a deep breath and started to run, down through the trees, half running through copses of ash and beech, half falling over ledges of green-gray stone.

Half an hour later, when she finally felt safe enough to slow down, she heard a chain saw chattering somewhere in the woods off to her left. The stuttering roar grew louder and louder until in front of her she could see a small pond encircled with stubby second-growth pines. Next to the pond, two men were bucking up logs for firewood.

"Lord," said the older man as she limped out of the trees. He cut off the saw and put it on the ground next to him. "Are you all right, miss?"

He was wearing a red and gray mackinaw coat over a flannel work shirt and green corduroy pants. The bill of his soft cloth cap, the kind with earflaps, was turned slightly sideways to keep the sun out of his eyes.

She ran up to him, breathing hard.

"I was out hiking," she mumbled.

"Take your time, now, miss."

"I guess I got lost."

"You sure did. I thought we had a sixteen-pointer crashing down on us, didn't you, Rod?"

"Something like that," the younger man said, looking at her curiously.

She said a small prayer. "Could you drive me back to town?"

"That all you need, miss?" the older man asked her. He was looking at her blouse. "We could run you over to the hospital."

She ran her fingers down to her breast. A splotch of blood the size of a man's hand had soaked through and dried on her blouse.

"No, just back to my car would be wonderful. I must have fallen down."

The older man nodded. "Why don't you give her a lift, Rod? I'll finish up here."

She followed Rod to a banged-up pickup at the far end of the pond. Ten minutes later she was standing beside her own car in the institute lot, waving good-bye to the receding tailgate of her Berkshire Samaritan.

★   ★   ★

At three o'clock, she came out of the bathroom of her suite at the Red Lion Inn, pulling the terry cloth guest robe gently across the Band-Aid under her breast.

Five after three now. No call. Damn, damn, damn. Maybe Santana didn't get through. What the hell should she do? She looked down at her hands. They were still shaking slightly. Should she call the police?

The buzz of the phone made her jump.

"Personal call for Abigail Mancini. Will you take it?" The bored voice of the hotel operator was as soothing as a Valium.

"Sandy," she said, trying not to whimper. "Is that you?"

"Right here, *principessa*."

"No, not here, you're over there," she said, blubbering now, the tears finally breaking over the dam.

"Easy," he said softly. "Santana told me about Sweeny. What's going on?"

"Everything's turning to shit, pups. I'm scared. I was coming back from talking to Dr. Hyduk and the next thing I know some freaked-out weirdo with a razor wants to give me a shave and haircut out in the woods."

Total silence at the other end. For one bad second she thought he'd been cut off.

"Are you okay? Where are you now?" No more pups. He sounded the way he did on the roof in Mogadishu.

"My hotel."

"How fast can you get out of there?"

"Tonight."

"Okay, here's what I want you to do . . ."

How wonderful. Did you hear him? He'd take it from here. She wadded the tissue and threw it toward the wastebasket. It went straight in. Two points. She felt her confidence trickling back.

"Wait, pups," she said. "Before we get cut off." She told him about Dr. Hyduk and his lost brother, the showdown at the bank, the short version of Rubber Jack.

"He was all naked, Sandy. He cut me . . ." Dammit, the tears were starting again. She forced them back. "But maybe it was just a coincidence. I went in his face when we pulled into the parking lot and I made him crazy. Maybe there's no connection."

"Yeah, maybe."

She heard him call out to someone. "Hey, isn't there a military hop to Frankfurt every morning at 0400 hours?" Then he was back on the line.

"It's all right, Abbie. You're going to be all right. Don't go dark on me now, okay? We don't have much time."

"Oh, pups, I think I kill . . ."

"Not over this line." His voice blotted out her confession. More gently, he said, "Please, Abbie, just meet me tomorrow at Dulles. I'll be there at two o'clock. The New York flight from Kennedy."

"How are you going to do that?"

"Leave that to me. I'm going to say this carefully now. There are a million flights west out of Dulles every afternoon. Book us as close as you can get to Hyduk. We'll figure out the rest when we get there."

"But your mission, your orders?"

"The mission just got changed. I'll see you tomorrow."

FORTY-FIVE

"Incoming. Watch your ass."

Plonk, plonk, plonk.

With a dull thud, the empty Jack Daniel's miniatures dropped one by one into the plastic bag extended by the Lufthansa flight attendant. Two from Nate's tray, the third from Sandy's.

"Danke sehr."

Sandy watched Nate as the blond Brünnhilde moved up the aisle. Clearly Sergeant Caldwell's tracking gear was on remote.

"You all right, man?"

Nate pulled the cobra-skin wallet out of his rear pocket. The plastic envelopes that held his photo gallery fell open. In the slot normally reserved for the pile of captured RPG launchers was a shot of Elena. She had on one of Nate's shirts, open at the throat. Around her neck was a small gold cross. Caldwell said morosely, "I think I'm in love."

Elena's expression matched Nate's. More shock than bliss. "So, even giants fall." Sandy laughed. "Worse things going around, dude. Just don't let it affect your aim."

The blonde returned with their lunch: bratwurst, scalloped potatoes, mustard and two bottles of Beck's. Even the sight of the chow didn't seem to cheer up Nate. "Hang in there, man," Sandy said, looking out the window. Seven miles below them, the Atlantic was sliding astern, blue with blinding flashes of white among the black shadows cast by clouds, immense, indifferent to small matters like love. He pushed his seat back and closed his eyes.

His mind moved back to what Abbie had told him about tracking down ODA 351. The living and the dead. Push the rock up the hill and every time you get to the top it rolls back and kills someone. First Perkins, then Sweeny. Now Abbie. Fuck coincidence. But if she was right about Hyduk, maybe they could find him before the next rock.

"What kind of a guy was Dan Perkins, Nate?"

"Good man. The best."

"I still feel like a shit for tearing his ass."

"Yeah, you were wrong, Hawk, but in case you didn't notice, you were kind of busy at the time."

"He thought I was off target about Alex, didn't he?"

"What's this *Alex* shit? You ever hear of 'Father'? Like what *do* you rich white boys call your daddy?"

"Never thought of him that way, Nate. I never knew what to call him. Chickenshit was the word that usually came to mind. That's what Perkins thought I had wrong."

"Yeah, he told me. Up on the roof. The night before he bought it."

"Look, Nate, I know you two were tight. I don't want to push my nose where I've got no business."

"Nah, that's okay, Captain. Like I said, Dan was talking about your daddy. That *is* your business."

"You mind telling me what he said?"

Caldwell rubbed his hand across his jaw as if feeling the stubble might help scratch away the past. "He told me he knew your daddy up in I Corps. Said your daddy saved his ass once."

"What happened?"

"Dan told me the NVA had him pinned down one time when he was pulling point, just waiting to grease him. Your daddy came bustin' in there all by himself and pulled his ass out. Hadn't been for Alex Caine, Dan wouldn't have lived twenty more years just to get his ass killed saving you and me. He told me you looked exactly like Lieutenant Caine."

"That Wolf shit he started to tell me—what was that all about?"

"He said the men started calling your daddy Wolf."

"Wolf?"

"Yeah, that's right. For the way he came bounding in that day and got Dan out. I gotta tell you, that don't sound like no chick-enshit I ever knew."

Caldwell tapped his fingers on the armrest. It looked like he had said all he was going to.

"What made them fight that way, Nate? Perkins, I mean. I still don't know about Alex. Maybe him, too."

Caldwell looked up at the ceiling.

"Okay," Sandy said. "I know they're dead, but you and I are still doing it. And I know I sound like a dork, but what about the whole Duty, Honor, Country trip? I'm serious."

"I used to think about that a lot, Hawk. Then I figured out why I really do it."

"For the pussy, right? I think you told me that once."

Nate didn't laugh. "In the beginning, it was for the pussy. And the shiny boots and the silver wings and riding up there in the front of the bus. All of that. But it ain't no more."

"What do you mean?"

Nate stared at him. "Okay, I'll tell you. But I'm only gonna do it once, so you need to take notes, you better start writin'. I did it for Perkins, I do it for Eddie and Kruger, I do it for Santana. Sometimes, I guess, I even do it for you. Could you shut the fuck up now, Hawk?"

He brightened as Brünnhilde came down the aisle with the duty-free cart. Sandy watched him pick out an Hermes scarf for Elena. No question, Nate was gone.

Above the north fork of Long Island, the plane dipped into the final descent. Over the marshes of Jamaica Bay, Sandy saw the plane's shadow racing them across the water. A gentle bump on the rubber-scarred runway, and they were home.

At the baggage carousel, they grabbed their bags and split up. Nate caught a cab and headed for La Guardia and his connection down to Fayetteville. Sandy rented a shower and soaped Bosnia out of his system. After that he spent more time than he had in months shaving, shining, shampooing. From his bag he took out a pair of slacks and a blue long-sleeved shirt. He also traded his boots for a pair of black Gucci loafers he'd picked up in Split, probably hot because they were so cheap. In the bar, he nursed a beer and watched replays of football on ESPN until they called his flight to Dulles International.

FORTY-SIX

She was wearing a reddish-brown parka that set off her curls. Her black stretch pants fit her like another skin. Hoping to take her by surprise, he tried to circle around and get behind her, but she saw him and ran to him, burying her face in his chest. After the stale air in the plane and the fast food smell of the airport, breathing in the clean fragrance of her hair was like a hit of pure oxygen.

And then her arms were around his neck and it was no longer possible to tell who was kissing whom because they were both making up for lost time.

"Are you all right?" he whispered, kissing her ear.

"No," she said, pressing against him. "But I'm better now. How did you get here so fast?"

"I did General Hunter a favor," he said. "He did one for me. We can talk about that some other time. The main thing is you're safe."

An hour to kill before the three-thirty flight to Salt Lake. In the lounge, he started to order a beer. "No way, dear heart," she said. "I need your full attention."

A few minutes later, when they were settled over coffee and tea, she said, "We are looking at some deep, deep weirdness, pups."

She was different this time. No cockiness. "It all started when I got back from talking to Janine. Patrice already knew about the trip. He also knew I'd been looking through the military records. Then I went down to see Santana and there was the stuff from Sweeny."

"What did he say?"

"He said, and I quote, 'Alex Caine was the most gung-ho sunuvabitch you ever seen.' End quote. He also said the men called Alex Wolf."

That made two Wolves in six hours. Where the fuck was Chicken Little?

"Anything else?"

"He was going to dig out a picture for you and I had the feeling he'd give us more. That's where the weirdness got weirder. Santana called. He sounded broken up, if that's the right word for it—you guys are about as emotional as fence posts—and he told me Sweeny was dead."

"Just like that?"

"That's right. Somebody came in that night, they got sloshed and Sweeny drove into the reservoir on the way home."

"Who was the drinking buddy?"

"Santana wasn't certain, but he sure sounded like Remy Fair."

"If it was Remy, he could have been passing through," Sandy said. "Just part of his job, maybe." He smelled peppermint and looked down at the table. She hadn't touched her tea.

"Maybe," she said. "Maybe not. Let's count 'em. First Patrice right after I talk to Janine, then Remy Fair after I talk to Sweeny. Then, after Dr. Hyduk, hello, it's Rubber Jack. I don't know what to think anymore."

"Plenty of time." He kissed the tip of her nose. "Where's Hyduk? Where are you taking me?"

"The Flathead Credit Union in Whitefish. Here, let me show you the note." She opened her purse and started to rummage around. "I *know* it was in here. I threw it in after we left the bank." Suddenly she began clawing through the side pockets.

"It's gone."

"Rubber Jack?"

"It was there before he conked me. It's not there now."

"One too many maybes," he said, putting his arm around her, drawing her closer. "Let's get going. We've got a plane to catch."

★   ★   ★

Below them, the Middle West went by in its quiltwork of sections, the country roads meeting every mile at the edge of dark brown fields stripped of the fall harvest. She told him about Janine and about Jeff's nightmares. "It's like it happened yesterday."

He nodded. "You never forget. I'm with Perkins and my guys almost every night."

Abbie rang for a blanket. They pulled the armrest out of the center seat and crawled under. Warmer, softer. Nicer. At the airport in Salt Lake, they split a peach Slurpee. She put her head on his shoulder and slept until they called the night flight to Kalispell.

It was well past midnight when they landed. There was a light on at the Hertz desk. The clerk gave them a map and directions north to Whitefish. Here and there in the darkness, their headlights picked up white crosses planted by the state where others like Sweeny had bought it on the road.

They pulled into the parking lot of the Grouse Mountain Lodge at 1:00 A.M. In the bar, the last embers were burning in a stone fireplace that rose up and disappeared through the ceiling. The kitchen had closed at eleven. But when Sandy asked if they could get a cold bottle of Chardonnay and a fruit and cheese plate sent up to their room, the desk clerk said, "You bet," and picked up the phone. Two minutes after they hit Room 258, he arrived with the food.

They had a sitting room downstairs with cathedral ceilings, a couch, chairs and desk. On the desk was an ashtray and a little bundle of candles. A card said "For Power Outages." Upstairs, a sleeping loft went all the way across the room. At its center was a king-size bed about half the size of the state of Montana.

They had toted their own luggage. Abbie dropped her backpack on the floor. Peeling the Saran Wrap back from the cheeseplate, she took a cracker and started nibbling. He fought with himself. He wanted her, but what could he say so soon after Rubber Jack?

So he took out his shaving kit, put his bag in the closet and draped his trousers neatly over a chair. "Gotta wash all that travel off my skin," he called across the room. Give her some time.

Stripping off the rest of his clothes, he went to explore the bathroom. The large tub had an equally large shower head. As he turned on the hot water, he could hear Abbie unpacking. He had seen her do it in Zagreb, enough to know she was slinging her things all over the room.

Sliding the glass doors open, he stepped into the tub. Steam began to fill the compartment. He closed his eyes, letting the hot water run down his neck, unknotting the muscles in his shoulders and back. And then he heard the shower door slide open.

"Hello there, big boy," she said huskily, vamping on Sharon Stone. "How about some room service you'll never forget?"

Floating through the steam, she slipped in next to him, her body glistening, her breasts firm, the water trickling down the red brush below her flat stomach. She leaned over and licked one of his nipples, then flicked a nail gently across the other. He felt himself stiffening.

"Not yet," she said, pushing his hands away. "Close your eyes. Don't move."

He felt a warm cascade down his chest. The sweet spicy scent of vanilla welled up into the steam. He opened his eyes and saw the bottle of Kiehl's body shampoo in her hand.

"You're cheating." She reached out a hand. Before her fingers drew down his eyelids, he saw her leaning over to put the bottle on the edge of the tub. Water and foam coursed down her shoulders, puddled on the small of her back, slid between her legs. Then he saw only soft circles of light projected backward against the screen of his closed eyes.

He felt her hands around his cock, a surging warmth, raising him hard through her slippery fingers. His breath caught in his throat. He groaned and bent his knees as she wrapped her arms around his neck and rose above him. Then she let her body slip down and he was in her and she kept sliding lower, squeezing, crying. He rose and pulled back, three, four, five times, until he didn't dare go for another. Slipping out of her, he picked her up in his arms. She let her head fall back and held him as he picked up a towel and carried her out of the steaming shower.

In the sitting room, a fluffy white rug lay on the floor in front of the couch. He tossed the towel across it, lowered her onto her back and kneeled over her. She bit her lip and then, pressing upward, wrapped her legs around his waist and pulled him into her until she had him deep, surrounding him, moving toward him, pulling back, slow, slower, forward, back until the white heat began to come and his back arched like a long bow and he shot his soul into her.

For five minutes he lay there on the white rug, his face in the nape of her neck, his breath drying the warm curves. He bent his head down, kissed where she'd been cut. She tasted like vanilla.

He heard the sound of running water and thought of mountain streams, sunlight, bubbling foam along dark wet banks. Then he realized they had left the taps on in the shower. Groaning, he got to his feet. The doors were pulled back the way he had left them in his sprint for the sitting room. Warm water was lapping at the top edge of the tub.

When he leaned over to pull the plug, he heard Abbie coming up behind him.

"Aspetta un momento," she said, looking over his shoulder. "I have plans. Big plans. Do not dare let that water out of the tub."

As he stood up, she went into the other room. When she came back, she had the cheese and fruit platter balanced on one hand, the Chardonnay, beaded with ice water, in the other, and the candles under her arm. "You first," she said.

He stepped into the warm water and sat down with his back to the taps. Officer and a gentleman, he told himself. Nothing that had ever happened to him with a woman had been so over the top. She handed him the Chardonnay and the platter of fruit and cheese. Then she lit the candles, dripped hot wax onto the counter next to the sink and stuck them into it. They looked like miniature torches when she turned off the overhead lamp.

In the flickering candlelight, her body was slinky, tawny. She climbed over him, leaned against the back of the tub and closed her eyes. Reaching down into the water, he ran his hands along her legs. She pushed forward and made little circles on his stomach with her fingertips, her fingers trailing lower in the warm water, searching for him.

"Welcome home, pups," she said. "Can I peel you a grape?"

FORTY-SEVEN

Whitefish ★ Montana

Sunup in Montana. Gray light filtering through the drapes, a white rime of frost on the window at the end of the sleeping loft. Abbie lay under the comforter listening to Sandy gear himself up for the day. Make love, not war? she thought sleepily. What a joke. With Sandy you couldn't have one without the other. She wondered how many women he had slept with. Last night he had come at her like a centurion returning from three years in Gaul. What would he be like if he fell in love? Assuming, of course, that he *could* fall in love. Not much chance of that, but hey, what about Antony and Cleopatra? Wasn't Antony a soldier, too? Right. But not Special Forces.

Turning on her back, she snuggled her feet into the down. A quick reality check. Something about Sandy still worried her. It wasn't just that he didn't seem comfortable in his soldier's suit. It was as if he wasn't comfortable in his own skin, something desperate in the way he made love, as if he wanted to lose himself, bury any sign of who he really was.

The sound of his voice broke the wobbling line of her reverie. From below only a word or two floated up to the sleeping loft, but it sounded like he was talking to Santana.

"Fucking zombie, man . . . Abella . . . scan."

He hung up and she heard him start up the stairs.

He was used to giving orders and she was used to blowing them off. Give it time, she thought. Maybe he'll change. Maybe she could change him. Work out a compromise. As he reached the landing, she closed her eyes, felt him leaning over her.

He touched her bare shoulder: "Reveille, Miss Vanilla."

★   ★   ★

Coming down from the loft, Sandy picked his way through the litter Abbie had left the night before. Her blouse and pants were on the floor next to the couch. Seeing his clothes arranged so tidily in the closet, he felt a twinge of embarrassment. Neatness before passion. What was it with him? He closed the door before she could see it, too.

He plugged the coffee pot on the counter into the wall. When the coffee was brewing, he went over and pulled back the drapes. Outside, the sun was just beginning to slant down through the tall green pines. He looked into the bathroom. The tub was empty, the candles had puddled out. Absently, he looked at his face in the mirror. He needed a shave. He reached for his shaving kit, then stopped. He was off duty, not going on parade. By the time she came down, a towel tucked under her breasts and across her hips, the coffee was ready. He handed her a cup, and when she took it, he ran his finger under the top of the towel.

"Don't," she said, smacking his hand lightly, like Melba protecting her cookie jar. "I'm recovering." Her tone was neutral, as if she were delivering an after-action report. "From the night of pillage and plunder. You ravished me."

"Who ravished who, Cat Woman?" He pointed his chastened finger at her underwear hanging from the entertainment center. "You want to check out the tracks you left on your way to the kill?"

Letting the towel fall, she wrapped her arms around his neck. "So what do we do now?"

He looked at the swell of her breasts. Touched the cut.

As he was tucking the loose corner of the towel between her breasts, she looked at him as if she were fully dressed. "I think we should go to the bank," she said.

The witch. She was in his head.

★   ★   ★

The Grouse Mountain Lodge was set on the side of a low hill that sloped down through a pretty valley to the village of White-fish. Off toward the east, partly hidden in a forest of dark green pines, was a blue lake surrounded on three sides by mountains.

To the right, the road sloped down in the direction of an old cemetery with a twisted wrought-iron gate.

"Boot Hill," Sandy said as they drove by. "Worse places to plant your bones."

"Thanks. I'd just as soon not."

They crossed a stream on the outskirts of town and shot past a commercial strip with a chiropractor's office, real estate agency and convenience store. Just before the decaying opera house, a traffic light stopped them. Sandy turned and cruised slowly, looking for a cafe.

Circling the railyard, he headed back along Center Street, past a saloon advertising poker and slots, a pharmacy, a shop with a window full of Native American jewelry. A pawn shop came into view not far from a place with a sign out front that said CHECKS CASHED.

At the end of the main drag he turned left and pulled up in front of the Buffalo Cafe. Inside, the customers were all men, a couple of ranchers in wool shirts and cowboy boots at the counter, a table with three guys in jeans and sports shirts discussing a school board brawl. Over in the corner, a sheriff's deputy sat stirring his cup and reading the sports scores in *USA Today*. The smell of bacon and eggs and steaming coffee was intoxicating.

Sandy ordered half the menu, the eggs and bacon, hashed browns, biscuits with gravy and a small eye of round steak. Rare. The waitress, a muscular blonde on the hard side of forty, looked like she wanted to throw Sandy and brand him. "You came to the right place," she said.

Near the cash register, a clock, the big and little hands tipped with flint arrowheads, put the time at twenty after eight. The bank wouldn't open until nine. Plenty of time to eat and think.

Sandy dug into the eggs. When Abbie had told him about Hyduk, his first impulse had been to call Jeff. But something had stopped him. If Hyduk was here—and if he could be found—the General and Jeff wouldn't be the only keepers of the past. For the first time in his life, he saw a tunnel to his father that he could move down alone.

Alone.

That wasn't quite the right word, was it?

He looked up from his plate. Leaning over her oatmeal, Abbie looked like a little girl waking up to her first morning at camp. How could any woman with such a motor drive and murder mouth look so innocent? He felt a pleasant twinge. Nothing like lust. What he really needed was to find somewhere safe where he could lock her up until he could figure her out.

Figure them both out. Stabbing his fork into a gravy-soaked lump of biscuit, he began to sop up the last of the eggs. "Do you think this guy Hyduk's for real?" he asked.

"His brother did. And he was not happy about it."

Digging into the oatmeal, she remembered the ugly scene in Pittsfield. Did Dr. Hyduk really want to help her? Or was he out to hurt his brother? "Doctor's Disease," she shrugged. "That's what M.D. stands for. Major Demento. All of them."

"But we're talking about this guy's brother. Why wouldn't he want to see him?"

"Let me ask you something, okay? Don't get mad. Just devil's advocate. You know the way you talk about your dad? How he was the greatest loser of all time?"

Setting the fork on the plate, he reached for his coffee.

"So what would you say if you could see him again? Would you even *want* to see him? Maybe the problem is you're scared shitless you share the same blood. Maybe the shrink is scared shitless the same way about his brother."

"Interesting theory," he said, waving for the check. "I'll think about it."

By the arrowheads on the wall, it was five minutes to nine.

"We're outta here," he announced, avoiding Abbie's eyes as he headed for the door.

★   ★   ★

The Flathead Credit Union was a new building with stone walls, shiny windows and a green roof the color of old copper and new money. Banks put Sandy on edge. They reminded him of the Putnams, their polish, their frigidity. It was the Putnam in him that made him practice automatic deposit and balance his checkbook every month, even on the days when he wished he could keep his pay in a jar with a screw-top lid, like Melba's uncle, the fisherman, saving for the next fiesta.

At five after nine, when Sandy and Abbie walked into the credit union, two tellers were standing behind a grill-less counter riffling through stacks of small bills. No bulletproof cubicles for Whitefish. In the loan officer's section, an older woman in a red sweater with a white lace collar looked up at them pleasantly. The name tag pinned to her bosom identified her as Mavis

Weller. She was wearing a Mickey Mouse watch with a red band that matched her sweater. A sticker on the back of her computer monitor said: NICE DAYS ARE FOR NITWITS.

"Want to open an account?" she said. "You up for it?"

"What can I get on five million dollars?" Sandy asked her.

"For five mil, cookie, you can have me, my dog and my motor home."

Sandy laughed. While he explained their errand, Abbie listened, wondering what the Berkshire Hills Bank crowd back in Pittsfield would make of Mavis.

"Good Lord, what a story," Mavis said when Sandy finished. "The man you want to talk to is High Preston."

She rapped sharply on the door behind her.

"That's High for high altitude, kids," she said. "You'll see."

Without waiting for an answer, she opened the door.

Slumped in a black leather swivel chair with his back toward them was a tall man—Sandy put him at about six-six unfolded—reading the *Wall Street Journal*. Facing him was a roll-top desk cluttered with files, ledgers and reports. On top of the desk was a brass name plate engraved on the flattened case of an artillery round. The name on the shell case said PRESTON LASSWELL, PRESIDENT.

From the wall above him, the head of a stuffed elk with eyes of brown glass stared out over the room. When Lasswell turned and stood up, his head grazed the elk's chin.

"Get your ears out of the antlers, High," Mavis told him. "This is Captain Caine. He's the Green Beret. The redhead is Miss Mancini. She's the reporter. They've got something they want to ask you."

The banker glanced at Sandy, then, more carefully, at Abbie. If this one was diddling somebody else's wife, she thought, it wouldn't be after bridge night.

Lasswell was wearing a brown suit over his boots. The braided leather tails of a silver bolo tie made two twisting black lines down his chest. Standing under the elk, he looked like a sight gag from Dr. Seuss. His long arms were heavy with muscle and he had a steamfitter's hands. Default on a loan, he'll have you stuffed, mounted and up there on the wall right next to Bambi's big brother.

"What's the story, Mave?"

"I'm not going to spoil it for you, High."

Mavis turned and went out, leaving the door ajar, like a

woman who knew she'd be back and didn't want to waste time on the return trip.

The tall man shifted his gaze to Sandy. Lasswell's bearing and voice sounded military.

"Okay, Captain," he said. "What's the skinny?"

"We're trying to locate one of your depositors . . . Mr. Lasswell."

Sandy hesitated. Dammit, he thought; he had almost called this guy *sir*. Recovering, he said, "The name is Hyduk. Larry Hyduk. Probably Lawrence in your records."

"Never heard of him."

Sandy looked blankly at the older man.

"How is that possible?" Abbie asked, breaking in abruptly even though she knew it would raise the hackles on both men. Put Sandy in front of a machine gun and the other guy was in deep shit. One flat denial from a source and he lost it.

"The Berkshire Hills Bank says he has an account here."

"No way."

"I've seen deposit slips."

Just a small lie—and white. Dr. Hyduk had seen the slips—all he'd given her was the note—but if she couldn't jar Lasswell they were dead.

"I make it a point of honor, Miss Mancini, to know the first and last names of everyone who does business with us. I assure you, we have no account under that name."

"I don't understand, Mr. Lasswell. He's been depositing roughly a thousand dollars a month for twenty or twenty-five years. I make that nearly a quarter of a million dollars. Are you saying you don't keep track of that kind of money?"

Lasswell eased his two-story frame back into the swivel chair.

"Needling me? Old fart? Memory shot? Alzheimer's? That what you're saying, Miss Mancini?"

Before she could reply, he held up his hand to stop her.

"Mave, will you get in here?" he barked. Mavis Weller immediately pushed the door open and stepped into the room. She'd been outside listening the whole time. Like Melba. Sandy smiled.

"Please tell these two young people here we have no account for any Lawrence Hyduk. They think I'm trying to buffalo them."

"Well, High," Mavis said slowly. "The problem is you're only half right."

Lasswell looked at her the way an irritable dentist considers an abscessed tooth.

"Which half? What the hell are you talking about?"

"You're not lying. You're right about that. Hyduk doesn't have an account here. Not really."

"What's the other half?"

"Miss Mancini is right about the money."

Lasswell's face reddened. Above him, the elk looked bored, as if riddles were just another service of the Flathead Credit Union.

"Goddamn it, Mave, you're talking in tongues again. What are you trying to tell me?"

Mavis came around to the side of the rolltop desk and put her hand on the banker's arm.

"That guy they're looking for?"

"Yes?" The banker's face went blank, like a monitor after a memory crash.

"It's the Night Stalker, High. Couldn't be anyone else."

★　　★　　★

Lasswell sank back in his chair. "You better take a seat," he told Sandy and Abbie, pointing to a couch. Almost longingly, he picked up the *Journal*, then dropped it back on his desk. "Close the door behind you, Mave," he said. "We could be some time."

When Mavis was gone, he didn't say anything for a moment or two, as if he had to choose what to put in and what to leave out. Then, ignoring Abbie, he leaned forward and said to Sandy, "I shouldn't be telling you this, Captain—the Feds would eat me alive—but I'm an old infantryman. Big Red One. North Africa, Sicily, Normandy. Before your time, but I'm guessing we understand each other."

"I think we do, sir." This time Sandy didn't kick himself for using the word.

"All right, then," Lasswell said. "Here's the deal. Like I told you, there's no account here under the name of Lawrence Hyduk. As far as I know, there's no Hyduk, period."

"But the money? I don't get it."

"There is a guy who calls himself Hyduk. He lives in Massachusetts, I believe. Every month he transfers about a thousand bucks to the account of one of our customers here. I always thought he was just a rich uncle, something like that."

"Who gets the money at this end?"

"The Night Stalker."

"Give us a break, High." Abbie said, risking a second interruption. "Are you saying you've got an account for Mr. John J. Night Stalker?"

"Shit, no. That's just what Mave calls him. She was here when the credit union first got going in Whitefish. Bob Hester ran the place then. Bob's dead now. He's the one who used to call him the Night Stalker, the one who set the whole thing up."

"So what's this guy's real name?"

Lasswell looked at his hands for a moment.

"Let's say it's none of your business. Let's say it's also against banking regulations for me to tell you."

"Okay. Let's say all that. What else?"

"Well, let me put it this way. Suppose you have a guy here in Whitefish who has a rich uncle back east named Hyduk. Lawrence, Larry, whatever. If I were you and if I wanted to get in touch with this guy, I'd go look for Henry Emerson."

"Henry Emerson?"

Abbie frowned. Then she saw a Buddha smile creeping across Sandy's face.

"As I understand it," Lasswell went on, "Bob Hester and Henry Emerson served together in Vietnam. The money from Hyduk goes into Emerson's account here at the credit union."

"Then what happens?"

"Our instructions from Emerson are to take the deposit from Massachusetts each month and buy ten individual money orders. Random denominations, between one hundred and one hundred ninety-five dollars. No more than that. The money orders are made out to cash."

"That's great, High. So where can we find Emerson?"

"Beats me. I've never seen the man. No one in the bank has, not that I know of. Not even Mave. That's why I got so scrambled when we started this party."

"But he's got to come in here to identify himself and pick up the money orders. Someone must know him."

"We mail them to a post office box. You won't find any Henry Emerson in the phone book. I've looked. The bottom line is maybe five thousand people live around Whitefish. The Night Stalker could be any one of 'em."

"Looks like we're chasing a ghost," Abbie said, looking at Sandy.

Sandy pushed back his chair and stood up. Sticking out his

hand, he thanked the banker. As they were leaving, he leaned over and kissed Mavis Weller on the cheek.

When they were back in the car, Abbie pulled the keys out of the ignition.

"Okay, pups, pal of infantrymen, lover of older women. What did you see that I missed?"

"Ectoplasm."

"Quit it. Stop doing that to me."

"Ghosts, Abbie. Two ghosts. Three. Ten if you count everyone in ODA 351 except Jeff." Then he shook his head, like an angry kid correcting an obvious mistake in his homework. "No fucking way," he said, starting the car. "I don't believe in ghosts. Let's get back to the lodge."

FORTY-EIGHT

★ Whitefish ★

The Whitefish cemetery loomed up in front of them. Sandy turned and drove through the old gate. In the older part of the graveyard, frost heaves had tilted the headstones winter by winter, inch by inch, until they looked like hats cocked back on the brows of the dead.

"Does this turn you on?" Abbie said.

"Looking for something," Sandy mumbled. Slowing to a crawl, he drove along the winding road, checking names and dates on the headstones. Under a tall green cedar, he parked the car. "Must be here somewhere," he said, taxiing off down a lane of graves. Toward the end of the third row, he suddenly stopped and waved her over. When she reached him, he was kneeling next to a marker that stood out distinctly from its neighbors. It was lower than the others, cut from green stone, rounder. Seen head-on, it looked more like a helmet than a headstone.

Sandy was brushing dust from the name. She bent down next to him and read ROBERT VICTOR HESTER—1934–1975. Above the name was the oak leaf of a major in the United States Army. Below it were the same words she had seen behind the bar at Sweeny's: *De Oppresso Liber*.

Centered under the crest of the Special Forces, Hester had added his own postscript: *Inter Fratres Unum*.

She looked at Sandy. "One of the Band of Brothers," he said, running his finger along the epitaph as he translated it. "One of us."

Us?

Almost as if he were including her. Or was he just referring to his Army boys' club? Stupid to push it. "So?"

"So it explains a lot."

"To you. Maybe it's a guy thing. In case you forgot, I'm out of the loop."

She was shivering. "The name on the account," he said, wrapping his arms around her waist. "Remember?"

"Henry Emerson? What about it?"

"That's what you didn't get back at the bank."

"How could I have missed it," she said. "I mean, an awesome name like that. Probably Ralph Waldo's second cousin twice removed, am I right?"

"It *is* an awesome name. You just don't recognize it."

"You've got me there."

"Let's go back to the car," he said, holding out on her. "It's freezing."

They walked back the way they had come. The first flakes of snow began to drift among the graves. Along the stone curb, the withered green grass, now flecked with white, felt cold and hard under their feet. When they were in the car, the heater going full bore, he looked at her.

"Okay, he said. "We've got the Night Stalker, Hyduk, and Henry Emerson. We're not talking about a whole squad." He gave a whoop and slammed his hands on the dashboard. "Yes!"

"What are you telling me?" Her hands made little circles as if she were trying to pull it out of him.

"They're all the same guy, Abbie. Hyduk, the Night Stalker, Henry Emerson. The name game must have been an inside joke between Hester and Hyduk."

"You'll notice I'm not laughing."

"Look, Henry Emerson was one of the fightingest, wild-horse-ridingest combat leaders in Vietnam. They called him the Gunfighter. Hank Emerson would have been a lieutenant colonel when Hester was a major and Hyduk was a grunt. When they needed a way to hide away Hyduk's tracks, they put the Gunfighter's name on the account."

"Wasn't that sort of illegal?"

"You could call it that."

"Why would Hester agree to do it?"

"Hyduk asked him for help."

"A lot of people must have asked him for help. He was a banker."

"They weren't in the Band of Brothers. I'm sure of it now—it's so clear Hester wasn't the only one, Abbie. Hyduk was a full member—all dues paid in Vietnam." Sandy started the car. Once through the iron gate, he headed back for Grouse Mountain Lodge, humming now, riffing to an old tune from the Lovin' Spoonful. She couldn't quite make out the words—but it sounded something like "What a Day for a Dead Man."

★　　★　　★

"Let's say you're right—we still don't know what Hyduk looks like."

"I'm working on it. What we need is a picture."

"Right. 'Wanted: the Gunfighter—Preferably Alive.' "

He handed her the computer. After letting her hang for a few beats, he said, "Why don't you check your e-mail?" She jacked the laptop into the wall. At the top of the list was a message from santana.net with an attachment she couldn't immediately decipher. The message was clearly meant for Sandy, not her.

Sharing her service now, was he? What next? Would she start finding her toothbrush wet in the morning? Well, what the hell. How bad could that be?

To: amanci@washchron.com
From: jose@santana.net

Hawk, Abella could only find one shot. Hyduk's class picture at Bragg.
Summer of '59. I've blown it up for you. Hope it helps.

She clicked on the attachment. It turned out to be a scanned photograph slugged "Hyduk." She watched it take shape line by line as it came up on the screen. The picture, enlarged and blurred from Santana's zoom, showed a jug-eared kid of about twenty. The lids of his eyes drooped like shades drawn against the world.

"Shit," Sandy said. "Picture must be thirty years old. Thousands of soldiers look like that."

Abbie closed the file. As the face disappeared, she remembered something Dr. Hyduk had told her. The fight in that busted-up saloon in Pittsfield.

She took out her notebook. Pulling over the phone, she asked Massachusetts information for a number. The automatic dialer connected her to the *Berkshire Eagle*. "Give me the morgue," she said.

The operator was a man. "Who are you, lady? Brenda Starr? We haven't had a morgue since 1981. The old stuff's with Computer Services now."

"Back issues, too?"

"No. The bound copies are in Al Justin's office. Al doesn't let anyone use them unless he's in the room. Says people are worse than silverfish. They eat the past. Pull it apart."

"Let me talk to Al."

"Sure. But it won't do you any good."

The *Eagle*'s librarian sounded like a guy who would never see seventy again, but perked up when Abbie told him she was calling from the Newspaper Preservation Committee at the Library of Congress.

"We're going through old morgues," she said. "We're trying to find out what's left now that everyone's moving away from paper. You won't believe what gets thrown out."

"Morons," Al muttered. "I'd believe it."

"Anyway, I was hoping you could help us."

"How?"

"I've been calling people, giving them a specific story from twenty or thirty years back to look up. I'm asking them to send us a copy as a quality control. If your search pans out, we can send someone out to discuss preserving your records. You interested?"

"Hell yes."

"Wonderful. Here's the test. Vietnam stuff. During the last week of August 1969, Vietnam vet named Lawrence Hyduk got into a brawl in Pittsfield. That's H-Y-D-U-K."

"Might take some time."

"How long?"

"Half an hour or so."

"I'm impressed. Could you scan the story and any photographs and send them to me?"

"You mean e-mail?" He made the phrase sound as repulsive as *toe jam*.

"I know how you feel," she said quickly. "I hate it, too. But it's the only way we can keep track. But to save the past we have to scan it."

"All right," he said. "Half an hour."

She gave him santana.net as her address. When the librarian hesitated over the odd handle, she explained that she had wanted to use the name of Santayana, the philosopher, for the project, but it was two characters too long. "Great mind," Al said. "You read *The Last Puritan*?"

"Loved it," she lied. God would forgive her.

Just before lunch, she checked her mail. For a man who hated cyberspace, Al had been fast. The story was only a few graphs lifted from the police blotter, but the picture was good. Very good. The war had carved Hyduk's face, his head was shaved, his eyes said nothing, as if his interior lights had all burned out, taking with them his soul.

The picture was black and white. Looking closely, Abbie thought she could see a difference in tone along the right side of the forehead. She imported the picture into Photoshop and blew it up. The difference was stronger now. She selected flesh tones and colored the photo. Then she clicked on the lasso tool and drew it around the paler parts of Hyduk's head. When she finished, she had defined an area about the size of a human hand. The hand had talons stretching back along the side of the head, across a dark hole where a kid's jug ear had been blown away.

She went to the paint tool and colored the ragged patch pale red.

It was as if something inhuman had reached over and torn away half of Hyduk's scalp. Moving back to the color palette, she picked a grayish white and used it to replace the red. Imposed over the pale flesh of Hyduk's ravaged face, she now saw his scar.

"Jesus," she whispered, pointing to the monitor.

"I think our ghost just developed a hood ornament," Sandy said. "Let's go find him."

FORTY-NINE

★ Whitefish ★

On the road into Whitefish, they stopped at a convenience store for gas and directions. The clerk told them they'd find the post office on Baker Street across from the Golden Spike.

They found the Golden Spike with no trouble. The place was impossible to miss. It was on the ground floor of an old dry goods store, two stories, with a wooden false front that lengthened its shadow. The windows were crammed with gear out of pawn: chain saws streaked with grime, shotguns and rifles, a scuffed saddle with the stiff loops of an old riata thrown over the horn. Up on the second floor, a large sign in the dusty window said SPACE FOR RENT.

The post office was modern, clean, soulless. Box 1093 was in the middle of the bottom row of mailboxes on a wall opposite the front window. It was big enough to hold a sheaf of checks and a case or two of whatever else Hyduk was sending himself through the U.S. Mail.

The postal clerk inside the building shook her black bangs when they asked who rented Box 1093.

"We don't give out names. You wouldn't want us to give out yours, now, would you?"

The clerk was a small woman, middle thirties, a formalist in a neatly pressed blouse and gray skirt.

"It's critical that we find this person," Sandy snapped.

"Well, Mr. Ness," the clerk said dryly, "since you're traveling without your FBI badge, why don't you do what any normal citizen would do?"

"And what might that be, ma'am?"

"Send him a letter. You've got the box number. Ever hear of 'Occupant'?"

"Great idea," Abbie said.

"Are you crazy? He'd flush like a sage hen. Two minutes after he slit open the envelope he'd be gone. We'd never get another shot."

"I wonder if we might talk to the postmaster?" Abbie asked the clerk. Offering Abbie a sisters-in-suffering nod at Sandy, the woman pushed a button behind the counter, and a small gate swung open.

"Bang on Tad Willey's door," the woman said, pointing across the mailroom. "Maybe he'll help you." Straightening the sheets of stamps in her drawer, she looked past them. "Next," she said.

They went through the gate. "You take point," Sandy told Abbie. "You're better at this than me." When they got to the office marked "Postmaster," she rapped on the door.

"Come in."

The voice was a deep bass, about two octaves below middle C. From behind the door, it sounded like an idling tractor. They entered and found the postmaster at the end of a long table sorting through bright posters splashed with Technicolor reds and greens, oranges, yellows and purples. The posters featured birds and flowers from the real world along with a celebrity cat, duck and rabbit from the world of cartoons.

"Some days I don't know if I'm running the mail or a day care center," Tad Willey said cheerfully, his voice grinding along in first gear. He was a short stocky man with massive shoulders, and a steel-gray crew cut, pushing sixty. "What can I do you for?" he asked them.

Abbie took out the retouched photograph of Hyduk. "We're trying to find this guy," she said. "He has a box here and we thought you might have seen him when he came in to pick up his mail."

Willey put on a pair of wire-rim glasses. "Don't believe so," he said.

"Are you sure?"

"All that stuff on his noggin. You don't forget a mark like that."

He pushed the photograph back across the table. Before she could figure out how to make a second run at him, Sandy blurted out: "He uses the name Henry Emerson. He rents Box 1093."

The postmaster looked at Sandy as if he had just dropped a toad on the table. "Well, now," he said. "I wouldn't know that, would I, unless I looked it up?"

"Why don't you do that? I mean, see where he lives? It must be in your records." The impatience had come back into Sandy's voice. Abbie shot him a warning glance. Too late.

"Nah, I couldn't do that. Against regulations. But I tell you what, you're welcome to stand out there and wait for Mr. Who-ever he is. Mail pickup's open twenty-four hours a day, seven days a week." He took off the glasses. "Sunday, you could take off a few hours and go to church. Try the power of prayer, pray for patience. Might do you some good, son."

*   *   *

When they were outside, Abbie took Sandy's arm. He was stiff with rage. "What now?" she asked, resting her cheek against his shoulder. "Should we go back to the lodge?"

Instead, he walked quickly across the street and into the Golden Spike. In the back, behind a glass counter filled with cameras and Indian jewelry, a fat kid in an orange flannel hunt-ing shirt that bulged out over his Levi's was cleaning a 12 gauge.

"Borrowing or buying?" He wiped the oil off his fingers with a clean rag.

"Renting," Sandy said. "How much is the room upstairs?"

"Man, you don't want that place. There's only the old couch Lester left when he moved to Seattle. Why don't you try Sleep Tite up the road? They rent half days."

"Two weeks. How much?"

The kid put down the rag and looked at the cash register, an old hand-crank number in polished nickel silver. A price tag of $350 was stuck below the crank. If you could buy the register for three or four bills, Sandy figured, two weeks' rent ought to come cheaper.

"I'll give you eighty bucks," he said.

"Hunnert."

"Eighty."

"Okay, eighty, it's yours."

The kid took two keys out from under the counter. "This one's for the front door," he said. The second was on a chain with a red rubber tag that said FISH, DON'T FUCK, a gift from some outfit called Montana Zero Growth. "The door back there goes upstairs." He pointed to the rear of the store. "Lock 'em both when you go out."

Sandy bent over the glass counter. In the case was a battered pair of field glasses. He pulled a twenty out of his wallet.

"I'll take those, too."

"You're kidding me." The kid pushed back the bill. "You got Zeiss lenses there. Two hunnert."

"Take it or leave it."

The kid reached for the twenty. "I bet you two know some tricks." He leered at Abbie.

"Whatever," she shrugged. No need to get Sandy going for this jerk's throat. The room smelled of spilled beer and ammonia. Pushed against one wall was a couch with cracked leather cushions. "Give me a hand," Sandy said. They nudged the couch in front of the window, just far enough back so it couldn't be seen from the street. Sandy dropped onto one of the torn cushions. It gave out a small sigh of stale air. Unwrapping the strap on the binoculars, he directed them out the window until the post office swam out of the blur.

"C'mere," he said. Abbie was still standing at the end of the couch, as if by closing her eyes she might make the whole room vanish. Sandy motioned for her to join him.

"What've you got?" she asked him. He handed her the glasses. Raising them to her eyes, she saw Post Office Box 1093.

*　　*　　*

The next day was Thanksgiving. When they came out of the lodge, the mountaintops across the valley were white with new snow. Abbie unlocked the two doors in the Golden Spike, and Sandy horsed a green cooler full of beer and provisions up to the second floor.

Dropping onto the couch, he popped a can of Coors. A little early in the morning, but what the hell, it was Thanksgiving.

Abbie was sitting at the other end of the couch. He pulled her over to him and began to nuzzle her. "I was just thinking . . ."

"Well, you can stop. Not here. Noooooooo way. This place's about as romantic as an Arab toilet."

Sandy tried to kiss her.

"I'm serious," she said, pushing him back. "This trip isn't

just about getting laid, is it? For you, I mean. Because it's not for me."

He looked at the ceiling. The place hadn't been painted for twenty years. Cobwebs hung from the moldings. Above the radiator, a curled strip of flypaper studded with tiny black corpses was twisting in the thermals.

"You know what?" he said. "Let's get out of here."

They spent the rest of the afternoon driving in the mountains. At the top of one windswept ridge, Sandy pulled over and they raced across a pure-white field of snow. They followed a bobcat's tracks that disappeared into a dark stand of fir. The air was cold. It was like breathing pure oxygen. She felt stoned. They were panting from the run when he kissed her.

That evening he took her back to the Buffalo Cafe. The place smelled of fresh bread and simmering stock. Great slabs of turkey arrived, arranged on their platters next to mashed potato mountains stained red at the foothills by cranberry sauce. They washed it all down with a bottle of Napa Valley Riesling they'd brought with them. At the lodge they made love twice, then slept like children.

Friday morning they took up their positions at the observation post early. For the first few hours, the watch was exciting. But when the day dragged on with only a few housewives and out-of-work loggers coming in to pick up mail, their nerves began to fray. It didn't get any better Saturday or Sunday. By the end of Wednesday afternoon they were hardly speaking to each other.

The next afternoon, just before four, Abbie was reading the editorials in the local paper, working her way through the moral calculus of how many broke loggers were equal to a virgin forest of spotted owls, when she saw Sandy jump up and grab the field glasses.

"So that's how the sonuvabitch does it," he said. "Come on. Move."

He was down the stairs and halfway across the street before she caught up with him. Ten yards up from the post office, Sandy slowed down to a walk.

A small figure in an olive-drab parka and cammo pants was just closing Box 1093.

His gloves were lying at his feet. The end of a green envelope stuck out from under the arm of his green parka. When he stood up, she saw that he was just a boy, no more than fifteen or sixteen.

Sandy motioned silently for her to get the car. Stepping behind a parked van, Sandy stayed out of sight until the boy came out, looked right and left, and took off up the block. When the kid had a 50-yard lead, Sandy started along the sidewalk behind him.

Abbie eased the car into low and shadowed them. At the corner, the boy turned right onto Railway Street and walked three blocks, past the rear of the minibrewery and onto the edge of the Northern Pacific freight yard. A Ford pickup, 1966, dark green, was parked on an oily strip of dirt next to the tracks. The tailgate was down. As the boy walked up, a man in matching parka and pants opened the door on the driver's side and got out.

He was smaller than Sandy expected, wiry, five-ten. He had pulled a black nylon do-rag over his head, the same kind bloods wore in Nam to keep their hair out of their eyes.

Sandy broke into a run. Before the driver saw him, he had closed most of the distance to the truck. For a moment, the guy hesitated. Then he called an order to the boy, who vaulted into the back of the Ford.

Sandy heard the engine kick over. He doubled his speed. Collapsing on the snub-nose hood of the Ford, his breath coming in ragged gasps, he held up his hand.

The driver leaned on the horn and gunned the engine. Sandy didn't move. Picking up speed, Abbie roared up and banged on the driver's window.

"It's okay, Larry," she shouted. "Be cool. We're friends."

The engine kept running, but the window came down slowly. For the first time, she could see his face. The pale scar tissue started below the bottom edge of the do-rag, the talons disappearing under the black nylon.

"Who the hell are you?"

"Your brother sent us," Abbie said.

"I got no brothers."

"Yeah, you do," Sandy said, coming up to the window. "More than one."

"Is that right? Like I said, who the fuck are you?"

"Sandy Caine. Special Forces. My dad was Lieutenant Alexander Caine."

Hyduk pulled back as if Sandy had taken a swing at him. "Prove it."

"You served with him in I Corps. ODA 351. Captain Taylor was the commander."

Sandy still had his hand sticking out toward the window.

Hyduk hawked a lunger and spit it on Sandy's open palm. He slammed the engine into gear. The wheels, spinning in the dirt, threw black grit over Sandy and Abbie.

Choking, they ran to their car. By the time they got it started, the Ford was already nearing the end of the freight yard. "No way, you bastard," Sandy said. The Ford wheeled away from the tracks and shot off down a dirt road that skirted the southern rim of the lake. After half a mile it began to rise along the shoulder of a mountain. Sandy tore after it, bumping, weaving, cursing himself for not renting a four-wheeler. The road narrowed to a logger's track. Sharp twists and secondary tracks shot off on both sides. For a while, rounding the longer curves, Sandy was able to get glimpses of the pickup. Then he lost it.

"Sonuvagoddamnfuckingbitch."

He pounded on the wheel as they came burning around a bend into a short straightaway that ended in a Y. A steel guard pole blocked the turn toward the left. Veering right, Sandy dropped into second and mashed the accelerator to the floor. The track rose sharply to a blind crest. Like a demented beetle, the little car shot over the top, its wheels spinning in the air.

Abbie screamed.

Sandy slammed on the brakes. Spinning sideways, the car smacked into a giant fir.

The logger's track led directly into a chute about eight feet wide and fifty feet long, its sides deeply scarred by sliding logs. The chute spilled over a rib of solid granite, slick and gleaming in the alpen glow. It was a straight drop of 200 feet to the lake.

"My God," Abbie whispered.

"As in nearer to Thee," Sandy said. "You get the feeling we're not wanted?"

FIFTY

★ Whitefish ★

"Morning, young soldier. How's the chow?"

Too early in the morning for small talk. Sandy was poised to demolish the Grouse Mountain Lodge's Rancher Wake-up: two fried eggs sunny side up, hash browns with a rare, eight-ounce rib eye bleeding into the spuds.

The man standing in front of him across the table was thin, almost gaunt, with a face that looked as if it had been cut from the local rimrock. The angular lines under his eyes and along his jaw were a shade redder than the rest, whether from sunburn or good scotch, it was hard to say. Draw poker eyes, the look of a man hiding his cards while he dopes out yours. He said, "Some folks came in last night askin' about a guy with whitewalls travelin' with a redhead. Reckon that's you two."

"I'm not military," Sandy said.

"If you're not a soldier, I'm not from Montana. Good Lord, it's written all over you. Mind if I join you? Name's Tim Grattan. I pay the mortgage on this joint."

Sandy leaned over the table and shook the older man's hand. "SF?"

"Left the business in sixty-eight. My wife, Darlene, couldn't handle me being a movin' target."

"Where was that?"

"Mostly the Highlands, sometimes Cambodia and Laos when no one was lookin'."

The waitress came back with the coffee. Grattan stirred it thoughtfully. "Look, these guys came in last night had a Ford with Avis plates, same as that vehicle of yours except dark blue and no dents. Three of 'em. Said they were looking for a Captain Caine. Alexander Caine. Travelin' with a redheaded gal."

Abbie checked him to see if he was trying to bait her. He seemed unaware of the slip. Maybe the news about women hadn't gotten all the way through to Whitefish.

"Did you tell them we were staying here?" Abbie asked him.

"Nope."

"How come?"

"They looked like fuzz to me. Government or military. I thought maybe the captain was up here overstayin' a leave."

"Why didn't you turn me in?"

"Don't care too much for the government and I guess you could say I never liked MPs." He smiled at Abbie. "You talk about pokin' your nose in other people's business, miss . . ."

"Abbie Mancini."

"Okay. You don't know what it is until one of those starched pricks with the armband and stick starts coming at you—if you'll pardon my French."

"Total amnesty, Mr. Grattan. Will you help us? We're out here looking for a guy. Viet vet. He disappeared back east sometime in the early seventies. His brother told me he was living somewhere around here. We're pretty sure we hooked up with him yesterday—for about thirty seconds—but he blew us off."

"What's his name?"

"Hyduk. Lawrence Hyduk. He answers to Larry. By which I mean, if you say, 'Hey, Larry,' he tries to kill you."

Grattan shook his head.

"You ever heard of a Henry Emerson?" Sandy asked him.

"Hank? The Gunfighter? You betcha. Best leader I ever served with. First time I went in country was sixty-two, back when we weren't there, if you know what I mean. But I did a second tour in sixty-five, that's when I met the Gunfighter—"

"I was thinking about someone else." Sandy paused. "Did you know Robert Hester?"

"Bullet Bob? Sure did. Good man. Silver Star at Plei Me. Sort of a local war hero. Why?"

"They said down at the bank that Hester knew Hyduk. Hyduk was using Hank Emerson's name to hide an account."

"The Night Stalker. That's who you're trackin'? You must've been talking to Mave."

"She told us Hester was willing to bend regulations to set up Hyduk's account."

"Look, Captain Caine, this is gettin' a little more personal than we like to be out here. Before we go any further can I ask you a question?"

"Sure. Fire away."

"That's a pretty hefty name you're carryin' for a guy who wants people to believe he's no soldier. You comin' from where I think you're comin' from?"

"My grandfather's John Pershing Caine."

"Only one way J. P. Caine could have a grandson—you'd have to be Alex Caine's boy. I'll be goddamned. I didn't even know he had a son. No wonder you're sneakin' around in dark glasses."

Sandy's jaw tightened.

"Look, no reflection on you. Goddamn it, sometimes I just can't control my own tongue."

"Did you know my father, Mr. Grattan?" Sandy's voice was as cold as dry ice smoking on warm ground.

"No, Captain. I only knew *about* him."

Grattan's eyes said "I raise."

"What—what do you know?"

"No way you get an outfit wiped out the way ODA 351 was without people wonderin' about it. The thing is, no one ever knew what happened, really. All you had was shithouse rumor. But one night, it must have been in early sixty-eight, after Tet, anyway, I was sittin' in the officers club bar at Bragg. We were gettin' our ass kicked. There was a lot of bitterness. Anyway, this major comes in and takes the stool next to me. He orders a double bourbon. I guess he saw the ribbon. Remember how that green and yellow Vietnam thing stuck out on your chest?"

"Still does."

"Yeah, for a few old farts. You got home, you didn't know whether to be proud of it or hide it under your mashed potatoes."

"Proud of it, I'd say."

"Yeah, well, you had to be there, I guess. Anyhow, the major sat there all evening knockin' back the bourbon. By ten o'clock he was shitfaced. Started mumblin' about it bein' our own damn fault we were losin'. Man, he took it from the top right down to the bottom. A fool in the White House, boot-lickin', brass-runnin' MACV, hurry-up trainin', too many incompetent officers into musical chairs.

"Then, I remember this because it interested me at the time, this major said, 'You could see the whole thing comin' right from the moment ODA 351 got greased.' "

"Now what would you say if I told you the story could be total, one hundred percent bullshit?"

"I'd say you have a problem."

"You know," Sandy said, pushing back the plate of cold death in front of him, "that's just what I've been thinking."

"I'd like to hear about it."

Grattan insisted on picking up the tab. He invited the two of them to his office. It was small, neat, unpretentious, with a stone fireplace cut into one of the walls. On another wall he had mounted half a dozen large topographical maps of the mountains and forests surrounding Whitefish, and on the wall behind his desk was a framed board displaying his Special Forces insignia, a Silver Star, a Purple Heart, jump wings and a Combat Infantryman's Badge, all pinned to a piece of dark green felt.

Grattan pointed to two plaid chairs flanking the fireplace.

Sandy ran through what Perkins had told him in Mogadishu. Abbie retraced the track that had led them from Pittsfield to Whitefish and their brush with Hyduk.

Grattan stood up and looked at one of the maps that showed a pale blue arc of lake cutting into green forests marked with wavy contour lines. "Let's say Hyduk and Henry Emerson and the Night Stalker are all the same guy, and let's say you got a piece of him yesterday. Didn't you say he disappeared in the early seventies?"

Abbie nodded.

"If he and Bob Hester were tight, he got here before April of seventy-five."

"Why?" Abbie said. "How can you be sure?"

"Because on May 1, Bob went over to the other side of the lake, put his sixteen-gauge shotgun in his mouth and pulled both triggers. They found him two days later minus his arms and legs. The bears had gotten to him. No note. Just a copy of the Missoula newspaper with that photograph of the choppers taking the last Americans off the roof at the embassy in Saigon. You remember. We had to boot off the locals to get away.

"Bob used to sit at the end of the bar every Saturday night. All night. Drinkin' brandy sodas. The early part of the evenin' he'd be okay. Around eleven he'd start talking to himself. I believe the operative phrase was 'Why the fuck did we do it?' That's all he said. Over and over. When it got to be somethin' like 'Wide-fuckdoodad,' around one o'clock, I'd put him in his Caddie and drive him home. Went that way for a coupla years. Until he killed himself.

"But he and Hyduk must've hooked up before that. You said this guy seemed right at home on those loggin' roads. You think he lives over there?"

"I didn't see any camp," Sandy said. "But he moved like he was on his own ground."

"Okay, they did some homestead grants out here in the early seventies. Most people wanted land they could farm. You couldn't give away that forest land over there. It's all up and down, steep, lotta rocks, deadfalls, all that stuff he dragged you through.

"But Bob told me he'd helped a coupla longhairs buy at the far end of the lake. Hermits, dopers, commune people, survivalists. Hyduk could have been one of them."

He went to his desk and punched a number.

"Louise, it's Tim Grattan. Need Libby up in Deeds."

There was a pause. "Courthouse down in Kalispell," he said, muffling the receiver with his hand. "If he bought, he's there."

"Morning, Libby. How's Travis? They fix his leg? I see the Bobcats lost fourteen to six last week without him. Junior, isn't he? Well, he'll be back in there next season, and you tell him I'll be comin' to see him. Listen, I'm tryin' to track down an old Army buddy who bought land up at the north end of Whitefish Lake, sometime between 1970 and 1975. Could you look at the book for me? Can't be too many deeds. Name's Hyduk. You might also check Emerson."

For several minutes, he stood holding the phone. Then he thanked Libby and rang off.

When he turned around he was smiling like a kid who's just pulled a silver dollar out of a window well. "Got him," he said. Pulling a pair of reading glasses from his pocket, he went over to the map.

"Here," he said, stabbing a pencil into a swatch of green webbed with contour lines. "Tract forty-seven. Four hundred acres. Twelve thousand dollars. Nineteen seventy-one. Financing by the Flathead Credit Union. Robert Hester cosigned the note. Purchaser, Henry Emerson."

Grattan went back to his desk, fumbled in the top drawer and pulled out a battered compass. "Baptized in I Corps," he said, handing it to Sandy. "Blood and beer. Take it. You're gonna need it out there. If it was me, I'd leave that guy the hell alone."

FIFTY-ONE

★ Whitefish ★

Big Mountain Outfitters was in a converted dry goods store next to a small strip mall at the opposite end of Baker Street. The cases near the cash register were filled with guns—rifles of every caliber, shotguns of every action and gauge, pistols and revolvers, little handguns you could slip into a lady's purse, hogshank magnums that would stop a charging moose.

Behind the counter, the owner, Richard Alexander, a guy with a truck driver's belly and a face like a side of beef, lifted a stack of bumper stickers. He was polishing the top of the case with Windex and a red bandanna. Abbie picked up one of the stickers. It said: I LOVE ANIMALS—THEY'RE DELICIOUS. The guns gleamed under glass.

"You folks lost?" Alexander said mildly, looking at Grattan's compass. It was dangling from a worn nylon lanyard around Sandy's wrist. Sandy shoved it in his pocket. "Do you sell topos?" he asked. "We're going north, beyond the lake."

"Three guys came in yesterday, I think they bought the last one. Elk hunters." Alexander led them to a large wooden case. "You're in luck. Must've misfiled this one last season. Supposed to be in with sections twenty to thirty, not thirty to thirty-six, but I get careless sometimes."

After they got back in the car, Abbie waited until they were past the freight yard and well down the gravel road next to the lake before she broke the silence.

"Rubber Jack?"

"Could be."

"The same sort of thing happened with Sweeny."

"Yep."

Two answers, three syllables. "I watched Gary Cooper movies growing up, pups. You're not him. That laconic shit—it does *not* turn me on. What should we do?"

"Find Hyduk. Fast."

"Thanks a lot, Coops."

★　　★　　★

The road was worse than a maze. At each side branch, Sandy got out of the car and checked for signs of the Ford. *Nada*. They rose through aspens, forded a shallow creek and moved into the jack-pines and fir. Above the ridgetops, dark gray clouds began ballooning up ominously.

Ten yards before the Y in the road where Hyduk had lost them, Sandy stopped the car. The guardrail had been moved. It now cut off the fork leading to the log chute. The long steel bar was set on cinder blocks dug into the earth. A small motor, like the kind used to raise and lower garage doors, was mounted on the blocks. Underneath, in a small steel box, were a series of old truck batteries that had been hooked up to power the motor controlling the guardrail.

"The nut job probably switched it from his truck."

Sandy headed back toward the car.

"He went that-a-way," Abbie said, pointing back to the left fork. "That was yesterday."

Instead of going up the road, he darted into the woods. The ground was rocky, but the trees were far apart, and they moved quickly, following roughly parallel to the logging road. After what must have been half a mile, Sandy stopped and waited for her to catch up.

"Okay, over there."

He set off for a gap in the underbrush. She found him a few minutes later sitting on a stump between a huge boulder and a dark wall of forest. In front of him, cutting across the road was a trench about two feet wide and three feet deep hidden under pine boughs and withered aspen leaves.

"A real axle breaker," she said, nudging the boughs with the toe of her shoe. She looked at Sandy. Sandy's hands were covered with dirt where he had dug out the car trap. He had dark smudges of earth and sap on his forehead and under his eyes where he had wiped away the sweat.

"Neck breaker's more like it."

"Maybe Grattan was right about leaving him alone."

"No fucking chance. This guy is beginning to piss me off."

"How are we going to get around this thing?"

Hyduk had filled the trench with jagged rocks and tree branches studded with nails.

"We're not."

The car was just down the road around another blind curve. Hyduk had obviously been counting on Sandy to keep driving at warp speed. They would never have been able to stop in time. Sandy put the map up against the driving wheel and looked at it for a long time, running his finger over the contour lines, looking for something he had missed on the way up.

"It's the creek," he said. Craning around, he threw the car into reverse and headed down the mountain. Twenty minutes later, he pulled over at the near side of the little stream they had crossed earlier that morning.

"Wait here."

She watched him disappear up the bank of the creek. The water had dropped with the season. It was about 10 feet wide, and no more than a few inches deep.

She was alone. The rushing water should have been soothing, but she was not a country girl—peace, Tim Grattan—and certainly not a mountain woman. The woods are lonely, dark and deep . . . Frost and snow flurries, she thought, trying to buck herself up. It didn't work. Below the surface she felt the first coppery tingle of fear.

She heard a tremendous splash in the middle of the creek. But when she looked up, all she saw was Sandy. He was wading down toward her, the water barely up to the ankles of his Timberlands. He came splashing up to the car looking like a Labrador retriever with soggy paws.

"You're making a lot of noise for a scout, Tonto."

"We're getting close to him now, Abbie. Real close. I *don't* want to surprise this guy. Be like waking a papa grizzly and telling him to get the hell out of his cave."

"What did you find up there?"

"I was stupid on the way up. I assumed he was using the logging roads. It didn't occur to me that anyone would go off road. *Could* go off road, for chrissakes. That old Ford of his has high clearance. The creekbed is dredged out for about fifty or sixty meters upstream. I should've figured it out sooner—it's an old Russian trick. He had it made. He just hung a right into the water and let us chase the road. Came out on the far bank. Come on, I'll show you. How're your boots?"

"Drier than yours."

"Mine are waterproof. Stay on the bank."

He ducked into the woods, making a wide buttonhook to the right and coming out about 100 yards upstream, where the creek flattened into a sandbar about 30 feet across. A narrow meadow ran from the sandbar over to a low, small promontory sticking out from the mountainside.

"Mine dump, silver, maybe gold." Gray tailings spilled away from the old shaft, creating a flat space out in front. Heavy timbers, black with age, lined the entrance. In the shadowy hole behind them, Abbie could just make out the snub nose of the green Ford.

Threading away from the mine, a path no wider than a deer trail came down to the creek. About 50 yards farther upstream, the meadow petered out, and the creek disappeared into a canyon. The trail crossed the creek, running along the far bank behind a tangled stretch of alders. Towering above them was a rock face of basalt, blackened by volcanic action and fractured into cubes of stone.

"Devil's dice box," Sandy said. "Let's roll 'em."

Abbie started for the path. Sandy grabbed her arm. "No more trails. He owns them. This way." He started up the near side of the stream.

The canyon walls closed in on them, growing more and more narrow the farther they went. Like receding wings on a small stage, the rock walls stuck out into the creek from both sides until they finally reached a spot so tight only one person could slip through at a time.

Sandy went first. The passage was about 10 inches wide and 16 feet long. Outcroppings of damp rock vaulted across the stream like the arches of a roof. He had to inch his way along, twisting sideways.

"Holy shit, look at this. Better get up here."

When she stooped under the last arch and came out, she saw him standing at the foot of a low crag looking upstream. By some freak of nature, the water had cut an expanse around 100 feet long and 40 feet high into the stone walls of the canyon.

They widened, curving upward to a crack of gray sky 500 or 600 feet above them.

Projecting out from a low shelf cut into the left wall, a ledge jutted into the stream. On top of the ledge was an odd structure made of basalt blocks and what looked like old timbers from the mine. The roof, impossibly, was solid concrete. Twining above and below the ledge and all along the banks up and down stream were endless coils of rusty barbed wire.

"Oh man," Abbie said softly. "What is it?"

"Command post. I'd say we just found ODA 351."

Suddenly she heard an odd whizzing sound, then the sharp report of steel ricocheting off stone. She felt a sharp pain in her arm. Her eyes shifted wildly to Sandy. On his forehead, just below the smudge of dirt, she saw a bright splash of blood.

As she fell, she heard a scream above her.

From the crag, a man dressed completely in black dropped on Sandy like a plummeting eagle, talons outstretched.

Not a bald eagle. This one wore a black do-rag. And he had a 6-inch trench knife in one claw.

She heard a soft whump as he landed on Sandy and put the knife against his throat. "Smokin'," he said.

"Smokin'," he said again, louder this time.

Suddenly, his hand dropped.

"Jesus Christ, Wolf, is that you?"

He slid the knife into a sheath hooked onto his web belt.

"Goddamn it, Lieutenant, Cap'n Taylor tole you 'bout forgetting the fucking password. I could've killed you."

FIFTY-TWO

It was like those freeze frames during an accident, the scream of the brakes, the steering wheel torn from your hands, the screech of tearing metal, the smash of shattering glass. Abbie watched it all. Within her body the last levee against panic washed out. A tremendous roaring filled her ears.

She was running. Running like deer, splashing wildly down the stream, plunging into the rock crack, scraping against the stone walls of the narrow defile. And then she was hurtling through the trees, branches whipping her face, tearing at her clothes.

Where the meadow opened up, her foot caught a snaggling root and she sprawled forward, falling like a wounded animal into the tall, wet grass.

Help. Get help.

For a moment she lay there facedown, her heart whumping against her ribs. Bastards. Crazy macho bastards. Damn bloody head-bashing heart-busting killers. All of them. Every damn one of them.

She looked up. Through the grass she could see the old mine not far ahead of her. Panting, she scrambled up the slope of tailings and stumbled over to Hyduk's Ford.

Locked.

Shit. Shit. Shit.

She felt a trickle of something warm run down her arm.

Looking down, she saw a small black blotch on her sleeve. She remembered the whine of the ricochet and the stab of pain in her arm.

I'm wounded.

For some reason, the recognition made her laugh. A long, wild, relieved burst of laughter. Reaching down, she pulled a small bit of steel from her arm. It came out as easily as a splinter from a child's finger. She pressed down on the cut for a few seconds and the bleeding stopped.

Okay, now, find the car. Get help. Save Sandy.

Jogging quickly now. Under control, though for the first few yards she had to force herself not to go flat out the way she had come down the stream. A few minutes later she came out to where the creek joined the main stream. Following the current, she moved on until she could see the bend up ahead where they had pulled off the logging trail. The car was there where they had left it.

Two cars.

She stopped. A second vehicle was parked behind theirs. Some logger must've thought they were lost and stopped. She started running down the road, waving her arms. The car was a blue Ford. Inside, she saw three men in dark green camouflage gear. Hunters, not loggers. Good. They wouldn't have to waste time going to town for the cops.

"Hey, you guys. Could you help me?" she shouted.

The driver's door swung open. "Hell, yes, Miss Mancini. We've been looking for you."

A man built like a bricklayer stepped out. Under his eyes, he had the same smudges of black she had seen on Sandy and his men in Mogadishu. In his hand he was holding a 9-millimeter pistol. The pistol was pointed at her face.

FIFTY-THREE

★ Whitefish ★

"Come on, Lieutenant. You gotta wake up now."

The water splashed over Sandy's head and ran down his scalp. Cold, freezing cold. Sandy spluttered, opened his eyes. He was lying on a field cot in a small room. Gray light slanted in from the slit windows cut through one wall. Hyduk was bent over him holding a canteen aloft, dabbing at Sandy's forehead with a blood-soaked rag.

"Hey, Wolf. You got any idea how lucky you are?"

Wolf?

"You should be dead. Password's *weed*. When I said smokin' you should've said 'weed.' "

Sandy sat up and touched his head. New knob to show Melba.

"You come sloshing up the creek like you never seen it before. Charlie's not that dumb. I started to pull off, but I slipped and the round went high. I had to go down to finish the job. Man, the knife was on your juggler when I saw it was you, Wolf. Christ, what would they give me for killing an officer?"

Wolf. No mistaking it now.

"Where's Abbie?"

"Who?"

"The woman. I had a woman with me."

"Oh you did now?" Hyduk looked again at Sandy's head. "Maybe you're confused. This ain't downtown in the ville, Lieutenant. You want to get laid, better ask Captain Taylor to send you down to Nha Trang and while you're at it, have 'em take a look at that scratch on your head. Piece of rock must've clipped you. Nothing that'll affect your dick, Lieutenant."

"What the fuck are you talking about, Larry?"

"Hey, look, Lieutenant Caine, I think—"

"It's Captain Caine."

"Is that a fact?" Hyduk was looking at him as if he were the one who had blown his circuits. "They promote you since this morning? What's Captain Taylor gónna say when he finds out this team's got two captains now? What about it, Wolf?"

"Who the hell's Wolf?"

"Who the hell's Wolf? You, Lieutenant Caine. You must be concussed to shit, man."

Hyduk's eyes had a dark haze floating in them. Sandy glanced around the bunker. It was clean and dry, surprisingly warm. One wall was lined with books. *Street Without Joy, Fire in the Lake*, the bulky volumes that made up a bound set of the Pentagon Papers on Vietnam. Beside the cot, the only other furnishings were a small handmade table and a wooden chair. The table was piled with neatly arranged stacks of books and notepads next to an empty shell case that held a fistful of pencils, pens and felt-tip markers.

Hyduk was living like a soldier in the cell of a monk.

Spooky. How whacko did you have to be to fall into this kind of time warp? "Get this, Sergeant Hyduk," he barked, sounding like a drill sergeant bracing a green recruit. "I'm not Lieutenant Caine. You're thirty years out of step. Snap out of it."

The words stung Hyduk. His hand shot toward his head. For a moment Sandy thought he meant to salute. Instead, he tore off the do-rag, uncovering the long fingers of scar tissue from the old wound. Even in the dim light, they were a deep purple. He sank on the cot where Sandy had been lying and buried his head in his hands.

When he finally looked up, the smoky haze was gone from his eyes. "It happened again, didn't it?" he said.

"Yeah, man. It happened."

Hyduk lapsed into silence.

"Larry?"

"Yeah."

"Know who I am?"

"No fuckin' idea, man." Hyduk stood up. Sandy saw the circuits sparking. "All right, got it," Hyduk said. "You're the guy who bushwhacked me in town. Chased my ass up the mountain. I forget your name."

"Sandy Caine. Captain Alexander Caine. I told you yesterday."

Hyduk sat down at the table. He looked at his hands.

"That must've been when I freaked out."

★　　★　　★

A mile down the canyon, Abbie started to raise her hands.

"No need, Miss Mancini," said the man with the 9-millimeter. "This isn't some western."

He laughed. The rear doors opened and two guerrillas in identical combat camo eased out. Both of them had Uzis.

"Hey, let's slow down here," she said. "I don't know how you know my name, but there's someone up the stream and he needs help."

"Is that right?" the first man said. "Sergeant Hyduk too much for him?"

"Put her down, Kip," said one of the guerrillas. "She'll get in the way."

The bricklayer reached into the car and pulled out a sawed-off shotgun. "If you want to see how it works, just open your mouth or run."

"I hear you."

"Good. Now let's just go on back the way you came. All together. It'll be more friendly that way. And, don't you say anything unless I talk to you first, got that?"

"Got it."

"Excellent." He turned to the other two.

"Cox, you take the point. Miss Mancini and I will be right behind you with the directions." He smiled at her. "Laneer, you cover our ass. I want you fifty meters back. If anything goes wrong, scoot around the flank and bail us out, okay?"

Abbie looked at the sky. Above the ridges the clouds were massing, much darker now. Snow began to swirl through the green firs.

"Move out."

When they got to the meadow, Cox peeled off to check Hyduk's pickup. "Which way?" the bricklayer asked her. "Don't fuck with us, hon."

She looked to the left and saw Hyduk's trail, the one Sandy had avoided. "That way," she said, pointing to the little path snaking up the creek. The four of them moved along the trail quickly, stopping every 40 or 50 yards to get their bearings. The snow was coming in light flurries now. She looked up and saw it dusting the top branches of the firs.

They reached the place where the little stream joined the main current. It was still a few hundred yards to where the canyon narrowed. She looked up the trail. For the first 20 or 30 yards it was bare earth, hard packed. Then she saw, crossing the trail, three splashes of green and pale yellow. Fir boughs, aspen leaves. A fierce joy rose in her throat. A sensation she had never felt before. Yes, she said silently. Yes.

★   ★   ★

The scream from down the canyon tore into the bunker like a mountain lion's wail.

Sandy's hand flew up to his bloodstained head. Was *he* cracking up? Then he saw the smoke drifting back into Larry's eyes.

"We got visitors."

Hyduk's rifle was hanging by the door. A 300 Winchester Magnum. Thirty caliber with a McMillan M-40 sniper's stock and a 26-inch Lilja barrel, topped off with a Leupold Mark 4 16-power scope. He took it off its peg and headed for the door. "Let's do it," he said.

★   ★   ★

At the sound of Cox's scream, Kip shoved Abbie in front of him.

"You first, hon."

Staying close to the alders for concealment, they inched their way up the trail until they could hear moans and a man's voice cursing. Kip jabbed the shotgun in the small of Abbie's back. "Here's what's happening, hon," he said. "You're going to go up there and see what's bothering Cox. Then you're going to bring the news back to me. Just like you do for the *Chronicle*."

He pointed to a tree a few yards ahead of them. "I'll see you and Cox will too. From the sound of it, he's not in a very good mood right now—neither am I—and killing you would probably make us both feel a whole lot better about our work. So, don't wander away."

Pushing aside the alders, Abbie stepped into the middle of the trail and started up toward Cox. Hyduk had been a busy boy. Cox was sprawled on his back, jackknifed into a man-size version of the tank trap Hyduk had dug on the logging road. He had fallen onto a sharpened punji stake driven into the ground and hidden under the boughs and autumn leaves. The point and about 10 inches of the shaft had gone into his right calf just below the knee, coming out a few inches higher on the inside of his thigh. The torn leg of his combat trousers was soaked in blood.

"Help me," he whispered hoarsely. "Where's Kip?"

"On the way."

Abbie kneeled to examine the damage. Cox's other leg was folded under him at an acute angle. Probably broken. She heard Kip's breathing as he came up behind her. "Cox, you're a moron," he exploded. "Oldest trick in the book. How could you be so damn dumb?"

Up the trail, a tremendous racket erupted. Two snarling bull mastiffs, chestnut brown, eyes wild, yellow teeth slashing at the air, came hurtling toward them. Cox shriveled. When the huge dogs were 5 yards away, their legs gathering in a blur under their heavily muscled bodies, ready to spring, Kip flicked the stubby shotgun upward, fired, pumped and fired again.

The leaping mastiffs hit a wall of buckshot. One of them ploughed into the ground at Kip's feet like a downed MiG. The second, blown sideways, fell into the trench with Cox, and died with a high-pitched cry that sounded to Abbie, not so much different from the man's.

Kip kicked the muzzle of the mastiff at his feet. His boot came away with a slick black stain on the toe. "Good team," he said. "Too bad."

Laneer came over and the two of them lifted Cox off the punji stake. Kip bandaged Cox's leg, and they propped him against a tree with the Uzi across his lap.

"Here's the deal," Kip said to Cox. "I'm gonna leave you with Miss Mancini. We might need her a little bit later today. We'll come back after we're finished with the other two."

Cox nodded weakly.

Kip reached into his pocket and slammed fresh shells into the shotgun. Laneer picked up his Uzi and he fell in behind Kip. The two men moved up the trail.

★   ★   ★

When they were gone, Abbie sat down across from Cox. He looked like a soldier, but he was much older than Sandy. She put him in his late forties. In his eyes she saw hatred so simple and complete she almost had to admire it. The guy obviously loved his job.

"What are you going to do with me?" she asked him.

"That's up to Kip."

"What if it were up to you?"

"It's not. So shut the fuck up."

Snow was drifting down, blotting out the pink Rorschach around the dead mastiffs. Cox shivered. "Who are you after? Captain Caine or the guy up the pass?"

"What difference does it make, we've got all three of you, don't we?" A wave of pain crossed his face. She started to get up.

"Stay right there, bitch."

She heard a metallic clink as the Uzi shifted against the buttons on his jacket.

"You set me up, didn't you?"

The voice lower now, barely a whisper.

"Like, 'That way, we went that way,' " he said, mimicking her voice. And then: *"Fucking bitch. You knew."* He pointed the Uzi at her stomach. His finger tightened on the trigger.

She felt something zip past her shoulder.

A purple moon appeared in the center of Cox's chest. He smacked back against the tree. For an instant, his eyes looked surprised, then they rolled up in his head as he slid to the ground, tracking the same deep purple down the trunk.

There had been no sound. A hand touched her shoulder. She cringed.

"Are you all right?"

Sandy's hand was on the nape of her neck. She buried her face against his leg. When she was able to stop sobbing, she got slowly to her feet and wrapped her arms around him. "I didn't know if you were dead." She pressed against him, felt the warmth of his cheek.

"Wasn't my time to go."

She touched the crust of blood on his forehead.

"Goose egg. That's all. Larry missed."

"But I ran away, pups. I clutched and I ran."

"Doesn't matter. We all get scared. We all run. Sometimes it's a good idea."

"You don't, pups."

"Yeah, well, stick around. We'll see."

Hyduk stepped out of the woods. He walked over and looked down at Cox.

"Pretty good shot," Sandy said. "What were you, four hundred yards out?"

"Five hundred. It's the Lilja, ten-twist. The Leupold helps."

He walked over and kneeled beside the mastiffs. For a few seconds, he shut his eyes. Then, cuffing the backs of their heads as if they were still alive, he got up and came back to where Sandy and Abbie were waiting.

"Two left?" he said to Abbie.

"That's right. How did you know?"

He pointed down the trail. The footprints of Kip and Laneer were etched in the inch-deep snow. "It'll take 'em at least two hours to get to my CP. Take us fifteen minutes my way. Let's patch you up. We got plenty of time to put down those dog-killing bastards."

★   ★   ★

The bunker was still in near darkness when they got there. Hyduk lit a Coleman lantern on the table.

"Who's the Wolf, Larry?"

Sandy asked the question softly, trying not to rocket Hyduk while he was dressing their wounds. Hyduk stood up and went over to his wall of books. When he got back to the table, he was holding a photograph. A bunker. The snapshot looked moldy and smelled of the jungle. One corner of the picture was gone, as if it had been ripped away. A dark brown stain that looked like blood covered the bottom part of the image.

The rest was clear enough. Leaning against the front of the bunker, nine men in tee shirts were hoisting cans of beer, mugging for the camera. Standing in the dark, sandbagged entrance to the bunker, a guy with captain's bars on his green beret was flashing a V sign. Hyduk pointed to one of the kids with the beer. "That's me," he said. "Captain Taylor's there in the door."

Sandy picked up the photo. "Who's this?"

Hyduk hesitated.

"The Wolf," he said. "Your father."

Father. My father.

Sandy's head throbbed where the rock had glanced off. "You ever meet a guy named Perkins?" he asked Hyduk.

"Dan Perkins? I replaced him when he got hit. Never met him, but everybody said he was a good man. Why?"

"We got into some bad shit in Mogadishu together. Last summer. He told me about the Wolf and then he got waxed. I didn't believe him."

"Believe it."

Hyduk got up and went back over to his case of books. Pushing aside a three-inch volume bound in buckram and marked *U.S. Foreign Policy, 1964*, he pulled out the bottle of Johnny Walker Black hidden behind it. When he got back to the table, he poured three inches of scotch into an aluminum canteen cup.

"Look," he said, "I need to know what happened to you guys. All of you. In that picture."

"Long story, man."

"If you've got the story, Larry, believe me, we've got the time."

"Ain't that easy. I mean—" He stopped himself and Hyduk sat down on the cot. Only a couple of feet separated the two of them. "Fuck it. Okay, here's what I know." Sandy looked at his eyes. They were clear. "ODA 351 was the best outfit I ever served in," he said. "Aces. All the guys were pros. I was just the other side of eighteen when I signed up. That would have been in fifty-nine. I kept my nose clean because there was a judge back home waiting to throw me in the slammer and melt down the key. They sent me to Benning for basic and jump school. After that I went with the 101st Airborne at Fort Campbell. I liked the jumping, the weapons shit. But I still had some serious problems over following orders.

"Then I met up with Master Sergeant Jesse O. Giddons. Tough old Irish bastard from South Boston. Been in World War II, Korea. First time I got wise with him about some order, he grabbed me by the scruff of the neck and dragged me out behind the barracks and told me he was going to kick the bejusus out of me. He made it sound like *beejaysus*.

"Okay, so a noncom's not supposed to hit a private, right? Sergeant Giddons says, 'Hyduk, you could be a good soldier if you weren't such a fuckup. I still think you're worth my stripes, so after I kick all that Pittsfield bullshit out of you, I'm going to be draggin' what's left of you back and you're going to be the finest soldier in this battle group or I'll eat me own jump wings.' I swear. He said 'me wings.' Like some freaking four-hundred-pound leprechaun. I figured I was going to wipe the floor with the old fuck.

"So anyway, the whole company was out there behind the barracks. I was fast and I got in the first good punches, but, oh man, I wanna tell you, after that he kicked the living shit out of me just like he promised. I went back to the latrine and looked in the mirror—I was all puffed up and covered with blood—and suddenly it hit me he would lose his stripes if anyone turned him in. If I ratted him out, let's say. And I realized he had done it because the old leprechaun fuck cared. And man, I lost it. Right there. I sat there on the toilet and I fucking cried.

"Guys started coming in and they thought I was crying because he whipped my ass. The funny thing was, I didn't give a shit that they saw me bawling. After that I got my shit together. Next couple of years I made corporal, then sergeant. No kidding, my father and brainy-ass brother couldn't fucking believe it.

"Then one day, I guess it was in sixty-one, after Kennedy got elected, they came into Campbell looking for weapons guys for a new outfit, Special Forces. I didn't even pay attention to the name. All I knew was you got to go jump out of airplanes and shoot bad guys and wear that cool green beret, and which is what I was born to do.

"They sent me to Nam the first time in sixty-three. Did two tours. Second year I was down at Muc Hoa in the Delta. They made me the team sniper. It was far out, man. I thought I was real hot shit. I had 111 kills. Every time I greased someone I cut a little notch out of my stock and after a while they started calling me Toothpick Charlie, nothing left of that stock but a toothpick and a shitload of dead VC.

"I used to go out in the bush and hunt. I'd lie there in the prone overlooking some VC trail, leaves and shit covering me, not moving for hours until Charlie showed up for me to wax his ass. It was perfect. I was happier than shit. Then one day I was out there and a column of dudes came out of the elephant grass. Seven of them. I was using a telescopic sight and a silencer. So first I picked off the last man in the column. Shhh. He goes down. Next guy doesn't even hear. I pick off the next, and the next. None of them fucking hear anything, man. I nailed five, then the sixth grunted and the leader started to turn around and I squeezed off a quick shot.

"I hit her between the eyes. A woman, man. A beautiful face, and I'm looking through the scope and it turns to chili fucking con carne."

He stopped. Sandy looked over to the cot. Hyduk's right hand was twitching. Without thinking, he jammed it under his thigh like a man who has mastered a little trick so long ago that he no longer notices it.

"I felt like a fucking murderer, man. But they gave me a medal. You heard of General Throckmorton? Throck the Rock? He called me down to Saigon and gave me the DSC and then they sent me back to Bragg as a sniper instructor."

Sandy stood up from the table. "What does all this have to do with Wolf, with ODA 351?"

"I'm getting there, man. I told you it was a long story. You want me to stop?"

"Shit, no, man."

"Right, so after I got the medal I went home. I thought maybe things would be different. Big mistake. In about two seconds my brother and father were all over me. Dumb fucks. I went out and got blistered and busted up two guys. So this time I was a war hero and the judge didn't give me jail time. But he fined my ass and sent the record down to Bragg.

"There's this sergeant major waiting for me when I get back. Sweeny. Sergeant Major Brian Sweeny. Tougher than Giddons even. 'Welcome home, Corporal,' he says, and rips off my sergeant stripes. Whole year before he gave 'em back."

"When did you go back to Vietnam?"

"About a year later. I got shipped over and sent to Team 351 to replace Perkins."

He pointed down at the table. Sandy picked up the photograph.

"See, the picture was after he got hit, which is how I met your dad. Perkins was the reason Wolf got his name. Your dad had this gray hair, even though he was only a kid. After he saved Perkins's ass, one of the sergeants came back saying, 'Did you see that stud? Sprang into all that fire like a fucking big-ass gray wolf.' The guy next to him says, '*Our* fucking big-ass gray wolf.' After that everyone called him Wolf. He used it for his call sign."

Hyduk was on a roll now. "I joined the team at Lang Vei." He got up and stoked his stove. His face glowed as he tossed in a chunk of wood. "We were dug in right across this big infiltration route for the NVA. Real thorn in Ho Chi Minh's ass. At first they hit us every few weeks, but it wasn't too bad. Between times it got real quiet." He laughed.

"I remember this one time, half the team got a little R and R and we went down to Nha Trang. The 5th SFG had its headquarters down there and you could get just about anything you wanted in the whorehouses. Pussy, booze, dope, lobster, steak, in that order. Anyway, we were all there. Your dad, all of us. We went to this place called Mama's Sweet Thing. Bargirls. Every-thing real wet, man, if you know what I'm saying.

"We're all sitting around this big round table and one of the guys, Shapen I think it was, says he wants to introduce us to something new. The Game of Smiles. We're sitting there drink-ing beer and a couple of bargirls are down under the table undo-ing our flies, slurping away and whipping us off. The first guy to smile had to buy the next round and pay the girls.

"So your dad was there, and this little honey grabbed his dick and tried to put it in her mouth. He didn't even blink. I saw him reach down, push her away. Then he stood up—he was so cool—and buttoned up his trousers. And he said, 'Well, gentle-men, I'm going to call it a night. I'll be seeing you at 0500 hours for a little run.' And he walked out. I hear one of the sergeants say, 'Shit. Our lieutenant is really a straight arrow, isn't he?' And another just laughed and said, 'Man, I don't blame him. You ever see the jugs on his wife?'

"That must've been your mom," Hyduk said, looking over at Sandy. "No offense."

"Forget it," Sandy said. "So when did the shit hit the fan?"

"Summer of sixty-six. The NVA surrounded the camp, started pounding our ass. Mortars, artillery, whole nine yards. Went on for a couple of weeks. Then the fog came down on us. They dug those fucking trenches of theirs right up to the outer wire. TAC air was off and on.

"The last day, Wolf was over in the outer perimeter running things. Man, he was everywhere. I remember, he had this French field jacket with the radio in it. Every time the shit came down you seen him over there running through the smoke, directing fire, leading counterattacks, bobbing and weaving like Muhammed Fucking Ali.

"Captain Taylor'd assigned me a squad of Montagnards to se-cure the inner perimeter. So I was up on the roof in the prone blowing away NVA. Things began to get fucking hairy. Captain Taylor was inside the command bunker and all of a sudden the Wolf came onto the net and they got in this big argument."

"Over what?"

"The Wolf wanted to call B-52 strikes starting right in front of the outer defensive wire. Taylor was saying no, it was too risky."

"What happened?"

"Nothing, at first. We had our go-to-hell plan. The bridge be-tween the outer and inner perimeters was all wired with demolitions. Ready to blow. The idea was that if the NVA overran the outer perimeter, Wolf would bring the guys back over the bridge to join the rest of us in the inner perimeter. When they were safe, we'd blow the fucking bridge.

"So I'm up there shooting so fast the sandbags are smoking under my rifle barrel and I see Wolf come running across the bridge, flames shooting up all around him, cool as if it was just some kind of exercise. But man, in my whole life I never seen one guy so pissed off. I saw him duck into the bunker and the two of them started yelling at each other."

"What did they say?"

"I heard Wolf tell Captain Taylor that if he didn't use the B-52s, he was going to kill him and take command. After that, I'm not all too clear."

FIFTY-FOUR

★ Whitefish ★

The bunker fell quiet. Abbie walked over and touched Hyduk's shoulder. He shrugged off her hand. "We got something else to take care of," he said. His rifle was propped next to the door where he had parked it when they came in. Picking it up, he ducked outside. They fell in behind him as he moved down the creek. "No way they're going up the defilade. They'll set up an ambush on the trail down along the stream."

He hesitated.

"What is it?" Sandy asked.

"Look, you mind if I take command here, Captain?"

Sandy laughed. "Are you kidding? You're in charge. It's your ground." Sandy retrieved Cox's Uzi.

"Know how to use that machine?" Hyduk asked him.

"I'd say so. How're we going to do this?"

"Hammer and anvil. They'll be waiting for you, so you gotta get past and down to the road. You set up in a good hide near their vehicle and I'll flush 'em down to you."

"The canyon's too narrow. They'll see my ass even if I make like a snake."

"You ain't gonna be doing no crawling."

"How, then?"

Stepping back, Hyduk pointed to the basalt pile rising above them. "No other way.

"See that?" he said, pointing to an angle up the incline. "The rocks are regular. Get it right, you can cut across and up almost like steps. You can do it."

Sandy turned to Abbie. "Wait back at the bunker. We'll come get you when it's over."

"No."

Sandy cocked his head at her. "You'll break your neck."

"I'm going."

"We could get killed."

"What else is new?"

Sandy slung the Uzi. "Okay with you if I pick the rocks?" Without waiting for her to answer, he started up the slope.

★   ★   ★

Abbie tied double knots in the laces of her running shoes and stepped onto the first block of basalt. Already 30 feet up, Sandy was waving to her. After five minutes she was sweating, but Hyduk was right, the route was easier than she expected. In half an hour they were at the top of a low ridge. Down one side, she could see the creek, the mine and Hyduk's truck. Down the other, a gentler slope with wispy patches of dead grass among scraggling pines, was the road.

Scrambling, sliding, skidding, they got to the bottom in five minutes. Through the trees on the far side of the road, they found the two rented Fords.

"Okay, you're a mountain goat," he said. "But not a shooter. You secure the rear. Just stay here, keep your head down and let me know if there's movement."

He crossed the road, working his way up through the trees to a ditch 10 yards above Kip's car. It gave him cover, concealment and a clear shot at the front seat.

An hour had passed since they split up with Hyduk.

★   ★   ★

The Night Stalker moved silently through the trees, following the tracks in the snow, toe down slowly, then ball of foot, then heel. Patrol mode, rifle at the ready. He allowed himself an hour to cover the first few hundred yards. It would take at least that long for Sandy to set up the anvil at the road.

The intruders were pros. They had seen the problem of their tracks and taken to the stream. Fine. It meant their boots were wet. Before they got a shot, they would have frozen feet.

At the edge of the meadow, he checked his watch. Sandy and

Abbie had been gone for an hour and a quarter. He got down on his belly and wormed his way through the high grass. About 10 yards down, there was a broad, flat rock. When he reached it, he crawled on top and steadied the Winchester Magnum.

Through the scope, he could see the entrance to the mine. Nothing at the foot of the tailings dump, nothing on top. He adjusted the focus.

They were inside the shaft. Under the pickup.

Shit.

He looked again at his watch. An hour and a half now.

He had fitted the Winchester out with a reworked Remington trigger that pulled off at a crisp two and a half pounds, less than half the normal pull. He was using a 180-grain load, one of the best for killing at distances out to 1,000 yards.

This time the target wasn't alive.

Fuck, he whispered, squeezing the trigger.

Ringing like a jackpot in quarters, the round blew the windshield out of his green pickup. Kip and Laneer came barreling out of the mine. Tumbling down the tailings dump, they sprinted for the trees.

He had time to squeeze off another shot. He thought it did some good on one of them, but he couldn't be sure. They were both on their way.

★　　★　　★

At the crack of the rifle, Sandy leaned forward in the ditch. A few minutes later, two men ducked out onto the road. One had a shotgun. The other, limping, still had an Uzi. Sandy fired a short burst. The limper fell facedown on the passenger side of the car. Flying lazily through air, the Uzi landed in the middle of the road.

The guy with the shotgun pivoted and charged the ditch. Sandy snapped off two more short bursts. Both went high.

One more time.

He rose to one knee and pulled the trigger. Point blank. The guy was huge.

The gun jammed.

Sonuvabitch. Sandy threw the Uzi at his face. For a split second it deflected the charge.

Springing from the ditch, Sandy took two low steps and tackled the guy. The shotgun boomed once, straight in the air, and followed the Uzi onto the road. Rolling over, he saw a flash of steel as the knife came out of the boot. Saw it coming down at his eye. Saw Abbie pick up the shotgun, smash the butt down on the hand with the blade.

The man howled. The knife went sailing into the trees. Swinging with his good hand, he caught her on the side of the head. Sandy saw her go down. She didn't move.

Kip jumped over her body and started for the shotgun.

Booooopaaaaaaah.

His head disappeared. The rest of him collapsed at the side of the road.

Sandy stood up. Screened by firs, Larry was sitting in the crotch of a tree. Lowering the Winchester, he shouted:

"That was for my dogs."

When Sandy turned around, he saw Abbie standing over Kip's body holding the shotgun. She had a cut under her eye. Blood was trickling down her cheek. When he reached her, she was nudging the dead assassin with the sawed-off barrel.

"Too bad," she said. "Hon."

Sandy took the shotgun from Abbie's hand. She smelled something acrid clinging to her hair. When she raised her fingers and sniffed them, the bitter smell was there, too, like the smoke off a Roman candle.

"Gelignite," Sandy said, touching her hair. "Join the club."

Grabbing Kip's body under the arms, he dragged it onto the road. He kneeled over Laneer, checking his marksmanship. The burst of automatic fire had hit just below the heart. Good shot group. Then the jam. Except for Abbie, he'd be dead now. Thank God Nate hadn't seen it. He took Laneer's feet and hauled him across the ditch, dumping him next to Kip. Breathing hard, he went through their pockets. All empty. He checked the backs of their pants, then their skivvies, then inside their collars. No labels.

"Who were they?" Abbie said, wondering what it felt like to grope a corpse.

"Pros."

As Sandy stood up, Hyduk came out of the trees with his rifle slung across his back. He had Cox over his shoulder like a deer. It occurred to her that they didn't know how many hunters Kip had brought on his expedition. Sandy rolled Kip over, pulled a 9-millimeter out of his waistband and handed it to her. "Hang on to this," he said, snapping on the safety.

The steel of the barrel was cold from the snow. A little runnel of blood had frozen to the trigger guard.

"Why?"

Reaching over, he took her hand and lifted her fingers to her nose. "Now you're in the club, you can pull security."

"You really think that's smart?"

"No problem, killer. I'll show you how to use that thing later."

In the trees, a branch snapped with the sharp, popping crack of a small-caliber rifle. Sandy grabbed Abbie's jacket and ducked behind Kip's car. He was reaching for the pistol when Hyduk started laughing like a kid watching those cartoons where the Coyote hits the dirt and sinks 6 feet under while the Roadrunner goes beeping down the road.

"About time, Zack."

Out of the underbrush stepped a boy carrying an old M-1 rifle. The kid from the bank.

"I thought I taught you how to walk in the bush." Larry snapped, sounding just like Sandy. "You sounded like a jail-house full of drunks out there."

The boy looked miserably at his boots.

"You had security detail. Do like that again and we could be dead."

"I was checkin' out the lake, Larry. Like you tole me. Heard the shots and ran my ass off. Never knew what slow was 'til I was tryin' to get back up those cliffs to you, Larry. . . ."

It looked as if the boy was going to cry.

"Okay, okay, at ease, soldier," Hyduk said to him. "We'll work on it." He looked down at the three bodies.

"Any ID?"

"Zip," Sandy said.

Hyduk put his hand down to his leg. Pulling out his knife, he slit open the seams at the bottom of Kip's padded vest. Two small items fell out of the lining where they had been hidden. The first was a set of car keys. The second was a single key attached to a plastic tag that said in hot pink letters—SLEEP TITE MOTEL.

"Better take a look," Hyduk said, tossing the key to Sandy.

"What about the roadkill?"

"Case of right way, wrong way, my way," Hyduk said, picking up the shotgun. "Right way and wrong way is to go get the sheriff."

"Your way?" Abbie asked.

"The trunk." Sandy tried the keys. Inside were three one-gallon containers of gas.

"Were they that worried about running out?" Abbie said, her voice trailing off.

Hyduk laughed. "The only thing worrying them was the best way to burn your butt. That stuff's their charcoal lighter." He turned to Sandy. "All right," he said. "Let's dump these stiffs."

The job was messy—it left smears of blood on the bumper—but easy with two men. "Okay, I'll drive, you follow," Hyduk said, slamming the trunk shut. "You know the way. Just don't get so close this time."

Hyduk and Zack climbed in the blue Ford and started up the logging road. Spotting them a dozen car lengths, Sandy followed. Their convoy wound through the forest along the route they had taken the day before. "See that?" he said, when they reached the Y and the guardrail, swung it around slowly to the left fork. They got to the top just in time to hear Hyduk gun the engine. The driver's door flew open and he came rolling out as the blue Ford picked up speed and shot off the edge of the cliff, nosing down to the lake. The black wheels spun in the air, churning up a giant rooster tail of spray as the car sank.

"How deep?" Abbie asked Hyduk, who came up whacking snow off his arms and legs.

"Some people say three hundred feet. Might as well be bottomless."

"That where you wanted us, too, Larry?" Sandy said. "Yesterday, I mean."

"That was sort of up to you, Captain," Hyduk said. "Think about it."

Abbie suddenly realized that Larry sounded a lot like Nate. His tone stopped Sandy.

"Let me spell it out for you," Hyduk said. "Remember what they told you at Infantry School . . . impetuous advance? All that hell-for-leather, let's-go-gettem shit? Gets you killed, not the enemy, right? Way I saw it yesterday, if you had any sense, you were okay. You pulled an impetuous advance right up my ass, anything happened to you was your own damn fault."

A smile spread across Sandy's face. "Spoken like a sergeant major, Larry."

"Thanks for the promotion, Captain."

Abbie nudged the two of them toward the car. "What about

the Sleep Tite? Shouldn't we do a bedbug run? What if there are more of them back in town?"

"Looked like full deployment to me," Hyduk said. "Zack and me are gonna work back to my place to make sure, you check out the motel."

Sandy frowned. Hyduk said, "Hell, Captain. No one down there. Tell you what, you keep the Uzi. Present from the dearly departed."

"You're giving me a jammer as a present, man? You sure you don't want me at the bottom of the lake?"

Hyduk thought about it. "You'll have the shotgun, too. I put it in your car." He pointed to Abbie. "Let her cover you. She ain't bad with the butt of that thing, anyway."

"Nah, Captain. Like I said, the Uzi's my present. Oil 'er up, take the mags apart, stretch the springs and give 'em a good oiling, you'll do better next time. Take these extra mags, too."

Sandy shut his eyes. Nate didn't have to be there. Now he had Hyduk.

They drove down the mountain. At the bridge, Hyduk and Zack got out and vanished into the woods after agreeing to meet them the next morning at 0700 hours. When they were gone, Sandy eased the car into gear and they started for town. About 20 miles an hour slower than they had driven the previous day. No more impetuous advances today. Abbie stretched out her hand and rubbed the back of his neck.

The Sleep Tite was a size-12 shoe box with half a dozen small rooms facing the road and four crumbling log cabins out back. The tag on the key said Cabin 3. The place was out of a bad film noir: a double bed with a sagging mattress and two singles, a rickety table covered with a red oilcloth, a couple of wooden chairs and a toilet with a rusting stall shower. It smelled of Lysol and bad sex.

Three small matching bags, black, heavy ballistic nylon, were tossed on the beds. The combination locks on the bags were made out of a lightweight metal Abbie had never seen before. Great luggage. She was working out the moral points of ripping off a hitman's carry-on when Sandy took Kip's knife from his pocket and slashed open all three bags. Out fell an assortment of radio gear and batteries, packs of cigarettes, and prescription bottle, a flashlight, a few keys. And three wallets.

Flipping two of them to her, Sandy started to go through the third.

They were all made of the same heavy black nylon as the flight bags. No photographs. Just a driver's license, a single credit card and a neat sheaf of $100 bills.

Abbie counted the money. Four grand in each wallet.

She was flipping bills. "Thirty-eight in here. He must have paid for the room."

"Two hundred bucks?" she said. "For this?"

"For shutting up."

The other two gunmen hadn't tapped their stash. The serial numbers were all consecutive. "They only dropped two bills, pups. Grattan said they were going around yesterday asking questions. That means they were here at least twenty-four hours. Let's say they dropped a hundred dollars on whoever changes the sheets and looks the other way out front. And let's say they had a steak and a few beers while they were getting ready to knock us off. That would have brought them pretty close to two hundred."

"So?"

"So how much did they spend on gas or cigarettes or those batteries or anything else you blow small change on when you hit the road? No way these guys flew commercial. And what about the guns? I mean, like I can just see them at the gate. 'Excuse us, ma'm, we'd like to check our artillery.' "

"So how did they get all those guns up here?"

"Beats me," Sandy said. "Maybe they have their own Air Force."

He tugged something from one of the wallets. "Look at this," he said. The driver's license was made out to Austin Kip, 1418 Jackson Terrace, Charleston, South Carolina. Height, weight, vitals looked accurate. "What do yours say?"

Abbie read from the licenses in her hand.

Howard Laneer, 1418 Jackson Terrace, Charleston, South Carolina.

Martin Cox, 1418 Jackson Terrace, Charleston, South Carolina.

She looked at the three credit cards. All were identical company cards in the name of Haskell Chemicals, also of 1418 Jackson Terrace, Charleston, South Carolina.

"No way they came from Charleston." Sandy shrugged. "Probably a vacant lot. Or some pet store with guppies in the window and Uzis in the cellar."

"Why did they need licenses anyway?" Abbie said.

"Minimum ID. They had to rent a car, this place. You can't put a car on a Lear jet and you can't fly a Hercules into Kalispell airport to offload a vehicle and a death squad without attracting a little attention." He stretched out his hand. "Let me see those again." She turned over the two licenses.

At the bottom of the three documents, a line in all but invisible type, said: *Issued in Halsted County, South Carolina.* "That should be a little closer to home," Sandy said.

On the wall next to the shower was a turquoise clock with a cord trailing down to the wall socket near the floor. About $125 at Back to the Fifties, a store one of Becca's pals owned. The clock said a quarter to seven.

"No way to fly out of here tonight," she said.

"No hurry."

Had she heard him right? "There's Larry in the morning. Here, let me show you something else." Drawing her over to the bathroom mirror, he rested his chin on her shoulder.

"Oh man," she whispered.

Her hair was snarled and full of pine needles. Under her eye, where Kip had whacked her, an indigo welt had spread across her cheek. Sandy's forehead was swollen. His hair was matted with dried blood, his own and Kip's. She was looking at Bonnie and Clyde.

Sandy took a washcloth, ran warm water on it. He dabbed away the blood on her face, as if he were a father patching up a child.

"You sure you're all right?" he said.

"No problem," she said, flinching as she touched the bruise on her cheek. "Do your dates always earn Purple Hearts?"

"Just you, Tiger," Sandy whispered, watching her eyes in the mirror. "Think we could use a shower?"

★   ★   ★

The next morning at six, they checked out of Grouse Mountain. Just out of town, a logging truck almost clipped them as it roared past them, belching black diesel exhaust. Abbie spilled her coffee. Sandy stopped and helped her wipe up the mess.

When they got to the bridge, Hyduk was sitting on a fallen log waiting for them.

"Thought you said oh-seven-hunnert."

His eyes wandered over the two of them as if he were patting them down.

Sandy looked at his watch. It was ten after seven.

"Sorry about being late, Larry. Had a little problem with a truck."

"Soldiers don't run late. Difference between life and death."

"Come on, Larry, you're the one who told me to slow down."

He felt Abbie's hand on his arm. Hyduk's eyes looked like L.A. smog on a bad day.

Sandy handed him the shotgun and the Uzis. They wouldn't exactly be assets at the airport. He kept the pistol. Then he gave Hyduk the three bags with the $12,000 from Haskell Chemicals.

"What's that?"

"Bounty on polecats. Buy yourself a new windshield."

Hyduk stuffed the wallets in his pocket. "You keep the bags."

"No, Larry," he said. "*You* keep the bags. Dump 'em. We have to get rid of 'em."

"Okay," Hyduk said, grabbing the bags and heading back into the trees. "Gotta show you some stuff." Where the stream ran into the little meadow, he pointed to a rotting tree stump just beyond a stretch of reeds. "That's my dead-letter drop. Friend used to leave money for me there."

"Bob Hester?"

"That's right. He died, I had to go to the regular post office."

"That was twenty years ago. Why'd you keep it?"

"Training sticks. A rock on top means mail."

Moving up the trail, they came to the deadfall where Abbie had trashed Cox. Hyduk had laid the bodies of the two dogs off next to a deep hole. Zack was standing over them, a one-man honor guard. Hyduk took off their dog tags and held them in his hands, looking at them for a long moment. They clicked together as he dropped them back into his pocket. Picking up the bodies gently, he lowered them into the hole. Then he handed the shovel to Abbie, nodding at the pile of fresh dirt next to the grave. "You first," he said. "You're the one Mike and Jake saved."

He watched as she dropped a spade full of black earth on the dark brown bodies. Then he took the shovel and finished the job himself.

When he was done, he whirled around and threw the shovel up the trail with all his strength. It sailed through the air, the handle spinning, the tip sparking off an outcropping of rock.

The sparks detonated Hyduk.

"Get the fuck out of my life. Both of you."

"Easy, man." Sandy tried to put an arm around him. Hyduk furiously shook him off.

"Fuck you. Everything was cool here until you came and made a shit sandwich out of my life. I don't care about you, your dad or Vietnam. Whole goddamn war was an abortion. Fuck all that shit. We shouldn't have been there in the first place. I don't want to remember any of it. Get out of my face, man. Leave me alone. I was okay up here until you came. Now everything is fucked up—and Mike and Jake are dead."

He looked wildly at Abbie.

"I've lived here twenty years and never had no trouble. You're here five minutes and it's World War Three. A bunch of dead guys with a whole lot of friends back at wherever the fuck they come from, and that means more shit coming down the track. Bad, bad shit. Whythafuck don't you just get outta here?"

"Can it, Sergeant. Lock your heels together." The same tone of command that had snapped Hyduk out of it the first time.

Hyduk fell silent.

"Those dudes weren't looking for me," Sandy said. "Or her, either. They could've taken us out back at the lodge between hoisting one at the bar and having a piss. It was you they wanted."

"What do you mean?"

"You been paying your taxes, man?"

Hyduk's belly laugh echoed up the canyon. His mood swing broke. He picked up his rifle. With Zack covering the rear, they loped the rest of the way back to the bunker.

When they got there, Hyduk told them to wait for him inside while he posted Zack. After a few minutes, he ducked under the low entryway. For half an hour he listened politely while Abbie told him everything she'd learned about ODA 351. Most of the time he looked bored. Finally, he stood up and started pacing back and forth across the bunker.

"Look, I see where you're coming from. I knew that stuff a million years ago. Nothing real new there." He picked up a brown felt marker and began fiddling with it absentmindedly. Abbie recognized the color. The marking on the after-action report at Suitland.

"What made you go chasing after it?" she said.

"It didn't make sense to me," he said. "I don't even know why. All I know is my brain kept telling me something was missing."

"Something was missing, all right—from your brain," Sandy said. "About half a quart of gray matter judging by those scars."

Abbie glared at him. Hyduk chuckled. "You're right, Captain, but that's not what I meant. I just kept having this feeling the picture played on past what I could remember. I tried everything. Checked all the reports, read all that stuff on the shelves, wrote down everything I could think of. But it won't come. Twenty years and the last of it won't come."

"Whatever the hell's missing," Sandy said, "we've got to figure out what it is before someone else finds you. They found you once, it's going to be easier next time. You're not safe here."

Hyduk shrugged. "Back to summer camp. I got two places," he said. "One for winter and one for the rest of the year. Only been here a week, but I guess Zack and I better pull back awhile."

"Good idea," Sandy said. "We'll leave our numbers with Grattan at Grouse Mountain Lodge. He's ex-SF."

Hyduk looked doubtful.

"Just in case you need to reach us. You can trust him. I get the feeling we're going to need each other. We've got to stay connected."

Suddenly Larry got up from the table. He was looking at Sandy as if he were someone he'd known a long time.

"Okay, Wolf," he said. "Siamese twins."

"I'm not Wolf," Sandy protested. He was no fucking menagerie. Hawk suited him fine.

"You are to me, man," Hyduk said. He smacked Sandy on the back. Then he walked them back to the brook.

FIFTY-FIVE

"Why don't you check in, pups? Better you deal with the pistol."

Before Sandy could say no, Abbie took off down the sidewalk in front of Glacier International Airport. On the way in, they'd passed a small hangar with a silver fuel tank and a dozen small planes tethered to the runway. Red and white Cessnas, mostly—one- and two-engine jobs—and one fine old Beechcraft Bonanza with an orange butterfly tail.

Glowering over them all, was an LS75 jet with two big fire burners aft and FC7-4502 lettered next to the door. Corporate. She'd jotted the numbers on her wrist. Leaving Sandy to handle their gear and turn in the rental, she backtracked through the parking lot, taking her bearings from the shimmering fuel tank in the distance.

At the far end of the lot, a gate led to the private section of the airport. Pushing it open, she stepped forward and headed for a shed near the silver tank. When she reached it, she saw a wooden sign posted next to the front door. In tall block letters, the sign said OFFICE. Below, in smaller letters, it said FLIGHT PLANS.

She knocked.

"It's open." The voice clear, high, came out of the metal shed like notes from a steel drum. Abbie stepped inside and found herself looking at a guy in mechanic's overalls. Very thin, very tall, very black. He was sitting at a small desk watching a micro TV. On the wall above his head was a faded poster of Bob Marley and the Wailers. In great swirls of black, the lettering, drooping like dreadlocks, spelled out the mellow moral: REGGAE RULES. An optimist.

"Don't get up," she said, as if that were even a possibility. "We just came in from Bozeman. My husband's over at the terminal picking up friends. We're heading right back."

"Flight plans in the basket," he said. Without taking his eyes from the tiny screen, he pointed a long finger to a table with two wire baskets. The one marked "Arrivals" was empty. Three or four forms lay on the bottom of the one that said "Departures."

"Will you sell me that Lear out there?" she said brightly. "God, I could get down to the Absarokas in ten minutes. Where did it come from?"

The thin man said nothing. From the TV, Abbie could hear Oprah doing her thing—how crash diets trigger binges.

"You mind if I check his flight plan?"

"Don't ask, don't tell, don't burn in hell," he said.

Abbie laughed. First time she'd heard FAA regulations delivered with a Montego beat.

"Sorry," she said. "I'll just drop off ours. I stick it in over there, right?"

"Mmmmmmmhhhmmm."

Shielding the two baskets with her back, she paged quickly through the forms in Departures. At the bottom was a plan filed by Earl Markham. Destination Rawlsville, South Carolina. The plane's number was FC7-4502.

Opening the door, she stopped and looked at the jet. A pilot in light khakis, too light for fall in Montana, was talking to an old man who was fueling the plane. Looking at his watch, he snapped something at the old guy, then swung through the aft door and stretched out on the last seat. He left the door open, as if he were expecting passengers.

The old guy topped off the aircraft and signaled to the driver to pull away. Abbie intercepted him as he headed for the shed. "Who do you have to be to come in on something like that?" she said, pointing to the Lear.

"Heavy hitters," he grunted. "Hunters. Least, *they* thought so. Come in here from the East Coast with enough guns to take out half the elk in Flathead County. Thought they could do it in forty-eight hours. Earl over there has been waiting for 'em since last night. I asked him just now where those other boys were."

"No kidding. What did he say?"

"He told me to mind my own fuckin' business."

"Nice guy."

"They're all the same. Damn shame if a bear got his friends."

★　　★　　★

Still half an hour until boarding. When Abbie got back to the terminal, Sandy was looking restlessly out the windows toward the waiting 727. She slipped past him to the bank of phones at the end of the terminal, jacked in her laptop, and searched Rawlsville, South Carolina.

The only listing was something called "Raw Raw Rawlsville, Lenny Fanning's Home Page." As the page came up with something called "Raw Facts," Sandy saw her and started toward her. No time to study the page. Flicking the pointer she downloaded "Raw Facts," as Sandy came bearing down on her like an Abrams tank.

"Jesus, Abbie. Where were you? We've got to go through security."

"I've been checking something before we talk. You're going to like this one."

★　　★　　★

An hour later, Delta Flight 1062 was at cruise altitude over the Rockies, the Saw Tooth Range falling behind them, the wheat and potato of Idaho and northern Utah heaving into view up ahead. Abbie opened the laptop and punched up "Raw Facts."

Who's Horny at Parham High?
Bad Dudes Corner
Artie's Lips
42-24-36 [Site Under Construction]

A gag bag of adolescent smut.

She read the Teddy-wants-to-finger-fuck-Sally rundown on the hornies at Parham High. Then she checked out the photograph of Artie's mouth, pursed as if he were about to blow up a balloon. The picture showed no evidence of anything that looked like kissing technique or experience. "Artie's Tits and Hips" page was down.

She sat back in her seat. Twenty thousand years of technological progress at the service of a teenybopper's hard-on. It was an effort to call up "Artie's Bad Dudes Corner."

Hanging out at the corner, she found a listing for Howie Mason, who had farted three times in October during the Pledge of Allegiance. Tanner Gorden was there because he had chugged three Buds and tossed his guts in the swimming pool and they had to drain it because Mr. Jefferson, the principal, believed it when Tanner said he thought he had mono. George Torrence made it for owning volume one, number one of *Wired* magazine, the one with the dweeby-looking guy in glasses on the cover who was in reality the supercool Bruce Sterling, the same Bruce who had "seen the future of war."

Abbie was reaching for delete when she saw the last name on the list: Artie Fanning.

Short-circuiting in contradictions as only a post-twelver can, Artie had chosen to list his own accomplishments as properly as if he were applying for his driver's permit.

Arthur Fanning
1849 Laurel Drive
Rawlsville, South Carolina, 11967
Phone: 208 453 862 2202
Fax: Don't I wish
E-mail lenfan@aol.com
Mom: Allegra Fanning, Managing Director, Charleston Ballet
Dad: Harold Fanning, Engineer, T. C. Johnson

How could she have missed it back at the airport?

T. C. Johnson. The merry messenger.

Oh shit. Oh yes.

She pulled the cell phone from the back of the seat in front of her. The desk clerk at Grouse Mountain Lodge put her through to Grattan.

"Tim, it's Abbie."

"Where you callin' from, the car wash?"

"No, from thirty-three thousand feet. Listen, I'm here with Sandy. We'll be in Charleston or Rawlsville, South Carolina, tonight. I'll tell you why later. You remember that story you told us about the major who got pissed to the gills and started bad-mouthing Sandy's dad?"

"Yep."

"The guy got a name?"

"Yep. Hard one to forget."

"What was it?"

"We were shitfaced and when the club closed we drove into town. Went to this great new place in Fayetteville. Special ops joint."

"Don't tell me. Was it the Valley of the Shadow?"

"How'd you know that?"

"I'm just an old camp follower, Tim. Who was the sloshed major?"

"I'll never forget. His name tag was sorta funny."

"What do you mean?"

"Well, here's this guy dumping shit on everyone, but the tag said his name was Fair."

"Remy Fair?"

"Yeah, Major Remington Fair. Like the rifle. Man, he was on full automatic that night."

In the seat next to the window, Sandy had his eyes closed, but she knew he was listening. Let him wait. She thanked Grattan and rang off, then pressed the button for the flight attendant and asked him for a blanket.

While the attendant was gone, Abbie pulled up the armrests between her seat and Sandy's. He kept his eyes closed the whole time. What would he try next? The fake snore?

The attendant came back and handed her two beige blankets wrapped in plastic. Abbie took them out, spread them across her lap and Sandy's. Then she reached underneath and grabbed his crotch.

"All mine," she whispered.

To her amazement, he didn't move. Then she remembered the Game of Smiles.

"I love you," he said. "And not just because you Number One Blanket Girl."

He opened his eyes. Abbie put her fingers on his lips to make him shut up.

"I do love you, Abbie."

She slid her hand up onto his arm. "Now that you mention it," she said, "I think I've got the same problem."

FIFTY-SIX

Rawlsville ★ South Carolina

Ed Train felt sleepy. It was 10:45 in the Game Room, 4:45 in Naples, nearly noon in Seoul. Train had a case of ragged nerves for every time zone. He was reading a report on metal fatigue in landing gears when Earl Markham mashed the button outside and stepped into the security lock.

Train glanced up through the bulletproof glass. Markham looked like shit. He hadn't shaved for three days, he had bags under his eyes, his shirt and pants looked like he'd been trying to screw all night without taking them off. And he was alone.

Seven hours earlier, when Markham's Code Red had come in, Train had relayed it immediately to Max. Now the reply was lying on the table in front of him, giving off a faintly radioactive glow. "Find those dipshits."

Train pressed the security lock release and Markham stepped into the room. He was walking with the stiff gait of a guy who had too much blood in his feet after a long flight at high altitude and a falling-rock landing.

"Where the fuck are they?" Train asked, dispensing with small talk.

"Jupiter, for all I know. Maybe Mars."

Train looked at Markham as if he were a bug that had just poked its head out of a rotting stump.

"Save the gags, I'm not laughing." He shoved the message over to Markham, who read it and slumped into a chair.

"Kip told me he figured six, maybe eight hours tops," he said. "When they didn't show up, I thought maybe his timing was just a little off. Nothing I could do but stay parked at the strip. When they got back we'd have to be leaving quick, know what I mean? Thirty-six hours. Zip."

"You just sit there?"

"Come on, Train. I don't like flashing Red any more'n you do."

"Okay, okay. What else you got?"

"I went into town, checked where they were staying. Room's empty. Gear's gone, beds made, toilets cleaned."

"You telling me they checked out?"

"Guy in the office says he never saw them split. He was back in Cabin Seven banging his old lady. Saw their bags were gone, twenty bucks on the dresser. Figured they just didn't want to screw up his good time."

Train rubbed his temples. He felt a migraine coming on. "What about the rental?"

"Disappeared."

"So where'd they go? Three men and a car don't just disappear from the face of the earth." Train didn't believe in alien abductions. What he believed in was the sanctity of contracts. When you took on a job, you fulfilled your obligation. You didn't flash Code Red and come crawling back with your tail between your legs.

"What about Hyduk and the others?"

"Them, too."

"What are you saying to me, Earl?" His voice dropped, but Markham didn't pick up on it.

"They're gone, too, all three of them."

"Any other good news?"

"Yes. It's a small town. People talk. I passed the word around the airport that our boys were staying on a few days and going out commercial if I couldn't get back in time."

"Good thinking. Better go get some sleep."

Markham stepped toward the security lock. "Uh uh, Earl," Train snapped. He nodded toward the bunk room behind him. "Crash back there. I get this feeling there'll be some questions."

Markham shrugged. Tossing off a mock salute, he went back and dropped into the rack. Within a minute, Train could hear him breathing deeply, zee-d away into dreamland.

Nothing for it. He sat down at the computer and banged out an advisory. "Team Beta MIA. Markham's back. Says they 'flat disappeared.' " He encrypted the message, sent it, then made a new pot of coffee and sat down to wait.

Half an hour later, a red light began to flash on the black panel that controlled the scrambler phone.

"Do I have it right?" The voice sounded as if Train had just called in with leprosy.

" 'Fraid so."

"Fix it."

"Look," Train said, scrambling for time. "It's gonna take me fourteen hours to bring Alpha back in from Bahrain. But I've already given them a warning order and we can move out again as soon as they get here."

He looked over at the light on the scrambler panel. The line was still open. It sputtered back to life. "Not good enough. You fly commercial to Whitefish today and have Markham bring me and Team Alpha out there tomorrow."

"Wilco."

"Find out what happened to our people. But what we really need to know is what happened to the targets. I don't care if you have to nuke the whole state of Montana—neutralize them."

FIFTY-SEVEN

Moncks Corner ★ South Carolina

The Inn at Moncks Corner loomed up out of the darkness like a set for *Gone With the Wind*. Along the lane running up to the white plantation house, lights tucked in the shrubbery played across the limbs of ancient oaks where the Spanish moss hung like pale green lace.

It was nearly 9:00 P.M. The backseat of the four-wheel Sandy and Abbie had picked up at the Charleston airport was loaded with their luggage and two grocery bags of junk food from a 7-Eleven in Mount Holly. A black bellman in white trousers and a white vest came across the veranda to take their bags. A full moon shimmered through the oaks. After Whitefish, the evening felt almost tropical.

"I need you, Scarlett," Sandy whispered. He ran his hand over the small of Abbie's back.

"Right now, Rhett, what I need is Tara. Let's check in."

Their room had soft old wallpaper with white camellias and a backdrop of dark green leaves. The crystal bowl on the dresser was full of dried flower petals. Between two tall windows looking out over a garden stood an old four-poster, French by its spindles, with a gauzy canopy and matching dust ruffle. Sandy looked dubiously at the bed.

" 'Fraid you might break something, pups?" Abbie asked as she dropped her blouse on a chair and headed for the bathroom. "Hope they have insurance."

He heard the sound of running water. Nearly ten hours since they left Whitefish. Washing the smell of peanuts and stale air out of her hair. She'd be in there a long time. He picked up the phone and dialed a number.

"Who's this callin' me in the middle of the night? Go bother someone else, man."

"Hey, Nate, don't hang up. It's me. It's only nine-thirty, man."

A pause at the other end of the line. "That really you?"

"Yeah."

"No shit. Captain Phantom himself? With your permission, sir, where the fuck are you?"

"Moncks Corner, Sarge. About a hundred fifty miles due south of your position."

There was a short silence, as if Nate were checking a mental map. "First good news out of you since Zagreb. So steal a vehicle and get up here."

"Can't, Nate. Not for a while."

A longer silence this time. "Look, Captain. Major Thayer called me in this morning. Wanted to know when your leave was up. It don't make him happy seeing my ass all around Bragg and no sighta yours."

"What did you tell him?"

"Told him you had four days left, but you might need more. Had to make sure your granddaddy was doin' okay with his busted leg."

"What'd he say?"

"Playin' nurse to a four-star got his attention."

Sandy looked over at the bathroom door. He heard Abbie turning off the shower.

"I'm in the middle of it."

"Yeah, sounds like you are."

"That's not what I'm saying. I was in a firefight yesterday that was serious shit. Abbie turned up this guy from my dad's old outfit in the Nam. The minute we get there, three guys packing serious heat tried to blow us away."

"Where they now?"

Over the line, Sandy could hear Nate's voice drop out of ass-kick overdrive. "Tell you when I see you. Let's just say we're okay, they're not."

Nate whistled. "Who the fuck were they?"

"That's what we're trying to find out. Whoever sent the Three

Amigos is still out there looking for us. We're guessing they had some kind of connection to T. C. Johnson in Rawlsville."

"T. C. Johnson? Guns 'R Us? If you don't mind my sayin' so, Captain, jivin' around Zagreb for a coupla days is one thing. I dunno about this shit."

"I'm in too deep."

"So now you got your own personal death squad on your ass, that what you tellin' me? Where'd you get your brains? The PX?"

Sandy smiled. He had Nate now. "Do we have any friends in there, Sarge? Half the Army must've left to get on T. C. Johnson's tit. I need someone in security."

Master sergeants don't sigh. The sound Nate made was more like the snort of an old cow horse watching a rider walk up in jodhpurs.

"All right, all right. Give me your number. I'll get back to you ASAP."

"Thanks, Nate."

"Don't thank me. Like I said, you're runnin' out of time faster'n I'm runnin' outta lies. You just lucky Thayer's one of the new breed of SF field graders, Hawk. Otherwise you'd be in a mean hurt."

★   ★   ★

Sandy put down the receiver. Idly, he poked his finger into the bowl of petals on the dresser. They gave off a faint scent of roses and violets. Behind him, he heard the bathroom door open. When he turned around, he saw Abbie, her hair still damp from the shower, coming toward him. She was wearing one of his tee shirts, nothing else. Must've pulled it out of his bag while he was on the phone. The brown cotton shirt covered her shoulders and breasts, stopping just short of her thighs. When she got to him, she took off his dog tags and slipped them over her head.

"Okay," she said. "Who am I?"

"Private Benjamin." His throat felt thick.

She frowned. "Pretty weak. That the best you can do?"

"The French Lieutenant's woman."

"Getting warmer."

Through the damp tee shirt he could see her nipples. He put his finger forward, but she pulled away. Her eyes were laughing at him. "You *are* getting warmer."

Dancing over to the foot of the four-poster, she picked up the bags from the 7-Eleven and emptied them onto the bed—Sun Chips, Cabot low-fat cheese slices, a can of walnuts, a loaf of raisin bread, half a six-pack of beer. The empty loops from the missing cans dangled from the rest of the pack like enormous plastic earrings.

"But first we eat."

He was washing his hands when the phone rang.

" 'Lo, Nate," Abbie said. "Wish you were here." She handed Sandy the phone and stretched out on the bed. The brown tee shirt rode up over the darker patch of her bush.

"I got someone for you, Captain," Nate said.

"Figured you would. Who is it?"

"Guy's name is Barry. Fen Barry. Fenton, but I wouldn't call him that. He don't like it."

"He any good?"

"Real good, sounds like. Special Forces, recon man. Left after Desert Storm. Little-bitty guy, but don't let it fool you. Third Dan black belt. Some of that kung fu shit. Kill your ass faster'n you can say mama."

"What's he doing working for T. C. Johnson?"

"Ask him. Gettin' by, I guess. Nuthin' bad on him I could find."

"You know him?"

"Nah, but I asked a coupla friends. They say you can trust him."

"Got a number?"

"Jesus, Captain, don't do that. The man says don't call him— he'll meet you in the morning."

"Where?"

"Davis Lodge outside Bonneau. Fishing place maybe ten miles from Rawlsville. He said meet him for breakfast at eight o'clock. His shift don't start until three."

"Thanks again, Nate."

"No problem, but you think about what I said. This whole thing's a bad idea, Captain."

"You got a better one?"

"Damn right, I do. Drop it and get back up here. Bring Miss Daisy."

"Won't work."

"Yeah, I know."

"I'm going to find out what this shit is all about, Nate."

Silence.
"Like I said, clock's runnin' against you."

★ ★ ★

Sandy replaced the receiver and looked at the bed. The moment had passed. Abbie's eyes were closed. Kicking off his shoes, he lay down next to her. No vital signs. He touched her bare stomach below the tee shirt line.

"Let's give it a rest," she said.

He moved his hand up to her breast.

Without opening her eyes, she took his hand away, dropping it on the dark green quilt between them. Then she turned toward him and nuzzled her head into his shoulder.

"Just hold me, pups," she whispered. "I need you to hold me."

They fell asleep on top of the covers.

FIFTY-EIGHT

Sandy pulled into the gravel behind the Davis Lodge. He parked between a greasy Peterbilt tractor missing its rig and a banged-up pickup hitched to a trailer with a bass boat. Except for one detail, the Davis Lodge was redneck pure. The detail was the Litespeed racing bike leaning against the wall next to the rear door.

It was a Vortex, the cold-worked-titanium frame a bright-brushed phoenix red. The bike had a Time Equipe fork and Campagnolo Record componentry: Record crank set, chainings, derailleurs and brakes with TTT Forma 2 handlebars, a yellow Avocet titanium saddle and alloy nipples. Not just another two-wheeler.

In the cafe, a bored waitress was behind the counter bent over an old copy of *Glamour*, smoking a Camel. She ignored them.

"That you, Captain Caine?"

The voice came from a half-hidden booth jammed next to an unplugged Wurlitzer jukebox on the far side of the room. The guy was short and lean, all muscle. Abbie put him at about five-foot-five. He looked like he had gotten lost on the Tour de France. Black bicycle shorts stretched tautly over his thighs. A matching jersey with the number 23 stitched on the chest and the word SECURITY on the back clung to his body. He had a red-and-black-striped racing cap pushed back on his head.

"Fen Barry," he said, sticking out his hand. "Heard you could use some help."

"Sandy Caine. This is Abigail Mancini."

"Abbie," she said. "That Vortex outside is yours, right?"

"Only one in Rawlsville," he said, grinning at her. "I kill 'em."

"I bet this place does, too." She studied Barry more closely. He had to be over forty, but he looked half that. His hair was light brown and his eyes were hazel. An average-looking guy she'd have trouble picking out of a lineup. "You won't find anyone from T. C. Johnson hanging in here," he said. "You ever see the face on a retired three-star if some pork chop calls him Bubba? Stars travel in packs."

Sandy took out his wallet and flipped the IDs from the Sleep Tite across the table to Barry. "These guys got anything to do with those generals of yours up the road? One of them was named Kip. That's what the others called him."

Barry examined the cards.

"His favorite word was 'hon.' " Abbie said, breaking into Sandy's rap. Barry banged his cup on the table. At the sound, the waitress clumped out of the kitchen to refill it. He handed the cards back to Sandy.

"Oh shit, yes, I've seen these guys around. They hang out with Ed Train. I saw Kip over in Loomis hitting on this young girl with giant jugs. He called her Hon, too—until she called him Grampa and told him to fuck off."

Abbie remembered the hungry eyes and creepy hands. "What did he do?"

"Popped her. Right across the mouth. Must've broken a couple of her teeth on his hand. He was bleeding like a stuck pig when he left."

"Anyone call the cops?"

Barry looked at her as if she were a Camp Fire Girl wailing "No fair."

"Not the way it works around here. T. C. Johnson owns this county. Everything and everyone in it. The girl wasn't exactly selling it that night. She wasn't a hooker. But she'd been around for a couple of weeks with those jugs hanging over the bar and that meant they weren't just hers anymore. Kip thought he owned shares in 'em. Like they was part of his 401K or something."

"So how did it come out?"

"She went over to the sheriff's office and bitched. Can't say I blame her for it."

"And?"

"Sheriff told her to find a new town with a good dentist."

"The bastard."

Barry shrugged. "Name of the game. You don't want to play, find yourself a new town."

"We need to know where Kip lived," Sandy said. "Can you get us keys, a rundown on his security system, password, number codes?"

"Jesus, you don't want much, do you?" Barry looked up from his plate. "Okay, no promises, but I'll try."

"What about Train?" Sandy said. "Any chance you're talking about Midnight Train?"

"Roger that. Midnight Train from Pleiku. Black ops. The Montagnards called him Big Train."

"You never hear him until he hits you, right?"

"That's what they say. Same guy."

"What's he do for T. C. Johnson?"

Barry looked into his coffee as if he expected Train to look back up from the cup. "Vice President—you're gonna like this one—for Special Projects.

"I don't know what kind of projects, but Kip works for him. So do the other two. You see them eating together, talking, know what I mean? Kip lives out by the golf course. The other two could be married, kids, live in one of the company crescents."

Sandy gathered the cards and handed them back to Barry.

"Think you could dig up anything more?"

"Maybe. Maybe not. Why should I?"

"Maybe it's better you don't know."

"You sound just like Train. Forget it." Barry finished off the dregs of his coffee and thumped the cup for the check.

"All right," Sandy said. "Day before yesterday your buddies tried to put Abbie and me into body bags. I'd like to see they don't get another chance."

Barry leaned back in his chair, absorbing this news. "Whyn't you say so before, Captain?"

"You didn't ask."

"You could go to the cops."

"Like you said, that's not the way it works down here. Besides, maybe when Kip grabbed Abbie, she popped him."

Barry broke into a laugh. "You're General Caine's son, right?"

"Grandson."

"Close enough. I've heard about you. Somalia, right? Tell you what. Give me a couple hours and I'll do some sniffing around." He stood up to go. "You get the check, man. Putting you two on the expense account sounds like a good way to get killed."

He started for the rear door, a little guy built like a taut roll of wire.

"Why are you doing this?" Sandy called after him.

At the door, Barry stopped and turned around. "The thing is, I don't like guys called Big." He pulled the door shut behind him.

FIFTY-NINE

"You ever see a town so clean?"

While Sandy drove, Abbie took in the well-scrubbed face of Rawlsville. Along Twining Avenue, the town's prosperity gleamed from the brightly polished store windows. Ann Taylor and the Gap, everything handsome, well made, middle class. She remembered the empty windows in Pittsfield, the opposite end zone in a zero-sum economy. For every winner a loser. Around Rawlsville, a lot of people were winning.

After Barry had pedaled off, Sandy had spent some time on the phone with Nate up at Fort Bragg. She'd called the *Chronicle* to check out Rawlsville. The company had moved its headquarters and main assembly plant to the eastern reaches of Halsted County. In the early eighties, surfing aggressively along the rising wave of defense spending during Ronald Reagan's first term, T. C. Johnson had bought thousands of acres of exhausted farmland and turned them into a model city with its own industrious soul.

The lawns were all uniformly green and neatly trimmed. No litter anywhere. The traffic flowed placidly. Everyone came to a full stop at stop signs. No one ran yellow lights.

"Do you believe this place?" Sandy said. "Disneyland's version of an Army base. Everything's new, even the people."

He turned onto LeMay Lane, where the two-story brick houses were arranged like an old-fashioned row of officers quarters. Paint them red instead of slate gray and downsize a little and you could be at Fort Bragg, he thought to himself.

"You're right. They're all young or middle-aged, Stepford types. Real scary," Abbie said.

She was reading names aloud from the company roster that Barry had left with them. Retired generals and colonels retrofitted as vice presidents for everything from systems analysis to research and development to public affairs. At T. C. Johnson, the revolving door was spinning at Mach speed.

Under Special Projects, she found Edward Scott Train, Lt. Col. U.S. Army, (ret.). Unlike the company's other divisions, Special Projects had no telephone extensions, no fax number, no e-mail address and no staff list.

Beyond the production facilities, Titan Crescent wound past the country club, wandering for a distance through the golf course. Sandy checked the clock on the dash. Eleven-thirty. He dropped into low. In front of the houses along the curving street, the names on the mailboxes were in small black letters, as if the owners didn't care for visitors.

The name on the box in front of the third house to the right was Cox.

Sandy parked and walked back to the Cox place. In the mailbox he found the morning newspaper and a telephone bill postmarked the previous day. Taped next to the buzzer was an overnight UPS advisory. The driver had tried to deliver a package at eight-fifteen that morning.

He got back into the car, made a turn on Freedom Drive and followed the bright green signs with the little carts on them to the golf course, the big clubhouse beyond the eighteenth hole, a caddy shack out back with rental clubs and spikes for drop-by guests. On the wall of the caddy shack, there was a pay phone. Sandy called Barry.

"Your party's not here," Barry said in a low whisper, as if half the company might be listening over his shoulder. "Sometimes he goes over to Bradley Park during lunch hour. You might get lucky and find him there." He rang off.

They wasted an hour exploring the rest of town. At a quarter after twelve, they drove through the white brick gatehouse into Bradley Park. The red Vortex was leaning against the side of the gardener's shed. Out back, invisible from the road, Barry was sitting on the grass. He looked up and handed Sandy a small envelope.

"Key's in there and the dope on the security system. Kip's place is off the fourteenth fairway."

"Thanks, man." Sandy pocketed the envelope and started to walk away. Behind him, he heard Barry scratching his shoulders against the wall of the shed. "Watch your back, Captain," Barry said. "I got a very bad feeling about all of this."

For a few minutes Sandy and Abbie sat in the four-wheeler studying their map. A red flash spurted past them, shooting through the park gate and out into Rawlsville. Abbie watched the Vortex disappear. "They teach you that in SF, pups?"

Sandy folded the map and started the engine.

"Roller blading, too."

They drove back to the golf course and parked behind the clubhouse. In the caddy shack, the rental kid fixed them up with shoes, a cart and two bags of clubs. All charged to Ed Train. No problem.

The cart scooted them along a neatly trimmed path to the fourteenth tee. Off to the left, about 200 yards down the fairway, Kip's house peered out from behind the rough. Squaring off with a driver, he sliced the ball directly into the rough in front of their objective. They piled back into the cart and rolled slowly down the fairway. Sandy hid the cart in behind a stand of scrub pines.

"Let's go."

Kip's front door was 20 yards in front of them. The key worked on the first try. He punched the six numbers into the security box, disarming the system. "We're in."

Shutting the door behind him, he waited until his eyes adjusted to the change in light. In front of him was a small living room with a long brown Afghani tribal rug on the floor. On the wall above the TV was a locked gun case with half a dozen rifles, American, Swedish, Soviet, Israeli. Something for every season.

Sandy snapped on the wall switch. The place was a trophy room.

Photographs covered three walls. The pictures were sharp, expert, the settings exotic: Kip with his arm around a Colonel Remirez, the younger man's face cratered by smallpox. A corpse in white cotton shirt and trousers lay face upward at their feet. By the face, the kid was about sixteen. El Salvador, probably.

The rest of the gallery expanded the theme. There was Kip, younger, standing behind Lon Nol, looking like an onion in a petunia patch. Kip next to Nguyen Cao Ky at the Citadel in Hue.

Kip bent over a Stinger missile, showing the ropes to half a dozen Afghani mujahedeen.

Around the walls it went, good causes and bad, all jumbled, hot days, terrible nights, all forgotten.

And then a prizewinner. A foursome: Kip and an Argentinean colonel standing on a landing zone in the rotor wash of an Argy Huey. Watching an older man unassing the bird, his face in perfect focus.

Gus Buell.

The picture was signed and dated *Valdos, Argentina, 20 Dec., 1983*. Below the chopper's skids, Buell had written, *For Kip. One of America's finest fighting soldiers. Keep slugging for freedom. Gus.*

Kip had decorated the last wall with two paintings. The first was a large picture of a naked Indian dancer. She had a red caste mark on her forehead and a green emerald in her navel. The second was an old chromo lithograph of Rembrandt's "Man in the Golden Helmet," mounted in a heavy gilt frame and tilted as if someone had been interrupted in the middle of hanging it.

Below the painting was one of those optical illusion statues soldiers and sailors bring back from the Far East. The subject was Don Quixote, the mad knight errant, in a sloping helmet. Turned slightly, the shape shifted into a giant, tumescent cock.

Abbie looked at it curiously. She hadn't gotten the sight gag yet. Give her time.

Sandy tossed the rest of the room and came up with nothing. The exercise was just beginning to annoy him when Abbie handed him Kip's Rolodex. Flipping through, he found numbers for Remy and Gus.

Before he relocked the door, he stopped for a moment to adjust "The Man in the Golden Helmet."

When he touched the frame, Kip's backup alarm shrieked like a banshee.

Screeeeeeeeewaaaawaaaaaaascreeeeeeewaaaaaawaaaaaaa-aascreeeeeee.

Sandy grabbed the Rolodex. "Come on, my love," he said. "We've got to get out of here."

"What did you say?"

"I said, move."

"That's not what you said."

Seizing her hand, he pulled her through the door and across the yard until her speed came up and she was running as fast as he was. Panting, they reached the golf cart under the pines. Ten minutes later, they dropped the cart behind the clubhouse and went into the bar.

"You members?" the bartender said, putting down his towel. "Don't think I've seen you before."

"Guests," Abbie said. "Ed Train's." Kurt would be proud.

"Didn't mean to hassle you," the bartender said quickly. "What are you drinking?"

"Dewar's. Two fingers. Neat." Abbie smiled at him.

"Where's your pay phone?" Sandy felt his hip pocket. Wallet in place. Plastic intact.

"Over there by the men's locker room. Whole bank of 'em."

When the barman returned with the scotch, Abbie knocked back half the glass and waited for the warmth to unclench her stomach. "Where did you learn to do that?" the barman said.

"Finishing school. You ever heard of the Valley of the Shadow?"

Sandy came back. His face looked like a Japanese mask.

"What's wrong, pups?"

"I called the General. Melba answered the phone, Abbie. Know what she told me?"

The bartender brought them two fresh glasses of scotch. "Compliments of the house," he said.

"Shoot."

"She said the General was over at Gus's office. He's been there all day. Remy Fair was the third member of their little party."

Abbie knocked over her glass. The scotch spilled across the mahogany bar like a bloodstain. "No way. No way, pups. I don't believe it."

"Believe it. The General knows everything. He's known since day one."

SIXTY

Delta Flight 217 made a sweeping turn to the north. Off the port wing, the sun dropped like a copper penny through a narrow black slot in the crimson clouds. Marv was waiting for them at National. She'd called him on the flight phone. His face fell when he saw Sandy walking down the sidewalk next to her. But by the time they hit the first light in Arlington, he'd recovered. He was whistling softly when they drove up in front of the General's house. Sandy pulled out his wallet and handed the cabbie a fifty. "Get my girl home."

Twenty minutes later, Marv dropped her in front of her own door. She reached for her bag. In the mirror, Marv was smiling. "You're covered. The guy's a spender."

The house was dark. In the kitchen, she turned on the lights and punched the button on the answering machine.

"Look, darlin', I know it's late, but I'm feelin' lonely and I got this quart of Ben and Jerry's and two spoons. Come on over, it's Cherry Garcia and . . ."

Oh Becca. She hit the skip button.

"It's Julian. Your senator wants to get moving sooner, not later. Call me."

She could let that one wait until tomorrow.

"Remembered something big. When you comin' back? Zack and me left the cee-pee. At summer camp now. First left past the log chute. See ya. *De Oppresso Liber*, folks."

She hit play again. "Abbie, darlin,' I beg you, save me from myself . . ."

Becca was starting to sound stoned. Punch, skip . . .

"Barry here. Something stinks. Guys you were talking about all work for Ed Train in Special Projects. The computer lit up like Las Vegas when I punched them in. I couldn't get access this morning, but I did a little hacking. Kip and Cox were both special ops heavies, Delta, CIA. Still trying to get a line on the third shooter. Train might be running some private ops. I'll keep you posted."

The pencil snapped in her hand. Upstairs, she heard a soft noise, like someone drawing a deep breath. She took Kip's pistol out of her suitcase. "Who's up there?" she shouted, trying to sound as butch as Becca. "Who's up there? I'm warning you, I've got a gun." When she reached the landing, she saw the window was open. The only sound was her curtains, rustling in the wind.

Four houses down, Trask watched his gear switch from record to standby. He touched the soft cotton pad taped to the back of his head. Damp. He'd have to change the dressing. Fucking lucky bitch. Wouldn't happen that way twice.

He reached up to his throat and fingered a key on the chain hanging around his neck. The key fit the lock on the STU phone on his table. Special Telephone Unit. Put in the key, scramble the message. Lose the key and you were in serious shit. He slipped the key into the slot on the phone, lifted the receiver and said two words. "She's back." Oh yes, the bitch was back.

How much could you scramble two words? In the darkness, he tried it. Probably sound like Donald Fucking Duck. *Ahh-hhsssssbbbbsssssseeeeekebbbbb.*

On the table next to the STU phone, his 9-millimeter was lying in its black goatskin holster. An old guy in Lisbon had made it for him one of the times when he'd stayed over on his way home from Angola. He checked the clip mechanically, clicking it back in with the palm of his hand, looking at the phone.

All he wanted was one word, he didn't give a fuck how they scrambled it.

Terminate.

SIXTY-ONE

★ Arlington ★

Sandy started up the long stone walk to the General's house. A light rain began to fall. In the darkness, he could hear his running shoes squeaking on the damp fieldstones beneath his feet.

Two old carriage lamps flanked the front door. In their glow, the door looked unnaturally white against the night. In his mind, betrayal was spreading like an oil slick. It was like stepping out onto a newly painted floor by mistake and not being able to get back. Each sticky step forward ruined the surface below your feet, each little skid threatened to take you all the way down.

Squeak, squinch.

He set down his bag and took off his shoes. No noise. Not tonight. Through his socks, the stone felt cold but reassuring. His balance came back. He knew what he had to do.

The door was unlocked. That surprised him. The General was a security freak. Melba must have forgotten to lock up. Silently he turned the knob and stepped into the hall. From the kitchen the smell of rosemary and roasting lamb. At the head of the hall, light leaking around the door to the library. He heard music, something old, slow playing on the stereo.

As Sandy got closer to the door, he heard Sinatra singing, young Frankie, not the old guy with the rug and the busted pipes.

The General didn't believe in tape recorders or compact discs. He had a three-speed Garard turntable from the early 1950s.

Museum piece. Still played 45s and 78s. The record was scratchy. The General was lost in his own blues somewhere in the thirties. The high trumpet of Harry James covered Sandy's final approach.

For the first time in his life, he didn't knock. The door was slightly ajar. Slowly he pushed it open.

The General was sitting at his desk, back to the door, staring out the French windows into the darkness. Immersed in the song. He always played it when he was feeling morose. One of the first big hits for Sinatra and James. August of '39. The Germans going into Poland. Elizabeth Putnam and John Pershing Caine trying to make love, not war. The new James Orchestra, only a year old, with this singing waiter named Francis Sinatra. A bit bottom drawer for Elizabeth. She loved opera. Lawrence Tibbett. The General was the one crazy for Benny Goodman. The Dorseys. So what would it be when Major Caine had leave and they could go up to New York? The Met or the Cotton Club?

Sinatra sang on as the old man sat in the night and dreamed of his young wife.

The jacket of the General's suit was draped over a hanger on the back of the door. The light of the desk lamp, set to low, played across his powerful neck and unstooped shoulders, softening the neatly clipped line of his steel-gray hair.

Sandy looked at the neck. How easy it would be. Two steps across the carpet, snap the cervical vertebra, crush the backbone. Two, three seconds . . .

He moved forward on the balls of his feet and put his hand on the General's shoulder, expecting him to jump halfway to the ceiling. The General didn't move.

"I've been expecting you," he said.

Slowly the old man turned his desk chair around. In his hand was a hog-shank .45. Pointed at Sandy's chest. A quick, reflexive look. The safety was off. The whole time the old man had been watching him in the reflection of the French doors. The light, the music, the turned back. An ambush.

"Sit down," the General said, pointing the barrel of the weapon at the big leather chair next to the stereo. "Over there where I can see you."

Sandy raised his hands and lowered himself into the chair.

"You can put your hands down. You won't be needing them, I'd say, unless you want to be out there in the garden on your back, watering the patio."

"How did you know I was coming? Remy tip you?"

"Why do you say that?"

"You were with him this afternoon, weren't you?"

"That's right."

"And Gus?"

"Right again."

"Then you know damn well why I'm asking. Fuck you, General. Go ahead, shoot."

He leaned forward, clenching the arms of the chair as if he meant to get up.

"Don't do it," the General said, wagging the .45 at his chest. "You think I want to kill you. Have I got that right, son?"

Son?

The word startled Sandy. He glanced across the room. The .45 was still leveled at him. The General was aiming just below the neck. "A guy named Kip just tried to take me down in Montana. Why did the sonuvabitch have a signed picture of Gus on his wall? Quit screwing around with me. Shoot." He no longer gave a flying fuck.

"No one's screwing around with you, son. Dr. Hastings is on his way over. I called him after you started ranting and raving to Melba. We've got a bed for you in a nice quiet little place over in Rectortown. When are you supposed to be back at Bragg? I'll buy you some time and we'll get you squared away. No one needs to know."

"Another cover-up, is that it?"

"If you want to put it that way—as I said, no one needs to know."

"Do they give ratings for cover-ups around here? You must be Sharpshooter by now."

"Easy, son."

The General was talking softly, soothing him, as if he were talking to a freaked-out combat case, as if . . .

"My God, you think I'm nuts. You don't know, do you?" He studied the old man's face. The General didn't know how to lie.

"I know you're not yourself. You call Melba and when she says I'm over at Gus's office with Remy you go off like a Cruise missile carrying on about people trying to kill you. What else am I supposed to know?" The General's expression didn't change. But he did lower the .45, resting it on his knee. "I'll give you exactly thirty seconds to explain yourself."

The .45 was the sidearm the General had carried all through

World War II, Korea and Vietnam. He kept it in the desk drawer for sentimental reasons. Sandy had always wondered if it was loaded, but had never bothered to check. He wasn't going to now. "Better put it back on safety, sir," he said. "Thirty seconds won't do it for this one."

The General snapped on the safety.

"I'm not trying to kill you, Alexander—how in God's name could you ever think something like that? The weapon was to slow you down long enough for Dr. Hastings to get here."

"What about the clinic?"

"You think I was going to check you into Walter Reed? If this stunt of yours gets out, you're dead in the Army."

"In or out, the last seventy-two hours I've been damn near dead twice. That's what I've been trying to tell you."

"You picked a hell of a way to do it. You are lethal, in case you forgot. The way you came in here wasn't exactly what I'd call normal."

"You're right. Let me back up. You remember that reporter from the *Chronicle*?"

"That Massina girl?"

"Mancini."

"Yes. What about her? I suspect Jeff could tell you far more than I."

A small subterranean jolt. Sandy let it pass. He'd ask later.

"She's been helping me check out Perkins's story."

"Oh, for God's sake, I told you to let that dead dog lie."

"It's been eating me alive. Do you want to hear this or not? Jeff wasn't the only one who made it out alive."

"That's impossible. The records are clear. Everyone except Jeff was killed."

"The records are wrong. Abbie tracked it down. She found another survivor."

"Come on, Alexander. One little girl stuck on a soldier and the soldier stuck in an obsession. It's all wishful thinking."

"You're wrong."

The General flushed. No "with your permissions," no "sirs." It was as if Sandy had just told him that his fly was open on parade.

"I've heard quite enough," he said icily, rising from the chair. Before he could say anything else, Sandy grabbed the .45.

"Now *you* sit down," he snapped.

The General laughed. Sandy glanced at the .45. There was no clip in the handle. "Sonuvabitch."

"All right, all right," the General said. "Now we've both got that behind us, what the hell is going on?"

For the next half hour Sandy poured out the story—the tip that had led them to Whitefish, Hyduk's fragmented story, the firefight. Staring at the French windows, the General took in all the details.

"Where does Remy fit in?" he asked.

"I don't know. But he's all over the landscape. Down at Sweeny's. At T. C. Johnson. Hanging out with Patrice. With you. What were you two doing this afternoon?"

"That can come later," the old man said. Rising, he went over to the bookcase and pushed aside six leather-bound volumes. Melman's edition of *The Decline and Fall of the Roman Empire*. In the gap was a small wall safe. The General swung it open and pulled out an envelope. "Read this," he said.

Sandy sat down at the desk and flicked the lamp up to bright. Inside the envelope was a letter typed on one sheet of age-yellowed stationery. The date at the top was 30 August, 1966.

Dear General Caine:

Sir, please allow me to say how sorry I am about the death of your son. When I get copies of the after-action report, I will send one to you. In the meantime, I was over the fight in my C and C chopper with Captain Fair that day and I know you will want the details. This is what we saw.

The NVA had been kicking hell out of Lang Vei for three days. Artillery, mortars, mass infantry assaults. The cloud cover was bad. We couldn't get in there with Air. On the fourth day, the weather lifted for a few hours. We got the tac air going. Air blistered the NVA. Charlie Beckwith was nearly there with a relief column. You know Charlie. He went through the jungle instead of up the road and that took time. But it was the only way.

The bird was holding at 1500 feet. I had a set of PeeVee 25 by 50s so I could see the ground pretty good when the clouds broke. The NVA were hugging the belt. They had themselves in there right up to the wire. Very hard to hit them without killing our own guys.

Jeff Taylor was everywhere, calling in artillery, leading counterattacks, pushing out enemy penetrations, standing on top of the command bunker to fine tune the air strikes, exposing himself to constant enemy fire.

I only saw Lieutenant Caine once. It hurts to tell you this, sir, and I hope you will forgive me. I saw Lieutenant Caine come out of the command bunker. He blew the bridge to the outer perimeter. It stranded half a dozen of our A Team on the far side. The NVA killed all of them. It was a shameful act. I wasn't going to tell you. But you're the one who drilled it into me that the thing a warrior fights for is the truth and his unit. So that's the way it was. I just wish to hell it wasn't me writing this letter.

Sincerely yours,
Colonel William Augustus Buell

Sandy put the letter down. The General came over and sat in the chair, reversing their earlier positions. "That is how your father died," he said. "I wanted to bury it forever. And I have buried it. For nearly thirty years now. I didn't want to believe that any son of mine could act so dishonorably. Only Gus and Remy know what really happened, and Gus swore Remy to secrecy. I've always been grateful to both of them. Now you turn up with this girl reporter and Hyduk, if it is Hyduk, back from the dead saying Gus and Remy are full of it. What do you expect me to do?"

"I guess that's up to you."

The General lowered his voice. "Right now, I suggest we put Melba out of her misery."

He pressed a button. Melba opened the door a little too quickly and came in, wiping her hands on her apron. "Your boy's all right," the General said. "Call Dr. Hastings and tell him we won't be needing him." Dropping the apron hem, she went to intercept the shrink. General Caine reached for his jacket. "If Gus's letter is right, I'll wear the disgrace," he said. "But if you're right, by God I want to set the record straight. I want the facts. Go get them."

SIXTY-TWO

★ Washington, D.C. ★

In Senator Taylor's office, the Bouvier clock began to strike eight, the bells tinkling like a wind chime. Patrice grabbed a file folder and a large manila envelope from the locked file cabinet behind his desk and knocked on the senator's door. The folder had poll results and focus-group summaries. In the envelope was the chart from Gus Buell on the ailing F-44.

"Come on in, Pat."

Senator Taylor was bent over the previous day's Congressional Record, his fountain pen in his hand, his reading glasses propped on the end of his nose. Old, Patrice thought. Way old. Get him contacts before the announcement. He pulls those out and starts to read, he loses two thirds of the Xers before he even hits the track. He dropped the file folder on the desk. "Second batch from Carver and Strong. Just in this mornin'. You're golden in the South, good 'nough for now in Illinois and California."

"Good enough to go?"

"No question about it."

"All right, here's what I want to do," the senator said. "I got the idea last night."

Patrice waited. First rule for a Chief of Staff is never to finish the boss's sentences or thoughts, no matter how transparent they may be. But this one surprised him.

"We'll make the announcement at the Wall."

"In front of a tombstone?"

"That's the way we're going to do it, Pat. So make it work, okay?"

Patrice nodded. He handed the senator a plain brown envelope. "Gus says they've been working triple shifts on the F-44. They should have it flying in three months. The second prototype should be up maybe three months after that. They have to start from scratch on that one."

"That's six weeks *after* the appropriations hearings, Pat. Not before, after. We'll have to vote before the flight tests."

"Gus says that's no problem. The computer simulations will all be complete. You'll have all you'll need to make the case."

"From the computers. No combat tests with a blood-and-guts guy at the stick. We're going to do this with a mouse and a monitor, is that what you're telling me?"

"T. C. Johnson *invented* full flight simulation. They wrote the software, they're writing new code right now to maximize the program for the tests."

Senator Taylor uncapped his pen.

"Here's my hardware, Pat," he said. He scribbled something on his desk notepad. "Here's my new code, Pat," he said, ripping off the sheet and holding it up. Written in large block letters, the note said BULLSHIT.

Somewhere within, Patrice heard a small voice saying why don't you give up, *chér*? You could be doing something worthwhile. Like shelling peas.

"I thought you might feel that way," Pat said quickly. He kept his voice in neutral. "I warned Gus."

"Good."

"Gus asked if he and Remy could get together with you sometime this week. After you'd read these reports. He hoped you'd find them reassuring."

Patrice paused. Some things had to be handled delicately. This wasn't one of them. "I don't have to tell you that they got T. C. Johnson to put up the seed money for the Carver and Strong samples. There's a lot more in the pipeline, Senator."

"I didn't hear that, Pat. Now, here's something I shouldn't have to tell you. The country doesn't believe in war heroes the way it used to. You need more than your old field jacket and a couple of medals to get elected. The country does believe the Pentagon is full of shit and it does believe in cutting taxes.

That's the bird we're going to fly in, my friend, not some cripple from Gus and Remy. Tell them I said so."

"You're the one who should tell them. Can I book them sometime? My place, maybe? We owe them that much."

Senator Taylor thought about it for a moment. The Bouvier struck the quarter hour.

"Sure, I have no problem with that."

He took his overcoat from the closet. Patrice watched until he had one arm in the coat. Then he said, "Gus and Remy say the reports were just teasers. There's more."

"Is that right? What's the main event?"

"You know Gus. He just laughed and said he had a secret weapon he wanted to try on you."

Senator Taylor stopped in the door.

"Fair enough. We ought to have one, too, don't you agree?"

"What do *you* have in mind?"

"Come on, Pat. This town is made of money. T. C. Johnson isn't the only game around. Go out and shake some other trees."

Out in the anteroom Adelle called, "The car's here." Senator Taylor winked at Patrice and left. Eight-thirty. Patrice listened to the chime. It sounded like fine crystal shattering on stone.

SIXTY-THREE

The General stood at the head of the table carving the leg of lamb while Melba served Sandy the oven-roasted potatoes. "All right, why were you with Remy and Gus today?" Sandy said after Melba withdrew to the kitchen. "You said later. It's later."

The General put down the carving knife. "We were talking business."

"What kind of business?"

"Their business. The F-44. They asked me to help them sell Jeff on it."

"I thought he was already sold."

"He was, but they fried the prototype out at Edwards. The backup has to be refitted. It won't be ready before the Senate votes on the appropriation. Jeff has the swing vote. They want me to persuade him that everything's okay."

"What did you tell them?"

"I told them I'd read the stats and performance reports and I'd think about it. Seems to me Gus has too much on his mind right now to worry about killing you."

The sarcasm grated. "I'm not making this up. Go out and count the shell cases around Hyduk's place."

"All right, all right. All I'm saying is that if there is something to this crazy story of yours, I don't see how you can be the primary target. If you're right, whoever is behind this was going after Hyduk. You and the girl just got in the way. Before we go any further, I need to know why you're pushing this mess so damn hard."

"Like you said, I want the truth."

"I want the facts."

Melba came in with a pitcher and refilled their glasses with ice water. When she was gone, the General said, "You want the truth and the reporter wants a story?"

"I guess you could put it that way."

"Do you think life's that simple? The truth. The big story. Where did you get that baloney? It didn't come from me. You're coming down on everyone like an old Sherman tank, all barrel and no brains. The truth and nothing but the truth. Get the hell out of my way and damn the consequences . . ."

"That's not fair, General."

"Fair? Not fair? Is what you're doing fair to Hyduk? You show up and the next thing Hyduk knows he's got a death squad on his neck. For the sake of the argument, let's say he did survive the firefight that got Alex. What good does it do him if you turn up thirty years later to finish him off?"

Sandy flushed. "He said something like that himself."

"That's the first thing you've said this evening that doesn't amaze me."

The General put down his knife and fork. They stuck out from the sides of his plate like sticks from a snare drum. "What we need to know is why anyone else would want to kill Hyduk. I'm the only one who wants to kill you, remember?"

At least he was joking about it now.

"Before you got so lathered up about the who, did it ever occur to you to find out the what of it?"

"Yes, sir. It did. There's something about ODA 351 we don't know. I'd say we've got the whole thing wrong. Dead wrong."

"Only if you're right, son. But I agree, it's worth looking into. So now, why don't you just take a closer look at the facts. Forget the truth. You may live longer."

*　　*　　*

If the General was a throwback to the forties, his kitchen was a monument to the fifties. The countertops were pale green tile, the double sink next to the ancient Amana range was white enamel, deep, with a narrow chromium trim; a circular window was cut in the swinging door. Melba was scrubbing the crust out of the roast pan when Sandy entered.

"*Qué tal, tiita.* My God, did you get me in trouble." He took the Brillo pad from her brown fingers and went to work on the corners of the pan.

"You sounded terrible, *halcón.* What else could I do? Are you sure you're all right?"

He didn't say anything. She listened to the rasping of pad on pan. The aroma of warm soap and charred lamb drippings filled the kitchen.

"Did he ever tell you anything about my father you didn't tell me?"

"*Nada.* Never anything."

He put the pad down on the counter, turned the hot water all the way up and ran the pan under it, burning his fingertips. "*Mierda, mierda, mierda.*"

She shook her head as he waved his fingers to cool them.

The gesture suddenly reminded her of the last time she'd burned her fingers. "Maybe there is something," she said. "I'm not sure. Maybe."

"What did he say?"

"Not something he said. Something he told me to throw out. Come. I'll show you."

She heard his footsteps behind her as she went down the wooden steps to the cellar. The ceiling was low. It grazed her hair as she walked over to the furnace, Sandy right behind her, bending like a gymnast.

The basement was very neat. It hadn't been that way the day she burned her fingers trying to relight the pilot on the furnace. Everyone thought the General was so tidy. That was because until she came he threw everything in the cellar. Old uniforms, tools, books, cracked pots from the garden.

The day she burned her hands, she had to move an old foot-locker away from the furnace to get at the pilot light. She could see that someone had stenciled a name and address on it. It said, *Lt. Alexander Grant Caine—5th SFG Group Nha Trang.*

The General heard her cry out. He came down and found her blowing on her hands. He took the matches and when he leaned over to light the pilot, he saw the footlocker. In the flickering yellow light of the match, she saw tears come to his eyes. "Throw that darn thing out. I don't want to see it again." He lit the furnace. After that, he blew out the match and went back upstairs.

It had taken her nearly a month to clean up the basement. She had thrown out all his junk. But not the footlocker. It was too important. It had made him cry.

So she had wrapped the footlocker in an old tarpaulin and kept it out of sight. Now she got down on her hands and knees next to the furnace. The pilot light was pretty, blue. Sandy was kneeling right behind her. In the closeness of the dim cellar, she could hear him breathing.

She opened a metal cupboard behind the furnace.

"There," she said, pointing to the box. Dust covered the oilcloth. Otherwise everything was the way she had left it in 1978. "Maybe you'll find what you're looking for in there."

*　　*　　*

The rain pelted down hard on the little Geo. Through the sweep of the windshield wipers, Rock Creek Parkway was a dark blur, red taillights streaming like tracers along the Potomac. Sandy glanced into the rearview mirror at Alex's footlocker on the backseat. Without the tarp, it reminded him of a small coffin, the kind they used for babies.

A flash of lightning backlit the Lincoln Memorial. Lumbering through the storm, he fought off a creepy feeling that he was riding alongside a box of old bones. Open it up and anything could come out. His destiny, maybe.

Lighten up, man, he warned himself. You are deeply full of it tonight. What about something a little simpler, like your destination? Where did she say her place was?

In the rearview mirror he saw the driver behind him flashing his headlights, prodding. He looked down at the speedometer. Forty-five, pretty sluggish even for Melba's little go-cart. He pulled into the slow lane and a burgundy BMW-in-a-hurry shot by.

Circuits smoking, Sandy turned into Rock Creek Park. The house was dark. Sandy parked in front and walked up to the door. He hesitated for a moment, then stabbed the bell. The porch light flashed on, and the door opened a crack. Behind the chain, he saw two frightened eyes looking out from a thicket of red hair. "Pups. Is that you?" Abbie was standing there with Kip's pistol. "There were noises when I got home, pups. I guess I'm jumpy."

He took the gun from her hand. She seemed happy to surrender it.

She was standing there in a flannel nightgown, ivory with small blue flowers, a granny gown with long sleeves. Even as covered as Old Mother Hubbard, she was beautiful. "Something in the car I need to show you," he said. She held the door open while he hauled the footlocker out of the car and carried it into the kitchen. "Over here," she said. "On the floor."

The footlocker was a steel and fiberboard number, olive drab with metal corners, scarred everywhere, covered with stains. It looked as if it had been tossed out of every truck and supply room from Nha Trang to Schofield Barracks to Fort Monroe.

Abbie handed him an old towel and he wiped off the metal. The key was stuck to the top with electrician's tape, the old kind before plastic, tacky black adhesive tape that stuck to Sandy's fingers as he pulled it back. The lock was jammed. For a moment he twisted the key carefully, then savagely until Abbie put her hand over his.

"Wait a second, caveman." She went to the drawer next to the refrigerator where she kept her junk, string and old rubber bands, pliers, a screwdriver and hand drill, and brought back a can fitted with a long nozzle that looked like a straw. She shot a stream of silicon into the lock, then gave Sandy back the key. This time the lock clicked open as smoothly as a German lighter.

When he raised the lid, the footlocker gave off a stale puff of mothballs and mildew, the smell of decaying cloth and damp paper, an essence of futility. Death.

The bottom of the box was crammed with tee shirts and shorts. He saw several sets of starched fatigues and a neatly folded khaki uniform beneath a faded red windbreaker with BOSTON RED SOX on the back. Running his fingers under the clothes, he felt a small metal box. Inside it were Alex's Combat Infantryman's Badge and a campaign ribbon for service in the Dominican Republic.

On top of the badge and ribbon, he found a soiled manila envelope marked "Personal Effects." The metal fastener broke when Sandy bent it back and dumped out the contents—a small clasp knife, a Zippo lighter, a unit coin and something that looked like a mummified roast beef sandwich.

He turned the coin over in his hand. On one side, the insignia of the Special Forces, on the other "ODA 351, 5th Special Forces Group, Vietnam." Lucky coin. Yeah, right. He flipped it onto the table. It clinked against the clasp knife, quivered, rattled down flat.

Death rattle.

Sandy examined the sandwich. Alex's wallet. On the back was a monogram in faded gold letters. AGC. Mark Cross. Fine fatted calf for the altar at Lang Vei.

Blood from Alex's wounds had glued the wallet into a lump. Sandy peeled back the darkly crusted leather. Inside, the piastres were wadded together like blackened papier-mâché. Stuck face-up to the bottom of the wad was a snapshot. Sandy opened the clasp knife. Working carefully, trying not to scrape away the emulsion, he used the small blade to tease the image out from under the rotted legal tender.

A woman in a bathing suit. Light hair. A face like a Polish saint's. Young, so very young. Not your ordinary swimsuit number. Breasts, yes. Enormous, swelling over the top of the one-piece suit. An even more enormous belly—a full, beach ball curve.

He turned the picture over. On the reverse side, he could just make out the last faint traces of the lipstick mark, the vanishing silhouette of a woman's full lips. Above and below the kiss were a few words, also faint, written in lipstick.

Bellies of Love from me and the Wolf Pup. Barbara.

He'd always been pups.

A convulsion.

It began in his gut and rose through his chest. He heard Abbie saying, "Pups, what's the matter?" He felt her hand stroking the back of his neck as he put his head on the table next to the wallet and picture. The sobs came with no sound. The only sign was his body, shuddering like a storm-blown aspen.

SIXTY-FOUR

★ Whitefish ★

An owl's cry floated through the small window of the cabin. Midrange. Alto. Like two soft notes from an oboe somewhere out there in the dark. Larry Hyduk stopped writing in the gray notebook. Putting down his pen, he cocked his head and listened.

Still not quite right.

He'd have to give the kid another lesson.

On the table, the hissing Coleman lantern gave off a bright white light. Leaning over, he closed the notebook, putting it into his field jacket pocket next to his knife. Then he cut the light. When his eyes had adjusted to the darkness, he picked up his rifle, slipped out the rear door and circled out and behind the owl.

"Who. Whhhhooooooooo."

The cry fell off into a strangled gurgle as Hyduk struck. Jamming the index finger of his left hand into the boy's throat, the soft spot where the collarbone met the neck, he pressed the back of the knife blade under his ear.

"You're dead, Zack."

His whisper hissed like a snake through dry leaves. The boy didn't move. "C'mon, Larry," he said. "It wasn't that bad. Gimme a break. I got news."

"You got a tin ear, boy. Get you killed. Your news more important than that?"

It was just short of midnight. Over the shoulder of the mountains at the far end of the lake, a full moon was beginning its climb. Across the dark water, the moonlight cast a reflection as wide as a freeway. "Down there," Zack said. He pointed to a small sandbank where a boat, partly hidden by low firs, was beached. "Someone pulled that thing in there a few minutes ago."

Hyduk nodded. Standing up, he headed back toward the cabin at a quick trot, the boy swinging in alongside him. When they got there, Zack took out the dummies and arranged them on the two beds. Two burlap bags filled with old clothes, a coupla mixing bowls for heads. They had drilled it dozens of times, until setting it up took less than a minute. When everything was in place, they slipped out the back door into the woods and made a swing around the cabin's outer security perimeter. They found nothing, heard nothing. At the end of the swing, they were back at the boulder overlooking the cabin and the lake. The boat was gone.

The moon was higher now. No one rowing on the lake. Hyduk didn't like it. For two hours they sat as motionless as deer hunters waiting for dawn. Finally, Hyduk stretched his legs.

"Shit, false alarm," he whispered, turning to Zack. "Maybe I'm getting paranoid."

"Getting?"

Beeeeeowwwwwwwww.

The shriek of the RPG ripped through the darkness like the scream of a small animal.

A dull thump rolled across the lake as the cabin exploded, the windows spraying glass, red flames shooting skyward. The crowns of the firs next to the cabin ignited like torches.

"Burn 'em, goddamn it," he yelled to Zack. "They're through the wire."

He fell to the prone and looked through his sniper scope. Two men, backlit against the flames, came into focus. The first was holding an RPG launcher, a new round ready to fire. In the hands of the second he saw the stubby stock and banana clip curve of an AK-47.

He pressed his eye against the scope. When the crosshairs met between the shoulders of the guy with the RPG, he slowly squeezed.

Pfffsssstttt.

The gunner pitched forward, the launcher falling to the ground and rolling into the flames. As they licked around the projectile, the guy with the AK-47 sprinted for the trees.

Pffffsssstttt.

Hyduk's second shot caught him in the throat. His hands rose to his neck, but his scream was lost in the explosion of ammo cooking off in the cabin.

Hyduk felt something cold sting his face. He reached up his hand. Pine needles, millions of them, blasted from the firs, were falling around him like spring hail.

Little needles, stinging his face. The explosions of the mortars crumping down. The timbers on the bunker splintering, peppering his face.

The roar of the second explosion still scouring his brain.

Behind the flames. Men moving. The green uniforms. The little helmets.

"Goddamn it, Captain Taylor," he bellowed. "Where the fuck are you?"

He saw the Wolf running through the fire, toward him, bent double, the Swedish K pulled into his gut, coming right toward him until he could see his face.

And then the little puff as the field jacket jumped and the body falling, spraying blood across the ground. Hyduk felt the hot wetness of blood on his shoulder and face. The body twitched violently for a few seconds, then lay still. Reaching forward, he turned the corpse face up.

Not Wolf. What the fuck?

"Colonel Train," he said in disbelief. "What are *you* doing here, Midnight?"

And then he saw Zack, the old M-1 hanging limply from his hand. Zack, face white, throwing up next to him.

Hyduk leaned back against the boulder. His mind was a washer on spin cycle, wild images, memories, the past and present overlapping, flattening against one another as they swirled. The spinning went faster and faster. And then, like a bandage ripped from a healed wound, he saw everything, remembered it all.

He reached into his jacket pocket and pulled out the gray notebook and pen. His fingers felt stiff, but between the full moon and the glow from the burning cabin, he was able to get it all down. Closing the book, he gave it to the boy.

"Mail this for me. Go call Grattan and tell him to get up here fast."

"I'm staying, sir."

"That's an order, Zack."

The boy's shoulders slumped, then he turned around and disappeared into the woods.

Hyduk got up and dragged Train's body behind the boulder. Then he walked toward the fire. His first kill was facedown about 30 feet from where the cabin had been. The round had bounced off a bone, glanced up and torn off his jaw. Wasn't much left to identify.

He found the third body impaled on a fir, neck broken, a jagged branch poking like the tip of a spear out from under the rib cage. Raising his rifle, he shot the branch off the trunk. The body crashed to the ground. Welcome to Montana, he muttered to himself. Scenic drives, hunting, boating. Bring the whole fucking family.

He went back to the boulder where he had stowed Train. Taking off his jacket, he broke two long branches and stuck them through the arms, improvising a crude travois.

At least it was all downhill.

It took half an hour to horse the first body down to the sandbank by the lake. Even though it was cold, low forties by the way the night felt on his face, he had sweated through his fatigues.

He covered Train's body with a few pine boughs, then walked into the firs wondering if he could get a boat with three bodies into the lake alone.

He found the boat tipped on its side behind the wall of firs. Where were the fucking oars? He walked around it and saw them lying under tree branches on the ground.

Three Stooges. What did they think? Someone was gonna steal their oars? He bent over to see how much wiggle room they had left him. His back was to the trees. A cloud drifted over the moon.

No shadow warned him. No sound came from the forest.

A tall, lean figure dressed in black—black boots, black combat pants, black sweater, black watch cap—stepped out of the trees. He caught Hyduk's neck in the crook of his arm.

"G'night, Larry," he said, sealing the carotid arteries like straws in a vise. "Time to close down the show."

SIXTY-FIVE

★ Rock Creek Park ★

Sandy felt a draft from the open window playing across his back. Reaching sideways, he touched empty sheets. Still face-down, he groped along the night table for his watch. Five forty-five. How did she do it? He still felt whacked.

After he'd stopped bawling, she'd taken him to bed. For half an hour he'd stared at the ceiling unable to move. The whole time, she lay there quietly until the warmth from her side of the bed thawed him, restored him to life. He turned and entered her like a man coming home. No pyrotechnics this time. "I love you," he said. "I know," she told him—that was all. Now she was probably downtown covering a riot.

He took a quick shower, pulled on his clothes and went downstairs. In the kitchen, he found a note with two black arrows. The first, pointing toward the microwave, said *Six minutes*. The second, pointing to a large bowl of oatmeal and sliced pears covered with Saran Wrap, said, *Eat me*.

He found an old jar of instant coffee hidden behind boxes of herbal tea. Lousy, but it had caffeine. It would have to do.

The footlocker yawned at him from the far end of the table. Last night he'd found himself in there. Now where was Alex?

Under Alex's uniform, he found a canvas-bound journal wrapped in a brown tee shirt and a small souvenir photo album.

The album was robin's-egg blue. On one side, in silvery letters, was the bargirls' international anthem. GOOD GUY GI. Turning it over, he saw WELCOME NHA TRANG.

He hesitated, not sure that giggling hookers and shitfaced grunts were what he wanted to face so early in the morning. He opened the book. No semi-pro porn. No tits and ass. No swollen dicks, no gaping beavers. Alex had purged the half-dozen plastic sleeves of their original contents and filled them with pictures from home.

There the young officer stood, in full dress uniform, his new wife in full bridal regalia clinging to his arm, his best man standing at his side. In the camera's flash, the new captain's bars gleaming on Jeff Taylor's shoulders matched the glitter coming off the 2-carat rock sparkling on Barbara's finger.

Behind them was the General, rigidly at ill-ease, standing under a giant banner that said SONS OF POLAND. Under the banner was the most all-American family Sandy had ever seen. Older men with strong faces, women with powerful arms, the younger ones from Alex and Barbara's generation innocent, fresh, a little blond girl with long braids clung to the bride's dress, a towheaded boy looking enviously at the uniform of the groom.

No coupon cutters in there, no cookie pushers. They were wonderful. Eat the Putnams alive. Maybe even the Caines. Why hadn't the General sent *Alex* to live with them?

Flipping through the other images, he saw another motif. Jeff Taylor was everywhere. The earliest shot showed Jeff and Alex in tennis shorts and Andover sweaters, Alex short, skinny, at the net, bending forward, peering intently through thick glasses, his face just cresting the tape, Jeff towering at the service line, back arched, undoubtedly smacking an ace.

A second shot showed Alex as a plebe, much taller now, but just as skinny. Jeff had him braced tighter than a two-dollar vise. Serious West Point stuff going down. Another snap caught the two of them in sweatsuits clowning beside the stone boot monument. Sandy smiled, remembering the old legend from the Point. If a cadet flunking a course went out to the boot at midnight and prayed his ass off, he'd pass. Alex must have put in plenty of time at the boot after he met Barbara.

Ancient history. Where was the real stuff? He flipped the sleeve and finally found what he was looking for. The SF camp at Lang Vei. Eleven men posed for the family portrait outside the command bunker. All wearing green berets, tiger suits.

Almost out of the picture, leaning against the side of the bunker, was a sturdy, alert-looking warrior in his early twenties. He had put his rifle next to him on the roof of the bunker. Even pushed into the background, the sniper scope stuck out above the timbers.

Intense eyes. Dark. Half crazy. No question. It was Larry.

Jeff and Alex stood on either side of the bunker door. Jeff had a briar pipe clenched in his jaw. Christ, he looked like Gregory Fucking Peck. Where did he think he was? Pork Chop Hill?

Alex was now only a bit shorter than Jeff, not so broad across the shoulders, still not much meat on his bones. Boots, tiger stripe, indistinguishable from the grunts. But he looked different. Quite different.

It was the field jacket. He hadn't noticed at first because none of the other men were wearing theirs. Too hot, probably, and Jeff had his OD jacket hanging from his shoulder.

Alex's jacket wasn't standard issue. Sandy had never seen one like it. The photograph was faded, but he could still make out the colors. It was green, brown and black in some kind of speckled arrangement. Very tight fit. He laughed. It reminded him of the jacket he had seen on Errol Flynn, leading guerrillas against the Japanese in *Objective Burma*. War movie shit.

The jacket had big pockets up on the chest, slash pockets down below. All of them were buttoned. Through a gap on the top left pocket, a long antenna stuck out. Examining the picture more closely, he could see the outline of something about twice the size of a cassette recorder bulging in the pocket.

Ground-to-air radio. TAC AIR.

He took another sip of the coffee. Cold, awful. He got up and dumped it in the sink. Picking up the photograph, he went to the phone and punched a number.

"Allo." A woman's voice. Syrupy accent. Thick as Turkish coffee.

"Elena? Is that you?"

"Yisss. I am Elena. Secretary. Sergeant Caldwell is in conferential."

"Elena, this is Captain Caine."

Short pause. "Sergeant Caldwell is not in office. Leave me his message, please. I get to him."

"Elena, it's me. Sandy Caine. Zagreb. What have you done to Nate?"

"Well, he is, you know, sleeping."

No doubt. At least Nate's woman was there the next morning.

"You roll him out of the sack and tell him Sandy's going to burn his ass if he doesn't haul it."

"Sandy? Sandy, darleeng," she trilled. "Is you? Why not you say?"

A low thumping noise, louder as it approached the phone. Then:

"This better be fucking good. You calling from the stockade?"

"Close. I can't explain everything right now. Just one question, then you and Elena can get back at it."

"Yeah, what?"

"I'm looking at a picture of a field jacket from Nam. Weird-looking. Not like one of ours. Lotta speckles, black, white, brown. Tight fit, very sharp."

He heard Nate grunt.

"Got pockets all over hell? Metal buttons? Very sexy?"

"Roger that."

"French. Paratroopers had 'em. Bad, bad motherfuckers. I think some of the ARVN Airborne got 'em from the French. You in SF, you killed to get one. It was like, if your best friend had got one somewhere you'd be saying, 'Yo, Jackson, you buy it, fuck your boots, I'm in your jacket and outta there, man.'

"It was like this. You want to be an SF stud, you gotta have your opal ring on the pinkie, the Montagnard bracelet on the wrist that didn't have the steel Rolex. That make you a stud. But you got one of those French jackets, you were King Fucking Kong."

"Thanks, Nate. Call you later."

He hung up the phone. Back at the table he slipped the picture into its sleeve and picked up the journal. The first entry was dated August 18, 1960. Alex's plebe year.

Beast Barracks. Week One
So you wanted to play soldier, be like Jeff, save the country, kiss the girls. How stupid could you get? Out on the parade ground two hours: "What are you, plebe?" "A worm, sir." "What was that?" "Worm shit, sir." And coming from Jeff.

Usual stuff. Might have written the same thing himself. He paged through the journal. In the beginning, the longest entries were on soldiering; Alex's dreams, induced by the General,

shaped around Jeff; also some doubts, sharp at first, sharper until
he met Barbara. Then they seemed to subside.

The philosophy and the love story would keep. He folded
back three fourths of the journal until Vietnam. Moving to fast
forward, he stopped at an entry marked with three exclamation
marks. Alex hadn't done anything like that before.

> *Lang Vei*
> *July 24, 1966*
> *Shit happens. NVA ambush near Lang Vei, another recon*
> *patrol. Too many of them. Can't get Jeff to stop going by*
> *the book. The gooks had our MO cold. Perkins had the*
> *point, they let him pass, then cut us up. No good choices.*
> *Hauled my ass in, hauled his ass out. Three WIA including*
> *Perkins. No KIA, thank God. Perkins one happy dude.*
> *Dusted him down to Nha Trang. Sorry to see him go.*
> *Good man. Very good man.*

A few pages later, there was a second entry, more terse:

> *I Corps*
> *July 31, 1966*
> *Note from Perkins, he's not coming back. Medevac USA.*
> *Sent a present: French cammo jacket, real beauty. Said he*
> *bought it off a Vietnamese nurse who got it from some*
> *shotup ARVN Airborne Captain. Replacement for Perkins*
> *reported tonight. Lawrence Hyduk. Think he could be*
> *okay. Weirdo. But great combat record. Word is he's one of*
> *the best snipers in S.F.*

The last twenty pages were blank. Backtracking, Sandy came
to the final entry.

> *Lang Vei*
> *August 20, 1966*
> *Things heating up. NVA probes. Intell predicting big at-*
> *tack. No time to send the Big P to Babs. DON'T FORGET.*

Some milk run. What was the Big P? He closed the journal.
The answer was in there somewhere. He'd track it down later.

He started to repack the footlocker. At the bottom of the personal effects envelope he felt a hard lump he'd missed the night

before. Something was stuck in one of the corners. He poked at it with his finger, and a ring dropped onto the table.

"West Point. Class of 1964. Duty Honor Country."

Alex's ring.

Sandy never wore his own. He couldn't stop thinking it was like wearing your pedigree on your sleeve, a bad form of pulling rank. Absently, he tried the ring on his finger. It didn't fit.

Of course, moron. Alex was a smaller-boned guy, a Powell-Putnam as well as a Caine. Just like Sandy was a Brakowski. Slipping the ring into the envelope, he put it back on top of the red windbreaker.

Sticking out of the pocket was the end of a faded ribbon. *P* for pocket, *p* for pitcher, *p* for pissed off—what the hell was Alex thinking about?

At one time in the past, the ribbon had been red and blue. But the colors had bled into one another, leaving only a darkish pink. When he reached down and tugged it, he pulled out a small jewelry box. The box was disintegrating, like the ribbon tied around it.

He opened the box carefully. Inside was something that looked like a flat napkin ring, black, pressed over a prune, also black. He poked the prune. It was rubber, dry on the outside, slightly tacky in the creases. It crumbled, the pieces sticking to his fingertips.

Suddenly he recognized this ring, too.

It was a pacifier. The nipple had rotted, but there was just enough of the tip left in the prune to give it away. A baby's pacifier.

Next to it was a sealed envelope marked "Maison Bleu" with a street address in Saigon. Inside he found a gift card with a note in the same handwriting he had seen in the journal.

Darling Babs,
This is for the son you've decided you're carrying. To free
up the real ones for me. Love you both. Yours forever,

Alex

The Big P. Lieutenant Caine's own pacification program. Ripping a sheet of paper towel from the rack next to the sink, he polished the ring furiously. It was metal, badly tarnished. He rubbed harder. Silver. From under the black tarnish, another monogram began to appear.

The letters were engraved. A fancy script, vaguely European.
AGC II Pfc

Name, rank, everything but the serial number for Babs and her beach ball.

Born to be a soldier.

SIXTY-SIX

The message light on Abbie's telephone was flashing. Not nice to snoop. Screw it. When the girl's away the guy will play. Sandy punched the play button.

"That you, reporter lady?"

Hyduk's voice startled him. Whatever the Night Stalker remembered had to be itching his ass. Nothing else would have gotten him within ten miles of town. He listened to the message twice and rewound the machine.

As he was considering it, the phone rang.

"Your wake-up service, pups. You okay? Steal any messages yet?"

"Gentlemen don't read other people's mail."

"Gentlemen, never. What about Green Berets?"

"Okay, okay, but it's your fault. I get evil when I wake up alone." He told her about Larry.

"What do you think he's got for us?" she asked him.

"Pulitzer stuff. No question."

"Come on, pups, don't be cruel."

"I can't see him leaving his tracks on your machine if it's not important. When can you leave?"

She didn't answer.

"It's on me. You bought the tickets last time."

"You go."

"Hey, I need you."

"You need a diversion, Sneaky Pete. Look, something's going on at Jeff Taylor's office. Patrice told me he got in at five. He was talking about turning the burner up on Jeff's future. And Julian's acting way over the top. He told me we could be looking at an announcement before the end of December."

"I can see it now, Patrice buying votes with beignets."

"Too true. But Patrice isn't a lurcher. This isn't like him. He's hauling Jeff out to the Korean War Memorial tomorrow afternoon for the dedication. I need to be there."

What was it the General had said? Something about Jeff knowing more about Abbie than he did?

"I think you should go with me."

Pause.

"I can't. But you can, you should."

"Yes, ma'am."

He rang off. No time to be jealous. He had two hours to catch the plane.

*   *   *

"Tryin' to love two soldiers is lahhhk a baaaahhhhl and chain . . ."

Becca was dancing behind Abbie's desk. Singing and dancing.

"Sometimes the pleasuhhhhh ain't worth the paaaaaiiiiiiin."

"I don't fall in love with prehistoric senators, so why don't you shut up?"

"Oooooh, ooooooh, ain't worth the paaaaiiiiiin . . . What about the other one?"

Abbie picked up the telephone and hit the memory button.

"I'm thinking about it."

Two rings, then the pick-up.

"Morning, Patrice. It's me. Just confirming tomorrow. Great. I'll catch you out at the Memorial."

As she was hanging up, Becca leaned down and whispered in her ear.

"You think about it much longer, darlin', you're gonna be one very lonely old thang."

*   *   *

The fire in the bar was down to a few red embers when Sandy came into the Grouse Mountain Lodge. He ordered a double Jack D. Down at the end of the bar, Grattan was playing liar's dice with a weather-beaten guy in a business suit and cowboy boots. Sandy listened to the thump of the dark leather dice cup and thought of Alex. Some men got to roll 'em, some men got rolled. All the rest was lies.

"Damn you, son."

"You lose, Pop. Pay up. Sixteen bucks on the barrel head."

As Grattan slid the cup toward the bartender, he noticed Sandy. Putting his arm around the older man's shoulder, he walked him to Sandy's stool. "Thought you'd be back, young soldier. Meet my old man. Roger Grattan. Worst dice player ever retired from the FBI."

The old guy had a grip like a pipe fitter. "Ten years in Butte," Roger Grattan said cheerfully. "Piss off Mr. Hoover, it's Butte for life. Am I right?"

"Never knew Mr. Hoover."

"Then what's an eastern slick like you doing here. *I* was born here. That's my excuse. What's yours?" He was a little tight, belligerent in a friendly Irish way.

"Just a little R and R, sir. I thought I'd check into the old soldiers home here and take some of that dice money off your son."

"He cheats." The old guy took his hat off the rack. "Doesn't help to watch him. Just pisses you off. Best bring your own dice."

A gust of wind blew through the lobby as Roger Grattan went through the door. "How's that make you feel?" Sandy said. Grattan took out a cigarette, thought better of it and tossed it into an ashtray unlit.

"Lying old buzzard. Taught me everything I know."

Sandy laughed. "Man, you don't know how lucky you are. Look, could I borrow the four-wheel again tomorrow? I gotta talk to Hyduk."

"How about I go with you?"

"Thanks." Sandy tossed back the last of the drink. "Going to see Hyduk, you need backup."

"A fire team, at least. See you at breakfast."

At 0600 the next morning, he met Grattan in the dining room. They stuffed away platters of bacon and eggs, then hit the road, Sandy driving, Grattan riding shotgun. At the log chute, he turned left, skirted Hyduk's tank trap, and rolled along for half a mile until Grattan signaled him to stop. "Open your window," Grattan said, rolling down his. The air had been cold and fresh when they started up the mountain. Sandy cracked the window. A dark, sour smell drifted into the four-wheel. Working up the mountain in second, he had missed it over the exhaust. No way to miss it now. "You, too?" Grattan said.

"Let's get there." Sandy jammed the four-wheel into gear.

The blackened embers of Hyduk's cabin were still smoldering. In the light breeze, the gray smoke curled around two bodies lying just beyond a ragged arc of burned brush.

Sandy crouched next to the corpses. The cammo outfits were scorched, and the bodies were stiff, dead a day or two at least, but no bears had been working on them. Pulling with both hands, he rolled them over.

Not Larry. Not Zack.

"Not too smart to get Hyduk pissed off," Grattan said.

For an hour they poked through the charred cabin. Nothing. They started working their way out from the burn, trying to pin down where the death squad had come in, where Hyduk and the boy had left. Again nothing. Until they reached a large boulder on the high ground.

"Got 'em," Grattan shouted.

On the backside of the boulder a long smear of blood pointed down to a gluey black mess of pine needles on the forest floor. The brush was broken in a narrow path leading off through the trees and down toward the lake.

"Look at this." Grattan opened his palm and held out three empty .30-caliber cases.

"Maybe he missed once," Sandy said.

"Maybe God's got one eye. Where's the other body?"

"Who gives a shit? Where's Hyduk? Where's Zack?"

Grattan stood up and blew out his lips in a travesty of a sigh. "You're right, we better get Wilbur on this." He pulled his cellular from a jacket pocket and flipped it open. "Hello, Agnes, Tim Grattan here. Tell Bob I got two missing persons and a load of charbroil for him up by Lolo Overlook. Tell him I'll meet him at the loggers' crossroad and take him in. He's gonna need the coroner and the bag-and-shovel boys. Yeah, Agnes, you, too. Have a nice day."

Grattan snapped the cellular shut and they headed back down the mountain to the creek leading up to Hyduk's command post. Sandy told Grattan to stop. Jumping out, he made his way up the stream, Grattan trotting behind him. "What's the big hurry?" he yelled as Sandy tore off the path into the brush.

About 30 yards up the path, Sandy found the rotten stump Hyduk had showed him. On top of the stump was a large flat rock. Before, there had only been the hole. He pushed the rock until it balanced on the edge of the stump then fell to the ground. The hole inside the stump was maybe three feet deep. Reaching in until his armpit grazed the rim, he groped blindly with his fingers. He felt soft moss, the slime of a slug. Then he touched something hard and flat wedged sideways at the very bottom of the hole. Prying it up with his fingers, he pulled it out.

A gray notebook. The cover was spotted. Brushing it off with the side of his hand, he saw that the spots were dried blood.

Grattan was standing next to him now, wheezing. Sandy opened the notebook. Block letters in brown. Hyduk. He looked over at Grattan. "Sun, rain, shitstorm, nothing stops the mail. Isn't that what they say?"

Craaaaaaaaaaaaaaaccccck.

The bullet ripped through the branches over Sandy's head. He hit the dirt behind a tree. Grattan smacked down next to him, pistol drawn.

Craaaaaaaaacccccck. Craaaaaaaaaacccccck. Two more rounds, well over their heads. Sandy peered around the trunk of the tree. From across the meadow, a small figure in combat pants and enormous boots was running toward them. Charging them. It was the boy.

"Hold your fire, Zack," Sandy roared. "It's me."

Craaaaaacccccccck.

The boy was nearly to the tree line now. As he pumped forward, one of his boots snagged on a fallen branch. He sprawled on his face. The rifle flew out of his hands.

Sandy tackled him, landing on his back, pinning him to the damp earth.

"Easy, Zack."

"You no-good shit. You killed Larry."

Sandy rolled the squirming boy over and sat on his chest.

"You got the wrong guy, Zack. I wasn't even here."

Grattan came up with the M-1, holding it barrel down. "What've we got here? Rambo Junior?"

"We're friendlies, Zack," Sandy shouted. "Friendlies." The boy squinted up at him. "Is that you, Captain Caine?"

"You're damn right it's me." Grattan checked the rifle.

"Where you been, sir? They got Larry."

"Slow down, kid. I'm going to let you up now, okay?" Lifting himself off the boy's chest, Sandy held out a hand, and helped him to his feet. "You all right, Zack?"

The boy looked sceptically at Grattan. "It's okay, this is Tim Grattan, he's one of us," Sandy said. Grattan ejected the clip and held out the empty M-1 to the boy.

Zack grabbed the rifle. "Grattan? You were the guy Larry told me to find. He ordered me to mail that shit you got there in your hand and to fetch Mr. Grattan. But I couldn't get the truck to turn over, so I went back. To help him. Larry." He wiped his nose. "I saw it. The tall guy, he took Larry down. I saw him put Larry in the boat and row into the lake. I couldn't take a shot. I was afraid I'd hit Larry."

Sandy put his hands on Zack's shoulders.

"It's not your fault, kid."

"Larry's gone, Captain. Whose fault is it?"

The boy sat down on a log. Laying the old rifle across his lap, he leaned forward until his forehead touched his knees. "I'm sorry, Larry," he whispered. "I'm sorry, I'm so fucking sorry." Sandy put his arms around the boy and rocked him.

"Come on, Zack," he said softly. "You've got work to do, man. We've got to find Larry."

SIXTY-SEVEN

★ Washington, D.C. ★

A gray sky over the Mall, snowflakes drifting across the temple to Abraham Lincoln. As Jefferson Taylor's limo drove up to the new Korean War Memorial, nineteen stainless-steel warriors loomed up in front of him like giants in a nightmare. Each man stood 9 feet high. A reinforced squad on patrol, advancing with weapons at port arms, flankers to the right and left of the point man, the leader clutching an old SCR 536—the radio that never worked.

Senator Taylor pressed a button and the rear window purred down. The grass was beginning to turn white, but around the monument's base, the TV lights cast a hot glare on the statues, warming the barrels of the rifles, melting the drifting flakes of snow.

The soldiers were wearing ponchos. You never wore your poncho into combat, no matter what the war. Get tangled in a poncho before you could shoot and it turned into your body bag. Interesting mistake, Senator Taylor reflected. Saving money, maybe. Steel poncho, the sculptor didn't have to do full justice to the men underneath. Cheat 'em, some. Just the way it was in Korea and Vietnam and every other fucking war.

"You think they're advancing or retreating?" he said to Patrice.

"What difference does it make?"

Patrice was sitting on the jump seat scribbling last-minute

talking points into the senator's speech. Senator Taylor pushed the button again, and the window slid upward, cocooning them snugly in the limo.

"Big difference, my friend. You should try it sometime." He leaned back in the soft black leather. As the window began to steam up, the warriors disappeared. Patrice looked worried, Taylor thought. Maybe it was the snow. Spoil the lighting.

Leaning across the seat well, Patrice handed him the speech. "Couple problems, I think. Take a look." The top of the text was clean but near the third paragraph there was a giant question mark, and one phrase was crossed out. But before Taylor could absorb the changes, he heard a tap on the window. Rubbing a little porthole through the steam, he saw Abigail Mancini.

"Read all about it," he said to Patrice, signaling the driver to unlock the door.

"I'd rather not." Pat opened his attaché case and buried himself in a batch of memos.

The reporter ducked into the limo and sat next to Taylor. With the dust of snow on her red hair and the cold reddening her cheeks, she looked stunning.

Yeah, sure. Who was he kidding? The girl was no Janine. There was only one Janine and now she was gone. He had driven her away.

"Where's the lap robe?" Abbie asked, smiling at him.

"I thought you didn't mix business and pleasure."

"I don't." She crossed her arms and hugged herself. "I just don't like winter."

He handed her the speech, enjoying the look of irritation on Patrice's face. The President was dedicating the new memorial. Count on him for the usual false pieties. His own remarks were scheduled for five minutes, no more. Plenty of time to float a balloon or two. Dry run for the Announcement. In his mind the phrase now came in capital letters, as if it were the Annunciation.

Abbie started to read the speech out loud. "We stand here today in the shadow of good men and bad weapons." She shrugged. "Not bad, Senator. Did Patrice write it for you?"

Patrice looked up from the open attaché case. "The credit's entirely his, *chér*."

"You'll have to cut Pat some slack today. He's trying to save me from myself."

She pointed to the third paragraph. It said: "The first lesson of Korea was never to neglect the basics of combat, the rifles, the helmets, the boots you see here today. The second was that we can't expect to win our next war with the weapons from the last. If you look behind me, today, you won't find an infantry-fired tank killer with these heroes. That wasn't just the sculptor's choice. Or theirs. They didn't have one. We are only getting an effective one now, forty years too late for these heroes, fifty years too late for the men who were ground into the tracks of German panzers in Sicily and France. It means death to forget the basics. Let's not forget that in this age of computers, satellites and fighter jets that go for two hundred million dollars a pop."

Patrice had crossed out the final phrase.

"I see your man has done some pruning." Abbie handed back the text.

"That he did," Taylor said, opening the door. "Come on with me. Patrice needs time alone so he can pout, and I could use an escort."

When he opened the car door, they could hear the Marine Band tuning up. The players, almost blue from the cold, were drawn up next to a small platform. Stamping their feet to keep warm, the reporters looked surly, bored.

Taylor's seat was six down from the President's, as far off as they could put him without shoving him off the platform. One by one the other dignitaries arrived, the Secretary of the Army first, then the Chairman of the Joint Chiefs, after him, the SecDef. Everyone in proper order, as if even the limos knew the protocol.

The President's motorcade, a brigade of motorcycle cops to the front, flanks and rear of the bulletproof limousine—arrived last. Taylor tried to remember what he'd read about Lincoln stepping off the train from Illinois alone after his first election, walking to his own inaugural. Not this guy.

"Afternoon, Senator," the President said as he mounted the platform. "I'm looking forward to your performance in this theater of honor."

Taylor smiled politely. Theater of honor. Who gave him that crap? The cameras rolled, the show went on, the President playing true to form. For ten minutes he talked about glory, sacrifice, valor, sprinkling clichés across the speech like toppings on soft ice cream. The SecDef got up to add a few more. Then the Secretary of the Army introduced Taylor.

"Hero in battle. Man of the Senate."

428 ★ David H. Hackworth

Also a cliché, missing only its final cadence: *and next President of . . .*

Adjusting the microphone, he saw that the TV cameramen were going to roll as soon as he began. The senator was the last speaker. Pat had alerted the network producers that the good stuff would come early. They could grab it and still make their feeds for the evening news.

Applause met his line about good men and bad weapons. The cameras were still running as Patrice's warning at paragraph 3 loomed like a detour sign on a stretch of washed out road.

Screw Patrice. And Gus. And Remy. He was the one with his dick on the block. On the battlefield, it ain't show, it's go. He launched into the offending paragraph.

"The first lesson of Korea . . ."

Safe boilerplate. Bulletproof.

"It means death to forget the basics."

The politicians and military leaders began to shift uncomfortably.

"Let's not forget that in this age of computers, satellites and fighter jets that go for two hundred million dollars a pop."

Clearing of throats. No applause. The SecDef looked astounded, the President amused. "Nice shot," he said on his way back to his car. "You should have thrown in campaign finance, Senator. Why not? Seeing you'll be running on five-dollar contributions."

"I'm working on it."

"You do that," he said. "Give you something to think about while everyone else rakes in the dough."

Taylor let the motorcade wind away from the memorial and shoot across the Mall before he left the platform. When he started for his limo, he felt a light, feminine touch on his arm. The reporter. He had forgotten about her. "That was great, Jeff," she said. "I didn't think you'd go all the way. What's Patrice going to do with you?"

"Why don't we find out?" he said, walking her toward the limo. "I'll drop you at the *Chronicle*, home. Whatever."

She hesitated as the driver jumped out to open the door. Taylor got in first, as if the car wouldn't start any other way, and then scrambled in beside him. The driver looked into the rearview mirror, the senator looked at the reporter.

"The *Chronicle*," she said quickly.

From the jump seat, Patrice was looking at the senator as if he had just announced his conversion to socialism.

"So, Pat. What do you think?" Abbie asked him.

Patrice closed the attaché case. "I preferred the war hero. I'm not sure I can handle the saint."

* * *

On the evening news that night, the networks devoted a minute twenty seconds to the story. There was nothing from the President's speech. The first few seconds showed his face darkening as Jefferson Taylor scored points with his line about men and weapons. Then followed a thirty-second soundbite showing Taylor's face close up, earnest, highly attractive in contrast to the pudgy profile of the man sitting on the stand with him.

As the finale, the cameras came in on the senator, the beautiful young woman on his arm, her flaming red hair, the great legs as she leaned over to step into the limousine.

The TV reporters, so surly before the event, seemed quite cheerful now. They made allusions to Jack Kennedy. *Senator* Kennedy. They pointed out how dangerous it had been for Dick Nixon to be such a lump when JFK was on the prowl.

"So what do you think, Pat?" Taylor said, surfing the rest of the newscasts. The versions were almost identical, as if a single intelligence, or perhaps none, had written the script.

Patrice looked at him stonily.

"Premature ejaculation," he said. "Too little too soon."

Taylor tossed the remote onto the coffee table. He was about to make an issue of it when Adelle stuck her head through the door.

"Call for you, Patrice."

"Not now, Adelle," the senator said.

"It's Janine."

Taylor looked at Patrice like a man reaching for a life rope. "I'll take it in here, Adelle," Patrice said, moving over to the phone at the end of the couch. "Put her through."

"*Bon soir, chér*," he said. "Jeff's on the floor." A white lie, Patrice rubbing his eyes tiredly, pressing his fingertips to his temples. "I do understand, *chér* . . . Yes, I'll tell him. Ummm hmmmm. Not really something we should discuss on the phone, don't you think? Why don't I come down there tomorrow and we can talk. Good, see you then."

"What was that all about?" Taylor asked him.

"Tectonic plates, seismic shifts, about nine point seven on the Richter scale, I'd say. About three points more than it took to wipe out San Francisco. Did the earth move for you, Senator?"

"What did she want?"

"She saw your little show just now."

"So?"

"So she wants to know why you sent . . . that 'cunt,' I believe was the word she used, down to suck up to her. She said she'd never felt so betrayed, even by you."

"Betrayed? Abbie went down there on her own. I didn't even know about it. You told me."

"Tell that to Janine. Lots of luck. She said you weren't just a cradle robber, you were a grave robber, fucking her right back into the ground just when she was starting to feel hopeful."

"That's ridiculous."

"I warned you this would happen when you let that reporter get near you."

"Dammit, Pat, Abbie's just working the story."

"It doesn't matter whether you are fucking that woman or not. This could destroy you."

"The Mancini girl means nothing to me. Janine's the only woman I give a damn about. I need her back, Pat. I don't want to run without her."

"Listen to me, will you? Janine says you're crazy if you think she'd keep going through the shit you put her through tonight. She says you know it would kill her."

"What's she talking about? Wasn't her last body scan clean?"

"That's not the point."

"What is the point?"

"The point, Senator, is that she says the deal is off."

"Christ, she said that?"

"That's exactly what she said. Are you looking forward to going home, opening a little military bookstore, maybe settling down? That's where you're heading right now."

Taylor picked up the remote and flicked on the *Lehrer News-Hour* to drown out Patrice.

"She agreed to see me tomorrow," Patrice said. "She blinked *last time*. Maybe I can get her to do it again. I'll go down in the morning."

Taylor listened, more closely now. "All right, you win, Pat. Call Julian and get us another reporter. Tell him you don't want to be politically incorrect or anything, but he should send us a guy. And, Pat, you're not going to see Janine. I am."

"Are you out of your fucking mind?"

"Maybe. But the only way I'll get her back is to go there alone." He held out his hand. "Give me the keys to that sweet little Porsche."

SIXTY-EIGHT

★ Whitefish ★

Sandy took Hyduk's gray notebook out of his pocket. At the stump he'd seen that it was Hyduk's after-action report, but the handwriting was barely legible and he didn't want to fight through it until he was alone. So he and Grattan had taken Zack home and left him with Grattan's wife. The kid hadn't eaten or slept in two days. Darlene fixed him a sandwich and he fell asleep at the kitchen table.

Now he hung up his jacket in the closet and ordered two bottles of beer and prime rib from room service. Then he sat down at the desk, turned on the light and flattened the notebook out in front of him. For a moment, he hesitated. He had spent a tough two weeks trying to capture this hill. Now, 10 feet short of the top, he wondered if he was better off not knowing.

Postponing the final assault, he turned on the news. The prattle was calming, like the radio when you were a little kid staying home alone. He left it on as he started to read.

The gooks pushed back the outposts and were into the wire. Mines were exploding and our guys blowing the 55 gallon drums of napalm we set up in the wire to slow attackers down.

The buzzer rang at the door. "Room service."
He tipped the waiter two bucks and had him set the tray back

on the desk. Leaving the slab of beef covered, he uncapped one
of the bottles of beer. Okay, Alex. This Bud's for you.

> *Wolf raced back to the command bunker. I was lying on
> top of it and I could hear him yelling at Taylor. "Let me
> bring in the B-52s. They're up there on station. It's the
> only chance we got to save the camp. . . ."*
> *Then Wolf draged Taylor out of the bunker . . .*

He stopped and read the line again. Hyduk had scrawled the
words in tiny letters, racing on. Racing the guns. It must have
been at night. But he had read it correctly.

> *Then Wolf draged Taylor out of the bunker and made him
> face the fight. I heard him saying, "We can hold if the B-
> 52s arklite the gooks. The attak will buy us time for the re-
> lief column to get here."*
> *Taylor was out of it . . .*

Sonuvabitch. Sunuvagoddamfuckingbitch. He turned the
page, heart hammering as if he were on top of the bunker.

And then, out of the TV set, he heard Jeff's voice.

"The first lesson . . . never to neglect the basics of combat, the
rifles, the helmets, the boots . . . It means death to forget . . ."

His eyes shot over to the screen. There was Abbie snuggling
against him and the reporter talking about "the game Jack
Kennedy gave the nation. Sex and politics. Politicians and sex."

He grabbed the phone and punched her number.

"This is Abigail Mancini. I'm not in right now, but leave a
message . . ."

Where are you, Abigail Mancini? Not with Jeff. Please, oh
please, not with Jeff.

SIXTY-NINE

★ Smith Island ★

The wind had whipped up whitecaps on Chesapeake Bay. Now, as Senator Taylor walked up to Janine's little yellow house, woodsmoke was blowing away from the chimney like a mane in the breeze. Good. She had a fire going. Maybe it would defrost her.

Before he could get through the gate, the front door flew open and she was out on the porch, one hand up, as if she were waving. But she was only shading her eyes against the sun.

He felt a panicky urge to turn around, retreat to the ferry. He shouldn't have come, it was still too soon. She thinks I'm Patrice. How's she going to take seeing me? As he got closer, he saw Janine take a step across the porch, then draw up short.

"Jeff?" she called out in surprise. "Is that . . . *you bastard.*"

"Janine," he shouted. "Wait." Bounding up the steps, he intercepted her hand on the worn brass knob. "Come on, give me a chance."

She slapped him across the face. The slap wasn't very hard, just enough to make his eyes sting. Still the old debutante. Was she still weak from the chemo? Was it that her heart wasn't in it?

Her eyes were blazing. How beautiful she is, he thought, even now with her red flannel shirt lying flat where the curves had been. Fighting to stay alive. He tried gently to pull her toward him. Hug her. Slow her down.

She twisted away.

"You son of a bitch. I thought Patrice was coming to clean up after you."

"Come on, Janny, it isn't what you think. We need to talk."

"Like I need radiation! You're poison, Jeff. Get away from me."

"Calm down," he said, touching her face. "This time I'm clean." She started to knock away his hand, but this time he sensed her hesitate.

"I saw her," she said. "Nuzzling up to you. Getting in the limo. Where did you go? Her place or yours? Not mine, dammit. I want you out of here."

Her hair looked thick and healthy with the gray threads shining in the sunlight. When he reached down to touch it, she pushed away his fingers.

"Look at me," he said, dropping his hands to her shoulders, eyes on high beams. They didn't melt Janine. She'd seen it before.

"Don't try to spin me, Jeff, there's nothing left to stroke. Remember?"

He followed her into the living room and sat down on the couch while she went into the kitchen. She returned with a tray, cups, a basket of herbal teas and a kettle of hot water.

"Why did you send that girl down here? She wanted to know everything about you. Everything."

"How much did you tell her?" he said, pouring hot water over a bag of Red Zinger. He watched the bag puff up and float, bleeding red into the boiling cup.

"Nothing that mattered."

Wrapping the string of the tea bag around his spoon, he squeezed the last red drops of tea into the cup. Janine never broke a promise, never welshed on a deal. The sanctity of sleaze, she called it: only a loser sells out another loser. And that wasn't her. "Thanks, Janny," he said.

"Don't thank me yet, Jeff. Who sent her?"

"The *Chronicle* sent her. She's a reporter. She was after a story, that's all."

"Don't give me that. How long have you been fucking her?"

"I'm not fucking her. I'm not fucking anyone."

"Don't lie to me. I know the weasel word twisting. When did you stop fucking her, or is she just blowing you, so it doesn't count? What's the truth, Jeff?"

"I swear to God, I never slept with her."

"Why not?"

"You know damn well why not."

"You're right, sweetie. I do."

"It's not the way you think. I don't want to run without you. I don't think I can anymore."

"What's the matter with you, Jeff? They will start with your personal life. When they get bored with that they'll go through every other drawer in your past. You think they're not going to find out?"

"Not if you don't tell them. I'm not interested in anyone. Except you. So why did you say all those things to Patrice?"

"Which ones?"

He saw the taut lines in her face beginning to soften. That was the way their fights had always run. The violent explosions, the afterspasms. Then calm. But they weren't there yet.

"That our understanding was off."

"I did say that, didn't I?"

"More than once. Over a girl who means nothing, an affair that never happened. With an ex-husband, I might add. And I stress the *ex*. You're the one who wants it that way. I don't. Never did. None of it makes any sense."

She pulled the red flannel shirt tighter across her flat chest, as if somehow hugging herself would keep away the past. "What you did to us, Jeff—did that make any sense?" She got up and started pacing the room in front of him, ticking off points on her fingers like a lawyer summing up a hopeless case.

"You're the one with the dreams, dear heart. Not me. You're the one with the guilty conscience. I never asked for your confessions. I didn't force you to tell me what happened. Like the spooks say, it was all need to know. And that includes Sarah Wilder."

Guilty as charged. He had dumped it on her the first night he woke up screaming and couldn't stuff it back. And she had told him it wasn't his fault and held him until he fell asleep. It had happened half a dozen times. She was always there, the cool arms wrapped around him, his head on her breasts. Then the cancer, the changes in her. And Sarah, who adored him, who made him feel young again . . . who was going to live. He was the one who had broken the deal.

She was crying now, no mascara to smudge, no foundation to run, the tears sliding down her fragile cheeks, dropping, disappearing into the soft red flannel. "Why did you have to do it? You never understood, did you?"

"Understood what?"

"You are a good man, Jeff. Who in that town could be your judge?"

He had arrived thinking she meant to take everything away. Now she was trying to offer him something. He curled his arm around her. This time she let it stay.

"You're too good for Washington, Jeff. I saw what you said yesterday about the F-44."

"I didn't mention the F-44."

She moved closer to him, put her head on his shoulder.

"Screw the White House," she said. "You don't need it, Jeff. You don't need it and I don't need it."

"You don't need it, Janny? So you're back in the picture?"

"Never left it, Jeff. You're the one who put Sarah between us. I was just getting even."

"What about now? Do you still want to get even?"

"What I want right now is to go to bed."

"You're right. I'd better go." He started to get up.

"That's not what I had in mind."

She took his hand and led him to the bedroom. The low yellow light made deep shadows on the familiar brass canopy. An Amish quilt lay across the bed.

She pulled it back, turned, faced him, started unbuttoning the red flannel shirt.

"What took you so long to get here?" she said.

He reached over and snapped off the lamp. The heavy old bed shook just slightly when they came together. In the darkness, they were buried under the warm quilt.

No bad dreams.

★　　★　　★

The next morning, as the sun came up over Chesapeake Bay, Senator Taylor sat among the schoolchildren on the Smith Island ferry, talking politics. "You really a senator?" one little girl in long blond pigtails who appeared to be about six years old asked him.

"That's right. Can I get your vote?"

"What'll you do for me?" she said, pulling her Lion King lunch pail closer to her side. So much for the people. Everyone trying for a piece of him before they even cut their permanent teeth.

But then, it was too nice a morning for cynicism.

The Porsche was waiting where he left it. He drove up the Eastern Shore, crossed the Bay Bridge, hit the Beltway and was back in Washington before lunch.

When he came into the office, Patrice was talking to Adelle. "How'd it go?" Pat asked, trying for the casual effect.

"Great," Senator Taylor said. "Come on in."

Patrice closed the door behind him.

Senator Taylor took off his jacket and loosened his tie. Then he sat down, put his hands behind his head and grinned at Patrice.

"I told you, you worry too much, my friend."

"What did she say?"

"She loves me, Pat. Never stopped."

"Wonderful. What about our deal?"

"We didn't really talk about that too much . . ."

"What *did* you talk about?"

"Us. The Kennedys. The smart thing and the right thing."

"You're speaking in tongues, *chér.*"

"Stay with me on this, Pat."

"We don't have a whole lot of time."

"Yeah, we do, more than you think. Like I told you, it went really well. You need to reach Gus and Remy before they come to your place tonight."

"All right. Anything else?"

"Yes." He felt good now. "The F-44 sucks, Pat. Tell them if they can't get that aircraft out of the hangar and into the air, I'm not going to get it out of the committee. If they can, we've still got room to talk. If they can't, that fucker's toast."

SEVENTY

★ Rock Creek Park ★

Message waiting.

When Abbie got up at four in the morning, the light on her machine was still flashing red with its bolt from the Grand Inquisitor. After she heard Sandy's voice, she had left it on. It had been that way all night. In the dark, when she got up to pee, she saw it there in the kitchen, blinking.

She couldn't fall back to sleep, so she phoned him. Two in the morning Mountain time. No answer in his room. She finally raised Tim Grattan. He'd been in the bar babysitting Sandy.

"I told him you were on the horn trying to find him."

"What did he say?"

"He said he wasn't lost and he wasn't talkin'."

"What's bothering him?"

"Don't rightly know. Been drinkin' here all night, drinkin' more than talkin'. I'll pour him on the early flight and you can find out for yourself."

"What's been going on?"

"Just what I was about to ask you. They had another crack at Hyduk. Sheriff thinks he's at the bottom of the lake. Your guy found something the Night Stalker left for him, came back here all worked up, sayin' he had to talk to you. Now he's bellied against the bar, mutterin' to himself. Reminds me of Bob Hester."

"Stay with him, will you, Tim? I should've come, too—to help with Larry."

" 'Fraid no one can help with Larry."

She had hung up feeling rattled. Why hadn't she straightened everything out? What was she afraid of? That she might set him off again? Or that she might lose him? Not knowing what else to do, she played the message again. This time she heard misery, not rage.

A jealous lover. A jealous lover who'd been anesthetizing himself with bourbon most of the night.

She could hardly wait.

*   *   *

When she got to the *Chronicle* there was another message for her, this one taped to her keyboard.

See me, please. Julian.

From across the room, Becca shot her a stricken signal. What did it mean? Another night in the arms of Ben and Jerry?

Great morning. Get hit by a car and it would be perfect.

Julian's door was open and for once he wasn't talking on the phone. He nodded toward the hot seat next to his desk.

"I'm taking you off Jeff Taylor," he said, smirking.

"Why?"

"The senator's asking for another reporter."

"You can't do that, Julian."

"I just did. You didn't tell me everything about you and Senator Taylor, did you?"

"What do you mean?"

"You didn't tell me you've gotten personally involved."

"You're kidding."

"No, unfortunately for you, I'm serious. Stroking a source is one thing. Fatal attraction is something else. Little conflict of interest, wouldn't you say?"

"Conflict of interest? Come off it, Julian. There's nothing going on except in your dirty mind." Lying, sexist prick. Oh God, don't let it show, Abs. Fucking old boy network . . . come on now, Abs . . . *grotesque—absolutely grotesque*—I can't believe this is happening to me.

"You're off the story, Abbie."

"You could at least listen to me, Julian."

"Who do you think is in charge here, Abbie?" He was studying her, as if she were a millipede crawling up his wall. "This is what's happening," he said. "You are going to go back to your gunrunning story. See if you can get someone around the CIA or

NSA to double source it for you. Play this one straight and I'll get you some space."

"What's really going on, Julian?" Her voice was too shrill, she could hear it. "Why are you totally ignoring everything I've said?"

"Because none of it matters, Abbie."

"How can you let them push you around?"

He ignored the question. "Taylor suggested I give them someone who wouldn't get so worked up around him. He wants a guy."

"Don't do this."

"Go chase those guns," Julian said. He reached for the phone. "I think I'll send them Becca."

SEVENTY-ONE

Abbie crawled into bed and slept for two hours. It was dark when she heard the sound of the door opening. Sandy didn't call her name. She could hear him rattling things in the kitchen. The smell of coffee floated up the stairs. For 10 minutes she waited, watching the clock beside her bed, her own anger growing in synch with the minute hand. Throwing back the covers, she stamped across the floor to her closet. *Thud, thud, thud.* She took out the red terry-cloth robe she used after workouts, the ugliest robe she owned. *Thud, thud, thud.* Back across the floor and down the stairs.

Thud, thud, thud.

He was sitting behind the kitchen table waiting for her. The coffee cup in front of him was still full.

A gray notebook was lying beside the coffee cup. He picked it up and tossed it across the table. "Read it," he said. "You're screwing around with quite a guy."

The voice of the eternal male. Arrogant, overbearing when hurt. She felt a current of rage, then, abruptly, she went cold.

Who needs this?

Why bother?

The brown lettering caught her eye. Hyduk again. Hard to decipher. Something about Wolf, the command bunker. Her eyes rose from the notebook. Sandy was staring at her.

"It's all there," he said. His voice was soft, but his eyes were bloodshot and he smelled hungover. "Go ahead, read it."

She opened the notebook.

The gooks pushed back the outposts and were into the wire. Mines were exploding and our guys blowing the 55 gallon drums of napalm we set up in the wire to slow attackers down. Wolf raced back to the command bunker. I was lying on top of it and I could hear him yelling at Taylor. "Let me bring in the B-52s. They're up there on station. It's the only chance we got to save the camp. Get out of your bunker. Take a look."

Then Wolf draged Taylor out of the bunker and made him face the fight. I heard him saying, "We can hold if the B-52s arklite the gooks. The attak will buy us time for the relief column to get here."

Taylor was out of it. No weapon, a total mess. He was just standing there. Then, before the Wolf could stop him, he ran to the bunker by the perimeter, pushed the detonator and blew the bridge. That cut off the rest of the team.

Wolf grabed him, whorled him around and smaked him across the face. Taylor fell down on the ground. Wolf booted him. He was lying there curled up like a baby, starting to cry. Wolf pulled out his pistol. I thought he was going to stitch the yellow bastard.

And that's when Wolf got hit. I saw his camo jacket jump—it had the radio and the SOIs tacked into it—and he fell.

I got down from the bunker, ripped off his jacket and tried to patch him up. I'm trying to stop the bleeding. The radio is blaring. The pilots are caling for targets.

Captain Taylor's hudled up against the wall of the bunker. I grabed Wolf's field jacket, with the ground to air radio and the SOIs, and tossed it to him. I said, "Get out there. Take comand. Talk to the forward controlers. Be a man." I pointed Wolf's pistol at him and told him if he didn't get moving I'd blow him away.

Then I draged Wolf into the bunker. I was patching his wounds. He was hit real bad. I was giving him morphene when Taylor came back into the bunker. He crawled over

in the corner and started to bawl. That was when I realy
wanted to waste him.

Then one of my security guys yeled and I ran outside
just in time to see the main attak. It came right thru the
approch Wolf had tried to clobber. It was just like he had
known where they were coming from.

But by then, it was all over. The gooks were wasting our
guys, killing the wounded. I took up a firing position in the
bunker near where the bridge was blown and started picking off the little mother fuckers. At first there was no way
they could get at us, because they couldn't get across the
ditch. I must have killed 20 of the little shits.

But then they turned their recoiless rifles and mortars
on us. Shit rained in. I saw the comand bunker take a hit
and colapse and figured Taylor had bought the farm.

Then I got hit and the lights went out.

Next thing I knew, I was in a hospital and it was 1969.

* * *

Abbie looked up from the notebook at Sandy.

He was staring at her the way he had looked at the kid on the
motorbike in Zagreb.

"Where were you last night?" What was this District Attorney
crap?

"Oh, c'mon Sandy. You're not my father, for God's sake."

"Where were you?"

"Since when did we start spying on each other?"

"I didn't need to spy. You were on fucking ABC, for Christ's
sake. You couldn't get into that limo fast enough. It looked like
you were going to wrap your legs around him before the door
got closed."

"Do you know how stupid you sound?"

"Cameras don't lie, Abbie. People do."

"Oh really? You think you've caught me with my pants down
giving Jeff a good time as we flashed down Pennsylvania Avenue? You don't believe everything you read in the papers, do
you? What makes you think it's any different with TV? Cameras
lie all the time."

"Fuck that, Abbie. I'm gone twenty-four hours, and look at
you."

"I was working."

"You sent me away. Why? Why were you so eager to get rid of me? So you two could get together again?"

Again? What was this *again*?

"You're sleeping with him, aren't you?"

"That's not true. What's gotten into you?"

"He told the General, Abbie. The General told me Jeff knew a lot more about you than I do. I didn't understand what he was saying, but I sure do now."

"Fuck the General, Sandy."

He looked as if she had fragged him. "Yes, right, nice girls don't talk that way," she said. "Well, pups, I don't feel nice right this minute."

For a moment, he seemed to hesitate, but she could see he was only regrouping. "I asked if you and Jeff were sleeping together." He was holding the coffee cup in both hands, as if he meant to crush it.

"I told you, no. No. *No*."

He put the cup down. His hands were shaking.

"I think you're lying to me."

"You don't want love, Sandy, you want unconditional surrender. I don't work that way."

"You're an asshole, Abbie. This isn't about war. I can't handle sharing you with anyone else." He picked up the coffee cup and banged it back down on the table. "No fucking way."

"Sharing? Is that what this tantrum is about? You're *not* sharing me. I'm not sleeping with anyone but you. Including Jeff. Especially Jeff. But if I were, it would be your fault."

"My fault?"

"Remember Fort Myer? Remember me? Standing there drooling over you? You were the whole reason I showed up— and you just blew me off. Don't say you didn't. You had your tongue hanging out all over that Carrie Perkins. And when you blew me off, it really irritated me, okay? So, yes, I went off with your precious Jeff. I even thought about road-testing him. But don't forget, *you* are the one who gave *me* the big miss."

"I was just trying to find out about her father."

"That's why your pink thing was sticking out of your pants? You crack me up. What did you two do when you left? Rush over to Vital Statistics and look up his birth certificate? How are hers, by the way?"

"Not as good as yours. How was the road test?"

"It doesn't matter. It never happened."

"I thought you were running out on me."

She took his hands and put them on her hips.

"Feel that, pups? What's the difference between that other woman and me?"

"Lotta differences. I—"

"What's the most important?"

"What?"

"I'm here. I mean, look at us, pups, duking it out. No quarter. Toe to toe. *That* is the point. *We're both here.*"

"So why don't you leave?"

"Because, you fucking idiot, it's my apartment. Not to mention that I happen to love you."

"What a way to put it."

"Best I can do."

He started to laugh. And then his arms were around her, carrying her up the stairs. She snapped off the light next to the bed. In the dark, he felt her cool body brush over his and she slipped under the sheets. His fingers touched the amulet dangling from her neck, moved to her breasts. He felt her nipples stiffen.

"Why are you doing this?" he said, as she kneeled over him and took him inside her.

"Are you asking what's in it for me?"

"Mmmmmmmmmm. Uh huh."

"You."

She kissed his eyes, tasted salt on his cheekbones. And when they made love this time, it was as good as love gets.

SEVENTY-TWO

Driving the T. C. Johnson meat wagon wasn't Barry's idea of good duty, but it beat checking IDs at the plant gate. He jammed the white ambulance into high gear and took the back way to the coast. It was four in the morning. No need to turn on the siren.

An hour earlier, he had gotten the call to pick up a company ambulance. When he drove it onto the airstrip two med-techs began horsing a stretcher out of the twin-jet. A man was strapped to the stretcher, his face and hands swathed in bandages as if he'd been burned. The restraints around his chest, wrists and legs were tight. To Barry's surprise, Remy Fair was supervising the transfer.

"Where's Ed Train?" he asked.

"You taking roll call this morning, Mr. Barry?"

"No sir," he stammered. Civilian life was making him slack, giving him a flap jaw.

"Train's been hurt, Barry. Gas stove blew up in his face." He nodded to the ambulance. "You're taking him to Crockett Plantation. We'll patch him up there."

"He don't look too good, Mr. Fair. How bad is it?"

"Bad. Better move on out—they're expecting you."

Mr. Fair didn't say who "they" were or why the med-techs had sidearms. But Barry didn't ask any more questions.

They hit the road, the techs in the back with the litter. Barry drove through Trio and Earles to Andrews and State 521, then went south, on through North Santee and down to Crockett.

Crockett Plantation was T. C. Johnson's corporate retreat. Barry had been there on a milk run two weeks earlier. Not a milk run, exactly. He had delivered a case of liquor and three cases of shotgun shells, 12s, 16s and 20s.

Mr. Fair had come down with a couple of senators and the deputy editor of the *Washington Chronicle* for a weekend in the duck blinds. The 12s and 16s were for them, two big dudes with heavy shoulders and fat guts, and one newsguy who wore some kind of English game coat. The 20s had puzzled him until he saw this little guy puttering around with the others, like he was some kind of mascot. Give him a 16-gauge and he'd blow himself back to the Beltway.

The next morning before sunup he had heard them out on the estuary shooting like there was no tomorrow. They fired off a few hundred rounds and came back with a couple of canvasbacks, three mallards and a blue-wing teal. Great white hunters. Gave them to the chef for dinner. So now they had used up the three cases of shells, they spent the rest of the weekend polishing off the booze and enjoying the pleasure of T. C. Johnson's imported good-time girls.

He saw the North Santee coming up ahead of him. Crockett Plantation was an island in the river, where the Santee widens out and heads into the Atlantic. Not precisely an island. A concrete bridge and causeway connected it to the riverbank.

At the security gate, he fished his ID out of his wallet. A guard checked it, then waved him on. No one said anything. The gate was made of some kind of wonder metal from the plant. It rose like a portcullis and he drove through it into the company castle.

Once he was across the causeway, the road twisted along the riverbank then turned and headed past several small clearings in the palmettos for the center of the island. At the end of a long alley of oaks, a fine old plantation house rose like Tara in the morning mist.

Off to one side were a dozen small houses made of brick, the old slave quarters. As he was driving up through the oaks, a tech dressed like the ones in the back of the meat wagon stepped out of the last hut and waved him over.

The three med-techs went into the brick hut together, and Barry climbed up into the back to take a look at the passenger.

Nothing to see but bandages. He heard a low groan.

"Water."

The voice was raspy, hoarse. The guy was awake, moving his shoulders against the restraints.

"Easy, Ed. You'll hurt something."

Another groan. More shoulder action. Barry pulled back the blanket and saw that Train was struggling to reach into his pocket. Reaching over to help him, Barry felt something metal, thin, like dog tags, and pulled them out. Lying on his palm now. Not dog tags. Dog licenses. Two of them.

Weird shit.

"What the fuck are you doing in there?"

The voice behind him didn't sound much like a medic.

"Just squaring things away," he said.

"Take a hike," the tech said. Nasty piece of work. The other two techs came out of the brick hut. "What's the matter, Phil?" one of them said as they walked up.

"He was in with the prisoner."

"Hey, I'm sorry," Barry said, stalling, thinking as quickly as he could. "I thought you had him out of there. I was just checking the rack, making sure it was secure. Didn't want it rattling around on the drive back."

"You ain't driving back just yet," Phil said. "Mr. Fair wants to see you. They got a room for you over at the slave huts. He'll be down later."

"I'll take the ambulance and lock 'er up," Barry said. Closing his hand over the dog licenses, he got behind the wheel. His cell phone was lying on the seat next to him. As he drove over to the house, he put in a call to the *Chronicle*.

The reporter picked up on the first ring.

"Abigail Mancini."

"It's Barry. I'm at Crockett Plantation down on the Santee, on the river between Sampit and McClellanville. Something weird's going on. Train's had an accident. Fair rolled me out of the sack this morning to drive the colonel down here. He's all bandaged up like a mummy. Anyway, Train's coughing and asking for water and when I try to help him he gives me these two things that look like dog tags. For-real dogs. All it says on 'em is Mike and Jake. I don't know what it's all about, but it doesn't add up. Fair says it's Train, but why'd the doc call him a prisoner?"

Barry pulled up to the curb just beyond the main house. No one in sight yet.

"The guard at the front gate's packing plenty of heat, and I saw a rover on security over behind the skeet range. Must be three or four other guys hanging around. Delta types. Bad dudes. I'll do another recon and call you later."

He shut off the engine and shoved the cell phone in the glove compartment.

★   ★   ★

Abbie put down the receiver and looked at her notes.

Mike and Jake?

She heard Hyduk's voice beside the grave in the woods— "You're the one Mike and Jake saved"—heard the clink as he dropped the dog tags into his pocket.

Had to be.

Grabbing the phone, she punched out a number. "Pups. Listen to this. He isn't dead."

"Slow down, Abbie. What are you talking about?"

"It's Larry, pups. Larry. As in H-Y-D-U-K. He's alive."

SEVENTY-THREE

★ Arlington ★

The General was standing in front of the Wall looking at the picture of Terry Grant Caine. Unhooking it, he put it on his desk. *'Til my trophies at last I lay down.* The line from the hymn welled up in Sandy's mind like a month of bad Sundays.

"I want you to have this," the General said.

The blank place on the Wall looked like a smile missing a tooth. "It belongs here," Sandy said. "You keep it." He crossed the room and put the picture back on its hook. Then he pulled out the gray notebook and tossed it on the desk. "Here's something for you."

The General opened the desk drawer. His reading glasses were next to the .45. Putting them on, he leaned over Hyduk's notebook.

"What is it?"

"You wanted the facts. I think you should read it."

The General examined the brown scrawl on the first page. As he started to read, Sandy watched his expression shift, the first flicker of surprise fibrillating into shock.

"Where did you get this?" Bewilderment in his eyes now, as if the notebook had been written in Greek.

"Perkins was right. Alex was not yellow. It was Jeff."

"I asked you before, what is this?"

"Bangalore torpedo. Right under the wire. I saw your face

when it went off. You know what you felt blowing past you right then? All your lies."

The General shut the notebook. "What kind of idiot do you think I am? That thing's obviously a forgery. Who did you get to do it for you? The newspaper girl?"

"Abbie's the real deal. Jeff's the fake. They gave the medal to the wrong guy. And someone sure as hell wants to shut me up. Shit happens. This time we can clean it up. You with me and my father or with them?"

He pointed to Hyduk's notebook. "You're the one who always played God with the Caines. All right, there's the gospel, chapter and verse. *The Caine Honor Redeemed*." He pulled the photograph of ODA 351 from his jacket pocket and flipped it on top of the notebook. "While you're at it, why don't you stick that on your goddamned Wall?"

"It's all so simple for you, isn't it?" the General said. For the first time, he looked defensive.

"What?"

"The truth. You go out and dig up Alex's body and bring it in here and dump it in front of me." He pointed to the photograph. "Now Alex is lying there between you and me and everything stinks to high heaven. You're telling me Jeff's a fraud and my oldest friend has been lying to me for thirty years. You expect me to pin another medal on you?"

From that zone beyond rage, where truth begets the furies, the answer came to Sandy. "You wanted Alex dead, didn't you? You've always wanted him dead."

"You're out of line, mister. Stand down. You're dismissed."

"Dismissed? I'm just beginning. Who said the truth was simple? Not me, goddammit. You think I'm enjoying this? Someone pissed on your son's good name, and now someone's out to get me."

"That's enough."

"How could you be so blind? All those years *you* were the one who painted Alex lousy, you were the one who wanted to believe the worst of him. You never did try to find out the truth, did you? You couldn't even open his footlocker. You hated him. If you'd spent all your time trying to invent a way to ruin his life, you couldn't have done it better. You dumped him on the Putnams when he wanted to be with you. He spent his life thinking there was something wrong with him because his father, General God, didn't want him around. Nothing he did was good enough for you. He got killed trying to meet your impossible standards."

"You're talking through your hat, soldier."

"Back off, General. Look at yourself. You think Alex killed Elizabeth. Just by being born. You told her you'd be with her and you weren't. So you blamed a baby and spent the rest of your life mooning over a stupid love song from 1939." Sandy went over to the phonograph and yanked the record off the spindle. It broke in his hands. "She died. It wasn't your fault. No one was to blame. But you ran away. You wrote off Alex and started running the day he was born."

"Stop it, Captain. Stop right there."

"You've been running since 1942. You never stopped running." Sandy dropped the two jagged pieces of the record in front of the General. "There's only one coward in the Caine family," he said. "You."

"Damn your soul, Sandy. What do you know about love?"

"You're the commander in chief of the Caines. Are you just going to buy another Sinatra record and keep on running, or are you going to do something?"

The General's hand shot forward. For an instant, Sandy thought he was reaching for the gun. Instead he picked up the two pieces of the record and held them in front of him like a shattered mirror. "Holy mother of God."

When he looked at Sandy, he had the eyes of a man with a cauterized soul. "Let's go talk to Gus," he said. "Gus is where we'll start."

SEVENTY-FOUR

They drove across town in the General's black Cadillac. With Sandy bringing up the rear, the General advanced on Buell's office like a HARM missile attacking a radar site.

Gus was on the phone when they came barging in. "Look, Remy. I said it can't wait. You get cracking now." When he saw the General he told Remy he'd get back to him.

"Morning, General," he said, trying to conceal his surprise. "I wasn't expecting you back so soon. How'd you like the reports? I told you that dog'll hunt."

"I'm not here to talk about the F-44, Gus." He flicked the notebook with a twist of his hand, as if it were a Frisbee. It hit Buell in the chest and dropped into his lap. "Take a look at that," he said. "I want you to tell me what it means."

Buell reddened.

"Jeff is a lying son-of-a-bitch and so are you, Gus," the General said. "I want to know why."

Buell scanned the notebook, then began to read it slowly. His dumbstruck expression looked genuine. "Where does this come from?" he said.

"Sergeant Lawrence Hyduk. The NVA didn't get him, Gus. They fucked up. So did you. You and that bullshit letter of yours. What was it you said, 'I'm sorry to be the one,' wasn't that it? What were you sorry about, Gus? The cover-up? The real cover-up?"

"Holy shit, John. I wouldn't lie to you. Remember *Bugle Notes* at the Point? Page twenty-nine. 'A cadet will not lie, cheat, or steal or tolerate those that do.' "

Buell stopped and looked at Sandy and the General. He's telling the truth, Sandy thought. The showdown began to go out of focus.

"Christ, John, I couldn't be wrong about this." A look of pure anguish. "When Charlie Beckwith came in with the relief force, I was on the ground in less than thirty minutes. Just as soon as he opened an LZ. The NVA had dropped a round right on top of the command bunker. We cleared the debris as fast as we could. I was first through the bunker door, the first to see Alex. He was so shot up someone had torn off most of his brown tee shirt to bandage him up. But it was him all right. The guy I saw blow up the bridge."

The General grabbed the notebook and shoved it in Buell's face. "Then how do you explain this?"

Buell looked ashen.

"I don't know, General. As God is my witness, I don't know. I cut Jeff out of the cammo jacket with my own knife. At first I thought he was dead."

The jacket.

It hit Sandy like an AK-47 round. The goddamn jacket.

"Why did you cut it off, Gus? Why didn't you just pull it off him?"

"That was the medic's decision. Jeff was an inch away from checking out. His chest must've swelled up from the wound—the jacket was that tight. Probably a lot of internal bleeding."

Slow down, Sandy. Rewind the tape.

The present from Perkins. Tight fit, very French. Remember the snapshot? Jeff so broad across the shoulders, Alex so narrow? Only a guy built like Alex could wear it.

"Did the jacket have a ground-to-air in the pocket? Up on the chest?"

"That's right. The antenna was sticking out. How did you know?"

"And Alex was lying there shot to hell. In the tee shirt?"

"Yes."

"When you cut the jacket off, what was Jeff wearing?"

"What do you mean?"

"Under the jacket, what did he have on?"

"An OD tee shirt and his dog tags. Covered with blood."

"That's it."

The blur suddenly took on a focus as sharp as death.

"Don't you see it, Gus? You and Hyduk are both right. You both saw the same thing. The jacket was Alex's, Gus. Perkins gave it to him. It was Alex who kept the ground-to-air radio in it. It was Alex you saw out there leading counterattacks, directing strikes, running the show."

"Then why was Jeff in the jacket?"

"That's what Hyduk was telling us. When Alex got shot he dragged him into the bunker. He said he took off the jacket and started to patch Alex up. He said to Jeff, 'Take command. Talk to the forward controllers.' The SOIs were tied by a cord to the jacket and the radio was inside the jacket pocket. Jeff must have put it on to talk to the air controllers. Exactly. After he pulled on the jacket, the bunker took the hit, and that's how you found them, Gus. The jacket was too tight because it didn't fit him in the first place. He's husky. Alex was a beanpole."

Buell looked as if the bunker had just collapsed on him. He went to the bar by the window and poured himself a stiff scotch. For a while he stood looking down Connecticut Avenue toward the White House. Then he poured a second glass and returned to his desk.

"What do we do now?" he said.

"Not *we*, Gus," Sandy said. "What are *you* going to do to fix it?"

"What's the point?" Buell said. "It's too late. Let it go."

Sandy swept the glass off the desk. It flew through the air and struck the wall, leaving a dark stain shaped like a star. "Fuck letting it go," he said. "It's not too late. You're the one who was sounding off as if you were running the West Point Cadet Honor Committee. What we're talking about here is honor. My father's, my family's, mine, the General's, yours. The U.S. Army's, Gus. You ever look at that West Point ring on your finger anymore? What's that written on it? *Duty, Honor, Country*. Why don't you pull your finger out of your ass and read it?"

"I'm going to let that pass, Captain." Buell turned toward the older Caine, the two-star to the four-star, expecting support.

"Come into the conference room, General. I've got something to say to you. Alone. This isn't personal. We are talking national security here."

The General didn't move. "General Buell, anything you have to say to me you can say in front of my grandson. What happened was a mistake. I would have seen it the same way if those glasses had been in my hands. Now let's put it straight."

The purple shot back into Buell's cheeks and jowls.

"Screw that cadet crap, John. Jeff is going to be the next President. We've been fucked since the Cold War ended. Every year the liberals go after the defense budget. Every year the Army gets smaller and weaker. Another couple of years we're going to be right back where we were before Pearl Harbor, only this time it's going to be the Chinese who kick us to hell and back. I know damn well you don't believe all that bullshit about peace dividends. Peace sellout's more like it. We have real enemies out there. Some of them right here in this country with the audacity to consider themselves good Americans. Jeff can change all that."

"How's he going to do that, Gus?"

"The people love him and we own him. Look at the polls. The people fawn on him. He'll draw his power from them and we'll do the rest. He's the only guy in Washington who can knock off that limp-dick liberal up the street."

"You're raving like a madman, Gus. Sure, we've got terrorists, but there are no big enemies out there. I'm not saying there won't be. But not now. Don't think there's any way I'm going to let this go."

The smell of spilled scotch floated through the room like methane over a garbage dump. "What are you going to do?"

"I'm going to ask for an investigation," the General snapped. "I'm going to the FBI and I'm going to ask the director to check out your T. C. Johnson and Company. We're going to find out if anyone around there thinks murder in the service of liberty is good for the bottom line. Then I'm going to pray that you and Jeff aren't that person." The General rose, wheeled around and left. Sandy grinned at Buell and followed him out the door.

When they were gone, Buell rose slowly and found himself a clean glass. He poured four fingers of milk in with the scotch this time and took it down in two swallows. Then he went back to the desk and picked up the phone. "You still there? I told you—get up here ASAP. We're in an end game."

SEVENTY-FIVE

★ Crockett Plantation ★

The afternoon sun streamed through the little window in the slave hut. Barry watched it play over his feet. Eight hours he had been waiting. Still no sign of Mr. Fair.

Click. Click.

He tapped the thin metal tags against his teeth. No way to tell what they were. Maybe the reporter and Captain Caine knew. His cell phone was about out of juice. He'd use the phone over at the main house.

Retracing his steps up the drive, he went into the house and climbed up to the second floor. Somewhere in the basement the furnace was rumbling. The guest wing was warm. As he approached 8A he saw the guard, a big man leaning back in a folding metal chair. The guy didn't look like a med-tech. He had broken the back of a paperback thriller and spread it across one knee.

"Got Colonel Train in there?" Shooting Barry a quick look, the guard nodded and returned to his paperback.

The billiard room was down the corridor and around the corner. The place was big enough for a Rockefeller, pool table, old sucker made of oak with leather sidepockets. Beyond the table was a rack for the cues and next to the rack was a wall telephone. He fished out the card with the reporter's home and office numbers on it. Three rings. No answer.

"This is Abigail Mancini. I'm not able—"

Okay, then, a message. "Barry, again. I'm getting a real bad feeling about this place. They've got Colonel Train in 8A up on the second floor of the main house. Guest wing. Very bad-looking guy outside the door. With an Uzi, instead of a stethoscope. Call you from Rawlsville tonight."

Barry hung up. Walking over to the billiard table, he picked up two cues and replaced them in the rack. Police the place. Mr. Fair hated a mess.

A hundred yards to the west of the big house, a tape deck in the security building automatically rewound, then beeped. *Whirrrrrrr, whirrrrrrrrs, beeeeeeeeeeeeeeeeeeeeep.* Tad Parsons, the duty officer, logged the call. Then he picked up his head-phones, transcribed it and slid the transcription into an envelope marked "RF Eyes Only." Sealing the envelope, he went into the next room and dropped it on the chief's desk. After that, he got a Coke out of the machine and returned to his copy of *Soldier of Fortune.*

★　　★　　★

Coming out of the drug haze, Hyduk could feel the bare metal of the bedsprings cutting into his back. The bandages were gone, but when he tried to sit up, pain sliced into his wrists and ankles. Opening his eyes, he saw the wire bracelets and anklets binding him to the bedsprings.

He tried to turn on one side. One of the med-techs was sitting on a stool behind a box, fiddling with a crank. Standing next to him was a tall guy with a microcassette recorder in his hand.

"Good afternoon, Sergeant Hyduk," the tall guy said. "Great day to be alive. For most of us."

"Where am I?"

"You're in shit, Larry, and if you don't play ball, it'll get deeper. That story you made up about Senator Taylor, who did you tell it to?"

"What story?"

The tall guy nodded at the med-tech, who grinned and cranked the box. An excruciating pain shot through Hyduk's balls. Just short of unconsciousness, he felt the current stop.

"Nice try, Larry. But I want you to stay awake." The tall guy kneeled next to the steel bed and pushed the microrecorder up near Hyduk's mouth. "Now you're going to tell me exactly what you told Captain Caine and that cunt from the *Washington Chronicle.*"

"What are you talking about?"

The white pain shot up again, then subsided to red, the red to black. Jesus, don't let it start again. The tall guy seemed to be thinking something over.

"Okay, Larry, we'll talk later. Maybe you'll be more in the mood. But right now, listen very carefully. Here's what I want you to say: 'My name is Lawrence Hyduk, Staff Sergeant, RA11242907.' Not so hard, is it? Just name, rank and serial number."

He put the microrecorder next to Hyduk's mouth while Larry began to say his name. "Thank you, Larry, that was wise. And here's something to help you remember I don't like to be kept waiting."

The tall man nodded to the guy with the crank.

White-hot ball bearings in his scrotum, a red rod of pain searing into his rectum. Darkness welling up. Let it come, let me go out, God, let me go out.

The tall man was smiling. He hadn't used the box since Vietnam.

*   *   *

Tad Parsons dropped the magazine into a steel wastebasket and looked at the clock. An hour since he logged the phone call. He was reaching for the phone when Remy Fair came in.

"Something you ought to see, sir. Straight off. It's on your desk."

"Thanks, Tad."

Fair came out of his office a few seconds later.

"Where is he?"

"Out in the hut."

Barry was laying on the bed, his head turned to one side on the pillow, snoring softly.

Remy slipped a 9-millimeter Beretta out of his holster and screwed on the silencer. He stepped to the bed, folded the pillow over Barry's face, and fired two shots through the soft down.

Psst, psst.

No more noise than a sentry's whisper.

He put the Beretta away and went back to his office. "I've got to go up to Washington," he told Tad Parsons. "Clean up the huts. Our phone boy's gone and shot himself. Handle it."

Easy assignment, Remy thought, heading for the chopper out on the lawn. Not much blood. The pillows and mattresses at Crockett Plantation were absorbent and highly combustible. The furnace could use a workout.

SEVENTY-SIX

★ Georgetown ★

The twin-jet touched down at quarter to eight. Half an hour later, the limo dropped Remy off in Georgetown. He got a quick hamburger at a little place just off M Street, then walked the rest of the way.

The lights were out. Pat was away at Remy's suggestion. No need to get him involved. Or Gus. Remy walked around to the garden and took the key out of a drawer in the elaborate barbecue grill. Letting himself in through the garden door, he got out the Jack D. and sat down on the couch in the dark.

At ten o'clock the light in the vestibule went on. Taylor stepped into the living room, groping for the switch. Remy pulled the chain on the lamp next to the couch.

"Evening, Senator."

Taylor's hand dropped. "Jesus, Remy, you scared me. You taking up a new line of work? Cat burglaries?"

"Nope. Just sitting here thinking."

"Where's Gus? Where's Pat?"

"We won't be needing them. You want a drink?" Remy tilted his glass toward the senator.

Taylor looked at him with distaste.

"I'll pass."

"Fine with me, let's talk about our little bird. Why don't you grab a chair? What do you think about the reports?"

Taylor walked over to the couch and looked down at Remy. "I think I'll stand. This won't take long."

"Suit yourself. What's the verdict?"

"Didn't Pat tell you?"

"Nope."

"I think you've got a lemon, Remy. I can't vote for it the way it is now."

"Is that a fact?"

"I can't do it, Remy."

From the couch, Remy's foot shot out, catching Taylor just below his game knee. With a searing flash of pain, the leg collapsed. The senator fell.

Remy rose slowly and pinned the injured leg to the carpet under his shoe.

"Are you all right, Senator?" he said. "Isn't it awful about accidents? They say the worst are the ones that happen around the house."

Taking the microrecorder from his pocket, he waved it in front of the senator's eyes, as if it were a remote controlling all his channels. "I'm here to tell your future, Senator," his thumb over the side of the recorder, feeling for the volume dial. "And I'm happy to say it's a bright future. Very, very bright. First, you're going to vote for our little bird and make sure all your friends do. Then you're going to be President of the United States."

Sliding the volume control all the way up, Remy leaned over and started whispering. "I know what you're thinking, Senator. You're thinking, 'Why should I listen to Remy Fair?' You'll just pretend to agree and deal with me later."

He put a little weight on the leg. "Don't think that." Taylor's face went white. Leaning back, Remy put the recorder on the side of the senator's face, resting it next to his ear. Then he pushed the play button:

"MY NAME IS LAWRENCE HYDUK," a voice roared. Remy rolled his thumb to soften the volume. "Staff Sergeant," the machine whispering now. "RA11242907. On August 26, 1966 I was in Vietnam on top of a bunker at Lang Vei Special Forces Camp . . ."

SEVENTY-SEVEN

Through the rear window of the kitchen, Janine could see the dinky skiff bobbing at the dock. Last pull of the season. She was sitting at the table nursing a second cup of tea before going to the boat. Raising the cup to her lips, she saw her fingernails and smiled. The morning Jeff left, she'd spent half an hour painting them. First time in years. A whim. It made her think of their first weeks in Washington, when Jeff was the flavor of the month in the House, the rush she felt dressing each evening for their next triumph. After midnight, the crescendo of sex.

Should she take him back? Help him? It had been good in bed. She pulled her hair back into a tortoiseshell band set with small bits of turquoise. A present from Jeff. For coaching him through his first congressional race. Maybe she could start coloring her hair again. The semipermanent stuff was supposed to be okay.

Outside it was warmer than she expected. The outboard started on the second crank. As the skiff veered toward the distant line of orange floats, she started to hum. Ah Janine, you incurable romantic. The truth was she would always love him.

From the pot under the first float, she pulled a gorgeous sook. For a moment she watched it scuttling in the well, red claws jabbing like boxing gloves, then she fished out the soft-bodied female and released her into the bay. Not today, she thought. Today she'd only keep Number One Jimmys.

She looked up and across the water. From behind the point at the far side of town, a Boston Whaler, 18-footer by the lines of it, was hydroplaning toward her, its engine cutting through the quiet morning like a ripsaw. Jerk in a black watch cap.

The cage was heavy coming up through the water. Two large males. Were they glowering at each other? Or her? Serves you right, she thought, flipping them into the empty well. Greedy guts. Turning her head to get a fix on the next float, she saw the Whaler veering toward the skiff. The guy in the watch cap stood up behind the wheel and raised his arms apologetically.

Oh, shit. Too nice a morning to yell at him. His arms came down, then he shot back up. She saw the funny-looking gun in his hand. It looked like a child's toy.

Paaah.

She felt a sharp pain in her chest and looked down. A dart was sticking out of her chest. In the middle. A wave of dizziness swept over her. ·

Where my cleavage used to be, she thought, giggling softly.

She heard a roaring in her ears. The bay turned black. And the sky.

She didn't hear the thud as she fell across the scarred thwart of the skiff. Or the sound of the hairband skittering off into the water. Working quickly, the man in the watch cap took the skiff's painter and tied it to a cleat on the Whaler, rafting the two boats. Reaching into the bow of the skiff, he grabbed the anchor line and wrapped it tightly around one of Janine's slender legs. She was pretty good-looking for a bitch her age. Then he dropped it over the side. It sank quickly, jerking her body forward until it jammed on the forward thwart. He put his arms around her waist and lifted her onto the gunwales. Then he lowered her into the water.

There was no splash. She sank into the shallow water, her windbreaker swirling around her like a moulting skin.

The man in the black watch cap stood up. When the stream of bubbles rising from the bottom stopped, he pulled the anchor line to make sure it had caught.

He looked at the sky. No clouds, no rain, not much wind. Stepping into the Whaler, he cast off from the skiff. The return trip would be easy.

SEVENTY-EIGHT

★ Arlington ★

The General couldn't understand it. All morning he had been at his desk working the phones. Getting nowhere. No answer from the Secretary of the Army. No return call from the Army Chief of Staff. Nothing from Jeff Taylor.

At ten o'clock, Melba brought him a fresh pot of coffee. "You look terrible," she said. "Don't you think it's time you got dressed?" He was still in his silk pajamas and robe, gray stubble spreading across his chin. He looked at her blankly. "What's the matter with you?" Melba asked him as she poured him his fourth cup of the morning. "Between you and Sandy, this house is becoming a crazy place."

He shrugged.

"Where is he?" she asked, frowning. "I haven't seen him since last night."

The General rubbed his hand across his jaw. First time in 10 years he hadn't been shaved and dressed by 5:00 A.M. "He's probably with that reporter."

"Not *that* reporter," she murmured, as if she were thinking out loud. "*Su corazón.*"

"What did you say?"

"*Nada.* What's wrong, my General? Are you all right?"

He put up a hand to silence her. "Not now. Not until I finish these calls."

Shaking her head, she picked up the dead coffeepot and left. In his mind, the General ran through everything again. Who knew about Jeff? Sandy and the reporter, their mystery man from Montana, Gus—and if Gus, presumably Remy.

And Jeff.

Jeff all along. Jeff the replacement son. Always. How could the miserable bastard live with himself?

Looking up from his desk, he caught a glimpse of his face in the mirror over the fireplace. Melba was right. He looked like hell. One more call and he'd go clean himself up.

Turning the pages of the old leather book next to the phone, he found the number he wanted. The White House operator put him through to Tom Grant. Early on in Vietnam, Grant had distinguished himself as one of the General's hotshot division advisors in the Delta. The President had made one or two intelligent moves, he thought, waiting on hold. One of them was making Tom his National Security Advisor.

"Good to hear from you, General," he said cheerfully. "What can I do for you, sir?"

"Got a hot one, Tom. I need a few minutes with the President."

"Everybody in the world does, sir. You know that. What's it about?"

"I can't talk about it on the phone. It's serious."

"How serious?"

"Like cost-you-the-election serious."

A pause.

"You just said the magic words." He put the General on hold. Five minutes later, he came back on the line.

"Four o'clock tomorrow afternoon. I'll leave word with security to bring you here."

"Thank you, Tom, I wouldn't . . ."

"I know that, sir. You can brief me when you get here and I'll take you in myself."

The clock was now running for them. Much better than the other way around. At the reporter's apartment, no one was answering when the General tried to reach Sandy. Just the machine.

Feeling like a fool, he forced himself to recite the morning's news.

"Sandy, this is your grandfather. We have movement. I'm seeing the President tomorrow at four. Gus called this morning. Said he feels like a louse. I'm beginning to believe that he didn't know. He said if Jeff couldn't explain, he'd just have to go out and buy himself another senator. Jeff's not returning my calls. I'll be at the stables from four to six, then home."

He showered, shaved and got dressed. The rest of the afternoon, he pored over his files on the F-44. What was it he'd been missing?

* * *

Trask put a drop of oil on the whetstone. When it had spread across the surface, he started rubbing the blade of his boning knife against it. German steel across a dust of industrial diamonds. The blade made a sound like a razor on a five-day beard.

Whiss, whiss, whiss.

Across his wrist. A new line of blood next to the healing scar.

He should have cut her tits off in the truck and dumped her in the woods. But maybe it was for the best. What would Mad Max have said?

Fuck Max.

The Germans knew how to make a blade that took a good edge. He preferred a boning knife for utility work. It was light, strong, reliable.

"Foooooollllllllllooooow herrrrrrrr." Mad Max, you asshole, what do you expect? She was asking for it. She gave me the finger, didn't she?

When the blade was ready, he picked up the apple sitting on the table next to the tape deck. Northern spy. Late for the season but still firm. Placing the edge of the knife near the stem, he began to turn the apple, slowly, slowly, the peel coming off in a slice that twisted down toward his feet like a curling red ribbon.

Hey, anyone could slip in a place like that. Wanna try again, bitch? Anytime you want it.

The single spiral peel fell to the floor, the apple stood out in all its fleshy nakedness like a flayed skull. The lights on his control panel started to blink. The cassette in the tape deck began to turn. He reached over and flicked on the monitor.

"Hey, Tim. Sandy. Your dad got anything for me yet?"

"Could be. You home?"

"At Abbie's."

"Tell you what. Go get yourself a bag of quarters. Call me from a pay phone."

Click.

Trask rewound the tape, beeped Mad Max and logged on to

"Hogs and Heifers." For twenty minutes he cooled his heels in the lounge, exchanging technoporn talk with someone named Happy Camper. Then he got what he was waiting for.

"Dear John, how they hanging?" Mad Max.

Trask looked at his notes and hit the keyboard.

"Pretty low, MM. New sound system sucks. Customer knows. Waiting instructions. DJ."

Happy Camper jumped in with a question about the First Amendment and censorship on the web. Trask blew him off with a hot link to the Library of Congress.

Then, Mad Max, back with the good word.

Terminate.

*　　*　　*

The morning shift was filling up the newsroom. Everything was still sluggish, the city's cynical heart had not yet started to pound. Abbie had been at her keyboard since five-thirty. Looking over, she saw she had forgotten to take her messages off the machine. She punched the button.

"Barry again. I'm getting a bad feeling about this place . . ."

She wrote down the message and put it aside for Sandy, wishing he'd check in so they could talk about Larry. Returning to her computer, she finished the last graph on her story and read it through one last time. The catastrophe at Lang Vei, the case of the wrong war hero, the new witness, the death squad in Montana, Rawlsville—it was all there. She printed out a copy and headed for Julian's office.

He was reading the stock pages when she came in.

"You back already?" he said, folding the paper and reaching for his coffee. Other people used Styrofoam cups. Julian got his from the wagon, then decanted it into white Limoges from the set on his sideboard he kept for the *Chronicle*'s owner and important guests.

She dropped the story in front of him.

"Tuzla at last. Shall we stop the presses?"

"Read it, Julian."

He started to turn the pages, dropping them one by one on his desk. When he finished, he stood up and closed the door. He was scowling at her.

"I don't believe you, Abbie. How could you do this?"

"It's all true."

"Why? Because you say so? You couldn't let Becca get a little leg up on you? Not even for one story? I thought you two were friends."

"Julian, that's holy shit stuff you're looking at. Get used to it. It's not going away."

"You're thinking with your box, Abbie. Use your brains. War hero versus some Unabomber clone who's lost his memory and his marbles, thinks people are trying to kill him. We'd be laughed out of town—besides getting the shit sued out of us. You want T. C. Johnson to own the *Chronicle*?"

"Back off, Julian. I'm not going to let you spike this one. Read the AP story on the shootout at Hyduk's. Bodies everywhere."

"No, kiddo, you back off. Get that cute little backpack of yours and clear out your desk. It's over. When I get back from lunch I want you gone."

She watched him push across the newsroom and disappear. Olivia Scott, the deputy foreign editor, was cringing beyond the door. "Who's he having lunch with?" Abbie asked her.

"I thought I heard someone say Mr. St. Jean was here—waiting downstairs."

*　　*　　*

Cunningham's Bar was a clean well-lit place down the street from the *Chronicle*. Malcolm, the bartender, was setting out glasses when Abbie and Becca walked in ten minutes later. "Little early, isn't it?" he said, looking at the clock. It always ran ten minutes fast, a small bonus for hard-core regulars who had trouble getting home to their mates on time. "I mean, even for you problem drinkers . . ."

The clock said ten-twenty.

"Shut up, Malcolm," Becca said. They ordered two Diet Cokes and took them to a booth in the rear of the bar. It took Abbie half an hour to bring Becca up to speed on the story.

"Pig fuckers. Every one of them," Becca said, stirring the Coke with the straw. "What do you want me to do, doll?"

Abbie handed her the folded hard copy of the story.

"Just hang on to this—and if anything happens to me, go with it."

"My, aren't we being melodramatic today? Nothing's going to happen to you."

"I've seen them, Becca. They scare the shit out of me."

"You need some insurance? Leak it to the *Times*. I mean, this time Julian has crossed the line."

Abbie shook her head. Becca got up, walked over to the bar and came back with a second round of Diet Cokes, two bright pink paper umbrellas sticking up through the ice. "Present from Malcolm. Mai tai surplus. He says to cheer up."

Abbie took the umbrella out and twirled it slowly in her fingers.

"I mean it, Becca. These guys are bad."

Becca pulled her handbag out from under the seat and started poking through it. Notebook, lipstick, credit cards, wadded tissue. Finally, an old key, nearly black with grime. She wiped it off with one of the tissues and handed it to Abbie. "Back door to my place. You go down there until we figure out what to do."

"I can't walk out on Sandy."

"I wasn't suggestin' divorce, darlin'. Take him with you. I cut off the phone for the winter, but there's one at Buzz Carraway's place over by the airfield. We're pals. Go see him. He'll turn on the heat and water and show you how to use the pump."

Abbie took the key. As they were pulling on their coats, she put her arms around Becca and hugged her, burying her face in Becca's warm collar. "You're a lifesaver," she said.

Becca rubbed her back gently. "Forget it, darlin'. Some girls will do anything to get laid."

*　　　*　　　*

The phone attached to the wall outside the Drug Fair on Connecticut Avenue looked like it had been dismembered. The receiver dangled six inches off the sidewalk, and the sidewalls were broken off. But a quarter in the slot still drew a dial tone. Sandy raised the operator and called Grattan collect.

"I'm back," he said. "Why the heads up?"

"This didn't come from me and it didn't come from Pop."

"And I never heard it anyway."

"Okay, they've been workin' on the shooters. The word from Butte is they were all pros. Former Delta, CIA types. Out of public service and into privatization. The three bozos we found were all on the pad at T. C. Johnson. Don't know about the others. They're still fishin' for 'em. You gotta get sharper. There's been too many grazin' shots. Listen carefully. Only guys on party lines get their fenders bent twice in one day. Do you understand me?"

"Got it."

"Okay. Keep usin' pay phones, stay in touch."

He called the *Chronicle*. Five rings, then Becca picked up.
"Deming."

"Becca, it's Sandy. Where's Abbie?"

"On the way home. She ought to be walking in any minute."

He felt a cold ball turn slowly in his stomach. One last quarter in his pocket. Dropping it in the slot, he punched out Abbie's number. Three, four, five rings. No answer. Then the machine. "You have reached Abigail Mancini. I'm not able . . ."

He looked at his watch. Five after eleven.

Abbie, Abbie, oh Christ, my love. Don't go home. He started to run. Behind him, the phone cord twisted slowly under its ruptured box.

★　　★　　★

Abbie tipped the driver $5 so she didn't have to wait for change and ran up the front path. Forget Larry. What she needed was to talk Sandy into a tactical retreat. How could she pull it off if she was shaking like a rabbit?

"Pups," she shouted. "I'm back."

Silence.

"Pups, it's me. You upstairs?"

She heard the television droning in her bedroom. MSNBC weather. She bounded up the stairs.

The room was empty. He must have left the set on when he went out. She snapped it off and went back downstairs. Walking over to the phone, she punched the message button.

"Sandy, this is your grandfather . . ."

Good news there. Maybe Becca was worrying too much.

Behind her, the door to the pantry opened. She didn't hear the soft soles cross the kitchen floor.

"Read all about it," Rubber Jack said softly, clamping his hand over her mouth and pressing the boning knife against her throat. "You ever hear of minding your own business, bitch?"

The knife was very sharp. It didn't hurt.

Whiss.

She felt it begin to slide, felt something warm begin to trickle under her chin.

The kitchen window shattered. A spray of blood hissed across the wall next to the phone. The floor suddenly tilted sideways, the phone was on the ceiling, the blood a cloud now, floating, all pink like high cirrus after sunset. And then night swallowed her up.

When she came out of it, Sandy was leaning over her, pressing his finger against the cut on her neck. "You're all right," he said. "It's only a nick." Next to the refrigerator, Trask was lying facedown on the floor. The shot from Sandy's 9-millimeter had blown off the top of his head.

Sandy leaned over and kissed her.

"Pups, I . . ."

"Shutting me up?"

He kissed her again. She sat up. Her throat was covered with a thin crust of blood. Sandy slowly took his finger away. The bleeding had stopped. He sat down next to her and took her face in his two hands and kissed her forehead.

"Where do you get your guts?" he whispered. "Don't leave me. Ever."

She rose slowly and leaned against the kitchen counter. Wobbly, but okay.

Trask was back in his Bell Atlantic gear.

"Who's that?"

"Rubber Jack aka your friendly neighborhood telephone man, Abs. Just paying you a little service call. Probably checking out his bugs. I saw him through the window. If I'd been here, it wouldn't have happened."

"If you'd been here you'd be dead. We both would."

She went into the pantry and took out a box of green garbage bags. Peeling a handful off the roll, she covered Trask's body.

"What do we do with him?"

"Leave him for the cleaning lady. Let's get out of here."

*   *   *

The little Geo tore down Rock Creek Parkway and crossed the Potomac at the Arlington Memorial Bridge. Up the hill toward the Kennedy Memorial, the white headstones in Arlington National Cemetery stretched off like rows of bleached dominos.

Quick or dead.

Sandy stepped harder on the gas.

As they headed down the George Washington Memorial Parkway, he checked the rearview mirror every few seconds. Abbie's head was down. She was still too shaken to talk. Just past the Pentagon, a black Dodge Ram with tinted windows fell in behind them. Through the tinted glass Sandy could see the shadows of four men. He picked up speed. At the turnoff for National Airport, the Ram closed the gap.

Sandy slowed for the gate to the long-term-parking lot, then mashed the accelerator. Spinning the wheel, he screeched to a stop next to the outer fence.

The Ram pulled in next to them. Slowly, the black window started to slide down.

Abbie whirled toward the door.

The window came all the way down. In the passenger seat behind the tinted glass, she saw Sergeant Santana, Sergeant Mayemura and Sergeant Kruger. At the wheel was Master Sergeant Nathan Caldwell, United States Army, Special Forces.

SEVENTY-NINE

The Truscott Stables were in Prince William County, out in the countryside between Manassas and Quantico. At three o'clock the General locked the F-44 files in his safe. Then he went up to the bedroom and changed into his riding breeches and boots. He parked in the lot behind the indoor dressage ring, Randolph Truscott's answer to the Spanish Riding Academy.

The tack room smelled of fine leather and money. It was like stepping into a Vuitton or Mark Cross showroom. When he came in, Calista Lewis, the stable manager, was replacing her saddle on the metal wall rack next to his. She was in her late twenties, a pretty blonde midwesterner. The General liked her. She knew more about horses than he would ever know about women.

Her saddle was an Hermès like his, buttery brown leather, perfectly tooled and stitched. A millionaire's indulgence. Miss Lewis was not rich. She called the saddle her engagement ring— her fiancé had bought it for her instead of a diamond. On her finger she wore the giant crystal rock the two of them had found on Wisconsin Avenue.

"Black Jack's not feeling good today," she said as the General took the bridle off its hook.

That made two of them. "What's bothering *him*?" he asked.

"Seems awfully jumpy. Probably nothing. Let me know if you want the vet."

He thanked her. Leaving the tack room by the side door, he

walked down the stable aisle until he reached Black Jack's stall. The stallion was a Morgan, a rich seal brown registered as black, head and neck arched in perfect balance, hocks, stifles, fetlocks and withers strong and graceful. He had paid $40,000 for Black Jack, named him after General Pershing.

The stallion was pawing at the shavings in the stall, tapping the floor like a furious aristocrat.

The General pulled back the bolt on the stall door.

"Easy, easy, easy," he crooned softly, slipping into the stall.

Black Jack tossed his head. His eyes were wide, crazy.

"Easy, Black Jack."

The General reached out his hand to pat the stallion's neck.

The whinny sounded like a scream.

Drifting back on his hind legs, Black Jack reared and kicked. One hoof caught the General on the temple just above the eye. A bright red splash of blood streaked across his forehead. He sank to his knees. And then the hooves came smashing down, wildly, again and again, until the General was lying still, his head pulped, silently bleeding into the white pine shavings on the immaculate stable floor.

* * *

Gus Buell got to Mona's at five-thirty. He had already finished the day's first bottle of scotch. He felt embalmed. The sauna would clean out his pores.

Mona was Sweden's contribution to the good life inside the Beltway. She was a tall blonde, six-feet-two, and quick with her powerful hands. Gus got undressed and lay facedown on the massage table. For 20 minutes he groaned blissfully as Mona worked out the knots in his neck and shoulders, the hard little marbles in the small of his back.

She tapped him between the shoulders. When he turned over, Mona looked at him professionally and started to pull down the sheet. He was limp as yesterday's linguine.

She started to bend over him. He pushed her away.

"Not today."

Shrugging, she stood up and left the room.

For a few minutes, he lay there reviewing the bidding. No way Jeff Taylor was going to get off this hook. The trick of it was not to go down with the senator, but right now, Gus felt in worse shape than the fucking F-44.

He got up from the table and went into the sauna. The door

swung shut. Breathing in the dry heat, he lay down on the cedar rack and closed his eyes. The scotch was coming out of him like water from a sponge. He'd be all right for tonight. Remy needed taking down a peg or two. Shouldn't have put it off so long.

The heat was beginning to make him dizzy. What he needed was a quart of ice water. He stood up and pushed the heavy wooden door.

Stuck. Shit.

He shoved again, harder this time. His hand left a wet mark on the red wood, but the door didn't move.

Sonuvabitch.

He hit the door with his naked shoulder as hard as he could. It was like slamming into a wall. He bounced backward.

There was a small window in the door. He pounded on it with his fist.

"Open the goddamn door," he shouted.

But no one came.

He felt a flash of panic. Both fists on the window now. *Bang, bang, bang.*

And then he felt another thud, this one deep in his chest. First a deep pounding, then wild, squirming spasms, as if his heart had turned into a tangle of worms.

He fell to the floor. A tank was crushing his chest now. He felt himself drawn into its searing belly. His eyes rolled up in his head. The squirming stopped.

An hour later, Mona looked through the window.

From the front of the door she pulled away a dolly with six boxes of new stainless steel free weights. 500 pounds dead weight. Rolling the dolly into the weight room, she unpacked the boxes and arranged the weights on her new steel rack. After that, she cut up the boxes, wrapped them neatly with string and put them into the Dumpster in the alley behind the massage parlor. Then she called the police.

EIGHTY

Swift Run Gap ★ Virginia

Abbie peered through the windshield of the black Ram. The dirt road tracking off the blacktop led up to an old farmhouse. White, early 1800s by the look of it, neatly painted, rust-red tin roof. Off to one side, at the edge of a cornfield cut back to stubble, was a matching barn; beyond the barn, a two-story henhouse.

She got out and unlatched the gate, leaving it open as she waved Nate on to the barn. To the west, the sun was dipping toward the mountains. She felt the chilly country air on her face. An hour of light left. Time to disappear. She'd feel better when it got dark.

Kruger and Mayemura were unloading the vehicle when she came up to the house. Behind the Ram, she saw half a dozen canvas duffels a little longer than her gym bag. Olive drab, zipped tight. Mayemura was handing Kruger the matching luggage: six MP5s. She recognized them from Mogadishu. It was amazing, really. Three months earlier she wouldn't have known the stock from the business end of a rifle.

She pushed open the front door. Inside, Sandy was standing next to the fireplace. Santana was kneeling, checking the draft. He already had a tent of Becca's fat wood kindling ready to torch.

Oh damn: the water.

"Hey, Nate," she said. "How about a ride? Got to go see a man about getting us some H_2O."

Sandy glanced at her. "We'll all go," he said.

"Six is a crowd, pups. We'll tip off the whole county."

"You think a white chick and a black stud won't be noticed? They'll probably lynch both of you."

"The way things are going now *that* would be an anticlimax." She headed for the door. "Come on, Nate. Let's go find Buzz."

★　　★　　★

They got into the Ram. Becca had said Buzz's place was on Route 810 about halfway between Charlottesville and Dyke.

"Dyke?" Nate said, looking over from the wheel.

"Don't turn pig on me. It's a town. An early influence, Becca likes to say."

"I've never understood them."

"What's to understand? Becca loves women. You do, too. Something the two of you have in common."

Nate laughed. "Never thought of it that way. Makes sense."

They turned off Highway 31 at Stanardsville and headed south down Route 810. The sun was behind the mountains now. Inside the Ram, the tinted glass made her feel invisible. An illusion, but comforting.

"There's something I don't understand, Nate."

"Go ahead. Lay it on me."

"Where did you guys come from? I've never been so glad to see anyone in my life. It was like Christmas morning." Nate reached forward and turned on the heater.

"Little chilly in here, wouldn't you say?"

"Come on, Nate. I won't put it in the paper. I can't anyway. Julian canned me."

"What for?"

"Nothing—I was set up. What made you guys show?"

"Coupla days ago, the Hawk gave me a heads-up. Called from Montana, I think it was. Said you might need some help. Yesterday he really started to yell, so we picked up a bunch of gear and hauled ass up here. There's a motel in Alexandria where we hung out until we got the word."

Abbie looked out the window for a while. "Why are you doing this, Nate?"

"What?"

"Don't give me that one-grunt shit. You're as bad as Sandy. You know what I'm saying."

"He'd do the same for me."

"That's it?"

"That's it."

"Guys," she said. "I don't understand guys."

Nate looked across the seat at her.

"What's to understand? The Hawk loves 'em, you do, too. Something *you* got in common."

Abbie turned off the heater. "The Army didn't just kiss you good-bye. What did you tell them at Bragg? No secrets. Tell Abbie."

"I told the major I was gettin' married."

"You *what*?"

"Yeah, that's right. Elena and me. We're gonna tie the knot. Moved the day up some and I told the major I needed a leave. Sort of cheated on her age a little, made it seem like a baby's on the way."

"What about Santana? Kruger and Mayemura? What did they say?"

"They didn't say nothin'. I don't want no lies on the record. I *am* gettin' married, and that's no lie. I told the major I needed them at my bachelor party and it was out of town. No lie there, either. We just didn't tell him what kind of party we was plannin'."

He eased up on the gas and slowed to 25 as they drove through the village of Dyke.

"You care 'bout somebody, you do what you gotta do. You know that."

* * *

The sign at the edge of the airstrip said BEN'S LANDING.

Caldwell cast a professional eye over the place. Paved strip, narrow but long enough. Not much company. One large hangar, couple single-engine jobs tied down to the field behind the hangar. Funky, real funky. He saw a light in a small window at the far end of the hangar and drove toward it. By the time he had the engine off, Abbie was already out and banging on the window. He fell in behind her.

The door next to the window swung open. A man in black overalls was standing there, midsixties, maybe, close-cropped hair. The eyes were wide set, practically over to the Dumbo-size ears. Sonuvabitch could probably see around corners. "Y'all lookin' fuh someone?" he said. Deep bass. Like something coming out of a 50-gallon drum.

"You Buzz Carraway?" Abbie asked him. "I'm Abbie

Mancini. Becca sent us. She said you could help us get things going up at her place."

"Two a yuh stayin' up there?"

"With some friends," Abbie said.

The guy looked about as friendly as a Ku Kluxer. Where'd he keep his hood and white sheet?

Over the bull's shoulder, Nate saw what was in the hangar. "Be damned," he said. "That what I think it is?" He stepped past Abbie. Behind the bull, filling most of the hangar, was an old CV-7 Caribou cargo plane, olive drab, homely as a preacher's mother. The cowling was pulled back from the starboard engine. Bull had oil on his hands. Must've been working on her.

"How d'yuh know about 'em?" Buzz was looking at him more closely now.

"Clocked a lotta hours in 'em in the Nam," Nate said quickly. "Great plane, that's all. That one still work?"

"Yeah, she flies. When she's not bein' temperamental." He pulled a rag out of his rear pocket and wiped his hands.

"Yeah, well, all right, let me clean up and I'll follow yuh."

"Can I use your phone? I'll put it on my credit card."

"Ovuh next to the can." Tossing the rag onto a workbench, he pointed to the back of the hangar.

"How come Ben's Landing?" Nate said. Warm the big motherfucker up some. "Ain't no water in thirty miles of here."

"Not 'sposed to be."

"So why?"

"Well, since you're so goddamn nosy, I'll tell yuh why. See that plane there? Flew one like her a long time ago. So did a friend of mine named Ben. Killed in Nam. Muh best bud. Worse pilot evuh got off the ground at Tan Son Nhut. They sent us up to the Highlands. Flops and drops. SF camps, mostly. We were flyin' out of this little strip outside Nha Trang. Ever' time Ben came back from a mission the air controlluh would yell, 'Ben's landin',' and ever' sumbitch on the field would get out of the way."

He looked at Nate as if he'd explained everything.

" 'Scuse me, Buzz. That all?"

The bull snorted.

"Nah, not all. I got back home, ever' chickenshit com-symp and peacenik in Albemarle County was shittin' on Viet vets. I wanted all those draft dodguhs to keep outta muh face. Had enough dough saved to foot a mortgage so I bought this place and called it Ben's Landin'. Works for me."

"Where'd you get the Caribou?"

No answer. Buzz stripped off the overalls and hung them on a nail next to the workbench. Then he took down an old leather flight jacket. The cuffs were out, there were tears under both arms. It looked like it had been dragged across every runway from the Delta to the DMZ.

Buzz pulled on the jacket and walked up to Nate until the busted nose was about 6 inches away and maybe 3 inches above Nate's own.

"You're Army, ain't yuh," he said. "Written all over yuh." The old bull whacked him on the back. "Come on, brothuh," he said. "Les get ovuh there and get you some runnin' watuh."

*　　　*　　　*

When the three of them got back to the house, Sandy and the others were still cleaning the weapons. Buzz looked at the OD bags piled next to the couch. "Yuh boys got somethin' in mind?" he said. "Or yuh jus' up here to play the U-Vee-A?"

"That depends. This stud here's Captain Caine," Nate said. "Buzz here's an airplane driver."

"You carry passengers?" Sandy said.

"Nah. Civilians are too fuckin' borin'."

"What about a mission?"

"Mission? Now *that* might be somethin' right up muh alley."

Old bull was practically pawing the ground.

EIGHTY-ONE

★ Crockett Plantation ★

Two hours before dawn, the Caribou lifted off the strip at Ben's Landing. In the velvet sky over the mountains, the crescent moon hung like a crooked smile. Just a sliver of light, not enough to give them away.

Buzz kicked the controls, the wing dipped and the plane wheeled like a falcon searching for a thermal. In the copilot's seat, Sandy watched the dark silhouette of the mountains falling behind them as they headed southeast for Crockett Plantation. On his lap was a small Polaroid camera and a Minolta equipped with a 1,000-millimeter lens.

At seven o'clock, the sky to the east turned from indigo to gray then to a pale salmon pink. Below the aircraft, hills and farmland appeared through the scattered clouds hovering over the Carolinas. Off the nose of the plane, they could see the great silver expanse of the Atlantic.

The sun rose on the horizon. Beams of yellow light fell across the brown wings and fuselage. As the sun eased upward, Buzz flew over Sumter, picked up Lake Marion, then followed the Santee River. Beyond Jamestown, where the river branched, he descended 3,000 feet and followed the north fork down to the coast. A few minutes later, he closed in on Crockett Plantation.

"Don't buzz the fucker," Nate muttered.

"Well, ah'll tell yuh," Buzz said. "You're talkin' 'bout my favorite thang. But I'll control myself." He eased back on the throttle.

On the first pass over the plantation, Sandy shot a roll from the Minolta: the main house with its balustrade and hipped roof, the security building, the golf course, the swimming pool and skeet range. The second time around he motioned for Buzz to come lower. Using the Polaroid he shot the causeway and front gate, then grabbed backup shots of the plantation house.

"All rightie," Buzz said. "Les go home."

*   *   *

Tad Parsons logged on to the security net at eight-fifteen. He saw three eyes-only bulletins for Remy Fair and picked up the phone. A few minutes later, Remy came running into the security center. Ignoring Parsons, he went into his office and closed the door.

The bulletins were from Rawlsville. Team Orange had arrived from Seoul and Remy had brought in Ed Liotta to take over Train's command. Remy respected Liotta. Wouldn't let a loon like Hyduk get the drop on him.

He deleted the bulletin, cranked down to number two.

Goody Two Shoes was down. Good. Always acting as if her shit didn't stink. The General was gone. Self-righteous old bastard. Gus too. Should've got me the stars, Gus. Fuck me, fuck you. Payback time.

Then a Claymore went off. Trask KIA. Sonuvabitch. Crumpling the bulletin, he smacked the wall with his fist. Stupid fool had moved in too soon. The backup had to haul his sorry ass out of the girl's apartment.

A small beam of light with bulletin number three. Something about a dipshit airfield in the Shenandoah Valley. A start, anyway.

He placed a telephone call to a number in his book, let it ring nine times. Then he repeated the call. Five minutes later, he logged on to America Online, clicked on the web browser and typed out the URL for "Hogs and Heifers."

It was only eight-thirty, but half a dozen early birds were already chewing the fat. Twelve Pack and Frodo, Front End, Libby and Blow. And Mad Max. Lurking.

Remy logged on as Lube Job. He invited Mad Max into a private chat room.

LJ: Score?

MM: Three of six. (You're only batting .500.)

LJ: Got one more here, last two in VA.

MM: Vaginal/Anal?

LJ: Right. Virginia loves lovers, but it's a big place. Albemarle County.

MM: Stand by.

Remy tapped the edge of the keyboard. Five minutes passed, and then Mad Max came back.

MM: Check Rebecca. Rebecca Deming. Dyke.

LJ: Will try anything once.

No answer. Mad Max was gone.

★　　★　　★

Becca saw Julian bearing down on her. The eyes looked deeply evil today. In his hand he had three sheets of wire copy.

"You see these?" He laid the stories out on her desk side by side.

"Grand Old War Horse Killed in Stable"—AP.

"War Hero Senator's Ex Drowns on Eastern Shore"—Reuters.

"General Turned Lobbyist Dies in Sauna."—Agence France-Presse.

"My God," she said softly. "All on the same day?"

"God works in strange ways, kid. I just tried to get Abbie up at your place. The phone's disconnected."

"What made you think she's up there?"

"I fired her. Where would a girl go to cry? I was in Cunningham's last night. Malcolm saw you give her a key."

She looked down at the wire stories, stalling. Julian was up to at least 75 percent on her Liar Meter, trying too hard to sound cool.

"I don't know where she is, Julian. The key was to my car."

"Yeah, sure. Well, if you bump into her, see what she knows about these three and feed it to Alterman. He's writing the obits."

"Julian, do I need to write it out for you? I don't know where she went. Not to mention that she doesn't work for you anymore, remember?"

"Did Abbie show you her notes?"

The voice at about 97 now, heading over the top.

"I do my own reporting, Julian. You said you wanted a fresh take. Three deaths like this. Don't you think it's a pretty damn big coincidence?"

"What difference does it make what I think, Becca? None of

our readers would believe it anyway. We're not a conspiracy sheet." He turned and walked across the newsroom. Voice-of-concern level at 103 on the Liar Meter. Heading for an all-time record.

EIGHTY-TWO

★ Swift Run Gap ★

The Caribou circled Ben's Landing once and came in from the southwest. It was a few minutes after eleven o'clock. They decided to split up. Buzz said he'd take the 35-millimeter film down to a one-hour developer in Charlottesville and bring it to the farm after lunch.

When Sandy and Nate drove up, Kruger was in the living room checking the medical kit. Santana and Mayemura were over in the barn with Abbie. They had all six of the green bags open; six HALO chutes, standard Double X HALO steerables, gray for night drops, were spread along the long aisle between the empty milking stalls. Santana was running his fingers along the shrouds like a surgeon examining tendons.

"We're good to go," he said.

Sandy nodded. "Almost. Come on back to the house." In the kitchen, he found the shank end of a roll of butcher paper Becca used to wrap venison for the freezer. She had shot an eight pointer in a stand of woods beyond the barn. The end of the roll still had bloody fingerprints where she had torn it the day she dressed out the buck.

Sandy ripped off a strip about 4 feet long. Stretching it out on the kitchen table, he drew a diagram of Crockett Plantation. Next to the buildings on his ground plan, he taped his Polaroids. When everything was ready, he stuck the chart to the wall of the living room with a half dozen thumbtacks from Becca's utility drawer. The A-team gathered around him as he chalk-talked the mission.

"They won't be expecting us," he said, tapping the map with his finger, "but it would be crazy to go in cold. We need a diversion." He looked at Kruger. He had noticed that Kruger was still limping, favoring the leg shot out from under him in Mogadishu. "You're too banged up to jump."

"*Nicht wahr,* Captain. I go vith you."

"Thanks, Sarge. But you've got a different mission."

Kruger looked crestfallen. "Vat's my job?"

"You are going to sing. Which is going to save our ass." He pointed to the causeway next to the security gate.

"The only way on and off the island is through this gate. That's where we stage the diversion. I want you to drive up banging off the rails all the way across the river. Sing 'Deutschland über Alles' as loud as you can. When the guard comes out to see what the fuck is going on, tell him you're looking for the German embassy, tell him anything you can think of. When he tells you to fuck off, get belligerent. Or cry. Whatever it takes to keep his eyes on you."

"Den I grease him, *ja*?"

"Nope. You leave him to Nate."

He pointed to the golf course beyond the skeet range. "Nate, you and I will come down here and regroup. Barry says medium security. One guy on the gate, one in the house guarding Hyduk, one out on the grounds, a rover. I'll find him and take him out. We got to crank in Murphy's Law, so let's plan for a couple more. And watch out for Barry—he's ex SF, friendly little guy, looks like an Italian bike racer."

He traced a line from the golf course to the causeway. "Nate, you work your way through here quick. Down to the gate. The guard will be busy with Kruger."

Nate nodded. "Catch 'em or hurt 'em, Hawk?"

"Rules of Engagement—use whatever force is necessary."

The Professor was polishing the lenses of his NODs with the tail of his shirt. "What about Eddie and me, sir?"

Sandy pointed to the big house. "We'll hit them high and low. You and Eddie are going to land on the roof. The slope's not too steep. You'll stick. There's a trapdoor up there to service all those brick chimneys. From what Barry said, they've got Hyduk on the second floor with a goon outside his door.

"Give Nate and me a little headstart so we can take out the rover and the front gate. Then go in from the top. Kruger links with Nate. They'll act as our reserves, preempt surprises. I'll come up from the ground floor, so the noise you'll hear coming up the stairs will be me. No friendly-fire casualties. And remember to keep an eye out for Barry. If everything turns to shit, the assembly point is here behind the skeet range."

Sandy turned back to Kruger. "One more thing. On the way in, check the nearest hospital. You need to know how to drive there quick-smart. Blindfolded. Okay, any questions? Anybody see any holes in the plan?"

"I have a question?" Sweet, from across the room. Abbie was raising her hand and wiggling her fingers at him. "What's my mission?"

"You're going to stay here until we get back." Sandy heard his own voice. He sounded like a school principal.

"No way, no fucking way, Captain, sir, Caine." She pounded the wall.

Nate laughed. Sandy glared at him. "Cut it out, Abbie, it's too damn dangerous. You've already earned three Purple Hearts in this campaign. Let's not go for four. You know what those dudes are like. You don't have to prove anything to any of us."

"Forget it, pups. I've stayed with this story since Mogadishu. You're not dealing me out now. Kruger's driving—that means there's an extra chute. I'm going."

"No way. You're staying right here."

Nate touched him on the shoulder. "Nah, she ain't, Hawk. Never happen. You ought to know that by now. Besides, think about it. The 'Dish, up that fuckin' road outside Sarajevo, out there in Montana. I ain't so sure who's the guardian angel around here. Bad luck to leave her behind." He turned to Abbie. "But listen to me, Mancini. You ain't putting on any HALO chute on my watch. You got me on that?"

"What am I supposed to do, Nate? Fly down on my gossamer wings?"

"No, ma'am. I'm your driver, remember? You wanna go on this mission, okay, you gonna ride down with me."

Abbie looked at him quizzically.

"We attach her to me, Hawk," Nate said to Sandy. "I done it before."

"Shit, I don't know, Nate."

"No shit. That's what we gonna do. Just don't tell Elena."

★   ★   ★

It was nearly two o'clock.

In the kitchen, Eddie Mayemura finished pre-rigging his 4 Wraps—four equal lengths of detonating cord with a *NONEL* instantaneous firing system. He looked at his watch. He'd also laid out six steaks he'd picked up that morning, along with the tomatoes and onions he'd been able to marinate while Nate and Sandy did the recon. The case of beer he'd stuck in the refrigerator was ice cold. "All right, you guys," he said. "Chow's on the table."

As they were sitting down, Buzz came back in with the photo enlargements. Abbie offered him half her steak, but he said a beer would suit him just fine. "Had muhself two Whoppuhs at Buhguh King on the way up." There was a loud hiss as he pulled the tag on a can of Bud, followed by the roar of an engine barreling up the road.

The A-Team dropped knives and forks, dove for their weapons. The door crashed open. Standing there, was Rebecca of Sunnybrook Farm. Behind her, steaming in the dooryard, was the yellow Land Rover. "Thanks, God," Becca said, leaning against the door. "I thought you'd all be dead."

EIGHTY-THREE

The black crepe drooped from the General's photograph like a shawl. From underneath the mourning cloth, he looked across the mahogany desk, surveying the mourner's book Melba had put out for family friends. Senator Taylor was wearing his uniform. For half an hour, he stood at attention in front of the picture. Tears streamed down his face.

Melba had called him the evening before. She had been crying when he came into the kitchen. He held her hand for a while, asked if she needed a doctor. When she told him no, he called a friend at Fort Myer and arranged to have the General's body picked up from the morgue and taken to Martin's Funeral Home.

The undertakers had already done their work, repairing the deep gashes in the General's head, stitching back the torn scalp. The service would be later in the week. Closed coffin. They were preparing for a big crowd.

He had sent Patrice down to Smith Island to retrieve Janine's body. He planned to meet the hearse at National Airport the next evening, escort her coffin back to Cincinnati and turn the rest of the arrangements over to her parents. Then he would shuttle between Arlington cemetery and Ohio for the two funerals.

When the half hour had passed, he saluted the photograph and signed the book. Then he spent 5 minutes in front of the Wall looking at the pictures for the last time.

When he reached the end of the long line of framed images, something suddenly caught his eye.

A new frame, silver, gleaming in the light of the chandelier overhead.

He put on his glasses and leaned forward to inspect it.

He saw Alex looking back at him, laughing, Alex and all the dead men from ODA 351.

The photograph had never been there before. He was certain of that. Where in God's name had it come from?

He retreated to the desk. For an instant, he almost sat in the General's chair. Catching himself, he stood up again. As he was rising, he noticed that the top right desk drawer was open. Reaching over to close it, he saw the handle of the General's .45.

Out in the kitchen, Melba was crying again. He heard the sobs, a crescendo of grief. On an impulse, he slipped the gun out of the drawer. Unloaded. The clip was lying next to it. Smacking the clip into the handle with the heel of his hand, he held it for a moment, feeling the heft, the solidity of it. He put the gun inside the waistband of his trousers, under his belt. Closing the door quietly, he went to the kitchen to see what he could do for Melba.

"Where's Sandy, Jeff?" she asked him. He put his hand on her shoulder. Without looking up, she lifted her own hand and put it over his. "I don't understand this."

"Neither do I."

Melba dropped her head in her arms to muffle her sobs. "Find him, Jeff."

He felt the steel lying against his waist.

"I'll find him," he said.

EIGHTY-FOUR

★ Crockett Plantation ★

"Their ass is ours."

Sitting in front of the computer monitor, absorbing the eyes-only from Liotta, Remy Fair allowed himself one small moment of pleasure. Why hadn't he put Train out to pasture sooner? Moot point now.

Liotta reported that Max had been right. The phone was at a little dump called Ben's Landing. Rummy old bastard ran the place. Couldn't get Vietnam out of his circuits. Tight with the *Chronicle*'s Rebecca Deming. The target was about 20 minutes up the road from the airstrip. Maybe two hours in the bird from Rawlsville.

Remy looked at the clock on the wall over Parsons's desk.

1430 hours. Two-thirty.

He picked up the red SPU receiver in front of him, punched in a number and got an immediate reply.

"Alpha. The doctor's in."

"This is Crockett, Alpha." The expression on Remy's face looked like a dog's grin. "Execute."

EIGHTY-FIVE

★ Swift Run Gap ★

"Hell's fire, Abbie, I gotta get you out of here."

Wheezing like a winded Saint Bernard, Becca collapsed on the couch. As her breath returned, she began to register the armed men standing all around her. "What kind of petting farm you running up here, darlin'?" she said. "Look at what they got between their legs—those little things are baby machine guns, aren't they?"

Nate was staring at Becca. She returned the look.

"You into guns or just scarin' people?" he asked her.

"Both."

A spark of interest came into his eyes. "You know how to use 'em?"

"Use 'em or lose 'em. The whole basis of evolution, stud. Buck or doe—it doesn't matter." She looked at Abbie. "Where did you find these specimens?"

"They come standard with that one over there," Abbie said, pointing to Sandy. Still holding the little MP5 in one hand, he walked across the room and poked the other hand out at Becca.

"You're the Sandy one, right?"

"Abbie's told me all about you, Becca."

"Lotta lies. We're too tight for her to be objective."

Suddenly Abbie saw a look she recognized cross Becca's face. Her mask for the bereaved. But this time it looked as if she genuinely cared. "I'm so very sorry to be the one to tell you your grandfather has had an accident. He's dead."

Before Abbie could reach Sandy, he was out the front door. Becca grabbed her as she started after him. "Wait, darlin'. He's gonna want the details."

Abbie stopped. "What happened?"

"He was about to saddle up. His horse went crazy and stomped him. DOA at Alexandria General."

"Just an accident? What you think?"

"No, darlin'. Thing is, the horse killed the General about five hours after Janine Taylor got her foot wrapped around an anchor line and drowned. And right about then, General Caine's good friend General Buell was in a steambath. Heart attack. Supposedly."

"How did you find out?"

"That's the cute part. Julian told me. The way he came running up with the wire copy, it looked like he'd written it himself. He kept trying to find out where you are, sugar. I gave him the business, but he didn't believe a word. I think he knows you're up here."

Abbie leaned against the door.

"If Julian knows, Taylor and all the rest of them know. Last time I saw Julian he was going out to lunch with Patrice."

"That's why I'm here."

"How long ago did you talk to him?"

"Maybe two hours. I tried calling Buzz, and when I couldn't reach him, I got up here as fast as I could."

"I better go find Sandy." Abbie squeezed Becca's hand. "I owe you big time."

Sandy was inside the barn sitting on an overturned bucket, his head in his hands. When he heard her come in, he looked up. His eyes were dry, his face looked awful. She gave him Becca's report.

"It's bullshit, Abbie. I'll never believe he couldn't control Black Jack. The man was tougher than any horse I've ever seen." He stared at the straw on the barn floor. "I got him killed."

"It wasn't your fault. He knew what he was getting into when he stuck it to Gus."

"I never should've listened to Perkins."

She slapped him across the face. "Goddamn it, pups, stop it.

You've got Nate and everyone else waiting on you. Are you going to get moody or get even?"

Without waiting for him to answer, she walked out of the barn.

* * *

When Abbie came back into the farmhouse, Nate was standing in front of the chart tacking up the enlargements. "Come on over here," he called to the others. "I got some things to say." Santana, Kruger and Mayemura crowded forward, Abbie, Buzz and Becca moved in behind them. "From here out, we runnin' a KISS operation. You understand me?"

"Keep It Simple Stew Pit," Kruger sang out.

"That's right. We gonna KISS those motherfuckers to death." He turned to Buzz. "How fast can you get the plane back in the air?"

"Muh baby's topped off and ready to go now. But we don't have neah 'nough fuel fuh gettin' down and back."

"Down is good enough. What's her ACL?"

" 'Bout seven thousand pounds."

"Okay, we got three vehicles and eight guys, including Mancini and Deming. Can you squeeze all of us into that sweet momma and still get out of here?"

"Six men, two women, one vehicle."

"Take mine," Becca said. "It's lighter than the other two and it's got a winch."

Nate grinned at her. "Deming, you jus' made sergeant." He looked at Kruger. "Kruger, you got another wife. Two of you gonna run the diversion. Drunken German, pissed-off wife. Even I'd believe it."

He was finishing the rundown when the front door opened and Sandy came in. He was swinging the MP5 easily at his side. "Let's roll."

Each man on the A-Team picked up his weapon and HALO chute. Buzz, Becca and Abbie followed them out to the vehicles. "Operation KISS," Becca said to Abbie as they got into the yellow Rover. She cranked up the engine. "Mmmmm, yes." Fifteen minutes later, the little convoy pulled into Ben's Landing.

The Caribou was still waiting outside the hangar. Buzz climbed into the cockpit and lowered the tail ramp. Nate came over to the Rover and motioned for Becca to roll down the window. "Better let me do this," he said. "I'm good going backwards."

"That right?" Becca said, climbing down to the ground. "I wouldn't have thought it about you."

Nate laughed and took the wheel. Craning out the window to follow Buzz's hand signals, he backed the Rover into the Caribou. While Santana stashed the other vehicles in the hangar, Buzz and Nate chained the Rover to the floor at the aircraft's tie-down points.

Santana handed Becca the medical kit.

"Better stick that in the back," he said. "Blood make you faint?"

"Chocolate makes me faint, soldier. Blood makes me come."

Even the Professor was laughing as they climbed into the old sling seats and fastened the safety harnesses. When everything was buttoned up, Buzz went back up to the cockpit to close the ramp. They heard a low hum, then, up front, a loud curse as the ramp refused to close. Buzz reappeared, a wrench in his hand. "Damn switch. Been havin' trouble with it all month." He walked over to the handle and gave it a whack. "Gotta do it man-u-lee," he muttered. The ramp didn't move.

By its side was a hand crank. He grabbed it and took two violent twists and the ramp began to move. Then the crank broke off in his hand. "Fuckin' metal fatigue."

Buzz was perspiring now. Looking out at the runway yawning beyond the open tail of the Caribou, he shouted to Sandy, "I'm not flying this sonuvabitch with the tailgate down. We may be goin' Greyhound."

"Vait."

The order came from Kruger. Unbuckling, he walked over to the sweating pilot. First he looked at the open ramp, then he looked at Becca's Rover. In the center of the ramp, up at the top, was a heavy ring. On the front of the Rover was the winch.

"Vatch."

Kruger crawled into the driver seat and turned on the power. Unrolling fifteen feet of cable, he slipped the hook into the ring on the ramp. Then he went back to the Rover and turned on the winch. Groaning like an arthritic patient, the ramp trembled for a moment. Then it came up and closed like a clam shell.

"Let us be on our vay," Kruger said to Buzz.

"Ah'll be damned," the older man said, smacking him on the

back. "Why din't I thinka that?" Shaking his head, he disappeared up forward.

In the cockpit, Sandy and Nate were strapped into the copilot's and navigator's seats. Buzz put on his headphones and pulled out a map. Nate looked curiously over his shoulder. He saw Texaco printed on one of the map's many folds.

"Shit, man. That's a road map."

"What d'yuh think you're flyin', Sarge? American Airlines?"

He held open the road map and stabbed his finger down on Florence, South Carolina.

"Got a friend ovuh there," he said, shouting over the engine's roar. " 'Bout two hours' run from here, forty-five minutes from Crockett. We can refuel. Give the German and Becca a head start down t' the coast. Hook up latuh."

Sandy looked at the map, nodded.

Buzz nursed the Caribou to the end of the runway. Checking the gauges one last time, he opened the throttle. The Caribou waddled down the runway and rose sluggishly into the sky.

EIGHTY-SIX

★ Crockett Plantation ★

Five P.M. in "Hogs and Heifers." Happy hour. Remy scanned the public lounge for twenty seconds, passing over all the Adolfs and Scarfaces, stopping briefly at Pop-my-Clutch—now there was someone with flair—until he found Mad Max.

Working quickly, Lube Job got Mad Max into a private room and tapped out the update.

LJ: Sitrep Alpha.

MM: Just my type.

LJ: Found pack. Jiving tonight.

MM: Drool. Just clean everything up.

LJ: Next sitrep: 0400.

MM: :)

When he finished the report, Remy logged off and took a walk around the plantation. He stopped to talk to the guard at the causeway, checked the perimeter wire. All quiet on the Atlantic front. He felt good, in full command at last. No more orders from Gus.

He spent an hour in the security center running through some backed-up intell from the Middle East and Southeast Asia. Then he went to make sure the night shift was set in the guest wing.

Hyduk was still upstairs in 8A. No need to keep him wired anymore. Feed him, keep him alive until after the Armed Services Committee votes, keep checking Taylor's temperature.

When the senator quit pulling his weenie, he could pull the plug on Hyduk. Right now, it made better sense to keep him alive.

Strange dude. Not eating anything. Couple more months until the vote. Wouldn't be much left for the furnace.

EIGHTY-SEVEN

★ Crockett Plantation ★

The yellow Rover strained at the quick releases as the Caribou bounced along over the Carolinas. In the cargo bay, the rattling chains did nothing to improve the atmosphere. Santana looked over at Mayemura, who had picked up the same vibes, as if some restless spirit had signed on for the mission.

The tower at Charleston International was reporting southeast winds of 10 to 15 miles and the probability of heavy overcast after midnight. Buzz decided not to tell the captain for a while. Might still clear up.

Shortly before six o'clock he saw the airport outside Florence. Double-checking his landing instructions, he touched down 10 minutes later.

Harry Foster, an old drinking buddy, ran a three-plane charter service out of Florence. His setup was off to the far side of the field, away from the terminal and hangars for the bigger birds. As Buzz taxied over to Foster's shed, Harry came out holding a hammer in his hand. When he saw the Caribou, he trotted over to the pilot's window.

Buzz cut the engines. "Fixin' to layovuh fuh a few hours," he yelled down to Foster. "Yuh got a solenoi handy? Ah need one fuh the ramp."

Sandy peered out the aircraft. The headquarters of Foster Charters was a small prefab modular, not much bigger than a house trailer. They'd stay in the Caribou.

Before Buzz went with Foster to organize the repairs, he lowered the tail ramp and snapped the quick releases on the yellow Rover. Kruger made a move for the wheel.

"Understand, Heinrich," Becca said. "You can get my wheels off the plane, but once we hit the ground, you ride shotgun." Sheepishly, Kruger tossed his gear in the back of the Rover, eased it down onto the tarmac. Then he shifted over into the passenger seat.

For a few minutes, the team minus Buzz huddled around the four-wheeler.

"You'll have plenty of time," Sandy said as they synchronized watches. "You ought to be down there before nine, even if you get hit with a lot of traffic. Moon sets at 2330. We're going to drop in at 0100 on the button. So Kruger," he looked over at Becca's passenger, "when we're on top of the plantation, give us two minutes, then you begin the diversion. Loud and long, guys. You'll be covering the roof noise, and Nate needs time to get over to you and take out the guard."

The two of them nodded.

"Watch your ass," Sandy told them.

"Always do," Becca said. "Never does a damn bit of good." She threw the Rover into gear and charged off the runway. Sandy put his arm around Abbie as the yellow Rover disappeared around the terminal. "I like your friend," he said.

"Must be mutual, pups. She says you're not so bad—for a high-testosterone type."

Once the ramp was repaired, Buzz left to organize some fuel. An hour later, a Texaco truck pulled up to the Caribou and they were back in business. "I see where Buzz gets his maps," Nate said as the driver hooked up the gas line to the aircraft.

But no Buzz.

Another hour passed.

Sandy posted Mayemura to stand security and began to pace the perimeter of Foster Charters. An AWOL pilot wasn't part of the plan.

Half an hour later, a brown Buick came rolling slowly across the taxiway toward the Caribou.

Sandy saw Mayemura stiffen and finger his weapon. The Buick was awfully slow. When the car was still 50 yards off, Sandy raised his hand to stop it. Mayemura had his MP5 at high port as the window rolled down and Buzz's purple nose appeared.

"Chow," he yelled, throwing open the door. Inside, he had a dozen bags from Taco Bell, Wendy's, Roy Rogers, McDonald's and Dunkin Donuts. Mayemura winced as Buzz started passing the bags to Sandy. Behind the wheel, Sandy saw a brunette in a satin bowling jacket that said FLORENCE LANES. She was in her late forties and in a lot better shape than Buzz. After the bags were all out of the car, Buzz went around to the driver's window and gave her a long wet one.

The Buick rolled off toward the airport's rear exit.

"She never goes ovuh thirty-five, on the road or in the sack," Buzz said, watching her disappear. "That's why I love her."

"Is that where you've been?" Sandy said.

"Yep. Figguh'd if I was goin' down, it bettuh be on empty."

★   ★   ★

At eleven o'clock Buzz went into Foster's prefab to check on the weather. When he came back, his expression was thoughtful.

"How's it look?" Nate asked him.

"Like Normandy on D-Day. Bad invasion weathuh. Wind's okay, five to ten miles per hour. But we got heavy cloud covuh down to one thousand feet, probably be gettin' some rain. Little thunduh and lightnin', maybe. Anybody sane would lock down and party."

"I don't see anyone sane around here," Sandy said.

"Yuh got a point. Let's go."

The Caribou was better without the Rover, but after it lifted off, it still snorted and bucked all the way up through the clouds. Buzz leveled off at 12,000 feet and headed southwest. Sandy unbuckled himself from the copilot's seat and went aft to organize the drop.

The cargo bay sounded like the hold of a ship. In the turbulence, every joint on the old aircraft groaned and squealed. They secured their NODs, ran through a final weapons check and inspected the chutes.

The Caribou lurched, then hit an air pocket and dropped 100 feet. Mayemura leaned over and puked across the floor of the cargo bay. Nate looked away. He figured he was maybe three or four minutes behind Eddie. Sandy fought his way back up to the cockpit.

"What do you think?" he said to Buzz.

"Not jumpin' weathuh, buddy. Yuh sure yuh got both oars in the watuh?"

"Let's not open that one up. How are we going to do this?"

"We got jus' one shot."

"Lay it on me."

"I got to get unduh the weathuh. Way down. Too low to jump. We take this bucket right down to the deck, and when we get there, I pop her up to one thousand feet. Like straight up. If the wings don't fall off, yuh guys have 'bout thirty seconds to get out. Yuh oughtta be okay after that."

"No other way?"

"Yeah, we could land on the causeway. Might give us away, don't yuh think?"

Sandy nodded.

"Now, yuh'll feel the plane go up like a fuckin' elevatuh. Soon's I level off, unbuckle and get ready to tailgate."

"How do we know when?"

"I'll flip on the green light and you go. Meet you at Flohrence. Y'all not back by sunup, I'm comin' back and droppin' bombs."

EIGHTY-EIGHT

★ Crockett Plantation ★

"You don't have to do this."

Sandy was watching Abbie watch Nate.

Nate leaned over and adjusted Abbie's tandem rig harness until it was snug. He showed her where her D-rings clipped onto his. She'd ride down in front of him, the back of her head against his chest.

"You can stay with Buzz," Sandy said. "Meet us back in Florence."

"Nope."

He reached over, pulled her close. For a moment she wondered if he meant to handcuff her to the plane's airframe. Instead, he kept his arm around her, and put his mouth next to her ear. "Okay, Tiger," he said. "I love you."

The plane began to climb, a fast, sickening climb. Mayemura puked again, sending the rest of Buzz's combination platter onto the deck. Sandy felt the elevator accelerating, the G's pulling at him. He cinched Abbie's seat belt tighter, then adjusted his own.

The Caribou made a sound like a death rattle. Everything in the cargo plane shook as Buzz pulled out of the climb.

Thousandth floor. Everybody out.

The ramp at the tail of the Caribou began to open like a giant clam.

Sandy took up position underneath the jump light.

"Santana, Mayemura, you're one and two. I'm three. Nate,

you and Abbie call your own jump. I'll be down on the ground to catch you."

"Ticket to ride, Mancini." Nate snapped her D-rings onto his.

"Jump," Sandy shouted, smacking Santana on the butt. The Professor fell into the darkness, then Mayemura. Sandy looked at Abbie, gave her a thumbs up, and followed them into the dark.

Nate wrapped his arms tightly around Abbie's waist. "Out we go, Mancini. Come fly with me."

They walked off the ramp, falling into the vacuum created by the fuselage. There was no lacerating wind, no prop blast. They were sinking backward into the night as if they'd fallen onto a giant, goosedown pillow.

Craaack.

She heard the chute open. Nate's arm was like a vise. She felt a jolt, and they were standing on the pillow, the coldness on her face sharpening all her senses.

Nate pulled the controls, the chute spilled air and they slid through flat blackness. Nate tugged again, and they were coming down 10 feet away from Sandy.

"Ready?" Nate shouted.

She nodded.

The ground came up toward them, faster than she expected.

"Now," Nate said, sharply pulling and releasing the two front toggles.

It was as if he had slammed on the brakes. Her feet hit the ground first; she stepped forward and found herself walking into Sandy's arms as easily as if she had just strolled across the ninth green to meet him.

"Perfect Hollywood," she heard him say, and then they were all on the grass, waiting for their hearts to reenter their heaving chests.

A horn sounded in the darkness, three times, then four.

Louder and louder.

Sandy and Nate pulled the NODs from their belly packs and adjusted them. What did they expect her to do, find a cane and a dog? Fumbling in his pack, Sandy drew out a second set of night goggles. Kruger's, she thought. Suddenly it was noon at midnight. "Go," Sandy whispered, touching Nate on the shoulder. Using the rough as concealment, Nate worked his way over to the skeet range. Sandy watched until he disappeared.

She saw a tiny pinpoint of light about 400 yards down the fairway, saw Sandy's head turn quickly as if he were tracking a grouse. He turned toward her.

"Stay here."

He formed the words silently with his lips. She started to protest. Not a good idea.

She nodded and shut up as Sandy started toward the light.

*　　*　　*

Harry Gustafson cupped the butt in his right hand. He could hear Remy reaming out his ass. Fuck him. Always so STRAC. Colonel Tightass had been on the rag three days.

He sucked in a deep drag from the Camel. Around the tip, a little circle of red, little circle of fire. Miniature, he thought. Like miniature golf. World's tiniest fire. No way to see it out on a real golf course in the middle of the night with clouds all over hell and the rain threatening to come down.

Fucking Brad Thomson. Fucking Tad Parsons. Thomson back in the big house, propped up outside 8A in the nice chair. Nothing to do but go in every four hours and stick the needle into the loser in the bed. Parsons shooting pool down the hall.

So fuck Remy.

He took another drag and closed his eyes.

Sandy broke his neck below the third cervical vertebra.

Harry heard the snap, saw a white flash. Funny. The light was on the backside of his eyes. Inside his skull.

Then Harry's little bonfire went out.

*　　*　　*

Two minutes after one.

Nate was lying on his belly behind a low hedge of shrubs. Through the thin patches near the roots he could see the front gate, the guard post, the causeway stretching off across the black water of the Santee.

He rose to his knee as Becca leaned on the horn again. The guard was coming out of the little house commanding the approach to the plantation. Slipping around the end of the hedge, Nate cradled the MP5 against his chest and began to belly crawl toward the gate. Looked like a fucking castle. Why was he always on the wrong side?

*　　*　　*

Abbie didn't hear Sandy come up behind her. When he touched her foot, her whole body started to shoot skyward. Then she was lying on her back and he was on top of her, his hand clamped over her mouth. "One down," he said softly, pulling her up.

On the second floor of the plantation house, a light went on. Sandy pointed toward it.

"That way."

*   *   *

Kruger took the safety off his weapon and leaned out.

"*Tannenbaum, O Tannenbaum*," he sang at the top of his voice. "Christmas tree, O Christmas tree."

Becca hit the horn in time with the words.

Three and four, three and four.

When she saw the guy coming out of the guardhouse, she flipped the headlights on high and started flashing them as she honked the horn.

The guy raised his hand to shield his eyes. She punched on the red warning flasher and started swerving, brushing the sides of the narrow causeway as she bore down on the blinded guard. When she saw him reach inside his coat, she slammed on the brakes. The Rover screeched to a halt 6 feet in front of the gate.

Kruger stuck his head out the window. "*Ich bin ein Berliner*," he shouted. "*Hilfe. Wir haben einen Notfall.* Ve haff emergency."

The guard started walking up toward Kruger's window. He had a 9-millimeter in his hand.

"*O Tannenbaum, O Tannenbaum.*"

Three and four, three and four. The horn still beating time to the Christmas carol.

Kruger started to yodel.

The guard was outside the window now. "What's the matter with you, asshole," he yelled at Kruger.

"*He da, ist hier das Deutsche Konsulat?*"

"You dumb motherfucker," the guard snarled. "The consulate's in Charleston. Do us both a favor and go home before you get hurt. You're not only in the wrong county, you're in the wrong fucking country."

Caldwell slipped up behind him. The guard whirled around. Caldwell's shot caught him in the heart. Becca saw his eyes widen as he dropped the 9-millimeter and crumpled backward, landing on the hood of the Rover.

Kruger grabbed him and threw him in the back.

Becca hit the release, ran around to the front bumper and peeled 15 feet of cable off the winch. Wrapping a 4-foot loop through the bars, she jumped back into the Rover and threw it into reverse.

The gate came out like a rotten tooth. Caldwell came pounding through the hole. "Shit," he said, landing on top of the dead guard. Becca jammed on the accelerator and the Rover shot through the gate and roared toward the plantation house.

Kruger's voice rose above the whine of the engine.

"Güten Abend, asshole, yourself," he shouted. *"How you like my Christmas tree?"*

*   *   *

On the roof, the Professor and Mayemura were crouched behind a tall brick chimney. The Captain had called it wrong. There was a trapdoor, but no way to get through it. They tried to force it, but it wouldn't budge. Sonuvabitch was nailed shut.

Mayemura reached into the cargo pocket on his leg and took out a 4 Wrap.

Motioning to Santana to stay put, he slid down to the flat place behind the balustrade and as quickly as he could make an omelet he taped the 4 Wrap to the door. When everything was in place, he took out an M-60 Fuse Igniter and double checked the adapter.

"Fire in the hole," Eddie said softly, signaling to Santana to get down.

There was a sharp click, then a flash of yellow light and the thump of an explosion. The door disappeared into a million splinters. Below them, they could see the guest wing corridor.

*   *   *

Sandy saw the flash of light. The sound of the explosion echoed off the berm at the rear of the skeet range. "Let's move," he shouted. No need to be quiet anymore. They were still 100 yards out, the gable end of the big house rising up in front of them. Fifty yards now. Make the gable, get around the corner, charge the front door.

*   *   *

Santana peered down from the gaping hole. No way left to be subtle about this one. Mayemura hit the landing and rolled to the wall just as Brad Thomson dropped his copy of *The Hunt for Red October* and came out of his chair.

Thomson's Uzi was parked on a side table. Mayemura looked up and saw the Professor's feet at the edge of the hole. Thomson lunged for the Uzi. Mayemura sprayed him. The rounds whizzed under Santana's feet a split second before the rest of him arrived on the landing. Thomson spun around and hit the floor, two rounds through the chest, two to the head.

Santana kicked the body aside and busted into Room 8A. The first thing he saw was Hyduk. Out like a child.

The next thing he saw was out the window.

★　　★　　★

Ten yards. They were at the corner of the gable.

"Stay here," Sandy shouted, signaling with his hand for Abbie to hit the dirt. He didn't look back as he jumped around the corner.

The front door opened like an exploding safe. Ted Parsons stepped out. In his hand he had a pistol. Sandy twisted and leveled the MP5. Every muscle of his body, every atom that had ever been trained, concentrated on Tad Parsons. Every instinct in him.

Except one.

Where was Abbie? Had she seen his signal? Was she exposed? He hesitated for perhaps two hundredths of a second.

A bright flash of red from the barrel of the pistol.

Sandy spun around like a boxer's heavy bag, his eyes fixed on Abbie. The eyes went dead as he fell.

Abbie screamed.

Parsons was running forward. He was standing over Sandy now. Raising the pistol, pointing it at Sandy's head.

Crrraccccckkkkkkkkkkkkkkkkk.

The sound of lightning hitting a tree. Abbie felt rain and raised her finger to her face. When she looked at it, it was covered with blood.

Everything in slow motion.

The glass spraying out of the second-floor window.

Santana flying through the air, diving at Parsons.

The pistol flying out of Parsons's hands as Santana landed on him.

No more shots. Only a splintering sound as Parsons went limp.

Santana had crushed his ribs, driving them through his heart like a handful of skewers.

"Saaaaaannnnnndy!"

Through the blackness, the scream needled into Sandy's brain, driving away the stupor, igniting a fight-or-flight center where flight had been trained away so long ago it was no longer a possibility.

He rose to his knees, then stood as the adrenaline kick kicked his body into motion. Off to his right and to the rear, he saw a man running through the dark toward the skeet range.

No more thinking. Sandy ran. Pounding across the lawn now. The distance to the target maybe 200 yards. He cut the gap to 150 yards, 100 yards.

Above and behind him, he heard a loud clatter. The white lights of a light observation chopper flashed from over his shoulders, picking up the man, who was standing on the skeet range, waving his arms toward the sky.

Fifty yards now.

The chopper hovered for a split second, then dropped down. A door opened.

Ten yards.

The man scrambled in, and the chopper began to rise. Sandy felt his lungs burning, sobbing for air.

Sonofabitching bastard.

The chopper was about 50 feet above him, now. No time left to take aim. He whipped up the barrel of his MP5 and blew the whole magazine into the engine. A single burst. Sparks flying through the black night. The bird hesitating, then pinwheeling down.

A pillar of flame shot up as the chopper hit the ground and crumpled. The passenger side door flew open. The sonuvabitch was out on the ground again and running for the trees.

Magazine empty. Do it the old-fashioned way.

Sandy pumped across the thick green turf. Five yards, one yard. He lunged forward, hitting the air. The tackle threw both of them to the ground.

The bastard was hard.

As they rolled, his bony elbow caught Sandy in the eye. Flash of red, then darkness on that side. But a good enough view from the other to see the hand shoot for the boot, the thin blade of the SAS knife slicing through the darkness.

Remy.

Sandy's arm shot up reflexively, knocking aside the blade. He heard the soft hiss as it cut, felt the hot blood coursing down his body. His body, shifting into automatic, arched, and he flipped Remy on his back. For an instant, Remy lay there bathed in an eerie glow from the burning chopper and the white phosphorous light in Sandy's brain.

The light fell on Sandy's hand, slashing down like the edge of a sword, breaking Remy's arm. The knife fell onto the thick green grass. Sandy picked it up and drove it into Remy's chest, lurching forward, falling on the handle with the full force of his entire body. He felt the blade press through the soft flesh under Remy's sternum and dig into the grass.

Then the white phosphorous light went out.

EIGHTY-NINE

★ Crockett Plantation ★

The Rover careened around the plantation house carriageway. Off to the left, Becca saw the two men backlit by the flames from the chopper. Jerking the wheel over sharply, she headed for the skeet range. When she reached the burning bird, she hit the brakes.

Nate was out before the Rover skidded to a stop. Sandy was lying on his back, eyes rolled into his head, chest covered in blood. Remy didn't move. In death, his eyes were still open. He looked surprised, as if it had never occurred to him that the game might end this way.

Mayemura came limping out the back door as Kruger ran up with the medical kit. Nate kicked Remy aside and knelt next to Sandy. Abbie was bending over him, rocking back and forth, whimpering.

"He's dead, he's dead, he's dead."

Nate put his fingers on Sandy's neck. When he looked up, he saw the T. C. Johnson ambulance drawn up at the edge of the slave huts where Barry had left it two days before.

"Kruger, get that fucker over here. *Now.*"

"It's my fault," Abbie wailed. "I killed him."

Nate held her head against his chest. "He's a long way from dead. We jus' gotta haul ass and get him out of here."

Kruger and Mayemura pulled the stretcher out of the ambulance and eased Sandy onto it. Kruger went to work. Stopping the bleeding. Stopping the shock.

"You okay, Professor?" Nate asked Santana, taking a quick inventory. Santana's eyes were still working, but he didn't look to be in much better shape than the Hawk. "You get in there, too," Nate said, pointing to the back of the meat wagon.

He took a quick body count. Guard, one at the golf course, two guys in the house. Now, Remy.

"How many you get?" he yelled over to Mayemura.

"One," Eddie said. Then he remembered something else. "We forgot Hyduk." He turned and double pumped up the stairs. Nate took off after him. By the time he caught up, Eddie was coming out of Room 8A with Hyduk draped around his shoulders, limp as a wet parachute. So doped he'd slept through the raid. Eddie put him in the ambulance with Sandy and the Professor. That made four within the vehicle Kruger was driving. If they could squeeze in Abbie and Eddie, they'd be cool for the extraction.

Nate returned to his body count. Guard, dude Sandy took out, two second-floor guys, Remy. Five stiffs. Jesus. Leave 'em and the whole damn county would be on their ass before they got out of there. He looked up. Becca was dragging Remy over to the yellow Rover. Picking him up like a doll with the stuffing falling out, she threw him on top of the dead dude from the front gate and Santana's kill. "That's three," she said. "You check out the bushes, I'll get the one upstairs." Before he could say anything, she grabbed Mayemura and they were gone.

Nate took a bearing from the front gate and the gable end of the house and trotted off in the dark. Five minutes later he found Harry. His neck was as bent as a dog-eared page. The cigarette had burned down, scorching his fingers. He threw the body over his shoulder and started back for the house.

When he came onto the carriageway, the ambulance had left.

Becca was standing alone beside the yellow Rover. She'd found a blanket in the house and tossed it over the corpses in back. "You want a hand, Nate?" She pulled back the blanket.

Long hump back from the golf course. Good this dude wasn't an extra-large. "Thank you, ma'am."

Becca took the feet, Nate took the arms. They swung Harry on top of the others. Becca replaced the blanket and got behind the wheel. For a moment, Nate stood looking at the dark black stains on the ground.

"You coming, stud?" Becca said. "Or are you going to wait for the lynching?"

Nate dusted off his arms and got in next to her.

"Screw 'em, Nate," she said, gunning the engine. "Let 'em do their own cover-up."

It took them over an hour to drive to Florence, Becca keeping below the speed limit for the first time since she was sixteen. At the airport, Buzz was standing by the tail of the Caribou. The door was open.

"Where's the ambulance?" Nate asked. "How's the captain?"

Buzz spit a stream of black Red Man tobacco on the field. "Sittin' up, last time I saw him. Laid him out in Fostuh's joint. Girl wrapped right around him. Lotta blood, not many holes. The knife didn't do much to his arm. Looks like the bullet ran along a rib and came out the side. They figguh to bring him back to Bragg with no sweat. Said to tell you—and ah quote—'He'll live to fight anothuh day.' "

Buzz jumped into the tail of the Caribou and motioned for Nate to back the yellow Rover into the cargo bay. After Nate got out, Buzz began adjusting the quick-release tie-downs on the axles and body of the four-wheeler. When he left, Becca sat in one of the canvas seats and fastened the safety belt.

Alone.

Ten minutes later, she heard the engines begin to rev. The cockpit door opened. Nate came back and took the seat next to her. "You ain't gonna hurt me now, are you?" he said, buckling himself in.

"Not if you mind your manners."

The plane started to roll down the runway.

"Listen," he said. "I need to ask you a favor."

"You really think I'm the one to help you, stud?"

"Yeah, I do," he said. "You ever been a maid of honor?"

*   *   *

The Caribou lumbered into the night sky, flying low, under the clouds. Between the two of them, there was one small port in the fuselage. Nate looked down. Buzz still had his landing lights on. No trees. Maybe farms. The lights were bouncing off something down there. Made no sense. Don't get reflection off plowed fields, trees. He looked again and saw whitecaps.

The Atlantic.

They were over the fucking ocean.

The cockpit door opened and Buzz walked back. "Who's flyin' this motherfucker," Nate shouted.

"Be cool, stud." Becca patted his knee. "Autopilot."

Buzz kneeled by the Rover. She heard the tie-down chains rattling.

"Give me a hand, Nate."

"What are you two doing?" Becca asked them suspiciously as the two of them pushed the yellow hearse to the very back of the aircraft and took off the emergency brake.

"Not to worry," Buzz said. "Ever'thin's gonna be jus' fine." He went back to the cockpit.

Becca leaned back and closed her eyes. The vibrations in the skin of the plane felt comfortable now, like the pulse of an old lover.

She heard a purring noise and sat up as the ramp of the Caribou slowly opened and Buzz's voice came over the intercom.

"This is youah captain speakin'. Y'all stay buckled up. Don't fuckin' move."

The ramp was all the way open now. A cold wind shot through the cargo compartment. The nose of the Caribou inched up, and the tail of the plane sloped down.

Slowly, as in a dream, the yellow Rover rolled aft. "Buzz," Becca shouted. "What in hell are you doing?"

The yellow Rover with its blood cargo in the back dropped out of the Caribou like a cub from a pregnant panda.

"Nooooooooooo," Becca cried, following its arcing path.

The yellow Rover did a long, slow somersault, the black wheels spinning against the yellow body as it dropped, turned lazily one last time and plunged into the sea.

A tower of water shot up as if the Atlantic had been hit by a 10,000-pound bomb.

Then the Rover was gone.

As Buzz leveled off, Nate reached over and patted Becca on the knee. "You can get a new one, girl. Get back, you report that one stolen. Sure as hell no one's gonna recover it."

NINETY

Four A.M. Witching hour for the Hogs and Heifers. At least one hundred in the lounge. Max peered at the screen of his computer monitor wondering how they did it. Up all night, stoned on biker fantasies, slopping beer all over the keyboard but still in there typing. What did they care about power, politics. The news, for godsakes.

Monsters.

For the tenth time he cruised the lounge.

No sign of the Lube.

A message suddenly flashed on his screen: "Mad Max. That you?"

No handle from the sender. Hell with it. He'd risk it.

"Could be."

"Don't play games with me faggot. You been lurking all night. You looking for closet action? H and H is for people who like to relate. Go suck your own pickle."

Flamed by a Neanderthal. MM logged off. He'd have to wait. He took a moment to consider unfinished business. With Sandy and Abbie dead, did they need to hang on to Hyduk? Not really. Why worry about the senator when it was so very clear he no longer had any choices?

Except to become President.

Max chuckled. All so simple. All those headlines. Perfect timing.

He stood up from the computer, tightened the cord around his dressing gown. A long buzz interrupted his revery. Four-fifteen. Becca Deming's place was only an hour or two away. Was Remy stupid enough to send someone here?

Bzzzzzzzzzzzzzzzzzzzzzzzzzzzzz.

Annoyed, he turned on the lights in the little vestibule and opened the door.

"I need to see you."

"What turns you out so early? Or are you on your way home?"

"We need to talk."

"You look terrible. Why don't you go home and sleep it off?"

"No. It won't wait."

"Okay, but let's do this in the living room. I've been sitting in a straight-back chair half the night."

So now they were facing each other across the coffee table.

"Why did you kill Janine?"

Was life going to be this way from now on?

"Correction, *chér*. I didn't kill Janine. She died."

"Someone helped her die, isn't that the way it went?"

"You could look at it that way."

"I'm in no mood to be fucked with."

"No, really. You could call it a . . . sort of . . . mercy killing. She was on her way out, actually, and someone just helped her along. Remember those reports? I had them spun just a little to spare you both the pain."

"A CAT scan. You're telling me you spun a CAT scan?"

"A very bad one for Janine, Senator. The doctor said four months tops. Look at it this way. She never had to know she was dyin'. No hospital, no pain, no morphine. It didn't hurt, you know. I made sure of that. The juice in the dart knocks you down immediately. She just sort of went to sleep and never woke up."

"You little bastard."

"Now hold on, *chér*. Are you sayin' you didn't have any hand in this?"

"I sure as shit didn't."

"You sure as shit did. Think on it a minute. This goes back a long way. Surely you haven't forgotten dear Sarah Wilder."

"Fuck you, Pat."

"You remember the part where you showed me all the pictures? And I said, 'Leave all that to old Uncle Patrice?' All on a need-to-know basis, remember? Because you sure as hell didn't want to know anythin', did you?"

"What are you trying to say?"

"You were so rattled you didn't tell me you'd already confessed to Janine. I swear to God, you actually sent me down there to try to talk her out of it and didn't tell me what you'd done. I was about to say, 'Look, Janine, America doesn't like its heroes bad-mouthed. Especially by women.' But I didn't even get two words out. You know what she said to me?"

"Don't, Pat."

"You know, that's exactly what she said. You two are a real pair. She said, 'Don't, Pat. He spilled his guts to me about Vietnam a long time ago. I know everything about ODA 351. And I'm not going to live with it anymore.'

"I didn't even know what she was talkin' about. So I asked her and she told me everythin'. So I said, 'Darlin', let's forget about heroes, then. Let's talk big picture. Your health, your future. Not only can you skin the goose, I'm goin' to help you do it right. Here's what's goin' to happen. We're goin' to give you everything that man has, includin' his full military pension. We're also goin' to put two million dollars in a new Swiss bank account for you. No-tax dollars, darlin'.'"

"You're lying, Pat."

"Nossir, I'm not. The two of us sat there lookin' at each other and I was holdin' up two fingers for that two million and do you know what she said to me? She said one word. Just one word. And you know what that word was, *chér*?"

"Cut it out, Pat."

"The word was 'five.' Like F-I-V-E. I figured fair's fair. So I gave her just one word back. And the word I gave her was 'done.' *Done*, as in done deal. Now, another thing, Senator, while we're at it. Where do you think that five million came from? Well, it came from good ole Uncle Gus, who had Remy collect it from good ole T. C. Johnson. So I'd say you had a pretty big hand in all this. To be honest, I'd even say you sort of owe them."

"No one buys me, you little prick."

"Is that right? Well, *chér*, I'd say we sold you down the Santee River a long time ago."

"What about the others, Pat? What about General Caine?"

"Cocaine. Injected in the hock. Never shows. They fix races now with fifty cc's. Black Jack was higher than John Belushi."

No point in not telling him. The more he knew, the deeper the hook. He'd never get off now. Hyduk was a luxury. Remy could delete him any time.

"What about Sandy and Abbie? And Buell?"

"Buell drowned in the sweat of his own fat gut; he choked on his own greed. Whatever turns you on, Senator. The young lovers? That's being taken care of as we speak. They're up at Becca Deming's place. She knows everything, so I'm afraid she'll be leavin' us, too. Not a serious problem. Reporters are a dime a dozen, we both know that."

"Call them off. Now."

"Too late, *chér. Pas possible.* Remy should be weighing in any minute. No witnesses. Witnesses would be very bad for your image, Senator. Bad for your polls. Bad for your future."

"Bad for T. C. Johnson?"

"That, too."

"Why, Pat?"

A hot surge of anger. Don't let him get to you.

"You have to look at these things with the third eye, Senator. It's all a question of the true nature of power. Use your imagination. When I was a child workin' in the kitchen I was an innocent, a regular little Keats of the scullery. 'Beauty is truth, truth beauty.' I was sure that was all you needed to know in life. What else was there? I had principles. Like I said, I was pure. But you know, I changed the day I discovered the way the world really works. In my innocence, I never understood that what counts is who's sittin' at the table, not what you put on it."

"Is that all you believe, Pat?"

"I believe it's safer to be feared than loved. Machiavelli, *chér.* I believe in power. That's where we started, wasn't it?"

"What the hell good does it do you? What do you want it for?"

"Nothin'. Power is about power, *chér,* nothin' else. Winnin' it is all that counts. Holdin' on to it. Why is this idea so hard to grasp? How many times have you heard liberals carryin' on about things like art for art's sake? Why not power for power's sake? It's honest. If nothin' else, it's the only thing that explains this town these days."

"Everything always under control, Pat? Is that it?"

"Well, I do like gettin' my way." Patrice pulled the silk gown tightly around his small shoulders. "But why don't you tell me why you ran off with Alex's medal, Jeff, why you stole his honor? These things happen."

Senator Taylor shot him once. The round from the General's .45 hit just below Patrice's widow's peak, dropping his soft body on the kelim while carrying the back of his skull across the room and arranging it on the far wall in an abstract pattern of blood, brains and bone.

Senator Taylor looked down at the body. The entry wound was very neat. It looked like a black quarter with smudges at the top and bottom like mascara.

Third eye.

"What do you see now, Pat?" Senator Taylor said out loud. From his pocket, he took a blue box 7 inches long and 3 inches wide and set it down on the coffee table next to the .45. He kneeled down and tugged the silk cord away from the dressing gown, placing the cord alongside the box. Then he went into the study and rummaged around until he found a pair of scissors and an envelope that carried his office postmark.

When he got back, he opened the box and took out his medal.

The ribbon fell across his hand like a caress.

Taking the shears, he snipped the medal off the ribbon and slipped it into the envelope. He took out his fountain pen.

No need for a note, really.

On the front of the envelope, he wrote, *For Lieutenant Alexander Grant Caine. US Army.*

Then he licked the flap, sealed the envelope and put it carefully on the dead man's chest.

For a while he studied the composition. There was a faint smile of surprise on Pat's face. Maybe he did have a sense of humor, after all.

Picking up the denuded ribbon and the silk cord, Senator Taylor crossed the room, opened the French doors and went out into the garden.

Cold now. Very cold.

At the end of the narrow garden Patrice had built a small pergola, just a few strong uprights and crossbeams with some trelliswork to keep off the summer sun. Next to the pergola was the small red wagon he used for moving plants.

The senator moved the red wagon until it was in the middle of the pergola. Then he took the silk cord and tied a Baker's bowline in one end. Standing on the red wagon, he tied the other end of the cord around one of the white crossbeams.

When the knots were done, he reached into his pocket, took out the ribbon and put it around his neck. The broken links where the medal had been attached snagged in his shirt. Pulling them free, he slipped the bowline around his neck.

He twined the ribbon around the cord, and tightened the knot. Then he kicked away the red wagon.

The fall was not enough to break his neck. He knew that. His feet stopped 4 inches above the ground. Pat's silken noose cut deeply into his throat, strangling him.

NINETY-ONE

It was nearly noon at Fort Bragg. The shades in Santana's apartment were drawn. Only a thin finger of light stretched across the floor to the chair where Abbie was sleeping. When Sandy woke up, the first thing he saw was the light playing in her hair.

"Abbie?"

Calling out made pain shoot through his body, sharp needles that followed his rib cage as if some demon seamstress was on top of him, stitching up his chest.

She stirred, opened her eyes.

"Is that you?" she asked drowsily, then, snapping awake, "I'm here, Sandy. Over here."

She sat on the edge of the bed and touched the bandages. "Better," she said. "You're not seeping anymore."

"How long have I been out?"

"Two days—you lost a lot of blood."

Before she could say anything more, Nate and Santana heard them talking and came in from the porch. "Where's Hyduk, Nate? Did he make it?"

"Yeah, he made it, Captain. We put him on the plane back to Whitefish this morning. He said to tell you he's through bein' Siamese twins. Too fucking dangerous bein' attached to you."

Sandy closed his eyes.

"What about the others, they okay?"

"All hands present for duty."

"Remy?"

"He ain't gonna be causin' no more trouble. 'Less you believe in the walkin' dead."

Santana leaned over him and felt his pulse. "Figured you wouldn't be real happy at waking up explaining those wounds to some T. C. Johnson–owned sheriff. We got a couple of pints of blood into you. Your arm's okay, but you busted two ribs. That's why you look so funny when you try to talk. No infection so far. We had a Special Forces doc come by and clean you up. He says give it a couple more days and you'll be packing a ruck."

Nate looked at Abbie, then nodded to Santana. They went back out on the porch.

"Jeff's dead, pups. Patrice, too."

"How?"

"Later, pups, you need rest now."

"I need to know."

She leaned over and sorted through the newspapers on the floor next to her, then read him the first wire service account. " 'Senator Shoots Aide, Hangs Self.' " The reporter had the gun and the silk cord, but the rest was police blotter stuff. No one had put it all together.

"Christ, it makes it sound like there was something kinky between them," Sandy said. "What a pile of crap."

"Sex, lies and politics, pups. What do you expect?"

"Jeff had nowhere else to go, Abbie. He did the right thing."

"I know."

"I loved him, goddammit. I still do. He did one dishonorable thing and spent his whole life trying to make up for it."

He looked over at her, studying her face.

"What is it, pups?"

"Thank God you made it. I couldn't live without you."

"Is that right, pups? Like forever? You know what? I think forever would last until the day you needed to do a little more research with Carrie Perkins."

"Oh forget Carrie Perkins, Abbie. You could've been killed. Don't you understand that?" She saw tears working at the corners of his eyes.

Okay, Abs, no more smart-ass. Reaching over she gently kissed his eyelids. "I'll tell you what I do understand, pups. Bad enough you were ready to die for me. I almost got you killed."

"No you didn't, Abs. I did a good job of it all by myself."

"I don't think so, pups. You had everything in the world going for you. You didn't need any of this. Why did you do it?"

"I did it for Babs."

"Barbara Ann Brakowski, bride of the Sons of Poland? I don't think so. You didn't know the first thing about her until last week."

He looked at the ceiling.

"All right, price of honor, I guess." He closed his eyes, as if saying the word had embarrassed him. "I had to get to the truth. It was like there was no choice. No truth, no honor. Fuck it. It's all a mystery to me. Let's talk about something else."

"All right, I think we should change jobs."

"You really want to shoot people? I could never write a story."

"Not what I meant. I was thinking about being your responsibility. I'd rather you were mine for a while, okay?"

"I thought I already was. And you're doing just great."

"You always think I'm doing just great. All this time, you never asked me to change. You didn't rattle my chains. Not once."

"It would take an eighteen-wheeler to rattle your chains."

"Very cute."

He touched his chest carefully, probing his ribs.

"Move over, soldier," she said, lying down next to him, snuggling against his good side. "You just don't get it."

"So enlighten me."

"I'm yours, pups. Totally yours. I've decided."

"Airborne, Abs. Glad you signed up. You're stuck with me, too."

Outside on the porch, Caldwell and Santana were playing cards. Sandy heard a sharp, ripping sound as Nate shuffled and dealt. The dead past tearing away. Royal flush. He pulled Abbie closer and closed his eyes. The hair, he thought sleepily, remembering the red curl he had slipped into the envelope in Zagreb. Now he knew why he'd kept it.

EPILOGUE

★ The White House ★

Six months later, during a small private ceremony at the White House, the President of the United States presented the Medal of Honor (Posthumous) to Lieutenant Alexander Grant Caine. The gathering in the Oval Office was attended by the Secretary of Defense, the Secretary of the Army, the Chairman of the Joint Chiefs of Staff, and the Army Chief of Staff. Captain Alexander Grant Caine II, United States Army, accepted the medal on behalf of his father, killed in action in Vietnam.

The other guests that day were Captain Caine's fiancée, Abigail Mancini; her colleague, Rebecca Deming; and Melba Casadero, a close friend of the family. The two reporters had just received the Pulitzer prize for their front-page series in the *Washington Chronicle* about the circumstances leading up to the murder-suicide of Senator Jefferson Taylor and his chief of staff, Patrice St. Jean.

On the same day, the Senate Armed Services Committee voted to kill the F-44 jet fighter. Six months later T. C. Johnson filed for bankruptcy. The A-Team was in Colombia on a covert mission. In the absence of Captain Caine, Chief Warrant Officer Nathan Preston Caldwell was in command.

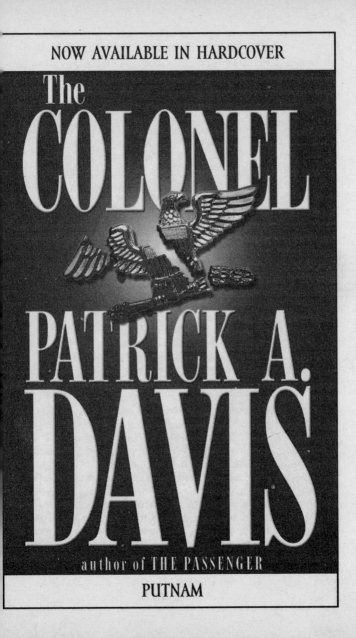

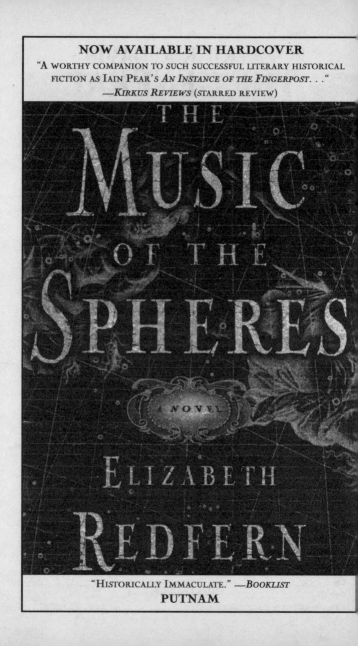

THE
MUSIC
OF THE
SPHERES

A NOVEL

ELIZABETH
REDFERN